"McMullen tosses us ... s plenty—rarely revealing ... t- ting us delightedly discover the fun story ... o. A captivating conclusion to a brilliant series."

—*Booklist* (starred review)

"This is great escape, and great fun."

—*San Diego Union-Tribune*

"Boisterously entertaining . . . the complexity of the book's plot is marvelous, like soap opera and Shakespeare, it is filled with fights, romance, wenching, revenge, greed, duplicity, and misunderstandings—a cacophony of schemery and slapstick that never fails to entertain."   —*Denver Post*

"Beamflash to North American fans: Australia Forwarding Huge Fun by Moonwing."   —*Kirkus Reviews*

"One of the best epics I've read. If you've read the first two books, no doubt you need little urging to read this one. If you read it alone, you'll probably enjoy it even without the back story, but you might want to start at the beginning with *Souls in the Great Machine.*

"The Greatwinter Trilogy is certain to become one of science fiction's master story arcs, and the author will no doubt continue to provide us with good reading for some time to come."   —Ernest Lilley, *SF Revu*

"Sean McMullen expands even further the busy, sprawling, and quite engaging series that began with *Souls in the Great Machine* . . . Not many thousand-and-a-half-page adventure epics have managed to hold my attention for the whole span, but this one has left me willing to read more."

—Russell Letson, *Locus*

The Miocene Arrow
Book Two of the Greatwinter Trilogy

"McMullen's prose is plain but lucid, and, nicely enriched with low human comedy, coincidence and farce, is perfectly suited to explication of his crowded story of heroism and cupidity in this cross between an old-fashioned air-ace adventure and Arthurian romance. The level of invention of *The Miocene Arrow* may be lower than its predecessor, but there's much to enjoy. . . . McMullen ties up the numerous plot twists with an admirable facility, and the final pages are imbued with the burgeoning sense that the diptych of *Souls in the Great Machine* and *The Miocene Arrow* is destined to become a classic."
—Paul McAuley, *Interzone*

"With remarkable imagination and insight, McMullen conjures factions, personalities, and plots, including well-placed glimpses of a lost, past America. A complex and lively story, rich with the action and reaction of human treachery, courage, battle-fueled passion, and quiet devotion."
—*Booklist* (starred review)

"The tale features labyrinthine politics, a large cast of engaging, thorny and occasionally rather cartoonish characters, and many well-depicted scenes of aerial warfare. The author's inventive use of several oddball technologies is particularly noteworthy, and veteran SF readers may well be reminded of the best work of L. Sprague de Camp." —*Publishers Weekly*

"Set in the same postapocalyptic universe as his groundbreaking *Souls in the Great Machine*, McMullen's latest effort elaborates on the evolution of a strange and, ultimately, mystifying future. Recommended." —*Library Journal*

"Every bit as much ingenious fun as the first book."
—Russell Letson, *Locus*

"A classic 'good read'." —*Analog*

"McMullen has fused the relentless pertinacity of Bruce Sterling with the stylized exoticism of Jack Vance, and, as his command of novelistic technique grows, his neo-medieval tapestry glows with an ever greater speculative intelligence."

—Nick Gevers, *Nova Express*

Souls in the Great Machine
Book One of the Greatwinter Trilogy

"A stunning idea—the Calculor's as real as if McMullen had built it in his backyard—with an utterly convincing setting, breathtaking developments, and a captivating narrative."

—*Kirkus Reviews* (starred review)

"Fast-paced and amusing, McMullen's latest novel is an action-packed adventure in the tradition of world-building SF. . . . McMullen's dramatic pacing and believable characters ensure that readers will enjoy Zarvora's quest through a well-wrought, richly imagined multidimensional world."

—*Publishers Weekly*

"Decidedly original, sometimes whimsical, and captivating, this is a genuine tour de force."   —*Booklist* (starred review)

"McMullen delivers a powerful tale of visionaries and schemers struggling to rediscover the secrets of their ancestors. Highly recommended."   —*Library Journal*

"A complex, well-crafted novel filled with action and adventure. . . . There is a marvelous inventiveness which pervades *Souls*. . . . McMullen has a wonderful grasp of action and is capable of vastly entertaining sequences. . . . *Souls in the Great Machine* is good fun and worth seeking out."   —*Locus*

"McMullen displays considerable cleverness. He's quite convincing, as he indeed is in most other aspects of this very satisfying saga of empire and technology. You'll enjoy it."

—*Analog*

"There is no shortage of either entertainment or intellectual stimulation in *Souls in the Great Machine*. McMullen offers readers a thrilling and thoroughly alien view of far-future earth, playing fiendishly inventive riffs on the postapocalyptic theme. . . . *Souls in the Great Machine* is an appealing book, crammed with gems that are sure to please almost every kind of reader. . . . Every time you think you know where McMullen is taking you, he swerves wildly, giving you a good hard laugh as you try to hang on."   —*Science Fiction Weekly*

EYES OF THE
CALCULOR

TOR BOOKS BY SEAN McMULLEN

The Centurion's Empire
Eyes of the Calculor
The Miocene Arrow
Souls in the Great Machine
Voyage of the Shadowmoon
Glass Dragons

EYES OF THE
CALCULOR

SEAN McMULLEN

TOR®

A TOM DOHERTY ASSOCIATES BOOK
NEW YORK

This is a work of fiction. All the characters and events portrayed in these stories are either fictitious or are used fictitiously.

EYES OF THE CALCULOR

Copyright © 2001 by Sean McMullen

Edited by Jack Dann

A Tor Book
Published by Tom Doherty Associates, LLC
175 Fifth Avenue
New York, NY 10010

www.tor.com

Tor® is a registered trademark of Tom Doherty Associates, LLC.

ISBN: 0-765-34512-9

First edition: September 2001
First mass market edition: December 2003

Printed in the United States of America

0 9 8 7 6 5 4 3 2 1

For Sensei Alexander Albert
. . . who is not a monk

The Greatwinter Trilogy
is dedicated to my friend
and production editor
Jenna Felice, 1976–2001

ACKNOWLEDGMENTS

Catherine S. McMullen, for constructive criticism; Trish Smyth, for research material; Jack Dann, for informed advice; John de la Lande, for checking my orbital dynamics equations

PROLOGUE

The Rochestrian Commonwealth, Eastern Australica

Deep within Libris, the vast and ancient Mayoral library of Rochester, the pulse of the electric calculor was the warm, regular gusts of air that blew through the corridors of its body. The heartbeat of ZAR 2 was less impressive than its pulse, sounding like heavy hail beating down on a vast slate roof during a windstorm. The air around it was warm with its life, and that life had never faltered in the twenty-one years since its commissioning. Attendants wheeled trolleys loaded with punched cards and reels of paper tape up to the toothed hoppers that were its many mouths, while far above, in the courtyards and gardens of the sprawling library that was its home, horses paced in treadcircles to turn the generators that powered its heart.

The display register in the operations room declared it to be the 13th day of September in the year 3961.

Twenty-one years was very old for a calculor; in fact, ZAR 2 had survived to twice the age of its predecessor, a human-powered calculor. ZAR 1 had never been called anything but the Calculor while operational, but after the assassination of its creator, Zarvora Cybeline, the calculating machines at the heart of the Rochestrian Commonwealth were renamed in memory of her.

All through the rooms and corridors that were ZAR 2's body,

the signs of age were clearly visible: Unpainted wooden beams, ripped cloth partitions, broken pulleys that had been bypassed instead of repaired; even the stone walls themselves featured holes roughly knocked through to allow easier access for cables and tubes. None of the electric calculor's attendants moved with any sort of animation, and nearly all looked as shabby and neglected as the machine that they tended.

In the sky above Rochester a great band of darkness blotted out a swath of stars, and at the point directly opposite to the sun was a small splash of orange light. The Mirrorsun band was a legacy of the ancient Anglaic civilization, an immense orbital sunshield to counter something called the greenhouse effect. It was also known to be intelligent. On this particular night there were odd twinkles and pulses of light in the darkened areas, and in patterns that seemed to be building in intensity. Astronomers excitedly took measurements, children pointed and laughed, lovers gazed skyward as they spoke endearments to each other, but most people were too lazy or busy to even glance up.

Franzas Dramoren was exceedingly tired, but the new Highliber of Libris did indeed bother to look up at the Mirrorsun band.

"Behind all great signs and portents may be found change," he said softly.

Somewhere nearby a clocktower chimed 2:00 A.M., and he turned away from the window and got into bed.

"And behind all small signs and portents may be found change," he added as he lay with his eyes closed, waiting for sleep to claim him.

Dramoren was the third Highliber to take charge of both Libris and the Dragon Librarian Service since the death of Zarvora Cybeline. A mere twenty-nine years of age, he had previously been head of the Espionage Constables for six years. Dramoren was, like Zarvora, a child of a noble family who happened to possess great talent and drive, and both had made the most of the rank, privileges, and wealth that they had been born with. Half an hour before dawn he awoke in the small but richly furnished Highliber's apartment, washed at a porcelain bowl, and dressed in the clothes and robes that had been laid out by his lackey. With each new Highliber came a new style of uniform for the Dragon Librarian Service, and in a sense Dramoren's aspirations were reflected in his choice of style. The black tunic, trousers, calf boots, and jacket were very similar to the style of Zarvora, but he had added his own special touch, with the wearer's rank displayed on the jacket's collar. Rank was now denoted by a pair of colored wings sprouting from a book, worn on the lapels of the jacket. Dramoren had black wings picked out in silver, for he was the only Dragon Black Librarian. Dramoren also wore a black skullcap. This was partly to acknowledge his monastic background, and partly to hide a bald spot.

Being not yet thirty, Dramoren was the second-youngest Highliber ever to take charge of the Libris. A five-inch scar emerged from the hairline of his left temple, passed through the edge of his eyebrow, and disappeared again into the beard that ran along his jawline. The scar was only as old as Dramoren's inauguration as Highliber, and the stiches had not yet been removed. He was buttoning his jacket when there was a knock at the door. He opened it to find his lackey, Vorion, had arrived with a chalkboard. Vorion's rank was Dragon Red, but he had forgone several opportunities for promotion to retain his position as personal lackey to the Highlibers.

"Highliber!" the middle-aged man exclaimed. "I thought you were still in bed."

"It is nearly dawn, Fras Vorion," replied Dramoren, gesturing to the window. "Most people have a tendency to get out of bed in the morning."

"But Highliber, I should be here with your breakfast before you rise, then help you wash and dress, brief you on the schedule for the day, and—"

"Fras Vorion, I can wash and dress myself, and I shall eat with my senior staff in the refectory."

"Highliber, do you think that is wise? After, well, what happened to Highliber Waramance?"

"After what happened to Highliber Waramance I think it is *particularly* wise."

Dramoren had already studied Vorion's file, noting that he had entered Libris as Highliber Zarvora's lackey and had worked in that position for the following thirty-three years. The two Highlibers since Zarvora had been over twice Dramoren's age, and had been given the appointment as a reward for a lifetime of inoffensive mediocrity. The first had died of heart failure after a single year in office. Highliber Waramance had then filled the position for four years without making a single decision of any consequence, then suddenly and mysteriously died. It had been made clear to Dramoren that certain reforms had been scheduled for the Dragon Librarian Service, and that the Commonwealth's Council of Mayors was less than impressed by Waramance's lack of performance—and even less impressed by his reluctance to resign when requested to do so. Dramoren had no doubt that the man had been deliberately returned to his Maker, and that as his successor he was expected to show considerably more initiative.

Vorion was looking a little crushed as Dramoren combed down his hair and beard, then put on his skullcap. He selected a flintlock from his wall rack, checked the priming pan, then thrust the weapon into his belt. Finally he picked up an ankle-length black coat.

"Er, Highliber, that is not part of the uniform."

"Ah, yes, but I am the Highliber," responded Dramoren, glancing out of the window as he put the coat on. "Have you looked at Mirrorsun lately?"

"I, ah, no, but—"

"There are faint lights dancing along its length, and they are growing more frequent by the hour."

"Oh Ah, what does it mean, Highliber?"

"It means change, Vorion." The master of Libris and the Dragon Librarian Service crossed the room and held the door open for his lackey. "One should be most alert when there are signs of change to be seen. Walk with me."

They began the trek to the refectory.

"What did you think of my two predecessors?" asked Dramoren presently.

"They were fine and learned—" began Vorion.

"I despised them both," interjected Dramoren. "Waramance was invited to attend the regional meeting of mayors at Rutherglen, so that he would be outside the protection of my Espionage Constables. There he was poisoned."

"Oh no, Highliber, impossible!"

"I have had my people make enquiries. The meeting had been convened especially to lure him out there, and a special poison was imported from the Northmoors."

"I—ah, how terrible," stammered the lackey.

"I quite agree; had they bothered to ask me I would have arranged his assassination with a lot less trouble and expense. Now, Fras Vorion, have you ever worked for anyone as ruthless as me in your three decades in Libris?"

"Frelle Zarvora Cybeline," replied Vorion without hesitation.

"Ah, really?" exclaimed Dramoren with a slight smile.

"Without a doubt."

"What did you think of her?"

"I would have cheerfully died for her, Highliber."

"Indeed?" said Dramoren, smiling again. "Well, I very nearly died to attain her rank, but here I am and there are going to be changes. The Dragon Librarian Service is like a beautiful, finely balanced, perfectly tuned flintlock. It looks magnificent, but it exists to be used."

"If my services are no longer required, Highliber, just tell me," mumbled Vorion, expecting the worst.

"That is up to you, Fras. I require assistance, not pampering. Be at my door as I emerge every morning, brief me on what is to come as we walk to the refectory, shield me from trivia, tend my files with efficiency, and keep an ear to the walls for rumors. Can you do all that?"

"Better than any other, Highliber."

"Then your services are required. What is scheduled for today?"

"A meeting with your Dragon Gold Librarians in the morning, and a tour of the book stacks in the afternoon. The Overmayor has invited you to her palace for a working dinner, and at the ninth hour you are to meet the Bishop of Woomera for drinks."

"Where I shall discuss what?"

"A new religious movement to redefine electrical engines as fueled engines, and hence prohibit their use. Finally there is a tour of the ZAR 2 calculor."

They are expecting change, thought Dramoren as he stood to address his Dragon Gold Librarians. *Who am I to disappoint them?*

"I have been appointed to oversee a profound change in the role of the Dragon Librarians," he began. "Until the spread of radio and wire artisanry, librarians were the controllers and coordinators of knowledge, information, travel, and transport. Once, the networks of beamflash signal towers used telescopes, mirrors, and flashing lights to relay messages, and human-powered calculors ordered, analyzed, and stored the information needed to run our mayorates. However, they were very large and expensive, and only the government could build and maintain them. Now, since the rediscovery of electrical essence, mere merchants can buy radio machines and desktop calculors, and networks of wire are replacing the old beamflash towers. What are we to do?"

Dramoren folded his arms behind his back as they thought.

"Restrict access to our boo—" began the head conservator before catching Dramoren's frown. "That is, preserve the glory and wisdom of the past."

"Encourage the use of our books by students and researchers," declared the head of Reference, fishing for Dramoren's favor.

"Through more rigorous cataloguing," added the head of Cataloguing.

"And acquire multiple copies of more books," added the Dragon Gold in charge of Acquisitions, not anxious to be left out.

"Research the control, storage, and spread of information," was the opinion of the Systems Controller of the electric calculor.

Dramoren stared down at the polished table before him. *They all want to say what will please me,* he thought. *They have no visions, neither have they dreams, and there is probably a shortage of backbones in the room as well. Would they do anything other than applaud politely if I drew my Morelac and shot the head of*

*Calaloguing's stupid hat off his head? If I dropped my trousers
and presented them with a full moon? If I announced the death
penalty for overdue books? Did I really leave the Espionage Constables for this?*

"Libris and the Dragon Librarian Service have had a role for
over a thousand years," said Dramoren. "I cannot believe that they
have ceased to be useful in just twenty. The Southmoors, the Central
Confederation, the new Kalgoorlie Empire, and the Alspring Ghans
are held together by their religions. The Woomerans and Northmoors
are no more than trade and defense alliances of small mayorates and
castellanies, while Avian's citizens have unity because they are
aviads and most humans are trying to kill them."

"Killing aviads is now prohibited under Rochestrian law," began
the head of Reference.

"Quite so, Frelle, but that is not my point. Only the Rochestrian
Commonwealth is based on the Dragon Librarian Service now."

"The Dragon Librarian Service nevertheless provides services
everywhere except Avian," said the Dragon Gold of Communications.

"Services which are becoming increasingly redundant, except in
our Commonwealth," Dramoren pointed out.

"In that case the Service is vital to the Commonwealth," said the
Systems Controller.

"So should we become the *Rochestrian* Dragon Librarian Service, and abandon our brothers and sisters elsewhere on the continent?"

"I am tracing a logical path, Highliber. Logic leads where it
will."

Dramoren nodded his agreement. *Perhaps Hawker has a brain
but has learned to keep quiet about it,* he decided.

"Your thoughts on this matter are very constructive, Systems
Controller Hawker," he declared. "I look forward to speaking
with you further this evening, during my tour of your electric calculor."

• • •

The day passed slowly, and Dramoren was deluged with agendas, petitions, and requests wherever he went. Late in the evening he called in at the refectory again and secured a mug of coffee, which he took with him.

"'Ere, who does 'e think 'e is?" demanded a servingmaid.

"The new Highliber," replied the refectory supervisor.

The Libris refectory was beside the dormitory wing of the vast library complex, and separated from the older buildings by a wall and bluestone plaza. The wall also separated the artisan workshops, bookstores, calculor hall offices, and armory of Libris from the lower security areas. Dramoren passed through a gate that was guarded by bluestone grotesques and live Tiger Dragon guards. Glancing up at Mirrorsun, he noted that the pulsing lights had by now become a faint, twinkling torrent of light across the sky.

"It means something," he said to a guard, who responded by saluting.

Dramoren entered the old central store where Hawker was waiting.

"Even after twenty years this place seems unnaturally quiet," said Hawker as they walked past a vast array of small, partitioned rooms packed with odd jumbles of woodwork and wire. "These cells are where the components were kept when they were not on duty."

"So, you saw this place when the components of the original Libris Calculor were housed here?" asked Dramoren.

"I *was* one of those components," replied Hawker.

"And which component was that?" asked Dramoren, quickly recovering from his surprise.

"MULTIPLIER 17. I was there from the first experiments until the upgrading to the electric calculor, ZAR 2."

"And what is all that rubbish in the cells?"

"Why Highliber, it's the abacus frames, desks, seats, and transmission wires of the original Calculor. Ironic, is it not? The great machine is now in the cells where its components used to sit."

"I read that it had been smashed up."

"About a quarter of it was destroyed, the rest was moved down here for salvage."

"And nothing has actually been salvaged?"

"When the space is needed, the salvage will begin."

They passed out into another courtyard, where two dozen horses were walking treadcircles while munching chaff from nosebags. They were powering gearboxes that were attached to generators, and from these ran wires wrapped in beeswax-soaked cloth spaced by porcelain insulators that led to the next building, a thousand-year-old cathedral to knowledge in red abandonstone.

"The courtyard used to be enclosed, but it got a bit smelly with the horses, so the roof was dismantled," explained Hawker.

"Have you noticed anything different about Mirrorsun lately?" asked Dramoren, looking up.

"Er, the moving lights?" said Hawker after staring at it for a moment.

"Yes. They worry me."

"They look harmless."

"So does a piece of paper with 'War is Declared' written on it."

One pair of horses near the door was driving a large reciprocating pump, which circulated air to cool the calculor. Inside the building, frame and canvas ducts carried air along the passageway just above their heads. It was like being within a vast, warm body as pulses of air dilated the ducts, relays sparked and clattered, and transformers hummed. Some artisans were clustered around patchboards, others heated soldering irons on charcoal burners, and yet more drew diagrams on portable chalkboards and argued about impedance, resistance, and capacitance. There were armed Tiger Dragons at every door, and the place was lit by flickering oil lamps.

"Two hundred souls are needed to maintain the ZAR 2 calculor," said Hawker proudly, "and it is still the largest anywhere."

A pervasive, hissing, clattering sound was gradually growing louder. They climbed one final flight of stairs, then Hawker opened a small door. A wave of sound surged out over them. Dramoren hesitated, then followed Hawker out onto a balcony of blackstone and marble.

Dramoren stood beside Hawker at the marble rail, looking out across the electric calculor. The air was warm, and laced with the smell of beeswax, oil, and ozone, while the clatter of many thousands of electric relays was as insistent a hailstorm. Compared with some of the rediscovered ancient devices now in use the old electric calculor was clumsy, noisy, and unreliable, yet it had one redeeming feature in the eyes of Highliber Dramoren. It was entirely comprehensible to mere mortals. Admittedly, not more than half a dozen mortals understood the workings of its seventeen thousand relays and the plugboard operating system, but they were sufficient to tend its maintenance.

"So, this thing was built in 1708 GW," said Dramoren above the din.

"Yes, and I was here when it was carried in through the door," replied Hawker. "I was still a component in those days."

"You must be a lot older than you look."

"I'm only sixty, Fras Highliber," replied Hawker, a trace of affront in his voice.

"Forgive me, Fras, but the prototype had been disbanded when I was eight years old, so to me it seems a very long time ago."

"This place was renamed Dolorian Hall when the ZAR 2 machine was moved in."

"Did you ever meet Frelle Dolorian?" asked Dramoren.

"Ah, yes, she was a regulator in the prototype. What a charmer, aye, and she sweetened the life of several components over the years. Have you ever heard of John Glasken?"

"Yes, he presented me with the Bouros Prize for mathematics when I was fourteen."

"Hah, well did you know he met Dolorian on the battlefield at the end of the Milderellen Invasion, and she bedded him?"

"I do know that, Fras Hawker. Dolorian was my aunt."

Hawker made a choking sound and turned bright red. Dramoren put his elbows on the railing and rested his chin on his clasped hands. The silence between them began to lengthen.

"The, ah, regulators are concerned about the electric machine," said Hawker awkwardly. "Parts are very old, and need complete rebuilding."

"What do you think?" asked Dramoren, looking down at two regulators replacing a bank of relays in one of the racks.

"I have been following the work being done at the University, Highliber. A whole new generation of relays is near to being perfected. They will be three times faster and a tenth the size of what is here, we should phase them in and simply discard this old machine."

"What about the regulators?"

"They worry that they may soon be lacking their jobs. So little has been spent on the calculor for so long that they think nobody cares about it."

"People care, Fras Hawker. Important people care. Libris is an arm of government. Librarians and libraries are the glue that binds the Commonwealth together, and the politics of control are what drives—"

Dramoren was cut short by a crackling cascade of sparks and violet fire from the relay banks, interspersed with cries of alarm from the regulators on duty. Smoke began to billow from all corridors of the huge machine.

"Is it supposed to do that?" asked Dramoren, but already Hawker had dashed out and could be heard shouting "Sabotage!" in the distance.

Down in the Dolorian Hall the regulators were running to and fro through the billows of acrid smoke with buckets of sand and fire blankets. Parts of the vast machine were already well alight. The system herald hurried across the floor calling "System Alert, Category 1, Class F!" and ringing a handbell. A technician ran shrieking out of the smoke, his clothing on fire, another technician chasing him with a pitcher of coffee.

"Attention all souls! Attention all souls!" shouted the supervisor of security. "Evacuate the calculor immediately."

"Prepare to initiate an orderly shutdown of the operating system!" shouted Hawker somewhere in the distance.

"Bring water!" shouted a voice. "There's no electrical essence now."

Obviously never tested their disaster contingency plan, thought Dramoren, *if they have one.* He was oddly calm in the face of this catastrophe. No electrical essence. Somehow that seemed significant. He turned away to look at the electric clock on the wall above him. It was smoking and had stopped at 10:36 P.M., barely a minute earlier. Standing on a chair, he lifted it from the wall mounting and noted that no wires trailed from it. After dousing it with the remains of his coffee, he saw that it was blackened within, and that its chemical battery had burst. The clock was quite independent of the calculor's supply of electricity, yet it had been destroyed at precisely the same time.

Implications began to tumble through Dramoren's head. Right across the mayorate all electrical devices might well be smoking, melting, and burning. Across the mayorate, the Commonwealth, perhaps even the entire continent. Perhaps all electrical devices everywhere had been struck down by some celestial sword that spared everything else.

"Mirrorsun," said Dramoren to himself, rubbing his hands together as he turned away from the ruins of the electric calculor and made for the door. "Well, fortune favors those who react exceedingly fast."

1

TOUCH OF APOCALYPSE

Twelve miles above Eastern Australica

Relations between Earth's intelligent species had been less than satisfactory for a very long time. For several hundred years humans had hunted whales and dolphins so intensively that many of their clans, attractens, and associons were wiped out. Those memories were fresh and raw when the humans managed to revive a cetacean warrior from a civilization older than the human race itself, a warrior skilled in the ways of warfare that had unleashed an undersea Armageddon nine million years earlier. There is nothing like a common enemy to inspire unity, and humanity was certainly that. The Call, a mind weapon, began to sweep over the land, permanently blanketing some areas, especially near the coast. Lured to the sea to drown, or held starving in a mindless reverie, the human population declined by nearly three orders of magnitude. The cetezoids could easily have wiped *Homo sapiens* from the earth, but then there would have been no common enemy left. Humanity was suffered to survive through sheer political convenience.

In the dying years of the Anglaic civilization, however, one last and desperate attempt was made to counter the cetaceans' weapon. Noting that birds were not affected by the Call, some of the last genetic engineers on the continent of Australia added tracts of bird DNA to the human genome. Overseas, frightened and confused armies flung nuclear weapons at each other, then chaos descended in the form of a nightmare winter that lasted centuries. As the world warmed again it was noticed that some people were immune to the Call, people who were also lighter, stronger, faster, and generally more intelligent than humans. These bird-people, the aviads, were slaughtered whenever they were recognized, and the genocide continued for two thousand years. Slowly, unobtrusively, the aviads began to organize their own nations in areas permanently blanketed by the cetezoids' Call, and their hatred for humanity was no less intense than that of the cetezoids. Within the Calldeath lands they were safe, secure beyond the reach of humans and their predilection to annihilate anything superior than themselves.

Then, on the 13th of September, A.D. 3961 the Call ceased to exist. Completely. Humans were free from the Call weapon that had ravaged their numbers and rendered vast areas of land uninhabitable for two millennia. The aviads of the continent now known as Australica were suddenly at the mercy of a human population a thousand times its number.

Fortunately this happened just as the only member of Earth's newest intelligent species decided to annihilate all electrical machines on the face of the planet. This was not entirely coincidence either, for the fourth intelligence had once been an aviad.

The sunwing *Titan* was a half mile in wingspan but barely fifty feet in length. It was pure wing, nothing more than a wing powered by electrical motors driven by direct or stored sunlight. Two thousand years earlier it had been designed to cruise the stratosphere forever, regenerating ozone to restore the delicate balance of Earth's atmosphere, never landing, self-repairing. It was an island of habitat in the sky. An air pressure of just below that of sea level was maintained by pumps to strengthen the *Titan*'s structure, and waste heat provided warmth for the cabins were where maintenance crews had been meant to live. The aviads had boarded the *Titan*, removed the ozone generators, and learned to steer it. Aviads could now cross human territory without fear of lynch mobs, torture, and inquisitions. They could even cross oceans.

The *Titan* was cruising twelve miles above southeastern Australica on the 13th day of September 1729 in the Greatwinter calendar of Australica, and 3961 in the Anno Domini calendar of North America. There were twenty-two aviad souls aboard the huge wing: three crew and nineteen passengers.

Captain Raffe Terian seldom steered the *Titan*. As captain he tended the running and security of the town-sized wing, managing the provisions, waste disposal, security, and maintenance of the living areas. He had a bridge from which he could adjust the course, but in practice this was little more than his office. This trip was quite routine, it was merely to transport aviad refugees from the humans' Carpenteria mayorate of the far north to Tasmania Island, where the mayorate of Avian was barely six years old. It was ironic that so many aviads were often born to human parents, so that the humans who hated them were their best source of recruits. Terian noted that they were above the Central Confederation's lands, but borders made little difference at a height of twelve miles. Even crawling along at an airspeed of just seventy miles per hour they would be above Tasmania Island in twelve hours.

"It is hard to believe that there is a battlefield down there," said Watch Officer Varel, standing at the observation plate with her arms folded behind her back.

"The Central Confederation and the Southmoors, I believe," replied Captain Terian. "It is nice to see humans killing each other instead of us."

"With respect, Fras, I never like to see anyone killing anyone," retorted Varel.

"Spoken like someone shielded from the tender attentions of a human mob, Watch Officer. What has been your background with humans?"

"I have been shot twice and raped once during the course of recruiting five dozen aviad brethren from among the humans. I have also killed eleven times."

Terian shook his head. "After all that, you still have a trace of compassion for the human exterminators?"

"They are just afraid of us, Fras Captain. Aviads are so much better in so many ways."

"That does not make it any more pleasant to be killed by them. Some factions say we should kill them all—"

The console before the captain suddenly hissed, then billowed acrid smoke. The light strips blackened and failed too, but clear panels in the roof allowed light from Mirrorsun to illuminate the interior of the *Titan*. Everything electrical had smoked, melted, or exploded at the same instant.

"What in all hells has happened?" demanded Captain Terian, fanning at the smoke between him and the ruined console.

"The nearest engine pod is trailing smoke, Fras Captain," reported Varel, staring through a roof panel. "Its propeller is just spinning unpowered."

"Get up to the navigation bubble, check if any others have failed."

Watch Officer Seegan burst into the bridge as Varel was climbing the steps. He reported that there was smoke everywhere, and that the passengers were beginning to panic.

"All engine pods are trailing smoke, Fras Captain," called Varel from the navigation bubble. "Some propellers have jammed, others are just spinning unpowered."

"All?" cried the incredulous captain.

"All that I can see from here."

"Then we are going to lose the sunwing."

By now the smoke was dispersing, but in the distance someone was having hysterics and screaming that they were all going to die.

"Even with total loss of power this thing will take over two hours to glide to the ground," Terian pointed out as he hurriedly thought through some figures he had learned for an examination years earlier. "That gives us space to breathe."

"Fras Captain, breathing could actually be a problem; we are also losing air pressure," reported Seegan, staring at a large mechanical dial. "We will be dead ninety minutes before the air can be breathed."

Terian closed his eyes and put his hands over his ears as he thought for a frantic moment.

"Perhaps not," he decided. "Draw your guns, come with me."

Although there had been safety drills aboard the *Titan*, there was no precedent for total failure of all electrical systems with no warning whatsoever. They were at twice the height of Mount Everest, although none of them knew of Mount Everest as anything more than a folktale.

The first thought of the passengers was to escape from the smoke, and the evacuation drills had made the location of the parachutes common knowledge. One of the musketeers strapped on a parachute, then led a group of passengers to the ferry bay of the *Titan*. The ramp was normally released by electrical relays when at lower altitudes, but now the switches remained firmly locked. Selecting an area of the low, sloping roof, the musketeer began slashing at the tough fabric. The already depleted air rushed out all the more quickly, sucking acrid smoke and fumes from the sunwing.

Eight of the passengers tumbled out through the hole, but within minutes five of them were dead, suffocated as they hung from their parachute straps in the rarefied air. Three others knew that survival depended upon reaching breathable air quickly, and did not open their parachutes. By the time they had reached denser air, however, they were dead from the wind chill. They had been dressed for the warm, comfortable cabins of the *Titan*.

Back aboard the crippled sunwing another three had died, suffocated by the smoke, but the captain had been quick to grasp what options were available for those aboard the doomed craft. Crippled the *Titan* might be, but it was descending in a long, shallow glide and would take a very long time to hit the ground. He and the two officers left the smoking control deck, shouting for all that could hear to make for the captain's cabin, and to ignore the parachutes. He got a mixed reception from the passengers, and even his authority could not convince them that true safety did not lie with immediate

escape. The captain seized a woman who was leading her two children aft, shouting at her to come with him. A confused man knocked
him to the deck and tried to lead the family away. Watch Officer
Varel shot the man dead.

Fifteen minutes after the catastrophic failure, three more passengers on the *Titan* were dead, asphyxiated in the corridors whose air
pressure had by now become equal with the rarefied atmosphere
outside. After half an hour the sunwing had shed six miles of its
height and was down to thirty thousand feet. In the captain's cabin,
two men, three women, and two children were huddled together in
the increasing cold, yet they could still breathe. The cabin was air-
tight, and had contained no electrical devices. Through the single
forward observation plate they watched as detail on the Mirrorsun-
lit ground gradually grew more distinct. They moved little. One of
the crew, a monk of the Avianese Gentheist Church, talked them
through meditative breathing exercises. They were down to eighteen
thousand feet at the end of the first hour. Slowly the captain bled
the air from the cabin, and breathing became more difficult.

"I thought the idea was to save air," said the mother of the
children.

"The *Titan* is descending more slowly in the denser air, so I don't
know how long it will take to reach a level safe for parachuting."

"What do you mean?"

"The pressure in here is that of two thousand feet above the
ground, and we are nine times higher. The air outside can be breathed
but it is very thin. Decompression sickness will soon kill us if we
open the door and jump now, so we need to slowly accustom our
bodies to the lower pressure."

"And if we are approaching the salt water before we are accus-
tomed?"

"Then we take a chance and jump anyway."

After two hours they were a mere mile above ground.

"We are over Southmoor territory," said the captain. "Not a good
place to jump."

"Fras Captain, will we reach the Rochestrian Commonwealth?"
asked the watch officer.

"Yes. In ten minutes, I estimate. Now listen to me, and listen carefully. The pressure outside must be nearly the same as in here, so I am about to open the door. Go to your cabins and collect all your money and papers. Put on the heaviest clothing and boots that you have, then come back here for your parachutes."

The air outside the cabin was cold but breathable as they merged, but Captain Terian discovered another problem. There had only been twelve parachutes aboard the *Titan*. Eight had been taken by those who had jumped at twelve miles.

The passengers quickly returned, dressed in coats and boots. The officers shed their jackets for bush coats.

"The mother, Watch Officer Varel, Frelle Tarmia, and yourself will have parachutes," the captain said to Seegan as he helped him into a parachute's harness. "You and Varel can hold a child each as you jump."

"That is only six of us, Fras Captain."

"I know. You will have to look after the group on the ground. Get them to Rochester and the safe house."

"You are going down with the wing?"

"In the absence of any realistic suggestions to the contrary, yes. I hereby surrender my authority to you, beginning when the *Titan* crashes."

Two hours and forty-five minutes after the invisible pulse of electromagnetic energy had crippled the *Titan*, the captain helped the six other survivors out through the rent in the sunwing's fabric made by the musketeer. In another five minutes all six were alive and gathering together on the ground in the darkness while the sunwing glided on, trailing smoke from the central section. Aboard the *Titan*, the fires set by the captain consumed sensitive documents and maps while he exchanged clothing with one of the dead passengers.

The ground was very close as the captain selected a bulkhead and put his back to it. A minute went by, another, then yet another. With a ground speed of fifty miles per hour, the *Titan* scraped trees, fences, and bushes, then ploughed into lush grass and rich soil. Branches, posts, and rocks gouged through living cellulose spars, ribs, and fabric. Bushes and small trees were torn from the ground,

and electrical engines were ripped from their mountings and wen
tumbling across the fields. Then there was silence and stillness.

The full span of the *Titan* lay like a crumpled blue ribbon acros
the green pastures of the northern Rochestrian Commonwealth, stil
complete to a distant viewer, but internally shattered, with its belly
torn out. Over two dozen sheep had died as they slept, shepherd:
had run screaming, mothers in nearby hamlets had dragged thei
children under the beds, the Kyabram town militia had been calle
out, and every dog that had been under the *Titan*'s glide path wa:
barking hysterically. It was dawn before anyone dared to approach
the immense wreck, and it was to be several days before it had beer
completely explored. No survivors were found.

Some distance away, Watch Officer Seegan quickly gathered the
survivors together and had the parachutes bundled and buried. He
led his charges across a field, then along a hedge-fringed lane, walking for a dot on a line map that he had salvaged. As they hurriec
through the darkness, they rehearsed their story and roles.

"So who are we?" Seegan asked the youngest child for the
third time.

"We're hikers, returning from a picnic."

"And where do we come from?"

"The Central Confederation. We're going to the paraline wayside, to take the pedal train to Rochester."

"Good, good. And what do you say if anyone asks you if you
saw the huge flying thing?"

"My mother told me not to talk to strangers."

"Excellent, you have it."

By now they had turned onto a cattle track and were picking
their way wearily among the muddy puddles and piles of droppings.

"How much further?" asked the child peevishly.

"According to the map five miles, but walk slowly; we want to
arrive after dawn. Now try to look as if you enjoy this sort of thing.
Remember, everyone, we are aviads and this is a human mayorate.
The actual killing of aviads has been illegal in the Rochestrian Commonwealth for the past twenty years, but a lynch mob of yokels will
not bother about fine points of legislation."

It took many hours of hard and determined tramping to reach the wayside. The dot on the map that denoted Stanhope wayside was transformed into an earth and timber platform, a rain shelter, the wayside master's cottage, some sheep pens, and a dozen cottages. As the sun rose the children sat sullenly, huddled together for warmth. The adults bought tickets and bread at the wayside kiosk.

"Did you see that thing that flew over?" asked the serving girl.

"The long thing, trailing smoke and flames, yes, we did, from our camp," replied Watch Officer Seegan.

"I was so frightened. My Garren and I, we were awake and, well, we were awake. He grabbed his birdshot musket and set off after it with the Stanhope town militia. Garren's so brave."

"But it was flying. How could they catch it?"

"Oh, it crashed. You can just see the wreck from the town's lookout tower."

"Oh. Does he think it might be dangerous?"

"Silly, it's not alive," the girl giggled. "It's like a paraline train, just a machine. Except that it's pushed by forbidden engines, not honest muscle. Garren says they might capture evil heretics in the wreck and turn them over to the Gentheist church."

"Ah, yes. Good, good."

"They're bird people, those aviads. Dirty folk, they sleep in big nests made of twigs, and lay eggs."

"Really? I have never met any."

"Strange things happenin'. Why, a couple of hours before that thing crashed, the wayside master's new clock and desk calculor both burned, and at exactly the same time, too. Both powered by electrical essence, they were. Electrical essence is really lightning, you know. What I says is that lightning is always lightning, you just can't tame it. My, we were runnin' about with pails of sand and water, we were lucky that the cottage didn't burn down."

"How amazing! We were far from all that. Close to nature. That is the saying of all hikers: Close to nature, close to Deity."

"Aye, yes, that's good. Where are you folk from? You don't sound like locals."

"Hah, you are very observant. We are from the Central Confederation, on a holiday. The Confederation Guild of Accountants Hiking Club. See, my papers."

"Oooh. Sorry, likc, I don't read."

"We have just hiked from Kyabram. Lovely city."

"You hiked from Kyabram? Gor, you're lucky to still be alive and carryin' your purse. Dangerous country, freebooters, you know."

"Really? We were not told."

"You should always check at the city constable's watchouse."

"Really? In future, we shall do that always. Now we are going to Rochester to see the sights."

"Rochester, eh? My Garren once went there. He were beaten up and robbed."

"Really? We must be careful."

Their accents were unusual to the gi l, but their Austaric was easily intelligible. Minutes later the white form of a pedal train appeared on the paraline tracks, and the *Tita* 's survivors gathered together as the long bentwood and canvas pedal train reached the wayside. The train's guards eyed the group carefully before deciding that they were harmless. They climbed aboard into the pairs of double cabins, settled into the benches, and prepared to push. The train's captain blew his warning whistle, then everyone aboard strained against the pedals as the brake blocks were released and the long, sleek train glided out of the wayside.

Seegan was alone in his cabin, and felt like doing anything but pedal for the two hours needed to reach Rochester. The *Titan* was gone, ripped from the skies by a disaster that should not have been possible. It had been built of independent modules, yet every system on the gigantic aircraft had failed. How? he kept asking himself. Sabotage? That was unlikely, as most of the *Titan* had been inaccessible. Somehow it had been just too big to crash, to be aboard the *Titan* was like walking on solid ground. He pushed listlessly at the pedals, thinking of the captain. He had gone down with the sicken giant, he had taken responsibility for the catastrophe that was none of his doing. Beyond the window slit the late winter sun was slowly climbing in the northeastern sky. The pedal train began to slow for the next wayside. They were to pass through Cooper and the junction town of Elmore before reaching Rochester itself. Cooper wayside was even smaller than Stanhope, and there was only a single figure on the platform. A shuffling, weary figure, bowed with fatigue, all muddied and—the watch officer scrambled to open his cabin's hatch.

"Fras Terian, over here!" he called, even before the pedal train had stopped.

He raced back along the platform, then escorted the captain up to his cabin, talking loudly all the way.

"How many times have I told you, stick together when we go hiking. There are freebooters in this country, you were lucky you weren't robbed. The rest of us were worried sick about you. In here, there's a space in my cabin."

In all, the captain of the *Titan* had saved seven out of twenty-two who had been aboard, including all of the women and children. His stricken craft had taken almost three hours to crash, but he had been there until the very end. Now he did not even have the strength to pedal. He sat listlessly, watching the sky, trees, and pastureland.

"So, the crash was not too bad?" asked Seegan.

"No crash is good," Terian replied.

"But it was good enough that you survived."

"What can I say? I stood with my back to a bulkhead and waited. There were a few lurches, then everything wrenched and collapsed around me. I burst through the bulkhead, hit the one behind that, broke it too, and ended up in the control cabin. Everything was silent. The forward canopy was smashed, and there was a dead sheep beside me. The crash had frightened all the local humans away, so I crawled out and made for some nearby woodlands. Once I was under cover I got my map and compass out and set off for the par-uline."

"By the sound of it you are not badly injured."

"My right arm is broken, and probably a few ribs too. There is a lump on my head and my ankle is twisted."

"Ah . . . but better than being dead."

"Not so!" moaned Terian with a hand over his eyes. "*I lost the Titan.*"

"Don't take it so hard, there was nothing you could have done."

"It must have been sabotage, I was not vigilant—"

"Stop it! I am your commanding officer now, remember? Listen to me! The serving wench at the wayside said that all electrical machines in the town burned, apparently at the same time as the *Titan* was crippled. Did that happen at Cooper too?"

"Cooper is a privy pit with a ticket kiosk. They had no electrical machines. Seegan, I lost the *Titan*! Nobody has *ever* lost a sunwing."

"I would imagine that all sunwings have just been lost, and I doubt that most people aboard were as lucky as us. We reach Elmore in a half hour; I wager that everything electrical has burned there as well, and the same will have happened in Rochester."

"But why? I don't understand."

"Mirrorsun; it has done similar things before. In 1708 GW it destroyed an army with some invisible power. Now it has decided that electrical essence machines are also annoying, so it has destroyed them too."

"But Mirrorsun built the *Titan*, out of things mined on the moon."

"Terian, I have a few facts, not every answer. What is certain is that you were not responsible for the *Titan*'s loss. Now, then, you were my commanding officer until recently and I need informed advice. What are we to do, Fras?"

Terian rubbed his eyes, then began to drag himself out of the miasma of self-pity, misery, shame, and pain where he had been wallowing. They were fugitives and refugees, but they were alive and free, and not entirely without friends.

"If our papers get us past the border post at Elmore, we must stay together and travel on to Rochester tonight. It is a big city, and if all electrical machines really have burned, there will be plenty of chaos for us to hide behind. The safe hostelry will welcome us."

"Terian, remember that none of this was your fault."

"That may be the truth, but history will be written by how I am judged."

The Rochestrian Commonwealth, Eastern Australica

In Rochester, the first official sign that the world had changed came within three minutes of the massive electromagnetic pulses from the sky that destroyed every circuit on the planet. Armed Dragon Librarians of the rank of Orange, Red, and Green hurried into the great, domed reading room of Libris, led by a Dragon Blue. The readers looked up uneasily, as did the duty librarian in charge. One student, Rangen, noticed that a new electric clock was trickling a streamer of smoke into the air. The Dragon Blue strode to the raised central desk and struck the gong for attention.

"The reading room will be cleared immediately!" she declared. "Gather your personal effects and leave."

The combined clattering, groans, and muttering of two hundred readers echoed up to the dome. Helicos and Rangen were a little slow in packing, and attracted the attention of a Dragon Green.

"Anything you can't carry by the second gong gets left here," he said firmly, his flintlock drawn and its barrel resting back on his shoulder.

"But, Fras, closing time is not until midnight," protested Rangen. "We have exams—"

"No readers allowed in the library, young Fras," replied the Dragon Green. "That's the order of the Highliber."

Nine minutes after the electric calculor had begun to smoke, there was not a single reader in the domed reading room. They were not ejected from the Libris grounds at once, however. The readers were made to form several queues in the plaza just behind the main gates, and the notes of every one of the annoyed and flustered readers were inspected at portable desks, by the light of lanterns. Dragon Green librarians questioned everyone about their courses and past studies, then they were allowed to go, although under the escort of Dragon Orange guards.

"Suppose it's the theft of some very rare book," said Rangen to Helicos as they stood waiting.

"Have you been stealing again to supplement your scholarship?" asked Helicos.

"Not from here," replied Rangen.

Rangen watched as other readers were cleared to go. Being a gifted student of mathematics who specialized in associative logic, he had a tendency to look for patterns in everything around him— particularly in the mundane backdrop of everyday life. He watched for any variation in the treatment of those being questioned, but there was none. Now he looked further afield. A student of ancient Anglaic dialects was marched away to the distant gatehouse by a Dragon Orange. They reached the gatehouse, walked beneath the arch, and turned left. Rangen listened to what several more students were saying as he neared the Dragon Green questioners. Economics, sciences, mathematics, law, history; there seemed to be no connection between the way that they turned at the gatehouse and what they studied— law left, but economics right—sometimes. All those taking history left. Those with mixed disciplines were turned in mixed directions.

Helicos reached the Dragon Green.

"Name and field of study?"

"Helicos Theon, University of Rochester, studying mathematics at the level of third year."

"But Fras, your notes are to do with Archaic Anglaic," he said as he examined the notes that Helicos had placed on his desk.

"I'm doing a short course of scholarly languages to assist my studies of ancient mathematical systems."

"Class C," the Dragon Green said to his scribe, then he turned back to Helicos. "You may go."

Helicos was already walking away beside a Dragon Orange when Rangen was chilled by a sudden suspicion. He began to unpack his notes very slowly.

"Name and field of study?"

"Rangen Derris, University of Rochester," began Rangen, who then dropped a sheaf of poorpaper to the flagstones of the plaza.

"Hurry, hurry, there's others who wish to be out of here," said the Dragon Green.

Rangen gathered up the notes, dropped some of them again—and out of the corner of his eye saw Helicos guided to the right by his Dragon Orange escort. The door to the right did not lead to the street outside. Rangen stood up and spread the papers on the librarian's desk.

"Rangen Derris, student of languages," he said quickly and softly, desperately trying not to stammer.

"Your notes are from the same texts as that last student," observed the librarian.

"Why, yes. He is my friend; I am helping him with his Archaic Anglaic for some mathematics examination."

"So you must know some mathematics as well?"

"Not at all, that was why I chose languages, Fras Dragon Green. I have no talent for figures."

The librarian glanced along the queue of restive students behind Rangen, then shook his head.

"Class R," he said to his scribe, then indicated the gate to Rangen with his thumb.

The librarian did not notice that Rangen had suddenly become suspiciously efficient while repacking his notes. Rangen began walking, a Dragon Orange beside him.

"What is all this about?" asked Rangen as the gatehouse loomed nearer.

"If you think a Dragon Orange would be told anything, Fras, then you have obviously never worked in a library. Turn left, and proceed to the outer gate down that corridor. No loitering near the gate when you are outside."

Rangen stole a glance at the door to the right. Four Tiger Dragons stood before a closed door, and two of them had their flintlocks drawn.

Rangen was no more relieved when he cleared the outer gates of the library walls and emerged into the darkened streets of Rochester. Knots of students were gathered here and there, obviously waiting for friends to emerge. Rangen kept walking, noting the time on a nearby tower's ancient mechanical clock.

Mathematicians! The Dragon Librarians were taking mathematicians into custody. This had happened before, years before he was born. Mathematicians had been slowly culled from the universities, streets, towns, schools, and even monasteries. They had worked for years in the first of the human-powered calculating machines, the mighty Calculor of Libris. Some had spent a decade in slavery before the early electrical essence calculors had been introduced. A few had been shot while trying to escape, and others had even been put in battle calculors and sent to war. Now it was happening again, but this time it was not a stealthy culling but the sweep of a mighty sickle that harvested everyone who could count with reasonable skill.

Rangen stopped at Wakefield's Electrical Essence Machineries, and was surprised to see lantern light inside. He glanced about for any suspicious watchers, then entered. He was immediately struck by the stench of burnt wax and paper insulation, and noticed sand strewn about on the floor and benches. Wakefield and two apprentices were gathered around a charred tangle that might once have been a bank of calculor relay switches.

"Fras Wakefield, I had an order for a custom relay rack due next week, I thought I'd check on it," Rangen called across the shop.

"Better come back next month, Fras," the artisan called back. "There was a freak lightning bolt. It roasted every circuit in my shop."

Much to Wakefield's surprise, Rangen thanked him and hurried away without so much as a single curse. Mathematicians were being taken behind heavily guarded doors by Dragon Librarians, and after electrical switches had suddenly burned to cinders and slag. Years ago the manual, slave-powered calculors had been displaced by electrical calculors, but now the reverse was happening. Rangen Derris was one of the few mathematicians in Rochester to have reached the correct conclusion before the Highliber's net ensnared him. He turned down a laneway, then another. Crouching down behind a pile of rotting garbage he discarded his notes. Next he took a knife to his clothing before rubbing it into the grime on the cobblestones.

Before long a filthy beggar emerged onto the street, leaning heavily on a staff made from splintery packing-case wood. A length of cloth covered one eye, and he had hacked his lush, neat beard down to an unkempt stubble. He watched as fifteen men and women wearing crests of the Guild of Accountants were marched past by the city militia on the way to . . . where? The watchouse was not in that direction, but Libris was. A few late-night revelers cheered to see the accountants being marched away. Nobody paid Rangen any attention.

Rangen sat down with his back against a wall, placed a broken pottery bowl beside his feet and sat in silence. For now he was safe, but what next? If he tried to flee the city there would be guards, inspectors, and Dragon Librarians at every gate. If he got past them, there would be more guards, inspectors, and Dragon Librarians in every regional city and town. A copper coin clinked into his bowl.

"Blessings of the Deity upon your house," said Rangen in a mixture of foreign accents.

Presently he fell asleep.

In the morning he awoke, and was dismayed to find that the past night had not just been a particularly harrowing dream. Again he sorted through his alternatives. If he fled to the frontiers, there would be bounty hunters waiting for anyone numerate enough to complain if they were not given the right change by a vendor. He would be safe enough in the wilderness, but he would not last long. He had only slept outdoors twice. Once had been when he had been too drunk to find his college after a revel and had spent the night in a flower bed in the university gardens. The past night had been the second time. Another copper landed in his bowl.

"Blessings of the Deity upon your house."

He had some silver in his purse, a gold royal concealed in the heel of each boot, an eating knife and the clothes that he was wearing. *Clink.*

"Blessings of the Deity on your house."

Clink.

Three coppers, collected in as many minutes. Admittedly that had been during the rush after the shift change in a nearby bakery, yet three coppers would probably buy a cut of bread. This was certainly easier than hunting possums in the forests. The weather was mild, and he could probably crawl into the stables at the university and sleep on the straw.

He started off for the university, displaying a limp and hunching his shoulders over. Before long a line of riders appeared ahead, escorting five covered wagons. Rangen cowered against a building as they passed, noting the faint, muffled sounds from the wagons as they passed. Gagged people would sound like that. Gagged people trying to attract attention before they reached the gates of Libris and vanished from sight forever.

When Rangen reached the university his worst fears were exceeded. Groups of students were huddled together, whispering, while cloaked editors scuttled between buildings as if afraid to be seen in the open. The doors to the Department of Mathematics stood open, and the latch had been smashed from the wood. Rangen looked longingly at his college dormitory, but he dared not enter it to claim the clothes, books, border papers, oddments, and money that were all his. Two mounted Dragon Librarians were observing the scene from near the gates, and more would surely be lurking about in disguise.

Rangen knew that without the protection of the Beggars' Guild he could be beaten up and robbed by any bully boy who thought that he might carry the price of a pint of ale, but to gain membership of the guild he had to be inspected by a medician. *That* was out of the question. He limped toward the laundaric and rapped timidly at the open door. The turbaned head of the washerman bobbed up from beneath the counter.

"Off, going away, out!" he shouted. "No beggarings!"

"Please, noble Fras, I'se wantin' work, like," replied Rangen.

"No beggarings. Out!"

"I can stoke tubs a-night, I'se lame, not weak."

The washerman of the laundaric pointed and opened his mouth again, but now Rangen was pointing—directly at him.

"Just a moment, now," he said, letting his new accent slip. "Northmoor sash tied up like an Alspring turban, a Kalgoorlie kaftan, and a very unconvincing Southmoor accent."

"I am Kamis bal-Krees, laundaric master from the distant mayorate of North—argh!"

Rangen had struck off his makeshift turban with his crutch.

"All the way from your father's estate in Rutherglen, by the look of your hairstyle."

"I surrender, I surrender!" the washerman cried, raising his hands. "Grand and merciful Dragon Librarian, master of disguise—"

"Shut up and keep your bloody voice down!" hissed Rangen, as he pulled the door closed. "Now, who are you—really?"

"I—I am Rhyn Ponsington-Taraven, student of general studies and youngest son of Lord Ponsington-Taraven, in the mayorate of Rutherglen."

"Ponsington-Taraven, ah yes, I have heard your name spoken among the mathematics editors. You took five years to pass some subject like Basic Arithmetic for Very Stupid People with Very Rich Fathers."

"I say, that's being a bit harsh. It was Introductory Mathematics and Commercial Methods . . . or was it Introduction to Commercial Mathematics and, ah, er—"

"And my bet is that you dashed in here when the Dragon Librarians arrived to abduct anyone who could count more than their allocation of fingers and toes, noted that the washerman had already been carted away, and tried to take his place."

"Why, how did you—"

"Have you a razor here?"

"A razor? Why, yes. The former washerman's effects were left behind when he was carried away."

Rangen hurriedly sorted through a rack of clothing.

"Take this, this, and this, shave your head, then come back here. You are now Bandilsi ba'Krees, a refugee Southmoor eunuch."

"I say, but I was calling myself Kamis bal-Krees."

"Which is a mixture of Northmoor and Alspring words, and which would get you arrested just as soon as you opened your mouth and moved your tongue. You are now working for me."

"Oh yes, I—what? I say, *I'm* meant to be running this laundaric."

"Where is the soap?"

"The soap. Ah . . ."

"That blue jar on your right with *soap* written on it. Where do you get water?"

"I—"

"By lowering a bucket into that hole beneath the sign that says Caution—Well. Where is the register of garments?"

"What's that?"

"That book on the counter in front of you."

"Yes, well, er . . . granted, I have had little time to familiarize myself with the procedures here, but—"

"Fras Rhyn, a dog wearing an academic cloak who tells customers that their laundry will be ready by 'Woof! Woof!' would make a more convincing master of the campus laundaric than you. If you want to stay out of the new Libris calculor for longer than it takes for the next member of the Libris Espionage Constables to walk through the door, you will work here as *my eunuch* and do *exactly* as I say. Agreed?"

"Well, I do concede that I am not sufficiently endowed with lower-class cunning to maintain this disguise for long, but—but do I have to be a *real* eunuch? I mean I'm rather attached to—I mean it would probably hurt to—"

"Fras Rhyn, *that* is *your* option, but you must at least shave your head. Oh, and rub in some umber brown to hide the paleness of the skin. Go now, hurry!"

Before ten minutes had passed a new customer entered the laundaric. To Rangen's eyes she was no more genuine that Rhyn or himself. By now Rangen was dressed in the former washerman's tunic and apron.

"Ah, pretty Frelle, how can I be helpin' ye?"

The woman frowned at him, hooking her thumbs into her belt.

"I was told that the washerman had been arrested."

"Aye, ye were told truth."

"Then who are you?"

"I be Skew."

"I—what?"

"I be Skew, the washerman's deputy. I were a musketeer, aye, and a corporal. Bone in me leg were broken by a shot, but healed skew, like. Tha's me name, Skew, 'cause I'm, like, skew. I'se strong an' willin', but, and I can do anythin' if its not ter be done at a run."

"Can you count?"

"Aye, yeah, ter ten, aye. Like the washerman did the countin' till today, but nothin' cost more than ten coppers in here, so I'se able ter take over."

"So, you can count coppers when students pay for washing?"

"Ah, aye. I can write names, too. If anyone comes in, I takes their washing an' chalks their names on a slate ter go with the bag. And I'se got a eunuch fer to do stokin'."

"A Southmoor? Is he educated?"

"Fras Bandilsi? Nay. Can't write or count, but he's strong. Now, what can I be washin'?"

"Only yourself," muttered the Dragon Librarian, who turned and walked out again.

Rhyn emerged from the back of the laundaric. His head was shaved, but he had rubbed the umber brown into his face alone, leaving the rest of his head gleaming white. Rangen shook his head.

"Your wages are fifty—ah, fifteen coppers a day, and you can lodge in the lumber room."

"But, I say, there's no bed there."

"Yes, there is, it's cunningly disguised as a pile of hessian sacks. Just evict the cockroaches and it will be just like home."

As Rangen stretched out on the former washerman's bed that night he contemplated his good fortune. In just twenty-four hours he had become a fugitive, commenced a new career as a beggar, changed careers to work in the university's laundaric, and given himself a promotion to laundaric master. Now he had accommodation and financial security, but best of all he had anonymity.

Mounthaven, North America

On the other side of the world, it was late afternoon when the electrical devices of the world had died. It had been a day after a massive air battle over the wastelands of central North America. A long and particularly brutal war had been won, a war engineered from a continent halfway around the world. The invaders and their allies had been crushed completely.

The following day, when dawn had risen over those celebrating victory in Forian, some scholars noticed that their experimental electrical devices had been reduced to char and metal slag. Few cared, for there were matters of much greater importance to deal with. The Call, the cetezoids' strange and deadly mind weapon, was gone. For two thousand years it had confined humans to tiny areas in the North American highlands, but with it gone there was suddenly a huge frontier to settle. However, the restraints of the Call had also shaped the American nations and royal houses, in fact it underpinned the very system. Already their rulers were feeling anxious.

It was late in the morning when the victorious Council of Mounthaven Airlords met to discuss the consequences of what had just happened. The walls of the Forian palace were still pockmarked with bullet holes and the glass was missing from many windows, but the jubilant Yarronese had cleaned away the dust and debris. In the Chamber of Deliberations tapestries had been hung over the worst of the damage to the frescos, and carpets covered the mutilated mosaics and tiles of the floors.

First there was the procession of airlords from the palace wingfield, where their tiny gunwings stood with the artisans and ground crews. Cheering, jubilant crowds flung spring flowers into their path while bands played marches and royal anthems, and for once the guards that marched with them were merely for spectacle. Wardens and other nobles marched too, all with their jewel-and-gilt-encrusted flight jackets sparkling and gleaming in the sun, although many wore bandages as well. Waves of louder cheers rippled out along the avenue as particularly well known heroes of the war passed. There was the invincible Airlord Sartov, who had transformed the Yarronese from being fugitives in their own domain to the leaders of a victorious alliance. Warden Bronlar Jemarial, with forty clear air victories, was the first and greatest of Mounthaven's female wardens. The bandaged Warden Serjon Feydamor who had bombed the royal palace at Condelor and killed the Bartolican airlord, came behind her. He had an unprecedented 104 victory symbols sewed in gilt onto the collar and shoulders of his flight jacket.

The vanquished Bartolicans were there too, having joined the alliance against the Australican invaders after Greater Bartolica was split into five lesser domains. Airlord Samondel of Leover, the Airlord of Highland Bartolica, was the only female airlord ever to engage in clear air fighting, and had the symbols for two enemy gunwings and three sailwings sewn into the throat of her flight jacket's collar. At nineteen, she was also the youngest airlord alive. Rather than cheers, a trough of silence and muttering trailed through the Yarronese crowd as the Bartolicans passed. It was not the place of commoners to heckle American royalty, but nobody was forcing them to cheer, either. Eggs, rotten fruit, and vegetable scraps were reserved for the shabby line of captured invaders from Australica, whose hair had been soaked in lubricant grease and smothered in feathers. There were only nine of them, all captured aviad artisans. Their warrior masters had fought to the death, or killed themselves rather than submit to capture.

As the parade reached the palace gates, each airlord broke out and marched through alone while the others in the parade streamed off to the right and left to be cheered by yet more crowds. When the last of the Bartolican airlords had entered the palace, the battered, splintered gates were pushed shut.

Airlord Sartov gave the keynote address, and his words were crammed with warnings. The whole of the North American continent was suddenly open for all humans to settle. Mounthaven had the most advanced technology in the known world, but Mexhaven had several times its population. Mounthaven was at the crossroads of destiny only a day after its greatest victory in two thousand years.

"We could maintain our traditional way of life in Mounthaven and defend our frontiers," concluded Sartov, "but in a decade we would be ringed by Mexhaven farms and warlords. In two decades we would be running a trade deficit with Mexhaven settler domains, and in five we would be losing wars with them. Our only possible course is to expand into the new and fertile frontier lands before anyone else. I favor claiming a vast stretch of frontier, and declaring that any Mexhaven settlers who enter it are subjects of the Mounthaven airlords. Palaces and wingfields can be built, and new domains can be proclaimed after a suitable time."

Sartov resumed his chair, and the herald announced that Airlord Samondel would now lead off the debate.

"As all of you know, much has been learned about Australican artisanry during the war," she began, standing at the podium with her arms folded and speaking without notes. "We know that humanity has split into two species there, the featherheads and humans like us. The featherheads' hair looks like long feathers under a microscope, but they are different in many other ways. The Australican humans have suffered just as much at the hands of the featherheads as we have, but there is evidence that some featherheads of goodwill are allied with Australican humans. Most Australicans support us, and I have interviewed one of the military advisors that they sent here to help us during the war. The linguist Darien has described how large animals have survived in Australica, large animals available to our ancestors when they began to settle this continent two thousand five hundred years ago. Horses, ponies, donkeys, camels, and cattle. They also have sheep and goats for the lush frontier grasses. Their kangaroos can thrive on near-desert forage, but most important of all are their horses. Horses can walk with loads over trackless wasteland, while eating whatever grows at their feet.

"Airlords can overfly any frontier, but it is those on the ground who control it. We could put in tracks for our steam trams and trains, but Mexhaven militias can tear up the tracks faster than we can lay them. Besides, according to my royal statistician, there is not enough spare iron in Mounthaven for such a venture. Squads of Mounthaven carbineers riding horses would be exceedingly fast and mobile, and could shatter the ranks of many times their number in enemy infantry. I propose that the entire wardenry of Mounthaven be sworn to both mapping the new frontiers from the air, and to procuring horses and other large animals from Australica. Thank you."

"Warden Drell of Montrass," called the herald as she sat down to a buzz of surprised comments and whispering.

"Saireme Airlord Samondel, I too have a royal statistician here," declared the young man, who was only months older than Samondel. "According to ancient maps, the overland route to Australica is over eleven thousand miles of ice, desert, forest, swamp, and jungle. It also involves crossing at least seven short stretches of salt water, and as we have been told by the Australican envoy, the sea intelligences have ended the scourge of the Call—but only as long as the seas are left to them. There can be no sea travel."

Samondel waved her interjection pennant.

"Darien said that on Australican shores, beached whale animals are rescued where possible, and in return they permit crashed flyers to swim ashore," she countered. "Semme Darien has assured us of this. It can apply to us too."

"Nevertheless, they are quite clear that no boats will ever be permitted," Drell countered. "Wingfields will have to be built to cross the stretches of seawater, transport wings the size of Yarronese super-regals will be needed to ferry humans and horses through the air, and fuel for the giant wings will have to be transported up to eleven thousand miles. My statistician estimates that the endeavor would take fifteen years and consume twenty-five times the money and resources that the war has cost Mounthaven. If hostile tribes are found anywhere along the way, it will add to the cost and take even longer. Besides, Darien also says that there are religious prohibitions against engines in Australica."

"Warden Samondel of Highland Bartolica," called the herald.

"My statistician concurs with yours," she announced, then paused for emphasis. The airlords glanced to each other, then looked back at Samondel expectantly. "I have, however, learned through my intelligence advisors of the capacities of the Yarronese super-regals. Airlord Sartov, do I have your permission to speak about the range of your aircraft, your marvels of Yarronese artisanry?"

Sartov glowered, but nodded.

"At a cruising speed of one hundred miles per hour, a super-regal can stay in the air for twenty-five hours. With all weapons and fittings removed to make way for extra tanks and five hundred pounds of load, a super-regal could fly for thirty hours. Using midair refueling from a second super-regal flying only part of the way, this could be extended to forty-three hours."

"True, but according to the ancient maps the largest gap over seawater is only three hundred miles," said Sartov, waving his interjection pennant.

"On Warden Drell's route, yes. Examine an ancient map of the Pacific Ocean, however, and you will see that wingfields could be established on three of the larger islands that are no more than two thousand miles apart. The route would be a mere seven thousand miles, and once the three wingfields are built we would need no more than a large volume of compression spirit for the engines."

"Seven thousand miles over water?" exclaimed Airlord Drell, holding his interjection pennant high in the air. "Madness!"

"Four leaps of two thousand miles or less."

"But each super-regal takes as much compression spirit as eight gunwings! Add the spirit burned to transport spirit to the island wingfields and each flight would take more compression spirit than Montrose, Senner, and Highland Bartolica normally use in a year."

"Yes, but with all of Mounthaven's compression spirit farms and distilleries working together, I calculate that we could establish three wingfields and reach Australica within four months. The cost would be *five hundred times* less than using the land route, and a hundred times quicker."

"But what about the Australican religious prohibition against fueled engines?"

"Semme Darien said *steam* engines. Our wings are powered by compression engines."

There is only one thing worse than an impossibly expensive scheme, and that is a realistically expensive scheme. The debate raged for another forty minutes. The airlords worked figures out on slates, waved interjection pennants, and shouted proposals and counterproposals. Sartov was curiously quiet for the entire time, although he did exchange a few words with the Cosdoran airlord. Suddenly he interjected.

"My current super-regals could carry only two horses each, based on their estimated weight. Even then they would have to be lying down."

"One might select only young horses," suggested Samondel.

Sartov thought for a moment then nodded.

"Very well, then. If the larger domains were to donate twenty gunwing compression engines, and a very large quantity of fabric, wire, and flight-standard wood, my artisans could build two super-regals that could remain in the air for fifty hours and carry six young horses," Sartov declared.

"While each gulps down as much spirit as ten gunwings for those fifty hours," scoffed the Montrassen. "Even that does not include the spirit needed to transport spirit to the island wingfields."

"But it could be done," said Samondel.

To the surprise of most present, Airlord Sartov agreed with her once more.

"Include a few bags of barley and sunflower seeds on each flight, and we could be growing enough compression spirit locally to halve the cost within a year," he suggested. "With a flight every week, we could have three hundred horses within a year."

"Airlord Samondel was saying that one horse carbineer is worth ten infantry carbineers," said the Cosdoran.

"Indeed!" exclaimed South Bartolica's airlord. "We had best introduce the death penalty for horse stealing."

"Or selling them to Mexhaven," added Sartov.

He gazed across at Samondel, stroking his beard, then leaned over to South Bartolica's airlord.

"How did a girl of nineteen with barely any flight experience until only months ago manage to think of this?" he whispered. "Where does she get such drive?"

"We grew up surrounded by engineers and artisans, Saireme Sartov. She also studied history and ancient languages—oh, and mathematics."

"Fine and suitable subjects for a well-bred girl, yet now they are the very skills that the rest of us do not have. I hear that Warden Feydamor plucked her royal flower."

"In exchange for his, yes. But last night he slept with Bronlar, and they intend to marry."

"On further thought, sense begins to emerge. Samondel loses a legendary hero to Bronlar, another legendary hero, leaving her as the airlord of a defeated, third-rate domain."

"True, and Bronlar has eight times more clear air victories than Samondel."

"But Samondel's were in a single day. This would be Samondel's chance to become a legend without having to wait for another war or fight thirty-five duels."

"Why? To get Serjon Feydamor back?" the South Bartolican laughed softly.

"No possibility. The marriage of Serjon and Bronlar has been announced for next month. Even the greatest of royal weddings in history will not rival it for sheer size and splendor. The Condelor palace will be the setting, with all airlords present. No, I think that Samondel's pride is at stake here. As Airlord Samondel Leover, who established a path over the greatest ocean in the world, her name will become immortal. In a hundred years people will say, 'By the way, did you know that Samondel treated a hero of the Great War to a couple of nights in her bed when he was feeling depressed? What was his name again?' "

"Point taken. How much would you say that she weighs?"

"When stripped for action with Serjon Feydamor? One hundred ten pounds at most."

"That's twenty more than Bronlar, but less than any male warden or airlord. I hear she asked the Australican agent, Semme Darien, to provide her with a common Australican language's basic grammar and vocabulary this morning. Austaric, is its name."

"Ah, so she definitely hopes to lead this venture to Australica."

"I think she may be the only one qualified to do so."

"How will you vote?"

"Affirmative, I should think."

All the time that they had been whispering, the debate on Samondel's proposal had raged on. When the division was called, the

vote was nine for Samondel's proposal and nine against, but as presiding airlord Sartov did not have a vote. Convention was that any
motion was lost on a tied council vote, but there was a single option
still left open.

"Is there any dispute against the count that declares this motion
lost?" called the herald.

Samondel waved her interjection pennant.

"Saireme Airlord Samondel of the house of Leover, you may
state your dispute with any vote."

Samondel rose from her cockpit-seat chair and strode across a
stretch of uncarpeted floor, her boots echoing like gunshots with
every step. She stopped in front of Airlord Drell, slowly removed
the glove from her left hand, then backhanded it viciously across his
face. Three of the gemstones on the jeweled and gilt-embroidered
glove tore scratches across his right cheek. Samondel offered the
glove to Drell.

"I say that you led the vote against my motion out of revenge
against me for the invasion of your domain," said Samondel clearly
and slowly. "You do not have the interests of either this council,
Mounthaven, or even you own domain, at heart. I challenge your
vote as an airlord."

Drell felt his cheek, regarded the blood on his fingertips for a
moment, then snatched the glove from her.

"I accept your challenge."

"What stake do you call?" asked the somewhat rattled herald,
who had not been expecting anything remotely like this at the victory
meeting.

"I demand that Highland Bartolica become a province of my
domain in the event of Airlord Samondel of Leover's defeat."

"Airlord Drell Darontien of Montras accepts a clear air duel challenge," the herald pronounced.

News of the duel caused an instant sensation throughout Forian.
There was no word about the cause of the dispute, but within two

hours of the meeting breaking up, the compression engines of the gunwings *Starflower* and *Dirkfang* were chugging evenly as they warmed for ascent. The airlords' reception to honor the newly engaged Serjon and Bronlar was scheduled to last all afternoon, and through matters of precedent and protocol it could not be canceled. After the official announcement, however, Samondel appeared before the honored couple. Her knee-length red hair was bound up tightly, and her violet eyes were alarmingly wide.

"Airlord Drell Darontien and I wish to take leave of your celebration," said Samondel tersely. "We may be back in a half hour."

"Granted," said Serjon and Bronlar together.

Drell and Samondel walked away across the wingfield and past the royal guards. In the distance artisans swarmed over their shuddering gunwings.

"Drell wears Princess Varelfi's colors on his arm, but Samondel wears none," said Bronlar, staring after them.

"Very unlucky," responded Serjon.

"You have colors," said Bronlar pointedly.

"You wear them," said Serjon.

"But I am not dueling today."

"You have already returned my colors to me once. That was one time too many."

The Conciliator spoke with both airlords, but neither was interested in a retraction. He stepped back from them, and the wingfield adjunct cleared his throat.

"Saireme Airlords, do you swear to fight with chivalry and dignity, in honor of the ladies whose colors you wear?"

The words were a formula, but the formula had never before been applied to a woman fighting a clear air duel.

"I do," replied Drell with a smirk.

"I wear no colors because I fight for the honor of all Mounthaven," replied Samondel.

The airlords and wardens looking on applauded, and Drell cast a sneer at Samondel before they turned away and walked for their gunwings. Moments later the two gunwings were in the air, speeding away for towers at opposite ends of the city. Both circled the towers correctly, at summit height, then climbed sharply as they closed again. Samondel climbed more steeply in the Yarronese tri-wing, but Drell climbed faster. Both were inexperienced, fighting with energy and ferocity rather than savvy.

After a head-on pass with reaction guns blazing, they got into a climbing chase, circling each other as they clawed for height. Drell's gunwing was faster, but Samondel was able to turn sharply enough to get several bursts of reaction gunfire his way. The adjunct noted several hits to Drell's wings, then abruptly *Starflower* seemed to lose power, stalled, and dropped into a dive. Caught by surprise, Drell broke out of his climbing circle and hurtled after her. Samondel dropped into a steeper dive, but Drell was not anxious to lose the chance to catch *Starflower* from behind. The Yarronese gunwing had already walked shots across his wings, and he was behind on points. As *Starflower* roared down at the wingfield, crews and spectators began to scatter. Samondel began to pull out, as if attempting a high-speed touch with her wheels. This would grant Drell a forfeit, but he wanted a clear air victory and nothing less. At extreme range he opened fire, the throttle of his compression engine wide open. Some thirty feet above the ground *Starflower*'s three wings provided just sufficient lift to break out of the dive. For several seconds of intense terror Drell realized that *Dirkfang* had too much speed and not enough lift.

Dirkfang ploughed into the Forian palace wingfield at over two hundred miles per hour, marking its own end with a mighty, mushroom-shaped plume of smoke, flames, and dust. *Starflower* made a single circuit of the wingfield, then descended to the ascent strip and taxied up to the pennant pole. There was blood trickling from Samondel's nose as her crew helped her from the cockpit. By then it had been confirmed that Airlord Drell was most definitely dead. Samondel gave her report to the wingfield's adjunct.

"*Starflower*'s guns jammed while I was in the chasing climb, Sair Adjunct. It was only a matter of time before Drell realized that I was not able to shoot back, and after that he could keep doing break passes until he hit me. I decided to tempt him into a dive, hoping to make him think that I had lost my nerve and fled to make a touch. I was successful."

From behind her there was cry of surprise from the crewmen examining *Starflower*.

"These cartridges, midway in the belts," shouted the armorer. "They're stuck in with resin!"

The result was awarded to Samondel, and the scandalized Forian officials launched an immediate investigation of the sabotage to her ammunition belts. The airlords took early leave of the engagement celebration and returned to the palace. The late Drell's vote was struck from the proceedings of the previous meeting, and Venture Australica was signed into law.

As the sun was setting Airlord Sartov found Samondel at the crater in the wingfield that had been blasted out by *Dirkfang*'s crash.

"The last time I was standing by such a pit was at a coronation in Condelor, just before the Great War," she said. "I never dreamed that the next one I stood beside would be that of my own victim."

In the fading light Sartov could see that there were tears on her face.

"Did you know him?" the Airlord of Yarron asked.

"Yes. Last year there was talk of an alliance between Montrass and Greater Bartolica. A marriage between a prince and princess would have greatly aided negotiations. I traveled to Montrass to meet Drell. He stole a kiss in the palace gardens one afternoon. I pinched his bottom, he squeezed my breast, and I accidentally pulled his codpiece off just as our chaperons returned to check on us. There was meant to be a big reception that night to welcome me to Montrass, but even as I was dressing for it in my newest gown a Bartolican regal arrived and flew me back to Condelor. I thought it was because the prince and I had been behaving in a rather too familiar manner with each other, but the next day I discovered that our domains were at war."

"I'm sorry. The duel was your choice, however."

"And I stand by my choice. Walk safely in the great blackness,

Saireme Drell," Samondel said to the sky. "You were diverting to be with."

They began to walk back to the tents at the edge of the wingfield, and their path took them past the strange wing that had arrived the night before. Its upper surface was charred and shriveled, and the inside of the cockpit was a blackened ruin.

"This is how the featherheads got here from Australica," said Sartov. "It was built by intelligent machines in Mirrorsun's mines and factories on the moon. Fantastically light and powered by the sun during daylight. Apparently stored electrical essence drove it by night."

"Who destroyed it?"

"Nobody. The guards said that it suddenly began burning in the early hours of the morning. Some electrical devices in the University of Forian also burned about the same time."

"Vandalism. Perhaps by the same enemy who tampered with my ammunition?" asked Samondel.

"The damage was spontaneous, it just happened. Perhaps it was something to do with the Call vanishing."

Samondel touched the tip of a wing. To her surprise she realized that she could move it easily.

"Unbelievably light, and the structure seems to be intact," said Sartov. "With some innovative repairs and a pair of conventional compression engines installed it could be of use in your Venture Australica. Its range could well exceed that of a super-regal, or so I am advised."

"When it is available, be sure to let me know. In the meantime, I had better get some experience at the controls of a super-regal."

They began to walk on.

"Airlord Samondel, do you have a feel for how far away Australica really is?" asked Sartov, bowing his head and folding his arms as he walked. "Sheer statistics say that one of my super-regals would have to fly for *three days continuously* to reach it."

"Legend has it that our ancestors took three days to fly to the moon. Three men flew in a spacewing, and they slept in shifts."

"I doubt that we can afford the luxury of three men in our crews. Two flyers only, and very small flyers at that. Flyers weighing less than one hundred and twenty pounds. Our wardens and flyers will have to go on diets."

"A half hour ago the wingfield physician weighed me, as naked as the day I was born. I was one hundred and five pounds. What was Warden Bronlar's registration weight yesterday?"

What Samondel had neglected to say was that she had drunk one mug of water and had not eaten at all for twenty-four hours, but Sartov did not need to know that. They stopped at the adjunct's office and being the presiding airlord of the council, Sartov could access the records of registration weights. Bronlar's kitted weight was 132 pounds, and a standard kit weighed thirty-five.

"A growing girl," said Samondel.

"Your weights are practically the same, and Warden Jemarial is known for her distance flying."

"Warden Jemarial is both unstable and insane, Saireme Sartov. Would *you* chose her as your *envoy* to the Australicans?"

Sartov would have cheerfully appointed the chicken that had laid his breakfast egg as Australican envoy before he would have appointed Bronlar.

"I am inclined to favor *you*," said Sartov, "but your lack of navigation skills counts against you."

"Navigation skills can be learned, and *I* am a scholar!"

"You will be looking for very small islands over very large distances," Sartov warned. "One little mistake in navigation could kill you and lose a very expensive multiengined wing that is sorely needed in Mounthaven. We don't even know the weather patterns over midocean."

"I shall find out for you."

"The sheer amount of fuel to get the first six horses back will be more than any one of my super-regals burned for the entire war."

"And how long will we have fuel in such quantities, Airlord Sartov? Just now we have reserves, but in a year or two the guild systems will be breaking down as people leave to hunt, farm, and build their own little empires in the frontier lands. With horses we can maintain civilization. Without them, you will soon be looking down upon a frontier filled with barbarians and anarchy from your carefully conserved super-regals. Either we move now or we are lost."

"Oh, I agree, Saireme Samondel of Leover, otherwise I would not have pledged my super-regals to your venture, as well as commissioning two more. This will be a more difficult feat than winning the Great War, but at least we shall be fighting on the same side."

"We are on the same side, but there will be no fighting, Saireme Airlord. My feeling is that all of the islands were scoured clear of humans when the Call began."

"Ah yes, I had forgotten that matter," replied Sartov, nodding.

Within a quarter hour Samondel was eating a dinner that would soon restore her body weight to a something more normal for her. At the same time Sartov was giving a secret audience to Serjon and Bronlar.

"You will be flying revolutionary sailwings," said Sartov. "Each stretch will be twenty hours or more, and you will be flying alone."

"We always fly alone," replied Bronlar.

The Rochestrian Commonwealth, Eastern Australica

Being under martial law, the citizens of Rochester were being particularly quiet and well behaved. During the night all electrical machines had burned and melted. Then the Dragon Librarian Service began abducting everyone who could count. Some people had noticed that Mirrorsun had stopped twinkling. Streetside preachers of the Reformed Gentheist Church Against the Electrical Essence Heresy loudly proclaimed that the Deity had just indicated that He did not like electrical engines any more than steam engines. Martial law was declared, and soon the preachers were being moved on by the city militia. Those who stopped and began preaching again were arrested. Those who resisted arrest were shot.

In his administrative chambers in Libris, Highliber Dramoren was pacing before a very nervous Dragon Green and flourishing a list of names.

"So let us go over it again," said Dramoren. "You signed off Rangen Derris as class R for Rejected, as opposed to class C for Calculor."

"Well, yes, I did just that, Highliber."

"Fras, Rangen Derris is not only a part-time edutor at the Department of Mathematics, he has topped the department's examinations five half years in a row. It is one hundred and thirty years since anyone else has done as well. He has even had papers on deductive logic published."

"His notes were all on languages, Highliber, and he said that languages were his field of study. He must have worked out what was happening and lied."

"Nobody else did."

"As you said, Highliber, the youth is truly exceptional and deductive logic is his greatest strength."

"Pah, and it is probably too late. The clever wretch probably bought a wig, shaved, then boarded a wind train wearing a skirt over a couple of oranges strapped to his chest and a pillow around his hips. No good will it do him, though. Every mayorate in the Commonwealth will soon be recruiting components for my manual calculor. We have depended on calculors for three decades, Fras. The need remains, even though the electrical calculors have melted, so we are returning to halls full of slaves with abacus frames. I want first choice of the best components."

The Kalgoorlie Empire, Western Australica

Jemli vil Amarana held high rank, yet was no more than a pawn in the politics of the Kalgoorlie Empire. Once she had been a mayor, but now she was merely the Kalgoorlie Overmayor's consort, cheated into surrendering her powers by the very man whom she had married. She had been promised the joint rule of a new alliance known as the Kalgoorie Empire, she had even betrayed Mayor Glasken, her former husband. And all for what?

She was in her early forties and had given birth to two more children by her second husband, but now he had other women to divert him. She remained attractive, but was well over six feet tall and had unfashionably broad shoulders. She admitted to herself that perhaps the Overmayor had always kept the dainty courtesans that were so much more to his taste than her, but had maintained discretion until his position was secure. Jemli looked up at the portrait of herself as Mayor of Kalgoorlie, painted when she had just been widowed. A single year, that was all that she had had in power, and she still had her mayoral robes, locked away in a trunk. There had once been pageants in her honor, royal receptions, tours of the provinces, but now . . . She picked up a petition from eleven members of the Reformed Gentheist Church Against the Electrical Essence Heresy requesting her to speak at their prayer meeting. Jemli had ordered a few steam engines smashed as part of a coup against her first husband, and she still gave streetside sermons against fueled engines to keep from dropping out of the public eye. *That's ecumenism for you,* she thought as she began to read the petition.

"New world order . . . cast down the sinners . . . raise up the righteous . . . lay waste the cities of iniquity with hellfire from heaven . . . Day of Judgment . . . tax concessions for the Reformed Gentheist Church Against the Electrical Essence Heresy . . ."

Jemli quite enjoyed public speaking, so she reached for a goose quill and scrawled her acceptance at the bottom of the petition.

"Why not; at least it's an audience," she said to herself.

From somewhere close by there was a giggle. Obviously her husband with some courtesan, but Jemli was not jealous, in fact she was relieved to be left to herself. She tapped some figures into her desktop electric calculor. Relays clattered, display wheels spun—and there was a crackling sizzle before acrid fumes belched out of the ventilation grille. Jemli stood up and backed away.

"Shyte, it's never done that before!" she exclaimed softly.

Now she noticed that the new electrical clock on the wall was smoking too, in fact it was actually on fire. Hearing cries of alarm,

Jemli went to the window and looked down to the pedal sheds. The generator navvies were milling around outside and gesticulating while smoke poured from the open door. She walked out onto a balcony and looked over the walls of the Overmayor's palace to the city. Everywhere smoke was curling up into the night sky, lit from below by hundreds of small fires.

Electrical devices were burning, Jemli realized. Everywhere. All across the city. If all across the city, why not all across the continent? The tirade against electrical engines in the petition from the Reformed Gentheist Church Against the Electrical Essence Heresy was fresh in her mind. She could recall it practically word for word. Jemli became aware that her heart was racing. There was a sickly sweet taste in her mouth, the type that came when one had just been propositioned by some ambitious but desirable young man at a mayoral reception and had thought "Why not?" It was the feeling of intense anticipation, laced with uncertainty and even danger. The end of electricity—again. The universe had changed, barely a minute ago. Old rules no longer applied, new rules were waiting to be written. Old rulers were only on their thrones because nobody had thought to push them off. Yet. Returning inside, Jemli went to her study, where the calculor and clock were still smoldering. She pushed a decorative stud on the wall, then twisted it clockwise and pressed it again. There was a soft click. She slid a nearby panel aside.

Relliana tumbled and giggled with the Overmayor on a pile of silk cushions as he sought to unlace her bodice from behind. The courtesan was lying facedown when the monarch suddenly rose clear of her.

"Hie, dummart, what do you think you're doing?" he demanded.

As Relliana tried to think what he might mean there was a blast, unbearably loud and percussive within the confines of the room. She rolled over and scrambled to her feet, trying to stuff her breasts back into her partly unlaced bodice as she backed away from the figure advancing through a cloud of gunsmoke with a flintlock raised. The last thing that Relliana saw was a flash from the left barrel of the

Morelac. It had been barely two minutes since the electrical machines had begun to burn.

With such an emergency as the clocks, calculors, and other electrical devices suddenly melting and burning it was not long before a lackey was sent to inform the Overmayor. He found the scene of a murder-suicide. Shrieking for the guards, he turned and fled. Jemli arrived with the first of those guards and watched attentively as the captain examined both bodies with care and an open mind.

"Powder burns on both of them," he concluded. "Both were shot from close range, the Overmayor between the eyes, the girl in the mouth. Both were standing when shot, facing the door, yet the girl's laces are undone and her breasts are hanging out. This Morelac was in her hands."

"I heard the shots," said Jemli. "Two shots."

"Someone walked in on them, someone with authority to be in this part of the palace and who knew where they were to be found. He shot them both, then tried to make it look like the courtesan was responsible. The bodies are still as warm as in life, so this happened only minutes ago."

"The lackey who found them must have come past very soon after the killings," said Jemli. "Did he see anyone?"

"He reported seeing nobody."

"How very convenient."

The captain's thoughts slid smoothly into a path in which everything fitted together very simply.

"He would not have been alone," replied the captain. "He had little rank or influence. By the Deity, look at what's inscribed on the Morelac's handle: 'Once the weapon of Lemorel Milderellen.' "

"That is mine!" exclaimed Jemli. "I reported it stolen months ago, it is a highly prized relic, a symbol of charisma and power."

"Aye, and I remember writing the report."

"The lackey worked for Sariach," Jemli pointed out.

That was no revelation. All the lackeys and officials of the palace worked for Sariach, and Sariach was the Overmayor's named successor. Overmayor Amarana had been in the very best of health, and would have had decades in office stretching ahead of him.

"These are very serious implications," said the captain, who was also within Sariach's chain of command.

"How loyal are the men of the palace guard?" asked Jemli.

"They are loyal to the Crown, but—"

"But who wears the crown, and with what right?"

The captain did not answer.

"Put the palace on invasion alert and have the overhand of the city militia proclaim martial law," said Jemli, gambling everything on the authority in her voice and bearing. "Have the lackey brought here, then send for Fras Sariach. Tell him that it is to do with the succession."

For a single, agonized moment the captain hesitated, his face alive with internal conflict . . . then he saluted.

It was now seven minutes since the electrical devices had begun to burn. Six minutes later Sariach arrived to inspect the scene of the tragedy that had elevated him to the highest office in the southwest of the continent. The bodies still lay where they had fallen, and present were the lackey who had discovered the deaths, six guards and the guard captain. Jemli was also there, the tall principal wife of the Overmayor. Sariach made to push past her, eager to check that the Overmayor was really dead.

Jemli's fist slammed into his abdomen, and he doubled over with a soft wheeze.

"*That* is for ordering this little rat to kill the Overmayor," Jemli said slowly and clearly. "Captain, have him bound, gagged, and locked in the south tower. Torture this lackey until he confesses to everything."

The guardsmen, the royal court, the militia—in fact, everyone—was more concerned with having a strong leader in a time of extreme uncertainty and danger than with questions of who actually had the right to the throne. The lackey was not suited to enduring torture, and had gathered that people suspected him of committing the murders by order of Sariach. He confessed accordingly.

By midnight over two hundred palace officials and courtiers had been arrested, along with the Overmayor's other wives and courtesans. Jemli donned her old mayoral robes and called a great meeting of Kalgoorlie's citizens in the square before the palace. Rocked by the events of only four hours past, over a hundred thousand people crowded together to hear Jemli speak by the light of lanterns. She was familiar to them, as she had ruled before. The year of her rule had been a quiet, prosperous one for the mayorate. She also had big lungs and a commanding voice; she sounded like a leader.

"Citizens, the Overmayor has been murdered."

Everyone knew this, of course, but they were there to hear it announced by someone in authority. Jemli knew that making the announcement gave her authority.

"Sariach was behind the plot, and he has been arrested. He will be tried by a martial law committee."

Now there were cheers. The Overmayor had not been unpopular, and people generally liked to see justice done.

"As your new Overmayor, it is my duty to warn you that the voice of the Deity has spoken to us all today."

Jemli enjoyed swaying crowds and she was very good at it; it ran in the family. After a major revelation she always allowed time for people to whisper to each other, to build up anticipation, to make them hungry for the answer that only she had. The voice of the Deity had spoken! Why had they not noticed?

"The Deity has cast heaven's fire down to burn all electrical engines. Those engines are hateful in His sight, but out of love and compassion He has allowed not a single one of us, His loving worshipers, to die in the conflagration."

There had actually been half a dozen deaths in the fires across Kargoorlie, but nobody was inclined to argue.

"All faiths—Gentheist, Christian, and Islamic—have prohibited engines that use fuel for two thousands of years. Those engines fouled the face of His creation and afflicted us, His people, with the blights of pollution, Greatwinter, and killing machines. For two millennia we lived happily without engines, but twenty years ago that evil band in the sky, Mirrorsun, struck down His angels. The electrical engines came back to scourge us."

She pointed up to the band that stretched across the sky, blotting out a strip of stars with darkness, and adorned by a splash of orange light reflected from the sun that was currently shining on the other side of the planet. The ancients' vast and powerful machine was an immense distance away in orbit, and was thus a safe target for invective and any accusation that came to mind.

"Tonight the Deity has made it clear that electrical engines are no less hateful in His sight than steam engines. We must go forth and destroy all devices that burn electrical essence, whether in the deepest tunnels or shielded cages. The Deity will smile on you, He will send a sign of His blessing."

Jemli stepped down to a thunderstorm of cheering and applause. The captain of the palace guard was waiting with an escort for her.

"I have important orders to give," she said as she strode away with them. "I want five dozen runners and couriers lined up at the door to the Overmayor's chambers in a few minutes. See to it."

Jemli's seat of power was the center of a wide, semicircular desk of bloodwood. She sat back in the padded, comfortable chair, glowing with energy and excitement that was virtually sexual in intensity. In four hours she had risen from mistress of her own study to Overmayor and Prophet. Although she had been quick with her planning and actions, one thought lingered before her like a divine vision. Surely she could not have risen so far and fast without the genuine favor of the Deity. The first of the couriers arrived.

"It is proclaimed that the beamflash signal tower service, which has been in decline since the advent of electrical machines, is to be restored under my control," Jemli said slowly as the scribes copied her words onto poorpaper. "Have this known in every city, town, and village."

After an hour of proclamations, declarations, and orders, Jemli had the captain called in. She told him to close the doors.

"Of all the people in the Kalgoorlie Empire, I know that I can trust you," she began. "You are to take a galley train west, to the capital of the Confederation of Woomera. I shall write out your orders and my message while you pack, and you must leave within the hour."

2

SOUL OF THE VICTIM

Rochester

Dramoren was the first of the continent's leaders to be given the unbelievable news about the Call ceasing. The message had originated at Seymour, a large township at the edge of the Calldeath lands bordering the Commonwealth. After being relayed through the flashing signal mirrors of the Rushworth beamflash tower, forty-five miles to the north, it had been sent another fifty miles northeast to Rochester.

The Call had ceased in the Calldeath lands. There was no longer any trace of it.

"Confirmation, I want confirmation!" demanded Dramoren, snatching the chalkboard bearing the message from his lackey.

"Highliber, the—"

"Get out!"

Dramoren slammed the door on his lackey and depressed the OVERRIDE lever at his calculor console. Nothing happened. Suddenly he remembered: the electrical calculor had burned the night before. He stood up, strode to the door, and flung it open.

"Vorion!" Dramoren shouted as loudly as he could.

"Yes, Highliber?" Vorion replied from beside the door.

Dramoren looked down at him. "I want all references to the Call ceasing. Now! Any new reports are to be sent to me as soon as they arrive."

"I have the current reports in this folder, Highliber."

Reports from Echuca and Darlington described moving Calls suddenly vanishing. Not stopping in the same place for the night but vanishing completely. Dramoren immediately sent out commands that the Bendigo and Inglewood beamflash crews check on the state of the Calldeath lands to the south of their towers, while putting in a request for confirmation at Seymour. Within a half hour the reports came back: the Call had ceased totally, and the Calldeath lands were safe to enter for the first time in two thousand years.

"An area the size of the Rochestrian Commonwealth itself has suddenly been opened up to human settlement," said the perplexed Highliber.

"Highliber, wonderful news!" exclaimed Vorion, clapping his hands together.

"Allow me to rephrase that. An area the size of the Rochestrian Commonwealth populated by heavily armed and very dangerous aviads has suddenly been opened up to human settlement."

"Oh," responded Vorion.

"Send a runner to the palace, get me an interview with the Overmayor. Request it with the Invasion priority code."

"Very good, Highliber, consider it done. And where will you be waiting for the reply?"

"At the palace gates, you idiot. Now run!"

It was a mere twenty minutes later that Dramoren was ushered into the audience hall of Overmayor Lengina. The young Overmayor had been installed in office a mere twenty days before Dramoren's appointment, and had only met the chief civil servant of her Commonwealth the day before.

"Grave and disturbing news, Frelle Overmayor," said Dramoren as he walked through the double doors of filigree relief mountain ashwood. "The Call has ceased completely."

The former mayor of Inglewood was more used to being told

grave news along the lines of hailstorms wiping out the year's grape crop before the harvest had begun. Having no Call sweeping over her realm was simply incomprehensible. It was like being told that dogs no longer had tails.

"Are your sources reliable?" she asked, leaning forward and pressing her chin against her fist.

"They are both reliable and independent," Dramoren assured her. "From Seymour to Inglewood, the Calldeath lands may now be entered by humans. What is more, reports have come in of active, moving Calls just ceasing to exist."

The monarch of the entire Commonwealth thought both quickly and deeply, but it did her no good.

"This matter has no precedent in two thousand years," Overmayor Lengina pointed out, quite correctly. "What do you recommend?"

Dramoren hoped that his relief did not show. He was obviously first with the news, ahead of her military overhands, economic advisors, and court nobility.

"The Calldeath lands are full of aviads," he replied. "We must keep them separated from settlers and adventurers, else there will be much bloodshed. Order that roadblocks be set up by local militias along the Calldeath borderlands, and suspend paraline traffic for a day. That will slow the flow of human settlers until we have had a chance to think."

"They are extreme measures," replied Lengina. "Commerce will be affected."

"Extreme measures show that we are taking the matter seriously, Frelle Overmayor."

"But how can we be sure they are correct?"

"We cannot, but then we only have to *seem* to be in control to keep the confidence of the citizens. Give people a firm order in difficult times and they will be relieved, not resentful."

The Overmayor frowned for a moment, staring directly at Dramoren.

"Your words might apply as much to me as to my subjects," she replied.

"Precisely, Overmayor, but notice that I have at least been honest with you."

Again Overmayor Lengina considered. Dramoren had given her a sensible course of action, but with no options. Lengina was uneasy when she had no options.

"Remind me of what will be achieved by your recommendation," she said.

"A lot of your subjects will be kept out of trouble and kept alive, Overmayor. You will also be given a few days to consult with your advisors and client mayors to determine a long-term policy appropriate to our new circumstances."

"Your advice seems both sensible and altruistic, Highliber."

"It is the role of librarians to keep government running in difficult times," replied Dramoren. "Librarians are the last line of defence against chaos."

Balesha Monastery, Western Australica

Two thousand miles to the west, the horse that Brother Martyne Camderine had stolen was rapidly tiring. It was better suited to the millwheel's treadcircle than desperate flight across the desert. The young escapee had managed to put fifteen miles between himself and the Christian monastery of Balesha before his escape had been discovered, but his pursuers were quick to run him down. Martyne had abandoned his horse in rolling, scrubby hills as soon as he saw dust being raised behind him, but this bought less time than he had wished. A riderless horse follows a less purposeful path, and the three monks soon turned back to search out the fugitive.

Martyne was just nineteen years and two months old, and had spent the past five and a half of them in Balesha monastery. He was clean-shaven, and the hair surrounding his tonsure was only a quarter inch long. Like all the monks of Balesha he wore just drawstring trousers, sandals, a cassock, and his belt. The black cloth belt carried a knife, flintlock, powder horn, and shot pouch: Balesha was a Christian monastery espousing devotion to God through the martial arts. Only the previous April had Martyne become Brother Martyne after enduring five years of study, training, sparring, prayer, ordeals, privations, examinations, and vigils. Until a day earlier Brother Martyne had been resigned to spending the rest of his life with the Baleshan Order, indeed he had no choice. The monks considered themselves to be so dangerous that none were allowed to walk free in the outside world, except in pursuit of fugitive monks.

Martyne found a soak hole by observing where the stubby trees and shrubs grew more lushly, and after drinking his fill he took out his knife and shaved his head entirely. This was his statement that he had left the order in spirit as well as body. He then began his stretching and sparring exercises. When his pursuers arrived they would be stiff from riding, and Martyne knew that he would need every edge and advantage that he could muster, no matter how slight.

When the three pursuers found him he was sitting in the shade of a low but dense tree beside a patch of smooth, red sand, his pack by his side and the twin-barrel Morelac across his lap. Two monks dismounted and flanked him as they approached, their muskets raised and the strikers cocked.

"Before these witnesses I claim trial by combat," said Martyne without moving.

"Raise your hands," replied the abbot.

Martyne complied. The abbot dismounted, approached warily, and lifted the Morelac from the fugitive's lap. He checked the flashpans and found them both primed for firing.

"Before these witnesses I claim trial by combat," Martyne repeated.

"Why is it that those who break our laws are the first to claim their rights under them?" replied the abbot.

"Trial by combat is nevertheless my right," said Martyne. "We could even have it here. You, the abbot, are present, the disputant is present, and there are two witnesses."

Abbot Leadbeater was two decades older than Martyne, but scarcely showed his age. He scowled at Martyne's freshly shaven head, annoyed at the show of symbolic defiance. Martyne had never been considered a model student or monk, but he had excelled in sparring and targetry contests. One day he would challenge to become abbot, one day when he had gained a few years of seniority, passed further examinations and ordeals, learned the nine hundred prescribed prayers, and experienced a divinely inspired dream or vision. When that day came he would be a fearsome opponent indeed. Abbot Leadbeater came to a decision, then twirled Brother Martyne's gun on its trigger guard and handed it to Gerian.

"What better place for a trial?" declared the abbot. "Brother Ortano, you will adjudicate."

Walking across to his mount, the abbot took a jar of water from a saddlebag and tossed it to Martyne. The monk caught the jar, then took his own water jar and offered it to the abbot. They uncorked their opponents' jars and offered them to Ortano. He drank from each in turn before pronouncing both to be pure and harmless. He returned the jars to Abbot Leadbeater and Martyne, who linked arms before drinking.

"Drink the waters of trust and friendship, then fight in the same spirit," said Brother Ortano.

They drank, then retreated seven paces each and set the jars down. Brother Ortano cut a crooked staff from the tree that had shaded Martyne and began to mark out a circle with the jars defining its diameter. Abbot and monk waited beside the jars until the circle was complete. Ortano and Gerian stood outside the circumference.

"This match of skills in the noble and holy art of Baleshanto is to try Brother Martyne by combat for his act of desertion from the monastery. A first attempt at desertion is punished by the cutting of the hamstring muscles in one leg, a second is punished by death. Either of these punishments can be reversed by God's will in the form of success against a superior opponent in trial by combat, and the trial will proceed until surrender, disablement, or death. Abbot Leadbeater, Brother Camderine, do you accept these terms?"

"Yes," said the abbot, and Martyne echoed the word.

"Re," said Brother Ortano.

The opponents bowed to each other.

"Hajime," barked Ortano.

They closed slowly and warily across the stretch of red sand delineated by the two jars. For some moments they circled each other, just out of reach. Their hands described slow, almost languorous paths through the air but their eyes were locked and unblinking. The abbot raised his leg and slashed across to sweep Martyne's leading arm aside before stabbing out with a flat kick at his face. Martyne arched his back and twisted, so that the abbot's foot merely brushed his cheek, then he retaliated with a rising roundhouse kick to the abbot's hamstrings. The blow was not crippling but it was damage, and instead of withdrawing his foot Martyne dropped it to the sand to step forward and punch the abbot in the lower ribs. Two ribs broke, but the abbot swung around with a backhand strike at the pressure point beneath Martyne's left arm, dropping the younger monk. The abbot raised his right foot to lash down at Martyne's head, but Martyne was already bringing his leg around in a flat sweep. He caught the abbot just below the knee, twisting to lock their legs as the abbot fell. For a moment the abbot's leg was locked between Martyne's, three inches above the red sand. In this moment Martyne's fist crashed down onto the side of the abbot's knee.

Martyne broke free and stood clear of the abbot. The ruler of Balesha got up slowly, but it was quite clear that he could put scarcely any weight on his left leg. Martyne circled him, giving him the opportunity to either attack or declare defeat. The abbot merely remained at the ready. Martyne stepped within range of the abbot's kick.

The abbot dropped while lashing out with a flat roundhouse kick to Martyne's knee, but Martyne merely drew his legs into the air to let the kick swing harmlessly past. The abbot toppled as he tried to regain his balance.

Ortano stepped in and barked "Yame!"

"I am not beaten!" insisted the abbot.

"Trial by combat is meant to be a fight, not a farce, Reverend Abbot," retorted Ortano to his superior. "I have declared an end, you have lost."

"He used witchcraft; I have five times more experience," the abbot shouted back.

"I am a student of history, not witchcraft," said Martyne as he stood back from the abbot. "I studied your fighting, then questioned your opponents. All said how blindingly fast you were, yet your speed never seemed more than unexceptional to me—as an observer. Do you know that I had to break into your chambers nineteen times until I finally discovered that hidden phial of slothwine in the hollow leg of your bed?"

The abbot showed no emotion at the accusation, but merely sat massaging his knee. There was a loud click from the joint.

"What I just drank was rainwater to which you had added yet more rainwater, and behold, you suffered your first defeat," Martyne concluded.

"But, but I drank the very same water as the abbot's opponents before many, many bouts and I was quite unaffected," protested Ortano.

"Ah, but you *were* affected, Brother," insisted Martyne. "An edge of perhaps one part in one hundred was taken off your reactions. Not enough to notice, but enough to give an evenly matched opponent an advantage."

Ortano did not reply, but the shock and confusion were plain on his face. The abbot got to his feet and dusted himself off.

"Brothers, bind him," he said firmly.

"But your rev—" began Brother Gerian.

"Do as I say! He may have beaten me, but he has now accused me of the most heinous of crimes. He may go free only after he has been taken back to Balesha and tried for this new accusation."

"When the hollow leg in your bed is considered beside the vinegar jar of slothwine that I concealed in the ornamental fish pool, I doubt that the trial will last long," warned Martyne.

"Bind him!" shouted the abbot.

Gerian and Ortano placed their muskets and Martyne's Morelac against the tree and seized the unresisting Martyne. They bound his arms—then looked up to see the abbot pointing Martyne's Morelac at them.

"Very un-Christian, the way you shot my two monks with a stolen gun," said the abbot.

The abbot fired the two barrels in quick succession. Ugly red patches appeared over the hearts of Brothers Gerian and Ortano. They winced, but remained standing. The abbot's jaw dropped open. He glanced from the gun to Martyne, then to the monks.

"Very un-Christian of me, loading my gun with beeswax pellets of red ink," explained Martyne.

The air was laden with the sort of silence that only a windless day in the desert can fashion. Intensely bright light and lurid colors to assail the eyes, baking, relentless heat for the skin, sulfur from the abbot's shot hanging in the air to suggest that this might be a foretaste of hell, the taste of fear on four tongues, yet nothing for the ears.

"You flout the will of God," snarled the abbot, flinging Martyne's flintlock to the sand.

"In your case I'd say it was the devil's will," replied Martyne, "and I do not worship the devil."

Gerian reached down and slipped the knot to Martyne's bonds. The abbot turned and hobbled for the horses, clutching at his injured knee. He had just reached his mount and drawn a small flintlock from his saddlebag when Gerian tackled him. There was a short but frantic struggle in the dust. The flintlock discharged harmlessly, then the abbot found himself with a knee on his neck, his face in the dust, and his wrist bent into an excruciating lock.

"Brother Camderine, you will have to return to the monastery with us," said Gerian to Brother Martyne as the abbot was being bound.

"But I defeated the abbot, I have the right to leave Baelsha."

"Yes, and after you have testified against him you will indeed go free. I do not shirk from sacrificing my life for my faith, but I draw the line at wasting my life as a result of some grubby little dispute. You will return with us, Brother Martyne, and you will testify. If we lose, you lose. If we win, you go free."

"Your logic has defeated me where the abbot could not," replied Martyne.

They rode through the night and into the next morning before reaching Baelsha. Within minutes of their arrival the trial of the abbot began, for it was prescribed in the Baleshan Order that evil must be sliced from its ranks on the very day that it is found. The trial began badly for the abbot when his bed was found to feature a hollow leg, and after the other evidence and testimonies were presented it became merely a question of whether he should be executed before or after lunch.

By noon the former abbot was hanging dead from the arch of the open front gate. Martyne spared him a glance through the dormitory window as he prepared to leave again, this time on foot. Brother Gerian came up behind him, carrying a pack.

"This will get you to the paraline, where you can flag down a wind train," said Gerian.

Martyne turned away from the window and accepted the pack in silence.

"From the moment that you step through the gate you cease to exist," warned Gerian, stepping past Martyne and pointing through the window. "You can never return."

"I know the rules. In fact, I got a distinction when examined on them five months ago."

"Why did you do it?" asked Gerian, rubbing at his tonsure. "You were hardly a model monk, but you had promise."

Martyne produced a scrap of reedpaper. Gerian saw that the words "Elsile" and "Murdered" were written on it in small, neat letters.

"How did this get into Baelsha?" asked Gerian in astonishment.

"A little bird brought it."

"I want the truth."

"Very well, a rather big bird brought it."

"Brother Martyne, do not jest. We are totally screened from the outside world, save what the abbot—"

"Abbot Leadbeater is disgraced and dead, Brother Gerian, and I have duties to attend."

"Who is Elsile?"

"My sister."

Gerian shook his head.

"You vowed to *renounce* your friends and family. We did not give you five years of the finest martial arts training on the continent to use in some family feud."

Martyne cast a glance to Gerian. Something flashed in the soft, chocolate brown eyes that nevertheless made the bigger monk step back a pace.

"The murder of my sister is not 'some family feud,' Brother Gerian, and I have won the right to leave."

"And by winning that right you have gained obligations. Chapter one, Section nine, Clause eleven: 'He who demonstrates the existence of corruption within the order is obliged to initiate reform, assuming whatever rank is required.' "

"Maybe so, but I have won the right to leave and I intend to exercise that right."

Gerian followed as Martyne made his way down the stairs and out into the courtyard where three dozen other monks were waiting in an arc. The rest of Balesha's community were forming a guard of dishonor, standing in two rows facing the path that Martyne would take to the gate.

"Obligation precedes right," said Gerian from the doorway. "Stand firm!"

Three dozen flintlock pistols were drawn from the robes of three dozen monks, and Martyne found himself at the focus of the line of fire of three dozen barrels.

"Once through the gate you cease to exist, but until then you are Brother Camderine and you are acting with the rank of abbot. Tell us, Abbot Martyne, what must we do to purge the corruption from Balesha?"

Martyne took in the sweep of barrels. There was no alternative but to obey.

"Isolation is our strength," he began slowly, "but isolation is our curse. We are an order of perfect swords that sit in racks, polished and honed to perfection but unused. In the east of the continent there is an order known as the Logisticans, who study God's universe and glorify Him by teaching what they learn to the laity. Go to them, beg help from them, offer help to them. Brother Gerian, there may be worthier souls than you in Balesha, but I have seen no better sense of justice or good heart than that you displayed to me. Now, as abbot I have given orders to purge Balesha's corruption and as abbot I name you as my replacement. Either order me shot, or let me pass."

The barrels of the guns followed Martyne as he walked to the ornamental pool in the courtyard and took a long drink. Finally he shouldered his cloth pack of dried fruit, waterskins, and bread, snaked his arms through the straps, then looked to Abbot Gerian.

"Pin your strikers, join ranks to banish this monk," ordered the newly appointed abbot. "Depart from us, Brother Martyne. Never return."

At that the two rows that flanked Martyne's path began chanting the Requiem Vitaren. As he walked between them nobody spoke a word of farewell or waved. He walked through the arch of the main gate, where the former abbot was still hanging, then stopped and turned. Now Gerian produced a flintlock, released the pin, cocked the striker and fired. The ball severed the rope, and the former abbot's body fell to the ground. Two monks broke ranks, stripped the body bare and flung it beside the track, just outside the gate. Nobody so much as glanced at Martyne, who was now no more part of the monastery than the body on the red sand. The gates were pushed shut, and the deep boom of their closing startled several crows into the air. One landed near the body, then cocked its head to one side and stared intently at Martyne.

"Ah, no, thank you, he is all yours," said Martyne.

He turned away off the track and headed south. Many days away was the paraline, but unlike earlier escapees from Balesha he had adequate provisions and no threat of pursuit.

Kalgoorlie, Western Australica

Given the dramatic circumstances of her gaining office, it was no surprise that Overmayor Jemli ordered a general mobilization of all musketeers and militias. Galley engines were sent out to all major centers to take control, and the bewildered librarians, officials, and citizens were not slow to accept the new overmayor's authority. Within a single day of the electrical machines burning, Jemli had sent twenty armed galley engines east along the paralines, dropping officials at each of the old beamflash towers. After crossing into the Woomeran Confederation, she pronounced that hers was an aid expedition after the catastrophe with the electrical machines, and that a council of mayors and overmayors would be called. Within eight days she had placed four thousand of her operatives all along the paralines, as far as the border with the Rochestrian Commonwealth. Here their help was politely but firmly declined.

The passing of ten days had transformed the political scene in both the Kalgoorlie Empire and the Woomeran Confederation beyond recognition. Jemli had been elevated to become a religious leader without even being ordained, and her followers had already begun referring to her as the Prophet.

"And as I warned you, so did it come to pass," Jemli shouted to the crowd that was hanging on her words. "I said that the Deity would send a sign if we began smashing all engines, and that sign is now with us. The Call has ceased, yes, and even the Calldeath lands are no longer the province of the aviads alone. The Deity has passed judgment upon them, He has stripped away the Call, their shield, and their armor. Engines of electrical essence He has struck down, and those abominations, the aviads, He has judged hateful in His sight. Soon He will smite the mighty band in the sky, Mirrorsun. What is a sign, except for us to act upon? If you want to go to Kalgoorlie and you see a sign which says Kalgoorlie—Fifty Miles, do you not turn down that road and prepare for a journey of fifty miles?"

She paused, and there was a scattering of cries along the lines of "Aye" and "Yes."

"And if you see electrical essence machines burn, then see aviads denied their protection, what do you do?"

"Smash them, kill them!" shouted a firebrand priest from down in the crowd.

Now catching on, the crowd echoed his words. Over and over

again, the words rolled like waves across the plaza and down the neighboring streets. Engines and aviads were excesses of the old civilization, brought back to life after they had nearly poisoned the world itself. The Deity was giving believers a chance to prove their faith, and His voice was the voice of Jemli.

Martyne was among the thirty thousand standing in the great square before the palace of Kalgoorlie, listening to the Overmayor's speech. Both of them were about to depart for the East, but he would be pedaling the engine that would be carrying Jemli.

"Remember that I promised you a sign, on the day that the electrical engines burned. Well, now you have your sign."

Jemli had actually promised a sign because it seemed like the right thing for a prophet to do. The last thing she had been expecting was a real sign.

"The Call has ceased," she repeated. "No more does the curse of the invisible allure sweep the land, no more may aviads walk free, stealing, murdering, and ravishing while we humans are insensible. We must now work to be worthy of His new blessing. Kill all aviads, destroy all engines not powered by wind, water, or muscle."

The crowd began to chant, generally along the lines of "Kill" and "Destroy," and Jemli let them have their way for a time. Presently she raised her arms and they were silent.

"My people, in our zeal, let us be sure to spare the innocent. Those in other mayorates must be *converted* to the truth, not have it forced upon them at gunpoint. To this aim I am about to leave for the eastern mayorates, to bring them the message of salvation. There I have called a great council, where I shall preach the truth."

Martyne waved his hat in the air for the sake of appearances, but did not cheer. For him, all this was just a means of taking him east all the more swiftly.

Five galley engines rumbled out of Kalgoorlie soon after the rally was over. Thousands of cheering believers flanked the paraline as the pedalers within pushed to drive the chains and gears, and Jemli waved from the hatch above the captain's cabin in the middle engine.

Martyne watched through the peephole beside his head until the crowds thinned and the city walls passed out of sight. Grassy, irrigated farmland presently gave way to open, scrubby forest.

"Your first trip?" asked the navvy beside him, a burly man with a broken nose.

"No, I came from the East by wind train, five years ago," replied Martyne.

"Nah, I mean as a navvy."

"Ah. Yes."

"You look trim enough."

"I work hard."

"Shifts are four hours on, half break, four on. Cruise at fifteen to the hour, we do. Battle conditions, hah. All out on battle conditions. Top speed is classified. Ever been in a battle?"

"A small one, a skirmish."

"Yeah? Yeah, well, only veterans aboard, I forgot. I been derailed in the castellanies, four or five years ago. . . ."

The man talked continuously for the entire shift. At the end of the second shift they were at Zanthus, over a hundred miles from Kalgoorlie, and on the edge of the Nullarbor Plain. By now night had fallen, and the navvies were changed. Inspectors went over the galley engines, checking for bombs, stowaways, and unauthorized cargo. The engines were very light and streamlined, but they were underpowered and their powerplants got tired very easily.

Nobody noticed Martyne slip away in the darkness and hurry east along the side of the paraline. The squadron captain's whistle pierced the night, and the five galley engines began to roll forward. Martyne crouched down as they went past, then sprinted for the last engine and clung to the side. Nobody seemed to notice, but he remained still for several minutes to be sure before crawling slowly down to the coupling skirt and settling in for the night.

It was still dark as they pulled into the Forrest railside. Martyne rolled from the coupling skirt before the train had stopped, then hurried along after it and mingled in among the fresh navvies. Martyne spent another shift pedaling until the squadron reached Maralinga Railside. By now it was early afternoon, so there was no question of sprinting unseen after the squadron again. Martyne settled down to wait for the next train east.

Overmayor Jemli was in no hurry to go on. Maralinga was a major railside of over a thousand people, and work was already under way to restore the beamflash tower after two decades of neglect. All but the guards on the engines were called to the base of the tower, where Jemli addressed them from one of the lower balconies. The theme was again the evil of electrical machines, the cessation of the Call, and the virtues of killing aviads. The onlookers cheered more lustily than those at Kalgoorlie, more because they were in the middle of the desert and starved for entertainment than because the prophet had an inspiring message. Jemli and the administrator in charge of the tower then walked back to the platform and stood a long time in discussion. The Overmayor was a head taller than he, even though the man was the same height as Martyne. Then, to the cheers of most of the railside, the galley engines rumbled away toward the eastern horizon.

Martyne had no cause to complain. He was nearly four times farther east than those who had remained at Coonana with the first shift change. He began a tour of the railside. There was a small temple to a Ghan saint who was buried there, with an inscription thanking Mayor Glasken of Kalgoorlie for locating her body in the wilderness. The area near the beamflash tower was cordoned off and under guard, but the market was open for the navvies who had just arrived. Martyne bought two flintlocks with damaged stocks, then found a suitable piece of wood at the railyard and settled down to begin carving new stocks while he awaited the next commercial wind train east.

The Central Confederation, Eastern Australica

Martyne's destination was Griffith, the capital of the Central Confederation. In Griffith, on that same day, the house of Disore was in mourning. It had been in mourning for two months. Glin Torumasen had been away at a war with the Southmoors for that time, but with the loss of all electrical essences within the known world, the war had wound down to a general demobilization. There would, of course, be more wars in the future, but for now there was a need to adjust to the vastly degraded communications that resulted from the loss of all radios and telegraphy.

"It was well before the Call ceased and the electrical essence devices melted," explained Harren Disore as the two men entered the bedroom. "Velesti had just passed her Dragon Yellow Librarian examinations and was walking home with her best friend, Elsile. Elsile was a Dragon Orange. With the war still raging, there were a lot of musketeers and lancers all over the city."

"And she was attacked?" asked Torumasen. "But she must have been wearing a Dragon Librarian uniform. Surely that would have deterred them?"

"The Dragon Librarians have lost a lot of authority in the Central Confederation over recent years. Besides, the penalty for rape is the same, whether the victim is a librarian or otherwise. Velesti wore no gun because she worked in a theological library. There was about a dozen and a half of them, mostly commoner musketeers, but three officers have been named also. She and Elsile were surrounded and gagged with so little fuss that nobody raised the alarm. They were then dragged off to a stable where they were ravished and degraded for hours. Elsile was murdered before they left. Velesti lost her mind."

Torumasen shook his head. "She always had a slender, delicate figure, and an even more delicate disposition."

"The experience turned her brain. Sometime before dawn the musketeers decided that they had done with them and it was time to leave. Apparently they set the stables afire and made their retreat, but luckily for my daughter, two passing lancer captains and their ladies noticed the flames. They broke in, thinking to save trapped horses. Instead they found Velesti in the straw, clothed only in blood and excrement, and quite without wits."

"Yet she was still able to identify her attackers?"

"No. At that moment one of the musketeers returned to fetch a saber that he had dropped, and he was shot in the leg by one of the captains as he tried to flee. In return for the guarantee of a life sentence he sang loud and long, but his officers were well connected so the trial has gone nowhere."

The girl was seventeen, on the high side of average height, and with long hair and a fine-boned but angular face. She lay with her eyes closed, and her brother, Reclor, was sitting on a chair beside her.

"Rector, Fras Torumasen is here to treat Velesti," said Harren.

His son looked up, then stood.

"Eleven other medicians have been able to do nothing," he said grimly.

"Then at least I can do no less," Torumasen replied.

Reclor left, and Torumasen examined Velesti. She was completely unresisting and limp, but Harren said that she would swallow when soup was put in her mouth.

"She has been like this since she was carried from the burning stables, and nothing has been able to stop her slow decline. Sometimes I think it would have been better if her throat had been cut, like poor Elsile's."

Torumasen straightened. "Harren, I want to give hope, but there is none to give," he concluded. "Her pulse is weak, she barely breathes, and her eyes are unseeing."

"Then what is to be done? Do you know anyone who can help? A doctor, edutor, sorcerer, priest?"

"No doctor or edutor can help. As for sorcerers or priests, I am in no better position to make judgments than you. Velesti may be aware of us from deep within her head, but she is retreating from life to escape the nightmare of what was done to her. Tend her well, give her absolute security and comfort. Try to let her know that the horrors of that night will never return."

"But we have done all that, Fras."

"Then you are already doing all there is to be done."

Torumasen bent over again and examined Velesti's throat. "Was there bruising on her neck?"

"There was bruising all over her body, her neck included."

"They may have tried to strangle her. Sometimes a loss of blood to the head can kill the mind while leaving the body alive."

Like most people, Torumasen had secrets to hide. He had once been the lover of the famous hero of the Milderellen Invasion, Dolorian, and had been with her when she had died over two decades earlier. Ten years later, Overmayor Zarvora had visited him in secret, about moving Dolorian's grave to a shrine in Rochester. Just before she left she had presented the medician with a flaccid, brown band, whose texture was rather like that of kid leather. "If ever again someone is as precious to you as Dolorian was, and is in the grip of death, put this around their neck," Zarvora had said. Now he was married with two children. He had intended to save the band for his own loved ones . . . but here was Harren, and his daughter was dying. Harren, his oldest friend. Harren, whose father had paid for Torumasen to go to university.

"I need to do one last test," said the medician. "Can you fetch a pitcher of cold water and a facecloth?"

As soon as Harren was out of the room Torumasen took the band from his pocket. Written on its inner surface in precise, angular letters were words in one of the ancient languages: SERIES 2 PROTOTYPE. He slipped the band around Velesti's neck and pressed the ends together. Almost at once he noticed that it was growing warm. Very warm. Velesti did not move. Within moments the band was too hot to touch. It was going to kill her! Its mechanism had probably failed in the two thousand years since it had been fashioned. He wrapped a handkerchief around his fingers and tried to tear it away, but it was changing color and melting into her skin. All that he could do was gently replace her head on the pillow. He felt for a pulse, but there was none.

Torumasen slumped to the floor beside the bed. What else could he have expected? The device had been two thousand years old, of course it would malfunction. Velsti was dead, he had killed her . . . but at least he had been trying to help. Harren appeared at the door, holding the pitcher and a cloth.

"Glin, what is the matter?" he asked.

"I applied a—a medicinal band to her neck, but to no avail. She is gone."

The pitcher fell from his hands, to smash and splash water across the carpet as Harren ran forward. He flung himself on his daughter's lifeless body, sobbing and beating the pillow with his fists. Torumasen slowly got to his feet, then took his friend by the shoulders and drew him away from the bed.

"Farewell, Velesti, it moved my heart to see you looking so beautiful," said the medician, gazing at the pale, gaunt, but strangely radiant face on the pillow before turning with his inconsolable friend and guiding him to the door.

Harren's wife, their son Reclor, Velesti's maid Julica, and the groom were gathered in the parlor when the two men returned downstairs. The circle of eyes was focused on Harren, but he said nothing as Torumasen helped him to a chair.

"Velesti is dead," the medician announced.

Harren's wife Elene cried out, then rushed to her husband's side and flung her arms around him. Julica fell to her knees, sobbing, but Reclor merely hugged his folded arms harder against his chest while his lips tightened to a thin, sharp line. The youth wore a medium bore flintlock at his right thigh. He was still too young to go armed in public, but ever since the attack he had strapped the gun on as soon as he returned home.

"Velesti has not suffered for many weeks," Torumasen explained. "Either through injury or revulsion, her mind probably fled to some dark corner within herself and slowly wasted away."

"But if her mind had fled, surely it might have crept back again," sobbed Julica, her eyes glistening as she wrung her hands.

"I have known that to happen. Folk have lain as dead for weeks, then returned to their senses for no obvious reason. Some reported that they heard their loved ones reading and talking to them, and that they journeyed toward the familiar voices through a strange and empty wasteland."

"I *have* been doing just that," cried Julica.

"But to return she had to *want* to return," explained the medician. "I only—"

Suddenly a piercing shriek echoed out from somewhere above them. Everyone froze for a moment, then looked to each other as if to confirm that the sound had been real. A moment later they were scrambling for the stairs.

Velesti was on the floor beside the bed, trying to raise herself on her arms and shaking her head as if to clear it.

"She's alive!" cried Julica, standing with her hands pressed to her cheeks.

Velesti looked up into her eyes, then hauled herself to her feet and stood for the first time in two months.

"Misar?" the girl whispered.

"Vel, you should be in bed," said Harren, stepping forward and taking her arm.

Velesti twisted out of his grip, spun him around and pushed him away. Harren staggered, stumbled, and fell to the thick carpet. For a moment everyone stood back, staring as Velesti stood swaying beside her bed. Her eyes were huge and round in her gaunt face.

"Misar?" she rasped again.

"Who is Misar?" asked Torumasen.

"I don't know," replied Julica.

"One of those who ravished her?" suggested Elene. "Or perhaps a secret sweetheart?"

Velesti ignored them, slowly bringing her hands up and staring at them. She ran her fingers over her face, then down her neck and chest. As she felt her breasts she screamed again and collapsed. Julica darted forward and caught her.

"Velesti, do you know me?" pleaded Julica over and over as she helped her back to the bed. "Julica, it's Julica! You're safe now."

Velesti opened her eyes again and stared at her. Her lips moved soundlessly, and she frowned with concentration.

"Julica?"

"Yes, yes. Don't you remember me?"

"Julica . . . soure mie . . . ah—my sister?"

Julica flung herself across Velesti, now sobbing with relief as the others crowded around the bed.

"No, no, but as dear to me as a sister. I have been your maid for five years."

Julica now sat up, but immediately Velesti seized her arm and drew herself up too.

"Do not leave!" she said with a subtle but distinct accent, looking fearfully around at the others. "Who are these?"

"Your father, your mother, your brother Reclor, Parrel the groom, and Fras Torumasen, your medician. He brought you back from the dead."

"So weak," said Velesti, still clinging to Julica.

"You've not eaten for two months," said Julica. "It was all that we could do to get you to swallow a little soup."

"Food," said Velesti.

"Are you hungry?" asked Julica.

Even as they watched, the fear went out of Velesti's face, to be replaced by something else. Something hard, sharp, and very, very cold. She held her arms before her, rotating them and frowning as if displeased.

"Food, yes, I . . . need it," replied Velesti. "So weak."

A bed tray was fetched, and a bowl of mutton soup followed within minutes. Velesti grimaced as the liquid reached her cramped stomach, but kept eating. Torumasen discreetly questioned the girl, and observed how she spoke with her family. An hour later Velesti was resting and the medician was at the door, preparing to leave.

"I have seen cases like this before," said Torumasen. "She retains language, manners, and such skills as writing or using a spoon, but she has lost all other memories."

"She did not recognize us at all," said Harren, his arms around his wife.

"There has been damage within her head that has taken until now to heal. Look after her carefully, do not let her become agitated over anything for at least a month or she may revert to being a beautiful but dying sleeper again. In time, her memories will slowly start to return."

"Even of the attack?"

"The attack? Possible, but unlikely. It was so traumatic that she will probably try to hide from it for the rest of her life."

"So those murdering rapists will go unpunished?" asked Reclor, who was standing back in the shadows.

"Well, I too would like justice, but at least we have not lost Velesti."

Julica joined them, looking worried.

"She is alive, but her brain is scarred," concluded the medician. "Let her do whatever makes her feel secure, and gradually bring her back into normal life."

"Anything?" asked Julica.

"Anything. For now it is more important to have her feeling secure. Absolute comfort and security, that will give her the confidence to come out of her shell. Be loving and kind, but do not press yourselves upon her. I shall be back in a few days, but if she has a relapse you must call me at once. Meantime, I have given her a list of light exercises to do, to restore tone to her muscles and build up her strength. I have explained that she must concentrate on doing them, it will provide a focus for her as she recovers. Julica, you must be sure to help her with them, and encourage her to persist if she appears to be giving up. This is a very important duty for you. Do you understand?"

"Yes, Fras Medician, I shall be diligent."

Julica hurried back up the stairs as Torumasen left, but paused as she reached Velesti's door. She had raised her hand to knock when she heard a slow, creaking sound, followed by a soft thump. It happened again, and again. Julica knocked. The sound stopped.

"Yes?" came Velesti's voice.

"It's Julica, Vel. Are you all right?"

"Yes."

"Can I help?

This time there was a longer pause, but finally Velesti said "Yes."

Julica heard footsteps, and the bolt slid back. As the door opened Julica saw that her mistress was dressed in silk pyjamas and Northmoor sandals, and had bound her hair into a makeshift ponytail. The room looked normal, and Velesti was now more steady on her feet.

"Sit on the edge," said Velesti, pointing to the bed, "and keep your legs up."

Julica did as she was told, then Velesti lay on the floor with her head just under the bed. *Do whatever she asks,* thought Julica, the medician had said something like that. Suddenly she felt the bed rising and she gasped with alarm.

"Sit still . . . or leave," grunted Velesti.

"But Vel, what are you doing? You're weak, you should be in the bed, not lifting—"

She caught herself, remembering what the medician had said about encouraging Velesti to do the exercises.

"Bed . . . too light," explained Velesti, pushing Julica up for the fifth time. "Need weight. You."

Julica clung to the edge of the bed, utterly astonished. Only two hours ago Velesti had been pronounced dead, and even after she had come back to life she had barely been able to stand. After eight lifts Velesti stopped to rest.

"Is that all?" asked Julica.

"Three repeats," panted Velesti. "Of eight."

"Oh. And then you rest?"

"No. Then there are other things to do. You can help."

To Julica, the exercises seemed onerous, even to a girl in good health, but then her mistress had come back to life under Torumasen's care so he obviously knew what he was doing.

Velesti began to push the bed up again. At the end of the exercise she was trembling like a frightened puppy and soaked in perspiration, but determined to go on. Two hours later she declared that she was finished. Velesti and Julica sat on the edge of the bed. Velesti was shivering, pale and haggard, but strangely alive with a cold, alien energy.

"And now will you sleep, Vel, darling?" pleaded Julica, almost in tears.

"Not until I eat," said Velesti. "Again."

"Oh, yes, whatever you say. There is some soup—"

"I want a *steak*."

"A steak. Yes, of course."

"And two eggs, carrots, lettuce, cheese, whole grain bread—and water, a pitcher of water."

It was two hours past midnight before Velesti was finally asleep, and even then it was on the floor, beneath blankets, and with an iron poker from the fireplace in her hand. Before dawn she was up again, back at her exercises.

Siding Springs Monastery, Central Confederation

Brother Tontare was not so high in status at the Siding Springs Monastery that he could requisition any telescope in the observatorium whenever he wished. Whenever he had a project that he wanted to pursue, a project that required one of the really large, ancient telescopes, he had to convince the Director of Schedules of its importance. This was generally no easy task.

"Why do you need the forty-inch telescope to study a mere lunar eclipse?" the director asked. "There is nothing to be learned that we do not already know."

"Not the lunar eclipse by the earth but Mirrorsun. I want to watch Mirrorsun's shadow pass across the moon's surface."

"That happens nearly every month. The orbital mathematics are interesting, but were worked out soon after Mirrorsun assumed its present form, twenty years ago."

Brother Tontare opened his folder and handed a sketch to the director. As artwork it was nothing special. The monk had placed certain key craters accurately but had paid no attention to fine detail. The shadow of Mirrorsun was an almost straight line along the lunar surface, slashed hurriedly across the disk. On this sketch, however, there were also three odd serrations.

"The sketch was done three days from full moon, so that some of the detail that we are seeing is from the back of Mirrorsun, the side facing away from the earth."

The director scrutinized the drawing again. The three serrations were evenly spaced, and one was right on the very edge of the lunar disk. Five more rough sketches with precise times appended showed more of the serrations. All had the umbra and penumbra clearly marked; Brother Tontare was precise with his observations.

"These have never been seen before," said the director. "Are you certain about them? Could they have been some distortion in the telescope?"

"I used the ten-inch waterwheel refractor, and have had the Regulator of Lenses and Mirrors check it subsequently."

The Regulator of Lenses and Mirrors was not known to be an idle dreamer, in fact he was one of the most cold, precise, pedantic monks in the monastery's observatorium.

"If this is a true and accurate observation, these shadows represent truly immense objects growing out of the back of the Mirrorsun band. You should look into the mathematics of the shadows, then report back to me."

"Learned Brother, I already have," Brother Tontare insisted.

He went to the door and opened it, then called to someone waiting in the corridor. The stooped, haunted, but smiling figure of Brother Nikalan entered. He was leaning heavily on a cane, and looked more to be in his eighties than the fifty-five years of his real age. The director was never comfortable in Nikalan's presence. The man had a past, and was not entirely sane. He was not a virgin, he had traveled, been a slave in the original Libris Calculor, and he had even been a favorite of the notorious warlord Lemorel Milderellen. Nikalan's life had been everything that the director's had not. In mathematics, the tragic man was without peer.

Nikalan limped over to where the sketches were lying on the director's desk and bent over at an even more alarming angle to peer down at them.

"Ah, Mirrorsun's paddles," he said with animation, as if recognizing an old friend. "Very significant."

The director leaned forward at the word "significant." Science was not his forte, but political intrigue, hierarchical precedence, and anything that anyone else might find significant was something that he could understand.

"You say the serrations are significant, Brother Nikalan. Could you explain yourself?"

"The paddles *may* be significant, Brother. I cannot comment upon them."

"Brother Nikalan, you just said that they were very significant."

"Ah no, Brother. I paused, to imply a full stop after *paddles*. *Very significant* was a separate sentence."

"So the paddles are not significant?"

"I did not say that; I cannot know that. Neither can you."

It was well known that the director had his position because nobody else wanted it, and because he had few skills in mathematics and no patience for observational astronomy. The less that people understood about science, the harder Nikalan worked to force them to think. The Director of Schedules took this as a slight to his authority. In this, the director was correct.

"Tell me what makes you say the word 'significant,' " he said, his patience beginning to fray.

"These paddles, of course," replied Nikalan.

The director closed his eyes, took three deep, slow breaths and forced a blank, black calm into his mind. He could register a disciplinary complaint against Brother Nikalan, but that was a sure path to humiliation in a monasterial tribunal. He glared at Brother Tontare.

"Please leave us, Brother Tontare," he ordered.

With Tontare gone, the director felt a lot happier, although one could not have described him as actually being happy. Nikalan liked to make people think in the same way that drill sergeants liked to make recruits run long distances carrying muskets and wearing packs full of stones. The director's prospects of enduring the next few minutes without being made to look like an absolute idiot were not at all good, so he had decided that he could at least make sure that it did not happen in front of an audience. In a silent act of grudging surrender to his mathematical drill sergeant, the director began to think.

"Are the paddles telling us something?" he asked.

"Oh yes, is it not clear?" responded Nikalan.

"Not to me, Brother Nikalan, no. Suppose that you explain it to me."

"But I already have, here," said Nikalan, pointing to a dozen or so lines of figures.

The figures bore symbols that were used in astronomical calculations. The words "orbital velocity" and "significant positive anomaly" appeared beside "3%" and all of them were on the last line of the calculations. Clearly they were a conclusion.

Unaccustomed thought was producing the feeling of uncomfortable pressure within the director's head. *What* was orbiting faster than it should have been? The moon? Mirrorsun? The earth? The shadows were of the Mirrorsun paddles moving across the face of the moon, and the monastic astronomers knew things about the moon, like its size and how far away it was, and even how fast it orbited the earth. Were Mirrorsun's paddles making the moon orbit faster? He opened his mouth to voice this opinion, then closed it again. The speed of the moon could be measured at any time. The paddles could only be seen from Earth when their shadows were cast on the lunar surface, so the paddles were what was moving too fast. All that was visible on Mirrorsun's inner surface was the distorted reflection of the sun, otherwise it was just a featureless, dark band; one could not directly determine what speed it moved at. Suddenly the director had his conclusion.

"Mirrorsun is spinning faster than it ought to be," he announced, beads of perspiration visible on his forehead.

"Yes, very good," said Nikalan.

"And it is accelerating."

"Even better."

"Why is this important?" he asked before he could stop himself.

"Mirrorsun might break," replied Nikalan.

Mirrorsun might break. Mirrorsun had an area bigger than the combined landmasses of the earth. Even though it was thought to be no more than inches thick, its absolute weight would be truly immense. It was also said to be intelligent, to be controlled by an immense, ancient calculating machine actually capable of reasoning. It was a weapon too, it had destroyed an entire army just over two decades earlier. Was it sick? Was it mad? Did those terms have any meaning for it? Would it endanger the earth?

"Were Mirrorsun to break, its fragments would fly away from the earth," said the director.

"But the dynamics of orbiting, flexible fragments of band are not well understood," replied Nikalan. "They could fly into highly elliptical orbits, with the aphelions near the orbit of the moon, and the perihelions below the surface of the earth."

Again the director had to think. A perihelion below the surface of the earth. This was clearly impossible, of course. The fragments would have to tunnel through solid rock at thousands of miles per hour. Yes, clearly impossible. The worst that might happen would be that a fragment of Mirrorsun the size of quite a large mayorate might slam into the earth. This would merely leave a large crater. A crater . . . farther across than the Director of Schedules had ever traveled in his entire life!!

"I am going to recommend to the abbot that every telescope in the monastery be turned upon the moon for the next eclipse," declared the director. "What is more, monks with portable telescopes must be sent to other mayorates in case of cloud. I shall also recommend that the observational monasteries at Cowra, Griffith, and Euroa be alerted to the danger and urged to make appropriate observations. It is vital to know whether the Mirrorsun band is rotating any faster at the next lunar eclipse."

"A very reasonable reaction," responded Nikalan.

The director dipped a quill into the inkwell and began to draft a note to the abbot. Nikalan stood peering over his shoulder, making occasional suggestions. After a half hour the Director of Schedules emerged with Nikalan, nodded to Brother Tontare and hurried off along the corridor. Tontare stood up and went after Nikalan as he shuffled slowly away in the opposite direction from the abbot's rooms.

"Was he sympathetic?" asked Tontare.

"Better still, he was actually frightened."

•   •   •

The abbot read the note carefully the second time. The first had been just a scan for the general meaning and importance. "Craters the size of entire mayorates" had secured his undivided attention. He read it a third time before looking up.

"Observations by Brother Tontare, analysis by Brother Nikalan, recommendation by Brother Disparon," said the abbot. "A very young and junior observational monk, a much older and very peculiar analyst monk, and an administrative monk not known for expertise in either of the aforesaid fields. How do you account for this?"

"We are a team," replied Brother Disparon with some accuracy, "but the importance is in the conclusion."

"Oh, I agree, but do we really have to turn every telescope in all four of the Logistican Order's monasteries to the moon on the night of October the seventh? Why not two lesser instruments here, with a third at Euroa? That would give us an indication of whether we have to look more closely the following month if the matter looks to be serious."

"By which time we would have two moderately accurate observations, to which a highly accurate observation would then be added on November the fourth. Better to have a comparison between at least two highly accurate observations."

Now it was the abbot who was being forced to think, for Disparon knew his politics as well as Nikalan knew his mathematics. Three decades ago the great observational monasteries had missed both the mining activities of the ancient automata on the lunar surface and the first signs that Mirrorsun band was forming in a much lower Earth orbit. The order had been severely humiliated as a result. As a further result, the abbot of the time had been forcibly retired by the Christian Church of Supreme Knowledge, the order's parent body and the largest Christian church on the continent.

"If I am wrong, what is to be lost by following my recommendations?" prompted Disparon.

"A half night's observations, resulting in some angry senior monks," replied the abbot.

"So what?" responded Disparon.

The consequences of inaction should Disparon be right did not even bear thinking about, the abbot was certain of that. He appended his approval to the note, and sent Brother Disparon away to implement its recommendations.

Griffith, Central Confederation

The light of dawn was spilling through the hallway's leadlight window when the bolt to Velesti's door was drawn back sharply. The door opened. Velesti stood before the waiting Julica, dressed in the uniform of the Dragon Librarian Service and with a splash of yellow on her sleeve. It was the old-style designation of rank in the Dragon Librarian Service, as Dramoren's decree on uniforms had not yet been implemented in Griffith. Velesti's long auburn hair had been chopped to shoulder length, and was again bound into a ponytail.

"For breakfast I want three eggs, grain bread toast, two apples, boiled oats with honey, and a pitcher of milk," she said in a hollow but steady voice.

"For you, right away, my dearest," Julica assured her. "But your hair, your long, beautiful hair!"

"It was annoying me," explained Velesti tersely.

"I—I—you look so pale. Perhaps some makeup, rouge and eyeshadow—"

"Nothing!" said Velesti firmly, with something almost like fear flashing in her eyes.

She walked slowly and with caution, but she was undeniably more steady than the night before. She descended the stairs without stumbling, although she held on to the banister all the way and had to rest at the bottom. Breakfast was served in the kitchen, and she slowly ate boiled oats with clover honey and goat milk. When she had finished she began stalking through the house, as if exploring. Julica followed. When they reached the dining room they found Reclor sitting at the table, cleaning a Cambrissen dueling pistol.

"Vel, you're walking!" exclaimed Reclor, springing up so abruptly that his chair toppled. "Here, sit down."

Reclor reached out for Velesti's hand but she flinched away. Behind her, Julica nodded to Reclor. He held his hands apart and backed away slowly. Velesti pulled back a chair and sat down. Reclor returned to his dueling pistol.

"In eleven days I turn fifteen," said the youth ominously. "Fifteen is the legal dueling age."

"What nonsense is this?" demanded Julica.

"In eleven days I shall fight for the honor of my sister."

Velesti seemed not to notice. She reached out and picked the other dueling pistol from its case on the table. She hefted it clumsily.

"Heavy," she observed.

"You have to get used to the weight of guns," said Reclor. "You will need to learn to shoot to gain your higher Dragon Librarian gradings."

Velesti stood up and walked over to the gun rack. She reached up and lifted a Morelac twin-barrel flintlock from its brackets. Turning it over in her long, pale fingers, she pulled back the left striker and checked the priming pan. It was empty. She pulled the trigger. There was an emphatic click as the flint in the striker sent a shower of sparks into the empty priming pan.

"Heavy," Velesti said again.

"Just what are you doing with that dueling pair?" Julica asked Reclor.

"I have a dispute with three officers in the Griffith Mayoral Musketeers," replied Reclor casually.

"What? You mean those who attacked Vel—ah, I mean—"

"Yes."

"Reclor, you cannot challenge those men to a duel," said Julica. "They're veterans, they have years of experience at fighting, they are real killers. You are not."

"I think you will be surprised," responded Reclor, frowning slightly.

"You're just a boy!"

"And a very dangerous, devious boy. I have already sent word to Martyne at Balesha. I told him that Elsile had been murdered."

"Who was Elsile?" asked Velesti.

"Martyne's sister, your best friend!" cried Julica, suddenly blind with anger and grief. "Don't you remember? Don't you care? She and you were raped by those sons of pig turds, then—"

Suddenly Julica caught herself and stood horrified with her hands over her mouth. Velesti turned to her.

"I do not remember, but I do care," Velesti said in slow, well-enunciated Centralian.

She turned back to Reclor. Julica gradually began to breathe again, almost swooning with relief. Velesti had not retreated back into herself upon learning the truth.

"An hour after Martyne arrives there will be nobody left to kill," said Reclor.

"Martyne has renounced our world, Reclor," said Julica, her voice barely above a whisper.

"If that is true, then it is all up to me, Frelle Julica. I must avenge both Elsile and Velesti, and I shall not fail."

"Avenge what happened to me?" asked Velesti, her words slow and evenly spaced.

"Come, Vel, let us walk in the garden," said Julica hurriedly.

"Reclor, am I your only sister?"

"Yes, Vel."

"And I was ravished? By musketeers?"

"Vel—"

"No!" shouted Julica. "Vel, trust me, do not ask or you might vanish back inside yourself and never return."

The North American West Coast

What flew out over the ruins of San Francisco were little more than two enormous wings with eight compression engines each. They were lumbering along at barely one hundred miles per hour, at five thousand feet and in a shallow climb. There were two crew in each wing, but the second super-regal was also carrying five passengers and their tool packs.

As they crossed the coastline the gangers crowded at the small viewing ports, but after that there was just unbroken ocean beneath a blue sky. Another half hour passed before the wing captain called to the navigator and unstrapped.

"Take over, Mardean, I am going back."

"Anything I can do, Saireme Airlord?"

"It is time the gangers heard what they are to do, and they had better hear it from me."

Samondel was dressed in her embroidered flight jacket, which by now had a symbol for her duel victory as well as the earlier victories in clear air combat. At the sight of her, the gangers all returned to their wicker seats and sat quietly. Samondel was by no means tall, but even she had to stoop as she stood before them in what had once been the super-regal's bomb bay.

"You all know what this venture is about," she began. "Sair Avoncor, would you like to tell us what you understand it to be?"

Overawed by his ruler, the burly man scratched at his stubbly hair as he composed his reply.

"Saireme Airlord, there's a big island off the coast, one that has really important relics of olden times. You'll cruise over the island and find a place that we can rough into a wingfield in two weeks. Then we'll parachute down to do the work, and you will return in two weeks with scholars and artisans. They will try to learn the secret of the relics. We'll not touch anything, except to make a wing-field and hunt game."

"That is quite correct, Sair, except for one detail. You are to make three wingfields, not one. You will be away for two seasons, not two weeks, and you will continue to receive six times your usual rate of pay for as long as you are away."

She allowed them to absorb this astonishing news. They would come home with three years' pay each, and the agreement was that the money would not be taxed at all. Avoncor raised his hand, and Samondel nodded to him.

"Where's the two other wingfields to be, then, Saireme? There's only one island, a couple of hours west. Hawaii, it's called on the old maps—I think."

"The *first* island is *twenty hours southwest*," said Samondel, her voice clear, slow, and precise above the drone of the compression engines.

"But Saireme, these things only fly for seven hours," replied Avoncor, a fact that all the others were also aware of.

"When loaded with bombs for combat, yes, but they have been stripped bare and given extra fuel tanks. My navigator and I have only a gallon of water between us and a pound each of dried meat and nuts to chew on for the whole forty hours that we will be in the air. Neither of us has a parachute, either. All of this gives us a cruising time of eighteen hours with your weight and tools added, but past midpoint we shall be refueled in flight by our companion super-regal."

"That leaves a very narrow margin for returning to the mainland," Avoncor pointed out.

"That is my concern, not yours. Are there any more questions?"

"The other two islands, Saireme. Ah, where are they?"

"One is two thousand miles further southwest, and is called Samoa. Nearly as far again is New Zealand. After that, well, we know the Australicans have their own wingfields."

"For the wings they stole from us, during the war."

"Correct, but we shall try not to hold any grudges."

It actually took a little less than nineteen hours to reach the main island of the Hawaii chain, as the winds were light all the way. There was cloud at the summit of an immense volcanic cone to starboard, but they came in low, over a coastal plain.

"That, there," called the navigator, pointing while he looked through his binoculars. "Seems to be part of an old road, and it's fairly clear."

"After two thousand years?" asked Samondel.

"The road was probably cut out of rock in the first place, so trees are unlikely to grow in its surface. It looks straight and level for about three miles."

"Do you think you could have half a mile of that made clear and firm enough to support this thing in a fortnight?" Samondel asked Avoncor, who was in the cockpit with them.

"It just has to be firm and level for the width of the wheels, Saireme. The trees and bushes to the sides only have to be felled and burned so that the wings and propellers have clearance. We can do it."

They climbed in a wide spiral until at parachute height, then the navigator wound the rear hatch open.

"Two weeks, mind!" said Avoncor as he stood ready to jump. "Come back with a bottle of Black Dirkfang for each of us, or don't bother to come back."

"You have the wingfield ready or I'll pour all five bottles into the reserve fuel tank," replied Mardean, slapping him on the shoulder.

Avoncor jumped. The others shambled after him and the navigator kept them moving, not allowing them to stop and think. Back with Samondel again, he could see five white parachutes already close to the ground. One by one they collapsed into the mottled olive green and dark gray landscape.

"Nineteen hours and twenty minutes," said the navigator. "We should reach the mainland with a big margin if we turn back now."

"Watch for a signal, keep watching."

"There, a flashing signal mirror . . . / ALL SAFE / ESTIMATE FOR WINGFIELD 3 WEEKS /"

By way of reply Samondel revved the engines, then drooped the port wing—and kept on rolling. The navigator cried out in terror, then they were level again for a moment before Samondel began a leisurely turn.

"I didn't know a super-regal could do that!" exclaimed Mardean.

"Neither did I," replied Samondel.

"You could have just waggled the wings."

"The very brave deserve a very special salute, Sair Mardean."

Rochester, the Rochestrian Commonwealth

Closter and Lermai had worked in Libris since they had been boys of ten, and both had recently been presented with their certificates of appreciation for eighty-five years in the service of the enormous mayoral library of Rochester. They had been relatively young men in their sixties when the legendary Highliber Zarvora had been appointed to run the place. They had seen the first Calculor of Libris built, and had been there when it had been commissioned, operating with only a few dozen human components. They watched it grow to be powered by several thousand souls, and for over a decade they had worked in the Calculor, sweeping floors, carrying meals, cleaning instruments, pushing book trolleys, and occasionally dragging out the bodies of dead components. They had seen it replaced by a calculor driven by electrical essence, and had helped to dismantle and carry away its furniture and equipment. Then, along with the former components, they had carried in and assembled the wires, relay banks, and register switches of the electrical calculor, ZAR 2.

"Told ye this thing would not last," said Closter as they pushed a trolley laden with blackened tangles of wire and melted relay switch banks.

"It lasted twenty-two years," Lermai pointed out.

"Ah, but how much of that time was spent broken? Downtime, as the regulators call it."

"Aye, but when it's up it's lots faster."

"Aye, but how often is it down?"

"Ah . . . sometimes."

They reached a guarded door, but the guards opened it for them without so much as a challenge. Outside in a cobbled courtyard, they began to heave the mortal remains of the electrical calculor onto a rubbish cart.

"The original Calculor ran from 1696 GW until '08. That's twelve years. Twelve years of continuous running."

"They stopped it sometimes."

"Like when?"

"Like when they used to take lazy components out and shoot 'em. All the other components were made to watch the executions. Made 'em work better."

"Aye, but that was not often. I'd say that if you looked at the registers of the duty regulators, you would find that the human calculor was running longer than the electrical essence one."

They pushed the empty trolley back inside the building but did not return straight to Dolorian Hall. Instead they shuffled to the component cells, where they loaded their book trolley with four benches, a dozen abacus frames, and a length of chain with manacles attached.

"Well, are ye?" asked Lermai.

"Are I what?"

"Going to look at the registers of the duty regulators for the past thirty-four years?"

"Aye, of course."

"But you're nearly ninety-five."

"So are you."

"You'll never finish."

"I have fifteen years until I even begin to think of planning to retire. I intend to be the first library attendant to serve in Libris for a hundred years."

"But I'm a month older than you are, and I joined a month earlier."

"So? You're going to work until only ninety-five. You've been saying it for years."

"I . . . might work on."

"What?" exclaimed Closter, thoroughly alarmed. "Why?"

"Well, I never realized that I might be the first to work a hundred years in Libris."

Closter shuffled the next few dozen steps in silence.

"Unless ye got beneath a very large, falling book," he muttered, more to himself than Lermai.

In Dolorian Hall the carpenters, clockmakers, and Dragon Librarians were all standing silent as Closter and Lermai arrived with their trolley. The elderly men began to unload, but were told to stop by a Dragon Green. Two dozen desks were already populated by components, all of whom had their abacus frames reset. A system herald and several regulators stood ready. A Dragon Gold who was the former system controller addressed them.

"The reference beat will be every two seconds at first," he explained. "For this revival exercise, we shall only be running the old SYKO operating system."

"That's Submit or You're Killed Otherwise," said Lermai.

"Aye, aye, I was there when it was first used!" Closter hissed back.

"We shall be running a precompiled decoding program written in SLAP."

"That's Simple Language for Assembly Protocol," explained Lermai.

"I know, I know!" exclaimed Closter.

Everyone turned to stare at the two attendants.

"Would you mind not distracting the slaves?" said the system controller.

"Components," the system herald added.

"Quite so," he agreed, but with a sneer at the system herald. "Now, at my beat . . . start!"

The system controller set a clock in motion that rang a bell every two seconds, and the components got to work on their abacus frames. Lermai had counted 317 beats when the only FUNCTION on the team held up his hand. The herald cried "System hold!"

The system controller walked over as the FUNCTION wrote down the output in the corresponding words in Austaric.

"The message reads / GET IT WORKING BY OCTOBER OR I SHALL ADD YOUR BALLS TO THE BEADS ON YOUR AB-ACUS FRAMES / HIGHLIBER DRAMOREN /" the FUNCTION read. The all-male team of components squirmed uneasily.

"Well, it seems that you are safe from becoming eunuch components," said the system controller. "For now. That is precisely what was in the test message. Three cheers for the new Libris Calculor."

Closter and Lermai returned to unloading their trolley as ZAR 3, the third version of the Libris Calculor, rattled into life again.

"Hch, just like the old days," Closter chuckled. "Wonder how long before the first component gets shot for negligence?"

Griffith, the Central Confederation

Reclor was in the garden, practicing his dueling turns when Velesti found him. He was walking in a straight line away from a melon impaled on a stick at the height of a man's head. With each step he counted aloud.

". . . eight, nine, ten!"

He whirled and brought the gun around in both hands and squeezed the trigger. There was a click-pop as the flint struck sparks into the charge in the priming pan, but there was no main charge or ball in the barrel. Velesti stood looking at him, her arms folded beneath her breasts.

"My brother, may I speak with you?" she asked.

"Well, yes."

"What happened to me?"

"You were sick for a long time. Uncle Torumasen cured you."

"Someone attacked me, and it turned my brain. You are training to avenge me in a duel. I have collected parts of the story and strung them together. Now I want to know the rest."

Reclor shrugged. "The medician said the truth might drive you deep into yourself again. Julica should have kept her tongue in better check."

"The truth might also free memories of the attack," said Velesti flatly. "You may be challenging the wrong man to a duel."

The thought had crossed Reclor's mind, but he had considered it too dangerous in the light of what Torumasen had said. Now Velesti had asked, however, and that seemed to change the situation. He indicated a garden seat with his Cambrissen. They sat down together, but at opposite ends.

"You had just passed the Dragon Yellow level librarians's examination, and had been walking home from the dinner with your friend Elsile. Both of you were set upon by musketeers, and some of their officers. They raped you both in a deserted stable for hours, then set the place afire. Two passing officers broke in to save what they thought were horses, but instead found Elsile dead and you unconscious. Her throat was cut, and you were both naked and covered in filth and terribly beaten."

"How do you know who the musketeers were?"

Relief coursed through Reclor. Obviously the story was nothing more than just that to her: a story. She had no memories at all of the terrible night.

"One of the musketeers returned to retrieve something, and was caught. At first he named everyone involved, then lawyers and magistrates got to him, along with the rich family of one the officers. The musketeer who was caught is still in jail, but the others are merely at the barracks and wear the yellow circle of inquisition at their collars. No trial, no justice, and honor definitely not satisfied. All that has happened has been a civil hearing."

Reclor took a key from his pocket and led Velesti into the house and to the parlor. Unlocking a glass-fronted library cabinet, he took a briefing box from one of the shelves and set it in front of Velesti.

"If you wish to learn a little of the truth, you will have to open the box and read for yourself. Enough hurt has been done to you, and I'll do no more—but neither shall I hide the truth if you ask for it."

Velesti opened the box. She took out three sheets of poorpaper, and a parchment declaring that further proceedings were suspended, awaiting the pleasure of the city magistrate.

"Is that all?" she asked.

"Yes. The declarations of witnesses, the statement from the musketeer, and finally an addendum declaring that the musketeer had withdrawn his earlier statement. It does, however, give me the names of eleven musketeers, two operations officers, and two commissioned officers. Seventeen is a standard squad, but the two other men have been accounted for as innocent. One was a sergeant who became involved in a brawl early in the night and was locked up by the Constable's Runners. The other met with a harlot and left the others just before you and Elsile were attacked. In general terms the musketeer's first statement is as close to the truth as anyone is liable to confess."

Velesti read the pages carefully.

"I do not know any of the men named."

"Of course not. You were set upon merely because you were female and chanced to stray within reach."

"Now you have challenged one of these men to a duel?"

"Yes. A lieutenant. I insulted him in public, quite deliberately, and he made a declaration of the aggrieved. In the eyes of the law, that makes me the challenger. Because I was still fourteen I had the option of naming a champion or waiting until I could legally duel."

Velesti put the sheets of paper back in the box and closed the lid.

"Now I understand," she said, her voice vague and flat.

He placed the box back in the library case and locked the glass door. Velesti now saw that the words "Martyne" and "Hearing" had been pressed into the leather and highlighted with gold.

"I did not see the name Martyne on any of the documents in the box," said Velesti, sitting with her hands clasped on the table.

"Martyne is Elsile's brother. Five years ago he left to pursue a vocation in the Balesha monastery, far away, in the West."

"Balesha," echoed Velesti.

"When he returns . . . well, let us just say that there will be no survivors left for me to deal with."

"True," responded Velesti.

She stood up. Her movements were smooth and careful, as if she were frightened of falling. She stared at Reclor, unblinking.

"You do not have to duel for me," she said, every word slow, precise, and deliberate.

"I was not there when you needed me, Vel."

"If you die, who will provide the family heir? It shall never be me. I cannot stand the idea of touching a man."

"Then the Disore name will die. Better that than shame and dishonor."

The afternoon became evening, and the evening began to fade into night. Harren and Elene Disore had dinner with their son, trying to persuade him to accept the services of a contract champion. Reclor was firm. Again and again he insisted that he wanted to fight, he had to fight, and he would fight.

"*You* had a chance to make a challenge and use the family champion," said Reclor to his father as he contemplated his very first glass of wine.

"Dueling is the final resort against injustice," pleaded Harren. "There has been no inquest or trial yet."

"There will be neither!" Reclor shouted back, slamming his glass down so hard that the remaining contents splashed dark red on the tablecloth. "Lieutenant Grammain is the city magistrate's son."

Reclor stood up, his shoulders back and his arms hanging by his sides.

"There is much to do, please excuse me."

This was the end of persuasion. Reclor was going to fight, and there was no more that could be done about it. His parents stood together and came around the table to where he was waiting.

"You bring honor to the family," declared Harren, grasping Reclor's right hand in both of his.

Elene embraced Reclor with a great rustle of lace and skirts. "I love you, and I am so proud of you," she said, her words forced and broken.

Reclor left without another word, for it was bad luck to say goodbye before a duel. He had his parents' blessing, which he had not expected. A thin, bright ray of optimism shone through the gloom that had been hanging about him all day. There was a chance that he might live. He was sure to fight with honor, but perhaps not to die for it. Good omens were the smiles of fortune, or so some old saying went.

"Fras Disore, have you spoken to Medician Torumasen?" asked Julica anxiously as she was clearing the plates away.

"About Velesti? Yes, I have."

"Is it—ah, is she crazed?"

"Between you and me only, yes. He thinks her behavior is predictable, however."

"Predictable? But Fras, she eats enough for three, and she has gained twenty pounds in sixteen days. She will be as fat as a prize sow by Christmas at this rate."

"Does she do Torumasen's exercises?"

"Well, yes, quite faithfully. More than faithfully, and every day, but—"

"Good. He thinks that she should have something simple to focus on, to cling to."

"But Fras, twenty pounds in sixteen days!"

"That brings her weight to just one hundred and ten pounds, which is hardly excessive. Frelle Julica, the medician says that victims of such terrible attacks can chose a number of paths. Some suicide, some lose their minds, some shelter behind the men of their households, and some even pretend to become boys. In the last case they seem to think that they have ceased to be girls, and so can never be ravished again."

"She will become ugly."

"So, what is worse? Ugly and alive, or the way she was—beautiful and dying? She may think that her beauty caused the attack. She may blame it for what happened."

"Fras Disore, that is not all! When she reads she turns the pages so fast that anyone else would have trouble just reading their numbers. Fras, she does not remember me, *she does not want* to remember me."

Julica fell to her knees beside the table, her hands clasped. The elder Disore patted her head gently but condescendingly.

"My dear, the medician says that she may be fashioning herself into someone new, and that she regards what she used to be as a failure. Please, try to be the new Velesti's friend and companion."

Julica slowly got to her feet, dabbing at her eyes with her handkerchief.

"I'll try, Fras Disore, but it will be hard."

Reclor washed, cleaned his teeth, then began to dress in the clothes that he had prepared weeks earlier. Everything had been meticulously, scrupulously laid out, polished, cleaned, or tuned to perfection. There was not a rule or protocol in the dueling or law books that he had not learned, attended to, or at least prepared for.

There was a soft rapping at the door. Reclor slid back the bolt, to find Julica waiting in the corridor.

"May I come in?" she asked after he had stood looking puzzled for a moment.

Reclor stood aside and she entered. Within his room were the birthday presents of his friends and family, but the youth showed no signs of settling down for the evening to enjoy them. He was dressed in a white shirt with fashionable puffed sleeves and a starched collar, a wide belt, blue riding slacks and calf-length boots. The pair of Cambrissen dueling pistols lay in a case that sat open on the table, and beside it was an authority to duel, signed by a magistrate that day. Julica closed the door behind her.

"So, you intend to go through with it?"

"Yes, it is arranged."

"And your parents will lose another child."

"Thank you for your faith in my skills, Frelle Julica. Besides, Velesti is still alive."

"Her body is alive, but the mind in it is only a few days old. She is a strange, cold thing now. It is hard to be close to her."

Reclor squared off in front of a full-length mirror, then turned slowly, checking his clothing for fit and stray threads.

"You look very fetching," observed Julica.

"Thank you. Do you think they will take me seriously?"

"Oh, yes. I presume the duel is tonight?"

"Yes."

"When?"

"In three hours. Don't try to stop me."

"Do what you will, I only want to protect you, Reclor. I have served you and your family for five years. I do not want you killed."

"I do not want myself killed either, but this is a matter of duty. You have duties to the family, and so do I. Well, time to be off."

Julica leaned back against his door and folded her arms. "So early?"

"Things to arrange."

"That is what your second is for."

"Some things a second cannot do."

"Like the Touch of Serenity?"

"Yes, well, bad luck to enter a duel as a virgin."

"Who is she?"

Reclor squirmed. "How should I know? Some whore on Hawker Lane, I'll try to chose one who looks sympathetic."

"You may get poxed."

"I'll wear a skin."

"Wearing a skin is bad luck."

"Then I won't. If I die, will I care about the pox?"

"That is not a good attitude to take into a duel. You should go in with everything to live for."

Reclor closed the case on the Cambrissans and snapped the latch across, then reached for his coat.

"I am open to constructive suggestions, but otherwise I would appreciate it if you would wish me luck and step away from the door."

Julica did not move. They stared at each other, unblinking. She unfolded her arms, reached up and undid the top button of her blouse.

"I have a suggestion," she said. "It is very constructive."

Reclor deduced the intent of her suggestion instantly.

"I, I, I—no!" he burst out.

She undid a second button. "Poking about with some strange whore will do nothing to steady your nerves."

"No! You're like a sister to me."

She undid a third button. "But I am not your sister, I am a servant. I am twenty-two, and you are fifteen. We are consenting adults in the eyes of Confederation law."

"I've known you since I was ten! You wiped my face, washed my clothes, even laid me over your knee and smacked my arse!"

She undid a fourth button, then pulled her blouse open to allow her breasts to stand free. "Maybe so, Reclor, but just now I am your friend and your lady, and nothing else matters or even exists," she said, now advancing on him. "I am going to make love with you, for there is no other man that I care for as much as you. Now get undressed and get into bed."

"Dammit, you've made that bed for five years!"

"And tomorrow I'll be sure to wash the sheets. Reclor, other youths are forever chasing and pestering their maids, and often bedding them. I am impressed that you have always behaved honorably toward me, but there is nothing unusual about a maid coupling with her master's son."

"I—I'm ashamed."

"Why?"

"I'm a virgin. A harlot might laugh, but then she would be out of my life forever. You work here, you—"

"It's bad luck for a virgin to enter a duel, Reclor, and I'm here to make sure that you're not when you leave tonight. I can provide the Touch of Serenity as well as anyone, and perhaps even better."

She began to unbutton his shirt as he stood with his coat in one hand and his case of pistols in the other. She slid her arms around him and pressed her quite high and prominent breasts against his skimpy chest.

"Reclor, Reclor, I want revenge for what happened to Velesti and Elsile as much as you do, and this way I shall be there, standing with you as you turn and fire. Lie with me, let me help, my brave and dashing lover. It is a mater of honor for me as well."

The mention of honor suddenly made all the difference to Reclor. He dropped his coat and placed his dueling pistols on the table, then wrapped his arms around Julica. She put a hand behind his head, drew his face close to hers, then kissed him. As their lips pressed together the memories of the previous five years faded away, and for a short time they became, truly, lovers.

It was only fifty-five minutes later that Reclor slipped from his bed and began pulling on his clothes. Julica sat up, hugging her knees against her breasts.

"You don't have to leave for another hour," she said.

"I have things to arrange. I had not reckoned on taking so long."

"So long? How long had you planned to spend doing. . . ." She waved her hand in circles. "Doing what we just did?"

"Ten minutes."

Julica shook her head, then rested it on her knees.

"When you get back, I shall have to introduce you to the idea of appreciating the pleasure of a woman a little more."

Reclor blushed and turned away.

"Julica, I could not possibly impose like that."

"Reclor, did it ever cross your mind that I might *enjoy* what we have just been doing? Sex is not something filthy that men do to women, it's pleasure to be shared. Look forward to spending the rest of this night with me, Reclor; survive the duel for it."

Reclor sat on the edge of the bed and embraced Julica again.

"I shall return," he whispered through her unbound hair and into her ear.

"What do you have to do? Your second should be arranging everything."

"Things unrelated to the duel, but things related to honor."

Here it is, twenty-five gold daras," said Reclor, counting out the coins.

"I might be cashiered for this," muttered the watchouse guard.

"The world is wide, and you are now rich. Now return to your post."

Reclor descended into the cells area, carrying a torch. The cells were all secured by doors of thick redgum, each with a tiny access slot bound with iron. At cell five Reclor put an iron spike into the lock and twisted. It gave a soft creak, then tore away. He drew back the bolt and opened the door.

"Musketeer Glarek?" he asked as he held the torch before him.

Three prisoners stirred, blinking up from their narrow bunks.

"Aye," said one, raising his hand.

"I'm here to free you, come with me."

Outside the cell again, Reclor slid the bolt back quietly. They ascended the stairs.

"I'll be wantin' coin fer those weeks in there," said Glarek as they entered the keeper's office. "All the others walkin' free, while I take the—"

Reclor pressed the baffle tube of his flintlock against the back of the musketeer's head and fired. There was a shark crack, like a swagger stick striking flagstones. Glarek fell.

"Consider yourself free," said Reclor as he began dragging the body over to the pantry.

Reclor walked slowly into the Gardens of the Commoners, his second carrying the case with the dueling pistols. The youth's legs felt as unsteady as those of a newborn foal, and he was sweating. The moderator was waiting there, holding a single lantern. Four other figures stood close by.

"You're exhausted, you can't shoot in this condition!" insisted Reclor's second.

"I had business on the other side of town, and some wastrel stole my pony."

"We can call a stay until—"

"No! We duel this very hour or not at all."

The medician examined Reclor and declared him fit to take the field. Both duelists now approached the moderator, who held up his lantern to formally identify Reclor and Grammain. Both seconds remained masked.

"You realize that this duel is not legally constituted, even though it is not actually criminal," said the moderator. "As the challenged party Fras Grammain can claim self-defense if he kills you, Fras Disore. If you win you will be charged with murder, and your only hope of cheating the gallows will be to prove just cause."

"I understand all that, but I am committed to the field of honor," replied Reclor. "Exceedingly committed."

The two duelists stood back to back in the dim light provided by Mirrorsun and the moderator's lantern. In the distance the gunshots of revelers and the glow of a bonfire added an eerie backdrop of festivity.

"This is a voluntary duel outside the rules laid down in Confederation legislation," the moderator said in a clear, sharp voice. "There will be no target shoot, and no right to call distance. I shall call the distance, and remember that I am only here to declare self-defense or murder. Understood, Fras Disore?"

"Yes."

"Understood, Fras Grammain?"

"Understood."

"I shall now begin counting. At the count of ten, turn and fire at will. One, two, three—"

A gunshot flashed beside a tree, directly ahead of Reclor. As the youth began to collapse he half turned, but managed only to fire into the air before oblivion claimed him. The moderator plunged a knife underhand into the back of Reclor's second, then ripped upward.

"Turn the boy to face the line," said the moderator, "then weight his second with stones and dump him in the lake."

"Damn, but it's good to see the end of this," muttered Grammain.

"Next time you go snatching free pussy make sure she's just a whore," hissed the moderator sharply.

The moderator stood in silence until the four others returned from the lake. He gazed at the glow from the bonfire across the city, and listened to the whistles of the Constable's Runners and the pealing of bells giving their alarm about something. Finally the field was in order and Reclor's substitute second was kneeling by the corpse with ten extra gold coins in his purse. The medician bowed to the moderator.

"Have you an outcome?" asked the moderator.

"Lieutenant Grammain's ball passed through Fras Disore's chest, killing him instantly."

"Gentlefolk, are you agreed that Fras Disore fired first?" asked the moderator.

"We are."

"Then summon a Constable's Runner. A death must be declared."

The moderator blew his whistle and they waited. The glow continued in the distance. No runners came. Eventually the medician had to be sent to find a Constable's Runner, and even then he did not return with one for another hour.

Julica had been extinguishing the lamps in the lower floor of the house when she entered the parlor from the antedoor. A single lamp burned in a wall bracket, and all was in order as she cast her gaze over the familiar room. All? Perhaps not quite all. There was the box with "Martyne" and "Hearing" in the glass-fronted cabinet, but "Martyne" was no longer on the right. Someone had replaced it upside down, perhaps someone in a hurry. Julica reached out and tugged at the glass door's handle. It was not locked. There was a soft clack as a key turned in the front door of the house. Someone had left in a hurry, presumably because he had heard her approaching footsteps. There was another clack as the door was locked from the outside. Julica drew out the box. It was empty.

Without even thinking Julica snatched Harren's spare cloak and pentacorner hat from the hallstand rack and unlocked the front door. From the drawing room came the drone of prayers. Julica had been told that Elene Disore was keeping vigil with a parson, Velesti, and some friends, waiting for word of the duel. Julica pulled the door shut behind her and pattered out to the garden gate. In the distance, a figure was striding away into the gloom. The moon was down, but Mirrorsun gleamed brightly, high in the sky. Julica set off in pursuit, unsure of what she was doing and not even armed. Who knew precisely where to find the box intended for Martyne Camderine, and who had a key to the Disore mansion's front door? The intruder had a thick-set chest and broad shoulders, but a very narrow waist, and he wore a sharply cut, tapering musketeer's jacket. It was definitely not Reclor.

Even though Julica's quarry had a head start, he was walking at an even, unhurried pace and was now making no attempt at stealth. The streets were not crowded, and those that they passed paid them no heed. The musketeer was moving in a methodical way, checking street signs at every corner and gradually making his way northwest. The buildings grew more crowded as the streets narrowed, then they were past one final corner and in Militia Square. Only a few yards away was the city barracks. Barely ten minutes since leaving the mansion, Julica guessed.

The musketeer walked on steadily toward the gates. Reluctant to be too exposed, Julica had stopped in the shadows at the edge of the square. A musketeer thief, she decided, he had stolen the records meant for Martyne. How had he known? Perhaps Reclor was dead, perhaps he had babbled out some boast about messages left for Martyne with his dying breath. Two guards sauntered forward to bar the distant figure's path—then Julica heard two muffled reports! Both guards dropped and lay still, and the figure paused to remove their pistols before walking on through the gates.

Julica stood leaning against a wall, barely able to comprehend what had taken place as she watched the musketeer vanish into a building. Someone had just shot down two sentries on duty in front of the largest barracks in the Central Confederation! He had apparently used silencing baffles as well. A warrior. Perhaps even more than a warrior. Someone trained in Balesha. The intruder emerged again, now wearing a cloak and holding what seemed to be a large book to the light of a lamp. After a moment he discarded the book and walked off to a nearby dormitory. Julica could see just the one figure for the next two minutes, slipping from one dormitory to another, apparently in search of someone or something.

At the sound of slurred cursing and shouting, Julica crouched farther back into the shadows. Some revelers were returning to the barracks, but were in an advanced state of intoxication. They were only yards from the bodies of the guards when they realized that something appeared to be wrong.

"Murder! Bloody murder!" bellowed a voice, then a whistle pierced the night air. Julica saw the intruder's distant form as he lifted a lamp from its mounting, carried it to a dormitory, and flung it inside. Flames lit up the windows from within, and cries of pain and alarm echoed out at once. People spilled from the dormitories, mostly in white flannel underclothing, and darted about calling for water. A cloaked shadow began walking for the gate.

One of the men at the gate called "Stop him, he did it!" The intruder swept his cloak aside and shot him with the silenced gun, then shot the musketeer beside him. Their companions scattered, drawing pistols and sabres. Three shots rang out. The intruder walked on steadily, firing as he approached the gates. Two more men went down, the other two turned and fled.

"You there, in the cloak!" shouted someone with an educated accent. "Stand or I'll fire!"

The intruder turned and shot down a man holding a musket to his shoulder. Someone else fired at him, then the musketeers and officers seemed to all open fire on each other at once. Through the billowing swirls of powder smoke, the intruder passed through the gates, still walking steadily and quite unhurried. Julica turned as the blast of an exploding powder store lit up the square for a moment. When the dazzles faded from her vision and she turned away again, the intruder was gone.

Julica reached the mansion to find all still as she had left it. No news had arrived from the duel, but Velesti was now in her bedroom and asleep on the floor. In the upstairs sunroom, Elene and the other keepers of the vigil were asleep in their chairs, in spite of the large, empty coffee mugs beside each of them. Sneering with disappointment, Julica pulled the door shut with a loud bang. Someone within woke, and began to mumble a prayer. Others joined in as they woke.

"Reminds me of Gethsemane, maybe it happens a lot," muttered Julica as she returned downstairs.

She replaced the hat and cloak on the hallstand peg. Although she collapsed exhausted onto her bed, she did not sleep at all. What had happened at the barracks had been completely beyond belief, and she replayed the scenes over and over in her mind. Two hours later she was awake to hear boots on the garden path and a knock at the front door that was somehow firm yet respectful at the same time. It was she who opened the door to the Constable's Runner who had brought news of Reclor's death in the duel.

3

SCENT OF THE HUNTED

Rochester, the Rochestrian Commonwealth

Rangen, like many other heroes, had not set out to become great. Greatness merely stole up on him. Being a strategic thinker, and having considerable sympathy for all of those numerate people who lived in fear of slavery within a new Libris Calculor, he had decided that a massive preemptive strike would be for the greater good.

"Is this place not guarded by a large and savage dog?" asked Rhyn as they crouched beside a wall near the university's administration building, waiting for the moon to set.

"That it is."

"Ah, but, ah, but, ah—"

"Please, come to the point."

"Does it not hurt a lot, being bitten by large and savage dogs?"

"So I am led to believe, yes."

"Then why are we here?"

"To secure our numerate brothers and sisters from oppression in the infrastructure maintained by the oligarchy that controls the destinies of us all."

"Er . . . does that answer tell me why were are here, at night, in the cold, risking being shot by the city militia and putting our bottoms in danger of having a very large dog bite them?"

"No, it doesn't, but the dog is not a danger to us."

"It isn't? In my experience savage dogs are notoriously difficult to negotiate with."

"I have been applying an ancient folk remedy to the dog's temper."

"You poisoned it?"

"No, I fed it chicken pie for several days. Good, that is dark enough. I am going to climb the ivy and break in to the records archive. If the dog comes to investigate, feed it this."

Rangen had no trouble climbing the vine, removing a few slates, and climbing down through the ceiling. From this he accessed the archives room by merely smashing through the lath and plaster. A tube of wormglow revealed the cabinets that he wanted, and before long he had emptied the wooden drawers and crumpled some of the poorpaper records within. Now he spilled a little gunpowder on the paper, pulled back the striker of his empty flintlock and sent a shower of sparks into the gunpowder. There was a puff of smoke, and red sparks were left among the papers, Rangen blew on them until flames began to lick and dance.

As Rangen emerged from the roof there was a sudden cry of dismay, followed by the sound of loud snarling through clenched teeth. From the vine he could see Rhyn running in circles with a large dog attached to the seat of his trousers by its teeth. Rangen scrambled down the vine and dropped the last ten feet to the ground, distracting the dog's attention for a moment. It released Rhyn and charged for Rangen. Rangen snatched up a stone and flung it into the nearby flower bed.

"Go for it, chicken pie!" he called, and catching the familiar and welcome scent of his benefactor the dog changed course in a frantic tangle of legs and went after the stone.

Rangen and Rhyn departed very quickly.

"What happened, was the pie rancid?" asked Rangen.

"I'm sorry, it smelled so good I ate it myself."

The following day the university administration regretted to inform the Dragon Librarian Service that the records for all students for the past fifty years had been destroyed by fire, and that the circumstances of the fire were considered suspicious. With no official records to go by, the agents of Libris had to rely upon the honesty of individuals when questioned about their training in mathematics. Predictably, they found that where confessing their mathematical backgrounds was concerned, people tended to be far less than honest.

Griffith, the Central Confederation

The enquiry by the Griffith city magistrate that was held on the afternoon following Reclor's death was out of all proportion to what he had been expecting. First there was the murder of Musketeer Glarek, whose body had been found when the watchouse pantry had been opened in the morning. The guard of that block claimed to have seen nothing. A rope was found dangling from a window.

Reclor had been declared to be a felon by the city magistrate, killed by Lieutenant Mattrel Grammain in self defense. Considering all that had gone on during that terrible night, both Mattrel and his fellow conspirators considered themselves lucky to be alive. The enquiry moved on to a more serious incident, one that had rocked the darkened capital of the Central Confederation as seriously as the approach of an invading army.

"Musketeer Charver, what were you doing before the attack?" asked the magistrate.

The musketeer stood as if at attention, although his right arm was in a sling and his head was bandaged. The observers and scribes sat attentive and alert.

"I were on guard at the barracks gate," Charver replied.

"Describe what happened next."

"I saw a man approaching, walking—"

"Walking how? Steady? Fast? Slow? As if tipsy?"

"Walking brisk, steady, no way was he drunk, exalted Fras. He were dressed in trews, tunic, and cloak. Musketeer Malger and I were relaxed but alert as he approached. He came straight for us. Malger said 'Ee, hope thee has late pass, chugger.' Then I asked, like, ah . . ."

"Yes?"

"I asked, 'Ye'd have got it in, then?'"

There were titters of laughter. The magistrate called for order.

"Do go on, Musketeer Charver. What happened next?"

"The intruder, well, like he had a twin baffle pipe mounted on a gun. He fired. It were like a thump, like a melon being dropped. He shot Malgar, he just went down. Then he shot me, like in the head. I . . . I . . . things went black until I woke and saw fire. Medician said it were a graze to the skull, I were lucky to be alive."

"That's all for now, stand down. I now call Lieutenant Trellik."

The lieutenant took the stand, took the oath and began his testimony.

"The barracks are not guarded within," he revealed sheepishly. "The evidence indicates that the murderer entered dormitory C2 first, the officers' quarters."

"Where you were sleeping."

"Yes, sir, I was off duty. He apparently emerged with the barracks register book and my cloak. He then, apparently, read the register by the oil lamp that burns a-night in the barracks plaza. He dropped that register beneath the lamp. He seems to have gone to B6. He walked in, went to the third bunk along, seized the head of Musketeer Or'Lin and slashed his throat. The murderer took Or'Lin's pistol and left without approaching any other bunks. He then entered B5 and killed another who had the yellow circle. In dormitory A1 he cut the throats of another four of the musketeers accused of raping that girl, the Dragon Librarian."

"Enough. Musketeer Charver, I call you to share the stand. Describe what happened as you woke up."

"Some revelers was returning along the street. They saw me and Malger lying there, and someone splashed wine on me face as someone else yelled 'Murder! Bloody murder!' I found me whistle and began blowing it. That was when I saw a figure lift the lamp from its mounting, take it over to dormitory A2 and throw it in."

"Was it the same man as shot you?"

"At that distance, who knows? He was wearing a cloak, though.

Flames, yelling and shouts all started, and people came running out of the other dormitories. People were yelling 'Murder!' as bodies were discovered in their bunks. I kept watching the man in the cloak, though, and he was walking back to the gate. One of the revelers who had helped to revive me saw him approaching too, walking away from the fire. He thought the same as me, like, and called 'Stop 'im, 'e done it!' The suspected man swept his cloak open and shot him with the silenced gun, then shot the musketeer beside him. Their friends backed away, reaching for pistols and sabres, but the suspect drew a musketeer's flintlock from his belt. By now I had me musket up, and I fired. Think I hit him, but like he didn't show it. Then he shot me, here. I blacked out, the pain—"

"Thank you, please stand down. Lieutenant, would you continue?"

"I was roused by a whistle, and I rose from my bunk and put on my boots. I thought it just some fracas at the gate, the guards struggling with a drunk. Then I heard the shouts and screams, and burning guns began to discharge in the dormitory that was afire. As I stepped outside with my long-barreled flintlock I saw a figure in a cloak by the light from the fire. He had a massive chest, and he shot down two figures at the gate. The other two turned and ran. He then flung his two pistols away."

"Yet you did not fire upon him?"

"Not at first; he might have been a fellow officer, shooting down intruders. But I did shout, 'You in the cloak, stop where you stand!' from the door of C2. He turned, I fired. I'm sure I hit him, then he shot me. The ball clipped me, it passed through the side of my neck and I fell, striking my head. As I heard later, the suspect flung that pistol away and shot a musketeer, taking a bead on him with the pistol in his left hand while drawing another with his right. The musketeer fell, but another musketeer fired his flintlock at him. The ball ripped harmlessly through his cloak, and then this musketeer was brought down by a confused officer who had just emerged from C2 and found me lying there. The intruder turned and continued on towards the gate. I woke as the blast of an exploding powder horn blew glass from the windows of the burning dormitory. 'The gates, secure the gates!' someone shouted. Five musketeers ran for the gates to carry out those immediate orders. They discovered the bodies there, then one of them fired at the intruder. All at once the others thought they were under attack from the gate and opened fire. The intruder's dark cloak presented little for eyes to seize upon, but the raw cotton nightshirts of those who had run for the gate provided excellent targets against the darkened town buildings beyond. Four dropped with the musketeers' volley, the other was apparently shot by the intruder."

"As far as we can tell, the intruder killed eighteen of those who died last night," the city constable explained next. "The other fifteen deaths took place as a result of the general confusion around the fire."

"You are sure that there was only one attacker?" asked the magistrate with just a touch of incredulity.

"The testimonies of the survivors point to it, Fras. Interestingly, all those who had their throats slashed were under suspicion of raping that Dragon Librarian girl some months ago."

"I—yes, but what are you implying?"

"From the testimonies of the two surviving drunks, there was no disturbance before they discovered the bodies of the sentries and began screaming foul murder."

"Are you trying to say that if those drunks had kept quiet then only two guards and the rapists would have been attacked?" asked the garrison commander.

"Alleged rapists," added the magistrate.

"In effect, Fras, yes."

"Quite so. And the girl's family?"

"The mother and daughter were at home," said the constable. "My wife was among those sitting vigil with them while their son went out to duel, and is willing to testify that they were there, praying, all the while. Harren Disore has vanished, however."

"He is too short to be the suspect."

"The son was later found dead in the civic gardens, five miles away. He had been shot once, through the chest, by Lieutenant Grammain. There can be little doubt that the lads accused in the rape case were the targets last night. They were sliced away just as neatly as boils on a buttock—"

"Constable, I'll thank you to remember that this is a legal inquest, not a tavern's taproom."

"My apologies, Fras Magistrate."

"So in your opinion, although thirty-three died only six were the attacker's targets?"

"I'd bet my badge on it, Fras."

"Thank you, step down. I call on the next witness, Constable's Runner Larken."

The man took the stand and was sworn in. Two court officials came in with a stretcher, and on it was a musketeer's jacket, a cloak, and a massive, torso-shaped thing of iron bands and leather straps. It bore several dents that were shiny with lead.

"Constable's Runner Larken, did you find these objects?"

"Yes, Fras, in the street about three hundred yards from the barracks."

"You reported that they may be related to the barracks attack."

"Yes, Fras."

"Why?"

"There is evidence of nine gunshot impacts on the metal, and through the jacket's and cloak's fabric. Three in front and six in the back. The armor is two-tenths of an inch thick and weighs one hundred twenty pounds."

"And why do you think he discarded it?"

"He probably wanted to run, and nobody could have run in that thing."

The magistrate made a note to himself. The armor and jacket were to be paraded before every metalworker in the city. The work was rough but professional looking. Some artisan was sure to have had a hand in building it.

The boy was fifteen, how could he have done all that?" the city magistrate fumed as he paced before his son.

"Where's the worry?" retorted Mattrel. "The little shit is dead."

"The worry is that he was probably *not* responsible."

"Harren Disore is missing."

"Harren Disore is fifty-five, very short, and weighs a hundred and thirty pounds. Someone else took on odds of over three hundred to one and triumphed."

"Papa, that's complete and absolute dog's drool. There were probably *dozens* of Southmoor terrorists swarming through the barracks. Why does everyone take the word of a few drunk or sleepy musketeers about there being a single assassin?"

The magistrate contemplated this for a moment, his chin resting on his fist.

"You may be right, but we still have a problem. The guard on this mansion is just six of the city militia."

"Our guards are awake and sober, unlike the musketeers—"

"Wake up to yourself, boy!" the magistrate shouted, suddenly losing patience with his son's smug confidence. "The musketeers were certainly awake as he shot his way out—and I *still* say there was only one assassin. I checked the records of the brother of that other girl you tumbled and sliced, Elsile Camderine. He went to Balesha five years ago."

"Balesha?"

"The fighting monks in the Kalgoorlie Empire."

"Oh, the mad monks, aye."

"They study all martial arts and weapons, and they pray and practice from dawn to midnight. 'Perfect blade, perfect edge, no handle' is carved above their gate. They consider themselves too dangerous to leave Balesha, except in pursuit of escapee monks. 'No handle,' Mattrel, they cannot be commanded or used. If one of them got loose . . . God in heaven, if one of them ever got loose . . ."

Mattrel did not display alarm easily, but his heart was now pounding and his hands were cold and clammy. His father was actually frightened. For the whole of his life Mattrel had never seen his father be anything but confident and all-powerful. Even the Overmayor of the Confederation deferred to his judgment where law and order was concerned.

"Have any ever escaped?" asked Mattrel, rubbing his hands together nervously.

"Only one, but technically he had not completed his ordination requirements and after pressure from the local mayor they let him go. *Your* problem is that Martyne Camderine does not have to stay ahead of his monastic hunters for very long. Just long enough to tear a rib from your chest and plunge it into your heart."

"I d-don't believe it," stammered Mattrel. "Balesha is two thousand miles away."

"It is two months and a few days since you ravished those girls. Yes, there has certainly been time for word to reach Kalgoorlie, and for Martyne Disore to return."

Mattrel forced a grin onto his face. "I'm not afraid. I've killed two dozen men in the past five years."

"Might I remind you that Brother Martyne Camderine killed nineteen men in less than five minutes?"

Mattrel's bravado cracked, and he began shivering visibly. "Damn you, Pa," he muttered, shaking his head. "Very well, then. What can I do?"

"The Disore and Camderine families want a public admission, apology, and restitution from those who watched but did nothing while their daughters were attacked, and death for those who participated. We can make up some story that you were too frightened to stop your men but did not touch the girls. I'll have the others shot—if Camderine does not get to them first."

Mattrel folded his arms very tightly and shook his head.

"For a city magistrate you are ignoring quite a lot of legal fact, Papa. Restitution means my entire inheritance going to their estate upon your death. A public admission that I was even a passive accomplice will draw a sentence of castration. That means no heir to carry the family name."

His father smiled maliciously. "We could pair you with some girl before—"

"No! You must guard me."

"Guard you? After what happened in the barracks? If all those musketeers could not stop Martyne Camderine, what good are six of the city militia going to do?"

"Then post a warrant for his arrest," cried Mattrel, the pitch of his voice now high with despair. "Set the entire city militia, the Constable's runners, and every musketeer posted to Griffith in search of him."

The magistrate smiled again. He had been slowly breaking down his son's bravado, and now it was the moment to strike.

"You will be bait, my son, and we shall catch a very vindictive and dangerous fox."

"What? No! Not when Camderine can hide and wait for years while I live as a prisoner. He may even *want* that. Just think: a guard killed occasionally, a scorpion in my bed, salts of nightwing slipped into my ale. One day I awake from a philter-induced sleep to find an ear missing, a finger lopped off—"

"Or worse," said the magistrate, verbalizing what Mattrel could not bring himself to say. "All right, then, there may be another way. Think! That's something you didn't do before you set your idiots onto those daughters of the upwardly mobile merchant class. Think! Why is Brother Camderine here?"

Mattrel thought. "Because of his dead sister? Revenge? Murder? Ripping my balls off with his bare hands, roasting them until they're medium rare, then serving them up to his grieving parents on a platter of wild rice and parsley, probably with a slice of lemon and a nice carafe of white wine?"

"If he has any sense of taste it would be a '26 cabernet from the Hunter Valley vineyards, but that is not the point. You forgot about honor—not that this surprises me, of course. If Velesti, that walking vegetable, were to vanish he would seek to rescue her as a matter of honor. That would distract him from his vendetta against you."

"For a very short time."

"Ah, but I doubt that the other monks from Balesha are far behind him. They are unlikely allies for the likes of you, Mattrel, but you know the old saying: take friends wherever you can find them."

•   •   •

Hallis Molor was no stranger to housebreaking, and his means of entry were as novel as they were varied. The Disore mansion was well secured, but presented no particular problem for a professional in his class. He merely crept into the gardens by night, and while an accomplice distracted the guard dog he scaled a wall, lifted the tiles, and entered through the ceiling.

Not long after dawn a cart loaded with firewood came down the street and stopped before the servants' gate. For Hallis this was his cue. He cut out an edge of Velesti's bedroom ceiling, then lowered himself to the floor. The girl was in bed, asleep. He took a small phial from his pocket and poured the sickly sweet contents onto a cloth. She was lying on her stomach as Hallis seized her, clamping the cloth to her face and pinning her to the bed with his weight. Presently she ceased to struggle. Slowly he took the cloth away, but she continued to lie still. Her buttocks pressed up very pleasantly against his loins.

The plan was to put her in a sack and deliver her to the carters downstairs, using the laundry chute. In a few minutes she would be on the cart, along with a dozen sacks of ash from the basement, but in the meantime . . . The girl's body lay beneath Hallis's, and her scent and feel were very enticing. He knelt on the bed, pulling the covers back from her, then leaned forward as he ran his hands along her legs and began to draw her night smock up, exposing her thighs, her buttocks . . .

A knee crashed down between Hallis's shoulder blades as a hand grasped his chin and another pressed against the back of his head. With a single twist Hallis's neck was snapped.

He what?" demanded the magistrate as he sat in the semidarkness.

The shadowboy was actually a man of about thirty-five. He was blindfolded, and had been brought to the magistrate's mansion in a covered cart. Nobody else wanted to deliver the news.

"Hallis Molor was found in a bag of ash collected from the Disore mansion. His neck was broken. There was no girl in any of the other bags."

"Does anyone else know this?"

"Only Red Man. He dumped the body, then drove the cart here."

The magistrate thought quickly and cannily. He had lost a skirmish, not the war. Now was the time to regroup his resources and attack again. He beckoned to his steward and pointed to the shadowboy.

"Take him back to the wagon."

Once they had gone the magistrate sat back in his chair, lit his pipe and blew a long, gusty streamer of smoke. Martyne Camderine again, and this time showing that he could be subtle as well as blunt. The killer monk had to be lured into view, one way or another. He picked up a report. No blacksmith admitted building the armor, but six of them recognized individual bands and plates as recently pilfered from their workshops. *Very resourceful, very clever, but not invulnerable,* thought the magistrate. A shot to the head would have—

A blow to his own head interrupted the magistrate's train of thought. As the room swam back into focus the magistrate was aware of a sharp pain at the back of his skull and a gag in his mouth. He was bound to a chair and someone was moving about behind him.

"Who was the moderator when Reclor Disore died?" asked a chillingly soft whisper behind him. "Nod when you wish to tell me."

The magistrate shook his head. There was a soft touch at his elbow, and white fire danced through his nervous system.

"Fras Poros Stal was named as Reclor's second in the magistrate's report. Poros Stal was a targetry instructor at the Griffith Weapons Academy. Stal had been training Reclor, but Stal was also known to have shadowboy associations. The name of the moderator in your report does not exist in any record in any library, yet you initialed his name as approved. Who was the real moderator?"

The magistrate shook his head. Again the soft but expert touch at his elbow, and again cold, silent fire crackled through his body.

"I really do want to know."

This time the pain was in both elbows. The magistrate jerked so violently that the chair nearly toppled.

"You must give me a very good reason to stop hurting you."

The magistrate nodded. The gag was loosened slightly.

"If you try to call out I can draw this tight again in an instant. Who was the moderator?"

"There was a conspiracy, a Dragon Silver from Libris—"

The gag was drawn very tight, and soft hands fluttered over the magistrate's neck. When the brilliant, clear wash of pain had ebbed away he was in such fear of further suffering that he was quite incapable of lying. Again he nodded. The gag was loosened for a second time.

"Me, it was me! I was moderator. My son, Mattrel, my only son was on the field. I wanted the duel to be fair."

The gag was hitched tight. The severed head of Poros Stal was now placed on the table before him by a gloved hand. Suddenly the magistrate of the great and powerful city of Griffith realized that Martyne had known all along what had happened at the duel—except for the identity of the moderator who had stabbed Reclor's real second. The monk's gloved hands were just visible as they attached a baffle pipe to the barrel of a flintlock.

The magistrate frantically shook his head from side to side until a hand seized his hair. The baffle pipe pressed against the back of his head. *He's just trying to frighten me,* thought the magistrate, *he wants—*

A muffled shot obliterated the thought. The intruder walked softly from the room, then went on downstairs, where the magistrate's steward was sprawled dead beside a desk where an accounts book lay open. One entry recorded a large payment to PS for "Services." A quill lay across the book, and "PS" had been circled with red ink, along with "Service," and the amount. He walked out to the cart, released the brake and flicked the reins, then tipped his hat to the militiamen at the front gate as he turned into the street.

Rochester, the Rochestrian Commonwealth

Lengina had never entertained any real hopes of becoming Overmayor of the Rochestrian Commonwealth, but a run of luck had
placed her on the throne. In most Australican mayorates the position
of mayor was hereditary, and her father had been Mayor of Inglewood. She had also been an only child, so when her father had died
she found herself mayor of a small but prosperous state. The overmayor at the time was a strong, healthy man, and seemed to have a
long reign ahead of him until he died of a sudden and exceedingly
mysterious illness.

A fierce struggle developed between two factions of the Commonwealth's mayors when nominations were called for the election
of a successor. The mayors of Tandara and Seymour were the two
groups' respective champions, but three of the four female mayors
of the Commonwealth decided that their opinions were being ignored. In her first speech before the Commonwealth Council of Mayors, Mayor Lengina of Inglewood had spoken of the power of
diversity and tolerance. She had gone on to introduce a variety of
controversial legislation in her own mayorate, the most controversial
of which banned the forced registration of aviads and prohibited the
use of guns in legislative duels.

As occasionally happens in preferential voting, the fancied candidates got ten primary votes each, and Lengina got four. This forced the
counting of secondary votes, of which the primary candidates got two
each, while Lengina got twenty. Secondary votes had half the value of
primaries, but Lengina had nearly all of the secondary votes. She suddenly found herself Overmayor of seven million souls, but presiding
over a council in which twenty of the twenty-three other mayors had
severe reservations about her ideals and plans for reforms.

It was not only the mayors who were unhappy about the young
woman's appointment. Although also young, Highliber Dramoren
was of the old school of librarians who believed that those in power
were there because they knew better than anyone else and should

thus be allowed a free hand. This was not the sort of attitude that Overmayor Lengina liked to see in her most senior civil servant.

"You may be wondering why I sent for you," began Lengina as Dramoren went down on one knee before his monarch.

"I suspect that it involves the right of Dragon Librarians to duel with flintlocks, Overmayor," said Dramoren as he straightened. "Personally I think swords are elegant and humane weapons, but librarians have been shooting each other for centuries and old traditions die hard. The Dragon Librarian Service is the backbone of the Commonwealth; you cannot afford to compromise its loyalty."

"This same organization also had the highest incidence of deaths by dueling in the very same Commonwealth."

"They accepted the *voluntary* use of swords if—"

"As important as this matter might be, Highliber Dramoren, I am more concerned about another just now. You can probably guess what it is."

Dramoren hung his head with studied humility and deference.

"There are so many matters afflicting the realm, Overmayor, I could not presume to guess which particular one is highest among your priorities."

"Walk with me," said Lengina as she waved her handmaids away and set off for a door leading to the Waterfall Courtyard.

The Waterfall Courtyard was smothered in mosses and ferns that thrived amid the cool damp stones and spray from the artificial waterfalls that gave it its name. Its aesthetics were truly pleasing, but it had been built because the sound of cascading water is particularly good for smothering conversations from nearby, unseen ears.

"The Libris Calculor is my concern, Highliber Dramoren," declared Lengina, pacing very slowly, and with her hands behind her back.

"Ah, but there at least I can give you good news," he reported with relief. "It is currently operational, with twin processors of two hundred components each, and almost a thousand more in the cells either in training or for use in the night shift. We run two twelve-hour shifts, but we are planning to change this to three eight-hour shifts in another month—provided a good rate of component recruitment can be sustained, of course."

"That is what I wanted to speak to you about. Petitions have been presented to me, petitions by respected citizens protesting about their spouses, children, friends, lovers, and even debtors being imprisoned and enslaved for no crimes whatsoever."

Highliber Dramoren stopped dead and folded his arms. Lengina walked on. When she finally turned they were twenty feet apart.

"I asked you to walk with me," said Lengina.

"I hope you are not even considering *dreaming* of having the components liberated, Overmayor," said Dramoren in a loud, level voice.

Any ears attempting to overhear their words would certainly have been able to make out what he was saying above the splash and gurgle of the water. Lengina covered ten feet back in his direction then stopped, also with her arms folded.

"My point is that the Calculor components are not all felons," she explained, just loudly enough to be heard by Dramoren.

Dramoren walked another five feet across to her, then stopped again.

"Rochester depends upon the Calculor no less than Rochester depends upon the Dragon Librarian Service, army, local militias, or Constables, and their runners. Young men—unless they are at university—have no choice when it comes to serving in the army or militias. *Everyone* who can use an abacus with any reasonable skill has no choice about serving in the Calculor, unless they are in a reserved occupation."

"I can operate an abacus."

"The office of Overmayor is classified as a reserved occupation."

Lengina considered. She was regarded as a reformer, so what would it matter if they were overheard while she was defending her own reforms? She took five paces away from the Highliber then turned again.

"I could send in the palace guard and set all of your components free!" she declared stridently.

"And you would instantly unify every one of the mayors in the

Council against you. They would send in the Commonwealth army in to restore the status quo."

"That would tear the Commonwealth apart!" Lengina exclaimed.

"So would attacking Libris. Overmayor, the Calculor runs our trains, generates beamflash code tables, calculates taxation schedules, catches financial felons, and even checks the troop movements of our neighbors for suspiciously warlike tendencies. The overmayorates to the north and west are in near-anarchy with the Call gone and all their electrical essence machines reduced to charcoal and melted copper. The Kalgoorlie Empire and Woomeran Confederation are now ruled by a religious fanatic and Alspring is on the verge of joining them. Rochester alone is intact and strong, but that same religious fanatic already has followers in the Commonwealth."

"I cannot allow slavery for the greater good!" said Lengina, taking a step closer.

"Compulsory service, not slavery!" said Dramoren, taking two steps toward her.

"Well even soldiers in the army can go home on leave. Prisoners in jails can have visitors. Why should components in the Libris Calculor be kept under such tight security? They might as well be dead."

"It's because I don't want outsiders spying on our Calculor programs and operating system design."

"Your operating system design is public knowledge! I read a book about it when I was at Rochester University."

"You—what?"

"When I studied mathematics."

Dramoren looked her up and down, taking in the frothy lace of her white gown, her classically pretty face, and fashionably low neckline. It had been many months since he had read her personnel file—and then it had been late at night, and he had been very tired. He had skimmed the paragraph headed "Education," and had only noted that she was bright enough to have gained a degree.

"*You* studied *mathematics*?" he exclaimed now.

By now they were only inches apart. Lengina's hand lashed across Dramoren's face.

"*That* is for even *thinking* that I am too stupid to study mathematics."

Dramoren took several deep breaths.

"For that and that alone I apologize, Overmayor. Hear me out now. I respect your courage and the wisdom of many of your reforms. That is why I fought the duel that made me Highliber with sabers instead of flintlocks, and I have this scar on my face to prove it! I supported you. Remember that!"

"Very gracious of you, Fras Highliber."

"Now I expect you to support Rochester!"

"So now hear my decision. Those serving in the Libris Calculor *will* be allowed visitors, and no less than once a week. If the visitors are kept out, my palace guards will storm Libris and shoot down any Dragon Librarians and Tiger Dragons that get in their way until they reach the Calculor. The visitors will be allowed a weekly audience with the components of their choice who are not actually on duty."

"The mayors will never stand for it!" shouted Dramoren.

"The mayors will ask why *you* met a more than reasonable request from *me* with violence that disrupted the working of the Calculor. Oh, and seeing as you compared the Calculor to the army, even conscripts in the army receive pay. See to it that the components receive the same pay as musketeer recruits."

A furious but constrained Dramoren strode out through the palace gates into the plaza that separated Libris from the palace. The four Tiger Dragons of his escort were hard-pressed to keep up with him without almost jogging.

"Pay for components, visiting rights!" he ranted as they walked. "What next? Abolition of the death penalty for disrupting the operating system? Leave of absence for maternity? Mark my words, let this sort of thing go too far and we shall be soon settling disputes by arbitration instead of duels."

"Oh, that could never happen, Highliber," said the squad captain soothingly.

"Don't bet money upon it."

Griffith, the Central Confederation

At the infirmary of the Griffith barracks there were two dozen musketeers and officers under treatment for burns. Some had been trapped in the A2 dormitory when the building had burned, others had been injured while trying to rescue those inside. Two of those from A2 had been put in a separate ward, and armed musketeers stood at each corner of the room. Nobody else was willing to share a ward with them, after what had happened to seven of their squad and twenty-eight other musketeers and officers who had happened to be nearby. More guards were outside, and only nurses and medicians were allowed to enter. Even then it was only after the oils and bandages had been inspected, and their meals tasted for poisons.

The first sign that anything was wrong took the form of groans, then screams, coming from the heavily guarded building. A medician and three nurses rushed to investigate, only to be stopped by the guards outside. They stood with their hands in the air while the screams continued. A guard from inside emerged to say that the two musketeer patients were writhing on the floor and vomiting. The guards conferred. At last one was sent to fetch the duty officer in command. By the time the lieutenant had arrived the screams had ceased. The medician and nurses were finally permitted to enter, muskets trained on their backs. The two musketeers were lying beside their bunks, covered in vomit and blood, their eyes bulging and their bodies contorted from their final agonies.

"Poisoned," was the verdict of the young medician, Haspen.

"That's as bloody obvious as balls on a bull," replied the lieutenant. "How?"

The corporal in charge of the musketeers within the ward was brought forward. A nurse had entered, carrying a tray with a jar of ointment.

"Some of it was rubbed on a test rat, but it still lives," he concluded, holding up a rat in a wire cage.

"It's dead," the lieutenant pointed out.

"No, it's not, it's . . ." The musketeer peered into the cage. "Dead. But it *was* alive, er, like, it did not die."

"Looks dead to me," said the lieutenant.

"I mean not as fast as the prisoners."

"I think I can explain," said the medician Haspen. "The poisoned ointment soaked only slowly through the rat's uninjured skin, but the nurse applied it the musketeers' burns, where it was absorbed more quickly."

The lieutenant studied him as he spoke. He was a very young and recent graduate, and had probably grown his neat beard to appear older. Nevertheless, he was an authority.

"She looked like a nurse," the corporal volunteered. "And her jar had the seal of . . . er, a medician."

"Duty Medician Norrel," said Haspen, holding up the jar. "He is unwell today. I am Medician Haspen. This seal bears his name, not mine."

"Oh," replied the musketeer. "Er, but I can't read."

"But hopefully you can recognize faces," said Haspen, indicating the three nurses who had been on duty. "Was the nurse any of these?"

"Er . . . no."

The sergeant in charge of the musketeers outside was now summoned. His story was identical to that of the corporal. During the incident the three nurses on duty had been changing the bandages of a musketeer in the other infirmary dormitory, in full view of all the other patients. There had been no other genuine nurse on the grounds at the time.

"I shall inform the magistrate," said Haspen to the lieutenant. "Meantime keep the three nurses on the grounds. Not under arrest, just . . . discretely confined. You never know."

A horse was fetched and the medician rode out through the gates at a brisk canter. The lieutenant was prodding the dead rat with the tip of his dagger when there was a scream from nearby.

"Would you like to bet a copper that the naked body of a nurse has just been found in a broom closet?" the lieutenant asked the dead rat.

Moments later a musketeer burst into the room.

"Medician Norrel's body were found in a broom closet, hidden under a nurse's uniform and wig," he shouted. "He were naked and his neck were broke."

The lieutenant suddenly had a pang of alarm that sliced through his abdomen like a saber blade chilled in midwinter frost. He buried his face in his hands. Norrel was the duty medician. Haspen was the reserve, but the lieutenant had never actually met the fresh-faced but bearded Haspen until that day. He spread his fingers and looked down at the dead rat.

"I owe you a copper," he muttered softly.

The news of the additional deaths produced something close to blind panic in the survivors of Mattrel Grammain's squad. Mattrel had found the bodies in his father's mansion. He fled at once, pausing only to raise the alarm before meeting with the other lieutenant, sergeant, and two corporals in their hostelry. They decided to flee in divergent directions, the corporals north, and the others south. The corporals hired horses and loaded their field packs with food and water. Forged passes for the city gates were not hard to buy.

Corporal Demitral was dressed as a journeyman saddler as he checked the harness of his horse. He had a flintlock in one hand and was glancing around constantly, determined not to be surprised from behind. Corporal Laharre was at the doors, checking the street outside.

"Damn you, we should just ride out!" rasped Demitral.

"Not until I'm sure it's safe."

"It's broad daylight."

"We can be shot just as easily in broad daylight."

"Do you even know what you're lookin' for?"

"Someone special. Someone out there, beyond the doors of these stables. Someone who took on the Griffith barracks alone and left four dozen dead. Someone like that is gonna look special."

"I want to get out!" insisted Demitral.

"Why? We're safe in here, nobody can see us, we're even disguised."

"It's bein' in stables. Like those girls, the last they ever saw was the inside of a stable."

"One. The other's alive."

"I keep thinkin' that it's gonna happen to me. Had dreams. Lookin' at straw, someone on top of me, light fadin'."

"Well, it's daytime now, so you're safe."

"Call's balls, but I didn't mean to do it. If they'd just jollied along an' not screamed about havin' us hung before we gagged 'em—"

"You gave 'em both hot iron, just like the rest of us! Just you remember that!"

"I thought they might be enjoyin' it! Some women plays reluctant at first, you know."

"Name me a woman who enjoys bein' done over by fifteen men, name me one who enjoys bein' pissed on, shat on, and kicked, and sliced. Then I'll call you innocent. You said nothin', 'cept how we shoulda killed both. Now hold those horses and shut up. I'm checkin' the street from the loft. If I were that mean fykart out there I'd hide on a roof with a couple of long barrels for a daylight hit. If it's clear we ride out, fast."

"And if it's not?"

Laharre held up a sniping musket. "Big reward out for the Barracks Phantom."

Demitral watched him climb the ladder, and Laharre called down that the loft was clear and safe. Demitral continued to glance about as Laharre's footsteps creaked boards on the loft's floor. He reached the loading doors.

"Seems clear," said Laharre after a moment.

"Then come down and let's be out of here. Damn all stables."

Demitral untied the horses and led them to the doors. Laharre jumped to the ground behind him—then Demitral saw his companion suspended in midair, his arms hanging limp and his head at an acute angle. A momentary gleam of harpsichord wire betrayed the real nature of the apparent levitation.

Corporal Demitral whirled and fired his flintlock. The horse directly behind him collapsed, shot between the eyes. A cloaked, hooded figure stepped out from behind the other horse. Demitral presented the pistol and fired but there was only an emphatic click. Taking the gun by the barrel, he raised it and swung the butt, but his wrist was seized and twisted, then his arm was wrenched up above his head and his wrist bent so acutely that the blinding pain forced him to drop.

A knee rammed into the corporal's back, his face was pushed into the straw. Soft fingers caressed the skin of his neck, then pressed firmly into his flesh. Corporal Demitral tried to struggle against the hold and wristlock, but he had no leverage. He began to feel drowsy. *The artery hold*, he thought. *Pass out, never wake up*. Darkness and lethargy clouded his mind. The light faded, he was held down as he once held Velesti down. Someone was banging on a door, asking if everything was all right, asking about a shot. Unlike Velesti, the corporal died.

Velesti was fetched from the reference desk of the theological library by two Constables' Runners. They were unaware that they were being watched and followed by a young man with stubbly hair and beard, all the way back to the Disore mansion. Velesti arrived home to find the city constable, ten runners, her mother, Julica, the cook, and the groom in the parlor. The argument that was raging was of such an intensity that they scarcely noticed she had returned.

"You are saying that nine of Elsile and Velesti's attackers have now been killed?" Elene Disore exclaimed as one of the runners tried to write down a statement and another stood by with a pair of lock shackles.

"Along with the city magistrate, his steward, a military medician, twelve additional musketeers and their officers, and ten members of the local criminal community," said the city constable.

"Who did this?" asked Elene.

"If I knew that, would I be here? The general feeling is certainly that it was done to avenge the ravishing and murder of Elsile Camderine, the death of your son, and the attack on this young lady here."

He gestured to Velesti. Velesti stood with her arms folded, listening to everything.

"*And* my husband," Elene Disore added, anger smothering her grief. "I have just heard that his body was found, and that he had been murdered. Nobody will tell me more."

"I know, *I* gave that order . . . but what does it matter?" The city constable sighed. "A paper found with the body of the medician in the barracks infirmary had the words 'Harren Disore' and 'Lake' written on it. That is why we trolled grapples through the lake's shallows. We found Harren's body, and it had a knife wound in the back. The cloth of a dueler's second was still pinned to his sleeve. He was obviously your son's real second—"

"And the duel was obviously a double murder!" concluded the enraged Elene.

"Well, that does seem possible. Lieutenant Grammain and his surviving comrades have meantime disappeared as well. Evidence suggests that a Balesha vigilante was responsible, and that he had some justification in taking vengeance on the city magistrate, but his actions are nevertheless criminal."

"Balesha? Are you saying that Brother Martyne Camderine renounced his order and came two thousand miles to avenge his sister?"

"Yes. Where was Brother Camderine of Balesha on the night of the twenty-ninth of September?"

Beneath the floorboards of the room Martyne listened to the conversation with great interest.

"How am I to know?" asked Elene. "The last we heard, he was still in Balesha."

"Then who is responsible for at least thirty-four killings plus an additional fifteen deaths that resulted from the consequent mayhem?"

"I don't know, but I approve," replied Elene.

"There is also a rumor that some secret lover of Elsile has been avenging them," said Julica.

"Then why did he wait so long?" demanded the city constable. "Was he intending to share a few killings with Brother Martyne, but got tired of waiting?"

"He may have been away at the war," suggested Elsile.

At this point a militiaman entered, dusting his jacket and carrying a dispatch folder. He presented it to the city constable.

"Ah, the statement of the river galley captain and extract from the Darlington immigration registers," said the city constable as he broke the seal. " 'Boarded at the free port of Mildura, mail galley Black Duck . . . twenty-ninth, Balranald . . . Fras Martyne Camderine, good character, strong and diligent rower . . . fifth of October, arrived Darlington. Extract of Entry, Darlington Inwards Register of Souls: Martyne Camderine, eleventh hour of the morning, fifth of October.' "

He handed the folder back to the militiaman, clearly disappointed.

"This means nothing. He could easily have paid some yoick to carry his papers and answer to his name."

"So, how many of the filthy swine are still alive?" asked Elene.

"Two members of the squad are under protective guard."

"Yes?"

"But both were proven to be elsewhere when your daughter was attacked. As I said earlier, the remaining five are missing. The squad's lieutenant, sublieutenant, a sergeant, and two corporals."

At that moment yet another militiaman arrived, wide-eyed and smelling of a horse hard ridden.

"Who is dead this time?" asked the city constable wearily.

"The two corporals, Fras."

"Why am I not surprised?"

"In a stable, about two miles from here."

The city constable looked around, his hands on his hips and an expression of exasperation on his face.

"Well, there is clearly no business to be done in the name of justice and the enforcement of the overmayor's law in *this* house," he said to Elene Disore. "Frelle Elene, Frelle Velesti, good folk, I must be off. There are three more bodies and one exceedingly dangerous maniac to locate within the city walls."

The Disore and Camderine families dined together at the Disore mansion that night, and the atmosphere was a curious mixture of sorrow and elation. The guilty were atoning for their crimes with their lives . . . yet Harren, Elsile, and Reclor were gone forever. Velesti sat in silence, eating a special meal of meats and salads.

"At last we see a modicum of justice, yet our rulers and protectors treat it like a disaster," said Elene.

"The question is, who is meting out the justice?" asked Graten Camderine. "My son, or someone else?"

"I have given the matter some thought. Those swine must have done such crimes before. Someone else may have lost a girl to them in like manner, and been trying to track them down. Then he heard what happened here."

Julica began clearing the dishes away, and had just turned from the table when the double doors were pushed open. Martyne stood before them, cloaked but with his hood thrown back to reveal short, black hair on his head and face. Julica dropped the armload of dishes and screamed, Velesti looked up without any trace of recognition, and the others bounded to their feet and rushed around the table to the former monk.

"There are none left," said Martyne in a remote, desolate voice as they crowded around him.

Another place was hurriedly set at the table by Julica as the groom cleared away the broken crockery, then the elder Camderines and Frelle Disore sat down with Martyne and Velesti for the first time in over five years.

"The servants will be discreet about your presence," began Elene, but Martyne waved her silent with a chicken bone.

"I have spoken with the city constable. My name is clear."

"Ah, well, that is good news," said his mother, Telsa.

"How?" asked Graten.

"I was very convincing," replied Martyne.

Velesti was munching her way through her salad, paying no attention to the conversation and ignoring Martyne completely. Martyne answered all questions with short, flat, economical replies.

"It is wonderful to all be together again," said Elene, attempting warmth.

"Those of us who are left," responded Martyne.

He drained his wine, then a thought seemed to cloud his features. He grimaced with pain. The silver goblet crumpled in his grip.

"It was not your fault, you were far way," said Elene.

"I should never have gone."

"You know there was no option but to send you to Balesha," said his mother.

"Reclor should have waited."

"He wanted to claim a couple of kills before you arrived in Griffith," explained Elene. "Family honor, you see."

"Very unlucky, dueling as a virgin," said Martyne.

Julica pressed her lips together as she set a new jug of wine on the table. Martyne put an elbow on the table and rested his face in his hand. Elene refilled her own goblet. There was a prolonged silence. Velesti placed her knife and fork together, then wiped her lips with her napkin. Elene called for another goblet for Martyne.

"I have registered to take the Dragon Color examination at Libris," Velesti announced.

"Libris?" exclaimed Elene.

"I booked passage on the galley train. I leave tomorrow."

"But— but Rochester is a wild and dangerous city," protested Elene. "You will not be safe."

Velesti folded her arms and glared at her mother. Elene broke eye contact very quickly.

"Is Griffith safer?" Velesti now asked, triumphant.

"But why?" asked Elene.

"Career."

Velesti pushed her chair back before the groom could walk across to her, then stood up.

"Career? But, but ever since you were a child you only wanted to marry. . . ."

Elene shot a glance at Martyne. Martyne joined his hands in the posture of prayer and raised his eyes to the candle chandelier above them.

"Well, to marry," Elene concluded.

"I have changed," replied Velesti.

Velesti walked from the room, and the groom pulled the doors closed behind her. Violating table protocol, Martyne poured himself more wine in the replacement goblet and drank most of it in a single gulp.

"I abandoned my vocation to avenge my sister," he declared. "But I returned to a circus!"

"Some people just don't appreciate the performing arts," said Graten.

Martyne selected several grapes from the fruit bowl and began to juggle them. Unaccustomed to even the small amount of alcohol that he had drunk, he lost control. One landed in his father's goblet, another in his mother's cleavage. Graten declared that Martyne had had more than enough to drink for one night. Telsa agreed, and angrily told Martyne that he was not too old to have his bottom smacked. Martyne promptly unlaced his trews, turned, and bared his backside across the table to his mother. Both of his parents promptly stormed out, slamming the double doors behind them.

"Fras Martyne is not in a state fit to be seen by servants," declared Elene to the groom. "You may retire for the night, but tell Julica that I shall send for her when the table is to be cleared."

The groom left. Elene Disore leaned with her back against the doors, folded her arms and shook her head to stop it spinning. Martyne attempted to bend over and pull his trews up again, very nearly toppled over, then pulled his shirt down to cover his loins instead before sitting back on his chair.

"Velesti's . . . lost her mind," mumbled Martyne, his head resting against the back of his chair.

"Yes, Velesti *has* changed since that terrible night," replied Elene. "She remembers nothing and nobody from before it."

"Not me."

"Not even me. Alas, there will never be an heir for the Disores."

"How so?"

"She cannot stand the touch of men."

"Understandable. Neither can I."

"All she does is eat, exercise, and study."

"She would fit in well at Balesha."

"Did *you* fit in well at Balesha?"

Martyne tilted his head forward, sat up, and was alarmed to see two images of Frelle Disore. He decided it was safer to stare up at the chandelier again.

"I seem to remember hearing a question, but not what it was," he confessed.

"Did you fit in well at Balesha?"

"I excelled."

"Would you go back?"

"No."

"No? You put five years into your vocation."

"Nonetheless, no."

"Why not?"

"Monks are . . . very wise in some matters but in others . . . a turkey accepting a Christmas dinner invitation couldn't be more stupid. F'rinstance, having relieved oneself at the privy, one is permitted to shake one's penis five times in innocence, but a sixth shake is considered masturbation."

"Not having a penis, I think it hardly my concern."

"Has to be confessed as a sin . . . forbidden pleasure of the flesh."

"I prefer my pleasures to be more substantial," said Elene, pushing away from the door. "What were the other monks like?"

"Some were there to perfect themselves physically and mentally for . . . the greater glory of God. Some were there to escape. The world, life, who knows? Some just liked having everything planned for them."

"None of those sound like you."

"Hated the place. Pushed myself harder and further to . . . to shut it out."

Elene reached the table, and put a hand down to steady herself.

"There was a time when Harren pushed harder and further, may his soul rest in peace."

"I hoped to die . . . in some sparring bout, or weapons accident."

"Not a good attitude."

"Once challenged the Dragon's Cough. That's when a flintlock's fired at you. See this scar on my palm? Struck the bullet aside. Trick is to move on the sight of the striker throwing sparks, not the blast. Somehow . . . survived every ordeal. Surpassed my teachers. Really wanted to die."

"Perhaps God was trying to teach you something."

"Well, He allowed me to leave. Now here I am. Elsile dead, Reclor dead, Fras Disore dead, and Velesti like a cage without the parakeet—ah, no offense, gracious Frelle."

"None taken," said Elene sadly. "But at least she is alive—and so are you. Once I had such great plans for our families, Martyne. Now I just take what comes my way."

Martyne reached for a wine jar, tilted it, then upended it. One drop splashed onto the tablecloth.

"Can't stay here," Martyne declared.

"Why not?"

"No prospects. Tomorrow I'll go."

"If not to Balesha, then where?"

"Rochester. I'll teach theology at the university."

"And watch over Velesti?"

"In Libris she won't need watching."

Martyne stood up, reached over the table for his mother's goblet, drained it, bowed to Elene Disore, then discovered that his trews were still around his ankles as he tried to take a step. He bent over to draw them up, felt giddy, and sat back on his chair.

"Thought I felt a draft," he explained.

Elene walked forward, then steadied herself against the table.

"You are mere weeks out of a monastery where you lived for five years," she said, with a hand on one hip. "How do you know the University of Rochester will have you?"

"I'm well qualified to teach theology," Martyne assured her.

"At least accept a promissory note of one Rochestrian royal to your bank tally every month."

"Why? I got here unaided."

"I worry about you."

"Just write to me, fair and gracious Frelle," said Martyne, standing to go again. "That's enough."

"Fair and gracious," simpered Elene. "Balesha taught you more than prayer and fighting."

Elene embraced him and kissed his cheek. She was neither a small nor svelte woman, and the sensation of being pressed against her warm, soft, scented body made Martyne's head reel more than the wine. Nothing in Balesha had prepared him for exposure to any woman under unchaperoned circumstances, even one twice his age.

"Look after yourself, Martyne, there is so much to do . . ."

"To my eyes, it already seems done," he replied, resentment again in his voice.

"Oh, no, there is more."

"Frelle?"

"So much evil has assailed our families. Why should it be evil to fight back?"

"Frelle Disore, all that I can promise . . ." began Martyne. His voice trailed away as he considered the unspoken question. "Obviously . . . this matter may resolve itself."

Elene pushed him back into his chair, then drew her skirts up and straddled him.

"Frelle Disore!" gasped Martyne. "This cannot be."

"Fras Martyne, this is very obviously in the process of being," Elene replied.

"But, but, but you're . . . Mother's friend."

"Charming woman, known her for years."

"I could be your son."

"But you *shall* be my child's father." Elene squeezed him all the more tightly.

"The maid might come!"

"But she will be too late. Our families will be united, Martyne Camderine, and we *shall* indeed have an heir."

Julica could not see what was happening in the dining room, but with her ear pressed against the door she had heard everything. Certain that Martyne was a less-than-willing participant in what was obviously going on, she rapped loudly on the door, then opened it and backed in, pulling a serving trolley after her. By the time she had turned around Elene and Martyne had their clothing more or less restored to normal and were standing beside the table. Elene was looking embarrassed and furious, but an outburst against Julica for entering without being sent for would be an admission of unseemly conduct interrupted. Martyne cast a despairing look to Julica, then looked back to Elene.

"Must go, thank you for . . . hospitality, Frelle Disore," he mumbled quickly.

"Hah, dinner was nothing," she replied. "Take this."

She reached up to a wall rack and took down a plain but sleek flintlock pistol, then presented the Morelac twin barrel to Martyne.

"You shouldn't," he mumbled weakly.

"Why not, you are practically family now," she replied pointedly. Martyne winced. "The other of the pair will be given to Velesti tomorrow, when she leaves for the paraline terminus. Julica!"

"Frelle Disore?"

"Fetch the groom."

"He is asleep, Frelle Disore."

"Then take Martyne to the stables and give him Harren's horse, harness, saddle, saddlebags, everything."

"You're too kind, Frelle Disore," slurred Martyne.

"Oh, nonsense, Fras Camderine. You gave up so much to avenge my daughter, I must show my gratitude. The night's compliments to you."

With that Elene swept out of the room. Martyne and Julica made their way outside and around to the stables.

"That was a fine thing you did," said Julica, to break the awkward silence. "You are more gallant than any of the noblemen who strut the streets of Griffith."

"I failed," mumbled Martyne.

"Nonsense."

Together they managed to saddle the horse, and Martyne mounted it. It quickly became apparent to Julica that unless the horse could find its own way to the Camderine house, Martyne certainly wouldn't. With Julica leading the horse, they set out on the short trip.

To Julica's mind, the situation was both sensitive and tragic. Martyne had wanted the murderers of his sister and friend dead, but he cared nothing for the glory of public vengeance. He had come in secret, taken the papers to identify the musketeers that were his quarry, wiped them out of existence, then somehow feigned innocence. He now had vengeance and Elene's unwelcome attentions, but nothing more, other than loss.

Martyne had just turned fourteen when Julica had begun working in the Disore household. He had been shy yet charming, strong yet gentle. He had once serenaded Velesti beneath her window for her birthday, and everyone had joked that he was in training to be a great seducer. At Christmas he had even saved his chocolates and presented them to a tired and disheveled Julica in the Disore kitchen on a little red cushion, but had fled back upstairs to the dining room when she tried to kiss him. Then the day had come when Elsilc burst into the Disore mansion in tears and announced that Martyne had decided to follow a vocation in the Church. He had left for Balesha with no more than a hurried good-bye and a kiss to pass on to Velesti as he climbed into a pony gig before dawn one morning. Like Velesti, he had once been so very charming. Now he had slashed away the lives of over three dozen men, and was terse, sullen, haunted, and desolate.

At the stables of the Camderine house Martyne toppled from the saddle into Julica's arms, rather than dismounting.

"Now, then, you left something behind, five years ago," said Julica.

She slid her arms around his neck and kissed him on the lips, then stood back from the astonished youth, holding both of his hands.

"Think, ah, I'd remember that, Frelle."

"Your Christmas chocolates were very welcome, Martyne."

She guided him inside and to his room, where she forced him to drink a pint of water and helped him to undress. Martyne gratefully crawled into the refuge of his bed, lay on his back, closed his eyes and felt himself spinning and tumbling through blackness, falling from nowhere to nowhere.

Another body abruptly invaded his reverie, a naked body with soft, warm skin and the hint of perfume.

"Julica—" managed Martyne before she smothered his lips with hers.

She lay on him for a long time, and did not free his lips until his badly coordinated struggles had ceased.

"In all conscience I could not let you end this night with Frelle Disore as your introduction to the female body," she explained.

"But, but should you get with child—"

"It is a little late to worry about that, Martyne, but do not worry. There is no problem."

"Frelle Disore will be very angry."

"And will dismiss me. Not to worry, I might even journey to Rochester with Velesti to seek my fortune. I have heard a lot about Rochester, it seems an exciting place. *We* might even meet there."

The following morning Julica arrived at the paraline terminus. A long, sleek, articulated pedal train was being prepared for departure, but Velesti was already aboard.

"Frelle, you want just one ticket to Rochester?" said the vendor at the registration window.

"Just one, I have the fare."

"But two fares are required, Frelle. What man goes with you?"

"None. I travel alone."

The man shook his head. "We are at war with the Southmoor Emirates, even though a truce is currently in force. Only women escorted by a man may travel through Southmoor territory, and from Narrandera to Rutherglen is indeed Southmoor territory."

"I happen to know that at least one woman is on this train unescorted," retorted Julica.

"So do I, Frelle, but that woman is also a Dragon Yellow. Librarians are not considered to be human by the Southmoors. I think it is meant to be an insult, but it does sometimes work in their favor."

"If it is a bribe that you want—"

"Frelle, I am no more above a bribe than a fish is above the moon, but just now I am powerless. Every ticket must be approved by that Islamic Fras over there, and you look exceedingly alone and female."

Julica watched as the train was cleared for departure. A Christian minister blessed the train, an Islamic cleric declared it to be approved, a Gentheist priest declared it not to violate the principle of engine prohibition, then the terminus master blew his whistle. The terminus band struck up the pedaling chanty "Ride the Rails," and the long, sleek shape glided softly away from the platform and out into the shunting yards. Julica watched, waving although she knew that Velesti would not be looking back.

Julica walked to a nearby artisans' institute, selected several books on mathematics, and copied some pages of exercises and tables. Next she went to the city gates and bought a place on a wool bale wagon bound for the Darlington river port.

There are more ways than one to cross Islamic territory, she thought as she watched the city walls of Griffith receding.

Siding Springs, the Central Confederation

Brother Disparon of Siding Springs might have been a political realist, but he had no way of knowing what the full consequences of his Mirrorsun Rotation Initiative would be for the entire continent. He sent out his request for the cooperative observation of the next lunar eclipse by Mirrorsun on the public beamflash network, and included the background information about the paddles and Mirrorsun spinning faster than was needed to keep it in orbit. He also included Brother Nikalan's speculations that should Mirrorsun burst, huge fragments could rain down on the earth, and asked for ecclesiastical orbital dynamics specialists to verify the mathematics. He had forgotten that the mathematically skilled beamflash operators could interpret his message about as easily as a dog could recognize a bone in its food bowl.

The message went out over the beamflash network on October 4th. By the night of the eclipse, nearly every set of lenses within a hundred miles of a functioning beamflash tower across the entire continent was trained on the moon. In addition to Brother Tontare's five sketches of the original eclipse, millions of sketches, paintings, projection tracings, and team drawings were made of the serrations passing across the face of the moon at the edge of the Mirrorsun shadow. Of all those doing observations, no more than a few thousand understood the mathematics of what they were seeing, but this in turn led to some quite wild rumors. Principal among them was the Prophet Jemli's opinion that the Deity had afflicted Mirrorsun with huge and terrible pustules.

At Siding Springs, Brother Tontare had access to the largest telescope for the first time in his life. He chose to do a projection tracing using a team of observers. The light from the moon was focused down onto a projection table, where a dozen monks stood ready with quills dipped in black ink. Tontare assessed the serrations passing across the lunar face, turned to the reciprocating clock on the wall, waited for the second hand to reach the precise time written on his slate, then called "Mark black!"

A dozen monks marked the precise location of the serrations, points where Mirrorsun's shadow met the edge of the lunar disk, and the central peaks of certain craters. Seconds ticked past. Monks in the background exchanged the quills dipped in black ink for quills dipped in red. "Mark red!" called Brother Tontare, the word "red" precisely on the second. A second set of observations was marked down on the sheet of poorpaper pinned down to the surface of the projection table. More quills were exchanged, blue ink was to be next. "Mark blue!" Outside the dome the tramp of neophyte monks on the treadmill driving the huge telescope sounded, just slightly out of syncopation with the clacking of the reciprocating clock. The operations monk kept the central peak of Thyco Crater precisely at the center of the crosshairs in his tracking refractor. "Mark green!"

The skywatch monk outside was watching scattered cumulus cloud with anxiety, continually estimating drift speeds and times. Mars gleamed brilliantly a few degrees from the moon, like a luminous spot of blood. Cloud drifted across Mars and smothered its ruddy light.

"One minute to cloud cover, estimate five to seven minutes of cover!" called the skywatch monk.

"Mark yellow!" called Tontare, reaching for a chalk. He wrote down a new time. Thirty seconds ticked by. "Mark violet!" Quills were exchanged again. Tontare wrote down another reference time.

"Ten seconds to cover," called the skywatch monk.

"Cloud contact, image fading," called the operations monk.

The image on the projection table began to fade. Tontare stared at the second hand on the reciprocating clock, willing it to move faster. "Mark orange!"

"Baseline lost!" called the operations monk at almost the same moment.

Brother Nikalan shuffled out of the background shadows, from where he had been watching proceedings.

"Seven out of ten, not a bad result," he decreed, although Tontare was muttering something that sounded like the words of an excorcism at the clouds visible through the slit in the observatory dome.

"Echuca reported clear skies in their last beamflash message," called the skywatch monk through the door.

"Good, we shall have an excellent baseline to work from, to make up for the brown, gold, and silver coordinates that the devil robbed from us here," said Tontare.

Using dividers and standard tables, Tontare began to call coordinates from the colored figures marked on the poorpaper. A neophyte scribed them down, while Nikalan listened, staring up at the blank slice of sky visible through the slit in the dome. Tontare took the clipboard and checked the figures from memory, but was satisfied that the youth had not made any mistakes.

"Brother Nikalan, you can commence work now," said Tontare.

"Mirrorsun has increased its speed of rotation by nine-tenths of one percent," said Nikalan, looking away from the sky. "The margin of error is two-tenths of one percent, due to these observations being so much better than yours of the previous month, but there is a definite increase in rotational velocity of no less than seven-tenths of one percent."

Now the abbot and Brother Disparon walked forward from where they had been watching and listening.

"Brothers Tontare, Nikalan, and Disparon, you have brought yet more honor and recognition to our monastery, order, and faith," declared the abbot. "Tontare for the discovery, Nikalan for the interpretation, and Disparon for convincing the rest of us to take it seriously. Brother Disparon, beamflash the results to the other three observatories, along with the results of Brother Nikalan's calculations. Inform the Bishop of Griffith, the Overmayor of the Confederation, the Mayor of Tenterfield, and the Overmayor of the Rochestrian Commonwealth as well. They were mightily annoyed to hear of this secondhand last month, so this time make sure that they are the first."

Had Brother Disparon died and been admitted to paradise he could scarcely have been happier than to have been sending a personal message to the head of the largest Christian church on the continent, and its two most powerful secular rulers. The moon was shining again as he stood in the monastery's beamflash tower, dictating his messages and appending "Brother Disparon, Project Coordinator, on behalf of Abbot Pelvar." So much had happened since Nikalan had forced him to think. He had made the most inspired judgment of his life, he had become famous, he had become a project coordinator for the first time, and his name would live forever in Church and secular histories. Yes, thinking was a good idea; he definitely had to do it more often.

As he stood on the gallery balcony of the beamflash tower, Brother Disperon looked up to Mirrorsun and thought again. Mirrorsun was speeding up, but nobody knew why. Mirrorsun might well burst and fly apart into fragments whose highly elliptical orbits would send them high into space only to rain down on Earth. Had he discovered the end of the world? Brother Disperon wondered.

An hour later an acknowledgment and personal note of thanks arrived at the monastery's beamflash tower from Rochester. Disparon read the operator's transcription listlessly, then called for a runner to take it to the abbot in the main observation dome. What good was being immortalized in history if the end of history was approaching? wondered Disparon.

Rochester, the Rochestrian Commonwealth

Martyne rode slowly to the Avenue Bridge, a long, multiarched causeway across the lake that divided Inner Rochester from the rest of the city. By now his hair was longer and his clothing dusty with travel. Rising above the walls was the mighty beamflash tower of Libris. Already the tallest structure on the continent, it was currently having another hundred feet added with a wooden extension. The clear sky of early spring was giving way to clouds, and all around Martyne people were hurrying to complete business before the rain began. Horses were barred from the inner city, except for the early hours of the morning, so Martyne signed his horse in at a stable and set out across the bridge on foot.

The walled island on which the inner city was built contained most of the really important buildings of Rochester: Libris, the palace, the University of Rochester, the cathedral, the main market, the city watchouse, and the paraline terminus, along with a fairly large proportion of the city's older housing. The mansions of the wealthy were in the outer city, sharing it with the warehouses, workshops, barracks, garrison, and most of the population. The inner city was in fact becoming a university town, but not all of it was picturesque academic cloisters and palatial towers. The Weapons Research Workshops had been established in an ancient walled citadel in the southeast corner ten years earlier and were under heavier guard than the palace.

The stableman advised Martyne about accommodation, prices, and good taverns to eat at, and his conclusion was that the best and cheapest living was to be found in the old quarter near the main gates of the university. Martyne walked the stiffness out of his joints and muscles as he crossed the long bridge, and presently he reached the university. The cloisters of the Guild of Students provided addresses of various rooming houses and hostelries, and the rates were generally reasonable.

"The Toad and Tankard has clean rooms and great discretion, Brother Camderine," advised a man to Martyne's right, who stood with his arms folded behind his back as he gazed at the notice board.

Martyne turned and regarded him carefully. The man was significantly taller than Martyne and had something of a military bearing, but was dressed as a university edutor.

"I do not believe we have been introduced," he replied.

"Of course not, you were pointed out to me no more than thirty seconds ago. Go to the Toad and Tankard, secure a room, have a bath, change into the best clothes you have, and then wait in the taproom."

"Wait? For who?"

"For my master."

"I do not see the Toad and Tankard on this board."

"Walk with me, I shall take you there."

"What are the rates like?"

"Reasonable. Your room has been paid for six months in advance."

Suddenly everything seemed obvious to Martyne.

"Dammit, I told Frelle Disore that I did not want help!" said Martyne, annoyance strong in his voice.

"Who is Frelle Disore?"

This was not the answer that Martyne had expected.

"Who are you? What is this about?"

"I am unimportant; you will probably never see me again. You are being offered employment, Brother Camderine of Balesha."

·　　　·　　　·

The Toad and Tankard was an alehouse that had taken over the hostelry beside it and been transformed into quite a large inn. It was clean, quiet, but crowded as Martyne entered, and true to the stranger's word there was a room booked in his name. A room with a very advanced, five-tumbler lock on the door. He bathed, changed into the cleanest of the clothes in his saddlebags, and went down to the taproom. A plaque on the fireplace declared it to be the Glasken Memorial Hearth, whatever that was. As Martyne turned to warm his back he found a serving maid before him.

"Fras Camderine, your guest is here," she said softly as she beckoned Martyne to follow.

The room that he was led to was small, and hung with tapestries. A thick Northmoor carpet stretched so precisely from wall to wall that it might have been woven for that very room. The maid's voice seemed dull and leaden as she told him to wait. The room was furnished to absorb sound, Martyne realized, even the chairs were padded and the tabletop covered with dark felt. The door opened again, and Martyne's patron entered.

The man had blue eyes, and a thin face that featured a very impressive scar. His rain cloak was wet from the rain that was now falling, and as he unpinned it and handed it to one of his escorts Martyne saw that he wore a long coat over the uniform of a senior Dragon Librarian. Martyne was on his feet by now, and as the door was pulled shut they bowed.

"Brother Camderine, I am most relieved that you agreed to this meeting," he said in a quiet yet sharp voice as they sat down.

"I have been expelled from Balesha and renounced my vows, so I am merely Fras Martyne Camderine now," Martyne pointed out. "Also, forgive me, Fras, but I have not yet had the pleasure of an introduction."

"Ach, my apologies, I am so used to people knowing who I am." He produced a black pass-card with silver script from within his coat: "Franzas Dramoren, Highliber of Libris."

There was very little that anyone could have said to that, and Martyne merely swallowed, and managed, "Delighted."

"My time is not my own, Fras Camderine, so I shall come straight to the point. Have you heard of the Espionage Constables?"

"They are spies. I believe that they used to be known as the Black Runners."

"Correct. They are an arm of the Dragon Librarian Service, and they do intelligence work for the Rochestrian Commonwealth. I wish you to join them."

"Me?" exclaimed Martyne, almost as surprised as when he had learned Dramoren's identity. "But I am a foreign national and not even a librarian. More to the point, I know nothing of spying."

"Five years in Balesha have given you a finer background in spying that anyone else in the Commonwealth. To be ordained a monk you had to study as hard as any student at a secular university, so the University of Rochester can award you a degree in theology at my word. With such a degree, you can in the Dragon Librarians at the rank of Blue. You can, of course, never wear the uniform."

"This seems reasonable. Having spies in uniform rather defeats their purpose."

"Nevertheless, you would need to be seen to be employed. I know that this afternoon you applied to the university to be employed as a part-time edutor in applied theology."

"Indeed, but because I have no degree my application was rejected. I was going to visit the cathedral tomorrow and—"

Dramoren dropped two scrolls in front of Martyne. Martyne unrolled the first. It was the testamur for a degree in theology, dated that day. The other was articles of edutorship at the university. Martyne placed the scrolls at the center of the table.

"My mother always told me not to accept presents from strangers," said Martyne, clasping his hands and staring Dramoren in the face.

"My mother always told me never to speak to strange librarians," replied the Highliber of the Rochestrian Commonwealth.

"Why this generosity?"

"You are from Balesha. You have martial abilities that other mortals can only dream about, along with an education. You could easily become a master of espionage and assassination."

"Monk I may no longer be, but man of principle and honor I still am," Martyne declared as he stood up. "I am certainly no assassin. Thank you for your hospitality and offer, Highliber, but I intend to apply to be a gardener at the cathedral tomorrow."

"If you are no assassin, why did you renounce Balesha and come two thousand miles to avenge your sister?"

Martyne sat down again. "That was a matter of family honor."

"This is a matter of family honor as well!" insisted Dramoren.

"I do not follow your words' intent, Highliber."

"I have known about you for some time, Martyne. I contacted the new abbot at Balesha. He gave you a character reference and security ratification that certainly meets the standards of the Espionage Constables. Your childhood medician, Glin Torumasen, is also a close friend of mine; he once falsified a medical record to protect my life. He also testified to your character and loyalty."

"Loyalty?" Martyne laughed. "I was born in the Central Confederation, and lived there for my first decade and a half. I then spent five years in a monastery in the Kalgoorlie Empire. I have now been within the borders of the Rochestrian Commonwealth for all of two days and you expect me to be a loyal citizen and work for your most secret espionage service! Forgive me if I find this a little strange."

"You were brought up in the Christian Church of Supreme Knowledge, Martyne. Tell me about it."

"What is there to say? Prayers every Sunday morning for tolerance, wisdom, and understanding within the world, projects in the natural sciences every month, some field of study to pursue for the greater glory of God and the betterment of my fellow man, then five years of learning to inflict everything between excruciating but harmless pain and instant death upon my fellow man—also for the greater glory of God. Except for Balesha, the CCSK is a caring and tolerant religion. It generally does not meddle in the bedroom practices of its members, which is a fairly good guide to tolerance."

"And that probably contributes to its large membership," said Dramoren. "Did you know that out of every twenty members of the

Dragon Librarian Service, five are agnostics or athiests, eleven are CCSK, and the rest are Gentheist, Islamic, and other faiths? What does this tell you?"

"That the Dragon Librarian Service has very close ties to one of the few constants in my life," replied Martyne, now nodding as he comprehended.

"Now how do you treat my proposal?"

"I still do not do assassinations on demand."

"Nobody in the Espionage Constables does that. All such assignments are voluntary."

Martyne locked stares with Dramoren again.

"It does not take any stupendous feat of deductive logic to show that I have no real choice here. I now know too much to go free, should I reject your offer."

"How so? I offered you a place in the Espionage Constables, in my capacity as their head's supervisor. Everything except my offer to you is public knowledge." The Highliber leaned forward over the table, his hands clasped. "Only truly free people can be expected to be truly loyal, Fras Camderine. What do you say?"

Martyne sighed quietly. This was almost like what little he could remember of being seduced by Frelle Disore: he was really not happy about it, but what could he do?

"I do believe you have a recruit, Fras Highliber."

Immensely relieved, Dramoren called in one of his staff to induct Martyne as both a Dragon Librarian and member of the Espionage Constables. When they were alone again the Highliber ran his finger over the felt on the table, leaving a faint impression. Martyne saw that he was drawing a picture.

"Can you tell me what that is?" he asked.

"It looks like a large fruit bat, the kind known as a flying fox."

"A fox that can fly, Fras Camderine. It stands for something that is of great concern to me, and also to you. Let me tell you all about it."

The rest of their meeting took two hours, and at the end of it Martyne returned to his room with two scrolls, a small drawstring purse of silver, several memorized code words and names, and a lot of astonishing revelations. His life suddenly had direction, even though his future was a lot less certain. The Dragon Librarian Service was the complete opposite of Balesha.

The Reformed Gentheist preacher had been touring through the Commonwealth for some weeks, and had converted many souls to the path of enlightened balance taught by Jemli the Prophet. Her message was that many of the methods used in both the Commonwealth and the Dragon Librarian Service were blessed in the eyes of the Deity. The calculor, the beamflash tower system, the pedal trains, and the river galleys were all human-powered machines that did not use fueled engines. Fueled engines were evil, they destroyed the balance of the Deity in the world. The preacher was in Rochester to give the Dragon Librarian Service the good news.

The audience crammed into the main auditorium of Libris was not quite what he had expected of the Dragon Silvers and Golds of the legendary civil service of Dragon Librarians. One in the front row was picking his nose and fashioning an increasingly large ball from what he was finding. Another had constructed a tiny ballista from a ruler and stylus, and was firing his uniform's buttons back up into the audience behind him. He could not determine which one was producing the particularly loud farts from over to the left, but he had managed to identify the woman three rows from the front who said "Quack" every time he used a gerund.

"So will you commit yourselves to the Word of the Prophet?" concluded the preacher.

"Yes! Yes!" shouted his audience, flinging fragments of torn paper into the air.

"Will you sign the pledge to destroy all abominations, whether living or machine?"

"Kill! Kill!" responded his audience, flinging more paper into the air.

Several of them attempted to kill each other as the preacher's lackeys circulated copies of the pledge, and the Tiger Dragons were constantly intervening to restore order. Several refused to sign. One woman presented the lackeys with a pair of bare buttocks with an eye drawn on each cheek in red ink, another leaped up onto his desk, insisting that he was the devil, that hell was a really a rather nice place, and that everyone should help him dig a tunnel down to it so that mortals could have free guided tours before deciding whether to be good or evil in life. At the end of the three longest hours of his life, the Gentheist preacher left Libris.

"I have heard that librarians here are peculiar, but I never, never expected *that*," declared the preacher as he strode away across the plaza with his assistants.

"Do those people really hold the Commonwealth together, Master?" asked one of his lackeys.

"If so, we have the Rochestrian Commonwealth conquered already. That crowd of idiots might have been a strain to deal with, but they were swallowing every word that I said like free beer. What a riot against their sinful rulers I have left behind us."

Back in Libris, Highliber Dramoren marched into the auditorium at the head of four Tiger Dragons and surveyed the rioting audience. He pointed. A man was seized, his arms were pinned, and he was frog-marched through the door. Once outside, he was stripped of his Dragon Gold uniform and forced into cotton pajamas and a straitjacket.

"It will be at least two hours before we have the last of them in the wagons and on the way back to the asylum," said Leometer, the deputy head of the Tiger Dragons. "As for cleaning and repairing the auditorium, who knows how long that will take?"

"Ah, but did you see how happy the Gentheist firebrand was?" replied Dramoren.

"I did. He certainly thinks that he has converted the rulers of the Dragon Librarian Service to the Word of the Deity with a single, inspired rally."

"Indeed."

They walked back into the auditorium and selected the man who was mining his nose. Jostled by the Tiger Dragons, the man dropped his ball of pickings, and became quite violent when they would not allow him to look for it. A few rows back the red eyes on the bare buttocks glared balefully down at Dramoren and Leometer.

"Only one thing worries me about this exercise," said Leometer.

"You think the preacher was suspicious?" asked Dramoren.

"No. It is the fact that he could so easily be convinced that this crowd of certified loons is the crowning glory of the Dragon Librarian Service."

"Actually I got the idea during last week's last meeting of the Council of Dragon Golds," Dramoren admitted.

A week after recruiting Martyne, Dramoren returned to the Toad and Tankard. His meeting was again in the soundproofed room, but this time with a man dressed as a Dragon Green Librarian. Upon pushing back the hood of his cloak, he revealed himself to have the tonsure of a monk. As Dramoren sat down, the monk began removing a number of elegant-looking brass stands and glassware objects from a wooden carrying case.

"Brother Leprasen, how long has it been?" said Dramoren once the door was closed.

"Nine years, Franzas," declared the monk, interrupting his work to shake the hand of the Highliber. "You seem to have aged and grayed rather faster than I have."

"And you have hair loss."

"Monastery-imposed hair loss, if you please."

"Can you visit Grandmother before you return to Euroa? She'd like that."

"On the way home, yes. But first I am charged to demonstrate this thing to you. What do you think?"

Dramoren scrutinized the instrument on the left of the table. It looked like a small, delicately made paddle wheel. It had been fashioned from foil and mounted on its side on a pin within a glass bulb. Half of it was shielded by a baffle.

"It has the look of a toy with an important principle behind it," said Dramoren guardedly to his cousin.

"Indeed it has. At the monastery workshops we have a decompression pump, and this was used to evacuate the air from the bulb before it was sealed. The thing is a stylized model of Mirrorsun in space."

"Very stylized. What does it tell us? It seems to just be sitting there and wobbling a bit."

"Just now the light is too dim, but fetch the lamp over from the wall and all that will change."

Brother Leprasen held the lamp's flame to a strip of metal held in a clamp.

"This is a strip of the increasingly rare magnesium," said Leprasen. "It represents the sun."

The metal caught fire, and began to burn with a brilliant white glow while releasing milky fumes into the room. To his astonishment, Dramoren saw that the paddle wheel within the glass bulb was turning.

"Light is theorized to be made of particles," said Leprasen. "They are quite tiny, but they do provide a slight pressure. Comets prove it with their tails, and this is yet more proof."

Dramoren bent across to watch the wheel spinning. He placed his hand in the path of the light and it slowed. Removing his hand set it spinning as fast as before. Presently the flame reached the clamp holding the magnesium strip and it winked out. Dramoren straightened.

"So simple," he said, shaking his head.

"This is one of two models we made with the aid of an old text. The other is back at Euroa, but this is yours. There are enough strips of magnesium for another ten demonstrations. Ordinary sunlight will suffice as well."

"Now I see why you predicted that Mirrorsun's rate of spin will increase, even before the latest eclipse."

"Yes, but since the eclipse we have been able to work out the total surface area of the paddles and make an estimate of the pressure of sunlight causing it to gather speed. This has in turn allowed us to calculate its actual mass as well. The figures need to be refined, but its lightness suggests that it is very thin yet immensely strong. Less than paper's thickness, we estimate, yet stronger than the steel in a gunbarrel."

"Were Mirrorsun to disintegrate, pieces might loop deep into space, then fall to Earth. My own staff have calculated that it could happen. Could Mirrorsun material survive a plunge through the atmosphere?"

Leprasen held up a finger, then reached into the wooden carrying case again. What he drew out was a crumb of black material about the size of Dramoren's thumbnail.

"From 1708 GW until the assassination of Highliber Zarvora, Mirrorsun had been sending us presents from its celestial workshops. The smallest of the containers were a yard across and contained little calculors. The largest could have enclosed a moderately big palace. They contained flying machines powered by sunlight, and released them on the way down."

"I know, I have seen one of those shells. It was crumbling to dust."

"As all of them did. Something in the air seems to degrade the material, but using diamond-point tools we cut a few samples from one shell while it was fresh. This fragment is coated in lacquer to protect it. Others are sealed in evacuated flasks, along with an entire parachute. It is light, Fras, lighter than poorpaper yet stronger than steel. This sample took two monks working in shifts weeks to cut away."

"So a piece the size of a mayorate plunging to Earth would be something to worry about?"

"Cousin, I have been worrying about the prospect a great deal."

"Mirrorsun may not be made of such stuff," Dramoren suggested.

"Then again, it may be made of something even stronger," his cousin countered.

Leprasen started to pack the model back into its case, giving Dramoren some simple instructions for its operation as he worked.

"I hate to be bureaucratic, but could you please sign for this thing?" Leprasen said as he handed a scrap of poorpaper to Dramoren. "It's not as if I don't trust you, but I'm not abbot yet."

"As if we do not have enough things to worry about already," muttered Dramoren as he signed with a char stylus. "Have you heard that Jemli the Prophet wishes to visit us next year?"

"That long-haired troublemaker from the backblocks?" said Leprasen.

"Go back four thousand years and that description could fit a certain Jewish carpenter who—"

"Yes, yes, and if Jemli the Prophet is willing to rise from the dead after three days I'll be sure to give her my undivided attention. Anyway, Franzas, she is Reformed Gentheist, not Christian."

"She is primarily Gentheist, but she has substantial Christian and Islamic followings as well. One of her messages is that fueled machines have been creeping back into use, and that they are evil in the sight of God. They once corrupted Earth and led to Greatwinter."

"So? Franzas, all major religions have a prohibition against devices outside nature's cycles."

"At the Council of Woomera in 1723 GW, the Christian Church of Supreme Knowledge defined the ban as applying to fuels that cannot be replaced. A steam engine can be fueled by wood but not by coal, for example. The Islamics are sure to follow that lead soon, and even factions of the Gentheists support the Council of Woomera's decision."

"Those factions' members are currently being hunted down, imprisoned, subjected to intensive reeducation, and in some cases even burned at the stake on a pyre of totally natural brushwood. That sudden annihilation of all electrical devices seemed to vindicate Jemli the Prophet. She's at least consistent. Years ago she denounced Mayor Glasken, her own husband, over some steam and electrical engines."

"Aye, and to marry her boyfriend," added Dramoren.

"Be that as it may, her actions of smashing the steam engines then seemed prophetic of what happened last month, when all things electrical burned."

"So do you believe in her?"

"Oh, no. We at Euroa now have working electrical machines in mesh cages, and they are powered by monks on treadmills. As you know, they did not burn. Electricity from muscle, can that be evil? Can God's wrath be defeated by wire mesh? I say that Mirrorsun is experiencing malfunctions, and that is where the damage originates."

"If I were you, I would hide those machines, cousin. In a few months, or even weeks, you might have rampaging mobs smashing your physics workshops and roasting you over a brushwood fire."

Hawaii

The sailwing was almost at stall speed as its wheels made contact with the new wingfield of Hawaii Brink. The surface was rough, but the *Dove's* wheels were well supported and the aircraft rolled to a stop in safety. Still unsure of her feet after nineteen hours in the air, Samondel nevertheless demanded a tour of the tiny colony of twelve men and three women. There was a wingfield, a compression spirit store, shelters built from local vegetation, and even a newly planted field of sunflower seeds.

"We were expecting the *Yarron Star*," said the adjunct as Samondel examined the barrels of compression spirit that had been dropped by parachute during the preceding weeks.

"*Yarron Star* will be arriving tomorrow. By then I shall be fueled from these barrels and in the air. Be good enough to fill the tanks and haul the *Dove* around for ascent in fifteen hours. I shall be flying south."

"Saireme Airlord, there are no islands of usable size for over two thousand miles."

"True."

"I know little about wings, Saireme Airlord, but would the speed of the *Dove* be perhaps ninety miles per hour?"

"The *Dove* can stay in the air for thirty-five hours at cruising speed, Sair Adjunct. That other sailwing, the *Gull*: have it fueled and tethered to assist my ascent tomorrow. My navigator will be its flyer."

As soon as the adjunct was gone she beckoned to two gangers who were standing nearby. Both hurried over and dropped to their knees.

"Get up, get up," Samondel said, looking them over. Both were short but strong, still in their teens. "What are your names?"

"Barek, Saireme Airlord."

"Karian, Saireme Airlord."

"Sairs, will you volunteer to fly with me tomorrow? There is one chance in three that we shall all die."

"We would fly with you to hell, Saireme Airlord," declared Barek.

"If one could fly to hell," added Karian.

"Excellent. Wear trousers and a jacket, and bring a pint of water, an axhead, and shovel. Eat and drink well tonight, for thereafter we shall be hungry for a long time."

The following morning the *Dove* struggled into the air towed by the *Gull*. The *Gull* had just a full load of compression spirit, but the *Dove* was so overloaded that it could not have ascended or even sustained level flight unaided. They banked to the south, and began a shallow climb.

By the time the *Yarron Star* made its descent the *Dove* was long gone. The super-regal's captain carried the news that Airlord Samondel had taken the experimental *Dove* on a test flight at Wind River's wingfield, then vanished. She was later found to have descended to refuel at the Oakland Waystation wingfield, then flown out to sea. The order was that on no account was she to be given any assistance.

After twenty-five hours the *Gull* returned, and Samondel's navigator reported that she had dropped the tether over empty ocean before flying on. When fifty hours had passed, all hope for the safe return of Samondel and the two gangers was abandoned. Prayers were said for their souls, then the *Yarron Star* returned to Mounthaven with the news that Airlord Samondel was dead.

Rutherglen, the Rochestrian Commonwealth

The pedal train carrying Velesti reached Rutherglen on the same day that Martyne joined the Espionage Constables in Rochester. Rutherglen was within the Rochestrian Commonwealth, just over the Southmoor border. Passengers desperate for anything alcoholic after the enforced temperance of countless Islamic waysides rushed straight from the immigration checkpoint to the nearest taverns, but Velesti was in no hurry.

"So, a Dragon Yellow from Griffith," said the immigration clerk.

"Yes," replied Velesti, reading the register upside down as he wrote.

"I see that you are staying some days in Rutherglen."

"Yes."

"Why?"

"Research."

"And your area of expertise is theology?"

"Yes."

"But would you have done any other studies, arithmetic for example?"

"Yes."

It was not an admission that sensible people made in the Rochestrian Commonwealth in the September of 1729 GW. Even Dragon Librarians were known to be abducted, stripped, dressed in other clothing, and then sold on the black market as calculor components. The mistakes were eventually discovered, of course, but by then the criminals involved had taken their gold and vanished.

The clerk caught the eye of an office boy. He nodded once. The boy slipped out. Velesti was given her papers with all the right signatures and stamps on them, and she emerged from the paraline wayside into the streets of Rutherglen carrying a light backpack. She went straight to the unitech library after booking a room at a hostelry. It was after dusk before she emerged from her researches, and she made for her hostelry through streets and laneways that had been abandoned by the citizens of the provincial capital for their dinners. Light rain had added a gleam to everything in the golden light of the tallow streetlamps.

An hour later Velesti arrived at the door of a room in another hostelry, not far from the town gates. She pressed the latch, and the door opened. The room was empty, and there were no blankets on the bed. She dropped her pack to the floor, then left again, pulling the door closed behind her.

The stables of the inn were large enough to accommodate two dozen horses, although Velesti noted from the inn's chalkboard that only five stalls were currently occupied by travelers' mounts. From one of the fodder bays came the sound of snoring, and by the faint light of a single tallow lamp she could see two oblong whiskey jars lying in the straw. A faint jingle came from one of the shadowed stalls, then a man of stocky build in his mid-thirties stepped out into the lamplight. He was holding a cavalry flintlock, and the striker was cocked back. Velesti raised her hands.

"Noticed you on the pedal train," said Sergeant Bruse dey'Tremmier. "How did you find me?"

"Find you?" replied Velesti, her voice like the hollow boom of a small gong.

"You're too fyk-arse smart for your own good. Your name would not happen to be Frelle Disore, now, would it?"

"Yes."

The sergeant appraised her, noting the gun in her belt and her Dragon Librarian Service uniform.

"So, the Dragon Yellow. And this time you have a gun."

"Yes."

The sergeant was the most professional of the fifteen who had attacked Velesti and Elsile the previous July. He had been two decades in military service and was very good at staying alive. Having checked and secured all entrances to the stables except for the main doors and rendered the stableman drunk, he had saddled another guest's horse in preparation for a flight that would not be noticed until morning. He had killed hundreds of men in battles and brawls, and when any woman that he fancied did not respond to his overtures, he forced them upon her anyway. In spite of all this he had not so much as set foot in a magistrate's court until the attack upon Velesti Disore and Elsile Camderine, and he was feeling mightily resentful about that. He had been close to being commissioned as a lieutenant but now all his prospects were gone, and merely because of a stupid musketeer and a girl who had no right to be alive. He had watched as the young lieutenant had squeezed Velesti's throat, but had neglected to check for a pulse afterward.

The idiot had had his commission bought, so he had probably never killed anyone with his bare hands before. No wonder she had survived.

"So, here we are again," said the sergeant, his gun level and steady.

Velesti said nothing, but kept her arms up and perfectly still. Her eyes were wide.

"Come, now, what about 'Don't hurt me'? No tears this time?"

Velesti continued to regard him steadily, her face blank.

"So, you think that you have a chance because you have a gun. Take it out of your belt, slowly, give it here."

Velesti did not move.

"Give it here, slut! I'll kill you!"

Still Velesti did not move. The sergeant advanced slowly, his gun held before him.

"Just the slightest nudge of my finger and this bores into you. Understand that? Eh? Better to have me boring in, just you believe it. Who would have thought I would again lie between your legs? Think about that while I—"

He had reached out to draw the flintlock from Velesti's belt. Those skilled in martial arts know that a well-trained and totally confident fighter can move faster than an opponent can react to pull a trigger, provided that the gun is within reach. Velesti's left hand swept down to bat the gun aside while her right chopped down into the side of the sergeant's neck. With her right hand she seized his collar and chopped the edge of her left into his throat. Now her left hand slid under his right arm and she bent him over with a straight-arm lock before bringing her knee up into his face. Unconscious, and with his windpipe crushed, the sergeant collapsed with the gun in his hand still ready to fire. Velesti put a knee into his back and gripped his head in both hands. With a brisk twist she snapped his neck.

It might be fair to say that the sergeant's dead body did, technically, lie between Velesti's legs as she stepped over it to walk away, but it was not the sort of technicality that would have given him any comfort, or one that she cared about.

Velesti set out for her hostelry. On the street ahead were two figures walking very slowly, and spaced so that with their arms outstretched they could have touched the buildings on either side. Glancing behind her, she noted a third shadowboy, this one hurrying along as if to catch up. She did not vary her pace, and closed steadily with the two ahead of her, walking to the left of the gutter in the center of the street. They closed. At the last moment she stepped to the right as if to give way.

The shadowboy sprang for her. Velesti took his arm, dropped her weight, spun him, thrust her hip into his abdomen, and flung him over her back to crash down on his companion. Picking up his swagger stick she spun and slashed it down across the face of the shadowboy who had been following her, then brought it up backhand into his crotch. By now the first shadowboy was back on his feet with his flintlock out. Velesti's Morelac went off in his face, placing a shot neatly between his eyes. The man he had come down upon did well to merely collect the side of her boot in his throat. Although it did not quite crush his windpipe, he suddenly became far more interested in merely breathing than trying to abduct any girl, no matter how good her background in arithmetic might be. Dropping the swagger stick, Velesti stepped over the bodies of both the dead and the severely distressed, then continued on down the narrow street.

A light began to shimmer beside her as she walked through the drizzle that was again falling, and within moments the light resolved itself into a striding human figure. The more detail the figure gained, the less it glowed.

"The evening's compliments, Frelle Zarvora," said Velesti without turning.

"You look wet," replied the apparition.

"Rain has that effect on me."

Zarvora's hair remained bushy and dry as the raindrops plunged straight through it unimpeded.

"That was a remarkably quick and humane pair of killings," Zarvora observed.

"Does that disappoint you?"

"No, but it does surprise me."

"I am not a cruel person. I think of it as culling an unhealthy characteristic from the human species, while at the same time giving a strong incentive for potential offenders not to offend."

They approached the awning of a tavern, where several galley engine navvies stood drinking. The burly men began to whistle and call unseemly suggestions. Zarvora walked straight through them. They dropped their tankards and scattered, screaming with fear, into the rain sodden darkness.

"I trust you have not forgotten our arrangement," said Zarvora, folding her arms behind her back.

"It is less than a month since you placed me here, and as you may have noticed, this body was not in the best of condition. I am on my way to Rochester and this is a scheduled stop. Is there a problem with any of the foregoing?"

"No. But remember that I have a deadline that is not subject to negotiation."

"I shall meet your deadline, Frelle Zarvora of Mirrorsun, and with no tricks. After what you did to me, I think that is an extradordinarily generous concession on my part."

"I had no choice, you know that as well as I do."

Rochester, the Rochestrian Commonwealth

One hundred seventy miles to the east in Rochester, Martyne entered a tavern and ordered a drink. This he sipped at so lightly that even the taste barely got past his lips. Before long he was accosted by a drinker with the mannerisms of an old friend rediscovered after many years apart.

"Fras Delta," his contact said as he slapped Martyne on the back and sat down at his table.

"Fras Gamma," replied Martyne softly, but with a wide smile.

Delta glanced about, but kept his own smile wide for the benefit of any interested onlookers.

"I hear that you are from Balesha, and have a contract to teach theology at the university," Delta said as if in congratulation.

"All true," said Martyne.

The Espionage Constable appraised him warily.

"Your background seems ideal, but you must realize that trust will take a long time to grow between the Constables and yourself. You must submit to tests of loyalty, and dangerous drudge work."

"I expect nothing less."

"A report has been made about you. You accessed certain registers to trace the movements of one Frelle Velesti Disore, Dragon Yellow and national of the Central Confederation."

"So? Is she under suspicion?"

"No."

"We grew up together; she is my friend. I wish to stay in contact with her."

"She should not be of concern to you, Fras Delta. You are one of us now."

"I have lived five years with colleagues instead of friends, Fras Gamma. *You* are a colleague. Velesti is a friend. Without friends a person's decisions become as cold as meltwater in a gutter after a hailstorm, and that is not healthy."

Velesti Disore was within the walls of Libris within fifteen minutes of arriving in Rochester. She regarded the Libris examiner steadily through cold, blue-gray eyes. He actually shivered, then stared at her application rather than lock stares with her again. Candidates for examination were meant to be nervous, or at least to be cultivating a cheery facade. This one could have been strikingly pretty with a little stylish makeup, yet she came across as merely wholesome: well scrubbed, lightly tanned, with hair cut straight at the shoulders and bangs at her forehead.

"So, you are Dragon Yellow level at the Theological College of Holy Trinity in Griffith," Sotel said brightly.

"No, I have resigned."

"Oh! That is . . . oh."

Librarians never resigned. Once one was in the system, one was part of the system. She was either insane, stupid, or very confident about something. He looked farther down her application. She had applied for regrading from Dragon Yellow to Dragon Blue.

"In order to be graded to Dragon Blue one needs a degree and a great deal of experience in library administration, procedures, and protocols."

"I have detailed knowledge of human calculor component training, discipline, and regulation, along with knowledge of human battle calculor functioning, communications protocols, and knowledge manipulation theory."

The fact that she even knew the terminology took Sotel's breath away.

"Where did you get such a background?" he asked, once he was able to speak.

"I knew Highliber Zarvora."

"You—but you must have been a mere girl when she died."

"I was a very precocious girl."

Sotel considered. Dragon Blue was the highest level that one could gain via examination. Higher levels came from ability, experience, or patronage—and generally the last-named featured most heavily in assessment. If she was all that she said she was, she would be the recruit of the year. She could certainly pass the examination. If she failed, he would lose face. He decided that he would personally escort her to the stocks, were that to happen.

"Well, then, I think that we can arrange an examination, Frelle Velesti. Is straight away too soon for you?"

"No."

Three hours later Velesti Disora had completed the examination, and ten minutes after that Sotel had finished marking her answers. Nine questions out of every ten were correct, and those that she had not passed were to do with fairly recent changes in calculor procedures. There was still the matter of weapons experience, however. Her papers showed that she had never taken a test or done training. Sotel took a Cambrissen flintlock down from a rack on the wall and presented it to her on the palms of his hands.

"You are required to demonstrate proficiency—" he began.

Velsti took the flintlock from him, twisted back the striker, laid the barrel across the back of her left wrist and turned to the window. She fired. When the smoke had dispersed a little Sotel looked through the broken window. A distant weather cock was now missing its head.

"I-I-I see," stammered Sotel, shakily writing "Proficient" in the space beside Duelist.

Two Tiger Dragon guards burst into the room. Sotel assured them that everything was all right and dismissed them.

"Well, then, that appears to be all," he said to Velesti when the guards were gone. "Do you have any preference as to where you would like to work?"

"As a calculor regulator or in the Espionage Constables."

"But, but the calculor does not exist—I mean, no calculor exists."

"I wish to work as a calculor regulator or in the Espionage Constables. If I cannot, I shall leave."

"Leave? But no, you cannot do that. Nobody with skill in mathematics may leave Libris—except with permission of the Highliber—and you have demonstrated very impressive skills with figures."

"If I cannot be a calculor regulator or an Espionage Constable, I shall leave."

"You would be stopped."

Velesti clasped her hands together on the desk and locked stares with Sotel.

"That would be a very, very bad idea."

Perspiring heavily, and somewhat unsteady on his feet, Sotel left Velsti in his office and hurried to his Dragon Silver supervisor.

"Good news, I have just taken a candidate through the Dragon Blue examination," he said, flourishing Velesti's application without actually laying it on her desk. "What is more, she has knowledge of human calculor systems as well as very advanced weapons skills. She wants to join the regulators or the Espionage Constables."

The Dragon Silver rose to her feet, beaming.

"Praise to the Lord!" she exclaimed. "She can join both! Draw up her articles, I'll present them to her, then take her to Dolorian Hall for the Highliber to meet. Was that her shot, just now?"

"Yes, at the weather cock."

"So, and she took the head off from at least sixty yards! Stunning. Where is she from?"

"The Central Confederation. The trouble is that she has no degree."

"Pah, a Tiger Dragon can be Dragon Blue without a formal degree; these days anyone with sufficient talent can be anything if the Highliber puts his seal on the paperwork. Well, don't just stand there, Fras Sotel, bring her here, I want to meet her!"

Velesti was escorted along numerous corridors while an entourage of lackeys and lesser Dragon Colors drew up scrolls on trays, pinned and sewed badges and colors onto her clothing, and had her sign registers and swear oaths. As the clock in Dolorian Hall struck three, Velesti entered as the second most rapidly promoted recruit ever to have passed through the Dragon Librarian Service examination system.

4

FIST OF FRIENDSHIP

Rochester, the Rochestrian Commonwealth

Velesti looked around Julica's little room in the attic of the tavern. It could very easily have been described as small and seedy, but Julica had a talent for making do with very little and the room actually seemed intimate and cozy even though its furnishings would not have cost more than a dozen or two silver nobles.

"After persuading the bargemen that I knew mathematics I was bound, hidden, and smuggled right through Southmoor territory to Rochester," Julica explained as they sipped tea from borrowed wine mugs. "Once in Rochester I was taken to Libris."

"And thrown out almost as soon as you arrived?" asked Velesti.

"You have it; figures are not one of my strengths. I got work in this tavern that very day. One of their jarmaids had been dragged off to Libris due to knowing a little arithmetic. So, here I am, building a new life. Harlotry pays better, but I am not that sort of girl."

"Are you the sort of girl to listen for suspicious conversations and report their content to me in return for payment?"

"You mean among the drinkers, Vel?"

"Yes. I shall pay you well."

Julica did not hesitate for very long.

"The money would be welcome. I may not be able to keep this job more than four or five months, being pregnant."

Velesti nodded at the revelation, but made no attempt to hug or otherwise comfort Julica.

"I heard about Martyne and you," she said.

"From who?" Julica gasped. "Surely not Martyne, he said he would not—"

"The Camderines' maid. Like you, she is prone to listen at keyholes."

"Girls looking obviously pregnant cannot work as jarmaids."

"That will not last."

"I have no family. How can I work and raise a child?"

"Libris has a nursery," said Velesti as if she was answering a very easy technical question. "I could arrange for the child to be placed there."

These words were worth a great deal more than any hugs or good wishes that anyone could have possibly given Julica. Dropping her mug of tea, she flung arms around Velesti and clung to her for many minutes, sobbing with relief and gratitude.

"Then you will be my spy?" asked Velesti.

"Anything, anything!" cried Julica. "You have given my future back to me."

The Rochestrian Commonwealth, east of Rochester

Barely a month after it had fallen from the sky, the remains of the *Titan* were crumbling and dissolving into the soil. Even its electrical engines and propellers had the look of being centuries old. The two riders dismounted and walked over to the nearest of the engine pods, waving to the distant farm laborers.

"Fully a half mile in wingspan, would you have imagined it without seeing this?" said Terian with a gesture to the wreck that stretched away across the fields like a long, bluish road.

"And you say it actually flew?" asked Shadowmouse.

"It could go so high that the air was too thin to breathe. It was dropped from orbit in a case the size of a palace, but the case split open ten miles above the ground and all this unfolded. It drank sunlight as it glided, then began to spin these propellers. It could even store sunlight to stay up during the night."

"So it had never touched the ground before it crashed?"

"Correct."

"Incredible," breathed Shadowmouse. "But you say that much smaller sunwings were used to ferry passengers and crew from the ground. Did they all meet with the same fate?"

"All three that we know about, yes. Two ferries were on the ground, one in the air. Its flyer parachuted to safety but died of thirst in a desert before he was found. Watch."

Terian reached out to an unbroken blade of the propeller and pulled. About a yard of it snapped off in his hand. Shadowmouse whistled.

"Just over a month ago a direct blow from an ax would have barely scratched the surface, and even the scratch would have healed over within hours. This machine was alive, with electricity as its lifeblood. Now it is dead and its body decays, just as ours will one day. As for salvage, the scavengers arrived within a few hours of the crash. We had made sure that everything of importance had been either burned or destroyed long before the crash, so they found only food, bodies, and a few oddments of no particular worth."

"You? You mean you were actually aboard?"

"I was the captain, Fras Shadowmouse. It took the *Titan* nearly three hours to fall out of the sky, but only one in three aboard survived that nightmare glide. It's strange to think that by going down with my sunwing, I turned out to have the best chance of survival."

They mounted their horses and began to ride along the edge of the *Titan*. Even though the thousands of other visitors to the site had worn a clear path around the edge of the huge aircraft's remains, it was an hour before they reached the point from which they had started. Shadowmouse took one last look along the wreck without dismounting, then reached out to touch the stub of a broken propeller.

"Saying good-bye?" asked Terian.

"Trying to tell myself that it is real, Fras."

"Oh, it is real enough as a wreck and as memories, but my queen of the dark and cold skies has been dead for many weeks now." He reached out to caress the propeller as well. "Good-bye, Your Highness. I did enjoy serving you."

They rode back the way that they had come, in no particular hurry. Because so many folk visited the monster aircraft's remains, none of the locals paid them any attention.

"I have been back to the wreck twice," confessed Terian as they rode. "The first time was by myself, the second was with the two crew. This will be the last time, I shall not return again. You, young Fras, are the first of us Airfoxes who has neither flown in nor even seen a sunwing, so I thought it important that you see and understand just what we are struggling to replace."

They had ridden out from Rochester and spent the night at Kyneton, then continued on to the wreck just after dawn. For the whole of the previous day Terian had kept his young recruit talking about himself, but now it was time to take him into the Airfox family. A low, bare hill commanded a good view of the sunwing's entire length, and they stopped at the summit, just as they had stopped as they had arrived. Other excursionists were arriving from Kyneton now, laughing and cracking jokes about bird people who could not fly. The pair quickly rode on down the other side of the hill, and back into solitude.

"The *Titan* and her sisters did their work well over the years," said Terian as they turned down the road leading to Rochester. "Twenty thousand aviads, Avianese citizens of Avian, now live on Tasmania Island. There are few adults left on the mainland, apart from agents like us."

"Yet aviad children are continually being born to human parents," Shadowmouse pointed out.

"Yes, but we have tracked down the main bloodlines and know most of those who are predisposed to occasional aviad children. Four out of five are smuggled away before the mobs come for them in the areas outside the Commonwealth. We feign their deaths and move them to oblivion on Tasmania Island. Even within the Commonwealth, under its new laws of aviad tolerance, we still move with stealth. Laws can be changed."

"With the sunwings destroyed, what can be done?" asked Shadowmouse. "Is the mayorate of Avian on Tasmania Island cut off forever?"

"Avian has other flying machines."

The revelation stunned Shadowmouse. To him the most advanced nonancient vehicle possible was a rail cart powered by one of the forbidden steam engines. To be able to build flying machines was almost beyond what he could comprehend. Visions of Avianese flying machines a half mile across glided through his mind.

"While we still had the giant sunwings we traveled the world, exploring other continents from the air," explained Terian. "In most places we found just wilderness, or at best feudal, subsistence communities of humans. On the North American continent it was different. Most of their civilizations were not as advanced as ours, but Mounthaven actually had small flying machines driven by compression engines. They were called sailwings, regals, and gunwings, they were tiny and underpowered, and only ten yards across. The biggest of them could carry no more than five or six people and could not fly very far. Still, we managed to, ah, obtain a few and tow them halfway around the world with our sunwings for our artisans and engineers to study."

Shadowmouse hung his head. The glorious dream of Avianese aircraft the size of small cities had crashed to earth, and all that they had left were unreliable toys.

"Can these American wings reach from Tasmania Island to the continent?" he asked.

"They can do that, and already some fifteen aviad children and babies have been flown from secret wingfields in the south to safety in Avian. There is hope, there is always hope. Only just before we left to come here I was given word that the first locally built wing has flown successfully. It is called a kitewing and is just a large box kite with wheels and a compression engine. Still, our people made everything from the airframe to the compression engine, so those skills can never be lost now."

"Will I be flying?"

The question was inevitable, as was the answer.

"No. Your work will be escorting aviad children to the hidden wingfields. The older girls will wear oranges down their robes and paint on their faces, and will carry babies supposedly their own. The boys will travel as your brothers or sons, and you will always go in small groups. Make no mistake, the work is as dangerous as flying, if not more so. Aviads are almost universally hated, and the flying machines are powered by compression engines that are just as reviled as steam engines by the religious authorities. The previous Shadowmouse was shot in an ambush, but she managed to kill the three bounty hunters and get her children to safety before dying of her wounds. A tragic loss; she had only been with us two weeks. Children are our hope and our future, yet there is no part of us which is so vulnerable or frail as them. We Airfoxes are the most dangerous warriors on the continent, because we are always fighting for our children. You have a camo name because you cannot afford to be touched or to feel while on duty. Can you live up to this standard, Shadowmouse, or shall I pass the name on to someone else?"

"All my life I have been isolated, Fras, lashing out at humans but never fighting back. Now you show me that I have another family. Do you really expect me to walk away when I can fight beside you?"

It took most of the day to ride the forty miles back to Rochester, and the sun was down by the time they reached the outlying area of the city. One of the virtues of traveling by horse is that it is very hard to have one's conversations overheard by anyone hiding nearby, and by the time Shadowmouse climbed into his bed his mind was filled with names, dates, times, code words, safe-house addresses, and contacts. Nothing marked him as an Airfox agent, although he now carried new border papers that declared him to be a young married Gentheist of twenty, with an unspecified number of wives and babies.

Rochester, the Rochestrian Commonwealth

For one who has always led a blameless life there is nothing quite so daunting as having to approach criminal circles. Rangen entered the Filthy Swine in his Skew persona, trying to disguise his nervousness as suave caution. He sat down to one side of the hearth, ordered ale, then rubbed his raw-skinned hands before the flames. The jarmaid returned with his tankard of ale.

"Ah, yer pardon, Frelle, but I were wonderin' where cheap paraline tickets could be found hereabouts."

"Cheap anything's available if you know where to ask," she replied. "Are your passengers illegal, or just short of silver?"

"They be folk who need cheap travel and no questions. It's their luggage, ye know."

"I could arrange introductions, Fras? . . ."

"Skew. Fras Skew."

"And my name is Julica. In ten minutes, bide ten minutes."

"Ach, ye be too kind, Frelle," he said, pressing ten coppers into her hand.

True to her word, Julica had a contact for Rangen within ten minutes. The man was also vending false papers, and specialized in moving those in dispute with the law to regional centers, or even to Woomera or the Central Confederation. His price was fair, if not actually cheap.

"Gotta finance risk, you see," Fras Garmal explained when Rangen questioned the price. "High-risk venture."

"Got three souls, they've a wish to see Rutherglen next week. Can ye get them papers and tickets?"

"Aye. Do they wish to fill in their names themselves?"

"That they do."

"Then be here tomorrow, at this hour."

Rangen limped from the tavern glowing with triumph. Already he had five of his fellow students hiding in the laundaric, and the logistics of keeping them fed was proving to be a strain. He had hit on the idea of an invisible paraline one evening when the bickering of his confined refugee friends had stretched his patience to the frontiers of reasonable limits.

"I say, any secrets to tell me?" asked Rhyn as Rangen returned.

"Were I to do so, they would cease to be secrets," said Rangen, stretching his legs.

"Oh, please. Things are such a bore in the laundaric. The liveliest thing that happened all last week was finding a condom in the University Constable's coat pocket."

"Very well, then. The good news is that our guests are soon to leave."

"What? Already? I've told them no more than a tenth of my favorite jokes and stories."

"Ah, then that's a bonus."

Martyne stared across the tavern crowd, looking for one of his contacts. Because he was concentrating on the door, he was among the first to see the girl enter. She was a little taller than average, wearing a rain cape, and she looked a little like Velesti. Her hair was dripping from the storm outside—she *was* Velesti. Martyne hurried across the floor and stopped before her, but she pushed past him with no more than a flicker of recognition from her eyes. He stared after her, rubbing the back of his head. It was definitely Velesti, but what was she doing in a lowlife tavern where sensible women never ventured and even the harlots only entered in pairs? She continued on toward a group of young officers.

"Lieutenants Vensig and Grammain?" she demanded.

A youth in the early stages of growing a beard, and a tall, rugged-looking man with a goose feather in his hat turned, both grasping for their weapons. Velesti's gunshot boomed like a thunderclap in the confined space, and Grammain's left eye splashed bloody. Velesti's second barrel misfired. Vensig's flintlock came free, but Velesti batted it aside with her own gun. Martyne's shot hit Vensig just in front of the right ear a moment before Velesti's knife slashed across his throat.

By now bedlam was fully established. Some drinkers dived under tables or through windows, while a group of officers scrabbled for their weapons. Three knives flew in rapid succession, and three officers fell. A fourth managed to get his gun clear but as he brought his arm around, Velesti stepped into it, thrust her hip into his stomach, and slammed him to the ground as his gun discharged. Martyne saw him lying on the floor, stunned by the fall.

Now people were firing at each other in a blind panic in much the same way as had happened at the Griffith barracks, and the air was rapidly clouding with gunsmoke. Martyne ran forward and seized Velesti in an armlock, then rushed her out through the door and into the rain. After a few steps she tripped him and twisted out of his grip, but even as he rolled to the cobblestones he lashed out at the glint of a descending blade, sent her dagger spinning into the darkness, then bounced to his feet again and squared off with the shape in the gloom before him.

"Daft birdbrain, it's *me, Martyne!*" he snapped as the rain hissed around them.

"Martyne?" replied Velesti uncertainly.

"Elsile's brother! Your *best friend's brother!*"

"Elsile? My friend?"

"Hurry, we can't stay here," he said, holding his hand out to her.

Velesti would not allow herself to be supported, even though she displayed a distinct limp. Together they slunk away into the rain.

They entered Martyne's lodgings through the back entrance, and he pushed Velesti into his room before dashing out with one of his shirts and wiping her blood from the passageway floor. He returned to find that she had removed her rain cloak, boots, and trousers, and was squeezing what appeared to be a long but shallow wound in her right calf. Martyne closed the door and dropped his shirt under her leg, from which blood was oozing through her fingers.

For a moment the room reeled before his eyes, then he was a Balesha monk again. He took out another shirt and ripped it into four strips, then poured whiskey from a jar onto one of the strips.

"Clean it," he ordered.

Velesti reached up for both the jar and strip of shirt with bloodied hands, then poured most of the spirits onto her leg and clamped the cloth over it. She did not even wince, thought Martyne. This was definitely not the Velesti that he had once known.

"I'm going to sew the wound up," he said slowly.

"No. Give me the needle."

Velesti began to sew. To Martyne it seemed nauseating, slippery, traumatizing work, but the five-inch gash was soon closed. Velesti bound it with strips of shirt while Martyne sat back on the floor taking slow, deep breaths. Except for the blood and bandages, her legs were as white as milk and almost hairless. Martyne had limited experience with naked, female legs, but even he thought it unusual that these particular legs had such pronounced muscular definition.

"You are Martyne," Velesti said. "You came to dinner."

"They said you lost your memory," panted Martyne.

"True."

Around Velesti was a bloody circle of torn shirts, spilled whiskey, a field medician's kit, and a pair of trousers with a burn mark and hole. Martyne crawled across the room, tipped some wood shavings into the grate, and struck a spark to them from his tinderbox. Presently he had a fire going, into which he fed the remains of his shirts after he had wiped the floor with the cleaner pieces.

Without a word Velesti put her trousers back on. Martyne had noticed that she was wearing a Libris uniform and the colors of a Dragon Blue, but he was largely beyond surprise.

"You shot Vensig before I cut his throat," said Velesti. "I should kill you for that."

"Try," said Martyne, who was by now disinclined to tolerate nonsense of any kind from anyone.

Velesti regarded him steadily. Martyne stared back.

"So much as think about reaching for that knife and you will be wearing a fang-star between your eyes, Velesti. Think about it. You are good, but only weeks out of a long stay in bed. I have just escaped five years of Balesha training. As you just may have noticed from our little altercation outside the tavern, I am a *lot* faster than you."

Velesti's sharp, alert gaze softened into a sullen glare. Like it or not, Martyne was right.

"Why did you shoot him?" she asked, a tiny suggestion of resentment creeping into her voice. "My blade was already moving, his throat was wide open—oh, I cannot talk about it."

"Your gun misfired, he had his own gun out. How was I to know that you could fight like that? Three weeks ago you were lying comatose in your bed. According to your parents and Julica, you had all the martial prowess of a cabbage. Now, I . . ." Martyne's eyes narrowed. "I suppose that it was you who destroyed dormitory A2 in the Griffith Barracks and killed eighteen musketeers?"

"Most of them just got in the way. I meant to kill only nine."

"Those who raped you and killed Elsile?"

"Yes."

"You killed all those innocent bystanders as well!"

"Innocent?" asked Velesti with surprise in her voice. "Think of the Bridge and the Thousand dilemma."

"It is a theological exercise in morality. You are guarding a bridge against a thousand warriors. You are also guarding one child, and you are a better fighter than any of the enemy. You kill them as they come at you one by one. They keep coming. Do you kill a thousand men, good and bad, brothers, fathers, sons and lovers, just to guard one child?"

"I did."

"It is a flawed, simplistic question, Velesti! The child may be a prince that you have captured, and who can be ransomed to stop a war."

"Every musketeer and officer in the Griffith Barracks was questioned about the attack on me. All three hundred. Every one of them swore that nobody had left the barracks on that night, except for the one caught red-handed. I kept killing until those who attacked me were all dead. Then I stopped. The others had been shielding rapists and murderers with their lies. Knowingly. Explain to me now why they were innocent bystanders."

Martyne ran his fingers through his hair. Morally he was in a difficult position. He had intended to kill all her attackers as well, but had also intended to take bit more care with those who blundered into the crossfire.

"But—but when I left for Balesha you could not even stand to squash a snail. You ate only vegetables, fruit, and nuts, and even then you mourned that the nuts would not grow up to become trees. Now you can shoot and fight, and, and you complain when I rob you of a victim!"

"Is this bad?" asked Velesti.

"Well . . . it is a little surprising. I mean, I like a girl who can defend herself. It shows independence and spirit, but really!"

"Really?"

"Really! I would be surprised if less than a dozen innocent drinkers have not been carried from the Filthy Swine feet first tonight, for a free night's accommodation at the morgue."

"If they were in that place then they deserved to die."

"*I* was drinking in that place."

"Then you deserved to die."

"I rescued you from the crossfire, and at great personal risk. Do I deserve to die for that?"

"No," conceded Velesti, then she stood up and limped over to the window. "The rain has stopped, I must get back to Libris."

"People are going to notice that limp," said Martyne. "Best to lean on me."

"I do not touch men."

"Except when you're killing them. Look, someone may have noticed that you were wounded, so the constable's runners will be looking for anyone limping tonight."

"So I'll kill them."

"No!"

"Then what do you suggest?"

"That I walk you back to Libris while you lean on my arm."

"But I do not want to touch you."

"Velesti! This is me, Martyne! Remember? We grew up together. Now I am trying to help. *I* don't like touching my own backside either, but I do it every time I sit down on the privy."

Hawaii

Twelve days after Airlord Samondel had disappeared, the *Yarron Star* descended with another load of fuel and Airlord Sartov. Venture Australica would continue, but from now on it would be managed by Yarron's airlord himself. Realistic goals would be the rule now, not suicidal bravery.

"Note, all of you, that as soon as Airlord Samondel departed from her own principles of caution she lost her life," Sartov told the gangers, farmers, artisans and their wives who were crowded around the nosewheel of the *Yarron Star* where he was standing. "The next phase will be . . ."

His voice trailed off. Nobody was looking at him. Instead they were staring out to sea, where a sailwing was approaching in silence.

"Ghost," said someone, and nobody else dared say more.

The apparition was gliding low over the waves and slowly losing height. It was the *Dove*, and it was trying to make for the beach. It began to skim the wavetops, and in the last few feet before the beach it suddenly dug into the water, tumbled, and collapsed. Spray flew high into the air, and the assembled human population of Hawaii rushed down to the beach of black sand to where a figure with long, matted red hair was crawling out of the water.

Sartov arrived to find the scratched, sunburned, and emaciated Samondel alive, with the wingfield adjunct kneeling beside her. Some yards offshore, the smashed body of the *Dove* was slowly drifting in with the waves. Sartov dropped to his knees beside Samondel.

"Is she all right?" he asked the adjunct.

"Apart from exhaustion and dehydration, yes. I've sent for a stretcher and water gourd."

"How in all names of hell and—I mean, what? . . ."

"Samondel, House of Leover," croaked Samondel. "Pleased to report . . . Samoa Wingfield . . . ready."

Over the following three weeks Samondel slowly recovered her strength, but only six days after her return the first super-regal flew out for what had officially been renamed Samondel Wingfield on

Samoa's main island. She had brought the *Dove* down on firm, wet sand at low tide. With a cleaver she and the two gangers had cut handles for the axhead and shovel, then set the brush and trees afire at her chosen wingfield site. The site actually turned out to be a two-thousand-year-old wingfield, and most of their time had just been spent grubbing out bushes, raking away sand on the ascent strip, and chopping down trees to give the wings clearance. They had lived on crabs and shellfish, foraged at low tide.

"What compelled you to do it?" demanded Sartov, visiting her the day after she had returned. "The *Dove* has been salvaged, but repairs will take weeks."

"My schedule was slipping. I saved us at least five super-regal flights."

"But why? The Council of Airlords is not unreasonably impatient with your progress, in fact they are quite sympathetic."

"Even the Council is hanging by a thread, Saireme Sartov, and support depends on results. We are now over halfway to Australica. In theory the *Yarron Star* could reach the Australican coast from *here* on a one-way flight."

The figures were true, but Sartov was not impressed.

"Then what? Are you going to leave the super-regal parked on some Australican farm road while you walk into the nearest town and try to teach them to distill compression spirit—provided that they speak Austraic on the northeastern coast. Semme Darien says that Austaric is only the common language of the southeast, by the way. When you arrive in Australica, you are to be an airlord representing the entire North American continent, not a wretched refugee crawling out of a crash-landed wreck. We shall continue with the original plan to establish a third wingfield at New Zealand, Airlord Samondel, then fly on to Rochester."

"The cost of the compression spirit burned in our engines alone has already exceeded my original estimate," insisted Samondel. "I have spies, I *know* there is disquiet in the Council."

"There is always disquiet in the Council. More money is sure to be found."

"Today. A week is a long time among accountants, and I have saved *four* weeks!"

"And practically wrecked one sailwing. Still, I thank you on behalf of the Council of Mounthaven Airlords, yet on behalf of that Council I now *order* you to lie there, shut up, and recover your strength for the next fortnight. All two dozen souls now in the Hawaii settlement have been ordered to take no more orders from you for that period."

Rochester, the Rochestrian Commonwealth

Although the clocktowers of Rochester were clanging out two hours past midnight, a history class was being held in a deep, soundproofed basement. The edutor was younger than many of those who were listening to her. These were adult aviads, those who had been recruited to the Airfoxes recently. Recruits tended to have a muddled grasp of their people's history.

"Until the day in last September that we call Black Thirteenth, humanity ruled most of the land, although we *Homo avianis* were gaining in strength. The oceans are forbidden to both humans and aviads, and are ruled by intelligent cetecians that also owe their existence to the technology of two thousand years ago. The great aviad leader Zarvora Cybeline managed to get in contact with that machine we see in the sky and call Mirrorsun, that huge band that circles the earth inside the orbit of the moon. She used primitive electrical essence machines, and discovered that Mirrorsun was a machine with intelligence. She persuaded it to send devices such as improved electrical communicators down to Earth for the use of we aviads. It was the greatest advance in our history; it had the potential to tip the balance between aviads and humans in our favor forever.

"For some there is no boon that cannot be improved upon, however. Frelle Overmayor and Highliber Cybeline was murdered by a faction of fellow aviads. She died sitting in her great reclining chair with an electrical essence machine encircling her neck and penetrating her spine with long, flaccid tendrils. The conspirators were exhilarated at first. Frelle Cybeline's electrical machine was removed from her neck and her body dragged away and cast into a stable. The leaders argued for many days about who should wear Frelle Cybeline's collar of electrical essence, and through it rule Mirrorsun and control its bounties. Finally Fras Dariar of the Radical faction prevailed. He lay back in Zarvora's chair and wrapped the collar about his neck, while all the leaders of the other factions stood in a circle with their guards flanking them and their flintlocks drawn. Not one of them left the room alive.

"From what was later deduced amid the carnage, the collar exploded with the force of roughly a fifty-pound barrel of gunpowder. Dariar's body was pulverized, and the others were smashed back against the stone walls of the room. All bounties from Mirrorsun stopped thereafter, and it would not respond to entreaties using old-style spark-flash radio machines. The goose that laid golden eggs had been killed.

"Still, Mirrorsun had already been sending its riches to a mainland aviad mayorate, Macedon, for eighteen years. There were goggles that allowed one to see in the dark, radio machines that would fit within your hand, small flying machines nourished by sunlight that could lift two heavy men from the ground, and huge flying machines that were a half mile in span and flew constantly. With these we began to lift pioneers to a colony on Tasmania Island, but our surviving leaders still had a hunger for very advanced machines that would magnify the strength of a few aviads against many humans. The huge wings that were powered by sunlight carried aviad explorers all around the world. On the North American continent they found a human civilization which had developed small, primitive, but effective flying machines and very advanced guns.

"Aviad agents were dropped to learn the Americans' secrets and steal their flying wings, reaction guns, and master artisans. The Americans guarded their secrets closely, however, and many lives were lost for every flying machine, artisan, and reaction gun smuggled the seven thousand miles back to the Launceston Technical Institute on Tasmania Island. Then Black Thirteenth happened, and we were cut off from North America once more. Ah, a question—and please state your camo name."

"Fras Shadowmouse. If you please, can the American flying wings not be used to cross the oceans as well?"

"Alas, they are small, heavy, clumsy and very limited in range compared to those from Mirrorsun. They also burn a mixture of alcohol and vegetable oil that is expensive to grow, harvest, and process, and each compression engine is the product of thousands of hours of work by countless artisans. Some are two, even three centuries old, and have been rebuilt dozens of times. For the Americans to build a flying wing to cross seven thousand miles of ocean would be impossible, our own engineers have calculated that. Another question?"

"Frelle Foxtread. What was the cause of the Black Thirteenth? Why would anyone want to destroy all electrical essence machines? Surely they benefit humans and aviads alike."

"There are as many theories as there are experts, Frelle. The one that I favor most strongly is that Mirrorsun, which is an intelligent machine of electrical essence itself, mistook the warlike uses to which our electrical essence machines were being put as preparations for an attack on itself."

"You mean to say all that was a terrible mistake?" asked Shadowmouse.

"That is my theory, young Fras, yes. The reason that you are here tonight is that for some reason the Call also ceased to act over land on Black Thirteenth. Our engineers and academicians think that the weapon that destroyed all electrical essence machines also damaged the mechanisms that the creatures of the oceans used to generate the Call. They are still formidable to deal with, of course. Avianese attempts to sail boats of even forty or fifty tons on the salt waters had been made, but all have been destroyed by shoals of sea creatures that boil up out of the depths and overwhelm them. Being immune to the Call, we aviads could live in Calldeath lands where the Call never ceased and humans could not go. With the Call gone, all we can do is retreat to islands beyond the reach of humans. For this we now use the few American flying machines that we towed over with the sunwings, and with some tiny kitewings that our own engineers have developed.

"All of you are part of a new, invisible paraline, one that moves aviads to the wingfields where they are ferried to safety on Tasmania Island. Babies, children, and those of small stature are given preference, because our wings are small and fuel is expensive. None of you will ever go to Avian, but you will ensure its future by giving it a population. Your work is dangerous, for most humans would gladly lynch us, but you have been selected as the cream of aviad warriors. Each of you is worth ten humans, but believe me, you will often be up against odds of greater than that."

Although the great reading room in Libris never closed, members of the public were compelled to leave at midnight, after which the staff moved in to clean, return books to their shelves, and then do their own studies if they wished. Few stayed more than an hour, but Velesti was one of those few.

The lower-ranking Dragon Librarians who patrolled the vast floor of the reading room knew that a ghost attended Velesti, a ghost in the image of the great and legendary Highliber Zarvora Cybeline. It hovered just behind Velesti as she sat turning the pages of some of the oldest and rarest texts, and they noticed that Velesti turned the pages about as fast as one could without damaging them. A few of the Dragon Yellows and Oranges had challenged the apparition, but it had either ignored them or vanished. Velesti denied all knowledge of it. By Velesti's second week in Libris the patrol librarians not only left her in peace, they actively avoided her.

"Derek Riplen, *The Principles of Plasma Magnetodynamics for Engineers*," said Velesti as she closed a slim volume bound in crumbly brown leather. "Eighty-two pages surviving out of five hundred twenty."

"What there was of it was very informative," replied Zarvora.

"I believe that it is my turn to read a book, Frelle Zarvora."

"We have scanned nineteen books, so the twentieth is yours," agreed Zarvora.

Velesti opened a large and heavy hardcover book and began to turn the pages. "Are you finding this interesting?" she asked.

"Why is it that so many hundreds of advanced scientific and engineering books have survived only as fragments, while Arnold Schwarzenegger's *New Encyclopedia of Modern Bodybuilding* has survived two thousand years without so much as losing a page?"

"I think I shall add these one-arm triceps extensions to my training scheme," declared Velesti.

"Why would you want to look like *that*?" asked Zarvora, bending down through Velesti's shoulder and peering at the photographs illustrating the exercise.

"Sheer vanity," replied Velesti.

"Keep turning, I have scanned that page for you."

"Anyway, it is a matter of impression and impressiveness. If people are impressed by you, they leave you alone."

"Are you trying to tell me that people do not already leave you alone?"

"Well, yes. Only last week a galley train navvy pinched my bottom. I do not want it to happen again."

"You cut off his hand, Frelle Velesti. It is *extremely* unlikely that it will happen again."

"He earns his living pushing pedals with his legs, it's not as if he was a watchmaker. Besides, if I had had better upper chest and shoulder development he would not have pinched me in the first place."

Within minutes they had leafed through the book.

"All right, all right, I have stored your stupid book and processed it for keyword search. Can we go on to *my* next book?"

"Brown and Kipple, *Basic Principles of Numerical Meteorological Modeling on Supercomputers for Global Systems*."

"For a change, it looks comparatively intact."

"It looks obscenely difficult," observed Velesti, flicking through it. "Why do the most demanding of books have words like *basic*, *introductory*, and *elementary* in their titles? Why not have a title like *Exceedingly Difficult Ways to Forecast Weather Using Giant, Complicated, and Stunningly Expensive Machines*?"

"So you did understand the title."

"Mostly. What is a supercomputer?"

"A very big and powerful calculor. Would you mind turning the pages?"

Velesti leafed through the ancient text while Zarvora scanned and stored the pages. Frightened Dragon Librarian guards watched in the distance.

"You know, I have reached a conclusion about you," said Velesti as she turned the pages. "You are no more intelligent than Zarvora."

"But I *am* Zarvora."

"You are Zarvora's image, stored in the structure of Mirrorsun. You now have a huge and perfect memory, you command powers that would frighten even the ancient gods of legend, and you can learn fantastically fast, but you do not come up with new ideas any faster than the rest of us."

"Should I be ashamed?"

"Not ashamed, but I know you are frightened."

"Frightened?"

"Frightened of your ignorance, and frightened that humanity could catch up with you. That's why you burned all electrical essence machines from the face of the earth, is it not? People were advancing too fast; in a hundred years they would have had spacewings flying to you, controlling you, threatening you."

"People are free to have electrical machines in shielded cages or deep underground."

"Unless machines are in common use and convenient to access they will develop infinitely more slowly."

"If they developed *infinitely* more slowly they would never develop at all," replied Zarvora smugly.

"Correct!" said a triumphant Velesti. "Relative to you, humans and aviads will never advance."

"Why is this bad?" asked Zarvora without a trace of guilt. "The world had access to electrical essence for a mere three decades after I destroyed the automated orbital battlestations and their EMP bombards, yet humanity merely spent those decades building better weapons, spreading lies and deceit by sparkflash and radio transmitters, and developing long-term plans to destroy *me*. I just struck first."

"Yet you need us, you need our knowledge."

"I need to stay ahead of you humans and aviads, Frelle Velesti. Were none of you here, I could easily live on forever, learning about the universe at my own pace. This is merely self-defense. Were I to wage war on creatures such as you I could be very bad company."

"Until six years ago you *were* one of us."

"We are all stuck with our relatives."

Bickering all the way, they scanned the pile of books and finally came to Velesti's next selection.

"*Australian Muscle*, September 2015," said Zarvora's hologram with a sneer of contempt.

"Yes, it is the special Ms. Olympia issue," said Velesti, eagerly, slowly leafing through the 1,946-year-old magazine. "Look at this! A free sports bra designed by Ms. Olympia 2014 with every dozen ten-pound packs of Hyper-Gro Concentrate . . . which has added ion exchange whey protein hydrolysate—"

"I think the offer has expired," Zarvora pointed out.

"A sports bra," said Velesti thoughtfully.

"They hold your breasts securely during training—"

"I know, it's obvious from the picture. I want one."

"If I help, will you promise to scan those other five piles of books tonight?"

"How can you help? You have no substance."

Without another word Zarvora sat down into Velesti, merging with her completely. A moment later she stood up, her body a green wire-frame mockup of Velesti from the neck down.

"Are we agreed that this is you?" asked Zarvora.

"Are my biceps really so small?"

Zarvora doubled the size of the wire-frame biceps.

"Happy?"

"Stop it!"

A white sports bra mockup materialized over the breasts and shoulders of the holographic figure.

"Is this what you want?" asked Zarvora.

"Well . . . yes."

"Then just relax, I am going to take over your motor functions."

Velesti's movements suddenly became precise and mechanical as she took a charblack stylus and began to draw precise lines and curves on a large sheet of poorpaper. After several minutes Velesti was free again, and a design pattern lay on the reading desk in front of her.

"In the morning, get a tailor to make up one of those," said Zarvora, morphing her wire-frame image into the Libris uniform of thirty years earlier. "In the meantime, get to work on leafing through my piles of books."

Velesti returned to her work, and the piles quickly shrank. By the time another hour had passed she had finished.

"I shall need some days to make sense of what I have scanned tonight," Zarvora admitted.

"Perhaps a week?" asked Velesti.

"Perhaps. I shall contact you, but for now, good-bye."

"Wait! I have questions."

"Questions? But I might not have answers."

"When you destroyed the electrical machines you caused deaths."

"True, but not many."

"Yet this thing around my neck is an electrical machine."

"Yes. I can spare areas as small as a circle ten feet in diameter. There were several of my own devices on Earth, devices that I cannot reproduce and which are of immense value to me. There were two collars such as yours in Australia and one in America, and there was a small sunwing ferry circling empty over the Pacific Ocean. These I spared, and for my own good reasons."

"And you burned the machines of everyone else."

"Yes. Good and bad, innocent and guilty, strong and weak, all of their electrical machines died."

"Why?"

"Survival. I am Earth's fourth species. A massive, space-bound calculor with an intelligence living inside it, and I am alone. I wield godlike powers to keep myself alive and free, and believe me, there are many who want me dead or constrained. I understand what and who I am up against, Velesti. I once walked the earth, fought for my beliefs and visions, ran Libris, built the first new calculor in two thousand years, gave birth to children, ruled half a continent—and was assassinated. I know what it is like to die."

"I do too," replied Velesti. "Very depressing."

"Agreed, and I do not want it to happen again."

Euroa, the Rochestrian Commonwealth

The Monastery of St. Roger at Euroa was highly regarded within the Commonwealth, and had a reputation for scientific research surpassing any university on the continent. While all scientific monasteries were by now taking the greatest interest in what was happening to Mirrorsun, the monks at St. Roger in particular now discovered themselves to have a great and powerful patron.

The abbot paced the stone stage of the open air amphitheater, occasionally glancing out over the four hundred faces that were his audience. In the distance the assembly bell continued to ring, but at last Abbot Ashman made a chopping motion with his hand. Moments later the bell ceased to ring. The abbot paused at the center of that stage, his arms folded behind his back, his body stooped a trifle as he faced the monks.

"As you and everyone else should know by now, Brothers, Mirrorsun is not only spinning faster than its orbit requires, it is still gathering speed. It appears to be doing this by making use of vast sails, each the size of the Rochestrian Commonwealth. Now, the idea of sails in the void of space would probably baffle the average citizen, but can anyone here explain how they would work?"

Four hundred hands shot into the air. The abbot called a monk in the front row to join him on stage. Brother Lartensen was exceedingly shortsighted and wore thick spectacles. He was not intimidated by his audience of four hundred because he could see them only as a brownish blur.

"From the observation of comets we see that the dust and vapors emanating from their surface is always in a stream that points away from the sun," Brother Lartensen cried in a shrill drawl. "This suggests that light from the sun exerts a pressure. This pressure is very small, but is as persistent as sunlight itself, although in my paper of 1725 GW, 'Quantified Speculations Concerning the Nature of Solar Radiation,' I suggested that it may also be due to the pressure of thermal radiation, better known as heat, which is thought to agitate the vapors and dust from the cometary surface in the first place."

"Thank you, Brother, that is enough."

"Actually the combination of thermal radiation and visible radiation, and possibly some other forms of radiation not yet discovered, may also account for the antisolar vector in the tails of comets—aagh!"

The abbot had by now marched Brother Lartensen to the edge of the stage and pushed him off. There was muted laughter, which quickly died away.

"I can now tell you that secret experiments in the Physics Cloisters have confirmed that sunlight—in fact any light—can exert pressure. Mirrorsun is indeed making use of this fact of physics, and this raises several questions. As a man of God, dedicated to His scientific truth, I am curious about this, but the Dragon Librarian Service also has an interest in the matter."

Considerable muttering and murmurs greeted this news, as the abbot had expected.

"The Highliber of Libris has been in contact with me through a secret intermediary, and has posed the following questions. Why is Mirrorsun doing this? How is it doing this? What are the consequences for Mirrorsun? What are the consequences for us? I now call upon Brother Nikalan of Siding Springs, who has been seconded to us, to supply what answers are currently available."

A gaunt man, even more stooped than the abbot, shuffled onto the stage and walked to the blackstone circle that marked the acoustic focus of the auditorium.

"Why? Don't know," began Brother Nikalan bluntly. "How? Sunlight. Consequences for Mirrorsun? Rupture. Consequences for us? Shower of fragments."

The abbot resumed possession of the focus point.

"Experiments with Mirrorsun materials show that it is exceedingly strong, and observations and calculations show that there is a vast amount of it," said the abbot. "Were it to burst, the fragments could do a number of things. The most likely is that they would enter a harmless elliptical orbit and not affect us. However, they could also enter a highly elliptical orbit, then crash down to Earth. If it is spinning even faster at the time of the burst, the pieces would fly off into space, like a comet. Now, this may seem like a relief, but the orbit of this Mirrorsun comet would intersect that of Earth, and one day it would return and crash down, again with catastrophic consequences. Mirrorsun is very big and very tough. A direct hit on our continent would wipe us out. Doomsday, in other words."

The abbot correctly anticipated a great deal of muttering, hand waving, and tracings of orbits in the air. He allowed a half minute to elapse before he called for attention again.

"Now, the Dragon Librarian Service is naturally concerned about this from a point of view of public order, and I have agreed that the librarians can work closely with us to—Brother Varlian, wipe that smirk off your face! Ah, to work with us to determine what will happen, and when. We have been promised gold, artisans, labor, materials, and access to any other resources that we require. Brother Nikalan has been sent here from Siding Springs to manage the calculation of orbits. Brother Varlian will manage experiments to determine the material properties of Mirrorsun. I shall manage all aspects of the observational astronomy."

The abbot withdrew from the focus stone, and Brother Nikalan again stepped forward to speak.

"An old-style calculor, a twin processor model, is to be built here," he announced. "Two processors, one hundred souls each, running in three eight-hour shifts. The same configuration as in the earliest form of the original Calculor in Libris."

"Six hundred souls required," called Brother Lartensen from the audience. "That does not add up."

"St. Roger's contains four hundred souls, of which one hundred fifty cannot be spared from the materials and observational projects. The Highliber of Libris has convinced the Bishop of Rochester to allow certain additional religious personnel to be in residence here for the duration of this project. One hundred of those will be monks from sundry other mayorates, to help with construction, catering, and cleaning. Fifty will be monks to help populate the sinister processor of the St. Roger Calculor. The three hundred souls for the dexter processor will be nuns from the convent of St.—"

The rest of the abbot's sentence was lost in the cries of astonishment, shouts of outrage, and not a few cheers that burst from the four hundred throats.

"The regulators of the St. Roger Calculor will be Dragon Librarians, supplied by Libris," shouted the abbot as the audience became orderly again. "These will all be veterans of the original Calculor built by Frelle Highliber Zarvora. All past the age of regular and frequent sexual activity."

"You hope," called someone, and titters rippled across the curve of the amphitheatre.

"The Emir of Cowra has generously agreed to donate five dozen eunuchs to preserve order and guard the good virtue of both yourselves and the holy sisters of St. Heloise. Now, then, dormitories must be built for several hundred visitors, and the chapel converted to a calculor hall. We have one week to have the monastery functional for these projects. You are dismissed, get to work!"

Rochester, the Rochestrian Commonwealth

Rangen stayed late at the Filthy Swine due to the rain that was lashing Rochester. At the hour of midnight the jarmaid announced for the fifth time that the establishment was closed, and this time she backed up her words by raking down the coals in the fireplace and snuffing all but one of the lanterns.

Singly and in pairs, the last of the patrons ventured out into the rain until only the lone cripple remained.

"A long run home, Skew?" asked Julica as she stood beside him in the doorway.

"Aye, 'tis sure. More water be out there than in your beer."

"Had I a copper for every time I've heard that tonight I'd never have to work again."

Julica closed the door and took Rangen by the arm. She put some kindling on the coals and blew on them until flames began to dance again.

"You know, I see a lot of bad lads here," said Julica as she knelt before the flames.

"And I do business with 'em," replied Rangen.

"But you are not like them."

"Ah, I were once an honest soldier, then my leg was—"

"I have been observing you closely, Fras, and I could not help noticing that you occasionally limp on the wrong leg. Your drawl also slips into quite educated Austaric on occasion, and you display refinements of manners to the jarmaids—including me—that no other patrons of the Filthy Swine have ever heard of."

"I . . . maintain multiple disguises," conceded Rangen in his normal speech. "Is this to be unexpected in a bad lad?"

"No, but bad lads tend to be cunning and shrewd, rather than educated as well."

"I am on hard times."

"You are not smuggling stolen gold and gemstones with your paraline passengers, are you? You are smuggling the passengers."

The crackle of the fire and the pattering of the rain outside greeted this speculation, answering yes in place of Rangen's silence.

"Not long ago I was abducted and sold into the current Libris Calculor," Julica continued. "I had feigned ability with arithmetic to get a free trip to Rochester. Upon arriving at the Calculor, I had my skills put to the test. I was thrown out within the same hour."

"Clever. Why did you want to come to Rochester?"

"To seek my fortune. I know that there's a lot of money in numerate souls."

"Aye," conceded Rangen.

"And I suspect that you are one as well."

"Frelle, you flatter me but—"

"But I'm right. I have been watching you, whatever your name is. I admire you. You could have fled to safety in the outlying mayorates or even farther, yet you stayed here to help others evade Libris and its librarians."

"I repeat, Frelle, you flatter me unduly."

"I know, I know. You cannot afford to admit anything." Julica took his hand and pressed it between hers. "Fras, I want to help, but you will admit nothing—and quite sensibly so. Still, I *can* help. Were you to hobble home in the rain you might well catch a chill and not work so hard as the fugitives need. The least I can do is prevent that."

"Gracious Frelle, I certainly would appreciate a night by the fireplace. The rain is sure to clear by dawn."

"Brave and dedicated Fras, I was thinking of accommodating you somewhere more comfortably than that," she said, releasing Rangen's hand and sliding her arms around his neck.

Julica was very pleasantly surprised to see what a comely and desirable body Rangen had once his disguise was removed, but while Rangen was initially an uneasy bedmate he was a little more trusting by the time the sun rose on a Rochester scrubbed clean by the deluge of the night. He did not reveal where he resided, but he began to entrust Julica with some minor errands, and presently he was spending two nights out of every three in her bed. She proved indeed trustworthy, and soon they were moving vastly more refugees to safety.

Peterborough, the Woomeran Confederation

It was a measure of Jemli's new influence and stature that she was able to have called the meeting of leaders at all. At the mayoral palace in Peterborough on the 20th day of October there gathered thirty-one castellians, seventeen mayors, four overmayors, and over two hundred religious leaders. The subjects under discussion were the cessation of the Call, and the destruction of all electrical machines.

In part the impressive gathering was related to desperation. The subjects of the leaders were both terrified and traumatized by the way that so much of the backdrop to their lives had vanished within just one day. Jemli's followers continually told everyone who would listen that she had predicted the demise of the electrical machines and had gone on to predict a major change in the Call. People were impressed. She had also predicted a great deal more that had definitely not happened, however, but religious believers tend to be selective in what they wish to remember.

From all over the region common people also gathered in Peterborough. They arrived by wind train, pedal train, horse, and foot. They camped in the open under clear but chilly spring skies, and they flocked to the walls of the city to listen for messages relayed from the palace. Rumors were rife among the faithful, and Reformed Gentheist priests welcomed thousands of converts into their religion. When disease broke out in the hundred-thousand-strong crowd, it was pronounced that demons of unbalance were assailing their faith and resolve. Within the mayoral palace, Jemli was not speaking to quite such a devoted audience. The priests, bishops, clerics, mayors, and overmayors wanted details. Jemli gave them sermons about faith. The Overmayor of Woomera finally led a movement designed to topple Jemli, forcing a vote to establish a commission of religious ecumenism that would draft a pronouncement on both the ends of the Call and the use of electrical essence. Jemli did not vote. When the division was called she strode from the palace hall and led her entourage to the palace wall.

A deep, reverberating growl went up from the crowd as Jemli appeared, and believers surged forward. Dozens were crushed to death, but this was scarcely noticed as the Prophet began to speak.

"Electrical machines are evil!" she shouted, raising her hands to the sky.

The crowd roared back, flinging an incoherent wall of sound at her.

"Fueled engines are evil!" she continued, and again the hundred thousand believers roared their agreement.

"The Word of the Deity is upon me! Will you hear the Word of the Deity?"

A third rumble of voices washed up to the walls of Peterborough and past the Prophet who stood there.

"I do not want to conquer your mayorates. I care nothing for who administers your religions. I care only that you heed the Word of the Deity. Smash fueled engines. Drown electrical essence. Crush those who use them, the academicians, the engineers, and worst of all the aviads. Who stood to lose most by the end of the Call? The aviads! Who is hateful in the sight of the Deity? The aviads! The former Calldeath lands are *covered* with the infernal fueled machines of the aviads, but the Deity in his wisdom has torn open their refuge. Yes, they use the machines of demons against us believers, but the Deity looks after those who are as solid as bedrock in their belief and faith."

The crowd responded by pouring in through the city gates. Back in the palace the vote went against Jemli, but by the time it had been taken, that vote had become completely irrelevant. Guards deserted or rebelled, servants and courtiers poured into the streets to shout praise to Jemli the Prophet, and by the late afternoon the Overmayor of Woomera was hanging dead from the arch of a gate in the walls of Peterborough while his successor swore fealty to Jemli.

The Rochestrian envoy regarded the body with disquiet as he stood with his aide in the street below.

"Alas, poor Bayjen, you were always the consummate numbers man," said the envoy.

"And he did have the numbers," his aide pointed out. "A three-quarter majority supported him."

"And a hundred thousand of Jemli the Prophet's supporters begged to disagree. Now the regions of Kalgoorlie, Alspring, and Woomera are behind her, and the western castellanies of the Rochestrian Commonwealth also pledged allegiance."

"Only in terms of faith. They do not want to be shot for treason by Overmayor Lengina's militias. Even the politics of Jemli's, ah, converted mayorates have not changed. They are independent, but worship under a unified theocracy."

"And with everyone bearing in mind what would happen if they tried to exhibit a bit of that independence in front of Frelle

Prophet," the envoy replied, arching his eyebrow in the direction of the corpse.

A group of bystanders began to fling stones at the dangling corpse of the man who had been the ruler of Woomera's mayors until only hours earlier. The Rochestrian envoy beckoned to his aide to move on.

"This could be very serious for Rochester," he said as they began to walk. "Rochester has always been seen as the most advanced of cities, and the Commonwealth has been held together by electrical calculors and radio machines for two decades."

"You are forgetting two important factors, Fras," responded his aide.

"I would appreciate being reminded of them," said the envoy.

"The Highliber got a human calculor and the beamflash network restored within three days of Black Thirteenth, last September. There is a lot less fear and disunity in the Commonwealth than elsewhere as a result."

"True. And the second?"

"Rochester has a very large number of religions."

"You call this good? Need I remind you that a religious nutcake has been given allegiance by three of Rochester's western castellanies?"

"But the Dragon Librarian Service holds the Rochestrian Commonwealth together, not the Christian Church or Islamic clerics, and certainly not the Gentheists—their largest followings are in Kalgoorlie, Alspring, and Woomera. Being run by librarians means that the Commonwealth is very robust, and cannot be conquered by some prophet winning over a few religious leaders. Our system is the best in the known world."

"There are Gentheists in the Dragon Librarian Service."

"But they are not unified, and they are small in number."

The envoy considered this for a time as they walked. Orators were declaiming support for Jemli the Prophet at almost every street corner, and members of the city militia were wearing Gentheist colors and pennants.

"The Highliber would be outraged to see all this," said the aide.

"Neither the Highliber nor the Overmayor wished to lend any legitimacy to this farce by attending in person. That is why *we* are here."

"And when can we leave?"

"Just as soon as formal proceedings are complete. That will be this afternoon."

The termination of formal proceedings was not quite so simple as the envoy had hoped, however. Late in the afternoon he found himself being granted an audience with Jemli herself.

"I note that Rochester did not choose to worship the Word of the Deity by sending the head of state," she began ominously.

"Frelle Prophet, Rochester is a secular commonwealth," replied the envoy, who had been expecting just such an observation. "We reacted to the Black Thirteenth crisis by commencing an adjustment of our secular structures, and that is taking all of the time and energy of both our Overmayor and Highliber."

"So they do not think that my word, the Deity's Word, is worth considering?"

"On the contrary, Frelle Prophet, I was sent precisely because Rochester does take you seriously indeed."

"Rochester could easily be described as a godless and evil wasteland!" rasped Jemli.

"But not accurately. We are a secular commonwealth where a diversity of religions coexist in harmony, just as the many religions of your followers coexist in harmony."

"You have a smooth and agile tongue, Envoy. You remind me of the former Overmayor of Woomera."

"My death, detention, or torture would result in the instant and unconditional declaration of war against the offending state. Forget that at your peril," replied the envoy firmly. "It is in the articles of exchange, of which I have a copy here. May I also remind you that Rochester's armies are completely intact, as are Rochester's paraline and beamflish networks? Can you say the same of yours?"

"Need I remind you that I am also Overmayor of Kalgoorlie and all its western mayorates?" declared Jemli with cold authority in her voice.

"Need I remind you that I am the Overmayor of Rochester's brother? With respect, Overmayor."

Jemli managed to contain her anger. She had wished to swamp the Rochestrian Commonwealth, to win it over through sheer charisma, but with no audience to perform to this was not an option. A war would be easy to provoke but hard to wage. Her forces were enthusiastic but ill equipped, and even less well organized and led. The difference was thanks to the Dragon Librarian Service that Jemli wished to control. Overmayor Lengina could definitely shatter Woomera's disorganized armies and cut the paraline to Kalgoorlie. Jemli chose tactical retreat.

"I am concerned only for the salvation of all Rochestrians," she declared soothingly, suddenly dismissing all the acrimony of only seconds earlier. "I wish to threaten neither you nor the Commonwealth."

"I am gratified to hear it, Overmayor."

"Return to Rochester, tell your Overmayor that I again request a conference with her. I shall travel to Rochester alone, with only the Deity to protect me."

"Consider it done, Overmayor," replied the envoy with immense but well-concealed relief.

Rochester, the Rochestrian Commonwealth

In the two months since her revival, Velesti had slowly come to trust Martyne with something approaching friendship, and even went so far as to be seen with him in public. Much of this public visibility consisted of blindingly fast sparring and applications training on the university lawns, however, and by late November they had a regular audience of students and academics when the weather was fair.

"I have noticed that many who watch are there regularly," said Velesti as she sat on a visitor's chair in Martyne's office.

Her Morelac flintlock was partly dismantled on his desk, along with a set of tools, jar of oil, and some cleaning rags.

"Some of them are my theology students," replied Martyne, who was preparing a lesson. "It leaves me a little self-conscious."

"I have been thinking about founding a new students' guild."

"In what? Blood-sports appreciation?"

"No, an actual sports guild."

"There are sports guilds already. Shooting, fencing, riding, and lawn bowls."

"Except for fencing, none require much exertion. I think I could start a Baleshanto guild."

The quill fell from Martyne's fingers.

"Baleshanto? As in the martial art? As in the martial art from Balesha monastery that no sane person could ever contemplate?"

"It has attractions. What other sports guild offers such personal contact?"

"Velesti, Baleshanto's version of personal contact involves beating the stuffing out of an opponent who is trying to do precisely that to you as well. This is hardly an attraction."

"It is for me. I would have more opponents. Will you approach the Academicians' Council on my behalf? You can be the head instructor; you have had formal training."

"And what training have you had?" asked Martyne, replacing his quill in a rack and placing his fingertips together.

Velesti tried to ignore the question, and continued cleaning and oiling the mechanism of her flintlock. The silence lengthened. Martyne waited. Velesti frowned. She began to replace the striker spring, lost her grip, and sprayed components into the air.

"Now look what you made me do," she said.

"What training have you had?" asked Martyne again.

"Adequate training."

"From whom?"

"I know Baleshanto. Is that not enough?"

"No explanation, no Baleshanto guild."

Velesti said nothing, but began to gather the gun's trigger components together and lay them out methodically.

"You are not Velesti," continued Martyne, picking the trigger spindle out of his hair and placing it on the desk beside Velesti's disassembled gun.

"I am still missing a screw, a retainer plate, and the spring. As for the Velesti of more than two months past, I have no memory of her. I am only two months old, Fras Martyne."

"Then let me tell you a little story. Years ago, in the days when Highliber Zarvora took control of Mirrorsun, a package was dropped to Earth. It contained four collars, just like the one you wear."

"And very stylish it is, too."

"The collars represented the very pinnacle of pre-Greatwinter science, they were not manufactured by Mirrorsun's machines. There were then only four in existence. Like much of what Mirrorsun has sent to Earth, they were in storage. They are two thousand years old, not newly built in the celestial workshops. Zarvora wore one of them, and discovered that it was a device to control distant machines using the entire body and brain. They are powered by nutrition in human blood, but they do not need much. They work equally well if worn on the wrist or neck. Two of them Zarvora gave to Abbess Theresla, who was meant to be her successor, and one just vanished."

"You have left out the one that Zarvora wore herself."

"Legend has it that Zarvora came to control Mirrorsun so very intimately with her collar that her very soul copied itself into its structure. When she was assassinated, she lived on in Mirrorsun. She later detonated her collar when one of her assassins tried to wear it, and bits of him are still being dug out of the brickwork of a certain tower in Libris. Theresla is known to have traveled to the North American continent on one of the sunwings, and has never returned. One collar was obviously kept in Griffith until it was applied to your own neck, leaving one more to account for."

"Perhaps the abbess took it with her to North America also."

"Perhaps, but she would have had to take Mayor John Glasken of Kalgoorlie with her, because I saw him wearing it when he briefly took refuge in Balesha after being denounced by his wife as a heretic."

A thoroughly poisonous silence gripped the room as they stared unblinking at each other. In the distance the university clock tower rang a quarter past the hour.

"Go on," prompted Velesti.

"A group of us monks and neophytes was sent into the desert with him, and for three weeks we toiled to level a stretch of ground, remove the stones, water the sand from a barrel cart, and pack the sand down to bake in the sun. At the end of this time we were sent back to Balesha, where a select few were loaded with stores of dried fruits, nuts, cheeses, and waterskins. Then we trudged back to the strip of level ground where Mayor Glasken was waiting. We arrived late in the morning, and were told to wait. When the sun was just passing noontime a great bird appeared in the sky. It circled us, losing height, and as it got closer I saw that its wings were at least a hundred feet across, and that two shimmering, whirring disks grew out of them. Then I realized it was a machine. It landed almost silently on our carefully leveled strip of desert and rolled to a stop.

"Mayor Glasken had us grasp the wingtips and turn it to face down the length of what he now called the ascent strip. It was only when the machine was ready to ascend into the sky again that Abbess Theresla opened a hatch and stepped out onto the ground. She greeted Glasken, stretched, then cleaned sundry bags of rubbish from within the cabin. I handed her the bags of new supplies, which she loaded with efficient haste. I remember that she smelled stale, as if she had not bathed in days, if not weeks. She wore a collar, just like Glasken, and as she worked she said in Austaric, 'I dropped Frelle Darien in a place called Veraguay, there to prepare our path and learn the local language.' He said, 'How long to reach Veraguay?' and she replied, 'Four days, if the weather is fair.'

"To us he now said, 'When we have gone, sweep the marks of the wheels from the ascent strip and strew stones and rocks across it again.' To the monk in charge he gave a handful of gold and said it was a gift to Balesha in thanks for loyalty. To me he said, 'Take the bags of rubbish, build a pyre of brushwood, and burn them to ashes.' Then he told us to stand clear. The machine's spinning blades whirled all the more quickly, and sped it along the ascent strip until it rose into the sky."

Martyne reached into his jacket and drew out a small fruit knife with a carved bone handle.

"I found this amid the rubbish that I burned. I imagine that it is from Veraguay, because the artwork and letters are like nothing that I know of from this continent."

Martyne placed the carefully cleaned and honed knife down beside Velesti's disassembled gun. After staring at it for a time she reached out, ran her finger along the handle, then picked it up.

"This says 'Theresla' in Veraguay's script," she said, holding it by the blade and stroking the handle. "May I keep it? I have nothing else to remember her by."

"Of course, Fras Glasken, to me it is just a curio—"

"*Frelle Velesti*, if you please," interjected Velesti with sad resignation. "Any other identity is pointless—no pun intended, of course."

They both snickered for a moment.

"Do you wish to tell your side of it?" asked Martyne.

"What is there to tell? Theresla did not wear her collar properly, and so her image was not stored in Mirrorsun. She was never strong on following orders. I was, however, and when I was shot dead I found myself to be an image in an immense lattice of memories and thoughts. Worse, I was sharing it with Zarvora. Needless to say, we did not get along harmoniously. After a time she told me that one of the collars on earth had been applied to a body whose heart was still beating, but whose brain had been deprived of blood too long as a result of strangulation. The soul had departed, but the ancient collar could let me live in the body from Mirrorsun. After a time of being forced to work by the band, the brain might heal itself and my consciousness would gradually be imprinted into it. It is still too early to know whether that will happen, but if it does I shall remove the band, and Zarvora will erase the image of me in Mirrorsun. Anyway, I agreed, with as much enthusiasm as a dead man can manage."

"Then you awoke to discover that Zarvora had omitted one vital detail?"

"You have the measure of her. I have felt a great number of

breasts in my former life, but none of them had been attached to me. You can imagine my dismay."

Martyne cringed and covered his eyes. "Well, yes."

"I teetered on the edge of insanity."

"Perhaps you did more than teeter?"

"Indeed, I actually fell a long way. My thoughts became exceedingly poisonous for quite some time. I suppose I tried to get back as much of a man's physique as is feasible, but after I had killed the last of Velesti's attackers I began to mellow. Do you know what I have discovered?"

"I'm afraid I do not have the benefit of your experience or insights," replied Martyne.

"I learned that I quite enjoy the company of women, just for its own sake. Take away lust, and I still like them. It was quite liberating to realize it. Men are still a problem, I cannot stand the touch of them. *You* are, perhaps, something approaching a friend."

Martyne swallowed. "The feeling is mutual."

"But nothing more!"

"Of course not! But I am still honored to be your friend."

Velesti sat back and sighed with relief.

"Thank you. So, now you know why I am so strange and twisted."

"There are plenty of people more strange and twisted than you. Me, for example."

"I . . . have been meaning to raise the subject of your relationship with my mother," began Velesti.

"You know?" cried Martyne, sitting bolt upright, pop-eyed with alarm.

"Yes, but let us not discuss it just now." Velesti absently stroked the little fruit knife, displaying the only real tenderness that Martyne had noticed in her since he had returned from Balesha. "Do you know what I hate most about being a girl?" she asked presently.

"The cost of makeup?" ventured Martyne.

"Being groped, fondled, and grabbed. I had no idea how much touching, seizing, and feeling is foisted upon us women. Nearly two-thirds of my fights have started with being grabbed, and often by someone stronger than me."

Martyne suddenly brightened. "Grabbed, as in by the arm?"

"Now that you mention it, yes."

"Excellent."

"Excellent? It's repulsive!"

"Ah, then recent developments in Baleshanto would interest you. There is a lot more emphasis on twisting, breakouts, and pressure-point holds."

"I have done twist dodges."

"No, more than dodges." Martyne stood up, came around the desk and extended his arm. "Pretend I am a girl and grab me."

Velesti warily stood up, then seized his wrist. "Now, notice if I twist my arm thus, only your thumb is holding me, and if I do it quickly, thus, I am in a fine position to give you a backhand fist to the nose."

"Or a chop to the throat," suggested Velesti. "Grab me, let me try it."

Velesti did several breakouts.

"Now, take it a stage further. What does the average yoick expect a girl to do when grabbed?"

"Scream?"

"She pulls away. The last thing a man expects is her to push forward. If she pushes forward while twisting out of his grip, he is still braced backwards for someone pulling away. Move in on him, and he will be off balance. Give it a try."

Several moves later Velesti was quite confident with the technique.

"You did an interesting block when we killed the last of those rapists," said Velesti. "You somehow got your hand under my arm and onto my shoulder, so that you could knee me in the cheek."

"I do apologize, my reflexes took over. You threw a punch for my groin, as I recall."

"I do apologize."

"Think nothing of it. Now throw the punch again, slowly. I did a low sweep block, brought my open hand under and around your upper arm, then pushed up onto your shoulder thus, and pressed down, thus. Notice how your face is now at knee level."

"So was that first block with an open hand?"

"Yes, a lot of the new blocks are with an open hand, so that you can grasp as well."

"I don't like grasping."

"Oh no, seize my wrist, right to right, now watch as I—"

"Arrgh!"

"Was that effective?"

"How did you do that?"

"I pinned your elbow while pressing your hand down to force you to keep holding me, then dropped my weight to bend your wrist sideways. Did it hurt?"

"Obviously! Show me again, I like that."

After an hour they had managed to smash a visitor's chair, practice a dozen moves, and gather together all the missing pieces from the mechanism of Velesti's flintlock. An overcast had covered the late afternoon sun as they strolled across the university lawns, arms folded behind their backs.

"This afternoon has been my happiest few hours since I shot up the barracks at Griffith," Velesti announced.

"I must admit I enjoy having a peer-level partner to practice with," replied Martyne.

"What do you think of me?"

"Well . . . you fight like someone two or three times your weight, and with a lot more reach."

"Really?"

"Yes."

"When I was in Balesha I was indeed twice this weight, and was a lot taller."

"You need to use more elbow strikes, and to concentrate on close-in fighting."

"I don't like being close to men."

"But you could hurt them a lot more."

"Hmm, point taken."

"I feel thirsty just now. What would you say to a beer?"

"I would say 'Afternoon's compliments, Frelle Beer.' "

At the gates of the university an orator in a green jacket was standing on one of the two stone gargoyles that guarded the gates. She was addressing several dozen students. Others dressed in green were handing out pamphlets to those passing by. Martyne and Velesti stopped to listen, although at some distance from the group.

"This is not about Islam, or Christianity, or Gentheism, this is about the Word of the Deity," cried the speaker, spreading her arms to the ground, where the god of the Gentheists was thought to dwell. "It is not our path to poison the sacred body of the Allcaring, we must care as we are cared for. Fueled engines poison the Deity, electrical machines torture the Deity's body, abominations disease the Deity. Do you care for your mayorate?"

"Yes!" shouted those Gentheists planted in the crowd, plus a few genuine converts.

"Do you care for your world?"

"Yes!" came a more unified and louder response.

"Then go back to your temples, churches, shrines, mosques, and cathedrals, remind your clergy of the principles that your religions are founded upon. Fight for the purity of your religions, and fight for your world."

"Two months ago I heard this in Kalgoorlie," said Martyne, "except that the orator was the Prophet Jemli herself."

"If the speaker knew *that* she would invite you up there to address the rally," said Velesti. "What are your personal thoughts on the matter?"

"Theologically speaking, it is a shaky proposition for Christianity and Islam. Nothing about engines or fuel sciences appears in their foundation Scriptures; all of that is in latter-day amendments that postdate Greatwinter. However Gentheism was founded on the Greatwinter Revelations, about fifteen hundred years ago."

"At the same time as the Christians and Islamics amended their own Scriptures," Velesti pointed out. "I have always believed that an ancient conspiracy is behind it all."

"So have many others. The Christians burned doubters at the

stake, the Islamics stoned them to death, and the Gentheists buried them alive in moist Mother Earth."

"So, you are a closet doubter, Fras Martyne?"

"Within the confines of a closet, and only between consenting adults, yes. Jemli the Prophet has developed a large and rabid following over a very short period, and she has done it by recruiting followers *within* other religions. Was she not once married to—ah, Mayor Glasken?"

Velesti raised her eyes to the sky for a moment, then slowly turned to Martyne.

"Yessss . . . but she showed none of this theological zeal in all *their* years of marriage. She was certainly ambitious—in fact it was she who was the driving force behind John Glasken being appointed mayor. Sometime after the appointment she suddenly denounced him for condoning the steam engines in the underground university. She then became mayor in her own right, married a local warlord after a year, then was deposed by him, and he became mayor and went on to unify the west as overmayor. Poetic justice, if you ask me."

"While I was in Kalgoorlie I heard that she went mad after her second husband deposed her as mayor. She began preaching against steam engines in markets, on street corners, even at the wind train terminus."

"What is madness, if not a virtue for prophets? After Black Thirteenth, people remembered what she had been predicting: the demise of electrical machines, a great disturbance to the Call, the destruction of Mirrorsun, and the return of Greatwinter if humanity does not heed the Word of the Deity. She has scored well so far. The first two have come true, and Mirrorsun really is behaving strangely."

"It is almost enough to make one a believer," said Martyne, looking up at the speaker and nodding his head.

"Oh, I could declaim far more accurate prophecy."

"Truly?" asked Martyne, turning away from the speaker to face Velesti.

"Truly."

"Then, Frelle Velesti, it is you who should be the Prophet."

"True, and just now I predict trouble," replied Velesti, pointing to the edges of the crowd.

Militiamen were gathering under the direction of an officer, and a Constable's Runner was endeavoring to keep a path clear past the university gates, which were almost blocked by now. There was a scuffle, and the Constable's Runner stumbled and fell. Two militiamen went to his aid, striking out with the butts of their muskets. Gentheists retaliated with swagger sticks. The rest of the militiamen advanced, but the crowd outnumbered them. Finding his men forced back, the officer panicked and fired his flintlock pistol at the Gentheist preacher. She clutched at her chest and toppled from the gargoyle.

Martyne and Velesati dropped to the lawn as the panicked militiamen opened fire on the crowd. Students fell and screams filled the air as some ran, but others charged the militiamen with swagger sticks, knives, and sabers. The Constable's Runner began to blow his whistle, but was quickly set upon and run through. Other Constable's Runners arrived from all quarters, but by now looters had joined the fighting and were at work among the stalls, houses, and taverns near the gates. More shots were fired, then a single, strident voice cut through tumult.

"That's an officer reading the Riot Act!" exclaimed Velesti. "Over to the fountain, take cover."

Moments later there was a disciplined volley of musket fire, followed by another, then another. Now the crowd broke and fled in complete panic, some into the streets, some back into the university. They were followed by guardsmen in skirmishing order.

"Dragon Librarian Service!" shouted Velesti, standing and spreading her hands wide. "Rank of Blue."

An officer came hurrying over as his men passed by the fountain.

"Did you see how it started, Frellc?" he cried as he reached her.

"It seemed to be a peaceful rally, but emotions were running high," she replied. "The trouble started when the numbers blocked the gates."

"May I have your name?"

"Velesti Disore, Dragon Blue with Libris. This is Martyne Camderine, edutor of the university. Both of us are paremedicians. Can we help?"

"Please, yes. There are fourteen dead and three times as many wounded."

Martyne was the first to the Gentheist orator, who had a bullet wound high in the chest and had broken her arm in her fall. He cut a strip from his cloak and pressed it hard against the wound.

"The ball missed your lung, you should be all right," he said as she looked up at him. "Hold this, press hard to slow the bleeding."

"The Deity watches," she whispered.

"Just lie still, if you move you will do more damage. Can you taste blood?"

"No. Aviad agents, they, they . . ."

"Don't talk, just breathe evenly."

The girl grasped his wrist with her free hand, her eyes shining. "Healers are blessed in the eyes of th Deity, Fras Edutor."

The young Gentheist priestess lived and was exonerated at the inquest that followed, mainly due to the testimonies of Martyne and Velesti. The dead and wounded were mostly students and militiamen, and the magistrate declared that the riot had been due to the ill-organized nature of the rally and the fact that it had blocked a public thoroughfare. The priestess responded that the Word of the Deity had attracted a larger than expected and highly excitable crowd.

"The Word of the Deity cannot be allowed to disrupt the public order in Rochester," the magistrate pointed out.

"The Word of the Deity will soon be the new law in Rochester," predicted the bandaged priestess.

"But meantime Commonwealth law is the law and it is my place and duty to administer it. I'm sure the Deity would not want more people to die in senseless riots."

Quite sensibly the magistrate ordered that henceforth any religious rallies within Rochester must be confined to the premises of religious institutions. This did not stop further incidents, but they were less dramatic.

Samoa

The islands of the Samoan archipelago were like luridly green jewels against the ocean as Samondel brought the sailwing around to land. On the ground were two strips of black with a brownish slash between them. White piles of coral marked the edges, and ten gangers stood waving palm fronds at the approaching aircraft. At the middle of the ascent strip was the *Yarron Star*, lying askew where a wheel had collapsed while it was landing. Samondel shed speed in the annoying, blustery wind that was blowing across the makeshift ascent strip. She hung just above the stall speed, keeping the stubby nose high, then passed so low over the *Yarron Star* that she heard one of the *Swallow*'s wheels clip a wing. Then the rear wheels bit into the rammed scoria surface and the *Swallow*'s nosewheel slammed down hard.

The surface was less than ideal and the sailwing slid awkwardly as it lost speed, sending up sprays of scoria gravel and sand. Samondel could hardly believe that she was down safely, even when all motion had ceased. She hauled on the levers that shut down the compression engines while the gangers ran up, cheering. Her new navigator, Alarak, lowered the hatch and stepped out onto the wingfield. As she followed him, Samondel noticed that she had overshot the ascent strip, and that the rear wheels were buried almost up to the axles in volcanic gravel.

"You should have circled," said Avoncor as they all stood looking at the wheels embedded in the surface. "We could have had *Yarron Star* clear in five hours."

"Five hours is nearly half of the distance to New Zealand," replied Samondel, "and a third of that to Australica. In any case, I am down. What work does the *Yarron Star* need?"

"We're going to lever up the wing, then build a frame underneath and roll it to one side of the ascent strip using the engines and rolling logs. Another three weeks should have it fit to ascend."

"Three weeks!"

"We have to do our metalwork with axes and knives, and none

of us are airframe guildsmen. But we'll clear the ascent strip by tonight, of course."

"Then do that, and draw off enough compression spirit from the *Yarron Star* to get the *Swallow* back to Hawaii."

The following day the *Swallow* ascended from the ascent strip named after Samondel, but instead of turning north she began a leisurely circuit of the wingfield. As the navigator watched she took a stick wrapped in paper from her jacket, and as she passed low over the ascent strip she flung it at the crippled *Yarron Star*.

"Can you see if they found it?" she asked Alarak.

"Yes, a group of them is gathered around whoever is reading it."

"That should not take long. It only says 'I Lied' and 'Lake Taupo.' "

"I know I have been saying this all the way from Hawaii, Saireme Airlord, but this is foolhardy."

"Far be it from me to accuse my fellow airlords of being fools, but let us just say that political pressures are being brought to bear on this venture. We are currently consuming two-thirds of Mounthaven's entire compression spirit production in establishing and supplying these wingfields, and monopolizing super-regals that could be put to use in dozens of other good causes. If there is a crash before the next two super-regals are complete, the venture may be ended."

"What can we do in New Zealand by ourselves?"

"With two helpers I prepared a temporary ascent strip for super-regals on Samoa, Sair. You and I must do as much again."

"And why Lake Taupo?"

"According to this ancient publication entitled *Five-Day Tours of the North Island*, Lake Taupo is the biggest lake in the area, and no matter how overgrown towns, roads, and wingfields become, lakes are like islands: they stay much the same over the millennia, and they stand out against their surroundings."

Lake Taupo, New Zealand

Lake Taupo appeared to be deep, and was bordered by several flat stretches of land that were many times the length that was needed for a super-regal to descend.

"Taupo, this is Lake Taupo," said the navigator, "but it is smaller than on the only map that we have. It is a volcanic area, and the volcano was marked as active."

"Some eruption must have changed things," replied Samondel. "We are lucky that there is any lake at all."

"You said islands and lakes do not change much with the millennia."

"I was lying, but you should have caught me. After all, many islands once on the map are now underwater. The sea level has risen."

The sailwing came down on the lake, on a skid that Samondel had had installed at Hawaii. They taxied rapidly along the surface, flinging two waves of spray aside.

"Go for that wide, flat sandbar over there and beach us," said Alarak.

"It's unusually flat, even for a sandbar."

"I know; it may even be firm enough for an ascent strip in itself. Slower, slower, steady, shut down—no! Throttle up, we're sinking, the sandbar's *floating*!"

One wingtip was already in the water as Samondel gunned the engine and drove the *Swallow* through the layer of floating, brown pumice. The navigator slammed the hatch back and crawled out onto the opposite wing, trying to weight it down. The submerged wing came up too fast, the navigator slipped off into the water, and as he came struggling back up through the surface and floating pebbles he saw the *Swallow* smash its makeshift skid into the real beach. By the time he waded ashore Samondel was inspecting the broken skid.

"Can you repair it?" he asked.

"Chopping down bushes is about as much carpentry as I know," Samondel admitted. "Even then all my experience is from Samoa."

"So what do we do?"

"The wheels are undamaged. We can worry about repairs when the next super-regal catches up with us. For now, we should start looking for a suitable place to build it a wingfield."

With *Swallow* tethered they stood in nearly complete silence on the shore, the only humans in a circle with a thousand-mile radius. Samondel closed her eyes and listened to the cool, fresh air rushing in her nostrils. The navigator presently broke the serenity of the moment.

"Sometimes I wonder if it is all worth it, Saireme Airlord. All this effort for a few animals."

"Have you stopped to look around on Hawaii and Samoa, Sair Alarak?"

"Well, yes."

"What are your impressions?"

"They are hot and steamy places, and their blood-sucking insects are delighted to see us. But I must admit that the fruit are wonderful, and the birds are better eating than anything in Mounthaven."

"Already gangers and farmers are growing settled there. As soon as I noticed that, I made sure that women were included among the planters and tillers who were sent out. Even if another super-regal never leaves Mounthaven for the islands, those already there can support themselves and live like nobility. Let a year pass, and Hawaii and Samoa will be producing enough compression spirit to satisfy one super-regal per month passing through. This place will be exporting it."

"But there are virgin areas of our own continent that are just as lush, and not nearly as dangerous and difficult to reach."

"But those areas do not have a large and powerful civilization only a thousand miles to the west. The Australicans will not just sell us a few animals, they can trade ideas and artisans. They do things with wind and muscle, while we use compression and steam engines. Their way of life is slower, but more efficient. We can learn a lot from each other."

"The last thing they tried to teach us was total war—with respect, Saireme Airlord."

"The Mexhaven peoples would have also done that eventually. Come, we had better start collecting brushwood for a beacon pyre. You never know when we will have to attract attention at short notice."

Rochester, the Rochestrian Commonwealth

Spring slowly matured in Rochester, and deciduous trees burst into leaf amid the eucalypti and other evergreens. In six weeks Velesti had put on somewhat more weight, all of it muscle, and had become an increasingly difficult opponent for Martyne as they sparred on the lawns of the university's cloisters. By early December Velesti had sat for assessment examinations at the university, and it had been determined that eighteen months of study in five subjects would be sufficient for her to be granted a degree. She would enroll in January, but in the meantime she continued her work in Libris.

It was 1:00 A.M. as Velesti sat surrounded by piles of some of the rarest books in Libris, none less than nineteen hundred years old. As usual, the hologram of Zarvora stood beside her, peering down as Velesti flipped through the pages.

"I was in an interesting riot recently," Velesti remarked as she turned the pages of a partly burned text on thermodynamics.

"Excellent—there is nothing worse than a boring riot," replied Zarvora.

"It was religious in nature. A Gentheist speaker had just told a rally that the destruction of the electrical machines was the work of the Deity."

"Gentheists are very excitable. I was brought up as a Gentheist."

"The Mechanists think you are a god, the Gentheists think you are a devil, the Christians think you are a machine but are theologically benign if you are powered by sunlight, and the Islamics wish you would go away and stop bothering them."

"A view which you doubtless share."

Velesti shook her head. "I do not mind your company; I just want to be free of you."

"In a few months that should be possible. What then?"

"That depends on what my current employer says. Speaking of Highliber Dramoren, here he comes."

The Highliber was approaching, flanked by two armed Tiger Dragons. All three had their flintlocks drawn. They stopped as Zarvora's hologram turned to regard them. The five figures stared at each other in silence for a time.

"I was expecting this, Highliber Dramoren," said Zarvora. "Please send your guards out of earshot so that we can speak freely."

Dramoren waved his guards back, then closed the gap between Velesti and the partly transparent figure beside her.

"Highliber Zarvora?" asked Dramoren.

"After a fashion, yes."

"Are you a ghost?"

"Yes."

"Oh. My Dragon Librarians say that you have been appearing to Frelle Velesti. For weeks."

"Velesti turns the pages so that I can read. I wish to study certain books that Libris holds."

Dramoren looked at some of the volumes on the desk before Velesti.

"These are all pre-Greatwinter books. My staff report that you appear twice a week, always in here and late at night. You read hundreds of books in just hours."

"Yes."

Dramoren took the chair beside Velesti. Unnervingly, Zarvora sat down in midair. Velesti reached out for another chair and dragged it over.

"Sit down in that Frelle, you will not put him at his ease by levitating," she said as she folded her arms again. Zarvora obliged.

"I can hardly imagine what you need from here," began Dramoren.

"I like to read nice books. Being dead makes that difficult."

"Oh. Highliber—"

"No, *you* are now Highliber—of Libris, its books, its Dragon Librarians, and its rebuilt human Calculor."

"Yes, but—"

"I am a ghost. Do you mind having me for a client?"

"Libris is for the use of scholars. You are a very unusual scholar, but a scholar nonetheless."

"That is a very civilized attitude, the very template of what a

Dragon Librarian should think. That is where the term Dragon Librarian Service comes from, did you know? Dragon for power and wisdom. Librarian for curator and keeper of knowledge, Service because we are all servants of the civilization that enriches and enhances our lives. How is your rebuilt Calculor performing?"

"Slowly, but increasing in reliability. Many of the skills and designs used in your first Libris Calculor have been lost."

"I can help. Send for Velesti wherever you are having trouble. Where she goes, I go too."

"Frelle Zarvora, that is a wonderful and generous offer," said Dramoren, leaning forward and rubbing his hands together.

"Does anyone remember me?" asked Velesti, waving a hand in the air.

Both hologram and human turned to her.

"I have a small but reasonable request."

"Speak," replied Zarvora.

"I want to be given every item of information known about a woman named Lemorel Milderellen."

"As in the Milderellen invasion?" asked Dramoren.

"The sister of the Prophet Jemli?" asked Zarvora.

"Yes. I want to see every record about her, every sketch, every report, and everything that she ever wore, fired, or used. Books have been written about her; I want to see them all."

"She died two decades ago," Dramoren pointed out.

"That is not a problem. I just need to know her as people remember her."

"But why?" asked Zarvora.

"Her sister, Jemli, profits greatly from her memory. It is in all of our interests to do so as well. Lemorel had an affair with Tarrin, a senior Dragon Librarian in Libris, then both of them betrayed you, Zarvora. I recall that you tortured three dozen librarians to extract the truth, nine of them to death."

"I was particularly cross," explained the hologram.

"Then tell me everything you learned. I want all of her campaign records while with the Alspring Ghans as well, *and* I want every gun that she ever owned."

"I have one more question," said Dramoren. "Why are you—that is, why is Mirrorsun speeding up its rotation?"

"To better myself," replied Zarvora.

"I don't understand."

"Another clue: Mirrorsun is a modern name for the ancients' sunshield in space. Their name for the project was Greatwinter, but that name was later hijacked for the stupid war that almost froze the world."

"I still don't understand."

"Then that is unfortunate, Highliber Dramoren. Two clues should encourage you to think. Three might spoil the surprise."

5

WINGS OF THE AIRLORD

Peterborough, the Woomeran Confederation

The first audience of Highliber Dramoren with Jemli the Prophet was made at the Highliber's request, and it was he who made the journey to meet with her. Peterborough was not a large city, but it was exceedingly ancient. It was a trade center on the paraline, with high, thick walls and splendid, ancient mansions, temples, and even a university. The larger city of Woomera had endured a long siege during the Milderellen invasion two decades earlier, and after it fell the carnage saw nine out of every ten citizens killed. That which could not be burned was blown up, and it was said that more gunpowder was used after the siege than during it. When Lemorel Milderellen's invaders were finally defeated the new Confederation was still named Woomera, but it would have taken a century to restore the ancient capital to its former glory. Glory, splendor, and imposing buildings to impress important visitors were what the newly appointed overmayor wanted and Peterborough had just that, so the city was declared to be the new capital.

The current overmayor had given Jemli his palace during the burst of religious fervor that had swept over the city since her arrival, thus strengthening his position with his own subjects. He moved into a smaller but more ornate palace, went about in a cavalry uniform, and gave himself the title Defender of the Prophet. Thus he retained control of his lands while siding with Jemli, yet Jemli gained the larger palace. True, it was no bigger than the palace at Kalgoorlie, but it was closer to the geographical center of the continent's southern mayorates.

As his wind train pulled into the terminus Dramoren looked through the window of his carriage and saw that he had a guard of honor from the Woomeran Mayoral Musketeers flanked by cheering crowds. He also noted Christian, Islamic, Gentheist, and other clerics among the dignitaries there to greet him. He was not surprised by his reception. The Commonwealth had no state religion, so the Dragon Librarian Service was what unified the richest region on the continent—and he headed the Dragon Librarian Service.

"Are you sure you want to go through with this?" asked his medician as he prepared to step out onto the platform.

"Of course. I planned it all myself."

"But it's mind-numbingly dangerous!"

"Ah, but that is why nobody will be suspicious."

Dramoren was put aboard a carriage after leaving his wind train, then driven through the streets to the palace. When he met Jemli, she was seated on her throne, with her hair brushed out cascading down over her shoulders and the armrests to the floor. The majority of those in the hall had ceased to cut their hair or shave, and while this was not something that Jemli had decreed to be the Deity's will, it was seen as a public affirmation of faith and solidarity. Dramoren stopped at the steps leading to the throne, gave a formal bow of greeting, then threw back his cloak and stood with his arms folded to signify that he was not reaching for a weapon.

"You are required to kneel," prompted a herald under his breath.

"I kneel to my monarch, I bow to all others," replied Dramoren, somewhat less softly.

There was an uneasy shifting among Jemli's courtiers. Slowly she stood up, standing well over six feet tall and enshrouded by her calf-length, meticulously dyed hair. She stared down at Dramoren. "Do you acknowledge the Word of the Deity?" she asked.

"I acknowledge the authority of the Christian Scriptures, the authority of the College of Abbots to interpret them, the authority of the Bishop of Rochester in general, and the authority of my abbot in matters relating to my personal behavior."

The reply caught Jemli by surprise. "You are a monk?" she asked.

"I am a laitor, educated as a monk, then sent out to work in the wider world."

So far the audience was going badly for Jemli. The visitor had refused to kneel to her and she had not known a very important aspect of his background. She changed to a new approach.

"Then you are the most powerful and highly placed cleric in the Commonwealth."

"I do not hold office as a cleric."

"But cleric you certainly are. Welcome to our number, welcome with honor."

A massed band in the gallery to the left immediately struck up at the keyword "honor," and was joined by a choir in the gallery to the right. *Very clever,* thought Dramoren. *She turns a diplomatic slight into a triumph by welcoming me without a chance for me to reply.*

Jemli descended the steps, held her hand out for Dramoren's arm, then walked back down the processional carpet with him as the entire court applauded and the music blared. Courtiers and clergy fell in behind them in order of precedence as Jemli took the Highliber out into the palace gardens. Sound did not travel so clearly, here as in the throne hall.

"My followers have been the subjects of some violence in your Commonwealth," said Jemli as they stepped onto the lawn.

"That very fact is why I am here," replied Dramoren.

Guards flanked them at a respectful distance, sketchers hurried along drawing outlines for the engravings and paintings that would soon be produced to celebrate the occasion.

"Is the Commonwealth hostile to the Word?"

"On the contrary, Rochester welcomes everyone who would support *or* oppose it. You must know the saying, two Rochestrians, three opinions."

"How can it be that you tolerate anyone opposing the Word of the Deity?" exclaimed Jemli.

"We tolerate all opinions, that is our strength."

"Then we must differ. My people believe in the Word that is Truth. We must proclaim it everywhere, we must denounce those who work for evil."

"It is my place to denounce evil as well," Dramoren replied firmly. "Where we apparently differ is in the definition."

They stopped beside a fountain and Jemli's large entourage began to spread out in a circle at a measured distance.

"The Commonwealth is unlike any other alliance of mayorates," said Jemli. "It has a secular heart, the Dragon Librarian Service."

"It is a powerful and reliable heart, one that has reconstructed the beamflash tower network. We have even assisted in the lands where you rule, Frelle Prophet."

"I do not rule. I declare the Word and it is up to the faithful to follow it. But it is not in the interest of the Word to have secular men and women transmitting it."

"Then what do you want?"

"I want all those in the Dragon Librarian Service to swear loyalty to the Word."

Dramoren did not react at once, for he had anticipated a demand along these lines.

"What you demand is not mine to give," he finally replied.

"So, you can enslave every numerate adult in the Commonwealth, yet you cannot order the Dragon Librarians to acknowledge what is upheld by every faith of any consequence?"

"I can tell them what to do, Frelle Prophet, not what to think. You are, of course, free to convince them yourself."

"Fras Highliber, my life is dedicated to convincing people of the Word."

"Then come to Rochester and preach to us. I have an invitation here from the Overmayor, and I have endorsed it personally."

Dramoren reached into his jacket and drew out a folded and sealed parchment. Immediately one of the guards raised his long-barreled flintlock and fired. The bullet clipped the invitation and struck Dramoren just behind the right deltoid. He dropped the letter and fell. The guards rushed up, dragged Jemli back, and seized Dramoren. One managed to strike the Highliber's head three times with the butt of his flintlock before Jemli shrieked for the others to release her. Her words also caught the attention of the guards holding Dramoren.

"Let him go!" demanded Jemli.

"But, Frelle Prophet, he—"

"Obey me or be damned and cursed eternally, ye disobedient servants who are foul and polluted in the eyes of the Deity," began Jemli, in a voice that carried clearly to everyone within a hundred yards.

Finally convinced, the guards backed away from Dramoren but kept their guns trained in his general direction.

"I thought he was trying to kill you," said one of them in a high, trembling voice.

Jemli snatched the letter from the ground. "And how might *this* kill me?" she asked. "Medician! Tend Highliber Dramoren!"

Jemli broke the seal on the letter and began to read it aloud. It was indeed an invitation to visit the Rochestrian Commonwealth and preach. Dramoren sat up with the medician's aid. Nobody else dared to approach.

"The Highliber has a bullet in his shoulder and is cut and bruised about the head, but his life is not in danger," pronounced the medician.

Clutching his shoulder, Dramoren shook off the medician's hands and got to his feet.

"Take him into the palace, to my own suite," ordered Jemli. "He must have nothing but the finest—"

"I am returning to my wind train," said Dramoren, blood seeping through his fingers and trickling down his face.

"Fras, you are in no condition to travel!" exclaimed Jemli.

"My father marched sixty miles with worse wounds than this during the Milderellen Invasion. Besides, there is a medician on my wind train, and a squad of more reliable guards than yours. Farewell, Frelle Prophet."

"But the invitation!"

"You may do with it what you will."

"I wish to accept."

"Well, then, I shall convey this to my Overmayor. When I have recovered from the attentions of your guards I am sure that we can arrange a suitable date for your visit. By beamflash."

Dramoren began to walk away.

"At least let me fetch a carriage!" Jemli called after him.

"I have had sufficient hospitality for one trip," replied Dramoren without turning.

Jemli snapped her fingers.

"Overhand."

The overhand of the city militia stepped forward.

"Have a thousand guardsmen escort him back to his wind train. Kill anyone who blocks his path, gets in his way, or even so much as heckles him."

"A thousand—"

"Instantly! That man's death means *automatic* and *total* war with the Commonwealth."

The overhand saluted, then ran, shouting orders.

"Medician."

"Frelle Prophet?"

"Escort him until he is in the care of his own medician. If he dies, do not bother coming back."

"Hospitaller!"

"Frelle Prophet?"

"Take twenty courtiers, pick up a fully laden feasting table, and follow the Highliber to the paraline terminus. Give him *anything* he wants. Have thirty priestesses walk beside him with feather parasols to shade him from the sun. Go!"

The captain of Jemli's personal guard was summoned next.

"Those five guardsmen who attacked the Highliber were possessed by the Polluted One," she decreed.

"Your word is the Word, Frelle Prophet."

"They are to be purified. See to it."

Dramoren walked the two miles back to the terminus with considerable difficulty. The guardsmen at the palace gate made the mistake of trying to demand an explanation for his condition before letting him pass. They were shot down by the overhand's men without so much as a single word in reply. Terrified crowds cheered Dramoren every step of the way, priests and courtiers staggered behind him with a feasting table, priestesses shaded him with feather sunshades on poles, several carriages had their occupants ejected and were following in case Dramoren decided he needed a ride, and guardsmen blanketed the area three hundred yards of him. Nevertheless, with blood soaking into his jacket and almost blinded by the blood trickling down into his eyes, Dramoren did not inspire confidence in the hospitality of the Gentheists' Prophet.

There was a light but steady wind blowing, and the rotors of Dramoren's wind train were spinning steadily as he came within sight of the terminus. Guardsmen had already informed the crew that he was returning, and with sudden inspiration, the city overhand ordered the Rochestrian medician and guardsmen to be brought out at gunpoint to meet and assist their master. Two hundred yards from the terminus Dramoren was met by his medician, and he stopped for a minute to have his wounds examined. Priests swarmed about offering the finest food and drink that the palace kitchens could produce to anyone who looked Rochestrian. Priestesses shaded and fanned them, crowds of onlookers cheered at gunpoint, members of the clergy offered prayers to the gods of a dozen major and minor faiths for Dramoren's speedy recovery, and a band came jogging up from the palace, playing as they went.

Dramoren refused to be carried, even by his own people, but before long he reached his wind train. The paraline had already been cleared all the way to the border, and Dramoren's train was bracketed by armed galley engines before and aft, and by a hundred lancers to either side of it. The captain engaged the gears and the wind engine and its single coach glided forward.

Jemli watched the Rochestrian wind train leaving from a tower of her palace. The captain of her guard stood beside her, watching a twinkling light at the terminus.

"The Highliber appeared to be strong as he boarded the train," he reported as he read the code in the flickering light. "An officer overheard the Rochestrian medician tell the Highliber that he was a lucky man as he treated him in the street. The priestesses shaded and fanned him every step of the way, of course."

"But he took no refreshments."

"No."

Jemli pounded the limestone railing with both fists. "Rochestrians can truthfully say that their Highliber was given no refreshments, was shot, and walked unaided and bleeding all the way from the palace back to the terminus."

"But he *chose* to walk, he was *offered* refreshments."

"You are a fool, Captain, and possibly under the influence of the Polluted One as well. See your confessor, have yourself cleansed. What of the guards who attacked Dramoren?"

"Four have been exorcised of the influence of the Polluted One by being buried alive," replied the thoroughly alarmed captain. "The fifth has gone into hiding."

"Offer ten thousand gold barters for his head on a platter."

"Consider it done."

The Rochestrian Commonwealth

The wind train reached the border of the Rochestrian Commonwealth the following day, and the lead Woomeran galley engine was shunted aside to let it continue onto home soil. A Rochestrian galley train was waiting to take over as escort, and as they continued into Rochestrian territory, Dramoren and a Dragon Librarian wearing no designator of rank stood looking back at the border post and two Woomeran galley engines.

"Well, Fras Cavor, we appear to have had a very successful mission," said Dramoren.

"It appears to be so, Highliber."

"That was a very good shot. I particularly liked the way you hit the letter of invitation as well."

"That was a fortuitous accident, Highliber."

Dramoren began to laugh, then winced at a twinge from his shoulder. "Do you have any observations, Fras Cavor?"

"It was a very, very dangerous act, Highliber. You could easily have died."

"So could you. The medician has removed the bullet, and he says that the injury is not severe—as such injuries go."

"Highliber, *any* such wound will make its presence felt for the rest of your life."

"I was wounded in the service of Rochester."

"Again."

"And probably not for the last time."

Dramoren left Cavor and walked through the carriage, crossing the walkway to the wind engine. Passing through the gearbox gallery he continued to the captain's cabin. The captain was in his fifties, but was weatherbeaten and looked older.

"I shall transfer to the galley engine once we are out of sight of the border," Dramoren announced. "I need to reach Rochester with more speed than the wind allows."

"Our place to serve, Highliber."

"While I have the chance, I would like to thank you again for all your help at Peterborough."

"That was the second time the Great Western Paraline has gotten a Highliber out of that place. 'Tis my honor to serve."

Dramoren stood watching the dials showing ground speed, wind speed, wind direction, rail inclination, absolute drag, and forward thrust. Every so often the captain would adjust a wheel, dial, or lever.

"We are tethering," explained the captain, noticing that Dramoren was taking an interest in operations.

"Tethering?" echoed Dramoren.

"Stealing a small forward vector from the slipstream of the galley engine in front."

"Ah, clever. Is it an old technique?"

"Goes back a ways centuries."

"Your Great Western people are sharp on ways to boost efficiency."

" 'Twas as Brunel taught."

"Ah yes, the pre-Greatwinter engineer that you worship."

"Not worship, Highliber. He was just the greatest of engineers, and we follow his way."

"I read that he built steam trains and steam ships."

"The world was different then."

"The Gentheists of Prophet Jemli have declared him an abomination."

"That they did."

"How did you react?"

"I moved from Kalgoorlie to Rochester and converted to Christianity."

That gave Dramoren pause for thought. The captain checked the rearview mirror, then began working the semaphore lever to signal the galley engine in front.

"We'll be docking in a few minutes," he announced. "You can cross to the galley engine through the forward hatch."

"Thank you. Tell me, how is the Prophet regarded on the paraline network?"

"We seniors say she treats us like a privy. She has to use us, but we're given no honor."

"So she is not in favor on the paralines?"

"She's in high favor by those toadies she's promoted, but all experienced and dedicated Great Western workers have been driven out. Most moved to the Commonwealth, like me. I'm lucky, I have a train. There's former captains who are tending gearboxes, or even pushing pedals in the galleys. Steady yourself now, we're about to dock."

There was a lurch and heavy boom as the engines coupled.

"Tell me, is the captain of the galley engine ahead also Great Western?" asked Dramoren.

"Oh, aye, and a fine, steady woman."

"A woman? As captain of a galley engine?"

"Aye, there's three of them, the first in history. The Great Western Paraline Authority is very progressive."

Dramoren was thoughtful as he transferred to the galley engine, followed by his medician, staff, and guards. A minute later the engines decoupled and the low, streamlined galley engine pulled away from the wind train, driven by the powerful legs of its team of human pedalers.

Rochester, the Rochestrian Commonwealth

Dramoren surprised the galley engine captain by ordering a stop at the maintenance yards in the artisan area of Rochester. It was evening, but the dismissal bell had not yet rung. There were both wind and galley engines under repair, and others being built. Windmills drove the lathes and forge hammers in the workshops, while smoke from wood-fired forges poured into the coloring sky. Dramoren made for the administration building, but word of his arrival had rushed ahead of him and the yard foreman met him at the base of the signal tower.

"Highliber, we had no warning of your visit—"

"I thought to make this visit only moments ago, Fras Foreman," said Dramoren, waving him silent with his good arm.

"Is there anything you'd like to see in particular? The drafting house library, the archive, the school for apprentices?"

"The yards and workshops themselves, Fras, and I want to meet as many Great Western refugees as can be mustered."

The dismissal bell rang, but everyone was too curious and excited to leave. Dramoren was no engineer or artisan, but he was certainly an experienced scholar. Many times he had managed to pass examinations on the strength of a day's study done after a term of stolen wine, drunken singing in the monastery walnut groves, nocturnal card sessions betting for raisins, and an incident with a female wine buyer that earned him twenty strokes of the abbot's cane and a month of cold baths. Thus the Highliber was skilled at becoming an instant expert. After broaching the subject of the Gentheists and the Great Western Paraline Authority with Captain Tarveran, he had been subjected to seventeen hours of her opinions on

Gentheist persecution, Great Western standards, Brunel, battles involving the Authority, and the evils of any paraline gauge other than seven feet and a quarter of an inch. In the Great Western circles there were two classes of people: the initiates and everyone else. Dramoren now knew enough to impress the initiates, and that effectively made him one also.

The foreman, the artisans, the apprentices, everyone who spoke to Dramoren was astounded by his knowledge, perception, and common sense. Many were refugees from Gentheist persecution, and they poured out their stories to him. At last Dramoren turned back to his galley engine, escorted by the foreman.

"There are long stretches of paraline in the former Calldeath lands, built by the aviads," said Dramoren as they walked over the rails. "The Overmayor has been thinking of enhancing and expanding them."

"They're piddling, three-foot-gauge thing; nowt can be done there," said the foreman bluntly.

"Well, indeed. But I have noted that there are many Great Western Paraline folk in the Commonwealth. I thought we might use their skills to do things properly in the new territories. They would be given a free hand, but apart from upkeep the payment could only be in land grants."

The foreman had already realized that a very senior member of the government was seriously sympathetic.

"Our people want only to build and maintain good paraline systems," he replied. "Given a free hand and resources, we'll build you the finest paralines in the world."

"Mind, I only want Great Western people," insisted Dramoren. "No riff-raff who have to be trained, or who would rather follow Prophet Jemli than Brunel's way."

"Ah, there's thousands of us, Highliber, we can spread the news and recruit the very best folk all the way to Kalgoorlie and beyond—"

"Discreetly, if you please. We must not risk persecution."

"The Authority has ways, Highliber. We look after our own."

Dramoren boarded his galley engine, which then slowly rumbled between ranks of cheering Great Western Paraline workers, artisans, gangers, navvies, and engineers. Soon they were among the cottages and apartments of the outer city, gliding through the smoke and cooking smells of thousands of hearths and stew pots. Then they rolled out into the clear air over the lake as they crossed the bridge to the inner city. The Overmayor was waiting at the terminus as the galley engine came to a stop. Dramoren stepped onto the platform, the white cloth of his sling standing out against his jacket and long coat.

"You could have sent an envoy," Lengina said as they set off down the platform.

"I carry more authority than an envoy. That which I had to present required authority."

"But it was just an invitation, it could have been sent over the beamflash. You were shot, you might have been killed."

"Ah, but I am alive. How has the news been taken here?"

"With outrage. The Dragon Librarian Service is held in high regard in the Commonwealth, it—and you—hold the Commonwealth together more surely than I do. That you should be shot while under diplomatic immunity is barbarism."

"Well, then, I obviously had more impact than an envoy, Overmayor."

The road to the palace was lined with even more cheering people than had been there to welcome him at Peterborough. Many had never before set eyes on the Highliber, but now he was highly popular, and known to be a hero.

Not among the onlookers for the Highliber's return from the west were Marelle Glasken and Velesti Disore. Marelle's tavern was open for the night, but the floor wardens were keeping the patrons away from one particular table. Marelle sat at the table alone, sipping at a drink and tapping her foot impatiently. A woman appeared at the door and made to enter. The guard at the door stepped across her path. There was a brief scuffle and a shriek of pain. The guard dropped to the floor. Velesti stepped over him, surveyed the interior, and made for Marelle's table.

"The night's compliments, Frelle Glasken; and your father sends his compliments," she said with a shallow bow.

"The night's compliments, Frelle Disore. Will you not have a seat?"

Velesti sat down.

"A drink?" asked Marelle.

"Actually, no."

The two women assessed each other across the table, Marelle with a generous cleavage on display and Velesti with her jacket and blouse both buttoned up to the throat.

"So, you say you knew my father," said Marelle.

"You were five years old when he caught you posing nude while Gerric Binkstym painted your portrait. He was six."

Marelle's mouth opened, and stayed open.

"When you were fifteen he surprised you with the Mayor of Cambala's son in the north tower's spare bedroom."

"But he had gone there with the Mayor of Cambala's wife."

"He thought fifteen was too young—" began Velesti.

"He was just *fourteen* when *he* first did it. John Glasken was a buffoon. Just what were you to him, that he told you so much?"

"We were on a long journey. He needed to learn my language, so we talked a lot as I taught him words."

"Including words of seduction?"

"Frelle, I could no more tolerate a man's embrace than Fras Glasken could have."

"*Could* have. So he is definitely dead?"

"Yes."

Marelle raised her glass and drank a toast to her dead father. Velesti sat motionless.

"He killed Warran," she added.

"My half brother is no loss. He was a monster."

"Fras Glasken said to seek out you and your mother, Varsellia, to tell you about many enchanting things he has seen."

"Doubtless all of them naked women."

"Oh no, they were snow-smothered peaks as far as the eye could see, canyons big enough to swallow cities, valleys carpeted in wildflowers, and strange civilizations."

Marelle shook her head. "He'd have traded it all for one drunken revel, followed by a night spent bundling into some wench."

"You forget that he mellowed. After all, he married, became a successful merchant, and was even Mayor of Kalgoorlie for a time."

"During which he established the Kalgoorlie Beer Festival, featuring such events as the stolen keg in the wheelbarrow gymkhana, vomiting contests, team drinking races, and tag mud wrestling for drunks—both in pairs and mixed doubles."

"Well, yes, he never let himself outgrow a little revelry with his mates."

"Unlike the long-suffering women associated therewith," added Marelle coldly. "Ah, but you are a woman, Frelle Velesti, he would not have told you of all that."

"Your words . . . do sour my memory of him," Velesti admitted reluctantly.

"If I asked you to name the ten most enjoyable moments of John Glasken's life—from what you now know of it—how many of them would involve getting a leg over some willing wench?"

"Then what are *your* best moments, if you are so superior to him?"

"Seeing my stepmother, Jemli, lose power as mayor, leaving home, establishing this tavern, being serenaded by a prince. All come before my most enjoyable night in bed with anyone. I treat sex the same as I do a bowl of whipped coffee cream and apricot liqueur sprinkled with chocolate chips. I hog it down when it is put within my reach, but I do not live for it." Marelle looked down at the table and shook her head. "Still, Papa was brave, loyal, generous, a good father to all his children, and—except for quite a few affairs—honest. That's why I love him still, and that's why he is still mourned by dozens today, if not hundreds."

Velesti's eyes had been flickering around as Marelle spoke, and now she fixed on someone. Marelle noticed that a young man wearing an edutor's cloak had entered the tavern. Velesti stood up and bowed to Marelle.

"I must go," the librarian said brusquely. "Glasken's compliments to you—and mine."

"As you will."

Without another word Velesti strode away, straight to where the young man sat at a table beside a window facing over the street. She said something. He looked up but did not reply. She spoke again. He took out a letter and waved it at her. Velesti held out her hand for it. He shook his head, put the letter back in his jacket and folded his arms very tightly. She tapped the table several times with her finger. He shook his head. She strode out without another word.

"May I get you another drink, Mistress?" another jarmaid asked Marelle.

Marelle inclined her head to the lone man seated by the window. He was by now cradling a glass flute of some golden drink in his hands and staring into space.

"What do you think of him, Nereli?"

"Looks lonely," replied the jarmaid.

"Fetch me a spiced wine," said Marelle as she stood up.

Marelle minced over to the youth's table, stopping before him with much of her left thigh showing through her split robe and with her arms folded.

"The evening's compliments, Fras Edutor," she said in a husky voice.

He looked up slowly. "Evening's compliments, Frelle Mistress."

"Something seems to weigh heavily upon you. Would you like another drink?"

"What I have is enough, but I shall buy another if you let me sit here."

"The drink was to be provided by the house."

"Ah, thank you. That was generous."

"I own the house."

"Oh."

"May I sit down?"

"It is your house, Frelle Mistress."

"I am Marelle."

"And I am Martyne."

Marelle was given her spiced wine, and she sat opposite Martyne.

"I realize that I'm intruding," she began.

"You are."

"But if you had not wanted company, you could have bought a jar at the market and brooded somewhere more private."

The observation caught Martyne by surprise. He had not realized that he tended to drink alone but in public.

"I have a lot of unwelcome thoughts, Frelle," he admitted. "Perhaps you do provide a distraction from them."

"Ah. So should you not share them with me, and ease your burden?"

"No."

"What burdens can an edutor have? Have you rendered some student pregnant?"

"No." Martyne laughed.

"Then tell me who you are."

"I am an edutor in theology at the University. Before that I was a monk for five years. I am nineteen years old, and not a virgin."

Marelle considered. "That all raises more questions that I can begin to ask. So you were a monk. Were you caught with some girl and ejected from the order?"

"Not quite. I renounced my vocation to avenge my sister, who had been most brutally raped and murdered. Then I discovered that fourteen of her tormentors had been killed. It was sheer chance that reserved just one for me to exterminate."

Marelle tried to weather the intense onslaught of misery with composure.

"Do you share a bed with a Dragon Librarian named Velesti?"

Martyne laughed. "Velesti? Even a flea would not dare to share a bed with Velesti. No, I just teach her some fighting arts and try to keep her out of trouble. She tours the taverns, hoping for men to grope at her breasts or bottom so that she can maim them hideously. Last week one of her victims died from her attentions, I had to testify to the magistrate on her behalf. Being an ex-monk, my word is respected. I *felt* like saying that unlike the five or six dozen others that she has killed, the latest slaying had in fact been an accident. Anyway, she was let off with a caution."

"Who does keep intimate company with you?"

"Nobody. Mine is a strange, twisted, but interesting existence."

Marelle began to laugh, but not loudly. Martyne shrugged, and took a delicate sip at his drink.

"Look about the room, Fras Martyne," she said. "What sorts of men do you see?"

"Prosperous men, happy men, drunk men, sullen men—"

"Most are in search of amorous adventures. Most would cheerfully leap through hoops of fire to be sitting in your chair, speaking with me."

"Oh, I'm sorry, I didn't realize," Martyne began, standing up.

"Sit down!" Marelle snapped, slapping her palm down on the table. Martyne slowly lowered himself to his seat again. "Fras Martyne, you are meant to be the hunter and I the hare, that is the way of things. This reversal business does not come easily to me."

"Am I to understand that you wish to seduce me?"

"Martyne, this is all wearing my patience a little thin—"

Her voice failed her in midsentence. Martyne had seized the rim of his glass and was squeezing it between his thumb and forefinger. Small standing waves were set up on the surface of his mead, then the glass snapped. Most of the shards fell into the drink, but one fell onto the table. Martyne flicked it with his finger, and it embedded its point in the back of Marelle's chair, just below where her arm was draped. Nobody else noticed.

"Just because I am pathetic, Frelle Mistress, do not make the mistake of thinking that I am not very, very dangerous. I am enchanted by your quite delightful body, I certainly do admit that, but there is seduction in my past that has caused a great deal of grief for me. I am in no hurry to add the tribulations of yet another to my already burdened mind. Now, then, I believe that I have created a small disturbance and the sign above the serving bench says that patrons creating a disturbance will be asked to leave."

Marelle cringed back as Martyne reached over the table, but he merely plucked the silver of glass from the chair and dropped it into his drink. As he stood up he took a silver noble from his purse and placed it on the table.

"That should cover the cost of your glass, and now I must—"

"No!"

"No? How much do these new glass goblets cost, then?"

Marelle stood up too, but she hesitated to touch him.

"Martyne, I—I can't pretend not to be frightened of you."

"No need, my manners are awfully good. Now I really must be going."

"Martyne, stay with me."

"Frelle, as I have said, I have more burdens than I can manage already."

"Silly Fras, I own this tavern, I am not some wench in search of a husband to support her. I want nothing from you but company. Interesting company."

"I am hardly interesting."

"Look about, how many men do you see without partners?"

"Ten—no, eleven."

"Do any of them deserve my company more than you?"

Martyne spread his arms wide, then shrugged. "Frelle, if I want to make a fool of myself I need only walk outside and bare my buttocks at the first Constable's Runner that I chance upon. That will earn me three days in the public stocks, looking very foolish indeed. You are Rochester's most attractive and alluring tavern mistress, and I have no interest in humiliating myself in your bed. The evening's compliments to you, lovely Frelle, but I have business at the night market."

Martyne turned to walk away, but Marelle strode around the table to stand in front of him. He halted.

"Secret, dangerous business involving Dragon Librarians?" she asked.

"Groceries, actually."

Not far away, out of Martyne's field of view, Velesti was back and watching. She was leaning against the jar rack and slowly shaking her head.

"Martyne, Martyne, do you know how hurt I would be if you stood me up for groceries? Come with me, let us talk easily."

At the word "hurt," Martyne's resolve buckled. Marelle took his hand and led him away. Velesti hurried out of the tavern but did not go far. Within moments she was on the roof of a building across the street, winding a light crossbow and looking at an upstairs window where lamplight was glowing. It was Marelle's room, and Velesti could see her with Martyne. By now his cloak and tunic were off and Marelle was running her fingers across the muscles of his chest. At a prompt that Velesti could not hear Martyne raised his hands to caress her shoulders. Marelle began to disrobe. Velesti raised the crossbow and took aim. She squeezed the trigger.

The tiny dart thudded into the frame junction of the window. The soon-to-be lovers looked around, startled, then went to the window and peered out. Velesti was given a quite intimidating view of Marelle's breasts for a moment as she drew the curtains. The librarian pulled a fine wire taut, a wire that reached all the way across the street to the dart embedded in Marelle's window frame. Velesti clamped the end of the wire to a metal diaphragm mounted in a conical earpiece horn.

For a long time there was only giggling, gasps, and moans in the earpiece, but they were gratifyingly clear. Velesti pulled her cloak about her and glanced to the sky, glaring at the gathering clouds. Presently a tinny scream overloaded the wire. Martyne said he was sorry, but Marelle assured him that he had nothing to be sorry about. For a time there was silence.

"Don't either of you dare go to sleep," muttered Velesti, rubbing her hands together.

"Tell me a secret," said Marelle, her voice low and barely audible.

"Would you believe that I have just been accepted as a member of the Confessors?" came Martyne's reply across the road through the wire. "It is a league of religiously inclined gentlemen who have arrangements with selected innkeepers. For a small fee we watch the cavortings of sundry unmarried couples in rented rooms through strategically placed spyholes. Thus we witness the sins before they are confessed, all very efficient."

"You dirty little boy," commented Velesti.

Marelle and Martyne were laughing, and their laughter led into another bout of rather familiar sounds. Velesti drummed her fingers on a tile, then took out her telescope and began to follow the activities of streetwalkers and their patrons in the dimly lit street below. Eventually there was silence on the wire spanning the street.

"You hardly know anything about me," chided Marelle.

Velesti lowered her telescope hurriedly and pressed the earpiece hard against her head.

"Er . . . so?" replied Martyne.

"Fras Martyne, really! The way to really charm a lady is to get her talking about herself! Only bores talk about how rich or strong or important they are. With some men you could probably put a cow in skirts and snuff the lamp, and they'd not notice the difference, but really suave men treat us as more than enticingly dressed flesh."

There was a brief silence as Martyne assimilated this lesson.

"I had actually wondered how you managed to buy a tavern while being barely older than me."

"Ah, flattery, wonderful—I'm actually years older than you. It was family money, I am the daughter of Mayor Glasken of Kalgoorlie by his second wife."

"So you are stepdaughter of the Prophet Jemli?" exclaimed Martyne.

"Unfortunately, yes. I came here in September, to get away from her. My mother provided me with some gold to go on with, and I saw the need for an establishment where single women of middling to high social standing could mix with a more refined class of menfolk."

"True, it is a setting that ordinary taverns do not provide."

"And it has been an overnight success. I turn a profit of eleven gold royals per month, after expenses and taxes."

"And your code name in the Espionage Constables is Frelle Orchid, but he does not need to know that for now," whispered Velesti to herself.

"I'm bored with talking of me," said Marelle. "What was the terrible deed in your past?"

"A sordid, messy, thing, Frelle. It was—no, you would despise me."

"Did the cow have a name, did she have nice, brown dewy eyes?"

"Oh, Godslove no! She was a woman!"

"Ah, see how hard it is to shock me?"

"Shock there still is. She is Velesti's mother."

"My, my."

"I had been drinking rather heavily."

In your position, I would have too, thought Velesti.

"A letter from her arrived some days ago," concluded Martyne miserably. "In it she said that I had been a most ardent and magnificent lover. I remember being neither ardent nor magnificent, but nevertheless she is now pregnant by two months."

"It happens," said Marelle, apparently not shocked at all.

"She wants to marry me."

Really, Mother, I am surprised at you, thought Velesti.

"She will visit Rochester at Christmas. You can guess what she has in mind, but marrying my best friend's mother is not to my taste."

"I'm glad to hear it," agreed Marelle.

Your best friend, thought a very surprised and flattered Velesti. *Why, thank you.*

"What can I do?" moaned Martyne. "She's twice my age!"

"Well, *I* certainly shall not become pregnant by you, neither shall I demand your hand in marriage," purred Marelle.

Spoken like a true Glasken, thought Velesti, pressing against the lee of a roof as rain began to fall.

"Now you can see what weighs upon me," said Martyne.

"Well, for tonight you can do no good by thinking on it further.

Lie at ease in my arms, Martyne. Pretend that a beautiful guardian angel is listening to your troubles, and that she will set your life in order as you sleep."

Best friend, now guardian angel, thought Velesti, whipping the wire to free the dart from the window. *Well, I probably should do something about Mother.*

The following morning Martyne returned to his lodgings, used the communal bath, then dressed and dropped a bag of clothes with the university laundaric on the way to the refectory and breakfast. At the Faculty of Theology he took a discussion class, and finally arrived at his study just as the clock tower was striking the tenth hour. Velesti was seated in his chair with her boots on his desk.

"Well, how was she?" she asked as Martyne stood gaping at her.

"Who?"

"Marelle?"

"Should I bother to ask how you know?"

"No."

"I have had more humiliating experiences in my life, but just now I am having trouble recalling them."

"As good as that?"

"Worse."

"Too demanding?"

"I think the men in her past have done rather more prerequisite fieldwork than I."

"She was brought up to demand quality."

"Now you tell me."

"But she is compassionate as well."

"I'd not like to see her vindictive."

"Actually I heard that she had a truly excellent time, and holds you in high regard. Too many men want to prove things, few treat their partners as equals and friends. She has invited you back. You accepted."

"How did you know that?" snapped Martyne.

"We girls talk," replied Velesti.

"She didn't!" exclaimed Martyne, suddenly discovering new extremes covered by the word *dismay*.

"Actually Marelle said you were strong, fit, of excellent wit, intelligent, and most important of all, sexually deprived."

"You set this up with her!"

"More or less. Her place tonight?"

"As a matter of fact, yes."

"And sparring with me this afternoon?"

"Why not?"

"Merely checking."

Euroa, the Rochestrian Commonwealth

The weekly meetings of the project masters of the Monastery of St. Roger were short and frantic, and run by the abbot. His position was one of absolute dictator. Five monks, one eunuch, and one Dragon Librarian hurried into Abbot Ashman's study, each with a chalkboard in hand. A scribe sat ready with a roll of poorpaper and a char stylus.

"Project masters' meeting for December seventh of the Year of Greatwinter's Waning 1729, and anno Domini 3961," declared Abbot Ashman. "Firstly, myself: astronomy. The twenty-inch telescope from Siding Springs has been installed, and is undergoing tests. It is expected to be operational in six days. A project has been initiated to make parallax observations of meteor strikes on the surface of Mirrorsun as a verification of the speed of rotation, but none have been observed yet. It is possible that only the biggest of the Siding Springs telescopes can resolve the flashes of such strikes. Project master Brother Varlian?"

"It has been speculated that the material used in a parachute from Mirrorsun, and preserved in an argon gas chamber for ten years, might be similar to that of Mirrorsun's body. A large frame to subject it to breaking strain tests is under construction, and will be ready by December."

"Why not cut off a small strip and test it in the laboratory?" asked the abbot.

"It cannot be cut. The parachute appears to be the strongest, lightest fabric currently on the face of the earth."

"Well, work as fast as you can, and call for laity help if you think it will speed up construction. Project master Brother Nikalan?"

"I have completed analysis of projected calculation completion dates for key computations by the St. Roger Calculor, at its current level of performance."

"And they total?"

"One hundred five years."

"Reduce that to one hundred days by the next meeting. Contact the Highliber of Libris about additional resources and techniques. Captain Andebaret, anything to report from your eunuch guards?"

"Five monks have been caught either at or within the perimeter of the nun's subprocessor. They insisted that they were repairing equipment, but there was no repair scheduled on the register."

"Seven days of cold baths and scrubbing privy barrels. What else?"

"One monk was caught within the Dragon Librarians' dormitory, with—or does that does that read within—a Dragon Librarian by the name of Frelle—"

"Thirty days of cold baths and scrubbing privy barrels, and deport the Dragon Librarian to Libris with a complaint."

"The monk was Brother Varlian."

The abbot winced.

"Brother Varlian, we can't spare you for thirty days of scrubbing privy barrels. Make that thirty strokes of the cane on your bare buttocks followed by one cold bath in salt water. Project Master Brother Pallock?"

"Stores are running down at a rate of fifteen percent faster than supplies can be—"

"Import the shortfall from the regional cities and send the invoices to Libris. Anything else?"

"No," chorused the project masters.

"Next meeting, this time plus seven days. Dismissed."

Bendigo Abandon, the Rochestrian Commonwealth

Shadowmouse was feeling edgy about the slow speed of the wind train. The winds had been weak and variable for most of the day, and the final short stretch to the Bendigo Abandon had taken five hours. Frelle Sparrow was keeping the children amused, but he did not like the party to be near the same humans for too long. The pair of them could certainly pass for a young husband and wife, but two of the children they were escorting were eleven years old. This meant that they could help to carry the babies, but they looked too old to be children of such a young couple.

"This is pathetic, we could walk faster," said Shadowmouse as he watched the gathering dusk.

"Our contact will wait for as long as it takes," replied Frelle Sparrow.

"The contact does not worry me. It's the yokel passengers who have been trying to be friendly ever since Rochester."

"You see spies everywhere. Look, if we were going to be arrested it would have happened long ago."

"True, but I still have the feeling we're being watched."

The sky was dark but clear as they arrived at the Bendigo Railside. From an unimportant loading point for farmers, it had suddenly become a major gateway for people moving into the former Calldeath lands. Most of the town was tents and vendors' stalls, and even at night the market was open and everything from muskets to horses could be bought. The prices were inflated, but they reflected what people were willing to pay. Shadowmouse bought a handcart and tent, then led his family through the dusty, bonfire-lit streets as if searching for somewhere to make camp for the night.

Eventually they reached the outlying woodlands and stopped at a marker cairn. A man stepped out of the darkness and sauntered over.

"We're hunting possums here, will ye be stayin' long?" he drawled.

"Tell us of a stretch of flat, clear ground and we'll be on our way, friend," replied Shadowmouse.

"There's two horses with saddlebags for the babies," the man now hissed, his drawl gone. "How many are there?"

"Two girls, three babies."

"That's seven on two, but you're mostly small. Frelle Finch is just down that track with your horses and her pony. Go, I'll take the cart."

They took only seconds to get mounted and riding, with dark cloaks thrown over their clothing. Frelle Finch led them along a track that seemed little more than a series of less dense patches of bushland, but at least there was no danger of meeting anyone else.

"How much longer?" asked the girl behind Frelle Sparrow after only ten minutes.

"About five hours," she hissed back.

The girl groaned.

"We had to build the wingfield far from humans," said Frelle Sparrow, "you know what humans think about engines—and aviads."

There was a distant, echoing pop. All three adults stiffened at once.

"Fras Possum, hunting his namesakes," said Frelle Finch.

There was another pop, then another, and another.

"Sounding bad," said Shadowmouse. "Those were large-bore muskets."

Frelle Finch increased the pace and they rode on in silence. Shadowmouse took the rear, with a girl riding in front of him. He kept his flintlock cocked and drawn. After the first hour there were no more distant shots, and at the third hour they reached a range of wooded hills.

"The wingfield is only an hour away, we've made good progress," Frelle Finch explained. "The hills reflect the sound of the kitewings' compression engines into the wilderness."

"But humans are pouring into the wilderness all the time," said Frelle Sparrow. "We saw at least a thousand settlers at the Bendigo Railside."

"Yes, but we have agents among them, listening for rumors of strange sounds and flying machines. So far there have been none."

"You should move farther away."

"This is five hours from the paraline. A wingfield on the coast would be ideal, but would you like to bring the children on a seven-day ride instead, hunted all the way?"

The wingfield was just clear, level ground beside the hills, but they were quickly met by two darkly dressed figures on ponies. The exchange was brief and terse.

"Finch?"

"Finch and escorts."

"Children?"

"Two, with three babies."

One of the men blew a sharp note on a whistle, then led them along the flat field. There was a faint scent of burning wood on the air, and Shadowmouse could hear a muffled chuffing in the distance.

"A still night, sound will carry," said one of the men to Frelle Finch.

"At least the babies didn't cry, they like the motion of horses."

Shadowmouse had never been all the way to the wingfield before, but there was disappointingly little to see. The chuffing got louder, then they were told to dismount. A mixture of some type of oil and alcohol was strong on the air, and what had seemed to be a grove of squat trees in Mirrorsun's light turned out to be a wide, low building. They were herded into a small, narrow room. The door was closed behind them, then Frelle Finch opened another door.

Two lamps lit the kitewing, whose engine was muffled by a long baffle pipe as it warmed up. A woman who was even shorter than the two girls was waiting beside the wing, and one of the ground crew hurried over with fleece-lined leather jackets. The babies began crying as they were strapped into their streamlined travel boxes, but noise no longer mattered by now.

"Pleased to introduce Frelles Coralen and Patrelle," said Frelle Sparrow to the flyer, who responded with a brief bow then took the girls by the arm.

"Do you know what is about to happen?" she asked.

"We're going to fly," said Patrelle.

"Do we fly in that?" asked Coralen, pointing to the kitewing.

"Yes, for four hours. Soon there will be no more humans hunting you, you will be in the Mayorate of Avian."

Shadowmouse watched as the flyer strapped the girls flat onto the lower wing, each behind a stubby windshield.

"Four hours is a long time for the babies to be unattended," said Frelle Sparrow.

"They come down just before the coast to refuel," said Frelle Finch. "That wingfield is more secure."

"And then?" asked Shadowmouse.

"It is ninety minutes over the salt water to King Gate wingfield." She seemed to gaze away into some vision. "One day I shall be a flyer, like her. I've been up once, and I have even worked the kite-wing's controls during ground tests. Terian says that I can qualify as a flyer when I turn eighteen."

Shadowmouse felt a twinge of envy. The flyer climbed onto the lower wing and lay flat, strapping herself behind her controls. Then the lamps were snuffed and the huge doors were pushed open. In Mirrorsun's light they could discern the flat expanse of the ascent strip as they walked outside. The baffle pipe was removed and the flyer opened the compression engine's throttle. The kitewing rolled out under its own power and continued straight down the ascent strip, the note from its exhaust steady but shatteringly loud to Shadowmouse, who had gone days keeping his charges as quiet as possible. Suddenly the woodland on the edge of the wingfield was lit up by a string of flashes.

The kitewing was saved by its very strangeness. The humans had never seen anything move so fast, had never seen a kite as big as a house, and had certainly never seen anything that size lift from the ground. The aviads were already returning fire as the kitewing's ungainly form rose, to be quickly lost against the dark sky.

"I *knew* there were too many friendly strangers about!" said Shadowmouse as he frantically reloaded in the darkness. "They must have been stalking us, even on the wind train."

"Fras Possum, those shots," said Frelle Finch.

There were two long blasts of a whistle.

"Fall back to the sheds!" shouted Frelle Finch.

Shadowmouse estimated that there were a dozen aviads gathered around him and lying flat in the grass. Fras Terian was giving orders.

"Forty or fifty humans," he estimated as bullets whizzed overhead. "Southwatch and Westwatch have whistled in, Eastwatch is silent."

"That means they followed us as we brought the children," said Shadowmouse.

"Trout, Wombat, proceed to Eastwatch and hold there. The rest of you, go with Finch."

Frelle Finch led them crawling to a scatter of low, bushy mounds. The human party had been working its way along the edge of the wingfield when the kitewing had ascended, startling some of their number into shooting and giving the aviads the alarm that the dead guard at Eastwatch had not been able to provide. A string of shots rattled out from where the kitewing had been housed, and was returned by a dishearteningly large number of flashes from the approaching humans. Shadowmouse could feel the body heat of Frelle Finch, who was lying beside him.

A fire began amid the woods, and there was a cheer from the humans as they hurried past, crouched over.

"Get down," hissed Frelle Finch. "Chain bombs."

A moment later there were five massive blasts, and a huge plume of flame erupted from the woodland. The aviads raised their heads to see the surviving humans outlined against the glow. They opened fire.

The humans lost fully half of their number in no more than seconds, but after that the fighting was both horrific and desperate. The aviads had better night vision and quicker reactions than the humans, but the humans were battle-hardened veterans. The surviving leaders rallied their men and charged back at the aviad position before the enemy could reload for another volley. Sabers flashed in the firelight against bayonets and skirmish knives. Shadowmouse parried with his empty musket, then cut with his saber at a human outlined by the fire. Frelle Sparrow fired her pistol past Shadowmouse at another shape, then Shadowmouse found himself in a fencing duel with a skilled opponent. Shadowmouse parried against a head cut, noted that his opponent was strong but had a much heavier saber, did a rotating half-parry, then lifted his leading foot and dropped into a lunge. The point of his saber found his opponent's throat.

Shadowmouse crouched, glancing around, saw a human with his foot on a body and thrusting down with a bayonet. He chopped his saber into the man's back. The other humans were now bunching together, their sabers and bayonets raised but defeat in their posture. Four humans faced three encircling aviads as Fras Terian came striding out of the burning ruins, his jacket smouldering and a double-barrel flintlock pistol in each hand. Shadowmouse, Frelle Sparrow, and one of the kitewing artisans had survived.

"Frelle Finch?" asked Terian.

"Under him," said Shadowmouse, with a wave of his saber. "I was not fast enough."

Terian put a pistol into his belt, then heaved the human's body off Frelle Finch and dragged it clear. He knelt beside the girl and felt for a pulse at her throat. He brushed a strand of hair from her face, then stood up and drew his other pistol again. The humans looked apprehensively from the body to Terian. The fire roared in the background, drawing a soft wind over them. Terian fired the four barrels of his two guns in rapid succession, and the screams of the humans were quickly silenced.

"My daughter," explained Terian, kneeling beside the girl's body again.

Forty-eight humans had died in the fight, for the loss of eleven aviads. Of the remaining humans, three were shot down as they guarded the horses and tracker terriers, and two more were killed as they tried to flee past Eastwatch. The terriers had been trained from birth to hunt aviads, and they barked and lunged as Terian turned on them. There were two more shots.

Terian called in the guards, and together with the others they stripped the humans of their weapons. The aviad bodies were tied to some of the horses, and barrels of compression spirit were loaded onto the others. What could not be carried was set ablaze, then they set off for the south. Each aviad was leading a line of packhorses.

Shadowmouse and Frelle Sparrow watched them ride out of the reach of the firelight.

"So, again we delivered our charges," said Frelle Sparrow.

"And lost all this," replied Shadowmouse. "She was only seventeen, did you know that?"

"Frelle Finch?"

"She wanted to fly. Now she's dead, tied to a horse and going to a hidden grave."

"But you have seen death before, Shadowmouse. You even killed the human who killed her. She's been avenged."

"It was not enough. Someone betrayed us, and I am going to go on a rat hunt."

They began riding, and were soon lost to the fire's glare amid the trees.

"I have noticed that those with glorious dreams are the ones that die first," said Frelle Sparrow after a time.

"Is that meant as a sneer at Frelle Finch?" asked Shadowmouse.

"No, it's a warning to *you*. The cold, cruel people like me survive in times and places such as these. Dreamers are creatures of peacetime."

The following day Martyne toured the burned-out remains of the aviad wingfield and compression spirit distillery. The human dead still littered the place, surrounded by carrion birds and wild dogs.

"They were a group of veterans from the western castellanies, allied with some Woomeran mercenaries," explained the Bendigo Constable. "As I heard, they attacked the place but got sponged."

"Not before doing some damage," observed Martyne. "How many aviads died?"

"Can't say, they always drag their dead away and bury them in secret. Maybe half as many aviads were fighting here as humans. They took all the guns and horses too."

"Any idea what they were making here?"

"Some type of oil to burn without smoke in their steam engines, I should think. They don't like to attract attention."

"And what do they use this strange, flat field for?" asked Martyne.

"It forces attackers to either approach over open ground, or through those trees where the chain bombs were planted."

"Clever."

They walked with two of the militiamen from Bendigo through the burned-out distillery. There was nothing more to see but twisted tubes and iron hoops amid the ash. The distillery had been designed to burn and leave nothing useful or informative. The skeletons of four of the men from the human vanguard lay white and powdery in the postures of agony and despair. The remains of flintlock muskets lay with them.

"Ach, I wish the Call was still with us," said the Constable.

"Why is that?" asked Martyne, surprised.

"The aviads never hurt us while they could hide here, they lived in peace. Now every human who dreams of a farm on the frontier is rushing in, and where are the aviads to go? I feel sorry for those aviads."

"Have you met any, Fras Constable?"

"Yes, I have, Fras Espionage Constable. A lot of folk wish them well, but they keep their opinions quiet."

"Which you had better do with your own opinion, Fras. This is a serious incident: people in high places will be very angry."

"What will you recommend?"

"Limits must be enforced on human expansion into aviad territory, else there will be more deaths on this scale or worse. The Overmayor will send musketeers in to clear paths and establish safe settlements."

Martyne heard a loud click as one of the Bendigo musketeers stepped on a buried chain bomb's trigger, then came a concussion so loud that he perceived it as silence. He was standing in the blast shadow of the Bendigo Constable, whose body was hit by enough flying metal to kill two dozen men. When Martyne awoke he was lying on the flat, grassy ground, fifty yards from where he had been walking before the blast, and the militiaman who had stayed back with the horses was kneeling beside him. His clothes were soaked in blood, but his only wound was to his right forearm. Parts of the Bendigo Constable were strewn nearby, and a haze of dust and ash was still on the air.

"Fras, Fras! You're alive!" cried the militiaman as Martyne stirred.

"Traps, left in rubble," gasped Martyne, squeezing his bleeding arm. "What of the others?"

"Gone, Fras, they're just gone!" the man shouted hysterically as Martyne rolled over and sat up. "He was a good man, a decent man, Fras, he hated nobody. There's no God, Fras, there's no God. God would never let a fella like him die this way."

With the explosion still ringing in his ears and aching from his wound and dozens of bruises, Martyne helped the militiaman rig up several charcoal-and-board warning signs before they returned to the Bendigo Abandon. It was another five days before two more chain bombs were found and detonated, and a week before what the bush scavengers had left of the bodies was gathered up for burial.

Rochester, the Rochestrian Commonwealth

Martyne returned to Rochester two days after Christmas. Much to his surprise, he was escorted from the paraline terminus to the palace by several members of the mayoral guard. There he was masked, then led into the throne hall, where he was awarded the Bronze Cross by the Overmayor. The ceremony was closed, but was attended by a few senior administrators from Libris and a dozen of the mayoral court. A public announcement was made, declaring that an agent of the Dragon Librarian Service had been decorated for bravery, having been wounded in a battle with aviads. Some time later an unmasked Martyne read the notice pinned to a public board, then fingered the Bronze Cross hidden within his jacket before walking on.

When he opened the door to his room Velesti was sitting cross-legged on his bed, stripping a Morelac target pistol with Martyne's service kit.

"I hear you make war on aviad children," she said as he closed the door behind him and leaned back against it with his eyes closed.

"Why do I bother to even carry a key?"

"Where is the Bronze Cross?"

Martyne tossed it to her. "I would have been given a Gold Cross, but they probably thought I would melt it down and sell it for the metal."

"But seriously, about those aviad children?"

"Would you prefer them fried or boiled, Frelle Dragon Blue?"

"What happened?"

"You mean you don't know?"

"Martyne, I am not in a mood for facile banter and mannered levity."

"And I have just come home from the frontier with a four-inch gash in my arm, more bruises than a tavern's doorman could accumulate in a lifetime, concussion, my ears still ringing, and memories of the bushland scavengers masticating pieces from four dozen bodies. I need a friendly ear, a welcome, sympathy. Do you know the meaning of any of those words?"

"You got a medal from the Overmayor, presented in the palace, before her court."

"I got stabbed in the left pectoral by the Overmayor, who had never presented an award before—and she fluffed her lines. I got three cheers from the courtiers and a trumpet fanfare, oh, and two little squares of toast smeared with emu liver pâté at the reception in my honor—at which I was not permitted to speak. Ever try to eat while wearing a mask?"

Velesti sighed. "All right, all right, welcome home, I'm sorry you were hurt and I'm sure you were very brave. Now, what happened?"

Martyne walked over to the bed, scooped up the carefully laid-out components of Velesti's gun, dropped them into her lap, then sat down.

"I was in the Bendigo Abandon, investigating the presence of a large group of veterans from the western castellanies and Woomeran Confederation. They had no women, children, or tools, but they were armed and mounted. On the night that I arrived there was a huge fire visible to the south, in the former Calldeath wilderness. At dawn I accompanied the Bendigo Constable and three militiamen as they rode out to investigate. We found over four dozen dead veterans and the burned-out remains of several buildings. One of the militiamen also discovered the hair-trigger to a concealed chain bomb."

"The hard way?"

"Yes. Aside from myself, one militiaman survived, but his grip on sanity is no longer all that it could be. The Overmayor was not anxious for it to be known that Gentheist vigilantes are hunting down aviads that her own lancers should be protecting, so I was made the hero of a battle that annihilated an aviad fortress in order to open bushland to honest Rochestrian farmers."

"So you fought no aviads?"

"I did not even *see* any aviads. For all we know that battle could have been between Gentheist veterans and some Inglewood warlord. The Overmayor wants it known that her forces are in control of the former Calldeath lands, however, so she has declared a great victory and I am a hero."

"A victory against aviads."

"Yes."

"Always the aviads, always the enemy," said Velest, shaking her head. "People still fear and hate them, even their protectors."

"They are stronger, faster, and more intelligent than us. These seem like quite good reasons."

"What a depressingly human thing to say. Speaking of humans, I was going to help with your problems with female humans, but now I am not sure that I want to."

"Help? What do you mean? The last time you helped me I ended up in bed with Marelle."

"Are you complaining?"

"Yes! I called at her tavern on the way home, but she yelled at me and threw me out."

"About?"

"About being away so much. I risk death in the wilderness, then get accused of being with another woman! Involvement with women and suffering are two expressions for the same thing."

"What about me?"

"Could you seriously describe yourself as a woman?"

"Point taken. Did you know that my mother is in Rochester?"

Martyne sat bolt upright at once. "I'm going to sleep in my study tonight."

"I showed her the sights, had long talks with her, and discussed family business."

"Family business? What sort of family business? Involving me?"

"Not saying."

"What? Why not?"

"Because I want to see you suffer."

"How Christian of you," said Martyne, rubbing his face in his hands.

"What is your plan now?"

"Hide from your mother, avoid Marelle, and teach theology at the university."

"And train with me?"

"Why not? It's as good an excuse as any to hit you."

"Speaking of hitting people, I have been thinking."

"Not again."

"It is about my self-defence guild. I have spoken with some of my sister students at the university, and many are anxious to be able to fend off unwanted advances without resorting to formal duels or keeping company with men just for protection."

"A worthy venture."

"You agreed to help, remember?"

"No," said Martyne firmly.

"Why?"

"I want to see you suffer."

"Martyne, seriously! We could emphasize locks, holds, and throws, teaching them to defend themselves without weapons."

"Me? Train a group of women? Velesti, I have been involved in one way or another with fo—er, three women over the past three months, and all three involvements have been absolute disasters."

"Even me?"

"Especially you. Now you want to involve me with training a couple of dozen of them!"

"Spoken like a true monk. You have skills with subtle fighting arts, better suited to girls and women not as strong as me."

"The answer is still no."

"What girl has not found herself alone with a much stronger man, and subject to unwelcome advances? Chivalrous it may be to defend a woman's honor, but even more chivalrous it is to give her the means to make her own choices at all times."

"You are talking to a man who has found himself alone with women and *also* subject to unwelcome advances—and superior strength was of no assistance. I still say no."

Velesti leaned her folded arms onto her crossed legs and batted her eyelashes at Martyne.

"Even if I was to free you from my mother?"

"I said no and I meant—"

Martyne made a choking sound, then seized Velesti by the lapels of her jacket.

"Now, let me see, what is the new Balesha method for escaping this type of hold?" asked Velesti with a wide and malicious grin.

"You're lying to me," Martyne rasped, his face very close to hers.

"No."

"How?"

"Do we have an agreement?"

"You bastard."

"May I interpret that as yes?"

"Not until you do the impossible. What is your solution to your pregnant mother?"

"I can say with some confidence that you were still a virgin when you left my mother's house for the last time."

"There is a God." Martyne sighed, releasing her lapels and slumping back against the wall.

"However . . ."

"However?"

"Interesting experiments were conducted in the cause of fertility and carnal pleasure."

"Spare me the circumlocutions, Velesti. So, I may not have rogered her, but I was in no condition to know or remember clearly what I was doing."

"Count yourself lucky."

"How do we confront her with your evidence, whatever it is?"

"We?" asked Velesti innocently.

"We!" replied Martyne very emphatically. "I am *never, ever* going to let myself be alone with her again."

"For now, just do nothing. I have the matter in hand."

"You are a saint."

"Please, no insults."

"And Marelle?"

"She's pregnant too?"

"No! But what do I do about her?"

"I shall tell her you are more than you seem, and that you were wounded in the service of the Rochestrian Commonwealth. She finds wounded men erotically stimulating, so expect an errand boy with Marelle's apology—and save it. Apologies from Marelle are not common."

"Velesti, I feel so light that I could float out through the window."

"Savor the feeling, Martyne. Within one sidereal day fate is sure to do something so pointlessly unspeakable that you will wish you had never left Balesha. Can we discuss a training syllabus for my Baleshanto guild now?"

"Is that all you want? Help with your bloody guild? For freeing me of your mother you could have asked for a thousand gold royals."

"I value your help more than that, Martyne." She pulled the striker back on her reassembled Morelac and pulled the trigger. There was a healthy shower of sparks. "And now I must be off to see Marelle. Make sure that she sees your wound, but don't show her that Bronze Cross. She is an aviad sympathizer."

•   •   •

Rangen and Julica were lying together, but not actually in the act of intimacy when the Espionage Constables burst into Julica's little bedroom. Predictably, they sat up in bed. Julica screamed. The intruders tramped around the room holding lanterns high. They looked under the bed, emptied the bags and baskets, and flung the shutters open and looked out.

"What's the meaning of this?" demanded Julica, summoning her courage. "We have done nothing wrong."

"There is a fugitive numerate in this building, a woman named Frelle Sharmalck," said the leader of the Constables.

"Never 'eard of 'er," said Rangen.

"What's a numerate?" asked Julica.

"Nothing here," reported one of the other Constables.

"There's a reward, three gold royals," said the leader as he left.

Rangen jammed a chair against the door, pulled the shutters closed, and returned to the bed. A woman emerged from a hollow in the feather mattress beside Julica.

"This building will be watched for some days to come," said Rangen. "However, in three days your name will be discovered on an emigration register in Deniliquin."

"But Fras, an unescorted woman cannot cross the Southmoor border," said Frelle Sharmalek.

"Ah, yes, but the gate register will show one *man* too many passing through. That gate will then be watched carefully by our friends in the Espionage Constables for a very long time."

"I regret that I have closed down a path in your most humane invisible paraline network," said the woman.

"No matter, Frelle, we never railed people out through Deniliquin in the first place. Now then, we must be disguising you as Frelle Julica here."

Lake Taupo, New Zealand

Samondel and the others watched as two sailwings circled the Taupo wingfield. The wings had immense spans, and were pushed by three compression engines between a pair of booms supporting the tailplane.

"In a storm those things would be torn to pieces," Samondel muttered to herself, but clearly there had been no storms for the past six thousand miles. With a stall speed lower than even the new super-regals', the first of the odd sailwings approached the new wingfield, did a single, shallow bounce and rolled smoothly to a stop. The eleven members of Lake Taupo Wingfield ran out to greet the new arrival. The hood slid back.

"Serjon!" Samondel shrieked.

Bronlar was in the second sailwing. It was quite some time before Samondel's former lover and his wife were able to tell their story. Over a meal of possum and wild potato stew he described how Bartolican artisans had been experimenting with extending the range of existing sailwings, rather than building the huge, heavy super-regals that had won the war for Yarron. Two of the sailwings had already undergone gliding tests when Bartolica had surrendered, and Airlord Sartov soon realized that they might have a range half again as long as his newest super-regals. The Yarronese took over the venture, and more were now in production.

"Those sailwings out there are wonders of the age," he said, pointing at them with a carved wooden spoon. "We could have by-passed Samoa to get here."

"I don't believe it!" exclaimed Samondel.

"True. They have a four-thousand-mile range, carrying one flyer, provisions for forty hours, and two reaction guns."

"Reaction guns?"

"Yes, with two hundred rounds."

"That must weigh at least a hundred pounds in total, you could have carried another six gallons of spirit," Samondel pointed out.

"Samondel, Samondel, we—"

"Compression spirit is worth its weight in silver here, and each gallon that you fly in is a miracle. What idiot authorized such a waste?"

"Gracious and beautiful airlord, have you forgotten what happened during the Great War, before the huge sunwings built by the ancients were destroyed? At least ten Mounthaven wings were towed to Australica by the aviads, along several of our artisans. They will have war flocks by now, make no mistake."

"I'm not believing what I hear. After all this time, distance, money, and effort, you just want to fight? This was meant to be a trade venture."

"And so it is, but we must approach in strength. Besides, our quarrel is not with the humans but the featherheads on Tasmania Island."

"When *I* approach, it will be in peace. So, the tanks of both your sailwings must be half-full—if they really have such a great range."

"Yes, we carried the maximum load of compression spirit, to build up the reserve here."

"Then transfer all fuel to one, and prepare it for flight. I shall leave for Australica in the morning."

"Impossible. You will need a conversion course first. The compression engines are quite different to the traditional designs, and the handling is tricky. Besides, they have been granted in lordship to Bronlar and me by Airlord Sartov, and you know what that means."

Samondel certainly did. A grant in lordship made the transfer of a wing absolute, and any use of it by another flyer would be an act of treason.

"Why are you here with those things, if not to make my work easier?" Samondel asked.

"When the first of the new super-regals flies out to Australica, we shall be flying an escort. That's what Airlord Sartov charged me with doing."

"Nothing was written to *me* about this."

"You are a long way from Mounthaven, and politics can change alliances and priorities very quickly. The aviads are known to be building wings and compression engines in the north of Tasmania Island, and these could be a very serious danger to the super-regals.

We cannot afford to lose either of the new ones. Only they can carry horses, and we need horses as quickly as possible. The Council of Airlords is desperate to stay in control, and the super-regals are needed to help them supply and rule our settlers in the wilderness. The fires of Mexhaven peasants can already be seen from Mounthaven's *borders* in places. We need results, Samondel, and very quickly. Horses and cattle must be standing on a Mounthaven wingfield within a month, if more compression spirit is to be ferried six thousand miles to here."

Samondel rubbed her face in her hands.

"Well, I cannot flout the will of Airlord Sartov and his Council. I did lose the war with Yarron, after all."

"These are not orders to humiliate you, Saircme Samondel. The other airlords are walking a tightrope of thinly stretched resources."

"So am I, except that my tightrope is six thousand miles long. All right, then, you can escort the super-regal when it flies west. In the meantime will you sign over your sailwings to me as adjunct of Taupo Wingfield?"

"Of course."

"There is a dormitory tent behind this one; I imagine that you are weary."

The following morning Serjon and Bronlar woke to the sound of a compression engine revving for an ascent. They rushed outside, then made for their sailwings. The two aircraft were neatly tied down and their engines idle. Out on the ascent strip the second engine of Samondel's sailwing belched smoke as the compression charge was fired, and it began to chug. Samondel was beside it in her flight jacket. Her navigator was kneeling on the wing, screwing an engine access hatch closed.

"Ah, good, I was about to wake you," she said as Serjon and Bronlar arrived. "I have decided to leave for the large Australican city of Rochester that the aviad prisoners told us about."

"In the *Swallow*?" exclaimed Bronlar. "Even with a full load of fuel you could only get there and halfway back."

"And last night you were saying that you have barely any compression spirit," added Serjon.

"That was before I drained the remaining spirit from your two sailwings. I can get as far as the city of Rochester and descend on one of the outlying roads."

"What?" exclaimed Serjon. "You had no authority to—that is—"

"Actually I did have authority to requisition your sailwing's compression spirit, as adjunct of the wingfield, while under orders from the most senior noble present—myself in both cases. If the humans are friendly in Australica, I should be back in a fortnight at most. They have seed oil and alcohol in Australica, so we should be able to distill compression spirit. If I do not return, fly your sailwing to a city farther north and parachute a diplomat down."

"And if that fails too?" asked Serjon.

"Then Project Tornado will be followed. By one means or another, we must have horses."

"But why all the haste?" demanded Serjon.

"Because you told me I am running out of time! Sair Vardy is hereby made adjunct in my absence, and I believe that you are the ranking noble, Serjon."

The *Swallow* made a long, labored run along the ascent strip, but rose smoothly into the morning sky and turned to head due west. Bronlar and Serjon examined their sailwings once she was lost to sight.

"Enough compression spirit for an hour and a half in the air for one of us, no more," reported Serjon.

"If we share it equally, we could fight off an attack by an aviad flock," Bronlar suggested.

"I would be surprised if the aviads are doing much more than learning to fly, just now."

"But they stole some very advanced sailwings and gunwings, not to mention guildsmen to maintain them."

"No more than ten, and their supply has been cut off. Bronlar, if I was an aviad mayor or airlord, or whatever they have to rule themselves, I would be learning to brew compression spirit and to build compression engines and airframes. If you ask me, the only aviad sailwings being flown are locally built. I doubt that any of those has a range of more than two hundred miles or a speed above seventy miles per hour. There will be no raids on Taupo Wingfield."

Bronlar climbed into the cockpit of her sailwing, rummaged for a few moments, then let out a shriek.

"My Clastini! My reaction pistol is gone. And all the ammunition clips too."

Serjon checked his own cockpit, but he knew that his reaction pistol would be missing as well. In times of peace some people seem unremarkable, but give them a crisis and they can perform miracles. Serjon and Bronlar had turned out just that way, but who would have suspected that a spoiled and indulged princess like Samondel could have been hiding so much drive? Underlying Samondel's bravery and determination was one additional factor that everyone had chosen to ignore or overlook: the Airlord of Highland Bartolica was more intelligent than any of her peers and opponents.

Rochester, the Rochestrian Commonwealth

Samondel looked down on the city of Rochester from a height of two thousand feet, noting that a large crowd was assembled in one of the plazas.

"A human city, even larger than Condelor," she said to her navigator. "Within the city, a lake, and on an island on the lake, an inner city. Look there, it must be one of their wind trains, the thing with rotor towers spinning and driving it."

"This is as far as I can take us," replied the navigator. "Now we need to be able to descend on a smooth, firm surface."

"There are outlying roads, Sair Alarak."

"There are indeed, Saireme Airlord."

"We shall—look, there!"

Rearing and plunging in their yards were horses and ponies, terrified by the noise from the sky. Pens with cattle were close by.

"Everything is here, everything!" said Samondel in triumph.

"Even horses. The *Albatross* could take four or five breeding pairs, provided they were juveniles."

"As many as that on the first trip?"

"Yes, while the price is low. The Australicans will soon realize that we have no horses or cattle at all in Mounthaven."

"Ah yes, and before you know it they will be demanding one diesel engine for every vole."

"I think the word is foal."

They circled the outer city at three hundred feet, the navigator hurriedly sketching and writing while Samondel called out things of interest. Samondel ordered that a parachute flare with a message be prepared to be dropped into the gardens of what looked like a palace on the central island.

"There are a lot of people crowded in there," warned the navigator.

"All the better, the message will be found quickly and taken to their, er, king. The smoke flare is harmless, it has guard mesh enclosing it."

"We have thirty minutes of compression spirit left for circling. Those headwinds over the salt water robbed us of a lot of margin."

"Indeed, but we are here and nothing else matters. Unseal that prepared message and attach it to the flare. I shall come low over that palace, just above stall speed."

The *Swallow* banked lazily to port, then flew out over the lake while slowly losing height. They passed over the island's ancient walls and the mansions, flying directly above a wide, straight avenue filled with people. They approached the palace.

Jemli had arrived in a train pulled by a galley engine, and under escort by two other military trains. Although her following was not particularly large or committed in the Rochestrian Commonwealth, a number of people lined the paraline trackway to see her pass. As she entered Rochester itself the numbers grew considerably, and an advance squad of organizers had distributed thousands of Reformed Gentheist pennons and flags for children to wave.

Jemli's train rumbled out onto the paraline bridge across the lake, and entered the inner city. Both the Overmayor of the Commonwealth and Highliber Dramoren were at the terminus to greet Jemli as she stepped down onto the platform. Trumpeters played a fanfare, and bombards thundered a response on the distant palace walls.

"Welcome to Rochester, Frelle Enlightened One," said the Overmayor, although she did not bow.

"I am always pleased to be among the faithful," Jemli replied.

"I believe that you have met Highliber Franzas Dramoren, head of the Dragon Librarian Service?" said the Overmayor with a gesture to Dramoren.

Dramoren bowed, and Jemli nodded in his direction and granted him the hint of a smile.

"Have you been to Rochester before?" asked the Overmayor as they began walking to the carriage that was waiting.

"Over two decades ago I worked here as a clockmaker, Overmayor. Hard work raised me above that, but the Deity raised me even further."

Forty of Jemli's own guard were with her, along with another nine dozen of her servants and priests. Many of these had already been in Rochester for weeks, making preparations. The carriage was driven through streets cleared of beggars, vendors, harlots, and refuse, then lined with cheering crowds. The square before the palace was already filled with crowds waiting to hear the Prophet's single, scheduled public oration. Once in the grounds of the palace she stepped down onto the pebblestone courtyard.

She stopped with a loud cry. Dramoren had just walked across to a line of ten Tiger Dragon Librarians who were standing with their long-barreled flintlock pistols held parade ready. Jemli strode over to the line of Dramoren's personal guard and stopped before one of the women.

"Your face, it is very familiar," said Jemli.

"We have never met, Enlightened One," replied Velesti.

"What is your name, where are you from?"

"Velesti Disore, Dragon Librarian Service, Dragon Blue."

"But where were you born?"

"Griffith."

Something about this answer and Velesti's lack of any recognition or familiarity seemed to satisfy the religious leader of several million souls in the middle and west of the continent.

"There is something about you, the Deity has been close to you recently."

By now Dramoren had joined them.

"Frelle Disore lay as dead from last July to September, Enlightened One," he explained. "Then for no apparent reason, she revived, only far more vital and hale than before."

"Ah, I was right," said the quite relieved Prophet. "And it was on the day that the electrical machines burned."

"It was eight days later, Enlightened One," said Velesti.

"It was on the Burning Day!" insisted Jemli, her eyes now wild and her demeanor unsettling. "The *healing* process began then. When you revived is not important." She raised her hands, her palms focused on Velesti's head. "Yes, and the healing process is still going on. The Deity has not released your full potential yet, it will take one calendar year."

Most who witnessed the exchange marveled at Jemli's sense of perception, others concluded that her agents had done their research well and prepared her skilfully. Jemli now swept away to the Balcony of the People, a point above the palace wall where Rochestrian monarchs had addressed their subjects since the palace had been built three centuries earlier. Jemli's handmaids were with her, changing her outer robes as she climbed the steps. The crowd fell silent as she walked to the marble railing and raised her arms.

"People of Rochester, however you worship the Deity, *all* of you worship the Deity. Through me the Deity speaks to all of you, because His message to you is the same. Smash the metal abominations whose hearts beat in mockery of our own hearts. Strike down the fleshly abominations who walk our lands in mockery of our own bodies. Fight those who would conspire against true and faithful servants of the Deity."

Like any good orator, Jemli paused for emphasis. Cheering began, a vast rolling wave of human voices. Jemli held up her arms again and the cheering died away.

"All of the amended Scriptures of the past two thousand years have denounced the metal engines that excrete poisons into the winds, waters, and earth, but we have just seen that electrical engines are cursed in the Deity's sight as well. As a Prophet of the Word of the Deity I denounced my own husband for the building of forbidden engines, indeed they were electrical essence generators driven by steam engines. Abominations wedded to abominations! People of Rochester, can you imagine anything worse? Even though he was my husband and the father of my children, I struck him down!"

She paused again, but this time another sound filled the silence that should have been filled by carefully prompted cheering. It was a continuous droning sound, not unlike that of a bee, yet no bee could have been heard equally well by everyone across the entire square. It was a sound that had been absent from the skies of Rochester for two thousand years. Two small diesel engines roared steadily as they approached from the southeast.

The crowd was by now in confusion, as were the palace guards, Dragon Librarians, city militiamen, officials, diplomats and priests. Descending over the city was one vast wing, like a giant bird with a tail but no body. The two engines roared, drinking alcohol and oilseed fuel, roaring the most flagrant and public defiance of theological orthodoxy that was possible. The thing dropped too low to be seen, as those aboard it examined the outer city, then it banked again and began approaching Inner Rochester, directly above the Avenue.

Jemli snatched a musket from the nearest guard, raised it to her shoulder and fired at the distant but approaching sailwing. The shot went completely wild, but it was the symbolism that was important.

"Fire on that abomination, bring it down!" she raged to the captain of her own guardsmen.

Forty flintlocks and matchlocks of Prophet Jemli's personal guard discharged in a volley lasting barely two seconds. Although none of the musketeers had ever before shot at an aircraft or even knew what points to aim at, there were so many shots that several of them hit the fuel tanks and engines. Samondel opened the throttles wide at once, but the response was sluggish. Almost together, the port engine seized and the starboard coughed fire.

"Trying to get clear of the city!" Samondel shouted. "We can descend in a field, then run."

"You run, Saireme Airlord, I'll have to limp," Alarak called back.

"You're hit? How badly?"

"Left thigh, bleeding."

"Losing power on starboard, port dead. Too low to fly the silk."

"Parkland ahead, ten points to port."

"Starboard seized!"

"We're still on fire."

"Going down."

"We're over houses!"

"Can't hold it!"

The stall speed of the sailwing was actually slower than the top speed of a galley engine, but the tiled roofs of the Rochester slums made a less than ideal wingfield. The *Swallow* clipped a chimney, then another, bounced off a roof, cartwheeled up again as it began to disintegrate, then flopped heavily into a row of terraced houses. Tanks split and diesel spirit splashed over the cooking fires below and ignited. The *Swallow* came to rest, and within moments both the wreckage and houses beneath were burning fiercely.

Samondel was aware of dull aches all over her body, and the scent of straw, wood resin, and something burning. She opened her eyes and saw hay all around her. She had landed in a wagonload of hay, with her parachute and field pack still strapped to her. Raising her head, she saw Alarak sitting against a wall not far away. Several armed men were guarding him, and as Samondel watched another two men came up with a stretcher and loaded her navigator onto it. She slipped from the wagon. Almost immediately she was accosted by another militiaman.

"You, clear off!" he shouted, waving his musket in the air

and gesturing away from the wreckage and fire. "Nothing to see here. Go!"

He seized her by the arm and ran her along the street, pushing her through a cordon of militiamen and sending her on her way with a whack across the backside from the barrel of his musket. Samondel stumbled clear to freedom, astonished at her escape. They had arrested Alarak but not her. Why? She was wearing the flight jacket, after all . . . but Australicans did not know about flight jackets. She had been thrown clear of the wreck but Alarak had probably been discovered crawling out of the wreckage. His jacket was dull brown, not the richly decorated masterpiece of embroidery that she wore. The parade! There were probably hundreds of elaborately dressed locals walking the city's streets.

Samondel walked steadily away, and soon only the pall of smoke from the fire was visible above the housetops. She reached an arched gate guarded by gargoyles in a long stone wall, and beyond it were rolling lawns, gardens, and ivy-smothered buildings. More to the point, there was a group of people in a variety of colorful robes and jackets milling about at the gate. Samondel found herself walking for the group even before her mind had decided that they would be a perfect cover for the next few minutes. Those around her smiled, bowed, and tried to speak to her in what even she recognized as very bad Austaric.

"Ah, the morning's greetings to you, Frelle, welcome to the University of Rochester," said a man with a clipboard and a char stylus. "Could I have your name, please?"

He was speaking very slowly and distinctly, unlike the militiaman. He obviously expected her to speak Austaric badly. The University of Rochester. This was a group of *foreign* students!

"Samondel Leover," she blurted out before she could stop herself.

"And your mayorate?"

"Jarbrovia," Samondel improvised on the spot.

The man smiled, thanked her, then stood back from the group.

"Good people, there are still six students missing, but they are probably caught up in the confusion across at the fire," he declared, speaking yet more loudly and slowly. "We shall begin our induction tour of the university now, and the others will be shown around later."

Within moments the young Airlord of Highland Bartolica, victor of several clear air encounters and commander of an expedition across over seven thousand miles of open ocean had become a young student in a foreign university, with nothing more to worry about than what to study and where to stay.

She was soon registered as a tenant of Villiers College Residency, and was assigned a room and key. While other students were registering, she shed her field pack, parachute, and flight jacket. The day was warm, so her shirt and promenade coat would be more than adequate. She was careful to conceal her reaction pistol beneath the coat, however.

The next stop was at the Office of Conversion, where five of Samondel's Bartolican gold coins were converted into rather a lot of Rochestrian silver after they had been weighed and assayed. Over lunch she listened as those around her discussed the mysterious flying machine that had been shot out of the sky.

"Blatant defiance of Prophet, while visit city."

"Use fuel engines. Big sacrilege."

"One heretic inside of machine."

"I have been told, not speaking Austaric, he is."

"Captured, he was."

"Was bleeding."

"Machine, burned, but not engines. Iron."

"Steel, am hearing."

"Brave man, to fly. Dangerous."

"Still heretic."

By the end of the meal Samondel had established that not just steam engines but *all* fuel-driven engines were under some manner of religious prohibition by the dominant religions of the continent. Darien's briefing back in Mounthaven had obviously been misinterpreted. There was also a famous religious prophet visiting the city, which had made her overflight seem like the very worst possible insult. By the time she reached the Registrar's Office early in the afternoon, Samondel already had her course of study mapped out in her mind. The clerk smelled strongly of wine, and was taking little interest in the responses to his questions.

"Name?"

"Samondel Leover."

"Mayorate?"

"Jarbrovia."

"Qualifications?"

"Certificate."

"From where?"

"Academy."

"Honors?"

"Yes."

"What will you be studying?"

"Applied Theology, Austaric Literature."

"Mathematics?"

"No."

"Wise of you. Sign the register, pay two gold royals or equivalent to the bursar, then see your mentor edutors for curriculums and reading lists. They are Frelle Kolbine in the Faculty of Austaric, and Fras Saresen in the Faculty of Theology."

The girl standing behind Samondel tapped her shoulder.

"If you please, Frelle Leover, I am studying those same subjects. Bide a moment and we can go over together."

Corien was plump, pretty, and had curly blond hair. Although she was from another mayorate she knew the language and had already been living in Rochester for a month. They were about to leave when three militiamen entered and spoke to the clerk. The enrollment papers of each student were checked hurriedly. Samondel was female, exotically beautiful, and had by now let out her long red hair. The militiaman questioning Samondel had a very different idea of what a warrior from a flying enemy war machine should look like.

"The flying thing, did you see it crash?" he asked.

"Bird machine, am very frightened."

"Did anyone jump out of it?"

"Fire, then boom, more fire!"

"Did you see it hit the houses?"

"Yes, liking your city, I am."

"You didn't see the crash at all, did you?"

"Boom. Big fire."

"Damn stupid wog," concluded the militiaman as he turned away from the Airlord of Highland Bartolica and reached for Corien's enrollment papers.

At Corien's urging, Samondel bought a slingbag from the campus market for the books and papers that she had acquired from the Faculty of Austaric. She glanced out over the city, to where the *Swallow* had crashed. The fire was long out, but the militiamen were still on the campus. Of all possible scenarios for contact with the Australican civilization this one was a good contender for worst, but on the other hand she had actually established herself in Australican society, could go about the city with impunity, and she even had a friend. There was no reason to flee Rochester; in fact, there was nowhere to go beyond it. The next attempt at securing horses was supposed to be well away from the city, and Samondel was not even meant to know the location that would be chosen. She was certainly marooned. Nonetheless, weeks, perhaps months as a student stretched in front of her, time during which she could learn about Australican society and religion in great detail. Eventually she would make her presence known to the authorities, but first she had a lot to learn. The first misunderstanding between their two continents had been quite sufficiently disastrous.

There was only one more thing to do before Samondel could leave Corien, retreat to her room in Villiers College, collapse onto the bunk, and try to assimilate the barrage of strangeness that the first six hours in Rochester had poured over her. She rapped at the door of her edutor in applied theology. A voice within said, "Enter."

The middle-aged man standing behind the desk was somewhat taller than she was, and wore a black academic cloak. He had a graying beard, and bushy hair that flared like the halo of an angel in the ancient paintings.

"Yes, Frelles? Can I help you?" he asked.

"Am seeking mentor edutor, Fras Saresen," Samondel replied.

"I—oh? Are you both students of Applied Theology?"

"Yes, I am Corien Meziar and my friend is Samondel Leover," Corien explained. "We have already enrolled and paid."

"Ah. I see. My apologies, Frelles, but female students of Applied Theology are not common. You are only the second and third that I have encountered this year."

"Is not allowed?" asked Samondel apprehensively.

"It is allowed," said Saresen. "Just difficult. Have a seat; I've just worked out a curriculum for Frelle Disore, a Centralian."

The curriculum that Saresen proposed seemed to suit their needs, and it did not take long to work through. He signed several more books out to them.

"There is one potential problem, however," he said as Samondel and Corien stood up to go. "Several students in the lectures and tutorials are from somewhat extreme acetic cults and sects, and are prohibited from having women as colleagues or associates. This includes attending lectures and tutorials with you two."

"Having suggestion?" asked Samondel.

"I could arrange for the academician to lend you his notes after each lecture. As for tutorials . . ."

"Yes. Day and time?"

"Ah, I suppose . . . I had arranged a private tutorial for Frelle Disore . . . yes, I suppose I could include you two as well."

Once out on the lawns again Samondel discovered that Corien was also living at Villiers College. They decided to have dinner together at the college refectory that night, but Samondel was wary of letting anyone learn too much about her and wanted a few hours to think through her new persona.

"For all the trouble, great thanks," she said as they reached her door.

"Think nothing of it, Frelle. I really admire you, coming here alone and knowing so little Austaric."

"You too, are being alone."

"Ah, but my uncle is Rector of Villiers College so I am not really alone. Your accent is odd. Where are you from?"

"Jarbrovia."

"I have not heard of it."

"Is long way north."

The charred remains of the sailwing did not take up much space once they were cut up and carefully bundled. Most of the wide and elegant flying wing had been just air enclosed by fabric and supported by lightweight wood strengthened by wire. The fuel tanks were of tin, and were almost as flimsy as the wings. The engines were another matter, but artisans were already at work dismantling them while Gentheist priests prayed and muttered exorcisms.

Meanwhile Jemli's guardsmen had been disarmed and bound, and a train to return them to the Woomeran border was arranged. Jemli remained free, but that freedom involved facing Overmayor Lengina.

"Nobody! *Nobody* gives an order for any organized force to fire in Rochester, except for myself or my delegated officers," Lengina shouted angrily as she paced before the much taller woman in one of the palace's parlors.

"I ordered fire upon abominations, both aviads and their machines."

"Why?"

"They are a danger, a pestilence. They used fueled engines to fly over the salt water where they cannot be followed."

"Considering that the alternative is public execution in some mayorates, and lynching by vigilante mobs in others, this is understandable."

"But if they are gathering and settling on some island beyond the saltwater there is nothing to stop them."

"Why bother? They harm nobody."

"They must be sponged away."

"You are the only one who needs to be removed, Frelle. The single thing that is out of place in a tolerant state is a person who preaches intolerance. You are such a person, and I want you back over the border with all possible haste."

•   •   •

The palace guardsmen had not been far behind the city militia at the crash site, and were quick to take control of the area. The wounded survivor was apprehended and hurried away, but the *Swallow*'s cockpit had been burned before anyone discovered that it could accommodate two. A search had found no trace of any other, so Alarak was assumed to be alone.

Within the palace dungeons it was quickly determined that Alarak spoke nothing remotely like Austarac, and that communication with him was going to be a real problem. He had, however, escaped with more than just the clothes he was wearing. The contents of his survival pack caused consternation in the highest levels of government exceeding that of the *Swallow*'s appearance over Rochester.

"This was found in the airman's pack," said the Overmayor to Dramoren, gesturing along a polished table where Alarak's survival equipment and supplies had been laid out.

"Ah, what am I to make of this?" asked Dramoren, unused to having his monarch give a technical briefing.

"A pack of dried meat strips, a tin canister of water, two packs of something resembling chocolate, one contraceptive device, one small utility knife with several small tools in the handle, one signaling mirror, one thumblamp and striker, the value of about ten royals in small gold bars, a dozen gold and silver coins of some unknown mayorate, what appears to be a pouch of medicinal powders and tablets, a phial of whiskey, those three boxes of tapered cylinders made of brass and lead, and this gun."

"*This* is a *gun*?" Dramoren said doubtfully, staring down at it.

"It is not only a gun, it is the most advanced gun on the continent, Highliber. It fires packaged charges, using the reaction of each shot to work the reloading mechanism. One palace artisan was killed in the course of determining its secrets. It has a rate of fire of several hundred shots per minute. A couple of dozen warriors armed with such pistols could take on the entire city militia and win."

"Where did it come from?" Dramoren asked.

"Beyond the continent, Highliber. This pistol is about two hundred years ahead of our flintlocks."

Dramoren could not disguise his astonishment.

"Is it safe to handle?" he asked, his hands hovering over the weapon.

"The remaining charges have been removed; you can pick it up."

"This would be a very attractive device for our musketeers," he decided presently.

"Technically, it is also an engine driven by fuel, and so proscribed by the Prophet's teachings."

"Oh no, you are . . . well, yes, perhaps you are right. Technically. Is the fellow from the wreck an aviad?"

"No, he has been examined very carefully. He appears to be from a distant human civilization of great power and energy. Come this way."

The Overmayor led Dramoren to a very old global model of the world, one with the ancient political divisions and names labelled.

"Even without language I managed to extract some sense from him," explained Lengina. "With some signs and prompting he traced a path from our continent here, across this blue area of water—"

"The Pacific Ocean."

"—to here."

"North America."

"He calls it Mounthaven, but yes, he is from America. Think upon it. The aviads can fly too, and they may have weapons such as this. If not, the Americans can soon supply them."

"Pah, why should the Americans side with a lot of admittedly clever but very poor Avianese when the wealth of Rochester could be opened up for trade?" asked Dramoren.

"Because we have just fired upon an American flying machine. The Americans and Avianese combined could wipe us out."

"But we treat our aviads well. Years ago we passed laws outlawing the killing of aviads, provided they register and then present themselves for chaining during any Call. Our laws are the most enlightened on the continent."

"Except for the aviad agents being hunted down by your Espi-

onage Constables as they try to smuggle aviad children to their feath-
erfields."

"Wingfields, Your Highness. And my Espionage Constables are
merely obeying your laws."

"You know I can't change them all overnight. The people need
to be coaxed to tolerance. Pah, what a dilemma. If we adopt Prophet
Jemli as our religious leader can we retain even the few tolerant laws
that exist? Food for thought, Highliber."

"In the meantime, Your Highness, all laws must be upheld. Remember, too, that organized aviads tried to take control of the
Dragon Librarian Service in the not-too-distant past. Aviads are
forbidden to organize or associate with any group other than family under pain of death, and marriage and procreation between
certified aviads is similarly forbidden. We are at war with aviads
as a group. My own Espionage Constables are your warriors, hunting their agents within the Rochestrian Commonwealth—in your
name."

"Do your Espionage Constables do anything to enforce the current laws *protecting* aviads when those laws are flouted by the occasional lynch mob?"

"When they are in the right place at the right time, yes. I enforce
all laws, Your Highness."

"Well, I suppose that having charge over such weighty issues is
why you live in Libris and I live in a palace. What are we to do
about the flying American? His name is Alarak."

"I can confine him in Libris with some of our best linguists so
that an exchange of languages might take place."

"Good, do it. We have some words unraveled already. He said
this thing is called a reaction pistol. My finest armaments artisans
have taken measurements and are even now duplicating its individual
components. Given perhaps two years, we may have a working prototype."

"A thousand aviads waving these things could conquer the Commonwealth within months."

"Very true, Highliber. Perhaps Jemli the Prophet could offer up
some prayers on our behalf."

• • •

Martyne watched as the goldsmith examined a gold bar that had been brought into the shop. It bore no stamp. In the front of the shop a man with a grubby, brownish coat, drooping hat, and lank, black hair was waiting.

"Worth eight royals," said the jeweler. "The gold is of a somewhat more pure type than is to be found in the Rochestrian Commonwealth."

"Offer him two," said Martyne quietly. "Then let him beat you up to something more realistic."

After ten minutes of haggling, the man departed with five royals added to his purse. He was even smiling.

"Are you not going to follow him?" asked the jeweler.

"I know who he is, and I know that he will not return to the one who gave him that bar."

"He has taken quite a loss on it."

"Yet he took it easily. He may have paid as little as three royals for it."

"What do you make of that, Fras?"

"I do not intend to tell you, Fras."

The Filthy Swine was a tavern frequented not only by militiamen and musketeers; spies and Espionage Constables were also numbered among its patrons. Martyne had many contacts who were regular drinkers there, and some patrons were wanted by the very same people who were unknowingly drinking beside them. Martyne leaned against a wall, having discreetly spilled enough of his drink on the floor to give the appearance of a genuine drinker. Another drinker strode across and clanked his tankard against Martyne's.

"Need a message, Hakara," said Martyne.

"Outward?"

"Yes."

"Text?"

"No."

Martyne slapped the man on the chest, as if to emphasise something, but slipped the little gold bar wrapped in grease paper into his pocket. Next he backhanded Hakara against the chest and laughed, as if they were sharing a joke.

"Tell the Highliber," said Martyne softly, "*this* is circulating, so there may be another man from the flying machine."

"The gold could have been gathered from the crash site."

"That is possible, but I want that to be *proved* to me."

Terror squads have arrived at night since time immemorial. At night people post more guards, lock secret doors, and leave tripwires attached to bells. The University's laundaric did nearly all of its covert business by day, however. As he waited in the queue, Dellar could see that many of the patrons were paying for very small amounts of laundry with quite large quantities of silver, while others were given packages and even things that looked like weapons wrapped in cloth mixed in with their clean clothing. Two features common to all laundarics were that they were open long hours and that everyone had a good reason to visit them frequently. This laundaric was apparently using those features to cover the laundering of far more than clothing.

Skew was a ratty-looking little war veteran who looked to be in his forties, while his helper had a shaven head and was much younger. The University of Rochester's laundaric had been established in 1337 GW, for the better hygiene of the sons—and now daughters—of gentlefolk while they went about their studies without the benefit of family servants.

Dellar waited patiently in the queue, and slowly worked his way toward the desk. Skew, the small cripple, was serving at the counter. At last it was Dellar's turn.

"Just this coat," said Dellar, putting a stained promenade coat on the counter.

Rangen reached out to smooth it flat—and Dellar snapped his ratchet shackle down around his left wrist.

The little veteran bellowed in a mixture of surprise, fear, and outrage as he tried to pull free. Chained to Skew, Dellar was dragged almost over the counter. By now the other students in the laundaric were screaming, shouting, and scattering. A crush of bodies jammed the door, but one of those from the queue was Martyne. The eunuch hurried in from the back, saw what was happening and drew a knife. Martyne cross-blocked the knife, twisted his arm around, doubled him over, and kneed him in the face. He collapsed. Dellar pointed a pistol between Skew's eyes.

"Best not to move," he advised.

Martyne presently had four other customers laid out on the floor. The rest had fled by now, but there was shouting outside. Martyne came over to Dellar.

"Good work, we had to catch this one even if all the others got away," said Martyne. "Now raise your scarf."

They pulled their scarves up to their eyes just as three militiamen entered. These began shackling those on the floor after a deferential bow to the two masked youths. Brindilsi was carried out on a stretcher, leaving Skew alone with his captors. Skew's wrist was skinned and bleeding where he had fought and struggled against the ratchet shackle.

"Only work 'ere!" protested Skew.

"You certainly do work here," agreed Martyne's fellow Espionage Constable. "It's the word 'only' that I take issue with. Lie on the floor."

Skew was stripped naked, and it very soon became apparent that he had no war injuries whatsoever. Furthermore he had the skin of a teenager—including acne. A wet cloth removed the pox scars on Rangen's face to reveal half a dozen very ordinary pimples.

"I do believe we have caught Fras Rangen Derris," said Martyne.

"There is a twenty-royal reward for him," said Dellar.

"Lucky us," said Martyne.

"Ten royals *each*."

"Correct."

All through Rochester there were raids by squads of Tiger Dragons, Espionage Constables, and even the ordinary Constable's Runners. For ninety minutes on that clear, warm, windless January day, law enforcement in the capital of the Rochestrian Commonwealth ceased altogether while the raids netted 340 unregistered numerates and dozens more sympathizers and associates. Rangen's invisible paraline had ceased to exist.

Martyne sat with Dramoren in the Highliber's study amid the towers and roofs of Libris, sipping coffee and munching on macadamia nut shortbread.

"Another piece of shortbread?" asked Dramoren, holding the plate out to Martyne.

"No, thank you, Fras Highliber, I have had two already."

"Are you sure? They're by mayoral appointment."

"My training partner has me on her lean-muscle-mass diet. She would be cross if she knew I had had more than one."

"Well then, more coffee?"

"Just half a mug—but no honey."

They sat back, looking out over the roofs at the clear blue sky of summer through the open leadlight windows. A warm, gentle breeze had sprung up around noon, moderating what would otherwise have been a fairly hot day.

"Well now, I can only say that I am overwhelmed by the complete and thorough perfection of your operation," declared Dramoren, raising one foot and placing the heel firmly on the list of names on his coffee table. "Most of the finest numerates known to us are now being prepared for training as components in the Calculor. Who would have thought that Rangen's invisible paraline was not to smuggle unregistered numerates out of Rochester but to disguise them and keep them in Rochester?"

"Did you hear about the fugitive numerate who said no?" asked Martyne.

"No," replied Dramoren, although he caught himself almost immediately, and laughed.

"Highliber, humor is all about looking at things laterally, and for that reason humor is the highest and finest form of human thought. Look at any problem laterally and you have generated a new idea. I did just that with the fugitive numerates. I am doing just that with several other potential threats to our Commonwealth."

"Oh ho, so what threats are these?"

"Some that you know of, others perhaps not."

"Name one."

"A second crew member from the flying machine."

Dramoren sat up instantly. "You—" He stared at Martyne, then allowed himself a shallow smile. "How soon can you bring him in?"

"Not so fast, Highliber. I have some observations to make first. In fact it may be more constructive not to make an arrest at all. Do you catch my meaning?"

Dramoren considered this option, settling back in his chair. "The man that was captured by the city militiamen does not speak Austaric, although my finest linguists have been putting in fourteen-hour days with him in an attempt to exchange languages. How is conversation with your man?"

"Who said that I had spoken with anyone?"

"Martyne?"

"Yes, Highliber?"

"Damn you."

"At once, Highliber."

"More to the point, Fras, I intend to have your authority within the Espionage Constables raised."

"I do not want a promotion, Highliber. It would cause me difficulties—"

"No, it will not. As Dragon Silver you shall have access to increased human and material resources on your own authority, rather than having to petition me directly as was the case with this morning's raids. Are you sure that you do not want any monetary reward for masterminding the operation?"

"Quite sure, Highliber."

"But why? Look, I can put a few hundred royals into a secret bank tally for you."

"No, thank you."

"I have never known anyone to refuse money before."

"Perhaps you need to know that I am beyond corruption, Highliber. I cannot be bought, I can only be trusted." Martyne stood up. "Be pleased to remember that, Highliber, especially if you hear anything strange about myself or my actions."

Dramoren now stood up. "Nobody is truly trustworthy, Martyne, and there is nobody but myself that I trust without reservation. Nevertheless, I am very curious to see what you can do for the Commonwealth. The afternoon's compliments to you."

"And to you, Highliber."

6

FACE OF THE ENEMY

Rochester, the Rochestrian Commonwealth

Velesti had been working hard to gather a big audience for the demonstration of her self-defence guild's way of fighting. Although she had only just met Frelle Corien at an orientation tutorial, she quickly convinced her to come along. When Corien suggested that her friend from Jarbrovia might be convinced to come along as well, Velesti agreed to speak with her.

"The quite notorious Mayor Glasken once stayed here," said Corien suavely, tapping a plaque beside the main doors of Villiers College.

"Ah yes, I have met him," replied Velesti casually.

Corien swallowed. "Ah, indeed? When and where?"

"An important diplomatic reception, some time ago. I was a lot younger."

Corien cast a suspicious glance at her.

"What was he like?"

"He was a big, fit man, around fifty. He had an eye for the ladies, especially ladies with substantial but shapely bottoms and breasts."

"All of that is public knowledge." Corien laughed as they made for the stairs. "What else?"

"Glasken had a pointy waxed beard, and while bowing to an important official's wife he dipped it into her cleavage. She seized his head and pushed his face into the very same cleavage, saying 'If you like them so much take a really good look!' He was a trifle misunderstood, but a dirty old man nevertheless."

Corien put a hand to her face. That sounded very much like the man who had struck her now-elderly uncle with a bag of stolen coins three decades ago. More than anything else, the words "dirty old man" convinced Corien that at least something of what Velesti had said was true. Most tales of the legendary Mayor of Kalgoorlie painted him as a great and romantic adventurer, but thanks to her uncle, Glasken was known as nothing more than a tasteless lecher in the Meziar family. Velesti's Glasken definitely sounded more like the Glasken of reality.

They walked down the residency wing's upper corridor. Corien rapped at Samondel's door.

"Waiting, please," called a voice from inside, then the latch clacked and the door was pulled open.

Samondel stood before them wearing a long promenade jacket over a calf-length skirt, with lace-up sandals on her feet. Her hands were demurely clasped before her, and her hair had been braided into a single plait that hung over her right shoulder and reached down to her knees. Her violet eyes were huge and winsome in the dim light.

Velesti gave a gasp of astonishment and scrambled behind Corien. Corien cast a puzzled glance back at Velesti, then looked back to the equally puzzled Samondel.

"Frelle Samondel, the afternoon's compliments," said Corien. "May I introduce Frelle Velesti Disore?"

"Frelle Disore, afternoon's compliments," said Samondel cautiously.

Corien stepped to one side and drew Velesti forward by the arm.

"Frelle Velesti is in our applied theology tutorial group. She is in the Dragon Librarian Service; and has just enrolled at the university to further her career. She . . . is also a little timid around strangers."

Corien was not sure whether that had been the cause of Velesti's reaction, but it did seem like a diplomatic thing to say.

"Er, greetings—and the afternoon's compliments!" said Velesti, slowly regaining her composure.

"Our first Applied Theology tutorial is at four P.M.," said Corien.

"Time, I have remembered," said Samondel. "Now is not time, also."

"Ah, but Frelle Velesti has a demonstration for a new guild she is establishing. It is on the cloister lawns, very soon."

"Ah, religious readings?" asked Samondel.

"Well, no. This guild is to help female students, ah—"

"To improve their confidence," interjected Velesti.

Samondel reached out and took Velesti by the hand.

"Is wonderful and worthy, Frelle. Believe in confidence, girls, having plenty."

"I'm sure you do," responded Velesti.

"Without confidence, long journey here, is impossible. Alone, I have traveled."

"I have no doubt of it," said Velesti.

"Shall come along, friendly faces in crowd, for you. Corien and I. Yes?"

"Look, this type of confidence development may come as something of a shock," warned Velesti.

"Oh, but learning, my purpose, here is."

The main cloisters of the university were three sides of a square, but with a curved stone amphitheater for the fourth side. There were thirty or so girls and a scattering of male students on the stone steps and as many again watching from the covered cloisters. Velesti watched as Samondel and Corien took seats near the front of the amphitheater. Martyne arrived just as they were seated.

"Time to start, Fras, are you ready?" said Velesti.

"Yes, Frelle. What about you? You look a trifle nervous."

Velesti had a great number of things on her mind, and was uncharacteristically ill at ease.

"Martyne, do you think they will laugh at me?" she whispered behind her hand.

"Laugh? Why?"

"Well, I feel so foolish, like, being a girl . . ." Her voice faded.

"Why is today different?"

"There are some very pretty girls watching, and some youths as well. I look, well, different. They might laugh."

"Gasp yes, laugh no," said Martyne. "Nevertheless, if any youth does laugh I shall haul him out here to demonstrate a few of the more painful armlocks. Come on, brave and deadly Frelle, let us start your guild."

They walked out onto the lawn, and the students began applauding. They both bowed to those on the amphitheater seats. Samondel and Corien clapped enthusiastically, then sat forward and gave Velesti both their full attention and wide smiles.

"I am Frelle Velesti Disore, Dragon Blue Librarian, and student of this university. Some time ago I was most brutally attacked in my home city, and as a result I have been taught certain arts to prevent this ever happening again. I now wish to teach other women and girls, such as yourselves, to use these arts so as to walk the streets and roads of this commonwealth without fear. This man is Fras Martyne Camderine, an edutor in theology in this university. Without further talk, I propose to demonstrate some techniques to you. Sensei, shall we begain?"

"Will you just look at her friend!" hissed Corien.

"Face, eyes, are showing kind soul," said Samondel.

"Never mind his soul, look at the rest of him."

"What arts are to demonstrate? Removing boots, they are."

"I'd like to remove more than his boots."

Velesti and Martyne took off their boots while the girls looked on attentively, Martyne then removed his tunic. There was a loud and collective gasp of surprise from the audience as Martyne stood before them, dressed only in black drawstring trousers. Edutors in theology were not supposed to look anything remotely like Martyne. He was heavily muscled rather than massively built. His abdomen looked like a quite a workable washerboard, and his pectorals cast shadows down his chest in the summer sunlight. It was also more than obvious that the ostentatiously padded shoulders of his tunic had not been padded at all. There was a bandage on his left forearm. Samondel's huge violet eyes were stretched wide, in spite of the bright sunlight.

"Imagine being in bed with him!" whispered Corien.

By now Velesti had removed her jacket, and as she slipped off her shirt Corien and Samondel involuntarily joined in the even louder collective gasp.

"Why did they gasp?" hissed Velesti anxiously to Martyne.

"Maybe they like that thing you are wearing," Martyne whispered back.

"The old language term is 'sports bra'; it does not translate easily."

"You may have started a new fashion trend."

The audience's surprise was not so much from the sight of the sleek, black symmetry of the first sports bra to be seen in two thousand years, as the sight of Velesti's upper torso. White silk stretched over a sculpture of heavy wire rope was the only comparison that Samondel could think of as she watched.

"Just imagine the two of them in bed together!" whispered Corien to the dumbfounded Samondel.

"Is self-confidence demonstration? Mistaken, perhaps?"

Martyne held an arm up for attention.

"Now I want you to think of me as a shadowboy, and of Frelle Velesti as a student for whom my attentions are unwelcome."

"Your attentions would be welcome to *me*!" called a girl behind Corien.

Everyone laughed. Velesti and Martyne blushed.

Martyne strode confidently up to Velesti and reached out for her. Velesti snaked her arm around his, stepping in close to him to lock his arm against her back as she doubled him over and brought a knee up to his face.

"The weakest girl's leg is stronger than the strongest man's arm," declared Velesti. "Had I followed through, he would not be getting up for a long time."

The audience clapped. Velesti released Martyne. He now attacked with a knife, overhand. Velesti cross-blocked with both arms, twisted his arm, and doubled him over again before bending his wrist and forcing him to drop the knife.

"At this point you can obviously knee him in the stomach," Velesti pointed out.

The audience applauded again. After several more practical demonstrations, the pair declared that they would now demonstrate free-form sparring. They bowed, then Martyne said "Hajime!"

Velesti and Martyne circled each other, their hands held out and their steps as smooth as those of the dancers of the Rochestrian Mayoral Ballet. Samondel could barely follow the first exchange of blows and blocks, but the whack of flesh on flesh came across very distinctly. There were kicks right up to head level, spinning back kicks, dodges, feints, and several blows that actually did get past the defenses of both fighters. Presently Martyne called "Yame!" The pair bowed to each other, then to the audience.

For the finale of the demonstration, Martyne picked up five terra-cotta roofing tiles and held them up for everyone to see. He looked across the audience, then pointed to Corien and beckoned.

Corien began to stand, but Samondel seized her arm.

"Frelle, no! Being hurting."

"Oh, no, I want to increase my self-confidence."

Martyne and Velesti held a tile while Corien sat on it, demonstrating that it could support her full weight. Corien held Martyne's arm, steadying herself, then she was set down. Now Martyne kneeled side-on to the amphitheater, holding the five tiles on his forearms. Velesti stood before him, her knees bent and her legs wide apart. She raised her open hand, held it perpendicular above him, the breath hissing between her teeth, then struck down at the tiles. They shattered. Martyne and Velesti bowed to their audience amid cheers, whistles, and cries for more. Martyne bowed to Corien, then led her back to her seat. Samondel looked up at him, then smiled tentatively.

"Fras, are hurt," she said, pointing to his arm where blood was seeping through the bandage.

Martyne looked down, releasing Corien's hand.

"A scratch, Frelle, no matter."

Just then there was a commotion from the northern archway of the cloisters. Watchers scattered to either side as the Yellowbird gang strode through the arch, through the cloisters, and onto the grass. There were five of them, all shadowboys from beyond the university gates.

"Now, here's a fine group to become Yellowbirds!" declared the tallest of them.

"Wear the Yellowbird badge, and you'll never walk in fear," followed the more authoritative voice of their leader.

Protection ventures were common around the city, and the university was a favored target. The students tended to be from affluent families and were seldom the most martial of people. Several gangs had been fighting for the right to farm the university for protection money during December, and the Yellowbirds had emerged as the winners. One carried a bag of yellow badges, another a register of names.

"Hey, then, Caelen, will you look at the woofters!" exclaimed the tall one, catching sight of Martyne and Velesti. Samondel put a hand to her coat, where her reaction pistol was concealed.

Even had Velesti brought the whole of her considerable will-power to bear she could not have stopped the smile that was spreading across her face.

"Can I have them, Sensei?" she asked. "Please?"

Martyne put his hands on his hips. "You will not show control. The answer is no."

"I'll owe you a favor. Anything you want."

"Anything?"

"Please, it's been months."

"Weeks, actually. Oh, very well, but don't kill any of them."

"Sensei, if I do, I swear on my honor it will be an accident."

"As you will. I shall guard their escape."

The Yellowbirds were not entirely sure of how to take this. Either it was outrageous bravado, or there was something very, very wrong. Velesti advanced briskly on the leader, who raised his swagger stick and dropped back a pace. Velesti brought a foot down, swung around with a flying, circular kick and smashed her boot into the head of the shadowboy beside her, then backhanded her fist into the leader's nose. Still turning, she lifted the tip of her foot into the soft flesh just behind what was protected by her next victim's codpiece, and as he doubled over she pushed his head down onto her knee. By now the leader was swinging his swagger stick down at her, but she cross-blocked with both arms, blunted the momentum from the blow, seized his wrist, twisted to double him over, then brought the edge of her hand down hard on the back of his elbow. There was a loud snap, followed by a piercing shriek of agony that was cut off as her foot connected with his face.

Something whizzed through the air, and a small-bore flintlock fell from the hand of a shadowboy who now had a wheelstar buried in his bicep. He toppled, his mouth open but silent. Another wheelstar was in his kneecap.

"Damn you, Sensei, stop doing that!" shouted Velesti, her hands on her hips. "I could have taken him."

Martyne shrugged and walked over to the remaining member of the gang, who was standing all alone, his swagger stick dropped and his hands raised. He turned him to face the astounded audience, then stood to one side.

"Now, here are some interesting thoughts on self-defense," he said, his eyes lingering in Samondel's direction. "With enough training you can withstand quite heavy blows."

He snapped his fingers, and Velesti slammed a roundhouse kick into his own abdomen that impacted with sickening force. Martyne appeared not to notice.

"On the other hand, there are certain pressure points that simply cannot be hardened."

He pinched the shadowboy between the neck and shoulder. He shrieked and dropped to the grass. Velesti hauled him to his feet as the audience applauded.

"Now, just here, at the center of the chest, there is another," she said, holding a finger up.

She thrust it into the center of the shadowboy's chest. He collapsed with an agonized wheeze. Martyne hauled him up again.

"Boxing the ears with cupped hands, very effective when you

are in someone's grip," added Velesti with an appropriate demonstration.

"Don't forget bending the little finger, when he grips you, also very effective."

"Or a knee to the testicles when in his embrace."

"Even a light blow to the throat."

"Pulling hair."

"Pinning his wrist to your breast if he grabs you there, then dropping to your knees, exquisitely painful."

"In fact there is a whole selection of really nice armlocks and wrist bends that you can do with practically no additional muscle development at all."

By now the shadowboy was incapable of standing unaided. Velesti released him and he fell to the ground. She walked over to the other shadowboys, none of whom had moved for the entire time.

"Ah, sorry, I killed the first one!" she exclaimed. "Got carried away."

Martyne knelt down beside her first victim, felt for a pulse at his neck, examined his head, then pulled his lips apart.

"He's alive."

"But I heard his neck snap."

"No, that was his teeth breaking. See?" He held up a broken tooth. "His pulse is strong." Martyne stood up and strode over to the shadowboy who had tried to shoot Velesti. With a determined tug, he pulled his wheelstar out of bone and muscle. Velesti kicked him delicately but firmly on the chin, then plucked her own wheelstar out of his kneecap.

"You did not have to do that," objected Martyne.

"But he was in pain, it was an act of mercy."

Martyne turned back to the audience. "We shall be taking names for both the lightweight self-defense course and the serious sessions on these fighting arts. There will be two lessons per week of ninety minutes each. Are there any questions?"

"What is the cost, good Fras?"

"There is no cost. Velesti will train you in basics, and I shall later take advanced techniques and conduct examinations when students move to higher gradings."

"Why do you have commands in that ancient language?"

"Because few understand Japanese here. If two students are sparring and someone passing by sees a friend in the distance and calls 'Stop,' one student may stop while the other fights on—and an injury could result. If they hear 'Yame,' they know that it is a command for them, from their instructor."

It might be fair to say that many of those who enrolled were merely interested in becoming acquainted with the remarkable pair of warriors who had just wiped out the scourge of the campus nightlife in a single minute, but there was a core of girls with serious intentions. Several youths also expressed interest. Velesti did not like the idea of including them, but Martyne seemed to think that it was a reasonable idea. In the meantime the Yellowbirds had staggered away, minus their weapons, register, bag of badges, and purse of silver. They were clinging to each other for support and in a great deal of distress as they passed through the campus gates for the very last time.

"So, Frelles, are you impressed by Martyne?" Velesti asked as she joined Corien and Samondel.

"I am looking blind, perhaps?" asked Corien.

"I meant his fighting."

"That too. Might I ask if he is, that is, are you and he—"

"Are perhaps sharing bedding," Samondel finished for her.

Corien elbowed her, but Velesti smiled instead of taking offense.

"Martyne is not free, but neither am I his girl, good Frelles. Would you consider joining our guild?"

"A strong and brave lover would provide good protection for far less effort, Frelle," said Corien.

"Ah, but do you have such a lover?"

"No, but two girls as alluring as ourselves will not be without lovers for long, is that not so, Frelle Samondel?"

"Is right."

"But see the time, we three have a tutorial in Applied Theology," said Corien, looking up at the clocktower.

"You go, tell the edutor that I was delayed," replied Velesti.

"This is not a studious attitude."

"But I have my own students to teach."

As they walked away Velesti returned to Martyne.

"Thirty-five enrollments, Frelle, and three of the girls wish to adjourn to a tavern to speak of the Women's Assertion League with you."

"With both of you," said one of Velesti's recruits. "What do you say to a beer?"

"I say 'Greetings.' "

"What about your tutorial in Applied Theology?" asked Martyne.

"You are an edutor in Applied Theology; give me a private tutorial in the tavern," replied Velesti.

"We are going to the Gaudeamus, you can see it from the main gates," said the girl.

"Are you sure you want a man present at such a meeting?"

"Fras Martyne, the Women's Assertion League is about equality and harmony between men and women, not domination by either or war between both. You are welcome, specifically."

"Well, why not?"

The Southeast Coast, Australica

Shadowmouse watched the kitewing curve away front the wingfield to follow a heading almost directly south. At this location the sea was only a few miles away, but the trip from the paraline wayside had taken more than a week.

"Now we go back," said Frelle Sparrow as they returned to their horses.

"Every time it takes longer," replied Shadowmouse.

"At least the vigilantes have left us alone since the great battle."

"They will just change their tactics. They always do."

The new wingfield was nothing more than a level strip of grass with a cache of compression spirit hidden nearby. With the kitewing gone it seemed just a grassy clearing. After farewells with Terian and his ground crew, they rode north. The aviads traveled by directions through the bush rather than paths, making themselves very difficult to track. Another tactic was to return by a slightly different route.

It was Frelle Sparrow who noticed the anomaly as they rode, something subtle in the background vista of the bushland. She reined in.

"The birdsong is not what it should be," she said to Shadowmouse. "Notice that sharp tweet, tweet, tweet of the suneye?"

"The male makes that call," replied Shadowmouse.

"But only when something approaches the nest. He's about a hundred yards away, so that something is not us."

They sat in silence for a time, listening, then Shadowmouse put a finger to his lips and dismounted. They tethered their horses and crept away, treading slowly and silently. The sharp, percussive tweets of the bird continued, then there was a soft snort from quite close by. Both aviads began to crawl. A party of five men had halted in a scrubby gully, and their horses were hobbled and grazing.

"Vigilantes," whispered Shadowmouse.

"And on our original path," Frelle Sparrow replied. "Tracking us."

"Why have they stopped?"

"They must have heard the compression engine of the kitewing. They want to find the wingfield, so they only followed us until they knew they were close."

"Five men, six horses!" Shadowmouse suddenly warned.

There was a sharp whistle somewhere away in the bushland. A sixth man, and he had found their own horses, Shadowmouse realized. The vigilantes froze, then crouched and drew their weapons.

Frelle Sparrow fired at the nearest of the vigilantes, then rolled to the left. Four shots blasted back at her cloud of gunsmoke, then Shadowmouse discharged both barrels of his Morelac. Frelle Sparrow sprang from her cover with her saber drawn, but was cut down by a fifth shot. Shadowmouse flung his dagger, then charged with his own saber held high. The foremost vigilante blocked the cut from Shadowmouse as he advanced, but the aviad punched his face as he dodged past, then brought a cut down across the back of his neck and rolled with the cut of another vigilante.

Vigilante and aviad exchanged parry and riposte amid the fallen for a few seconds, then a gunshot blasted out from the bush beside them. Shadowmouse dropped into a lunge, taking the vigilante in the throat with the point of his saber. As the human fell, Shadowmouse noted a sixth body slumped at the edge of the gully. He returned to where Frelle Sparrow had fallen.

"Reloaded," she explained, frothy blood trickling from her mouth.

"Can you ride?" asked Shadowmouse, cutting open the blood-soaked cloth above the wound in her chest. "The wingfield has a medician."

Frelle Sparrow just coughed and let her flintlock fall from her fingers. Shadowmouse began to tear bandages from his trail cloak.

"Live well, it's all there is," whispered Frelle Sparrow with her last breath.

It was the evening of the same day that Shadowmouse, Terian, and two other aviads stood beside Frelle Sparrow's grave. Terian read a short Mechanist service, then they piled stones on the grave and returned to their horses.

"The vigilantes have changed their approach," said Terian. "One vigilante commanding four or five musketeer mercenaries. Small squads, but very effective."

"And all in the pay of the Gentheists," added Shadowmouse. "She loved life so much. I should be down there, not her."

"If you want to bring her back from the dead, young Fras, live life as she did."

Rochester, the Rochestrian Commonwealth

The dragon Gold Chamber was the most secure and secret of rooms in Libris, other than the study of the Highliber himself. It had no windows, the lighting was minimal, there was half-inch-thick carpeting on the floor, the ceiling was covered with small cardboard and felt cones, and the walls were smothered with thick tapestries into which had been woven everything from abstract mathematical designs to portraits of past highlibers. Speaking in there was like having the words sucked out of one's mouth and smothered.

The large, oblong table was entirely covered in burgundy leather, while the high-backed chairs were smothered in green felt and crushed velvet. There were fourteen chairs in the chamber, but today only six were in use. The Highliber, Velesti, Martyne, the Calculor's System Controller, Rangen Derris, and Frelle Halen, the Dragon Gold in charge of the Espionage Constables, sat clustered at one end of the table, circulating a clipboard with several reports attached. Dramoren could not help but notice that reports with bad news tended to have the best calligraphy and illumination, and these reports almost glowed from the poorpaper.

"Let me try to summarize my understanding of this situation," said Dramoren quietly, adjusting his skullcap, then pressing his fingertips very hard against his temples. "Fras Martyne Camderine, you recently smashed a smuggling underground for numerate people who would otherwise be destined for the Libris Calculor."

"Yes, Highliber."

"Fras Rangen Derris, you were running this underground."

"Yes, Highliber."

"Frelle Halen, since that raid you have reported a ninety percent reduction in new components recruited to the Libris Calculor."

"Yes, Highliber."

"Fras System Controller Hawker, since Fras Derris was inducted into the Calculor you have reported no less than five assaults or attempts on his life by very angry components."

"Yes, Highliber."

"Frelle Halen, where do most Calculor components come from?"

"Certain, ah, criminal sources, Highliber."

Dramoren sat in silence for a moment with his eyes closed.

"Am I to conclude that the Libris Calculor's primary supply of numerate components has been an underground operation designed specifically to keep them *out* of the Calculor?"

Silence was their only response. Dramoren considered shouting at them at the top of his voice, but decided that his head was hurting far too much for that.

"Who was your contact with the criminal sources, Frelle Halen?"

"Frelle Velesti Disore, Highliber."

"Frelle Disore, were you aware that Fras Derris was at the other end of your source of components?"

"A mercenary contact named Frelle Julica was my informer. I had not originally employed her to find Rangen, she did that on her own initiative. She is a bright girl who—"

"Answer the question! Were you aware that Fras Derris was at the other end of your source of components?"

"Yes, Highliber."

"Why did you not arrest him?"

"There was no arrest order, Highliber, only a reward. I thought that a good supply of components was of more value than one brilliant component. I did not pocket the commissions, all that money went to Julica. She needs it because she is—"

"Did you tell anyone else, Frelle Disore?"

"No, Highliber."

"So we are now getting one recruit for every nine that we used to get, and the single best recruit that Fras Camderine did manage to apprehend for the Calculor is unusable because the rest of the Calculor's components want to kill him—or at the very least hurt him a great deal!"

"True, Highliber," responded Halen and the System Controller together.

"Do *any* of you *ever* talk to each other?" demanded Dramoren at the top of his voice.

"Fras Camderine and I discuss Baleshanto training—" began Velesti.

"Shut up."

"Yes, Highliber."

"Get out. All of you."

"Yes, Highliber," they answered together.

As the pleasantly warm days of January merged into the blazingly hot days of February, Samondel's life settled into a routine. She attended her lectures, and studied in the university library. Interminable talk with new friends in the university refectory, the student taverns, and even on the university lawns quickly improved both her Austaric and her grasp of Australican religious and political issues to a degree that the Mounthaven airlords could never have dreamed possible.

All the while she was being watched, and her opinions and questions were noted carefully.

By now Martyne had problems of a very different nature.

"This morning I was watching you with a telescope, from the tower of the Gaudeamus Tavern!" cried Marelle, humiliated, furious and in no mood to hide it.

"Watching what?" asked Martyne wearily.

"Watching you and that half-naked, melon-breasted tart on the campus lawns just after sunrise. I wondered why you were so anxious to get out of bed early. You were flinging her through the air and then lying on top of her!"

"I was teaching her to defend herself."

"Well, she was not doing a very good job of it!"

"How else was I to teach her, except by example?"

"And what else do you teach her by example? All the things that *I* have been teaching *you* for the past weeks?"

"Marelle, there were thirty others looking on."

"Aye, and nearly all of them were nubile young whoopsicles with only a strip of black cloth between their tits and indecent exposure. I saw how they were ogling you."

"They were just being attentive. It's Velesti's guild—"

"*Don't* try to bring Velesti into this! And another thing! Over the past month you've been away eighteen days in total."

"I was touring the rural monasteries, I had a seminar to give at Kyntella—"

"Well, I checked on the Kyntella Monastery. It has been a ruin since 1497 GW."

"The ruins are a place of pilgrimage."

"The only pilgrimage that you have been making has been to the bed of that vixen with the huge tits and short black hair. What has she got that I don't have—apart from six fewer birthdays?"

"A longer fuse on her temper?"

Martyne fled from the tavern amid a shower of pots, mugs, and wine jars, not all of them empty. It was the evening of the first night of February, and there was now a cool, blustery wind blowing while clouds gathered in the sky. It was painfully obvious to Martyne that he would not be getting dinner from Marelle, so he called in at the Gaudeamus. No sooner was he through the door than he was hailed by a chorus of voices. It was five of Velesti's students, two boys and three girls.

Martyne was pleased to join them, and was soon washing a flatbread and bacon salad down with light ale. The other five had been drinking and talking for the better part of the afternoon and had been reduced to a rather serious state of frivolous philosophizing.

"And just why should I worry about producing an heir for my father's dry goods importation agglomorate when Mirrorsun is spinning out of control?" asked Kenlen with a vague gesture to the rafters. "He wants a schedule for my courtship and marriage, can you believe that? I'm twenty, you know? But I'm expected to be an old man."

"Mine is arranging a marriage for me when I return with my degree," said Rositana, swirling her hair out in a fan. "The merging of two great highland sheep dynasties. I refuse to be the paper on which some contract is written."

"So how old are you?" asked Kenlen.

"Twenty in three months. My mother's been forty ever since she was fifteen—that's when she was married. Life of luxury, but eleven children! Before I graduate I'll be in the Dragon Librarian Service, then let them try to barter sheep for my body. Say, Martyne, how do Highland shepherds find their sheep in the mountain forests?"

"I can't say, I've never been to—"

"Very satisfying."

They all hooted with laughter, and Kenlen called to the jarmaid for another round.

"My parents think the university edutors are chaperones," said Cherene, a thin girl with mousy brown hair. "I'm twenty-two, the oldest child of the family, yet they'd have hysterics if they realized that I had ever tasted wine."

She put her head back and drank from a small jar of wine, then passed it to Rositana, who drained it, then tossed it over her head into the empty fireplace, where it shattered. The other drinkers in the taproom cheered.

"If only they really knew about the edutors," said Rositana. "Like that it's only safe for female students to enter their offices in pairs."

"I resent that," said Martyne with his mouth full, waving a fork in the air.

"Present company excepted," called Rositana.

"That's very generous of the sheep."

"Baaa."

"What do you think, Fras Martyne?" asked Bastirrel, who was twenty-one and fancied himself a more serious philosopher than the others. "You've seen life, when has a person seen enough?"

"What have *you* done, Fras Edutor in Applied Theology?" asked Sembelia, who also had short, dark hair, and whose tunic featured a large orange star at each breast.

Martyne sat back from his empty dish and thought for a moment. There was so much to say that could not be said, and so much more that he should not have to say.

"I was in a monastery for five years, and I was ordained as a monk. I killed a man who raped and murdered my sister; in fact, I have killed eleven men in five incidents. I have worked as a wind train rotor-jack, a river galley rower, a mercenary guard, and sundry other jobs that I really cannot talk about. I have looked upon the salt ocean, walked the streets of distant Kalgoorlie, stood beside the grave of the legendary Ghan princess Ervelle, slept with a mayor's daughter, serenaded a girl on a balcony with a lute—oh, and been wounded in a small but murderous battle that I may not speak of." He displayed the month-old wound to his left arm. "What else would you like to know?"

There was silence. Martyne looked very, very tired after recalling his turbulent life.

"Fras Martyne, I—I think that you have borne your long and incredible life very well," said Sembellia. "You are still good-humored and free of wrinkles and gray hair."

"Aye, Martyne," said Rositana. "You could well be one of us."

"I turned nineteen last September, generous Frelle," said Martyne.

There was a more extended silence as the fact that Martyne was younger than any present dawned upon them. The moment was abruptly broken by the arrival of Velesti.

"So, you survived being ejected by Glasken's daughter?"

"As in *Mayor* Glasken?" asked Rositana.

"She hit him on the shoulder with a full jar of clarek hermitage, but luckily it didn't break when it hit the cobbles."

Velesti placed the sealed jar on the table. Martyne scowled at the jar, then at Velesti.

"Well, don't just stand there, open it!" snarled Martyne.

Later that evening Martyne walked through the university grounds, escorting Rositana back to Korvarin College. Mirrorsun was high in the sky, shimmering and twinkling through scattered cloud and turbulent air. Rositana stopped, staring up at the sky.

"Do you really think it is the end of the world, Fras Martyne?" she asked.

"The world has never ended, Frelle Philosopher. *People's* worlds have ended countless times, but the world itself has gone on. Live well or live ill, we shall all die."

"I am the first girl from my province to attend this university, and I shall die with that carved into my headstone. Why did it take two thousand years?"

"They probably thought you would miss lectures to graze on the lawns."

Rositana aimed a roundhouse kick at Martyne's buttocks, but he caught her foot smoothly and stood holding her at leg's length.

"Well, how long will this dose of humiliation last?' she asked, hopping on her other leg with her arms folded.

Martyne released her.

"So sad to think of all the talent and energy of highland girls being wasted for two thousand years," he said, looking up at the Mirrorsun again. "Are you serious about joining the Dragon Service?"

"Oh, yes, I have applied already. There is a long waiting list, but I have two years of study to go, so there is plenty of time. Secure income, that gives women freedom."

"That gives everyone freedom."

"Will you sleep with me tonight?"

"Well, it depends on how long it takes to prepare my tutorial questions on—will I *what*?"

"Will you sleep with me tonight?" asked Rositana, standing beside Martyne and putting an arm around him as she looked up at Mirrorsun.

"Lovely Frelle, I am honored, but, but, but . . . I have just been ejected from my former lady's favor in quite violent circumstances and—"

"Martyne! Stop it! I said sleep with me for one night, not marry me. You are not the first, and besides, I like you—even though you have suddenly become a bit old-fashioned. Years from now, Fras Martyne, I shall be a Dragon Silver and you shall be dean of this university. When we meet at some fabulously important mayoral reception we could smile suavely at each other, and think, *Ah, the summer of 1730 GW, what a splendid night.* Or you could say, 'Frelle Rositana, why have I not seen you at training for the past twenty-five years?' Then I would think, *Boring old zot, he never changes.*"

"Putting it like that, you give me little choice," replied Martyne, putting an arm about her shoulders.

"Diplomacy is my finest skill."

"Then it's the Libris Diplomatic Corps for you."

"My average is second-class honors, and the waiting list is years long for that particular Corps. My next option is the general Dragon Librarian Service, then an edutor post at some provincial university or academy, and lastly—"

"Baaa!"

"Never!"

"Cheer up. Tomorrow afternoon you will be offered a cadetship exam at Dragon Orange level in Libris' Diplomatic Corps. Accept. It is three hours in length, beginning at one P.M."

She gave a light, tinkling laugh.

"I'll not be on the Orange lists for five years, three if I'm really lucky. I've applied for White."

"Fact: The examination is scheduled for one P.M. tomorrow."

"Public knowledge."

"Fact: I was asked to give you a character reference by the Inspector of Cadets, in my capacity as a theological tutor. *Not* public knowledge—and I gave you a very good reference, as a matter of fact."

Rositana stared at Martyne in Mirrorsun's light, both eyes and mouth wide open. She was a good intuitive judge of character, and this intuition told her that Martyne was neither joking nor lying.

"Didn't you get a letter?" asked Martyne.

She shook her head.

"Oh dear. Now, given that you have a mere fourteen hours to prepare for the examination, and given that you have several hours of solid drinking behind you . . . if I were you I would begin munching my way through a couple of pounds of chocolate coffee beans in preparation for fourteen hours of solid study."

"But why?" she whispered. "I know the politics of the cadetship lists; I applied as a gesture of defiance rather than in real hope."

"Well, that was a bit dim of you. There are too many bad diplomats being appointed as political favors, and the Dragon Librarian Service has adopted a covert program of reform."

Rositana suddenly remembered something fairly important.

"Martyne, I—I was serious about wishing to, well, you know—"

"Frelle, how would I feel if you failed by some small margin because I wasted even an hour or two of your study time in bed? Up to your room, get to work. Go! Go!"

The following morning Martyne paid a visit to a house where he dropped a message, then he went straight to the paraline terminus and vanished from the city. Three hours later the Inspector of Cadets at Libris was paid a visit by Highliber Dramoren.

"Make sure that an applicant for Dragon Orange named Rositana Seubel from Highlands castellany is on this afternoon's examination posting, and make sure that she is marked and passed on merit alone," Dramoren ordered.

"Merit *alone*, Highliber?"

"Yes. The Espionage Police are involved, so be sure to take care."

Dramoren was not sitting in his usual presiding chair at the weekly meeting of the Dragon Gold Librarians. It was occupied by an observer. This observer was the one person in Rochester who had a higher rank than that of Highliber. Out of courtesy and deference to Overmayor Lengina, Dramoren had given her the presiding chair and removed himself to the other end of the table.

"And next we have a report from the Monastery of St. Roger at Euroa," said Dramoren. "Calculations regarding possible scenarios when Mirrorsun might burst cannot be completed under a minimum of twenty-six months, and even that is an improvement on earlier estimates. Instead Brother Nikalan has proposed that all resources be put into testing the strength of the Mirrorsun material in storage at the monastery."

"I thought that was already being done," said Lengina.

"The rig is complete, Your Highness, but the crossbar beam broke at sixty tons. Both it and the weight box need to be strengthened to carry up to five hundred tons."

"One scrap of fabric can support five hundred tons?" exclaimed Lengina.

"We do not know, Overmayor. However Brother Nikalan's calculor programs have calculated that a break at four hundred ninety tons is good news for us. The Mirrorsun band would then have the velocity to escape the gravitational pull of the sun completely."

"It would never return," added the system controller.

"Precisely. Once the strength of Mirrorsun fabric is known, we can calculate when it will burst, if it will be a danger to Earth, and when that danger is liable to materialize. That calculation will need no more than two months, with the Libris Calculor helping."

"Jemli the Prophet predicted that Mirrorsun is being punished by the Deity for being an abomination, she says that it will be 'flung into the blackness, never to return.' How can she predict with prayer and visions what we have spent two million gold royals trying to do—so far with no answer?"

"Overmayor, she has made no verified predictions so far," Frelle Halen of the Espionage Constables pointed out. "She has only interpreted events that have taken place and predicted what has not yet happened."

"But people *believe* that she has foretold the future with accuracy," said Dramoren.

"All the more reason to have our own prediction," Lengina replied. "Highliber Dramoren, do you have faith in your librarians, and in the monks?"

"I would trust them with my life, Overmayor."

"Splendid, then I shall trust them with my reputation. Spread a message across the realm and beyond, say that I shall make a pronouncement on the danger from Mirrorsun in—ah, when will the tests on the fabric be done?"

"In ten days."

"So in ten days you will be able to say if there is a threat, and in two months you will be able to say what the nature of the threat is?"

"Yes, Overmayor."

The meeting broke up, but Dramoren and Lengina stayed on in the room after the others had gone.

"You realize that this is science against religion, Highliber Dramoren?" said Lengina.

"It is actually engineer against priest, Overmayor. The people supplying our science are monks, after all."

"Whatever. I am in your hands, Highliber," she said with a coy smile. "A daunting prospect, is it not?"

Dramoren spent three frantic seconds searching for a witty yet respectful reply.

"I shall try not to drop you, Overmayor," he managed.

"I have the greatest faith in you, Highliber."

Two days later the lists for the Dragon Orange Diplomatic Corps cadetships were presented to Highliber Dramoren. He ran his finger down the list. The name Seubel was absent. Two minutes and forty seconds later the Inspector of Cadets was marched out of his office by two Tiger Dragons with a gag between his teeth and his hands shackled behind his back.

The Deputy Inspector of Cadets was a mature, ruthless, and politically canny administrator, and not the sort to cower before even the Highliber. She was, however, cowering as Dramoren stood before her desk. Beside the chief of the Dragon Librarian Service was a strange Dragon Blue; in her eyes was a suggestion of something that lacked sanity and ate live meat.

"The Highliber wishes to speak with you, Frelle," said Velesti in a voice with the bite of a south wind in midwinter. "Please do not make him repeat anything, I am *very* anxious to begin a private interview with the former Inspector of Cadets."

The Deputy Inspector's bladder failed her, but she nevertheless sat upright and attentive with her hands clasped on her desk as Velesti took a step back.

"Candidate Seubel was to be marked on merit, why did she not pass?" asked Dramoren.

"Highliber, the candidate Seubel scored eighty-one percent in her paper, but the pass mark was raised to eighty-three percent in order to accommodate certain assisted passes from the diplomatic lists."

"Who authorized the mark to be thus raised?"

"The Inspector of Cadets, Highliber."

"What was the unadjusted average mark of the successful candidates, Frelle?"

"Sixty-one percent Highliber."

"Frelle Deputy Inspector, if I said the words 'marked and passed on merit alone' and 'Espionage Police' to you, would you have failed Frelle Rositana Seubel?"

"No, Highliber."

Dramoren turned to Velesti and nodded. Velesti folded her arms. Dramoren turned back to the Deputy Inspector.

"Congratulations on your appointment to the position of Inspector of Cadets, Dragon Silver," declared Dramoren. "What was Frelle Seubel's absolute placement?"

"Third out of ninety, Highliber," responded the new Inspector of Cadets.

"Post all the results on absolute merit."

"There will be protests from the nobility, Highliber."

"Deal with them. If any persist, arrange an interview with my new Inspector of Espionage Constables, here, Frelle Velesti Disore."

The new Inspector of Cadets looked from Dramoren to Velesti, then back to Dramoren.

"Would it not be more humane to just shoot them, Highliber?" she asked.

"It would indeed, Frelle, but I am feeling particularly vindictive today. Favors to the rich, influential, and stupid have become a blight upon the service; it is time for some merit to be flushed through the system."

•   •   •

Precisely thirty hours later, to the very minute, Rositana was in her Libris uniform and orange colors and dancing on a tabletop in the Gaudeamus Tavern, shouting "Bronze Scholarship!" and buying drinks for the entire taproom.

At the very same instant Martyne was far away, shivering with shock and soaked with blood. Fortunately most of the blood was not his.

Euroa, the Rochestrian Commonwealth

Rangen stepped down from the cart as the monastery gates closed behind him. Waiting for him in front of the ancient stairway leading to the monastic hostelry was a stooped monk in his fifties with his hands clasped before him. The cart was driven off to the stables. The two men faced each other.

"I was told by the Highliber that Brother Nikalan would be meeting me," said Rangen.

"And Brother Nikalan has met you, if you are Fras Rangen Derris. Even if you are not Fras Rangen Derris, Brother Nikalan has still met you, but seeing that nobody else would have been told that Brother Nikalan is meeting him, then you must be Fras Rangen."

Rangen lifted his bag from the ground.

"Well, take me to your calculor."

"Uh-uh, we cannot waste the talents of one such as you in a calculor," replied Nikalan, waving a finger. "We must have a tour of the monastery. Leave your bag there, someone will collect it eventually. But first, why are you here? Why is not Highliber Dramoren using your talents?"

"Because of a woman," admitted Rangen sullenly.

"Only one?" asked Nikalan sympathetically.

"I was running an invisible paraline, smuggling numerate refugees away from the reach of Libris. She seduced me, charmed my secrets from me, then sold them to the Espionage Constables. She made over three hundred gold royals from the venture."

"They arrested you?"

"Worse. They intercepted my numerate fugitives by the hundreds. By the time I was caught the Libris Calculor was overflowing with components—people—who were desperate to kill me. Preferably slowly, and as painfully as possible. I was sent here to be out of harm's way."

"You will like it here, a mathematician of your talents. St. Roger's is dedicated to the pursuit of science."

"Good. I have been seriously contemplating holy orders and celibacy anyway, as a new lifestyle."

"You wish to become a monk? Even better. That is the chapel, where the Calculor is housed. The observatory is on that low hill off to the north, and that very strange framework to our left is a machine to predict the end of the world by the application of physics and mathematics to observed phenomena."

"The end of the world?"

"Well, perhaps not the world, but the end of conditions under which we could live."

"Is it something to do with the speeding up of Mirrorsun?"

"My young neophyte, it is everything to do with the speeding up of Mirrorsun."

Behind them, out of sight, two Balesha monks were watching. One of them had been driving Rangen's cart.

"Killed two," reported the carter monk.

"Gentheists?"

"Aye. Everything still on schedule?"

"Aye. Everyone is so grateful for our guard and security services in this endeavor."

"Isn't it nice to be appreciated?"

"That it is."

Lake Taupo, New Zealand

The wingfield at Lake Taupo was of a higher standard than those at Hawaii and Samoa, even though it had been prepared with less labor. Two thousand years earlier there had been a road running beside the lake, a wide, straight road on firm ground. Sometime in the mid-twenty-first century of the old calendar, there had been a volcanic eruption that had deposited a layer of ash over the road, and this had protected it from erosion by weather and vegetation. Although digging three feet of ash and pumice away from a strip several hundred yards long by ten wide had been depressingly hard and dirty work for Samondel, Alarak, and the first four navvies, at least there was little preparation work needed on the surface. Since Samondel had left, a lot more of the road had been exposed and crude shelters of poles and brush thatch were even being built.

The limiting factor was fuel. The new super-regal *Albatross* had enormous range, but it was the only wing of its kind yet in service. Oilseed, barley, and other compression spirit crops had been planted in the rich, volcanic soil but they were months from producing anything, even had processing equipment been on hand. By February the *Albatross* was making a trip every four days, however, and compression spirit barrels were piling up in the shelters. Serjon decided that it was time for the *Seaflower* to fly due west.

It had been three weeks since Samondel and her navigator had flown west in the *Swallow*, and it was no real surprise that they had not returned. They had achieved miracles by establishing wingfields on three islands, but none of these had been inhabited. The question of most concern to those on Lake Taupo was not the fact of the *Swallow* having gone down but where and in what circumstances. Serjon's flight plan was a lot more ambitious than Samondel's, yet it left a lot less to chance. As the light of early morning began to color the sky, lake, and wingfield, Serjon, Bronlar, the wingcaptain of *Albatross*, and the adjunct discussed procedures.

"First the *Albatross* ascends and circles, then the *Seaflower* ascends and both turn west-," said Serjon. "*Albatross* will then drop a tube line to the *Seaflower*, and top up the tanks."

"I cannot understand why the wing's tanks were built to take more compression spirit than it could get off the ground," said the wingcaptain.

"Normally it can, Sair Wingcaptain," replied Serjon, "but the *Seaflower* will also be carrying Semme Bronlar and provisions for two days. Even as little extra weight as that makes a difference.

"When the *Seaflower* is gone, the *Albatross* will return here. The *Seaflower* will proceed to the edge of the Australican continent, where it will overfly the southeast region at extreme height until the major cities are found. I will then parachute down to a suitable rendezvous point and Bronlar will return here. In fourteen days she will return to the rendezvous point, and if I signal with a mirror that it is safe she will descend. If not, she will survey the Australican farms for one with horses and we shall proceed with Project Tornado."

"It strikes me that we should have gone to Project Tornado in the first place, rather than risking the lives of an airlord and navigator first," said the wingcaptain.

"That was considered, but it was thought that diplomacy should be given a chance first," explained Serjon. "Besides, we would have the results of two overflights to plan from by then, which could make the difference between success and failure."

"Serjon has the basics of the Australican tongue, and a small pouch of old-civilization gold coins, crucifixes, and chains, such as might be dug up by chance in ruins," said Bronlar. "As you can see, he is dressed in leather trousers and tunic under his flight jacket, such as a wilderness trapper might wear. He will also attempt to learn Airlord Samondel's fate, and if it seems safe will try to establish diplomatic contacts. Otherwise, Project Tornado will proceed."

The *Albatross* was lightly loaded, and it ascended from the wingfield without difficulty. By contrast, the much smaller *Seaflower* needed the entire length of the strip to struggle into the air, and Serjon dropped his disposable wheels while less than a foot off the ground. Bronlar wound in the ski as they slowly rose into the brightening sky, then the *Seaflower* banked to take up a heading due west and rendezvous with the *Albatross*. The tube was already trailing for them as Serjon approached and matched speeds.

"*Seaflower* is already near its limit," Bronlar pointed out. "Two hundred pounds of extra compression spirit may be enough to drop us out of the sky."

"With the wheels gone and the ski wound in we have saved a little weight and drag. Prepare to open the nose hatch and grapple the tube."

Twenty minutes later the *Seaflower* detached the tube and the *Albatross* began to bank around for its return to Lake Taupo wingfield. They were still over land, and the ocean was not even in sight. Bronlar studied the chart, then took out a folder from her flight jacket.

"We need a fifteen-degree correction to the south when we reach the coast," she said.

At the west coast Serjon adjusted their course accordingly, then began to remove his leather tunic. It was very cramped in the *Seaflower*'s cockpit, and they had been over water for thirty minutes before Serjon was wearing his quilted shirt, embroidered flight jacket, rhea leather trousers, and down-lined parade boots.

"Bundle up that rubbish and dump it through the hatch," he said as he strapped in again. "Every ounce of weight saved is airtime that you might need."

"Even the gold?"

"Especially the gold. I have Yarronese money in my flight jacket."

With the disguise gone, Serjon checked the heading, airspeed, wind vector, and solar elevation, then did an audit on the compression spirit, engine temperature, oil pressure, and trim balance.

"Eleven hours in calm air, fourteen in the current headwind, with a five-hour margin. From what I have seen of the current weather patterns flowing over Lake Taupo, I would say you could return with a third of the compression spirit unused."

Bronlar patted his shoulder, then stretched out along the narrow access shaft through the center of the *Seaflower*. It was padded with cotton quilting and she had two blankets, but it was still hard, cold, and noisy. Once Serjon was gone there would be a long, lonely, and exhausting trip back to Lake Taupo, and possibly even a night descent. The only sleep she would be getting would be on the westward leg, so even though she was not at all drowsy she closed her eyes and tried to blank her mind.

Launceston, Tasmania Island

Serjon and Bronlar had been over land for thirty-five minutes when they saw fires burning fifteen thousand feet below. Through her binoculars Bronlar could see that they were in virgin wilderness, and were in a series of regular patterns.

"Fires for clearing farmland," she said above the sound of the engines. "And I can see cultivated fields to the north."

"There should be a small capital nearby," said Serjon, unbuckling his straps. "Time to hand over."

Changing places in the confines of the sailwing's tiny cockpit was not much easier than changing clothes, but they had practiced it before. By the time Bronlar was at the controls the haze of a small city was visible, as were the softened angular patterns of overgrown ruins belonging to a much earlier and larger city.

"That is our target, you can tell from the river," said Serjon.

"Any signs of Avianese gunwings?" asked Bronlar, reaching forward and arming the two reaction guns.

"This is not Bartolica. There has not been a clear air duel in these skies for two thousand years, and besides, only the Avianese have wings of any sort here. Because we are flying, we shall be assumed to be aviads. See those mountains to the west? Drop to about two thousand feet over them, then return to the capital and circle once."

"Have you chosen a rendezvous point?"

"Sketching it now."

As they came back over the capital, Serjon could see nothing as he crouched behind the flyer's seat. When Bronlar slid the hatch back he began to clamber in beside her.

"I'll always love you!" shouted Bronlar above the slipstream, reaching across to squeeze his arm.

Serjon took her gloved hand and kissed the leather. "No dramatics, if you please," he shouted back. "I'll be in less danger than you."

The sailwing rocked as he squeezed out of the hatch with his parachute. He turned, blew Bronlar a kiss, then jumped.

Bronlar slid the hatch shut, then banked around sharply. Serjon's parachute was open by the time she caught sight of him, and he was almost down. Too low, that was too low, she thought, yet jump too high and some idiot might decide to shoot at the lingering, tempting target. Serjon came down in a wide field, not far from some hand-carts with barrels. Figures were running over to him even before his parachute had collapsed. Bronlar circled, dropping lower. The figures surrounded Serjon, they appeared to be talking. There were no rapid movements that might indicate a struggle, no puffs of smoke from their primitive flintlocks.

The Seaflower circled, then circled again. Bronlar caught sight of a twinkling light as Serjon signalled with his mirror.

/ NATIVES FRIENDLY / HAVE SEED OIL / RETURN WITH ALBATROSS 3 WEEKS / LOVE YOU /

Suddenly exhilarated, Bronlar dipped her wings, then began to climb as she turned east. This was perfect, absolutely perfect, she thought, but nevertheless she kept scanning the airspace for Avianese gunwings. She had been over the Tasman Sea for five hours before she finally disarmed her reaction guns.

Euroa, the Rochestrian Commonwealth

By the 15th of February the material-testing venture at St. Roger's Monastery was already five days behind schedule, and very few of those who were directly involved had slept throughout the previous two days. The lead casket containing the ancient parachute was carried out on a litter borne by four monks and set down beside the strength-testing frame. Prayers were said as the seal was cut open, and a choir sang "Hail, Thou Glorious Light of Reason" as the parachute was lifted out. One end was quickly fastened to the crossbeam of the frame and the other to weight-box, then the jacks were removed from beneath the box. The fabric held the twenty tons of the box without any sign of strain.

Brother Varlian ordered the crane to swing the first stone into the box. The monks of the monitor team reported that no measurable stretch was visible on their gauge. Another ton was added. No strain was recordable. At the tenth ton a slight stretch was measurable, and a cheer went up as this was announced. The weight reached thirty tons, then forty, fifty, sixty, and seventy.

"At this strength a burst will return the band to Earth in a highly elliptical orbit," said Nikalan to Rangen.

"Which gives us Armageddon within a year," replied Rangen.

"Oh, yes, even before Christmas."

The weight crept up further, and the audience and workers watched the tally weight on a large chalkboard. Another chalkboard displayed the critical strengths, and another cheer went up as eighty tons was passed.

"It will escape Earth." Rangen sighed with heartfelt relief.

"But orbit the sun on an intersecting path," Nikalan pointed out. "Someday it will be back."

"You sound like you enjoy the prospect."

"It may not happen for decades, by which time I shall be dead."

"And it might happen sooner."

"Oh, then it will be a very exciting way to die."

"Spoken like a man with most of his life behind him," retorted Rangen.

At 206 tons the fabric burst apart. There was a sharp blast and flash of light as the material gave way, then a thunderclap of sound as over two hundred tons of box and weights hit the ground after a fall of three feet. A collective gasp went up from the crowd and workers, and Varlian climbed out onto the frame and reported that the fabric was too hot to touch at the break point. Nikalan and Ran-

gen hurriedly conferred, working quickly on an abacus and chalkboard. As they stood up to speak with the abbot, Nikalan was still
obviously thinking about something, but Rangen was smiling
broadly.

"The Mirrorsun band should burst with enough speed to orbit it
about the sun like a long-term comet," Abbot Ashman announced.
"Depending on the point of breakage, the orbit will be no less than
three hundred years."

The cheers from those gathered around the frame quickly spread
across the monastery grounds to those in the Calculor, the kitchens,
the workshops, and the fields. The monastery beamflash tower was
already relaying the news to Echuca, from where it sparkled into the
eyepiece of the Rushworth tower, before being retransmitted to
Rochester.

Rochester, the Rochestrian Commonwealth

Dramoren and Lengina were waiting together in the Highliber's
office. A metal rabbit in the Calculor's display rack rang a bell, and
Dramoren bounded to his feet. Rushing over to the paper-tape mechanism, he watched the mechanical hens begin to peck out the words
/MIRRORSUN BURST 300 YEAR SOLAR ORBIT / in a tape, then
freeze again.

"Three hundred years!" he shouted, tearing the tape from the
ornate machine and waving it in the air. "No Armageddon for three
centuries, maybe not even for thousands of years, perhaps even
never."

To his surprise Lengina showed no more elation than a weak
smile.

"Good news for the world, and better news for Jemli the
Prophet," she said.

"What do you mean? She did not predict this."

"She has predicted that Mirrorsun will be cast into the darkness, and that the earth will be safe. This is precisely what will happen. We have spent two million royals proving her right, and giving her massive credibility with her followers among my citizens."

Dramoren dropped into the chair before the Calculor's console rack and held up the paper tape containing the good news.

"So, shall we tell people that the world has been saved for Jemli the Prophet?" he asked.

"When will the burst take place?"

"Just a moment."

Dramoren typed in several command strings, and after a minute the mechanical hens began pecking again. He heaved himself out of the chair and walked over to the paper-tape machine.

"If the bulk of Mirrorsun's band material is identical to the parachute material, and of similar thickness, then within two years."

"Then make an announcement as follows," said Lengina, who now sat pressing her finders against her eyelids. " / MIRRORSUN BURST WITHIN TWO YEARS / ARMAGEDDON NOT IN OUR LIFETIMES/ "

"As true as can be managed, but without admitting that Jemli was right," said Dramoren.

"It is the job of leaders to turn fact into politics," responded Lengina.

"Still, she has won."

"Indeed. Perhaps the Deity really does speak through her."

"What a repulsive prospect."

Euroa, the Rochestrian Commonwealth

Back at Euroa, Nikalan and Rangen were clambering over the rubble beneath the frame when they noticed that the crowd of onlookers was parting. A tanned, barefoot man wearing only a burlap kilt was approaching, bowing and smiling to all as he passed. His hair and beard were very long, but both were neatly bound up with leather lacing. In general he seemed to be considerably cleaner than the average hermit.

"Brother Nikalan, congratulations," he said genially, "I heard your apparatus discover Mirrorsun's measure."

"Liaisary Ilyire, what are you doing so far inland?" asked Nikalan.

"I have been communicating with the cetezoid creatures of the oceans too long, old friend, and what is a liaisary who does not liaise? It is time that I spoke to humans."

The abbot considered ushering the two men away to the privacy of his office, then decided that what Ilyire had to say might be intended for as many ears as possible.

"And how is your sister, the Abbess Theresla?" asked Nikalan.

"Dead, I am sad to say. The cetezoids brought her body home from the coast of North America three months ago, but by then she was two months dead and in less than wholesome condition. Still, I welcomed what was left and buried her with all proper observances. What news of Armageddon?"

"Not in our lifetimes, but it is more complex than merely that. What news of the Call?"

"The cetezoids have obviously ceased its generation, but it is more complicated than that."

"Then the Call was not stopped by God?"

"It was stopped by conscience and shame among the cetezoids. Whether the Deity was thus involved is a matter for debate, but there was no direct intervention."

Rochester, the Rochestrian Commonwealth

The mechanical hens began pecking at the paper tape again just as Dramoren and Lengina were raising their sixth tumbler of macadamia mash brandy in a toast to their adversary's victory.

"Vorion!" shouted Dramoren, and the lackey opened the door moments later.

"Highliber?" asked Vorion, taking in the empty brandy jar, the Overmayor lying back in a reading chair, the Highliber draped over the console, the strip of paper tape on the coffee table, and the second strip still in the hole-punch machine.

"Fetch that message, I am unsatable," said Dramoren.

"He means unstable," added Lengina.

Vorion ripped off the tape and presented it to the Highliber, who regarded it for some moments.

"Better read it too."

Vorion scanned the pattern in the holes, his eyes widening. He passed it to Lengina. Lengina's crystal tumbler fell from her fingers to bounce on the thick carpet as she read the message.

/ ILYIRE APPEARED AT EUROA / REPORTS THERESLA DIED AFTER CONVINCING CETEZOIDS TO END THE CALL / ILYIRE TO PREACH TRUTH ABOUT CALL ENDING AND TOLERANCE OF ALL INTELLIGENT CREATURES /

"There is a God," mumbled Dramoren.

"Extend Ilyire my mayoral welcome, patronage, and invitation to preach wherever in the Commonwealth he feels inclined," declared Lengina, slowly, with considerable care and concentration.

I have been propositioned by three girls from your damnable martial arts guild in the past fifteen days," Martyne began as he faced Velesti across her desk in the Libris administration wing. "Would you like to explain why?"

"You have very nice pectoral and abdominal development, although your deltoids could do with some improved definition and   "

"Velesti, stop it! You are trying to set me up. Again."

"Me?"

"Yes, you! A week ago Cherlienne visited me in my office and poured out a long and depressing tale about being a skinny little girl who nobody took seriously and men shunned. When I tried to tell her that she was beautifully exotic, she was all over me, and right behind my own desk. As for Sembelia—"

"Yes, I heard."

"If ever again any of your students come to me with fears that they might be lesbians, I shall send them straight back to you!"

"I am not that sort of girl. That was rather clever, what you did for Rositana."

"She is a bright girl, she deserved to compete on level ground."

"Your trick to stay out of her bed ca sed the entire examination of Libris to be restructured. You are a man of influence."

"Thank you. Now stop setting me up?"

"Only when you stop acting like a monk."

"I *am* a monk."

"Martyne, when you go on those 'tours,' I now know perfectly well what happens. You come under fire, and you have been wounded once. Five of those around you have been killed."

"It is my work, my duty."

"Martyne, you are still a monk, within yourself at least. You eat plain food, drink light ale, sleep in a bare, undecorated room, and are so frightened of emotions that—"

"I could say the same of you."

"Yes, but I am mad and you are not."

"Velesti, I am at least as mad as you. I am merely less flamboyant about it."

"Those girls are in awe of you, Martyne, they are curious about you. Why not you, rather than some dead-wit student with a small brain, rich parents, and a large purse? They are at an amourously inquisitive age, Martyne, and so are you."

"*You* are living *your* amourous life through *my* body. Stop it."

"Do you prefer celibacy?"

"Of course not, but celibacy has a place in my violent and dangerous circumstances. I need to be cold and focused, I need to be ready to attack and possibly die rather than hold back because someone loves me."

"The musketeers who rode me were cold and focused, for all their lust. Do you aspire to be like them?"

"No!"

"Then tell me how you are different."

"I fight the enemy. Nobody else."

"The enemy, you say. Well, then, let me turn an enemy over to you, one who I discovered last January and have been shadowing ever since. The second member of the flying machine's crew, a flyer of fighting air machines from North America."

Martyne was suddenly a concealed cat watching a careless bird, eyes gleaming, perfectly still, muscles tense and heart racing.

"Their gunwings use fourteen millimeter reaction guns that fire hundreds of shots per minute, centuries ahead of our flintlocks. They spanned the largest ocean in the world with flying machines; the cost of the venture would have almost bankrupted the Rochestrian Commonwealth."

"Give me a name, I shall have him dead or detained within the hour," replied Martyne.

"*Her* name is Samondel Leover."

Shock flickered over Martyne's face like distant lightning, but passed to leave his composure intact. He rose to his feet.

"Is this some very sick joke, from the dregs of your very sick mind?"

"She is a deadly warrior, and she carries a reaction pistol that can fire hundreds of times more rapidly than the best Morelac. It is the slight bulge near the waist of the promenade coat that she always wears. Here is a reaction pistol bullet; I took several when I broke into her room in Villiers College."

Martyne examined the bullet. It was as precisely wrought as if some Rochestrian jeweler had made it as a pendant. Velesti held up a very strange contraption that was barely recognizable as a gun. A flintlock striker was positioned so as to strike with a blunt pin at the end of an open barrel. Taking the bullet back from Martyne, Velesti inserted it into the breech of the barrel, locked it down, cocked back the striker, and aimed through the open window at a nearby headless weathercock. There was a sharp, loud crack, like a swagger stick hitting the top of a desk, but no smoke or flash. A neat hole appeared in the weathercock's body.

"Very, very advanced," said Velesti. "The winsome and beautiful young Samondel is yours, Martyne, take her. I said I'd owe you a favor for being allowed to crunch those shadowboys at the demonstration."

Martyne could feel himself hardening from within. The enemy was within view. The enemy was to be dropped with a clear, clean shot. No torture, no gloating, no rape, no looting, no boasting, just a clean capture or kill. Samondel had become a thing.

"What has she been doing? I need to make a report."

"She is studying us. Our religions, politics, customs, laws, jokes, food, and machines. She is trying to understand Rochestrian society, especially the Dragon Librarian Service. Thankless task."

"Spying."

"She approached us openly, Martyne, but we shot her down and forced her into hiding."

"Are you trying to apologize for her, Frelle?"

"That would be treason, Fras."

"Well, then, I shall have *her* dead or detained within the day."

Samondel was not in her room at Villiers College when Martyne knocked at the door. Going to Corien's room, Martyne found her in. She did not know where Samondel might be, but she said that her friend was due any minute, and invited him in to wait. After a half hour it became apparent that Corien was rather strongly interested in experiencing Martyne's muscular development while gazing up at the ceiling, and that Samondel was probably not due to call at all.

Martyne set out across the university lawns for the faculty buildings. It was a blazing hot February day, and being a curriculum holiday the university was closed down. Martyne went to the applied theology annex and made for his study to add some coded notes to his private files of people that he was monitoring. It was only now that he heard a thin, muffled scream. He walked in the direction. There were more screams, and pleas to be let go. They were coming from behind a fellow edutor's door. Saresen's.

Martyne shouldered the door open without either knocking or drawing his pistol. Saresen had Samondel beneath him on his couch with her arms pinned. Papers were scattered across the floor, and

Samondel's skirts had ridden up around her thighs. In a panic, Saresen rolled off at once, drew a knife, and lunged for Martyne. Matyne blocked the knife cross-handed, wrenched his arm around and up, kneed Saresen in the face, then bent his wrist until he dropped the knife with a shriek of pain. He pushed the edutor away from him, and Saresen crashed into his own desk and fell heavily. Samondel was now on her feet and had snatched her jacket from a peg. One breast was showing through a tear in her clothing, Martyne noted with involuntary interest.

"Martyne! Gun!" she shrieked as she tried to pull out something that was tangled in the inner pocket of her coat.

Martyne whirled and flung a wheelstar, pinning Saresen's hand to his flintlock. The gun discharged and Saresen fell to his knees, howling with pain. Samondel hurriedly put her coat on and began to button it.

"Did he violate you, Frelle?" asked Martyne, putting an arm around Samondel.

"Dignity only," she replied, "but had intent."

"Then I'll not kill him. Gather up your books and papers, then come with me. You now have a new edutor in Applied Theology."

Leaving Saresen to tend to his own wounds, they left the annex. Samondel kept her coat buttoned to her neck all the way to Villiers College, where they reported the incident to the Rector.

"Are you sure you did not, ah, encourage Fras Saresen?" he asked.

"Never!" she spat.

"Misconduct charges cannot be pressed in this university unless there is a witness. Girls do try to blackmail edutors, you know."

"I was a witness," Martyne pointed out. "Besides, he attacked me, too."

"But you broke into his office. He will claim he was defending this young lady from you."

"Why would I know she was in there if she was not crying for help?"

"Why, you, er, might . . . you might have a case," the Rector conceded reluctantly.

Samondel went to her room, still escorted by Martyne.

"He not caring!" she fumed.

"The academic community defends its own," he explained. "There are unwritten rules for students to learn, like girls must always go in pairs to visit an edutor. You should change, then see Corien. The Rector is a relative of hers, she will make sure that he takes action on your behalf. Besides, talking helps sponge the poison of such unpleasantness from the heart."

"No! Staying, Martyne. Must talk."

He stood with his back turned while she undressed and changed into clean and undamaged clothes. She was washing her face when Martyne noticed that her promenade coat was now hanging on a peg. She had dressed in drawstring trousers under a green leafprint tunic, and after drying her face she reached into her bag and drew out a sheaf of poorpaper on which she had neatly written her first essay in Austaric: *Engine Prohibition Theology Prophets of the Late Greatwinter Period.*

"Am not skilled in Austaric," she began as she held the essay out.

Martyne scanned it, noting that while she was indeed not fluent in Austaric, she had addressed the topic in a logical, well-researched way.

"I would pass this," he concluded. "I would even pass it without trying to rip your clothes off. Do you wish to transfer to my supervision?"

"You are needing to ask, even?" she replied.

Quite casually, Martyne stood up and reached for her coat.

"No!" Samondel gasped as she stood up, but she dared not approach him.

Martyne removed the reaction pistol, turning the unfamiliar but very advanced weapon over as Samondel stood wringing her hands.

"What do you have to say for yourself?" asked Martyne.

Samondel could not even hope to explain, even were her Austaric as good as Martyne's. The gun was just like the bullet that Velesti had shown to him. Polished, functional and very finely made. Martyne stared at her intently . . . but there was something about her face that disarmed him, a cornered and hopeless expression. Back in his office, on the wall, was a char stylus sketch of his sister Elsile, done only a fortnight before her death. Drawn by Velesti, as she used to be. The face was proud and full of enthusiasm, not desperate and hopeless as it had certainly been in her last hours alive. Martyne blinked and shook his head. Huge, violet eyes regarded him steadily, and hair as red as late sunset cascaded down over one shoulder.

He placed the angular, unfamiliar weapon on her little writing desk.

"Frelle, please throw this stupid toy away and get a proper gun," said Martyne, now looking at her with an earnest, helpful expression.

"Toy?" echoed Samondel, glancing doubtfully down at her reaction pistol and its clip of ammunition.

"I have seen combat, Frelle. Serious combat. I am only alive today because I have learned to react quickly to concealed threats— like a gun's outline in a coat."

"Ah," said Samondel. "Very sorry."

"Misunderstandings happen so easily. Carry a real gun, if you are going to carry one at all." He scribbled out a note and handed it to her. "Here, show this to Frelle Larchfeld in the University's administration. I am your edutor in Applied Theology now. You may have a high pass for your essay. In your native language it might have been honors, but the subject must be conducted in Austaric."

"Ah. Thanking you."

Martyne returned to his office and sat behind his desk, his face in his hands, propped up on his elbows. He forced himself to breathe evenly. Eventually his cramped muscles began to relax. A bell tolled the hour in some distant clocktower. Five clangs. No appointments. Just as well. Martyne's mind held a pleasant blank. He thought of moving to a meditative state, but it seemed like too much effort. Various feet strode up and down the corridor. Someone laughed. The relief of thinking about nothing was almost as pleasant as surrendering to his first seduction by Marelle. A confident, brisk pair of feet sounded on the bare floorboards of the Faculty of Theology's edutor annex. Feet with an almost military bearing. Someone knocked.

Martyne did not reply, he did not even move a muscle. Another knock. Silence. Martyne remained sitting with his hands over his eyes. The latch of the door clacked, the door creaked open. He had neglected to slide the bolt over. *A good way to get killed,* thought Martyne. *I should be so lucky.*

"As the ancients used to express it so very eloquently, Frelle Velesti, fuck off!" said Martyne between his hands.

"Am not Velesti."

Martyne looked up, blinking in the bright sunlight streaming over the modesty curtain. Samondel was not wearing a promenade coat, nor did she have the reaction pistol.

"Was there a problem with Frelle Larchfeld?" asked Martyne.

"No."

"Then why are you here?"

"Ah, advice, flintlock, purchasing, required."

Samondel closed the door and sat on the edge of his desk, hunched over with her hands clasped.

"Having no friends, knowing weapons, here. Isolated."

"Know the feeling."

"You. None friends, real friends, except Velesti."

"True."

"But Velesti, being, ah, something of strain."

"Frelle Samondel, just how do you put so much meaning, perception, and wisdom into so very few misarranged and misused words?"

Samondel frowned, for a moment, then brightened. "Compliment? Yes?"

"Yes."

"Lady on wall. Is dear to you?"

"My sister. Her ghost haunts this room, and she is very cross with me. I was not with her . . . so she died."

Samondel put her hands on Martyne's shoulders, shaking him gently.

"Martyne, looking at me. Looking up. Not long ago, facing defilement. Saved. Now what? Next time, you are not there, for me, perhaps. Better buy real gun, for wearing, nice redwood handle, matching hair. Yes?"

"Yes, but you had better learn to fight without guns as well. Take some instruction from Velesti and me. Promise?"

"Ah . . . yes!"

Crashing in Australica had seemed to Samondel no less final than crashing in the ocean: one simply did not expect to survive. Now she was sitting in a tavern whose cuisine was even better than what one might find in a palace at home, in an exotic sort of way. Rochester even reminded her of Condelor. She might well be a student girl being shown the sights of Rochester by a quite gallant and handsome chaperon . . . but in a real sense, all of that was true! An oddly acute wash of pleasure passed through Samondel, in spite of the danger and distance between her and home, and she smiled at the strange but charming edutor sitting across the table from her.

Samondel and Martyne left the tavern and wandered the nearby market. Determining prices, change, and rates of currency exchange was particularly entertaining. Rochester was trying very hard to be normal, in spite of the extraordinary circumstances that currently assailed it. In public, everyone assiduously denied any knowledge of arithmetic at all, because gangs of shadowboys lurked at markets, taverns, and even the paraline terminus in search of anyone numerate enough to get into an argument about being short-changed—whether vendor or customer. Strangest for Samondel, was being in summer during February, while half a world away her friends and subjects were enduring winter.

A squad of lancers rode past, colors flying from their lances and their helmets polished. The horses were so huge and strong that Samondel cringed away by reflex, yet they were so docile as well. Mighty beasts that loved humans and worked hard for no more than fodder, yes, they were definitely worth coming seven thousand miles to buy. Even stranger was the lack of class distinction that was so evident on the American continents. There was a local nobility, but the Dragon Librarian Service added an avenue to power and influence for those with intelligence and education, regardless of social background.

"About yourself, no hearing?" Samondel asked, noticing that Martyne had been saying little for some time. "Clergy, yes?"

"Former clergy, a monk, actually. I left my order to avenge my sister's murder."

"Oh. Tragedy. Doing it, as yet?"

"Someone else beat me to it. Mostly. A bit annoying, really. I give up everything for honor and revenge, then I arrive and it's already done. I really felt quite a fool. Now I teach theology in the university, and teach girls to fight back when cornered."

"And are betrothed?"

"You might say that," Martyne replied unhappily.

"Not love?"

"Duty."

Samondel was amazed at how many of the pistols for sale had been supposedly salvaged from the wreck of the "air machine" that had crashed in the city earlier the month before. Martyne stopped at a stall that seemed little different from all the others and spoke a few words of some quite unintelligible language to the owner. The vendor presented Samondel with an attractive double-barrel flintlock, which had one barrel mounted above the other. The stock was of beautifully carved and oiled red rivergum.

"Always best to have two barrels," said Martyne. "Shoot to maim with the first barrel, then everyone else knows that you are not afraid to fire the second."

"Two shootings, only?"

"Yes, I'm afraid so."

"Wear always?"

"Ever since the Women's Assertion League grew out of the Dragon Librarian Service, all young professional girls and female students have been encouraged to carry a flintlock."

Samondel examined the weapon.

"Loading?" she asked presently.

"Loading is tedious. You pour gunpowder into the barrel, ram a lead ball down with poorpaper wadding, pour a little more powder into this flash pan, then twist the sparker down to hold it in place.

When you want to shoot, twist the striker with the flint back and pull the trigger. Sparks from the striker ignite what is in the flash pan, which ignites what is in the barrel through a little hole. This shoots the lead ball out of the barrel."

For a moment Samondel was lost for words.

"Is much bothering."

"I admit there is probably scope for improvement, but it is better than throwing rocks. Do you like it?"

"Yes. Magnificent. Is priced?"

Martyne turned to the vendor, they exchanged a few words, shook hands, bowed, huddled over the stall, then exchanged a few more words. They clapped their right hands together, then their left hands. The vendor's wife came out from behind the stall. The vendor kissed her on the cheek, and she passed the kiss on to Martyne. There was yet more talk and waving of hands. The vendor burst out crying, wailed something incomprehensible, then dripped tears onto the stock of the gun and rubbed the tears into the wood with a cloth. Four tiny ceramic thimbles were produced, and something exceedingly sharp scented was poured out from a small jar. They tossed back a liquid that left Samondel coughing for nearly a minute. Martyne embraced the vendor's wife, the vendor's wife embraced the vendor. Martyne and the vendor strode away into the crowd, leaving Samondel with the vendor's wife. She discovered that the vendor's wife did not speak Austaric, and certainly did not speak Old Anglian or Bartolican. Martyne returned. He now had a belt of scarlet leather whose buckle was cast ironblack in the shape of interlocking wings. Samondel complimented Martyne on his good taste and buckled on the belt. The vendor's wife arranged the twin barrel pistol in the left side of her belt with the stock facing right. There was another round of bowing and incomprehensible talk, then Samondel and Martyne walked away.

"Buy for me? This?" she asked.

"Just a moment, Frelle," responded Martyne.

There was a great shouting and commotion behind them, and the vendor from the gun stall came running after them with the utility case for the pistol. They bowed, the vendor knelt and placed it on the ground, Martyne knelt and picked the case up. They clapped the right hands together and bowed, then Martyne and Samondel continued walking.

"The sale has been concluded, do not ask me to even attempt to explain what just went on."

"Paying, you have?"

"I am owed a favor by the vendor, so he has been trying to give me one of his wretched guns for months. I will show you how to use it tomorrow at the public firing chambers."

"Most real thanks, Fras Martyne."

Dinner was shredded roast lamb and pine nuts rolled in layers of flatbread and lettuce, and eaten as they walked. By the time they reached the doors of Villers College the air was cooler.

"Waiting, be back," said Samondel.

She hurried inside. Presently she emerged with the reaction pistol and a brown drawstring bag.

"Toy is yours. Fun, yes? Put on wall."

Martyne forced himself to laugh as he accepted her gift.

"Gracious Frelle, I am honored."

Martyne bowed, but Samondel did not respond with the subtle curtsy customary among well-bred women of his homeland. Feeling foolish, he turned and walked away into the night without another word. For a moment Samondel stared after him, a hand on her hip, the brown bag hanging from her other hand, affronted that he had left without a farewell. Perhaps it was something to do with being a monk, she decided, some religious protocol. After tossing the bag of bullets into the rubbish cart behind the refectory kitchen, she returned to her room.

Martyne unlocked his door to find Velesti sitting cross-legged on his bed with Samondel's brown bag. She was counting out the bullets.

"A cunning ploy to say that you have been in my bed, Frelle Cat Burglar?" asked Martyne.

"I just happened to be foraging for fisheads in the university's garbage wagon when this landed on me."

"Can you walk through walls, or is there something wrong with my new and very expensive lock?"

"I told the landlord to let me in. He did."

She bared her teeth.

"Can I get you anything? A saucer of milk? A nice fat mouse?"

"Meow. Look on your table."

On it was a somewhat more streamlined version of the single-shot pistol that Velesti had demonstrated to him that morning.

"What is this for?" asked Martyne, picking it up and checking the mechanism.

"For not arresting Samondel."

"I changed my mind. I am going to keep her under surveillance."

"Even that is worth a reward."

"Thank you, I am touched. Really."

"My new, lever-action pistol can be reloaded fifteen times faster than a flintlock. There are only two in existence, and until I learn to make bullets I would advise you to use these American imports sparingly. You can have half, and the spare ammunition clips. Where did she dispose of the reaction pistol?"

"You are asking *me*?"

"Are you not Martyne Camderine, master spy?"

"Hah! Even when some girl propositions me you seem to know before I do."

"Point taken. I'm surprised that she kept the gun as long as she has. It marks the owner as being someone exceptional. This is not wise, when one is trying to be inconspicuous."

Velesti got off the bed, then scooped up her share of the bullets and dropped them into her jacket pocket.

"I knew you would come back here alone."

"What do you mean?"

"Any other lad would have taken Samondel out for a few drinks, invited her back, and rolled her. *You* merely bought her a gun and a walkalong dinner, then escorted her back to Villiers."

"What would you suggest?" asked Martyne, pressing a bullet into his prototype lever-action gun.

"What about looking into her eyes and telling her they are like clear, violet sapphires that reach into you and draw the heart and soul out of your body?"

"She would think I was trying to get her into bed!"

"You should be."

"No!"

"Call yourself a man?"

"I call myself a gentleman!"

"Well, even as a gentleman you need to speak to women as a gallant valiant. You must suggest great strength, even though you win their admiration with charm alone."

"How would you know?"

"What are these?" asked Velesti, hefting her breasts.

"*You* are not typical."

"Practice on me. Look into my eyes and tell me that you see the soft, delicate glow of a sunrise in early spring."

Martyne peered at Velesti's eyes.

"Velesti, as I look deep into your eyes . . . I see the dangerous glint of a violent and unstable psychopath."

"Oh, really?" she responded, batting her eyelashes and giving him a coy push. "You're not just saying that, are you?"

"Velesti, just how much did you bet with your scabby students of Baleshanto that you could get me into bed with Samondel?"

"Thirty silver—" began Velesti before clapping her hand over her mouth.

"Why is that amount so significant?" sighed Martyne.

"What is wrong with sex?"

"Nothing, but just now I feel like some sort of sex slave."

"I'll see what I can buy for you."

"Stop it! Follow your advice and I would end up looking like a fool."

"You are a fool already, Martyne. Whether you look like one or not is up to you."

•   •   •

Samondel did not go Corien's room to tell the day's story, but went straight to bed and lay thinking of Martyne for many hours. A great number of men had paid her attention in the five weeks since she had crashed in Rochester, but unlike the others Martyne did not swagger and posture, and had no sense of self-importance. It was almost as if he were trying to cover up much of what he was. Over and over she played through the scene of Saresen kneeling in agony on the floor, his gun pinned to his hand and Martyne standing with one arm protectively around her shoulders. True, his heart was not free to give, but it was no crime to dream.

The following day she met Corien in the refectory during breakfast. The girl was always surrounded by friends, but Samondel soon took her aside and arranged a rendezvous beneath one of the ancient eucalyptus trees on the lawns.

"Saresen had suggested, tuition of privacy," Samondel explained as they lay in the early morning heat. "My Austaric, lacking quality, having special needs."

"All of that is true," said Corien.

"Meeting in his room, sat together, discussing my writings. He was friendly, joking, patting hand, patting knee. Were discussing regeneration vectors for power for things, I asked, what is example of regeneration vector. He said, for humans, I show. He showed. Am shocked. Slap face. He seizes me, rolls on me, pins arms. I scream, he says nobody to hear. Regeneration lesson, he says. Make baby human. Pulls me along, dress rides up."

"Sounds like he's had practice, poor Frelle."

"Was helpless, but screamed, screamed. Suddenly door smashed open, Martyne there. Fought Saresen."

"It must have been a one-sided fight," said Corien.

"True. Few seconds, all over."

"Perhaps Velesti was right. Sometimes we can't rely on chaperons, lovers, or even weapons to be with us when we need them. Strange, Saresen never tried such advances with Velesti or me."

"Important relatives, are having. Also I am looking vulnerable, perhaps."

"Yes Frelle, you do have a timid bearing about you. We should definitely get you a lover."

"Not needed, have Martyne."

"What? But he's betrothed already!"

"Have Martyne, as Baleshanto instructor. Only."

"Oh. Of course. Silly of me. Well, my dear Frelle, I think we should see my uncle and the Academician General of the Faculty this afternoon to press the complaint. Edutors like Saresen cannot be allowed to go unpunished. We can get the League behind us."

As it happened, Saresen was found dead in the university's ornamental lake the following morning. A statement from the Espionage Constables quickly cleared Martyne of any involvement.

Siding Springs, the Central Confederation

Overmayor Lengina declared a fortnight of public revelry and feasting to celebrate the news of both Mirrorsun's threat passing, and of Ilyire's revelation that the cetezoid elders had decided to end the Call as long as humans never again returned to the sea or killed whales. After two thousand years without contact with the sea, it was hardly a factor in human society or economics. The Avianese had flight technology, so apart from accidents they had no reason to come in contact with the sea either.

Farther west, Jemli considered the news about Mirrorsun as merely confirming her teachings, while condemning Ilyire's pronouncement on the end of the Call as heresy by a fellow Gentheist. Overmayor Lengina immediately declared that Ilyire had the unconditional support of the Commonwealth to preach what he wished, and ordered that he be protected from violence wherever he went. This generated outrage among the local Reformed Gentheists, which in turn produced tension between the Rochestrian Commonwealth and the Woomeran Confederation. At last Lengina's fondest political wish was coming true: international relations were deteriorating, but she was holding the moral high ground.

To the north, science stepped in to confuse everyone's political and religious agendas. Using the largest of the telescopes at the Siding Springs Monastery, Brother Torumasen had been studying the inner surface of Mirrorsun. This was generally featureless, except at the reflection point, but it was known to have very occasional meteor strikes. These appeared as tiny flashes that faded after a second or so, just long enough for the velocity of the band to be measured. Over the months of his study, he had been able to observe five strikes, and they provided him with a confirmation of Mirrorsun's increasing speed. They also revealed something totally unexpected.

"There is an inner band, about a quarter of Mirrorsun's width," he announced as he stood before the abbot's desk. "It is rotating at just sufficient speed to maintain itself in orbit."

"There are *two* bands?" gasped the abbot, rising to his feet.

"Yes. I checked the actual Mirrorsun reflection itself, the reflection of the sun on the inner surface of the band. Once I knew what to look for I found it quickly: a slight, sharp line through the reflection pattern. Parallax estimates with Euroa put the bands about ten miles apart."

"This . . . is . . ." Words failed the abbot. He sat down again. "What does it mean?" he finally asked.

"I cannot say, Reverend Abbot, I am an observer, not a theoretician."

"Just as long as you are not a prophet. Bring a chair over, sit down. You must help me to compose a very creatively worded announcement."

Rochester, the Rochestrain Commonwealth

In all of her life, Samondel had never been so very close to such an enormous animal as a horse. The stables were on the edge of Lake Rochester, and a selection of docile, placid mounts were available for riding lessons. Martyne hired two horses for the afternoon, then took Samondel firmly by the hand and led her to the stalls. He had selected two geldings and had them saddled.

"Why are so big?" she asked, trying to keep Martyne between her and the two mountains of flesh and muscle that he was leading.

"They eat lots of grass."

"Am frightened."

"That will pass once you are riding one."

"Ride? Too frightened."

"They expect to be ridden. It's their job. How else can they earn their grass, hay, and oats?"

Samondel was unsure whether or not he was being sarcastic.

"Which mine?"

"The brown one. Take this apple, introduce yourself."

Samondel stood before the horse with the apple in her hand.

"Ah, compliments of noonday, I am Samondel Leover and I—"

She shrieked. The horse had neatly removed the apple from her hand and begun munching it.

"Took apple!" wailed Samondel, hiding behind Martyne again.

"It thought you were offering it."

"Never said thank you."

"Horses can't talk."

"No? Then—Martyne! He looked at me!"

So this is the deadly warrior airlord from North America, thought Martyne. He would be having some very sarcastic things to say to Velesti after Friday's Baleshanto training.

Persuading Samondel to get into the saddle took a rather considerable time, even though the horse was tethered and munching on a pile of hay. Martyne was not entirely sure how she managed to get on backward the first time, but after another ten minutes she was in the saddle and facing forward. He led her mount around the dressage track.

"Martyne! Too fast, am frightened."

"I'm only walking."

"And too high! Might fall, want smaller horse."

He would never, *never* let Velesti hear the end of this, he swore to himself. At the end of another hour Samondel's bottom was aching as she hobbled out to a limewater vendor by the front gate. They had still not left the yards, and Martyne had done no more with his own horse than pat its neck.

"Daft bird ye got there, Fras," said a stableboy, who had been observing proceedings from time to time.

"You think this is news to me?" replied Martyne.

At the end of the third hour Samondel was riding the horse around the dressage track by herself and could persuade it to start walking, but not to stop. When it did stop—to eat an apple that Martyne had dropped—Samondel tumbled right down its neck and to the ground, then was dragged three feet by the stirrup as the horse sauntered over to a second apple. To Martyne's surprise, she got straight back into the saddle. By the end of the fourth hour Martyne was riding beside her along the lakeside esplanade, and she was generally guiding the horse herself.

Only after six hours did Samondel give up and limp back over the long bridge to Inner Rochester, her hands and knees bloody, her clothes filthy with dust, and smelling little different from any stable hand.

"When returning tomorrow, no damn nonsense from any horse!" decreed the Airlord of Highland Bartolica.

"Samondel, I have to work tomorrow," said Martyne.

"No matter, know procedures now. Shall practice. Solo."

Suddenly it was the warrior of the skies speaking, after a very bad day testing a particularly awkward new prototype. In six hours she had gone from hiding behind Martyne and screaming to seriously considering the idea of riding alone.

"On Saturday we can ride to Bektyne Forest—" he began.

"Ah! Yes, and musket to hire, shoot from saddle. Must learn."

Samondel bought them rice pies at the Gaudeamus Tavern, although she was nearly ejected for violating the establishment's minimal dress and hygiene standards. For courage, determination, and raw dedication she could have given any Balesha abbot serious competition, thought Martyne. He also noticed that his mouth was dry, his hands were trembling, and that the prospect of leaving her at the Villiers College door was filling him with genuine anguish.

"Shall not be beaten!" declared Samondel, snarling down at her tankard. "Is *war*. Objective: learn to canter."

Martyne looked around the room. Samondel was at the focus of a least a dozen admiring stares. *The most beautiful woman on Earth has just bought me dinner*, he thought.

"What is horse command, Do not shyte?" asked Samondel, who had experienced a particularly unpleasant incident involving that function late in the afternoon.

"There is none."

"Ach, bad design."

After seeing Samondel to Villiers College, Martyne started out for his own room. He was surprised, but not unduly surprised, when Velesti fell in beside him. Mothers scooped children out of her path. The occasional shadowboy turned and fled.

"How is Rochester's newest lancer progressing?" she asked.

"Amazingly well, she has the dedication of a roomful of chief librarians, the willpower of a Balesha exam candidate, and the drive of a galley engine. Six hours, torn clothes, bloody knees, yet not a complaint—and she's going back by herself tomorrow."

"Tomorrow? Look at that sunset, she might be riding in rain."

"Yes, yes, and have you noticed the way her hair glows red, just like that sky?"

"Speaking of tomorrow, how is the register analysis going on the smuggling syndicate case?"

"I'll do it tonight, have it at Libris by the tenth hour."

"No hurry, my people don't need it until the afternoon market checks."

"No, I'll do it tonight. I was thinking of helping Samondel with her riding again."

"Martyne, you are in love."

"I—what?"

"Not a pretty sight. Enough to make strong men vomit and women run screaming."

"You have done neither."

"I'm trying not to look."

Six weeks of particularly intensive language classes had given Alarak a working command of the Austaric language, but neither the navigator nor his edutors had learned a great deal. The American's aircraft had been shot down, after all, and by mere commoners. Although not of the nobility, the little American had a very strong sense of class distinction and quite definite ideas on matters of chivalric behavior. The problem was that of just how nobility was defined in Australica.

In the Mounthaven domains, librarians were just people who looked after rooms full of books and took orders from artisans and engineers—who were the right hand of the nobility. In Rochester, librarians ran the state and gave orders to artisans and engineers. Worse, the nobility did not fly or fight, they just ran their estates and lived comfortably. The more dynamic of them acted in various public positions, such as magistrates, senior academics, and inspectors of taxation. True, surplus sons tended to be sent off to the military and surplus daughters to the Dragon Librarian Service or nunneries, but Alarak did not find himself viewing these people with anything like the respect that the flying wardens of America commanded.

Dramoren had ordered the prisoner moved up to one of the Libris towers, after having the windows securely barred. The American was provided with a comfortable bed, the same food as the Dragon Librarians, a selection of carefully chosen books, and clothing that would not be out of place on a reasonably prosperous merchant. His reasoning was that the man must have been a member of the nobility wherever he came from, and should be treated accordingly. After another six weeks the Highliber decided that Alarak's interrogation and education were going nowhere.

Alarak was roused by the jangling of a bell, which was more of a signal that the door was to be opened than a request to enter. The Tiger Dragon on duty drew back the bolt, and a young man with an impressive scar down his face entered. He was wearing the jacket of the Dragon Librarian Service under a long coat, and the insignia of rank that he wore was black. Alark remained seated beside the window, and after favoring Dramoren with a glance returned his gaze to the rooftops of Rochester.

Dramoren raised his hand and snapped his fingers. Two Tiger Dragons entered, followed by an edutor.

"Has this man been instructed about the ranking and peerage conventions in Rochester?" asked Dramoren.

"Yes, Highliber."

"So he knows who I am?"

"Yes, Highliber."

"Guards, do your duty."

The Tiger Dragons holstered their long barrel flintlocks, then marched over to Alarak. One hauled the navigator to his feet and pinned his arms, then the other backhanded him across the face. This was not just a formal slap meant to signify an insult but a blow delivered with all the strength of a very strong man. Stars flashed blue before Alarak's eyes, and he would have reeled with the shock had he not been held. Being a person who liked symmetry in everything, the guard now delivered in identical blow with his other hand. Blood began to flow from Alarak's nose. The Tiger Dragon placed his face very close to the navigator's. Dramoren had given him a raw clove of garlic to munch and swallow just before they had entered.

"Do I have your complete and undivided attention you *filthy, insolent* little man?" the Tiger Dragon shouted in Alarak's face.

"Y-yes," replied Alarak at once.

The guard delivered another two backhands to his face.

"That's yes, *Fras Tiger Dragon!*"

"Yes, Fras Tiger Dragon."

"What do you do when the second most senior noble in all of the Rochestrian Commonwealth enters your presence?" shouted the guard with undiminished volume and ferocity.

"I, I, I—"

"Let me remind you! You stand! You face him!" Alarak was hauled around to face Dramoren. "You bow!" Before Alarak was even given the option of defiance or a bow, the guard kneed him in the testicles. He doubled over. The other guard tried to haul Alarak straight again, but his feet merely came off the ground and he remained doubled over. "You say, 'The afternoon's compliments, Highliber!' "

"The afternoon's compliments, Highliber," wheezed Alarak.

The other guard released Alarak, who fell to the floor. The guard kicked him in the ribs with a resounding thud that made even Dramoren wince.

"Now get up and greet your patron, protector, and benefactor with the deference due to his rank!"

It was not as if Alarak were lacking in courage, but the sudden, catastrophic change in treatment had shattered his determination in a way that weeks of slowly escalating torture could not have. With his chest on fire from three broken ribs, his genitals feeling as if they were being massaged in broken glass, with blood pouring down over his lips and dripping from his chin, he got to his feet, straightened a little, bowed, and greeted Dramoren exactly as the Tiger Dragon had demanded. Dramoren began to circle him.

"Now, then, Fras Alarak, for six weeks we have lavished care upon you and in return you have given us your name, rank in the navigator's guild, and artisan's serial number—not to mention quite a lot of insolence. In my experience, this is the way of particularly stupid commoners when faced with exotic, foreign manners, and nobility. Having determined that you are a commoner, I have decided to have you flung into our lowest, most squalid dungeon and to have Fras Dangerdrine here put in charge of your interrogation. You will be most savagely abused, but kept alive for a long time nevertheless. I no longer care whether you tell me anything about anything, I just want you punished for the rest of your miserable life for insulting me. Occasionally I shall come down to listen, but only when I am in a bad mood and require cheering. Take him away, then have his smell scrubbed from the tower."

Dramoren broke off for the door without another word. Alarak was by now broken, but not only in the physical sense. He suddenly realized that he had grossly insulted one of his betters, that he had been rude to the equivalent of an airlord, and worst of all that he was being regarded as a commoner. Should Samondel learn any of the foregoing . . . A hand seized his collar.

"Highliber, pardon, pardon, pardon!" babbled Alarak as he attempted to drop to his knees.

Dramoren turned in the doorway to see Alarak suspended in midair, Dangerdrine holding him by the collar.

"Well?"

"Highliber, most apologies. No excusings insult. Deserve beatings more."

"Oh, that will be done, have no fear of that."

"Ask all. If say I can."

Dramoren walked back into the room. The Tiger Dragon put Alarak down.

"Where are you from?"

"Mounthaven, glorious Council of Airlords sending."

"Mounthaven in North America, I know the place. Why are you here?"

"Wishing trade—pardon, please."

"Trade? In what?"

"Horses trading. None, are having. In America."

This took Dramoren by surprise. Horses were seen as useful in the Commonwealth, but the idea that an air-going power might value them was not at all expected.

"Good, the Rochestrian Commonwealth is founded upon trade, and we have the finest work and cavalry horses on the continent."

It was now Alarak's turn for surprise.

"Honor, honor, honor," he said to Dramoren's boots.

"Why were you so insolent to my Dragon Librarians?" demanded Dramoren.

"Monthaven, librarians nothing. Flying noble everything. Stupid am, I being. Noble librarian, mighty librarian, wise librarian. Now know. Here no flying."

Dramoren returned to the door, glanced out and snapped his fingers, then turned back.

"Plug his nose, clean him up, then march him down to the Promenade Courtyard," he ordered. "Oh, and one last thing, what is your rank in your North American peerage?"

"Ah, ah," began Alarak, wondering whether or not to confer rank upon himself. His nerve failed. "Like edutor, important edutor. Not warrior. Know maps, finding stars, using for direction."

"Ah yes, I see. A respected calling, but not nobility. Just as it is here."

"Wise Highliber, very right."

It was a half hour before Alarak was clean and sufficiently straight to walk down the three hundred stairs to the Promenade Courtyard. The place was a two-hundred-yard oblong, bordered by Libris buildings, and was alive with men and women engaged in fencing, flintlock practice, and general strength and fitness training. While they were all in exercise tunics, they still wore their colors of Dragon Librarian rank. Alarak was walked the entire length of the place, to where Dramoren was waiting beside a cloth practice dummy that was being used for knife throwing targetry.

"Fras Alarak, until six weeks ago the Commonwealth had no air machines at all, apart from tethered hot air balloons," Dramoren declared as he held up his hand.

All at once the general activity in the long courtyard ceased.

"Look to that tower behind you, the tall, central one."

Alarak turned in time to see something detach from the great beamflash tower, something in the shape of a wing. It gathered speed, flying straight, then banked to circle the tower once before approaching the square. Alarak realized that a man was suspended beneath the wing, but that it had no engine and was just gliding. It flew the length of the courtyard, losing height all the time, then at about thirty yards distance there were two gunflashes from above the flyer's head. The glider swooped over them, then the flyer's feet touched the ground and he ran along until he had lost momentum. Two holes had been drilled through the cloth targetry dummy's head.

"We may be primitive, but we learn very, very fast," said Dramoren.

"All that, six weeks?" gasped Alarak.

"Less," said Dramoren.

Alarak could see that the flyer appeared to be a monk. This was not a surprise, for Mounthaven's monastic clergy also engaged in fundamental research.

"Like centuries past, warden duelwing gliders," said Alarak, realizing that the wing was armed with just fixed flintlock pistols. "Amazing. You are learning all, just having wreck. Sailwing of?"

"Yes," replied Dramoren.

"All this, such wonder."

"Come, talk as we return to your tower," said the Highliber, and again the groups of sweating librarians parted to let them pass. "What are wings used for in Mounthaven?"

"Dueling. Noblemen—and women—only. Gunwings. Have sailwings, carry important things."

"Important things?"

"Messages, gold, treaties, greetings. Sailwings, regals, using for."

"And you came in a sailwing."

"Yes."

"Tell me, what of your antiengine movement?"

"Pardon?"

"Your antiengine movement, the Christian Gaia Crusaders. Certain of my spies have reported that they oppose all fueled engines, like our own Revivalist Gentheists."

"Pardon? Mounthaven?"

"Yes."

"Is not exist. Compression engine, holy machine. Right hand of God, defense against darkness. Engine opposition heresy! Anti-God, anti-American, antimorals, anti-airlord. Not exist."

"You do not have to lie, just refuse to answer and be civil about it."

"Is truth. Christian Gaia Crusaders not existing. Cannot existing. Heresy, treason, abomination, attacking engines, is."

Dramoren stroked his beard as he walked. "Interesting," he said. "Thank you, Fras Alarak, I'll send a medician to tend you. Your words have saved me a great deal of confusion."

"Excusings? Is all, you are wanting?"

"Yes, as a matter of fact. But is there any question you want to ask me?"

Alarak thought carefully. This noble was being gracious, but possibly this was some test. Would he prove something by asking a stupid question? Would he betray Samondel, about whom they appeared to suspect nothing?

"Shooting down of me: why?"

"Fras Alarak, had I appeared on horseback in a Mounthaven city, riding for the, ah, airlord's palace as fast as I could, would not the palace guards have opened fire upon me?"

Alarak nodded. "Ah. Explains all."

As the door closed behind Alarak he felt curiously secure. Although he had been subjected to quite a brutal beating, he had established his place in Rochestrian society and at least achieved a meeting with someone very senior. He realized that while they did not have much flight artisanry, they were a very advanced and skilled people. Questions remained, however. What to do next was clearly of most concern, but for now there was no alternative to nothing. The existence of the Christian Gaia Crusaders and the fact that they claimed to be American was quite beyond comprehension.

7

HEARTS OF THE LOVERS

Traralgon Castellany, Southeast Australica

Serjon found that riding a horse had some similarities to controlling a gunwing. Even after a mere five days of lessons and experience, he could manage a walk, trot, canter, and gallop, and had overcome his fears of an animal that was an order of magnitude heavier than anything on either of the American continents. Samondel had been right. Horses had the strength of a small steam engine, were fueled on grass and water, could go almost anywhere, and needed no artisans to build them. Whoever had horses would rule the Americas.

The Warlord of Traralgon was riding beside him, a big and powerfully built man dressed in a shaggy hide coat, leather kilt, and horned helmet. He reeked of horses and sweat, but he knew horses like Serjon's father knew compression engines. He also knew mounted warfare.

"There, watch the apple," said Galdane as one of his lancers came about at the end of a field beside his fortress. "It is the size and color of a heart, and at heart height."

A peasant was standing a few feet away, holding up an apple on his open palm. The lancer urged his horse into a gallop, bearing down on the peasant. The man did not seem concerned, although he was not actually smiling. The lancer thundered past in a flash, and Serjon realized that the apple was now on the end of the lance. The lancer returned and tossed the apple to the peasant. The peasant began running, again holding the apple in his outstretched hand. Again the lancer skewered the apple. Galdane and Serjon rode over and examined the lance, the apple, and the peasant's uninjured hand.

"Time? Learn also?" asked Serjon slowly.

"To be as good as Fras Canavar? Years. To just kill peasants without style, a month if you worked hard."

They rode past the village, which lay beside the fortress and behind a stagnant-looking moat and low earthwork wall. Twenty lancers were with them, all armed with lance, saber, and musket, and wearing light plate armor that seemed more decoration than protection. Presently they came to a long, ancient wall, where two peasants had lined up a number of pottery jars. As Serjon and Galdane watched, a lancer suddenly left them and charged the wall with a musket in his hands. At about a hundred feet he fired, shattering a jar, then he drew his saber and chopped another jar as his horse jumped the wall. Serjon was so impressed that he clapped.

"Horses are the most treasured of animals," said Galdane. "The price is high, but the worth is returned many times over."

"Pricing, ah, much?" asked Serjon.

"Fifty gold royals each," replied Galdane.

Serjon considered carefully. According to his contacts, a foal could be bought for a hundred times less than that, but Galdane knew that his horses were desired by someone who wanted complete discretion and a long, hard strip of ancient road within his land's borders. He assumed aviads were involved, and he was charging accordingly.

"Just say you had four enemies," said Galdane, then he spurred his mount and charged the wall.

With a double-barrel pistol in each hand, Galdane bore down on the wall, firing as he went. By the time his horse leaped the wall, four jars had been shattered.

"Would you like to try, Fras Serjon?" asked Galdane as he rode back.

"Trying, yes."

"How many jars?"

Serjon held up all ten fingers. Roaring with laughter, Galdane gave the order for ten jars to be set up, thinking that Serjon hoped to hit at least one if they were close together. Serjon reached into his f'ght jacket and drew out a Clastini reaction pistol and held it out for the warlord to inspect. The weapon was passed from hand to hand among the lancers, and jocularity about the small bore of the barrel reached his ears. It was returned to him. He flicked off the safety catch and urged his mount to a trot. This inspired yet more laughter. Serjon opened fire.

With a rate of three hundred rounds per minute, the reaction pistol produced a sound that Serjon's placid training horse had never known. It reared by the time five jars had been shattered, and Serjon half slid, half fell to the grass. As his mount galloped off in terror Serjon got to his feet, hurled curses at his supposed enemy and charged the jars on foot, firing as he went. There were still two rounds left in the clip by the time the last jar shattered. The astonished Galdane dismounted and walked over to Serjon while a lancer rode off to catch the fleeing horse.

"What is that thing?" asked Galdane in wonder.

"Gun," replied Serjon simply.

"But—but it shoots like a dozen lancers."

"Is why, ah, worth dozen horses."

Galdane scowled, but was not slow to accept when Serjon offered him another demonstration. After shattering a dozen jars at his first try, the warlord realized that the effectiveness of his cavalry would be improved twenty, fifty, even a hundred times over if each man had a Clastini 9mm reaction pistol and several spare clips of ammunition each. His three hundred musketeer lancers could even take on the Rochetrian Commonwealth with a fairly good chance of carrying the day.

"Maybe five horses for one, ah, how is it named?"

"Reaction pistol," replied Serjon.

Rochester, the Rochestrian Commonwealth

Manden Reppan walked through the power room below the Calculor, nodding to the drivers and waving his security pennant at the guards. It was here that the horses plodded in treadcircles, munching from their nosebags as they turned the gearboxes to the Libris Calculor's attachments that required more than mere calculating power. Reppan climbed the stairs from the power room and entered the cool, clean brightness of the Voice Chamber, a room alive with the clatter of machinery and smelling of machine oil rather than horse manure.

Here tape machines punched holes in thin paper tape, providing answers that could be read by either humans or other machines. Five giant turtles carved from red rivergum ate tape from reels held by carved kangaroos, then expelled punched tape through the mouth of a second head. Beneath the body of each, a drive spindle powered the mechanisms while levers triggered the spring-loaded punches that were the voice of the Calculor. Reppan knew something was wrong as soon as he opened the door. The polished carapace of one turtle was raised, and several Dragon Librarians were examining the machinery inside. He strode over, his face flushed with anger.

"Are any of you members of the Guild of Clockmakers?" demanded Reppan as he stopped before the disabled punch machine.

"I am the duty controller," replied a short, slightly harassed-looking woman.

"And is your name on the maintenance contract?"

"Her name is not, Fras, but I designed this machine," said the lanky, balding man who was sitting on the edge of the output head of the turtle and looking inside. "My name is Bryn Barwon."

Reppan swallowed.

"My pardon, learned Fras, but the service history on these machines must be kept accurate and consistent. My guildmaster holds the contract for the maintenance and tuning of them."

"But not the upgrades?"

"Oh no, Fras. That is done by your Libris artisans. We are only given the altered diagrams and specifications."

"Of which we keep one copy. I have my copy here, and my copy does not include that little box down there, you can see it in the mirror that I have placed beside the bulkhead."

Reppan pulled out his folder of diagrams, looked carefully at the object in the mirror, then checked the appropriate diagram.

"That is an unauthorized modification!" he exclaimed.

"My opinion entirely," replied Barwon.

"Then I must seek out my guildmaster and bring him here," said Reppan, replacing the diagram in his folder and picking up his bag. "This is an unauthorized change, it has probably disturbed the tuning of the mechanism. I shall be back within the hour."

Reppan turned to find himself confronted by a slightly shorter-than-average man wearing a silver mask that covered his face, except for eyeholes and a grille over his mouth.

"According to the records, you have serviced this unit since it was returned from the palace museum in November. I noted that the seal was intact on this unit when we opened it a few hours ago."

"Seals can be duplicated."

"They can indeed, but a life cannot."

"What do you mean?" asked Reppan slowly, wondering whose life might be involved.

"You have never seen that box?"

"Absolutely not—"

"Seize him."

Reppan's arms were pinned by two of the Dragon Librarians while a third put ratchet manacles on his wrists. The masked man ordered him brought to the edge of the open tape-punch device.

"This is an outrage to the guild!" cried Reppan.

"This certainly is an outrage," replied the masked man. "Hold him right down with his head inside the shell, tie him fast."

"Stop this! I demand my rights, you're in serious trouble! The guild will sue, Libris will be fined thousands of royals."

"One of us is in serious trouble, Fras. Or possibly both of us. Ladies, gentlemen, please retreat to a safe distance while I remove the unauthorized device."

"No! You can't do that!" shouted Reppan, frantically struggling against his ropes.

"Why not?"

"It may be a trap."

"It may, but it may not. We are not to know."

The masked man reached in. Sweat beaded Reppan's forehead.

"I feel wires, linked to the punch-driver rods. My shears are cutting through them easily enough, however. Now, then. Three bolts with wing nuts are securing it, and a little spindle, presumably linked to the gearbox to drive it. There, it should lift free now—"

"Stop! Stop! The spindle trips the flintlock trigger to a bomb!" screamed Reppan.

The masked man lifted the box clear.

"The spindle certainly does, my friend, but the trigger is currently jammed with a very large blob of wax. Now, what we all want to know is how you knew exactly what was inside this little box?"

Reppan quickly realized that he had just exchanged death within seconds for death in a few days, probably as a result of an enthusiastic bout of torture.

"I guessed it was a bomb!" he nevertheless snapped, his nerve returning.

"Ah, good. Well, I hope you are a brave man, because you are about to be interrogated until you guess exactly what else is in this box. After that, you will most likely find yourself in about as much trouble as a bull caught dancing a highland reel in a china shop owned by the local butcher's wife. On the other hand, you could be candid with us from the beginning."

Guildmaster Larjerra was seated at his design bench when the loop of wire was dropped around his neck from behind and drawn tight. He stood up, reaching back and grasping it, but the wire extended up beyond the length of his arms. The pressure kept increasing. The guildmaster climbed onto a chair. The pressure eased slightly.

"I may be only a filthy, perverted aviad agent, but I do have a few contacts in Libris," said a soft, well-educated voice behind him.

Shadowmouse walked around into the guildmaster's view.

"The wire extends all the way to the rafters, Fras. Now, then, I have heard that Fras Reppan has been taken into custody over devices placed within certain key mechanisms of the Libris Calculor. Soon the Espionage Constables will be here, but then, I am not an Espionage Constable and I want to know the truth as well. Each of those boxes contained a beautifully made little paper-tape punch, tissue paper reel, and pins, and it was set to record only certain transactions and data."

"Selling," gasped the guildmaster. "Merchants."

"I think not, the data has been analyzed. It contains only the movements of certain families, paraline train times, and various border clearance records. I think you have been gleaning data on the smuggling of aviad children to their safe lands, the Mayorate of Avian."

"Rochester. . . . should be doing it," whispered the guildmaster. "Cursed abominations."

"You are a Reformed Gentheist, I have checked certain records in very dangerous places. Smell the fragrance of horse manure in my robes? I work as a driver in the power rooms of Libris when I am not smuggling children, and in my spare time I have slipped into places where I am not authorized to go. Hence my name, Shadowmouse. As silent as the shadow of a mouse. I can get into places without anyone knowing—but then, you are most painfully aware of my talents in that regard, are you not?"

Shadowmouse held up a folder.

"I have compiled a list of every Reformed Gentheist in your guild, using a list from your own records. But who are the others, the contacts that you passed the aviad movements to?"

"Live by the Word, die for the Word."

"Ah, I suspected that you might say as much, that is why I took the liberty of liberating some of your records in advance. Some very dear friends of mine have died because of you and your kind, Fras Larjerra, and I am very angry about it. Still, I am not a vindictive man, and I recognize the way that you have lived for the Word as a man of genuine faith. Allow me to help you die for it."

Shadowmouse kicked the chair from under the guildmaster's feet.

When the Espionage constables arrived ten minutes later they found a note on Larjerra's desk that said "Flee. Reppan taken." Charred fragments of diagrams and notes were found in the grate.

Martyne had met Overmayor Lengina before, but was still not sure whether or not to be in awe of her. Although she had a regal bearing and demanded deference in line with her rank, she spoke more like the captain of a polo team in the lancers, and expected people to think and act intelligently while carrying out her orders. He suspected that advisers who gave her only the answers they thought she wanted would soon find themselves in serious trouble.

"So, you have connections among the aviads, Fras Camderine?" she asked as she paced between rows of ornamental wind chimes in her meditation suite, setting them tinkling each time she passed.

"I have connections among many people, including those who drink lamp oil and sleep beneath paraline bridges, Frelle Overmayor. I am a spy."

"I am not censuring you for knowing aviads, Fras, I merely wish to know more. For example, what laws do they break, who suffers through their activities, and how many children are abducted by them each year?"

"Frelle Overmayor, the aviads remain invisible by breaking no laws and exploiting nobody. They do take aviad children from human parents, but only after those parents decide that they want their children to grow up free and safe. They pay all taxes and dues, even more scrupulously than most humans. They stray beyond the law only when issuing false travel papers and names."

"So they hurt nobody?"

"They hurt anybody who attacks them."

"And so would you. So would I. But before the Call ended, they used to take advantage of their immunity, did they not?"

"That is the case. They were, in turn, lynched or imprisoned whenever caught."

"But with the Call gone they are still persecuted."

"The Commonwealth's laws require them to be registered, Frelle

Overmayor. They are faster, stronger, and brighter than humans, and have strong traditions regarding work and education."

"Have you ever spoken to them—as in intimately, philosophically, as friend to friend?"

"I have spoken to a few at length, such as while riding together."

"What do they think of us?"

"Humans? Many aviads hate us. Not one alive has not lost a relative or friend to the mobs or prisons, but most just want to live apart, to get away."

"Truly, Fras Camderine?"

"As I am your subject and servant, Frelle Overmayor."

Highliber Dramoren entered as soon as Martyne had been shown out. Lengina continued to pace between her wind chimes.

"Can he be trusted?" she asked.

"About as well as I can," Dramoren replied.

"Then the aviads are no real threat to the security of the Commonwealth."

"Corruption among your taxation officials costs us more, according to the Libris Calculor."

"Were I to revoke the Commonwealth's Aviad Registration and Control legislation, and declare safe passage for aviads who wish to leave for the wilderness of the Otway Mountains, what would result?"

"Materially nothing. Religiously, the Reformed Gentheist extremists would scream hellfire. The Aviancse are known to use fueled engines because they have very small numbers—quite apart from being what the Gentheist Scriptures call abominations. You would split the Commonwealth."

"Splendid, splendid," said Lengina. "I want you to join me in a meeting with my most senior legislative advisor."

Traralgon Castellany, Southeast Australica

Dusk was long past as Serjon and Galdane stood waiting at the edge of a stand of trees. Behind them a dozen of Galdane's warriors stood ready with five blindfolded young horses, all recently weaned, and behind them was yet another group.

"I hear nothing, I see nothing," Galdane said yet again, scanning the dark skies.

"Approaching unpowered," said Serjon, "not want to be noticed."

"Why do they worry? The Rochester Overmayor has changed the laws about persecuting birdmen."

"Changes in law not stop Gentheist terrorists and vigilantes."

Off to the south a brilliant point of light appeared, dropping rapidly and leaving a trail of smoke. Serjon pointed.

"There! Light fires."

Eight bonfires lined the edge of the makeshift wingfield, and at Galdane's call these were ignited. They were made of dry brushwood, and they blazed up quickly. The light in the sky winked out, but nothing else happened. They waited.

"Is your flying machine so small that we might have missed it?" Galdane laughed without mirth.

Serjon knew what to look for, and in Mirrorsun's weak light he gestured to the enormous shadow that swept past them and on down the wingfield. Galdane fell over his own feet as he attempted to duck, turn, and run all at once.

Galdane's initial shock was not lessened by closer inspection of the super-regal. This was one of a pair especially built for the transport of horses, and featured a huge, oblong bulge beneath the main wing structure. It was driven by ten compression engines, but all of these were currently silent.

"Have horsemen ready to turn wing," said Serjon. "Is clumsy on ground."

"You said it would have to be pulled all the way back along the strip," replied Galdane.

"Tonight is no wind. Must descend and ascend facing wind."

Serjon entered the huge aircraft as it was being turned by a team of uneasy horses. Aboard were just the wingcaptain and navigator.

"Here we are, and with very little compression spirit in the tanks," said the wingcaptain. "I've never flown this thing so lightly laden before."

"All is safe enough here, both cargoes are ready."

"Then we need to open the doors. Come, you know what to do."

The aircraft was still moving as they began to wind the frame and canvas doors open. Once it stopped, Galdane's men fearfully advanced with a wooden ramp and placed it on the lip of the decking, then the first of the horses were led aboard.

"They're smaller than I've been told, Sair Feydamor," remarked the wingcaptain.

"They are very young, it saves weight."

They watched as the horses were strapped into their stalls and given nosebags. One defecated copiously, and Serjon ordered the pile of manure to be removed.

"Anything to save weight," he commented. "Ah, here are the extra items."

The aviad children began to file aboard, each carrying a sedated baby in a sling. The navigator hurriedly took them to a number of padded recesses in the structure of the super-regal and helped them to strap themselves in.

"Eighteen children and babies for delivery to the Launceston Wingfield, Sair Wingcaptain," said Serjon as they began to wind the doors shut. "Then you can replace their weight with compression spirit and return to Lake Taupo."

"It goes against the grain, Sair."

"Maybe so, but it means that we are supplied with a vast amount of compression spirit that does not have to be flown over from Mounthaven. Safe flying."

"Sair Feydamor, the Mayor of Launceston gave me this message just before we ascended," he said as he handed a sealed fold of poorpaper to Serjon. "He said to burn it, then take whatever action you would."

"Thank you. Do you know what it concerns?"

"He said it was personal."

Serjon and the navigator made their way along the top of the vast wing, firing compression charges to start the engines. When all ten were chugging steadily and warming up, Serjon slapped him on the back and dropped to the dark grass. Galdane was waiting for him.

"Would that I could see this in daylight," Galdane sighed.

"Unlikely," responded Serjon. "Too many think engines instruments of devil."

"Hah! Pale, cowering city mice! We of the grasslands believe in gods, not devils. Good gods and bad gods, great gods and weak gods. Your sky machines are free to come down here, in Traralgon. My castellany will keep the Gentheist vermin in their place."

The wingcaptain now brought the ten compression engines up to a steady, uniform speed, checked that all were in balance, then pushed the main throttle forward. The super-regal began to roll, and a great moan went up from the horse handlers to see their beloved charges taken away in such a strange monstrosity. The black super-regal merged with the darkened trees at the end of the wingfield, then lifted clear and was faintly visible for a moment before it turned south. The Traralgans all cried out, then began to cheer.

"Feldar Harg!" roared Galdane, waving his gun, "Feldar Harg, fil'dar."

The others took up his cry.

"What are shouting?" asked Serjon.

"Thunder Horse!" he replied in Austaric. "The flying steed of our greatest god, who flies with a roar like thunder. Our foals have become the children of Feldar Harg."

Serjon walked over to the smoldering coals of one of the bonfires, fanned it into brightness, then broke the seal on his message and opened it.

Fras Feydamor, one of our agents has reported that a girl going by the name of Samondel Leover is enrolled at the University of Rochester. She has red hair that reaches down past her knees, and eyes of a very strange shade of blue. We have also been told that a man was pulled alive from the wreckage of the Swallow, and is being held in the Overmayor's palace. Cleren, Mayor.

Serjon read the note twice more, then dropped it among the coals where both paper and wax seal blazed up for a moment. Straightening, he returned to Galdane and his men.

"Need travel to fringes of Commonwealth, are certain devices I need artisans build."

"But my blacksmiths are at your command!" exclaimed Galdane.

"No, need fine clockwork and gears."

"What sort of machine are you building?" Galdane asked suspiciously.

"Machine make little bullets reaction gun fires."

"Hah! You should have said! When would you like to leave? Tonight?"

Rochester, the Rochestrian Commonwealth

Word of the first ferry flight of the super-regal reached Rochester's aviads a few days later, and with it came a coded message from Serjon. While no aviads went about flaunting their identity in public, they were celebrating in secret. Terian and Shadowmouse walked together in the market, talking quietly and taking no interest in the stalls and vendors.

"The first American super-regal made its visit three days ago," Terian reported. "It took eighteen of our young, even laden with five horses."

"Four times what can safely go on a kitewing," replied Shadowmouse. "Without the horses they could carry perhaps fifty."

"Such feats are being negotiated. The Americans want horses, but they need fuel as well. Avian can provide fuel, but not as much as the Commonwealth."

"Have you some scheme?"

"I have exchanged beamflash messages with an American in Seymour. They are using fuel faster than Avian can produce it, but the distilleries of Rochester's mayorates could produce unlimited amounts. At present they have one spare super-regal, they expected to lose a few to accidents by now but they have been fortunate. They are willing to dedicate it to flying our people to Avian if we can supply fuel at Traralgon when Avian's stores run out."

"That can be done easily enough. The castellanies are anarchic, lawless places where the Reformed Gentheists have little influence. We could move wagonloads of spirit out there."

"And we could have those wagonloads being produced by un-suspecting human distillers by May. For now, you will begin re-cruiting trustworthy people for a dummy spirits-and-cooking-oil merchant house in Seymour."

"As good as done. Anything else?"

"The Americans want their people back, those flyers from the sailwing that was shot down over Rochester."

"Flyers? Word is that only one was involved."

"The Americans say there were two. The navigator was taken prisoner, but the venture's leader escaped unseen. That leader is also the envoy of their overmayorate, and a mayor of one of their states. Their mayors are called airlords, by the way."

Shadowmouse whistled and shook his head.

"A brave, resourceful, and important man," he said with genuine admiration.

"Woman."

"You jest!"

"I do not. She has been going openly by her American name, hoping that any rescue attempt would hear of her. Frelle Samondel Leover also has long, flame red hair that reaches past her knees, and her eyes are of a violet color."

Shadowmouse walked on for a few paces, his head bowed.

"Yes, I do know her. She is a student of theology and Austaric at the university. Do you want her taken to Seymour?"

"No, just ensure that she remains safe. In a fortnight an American spy will arrive to escort her to the Traralgon wingfield. From the sound of it she is like our Dragon Librarians, brilliant, educated, brave, and deadly. She had shot down six other warriors in airborne duels, and is known as Red Death. Once she is safely away, we are to rescue the navigator. You will participate in that as well."

Shadowmouse stopped at a stall selling sabers and tried one for balance. After executing several vicious cuts and thrusts on a practice dummy he tried another, then another. He haggled with the stallholder for some minutes, then drew his own weapon and pointed to a deep nick in the blade. He tried his preferred choice in his own scabbard. At last some coins and the damaged saber were exchanged for the new weapon.

"I have been talking to our own flyers at Apollo Wingfield," said Shadowmouse as they walked on.

"Fine young women they are, too."

"Indeed. One of them told me that Avian has a strange weapon of the ancient technologies. It is called Skyfire, and only men are allowed to operate it. What do you know of it?"

"What I know I should not be telling you."

"But will you?"

"In a fashion. I do not know the nature of Skyfire, but I do know that it tends to kill its operators."

"My informant said that it sounds like thunder. Her lover was an operator, and it killed him. When she saw his body it was burned hideously."

"Yes, I know that too."

"Can you tell me something I do *not* know?"

"Fras Shadowmouse, Avian can produce a new compression engine every three months, and even then many parts are made by unsuspecting human artisans on the mainland. Our spies have reported that hot air balloons shaped like vast sausages and driven by pedaling musketeers have been tested in the deserts of Kalgoorlie. They are sound in terms of Reformed Gentheist dogma, but currently can travel only ten miles before the fuel to heat their air runs out.

Still, calculations show that in the near future these things could cross the salt water to Avian."

Terian let the implications register with Shadowmouse, but this took only moments.

"Surely our kitewings could destroy them."

"Yes, but our kitewings are very expensive to build and maintain, and they are needed to transport people and supplies to Avian. The Skyfire machines are extremely cheap to build by comparison, and they can spray their fire up to ten miles. More than that I cannot say."

"How can I volunteer?"

"You?"

"Me."

"Have you not been paying attention? The device is almost as deadly to the operator as to the victim."

"But I meet all the criteria. I am a young male, I have no sweetheart, and I want to serve Avian and my people."

Terian thought for a few steps.

"You are of too much value here."

"After I have done all of my current assignments, what then?"

"There will be more assignments. Fras Shadowmouse, there are plenty of young men in Avian already, and there are many more worthy passengers than you to ferry over the salt water before a case could be made to take you as well."

"But will you at least send my petition to the people in charge of the Skyfire weapon?"

Terian sighed. "That I will do, but nothing more. Are you happy now?"

"That much is better than nothing. Yes indeed."

Samondel said I have soulful, dreamy eyes today," Martyne told Velesti as she read his analysis of the market extortion reports.

"No wonder, you stayed up all night doing these reports."

"So, when else can I do them?"

"What about during the day, like the rest of us?"

"I'm busy during the day. Surveillance."

"You mean shadowing Samondel and looking for any possible excuse to meet her by accident."

"She could be under threat. The Gentheists—"

"The Gentheists could not organize a beer festival in a brewery, let alone an abduction in Rochester."

"She held hands with me in the refectory today."

"I arrested that Dragon Green from the Calculor dissemination register team today. He was selling half-price bookings for wind train trips that end outside the Rochestrian Commonwealth. The verification system for those is not at all rigorous."

"Samondel asked me to go to the University Music Festival with her."

Velesti drew her Morelac and pointed it between his eyes. "I could put you out of your misery," she speculated.

"Samondel's flintlock practice is coming along very well. She has a natural talent."

"She's a professional warrior, Martyne! What do you expect?"

"She has such smooth, white skin, and have you noticed that her hands—"

Velesti slammed fifteen silver nobles down on the desk in front of her. "Martyne, take this money, leave this office, and do not come back until you have taken her out to an expensive café and told her at least a thousandth of the things that you have been telling me. Oh, and our parents are traveling here. They arrive on March sixteenth."

Martyne shrieked with dismay as he jumped to his feet. "Oh, no!"

"Oh yes, and my spies in Griffith say that my mother is looking rather pregnant."

"But you said—"

"I have done some research, which indicates that after you escaped my mother you spent the night with Julica, you randy little devil. Now, when I took my gun barrel out of her medician's mouth yesterday he was good enough to tell me that she is due to give birth in June."

"Julica?" Martyne shouted. "Pregnant? But she said it was not a problem."

"What specifically?"

"You know, amorous activities."

"Not a problem because she wanted to bear your child, no doubt."

"She sees me from time to time, I sometimes drink in the tavern where she works. She's never mentioned this."

"I have a feeling that she soon will, she's due in four months. My condolences, she was probably more fun than Mother—whatever went on there. But cheer up, Martyne, it may not be you."

"Velesti, even *you* could get pregnant and insist that I am the father. If you had a sufficiently good lawyer you could also convince a magistrate. There would then be exceedingly strong legal pressures to marry or pay ruinous fines, be indentured for the next twenty years, and so on."

"True."

"So I must get myself killed, flee, or marry her."

"Who? *Two* women are pregnant; it must have been quite a night. Just be thankful you're a Christian instead of Gentheist, otherwise you would have to marry both."

By now Martyne was kneeling and banging his head against the floorboards.

Velesti hauled him to his feet. "Here is a little free advice, Martyne. The nightmares are bearing down on you as fast as their wings can carry them, but they are not here yet. Now get out there and do something, anything, romantic with Frelle Samondel while you are still a free man."

Samondel was walking alone in the market, buying fruit, when the stranger accosted her. He did not seem strange or suspicious, just a well-dressed, prosperous-looking man of average height and perhaps in his sixties. He bowed to her. She blinked in surprise, then returned his bow.

"Frelle Leover, Serjon will meet you here on the sixteenth day of March at this exact hour," he said in Austaric, then bowed again and turned to go. Samondel darted after him and grasped his arm.

"I—what? Waiting! Who—"

He gently detached her hand from his arm. "I was told to tell you as much, Frelle. I know nothing else whatever, and on that date I shall be a very great distance from here. The compliments of the day to you."

He was quickly lost amid the shoppers, leaving Samondel speechless. She had done the impossible and survived. Now Serjon had done the impossible and found her.

Ilyire was dressed in just a kilt as he preached, but although his hair and beard were long, they were well brushed and clean. Martyne and Samondel stood listening near the front of the crowd of students.

"My word is a true word, as true as my name is Ilyire of Glenellen. The Call has ceased as a sign of goodwill from the cetezoid creatures, they have realized that we all have to share this world. This I say to you, intelligence is intelligence no matter what color or shape the body that harbors it. I also say to you that I am an aviad."

The crowd murmured, but did no more.

"I say to you that my sister, the great Abbess Theresla of Glenellen, spoke with the cetezoids just as easily as I speak here today. She preached to them that rogue aviads were harming the humans, she preached to them that soon those rogue aviads would turn upon the cetezoids. That is why the Call ceased. The rogue aviads have now been vanquished, and the cetezoids are content to leave the lands to humans and aviads if we will leave the seas alone. Our world has changed very much in a mere six months."

"But Learned Ilyire, what of the doom from Mirrorsun?" called an intense, wild-eyed girl close to the front of the crowd.

"Mirrorsun I do not speak with, but let me ask you this: When did all electrical essence machines burn, and when did Mirrorsun grow those great light sails and begin spinning?"

Incredibly, nobody else had made that connection thus far. Again there was a great deal of murmuring.

"Mirrorsun is like humans, like aviads, like cetezoids. We are all intelligent. If you piss in a river, does that not eventually foul the water that the cetezoids inhabit? If the cetezoids drive shoals of fish ashore while hunting, does not the stench of their rotting render the air that we breathe foul? If Mirrorsun drinks sunlight to spin its body, might it not somehow foul the electrical essence that we can use but really do not need? I say to you that there is no doom other than what we fashion for ourselves. God, Allah, Deity, whatever and whoever you worship, is not involved in the issues that trouble your hearts. Open your hearts and live well, do not hate, take glory from diversity, and strength from your own kind."

Ilyire now held out his hand. "Will anyone here lend me a knife?"

Several knives were proffered, handle first. He selected one.

"I have come here from the coast because I have heard of heresy preached, hate spread, and lies offered to you as the Word of the Deity."

He held up the knife.

"Here is a tool of intelligence."

He grasped his long hair.

"Here is the hair of my head and the gift of the Deity."

He sliced his hair off just above shoulder level. There was a loud gasp from the crowd. He held the severed hair high.

"Bring me a lighted torch."

Moments later a student came pushing through the crowd with a torch that had been stolen from a wall and lit at the laundaric. Ilyire set the severed hair afire.

"Here is fuel that might drive a steam engine, fuel that is a gift of the Deity and which the Deity will grow back. It is not evil to burn what can be grown back, it is only evil *not* to grow it back. Burn the Deity's bounty in whatever grate, furnace, or engine you will, then glorify the Deity by planting a thousand seeds. That is all that I have to say to you, my fine and clever young people. Go your way and think, but before you do, come to me, whisper your concerns and have your hair trimmed. After all, why look as old and ugly as I do when you are forty years younger? Indeed, and who would be weighed down with as much hair as Jemli of Kalgoorlie wears?"

From a nearby building the Overmayor was watching, flanked by Highliber Dramoren and the University Librarian.

"I am strangely moved by his words," she admitted quietly.

"He has a good heart sharing his body with a good mind," replied Dramoren.

A pair of scissors was fetched for Ilyire and a bonfire was made of wood stolen from the refectory kitchens. Ilyire began to trim beards and cut hair while the students gathered around.

"His words, are noble, sensible," said Samondel.

"Speaking as a theologian, I say they are the most sensible I have heard preached in the ten years past," replied Martyne.

"Am agreeing. Never had hair cut. Must have hair cut."

Just then there was a disturbance at the edge of the crowd, and Martyne feared that another riot was beginning. Velesti marched through as the students parted before her, leading a group of her Baleshanto students. The tension evaporated as she bowed before Ilyire.

"Master, will you cut my hair?" she asked, then went down on one knee.

"Friend, people have been telling me their concerns as I have barbered them," he said as he trimmed a lock of her hair.

"In that case, thank you for the brief and frantic lesson in camel riding."

Ilyire struggled to hide his astonishment. He had only ever taught one person to ride. That had been Lemorel Milderellen, and he had seen her die.

"But you were killed, shot dead," he whispered.

"I was called back for the same reason that you are here, Ilyire of Glenellen. Are you finished?"

Ilyire cast Velesti's hair clippings into the fire.

"What is it like, in the grave?" he asked as she stood up.

"Very dark and very cold, but then that was the way I lived. This is my chance to make up for all that."

Samondel had her hair trimmed to halfway down her back, indeed more hair was cut off than remained.

"I have been sleeping with a married man, but I love another," she whispered.

"These matters are your own business, do not let others preach to you," he advised.

Ilyire's answer was not what she had expected, but was curiously reassuring. The crowd cheered as her hair was dropped into the flames. Martyne knelt before Ilyire.

"Not much hair," said Ilyire.

"Not much sympathy for the Prophet," Martyne replied.

"Have you concerns?"

"Two woman are pregnant by me and two women have died for me. I love another, but I am afraid of cursing her with misfortune, like the others."

"Then protect your beloved, and the future will happen."

Again there was a disturbance at the edge of the crowd. People rushed to get out of the way and Velesti and her students formed a line as a group of guardsmen marched for the center of the gathering. Martyne hurried to stand with his friend, and Samondel came after him, drawing her flintlock. Other students began to rally behind the Baleshanto students. The guardsmen stopped.

"You have no business here, this is a peaceful rally," said Velesti.

"We have orders—" began the guard captain.

"Ilyire of Glenellen is a holy man, we shall not let him be harmed or imprisoned," said Martyne.

"We have orders to escort the Overmayor to Ilyire of Glenellen," explained the guard captain. "She wishes to have her hair cut."

A path was cleared for the Overmayor, who walked up to Ilyire and knelt before him.

"Master, my motives are less than altruistic," she whispered as he trimmed her hair to shoulder length.

"As are mine, but they are more altruistic than those that I oppose. Is this bad?"

The Overmayor stood and turned to go, and found that her squad of guardsmen were lined up behind her with their helmets removed.

There were loud cheers as her trimmings were dropped into the flames. When Martyne and Samondel left for the day's riding lesson the crowd was still swelling.

This time Samondel managed to urge her mount to a canter as she and Martyne returned to the stables at the end of the ride. It was evening as they walked to the inner city over the stone footbridge that was reserved for pedestrians.

"Am wondering," she said as a barge with about twenty revelers, a small band, and one weary-looking poleman passed beneath them, "Few horses, seeing at inner city."

"The inner city is small and the roads are narrow—except for the Avenue, that is. It is not hard to walk from place to place, and the paraline has a terminus just inside the walls. Horses are not needed, and would only add to the crowding. There are moves to ban horses from the inner city altogether, but there are religious objections to that."

"Religious? Are serious?"

"Oh, yes. The Prophet says that horses are a symbol of natural muscle that the Deity has provided for us to use. The Highliber says that they poo in the streets, and that if people want to live in inner Rochester they can put up with handcart deliveries and higher prices. It is likely that the Highliber will soon only allow horse transport there between midnight and dawn every second day, for the sake of good economics and religious tolerance."

"Confusing. Where, ah, I am coming from, issues decreed. Centuries pass, no change."

"This place must be confusing for you, and distressing."

"No. No, no. Most romantic city, anywhere."

Romantic! A surge of adrenalin slashed through Martyne's body, almost doubling him over.

"A lot of people love Rochester," he responded, his voice almost cracking.

"Is me also, loving it."

Slowly Martyne's physiological state began to return to something resembling what was generally called normal in textbooks. They reached the city gates. Samondel bought a packet of roasted chestnuts from a vendor, and they shared them as they walked along toward the university. They talked easily, working to improve Samondel's grammar, and as the sky colored to darker shades Martyne suggested that he buy them dinner. With a stroke of boldness that he did not realize he was capable of, he lightly placed a hand on Samondel's shoulder and gestured to Café Marellia. The door was painted green, and there were two red hearts encircled by a ring of silver stars. Beneath this was a brightly polished brass plaque. Samondel leaned over to read it, her hands on her knees.

" 'By Appointment to Overmayor Cybeline.' Is famous ruler?"

"She is the one known usually as Zarvora," said Martyne as he pressed the latch down and pushed the door open.

"Ah, the great leader. Highliber, and first overmayor."

They were greeted by a waiter with heavily waxed silver hair, and a long, waxed mustache.

"Most beautiful young Frelle," he said with a wide smile, taking Samondel's hand and kissing it. Then he turned to Martyne and bowed. "Dashing young Fras, welcome, both of you."

"Fras Manuel, it delights me to visit your legendary house instead of merely hearing about it," said Martyne.

Martyne blinked. Had he really said that?

"Delightful Frelle, eyes like violet sapphires, hair like sunset when a storm has just passed. What is your name?"

"I—I—Samondel Leover," Samondel stammered softly.

"Samondel," said the waiter, as if savoring the word in his mouth like a delicious pastry. "A name almost as beautiful as yourself, most enchanting Frelle. Please, this way. I must apologize, but the lute player is sick tonight. Only my humble self to play a little harpsichord for the mood of—"

"Asti!" Samondel exclaimed as she caught sight of the instrument in one corner. "*Fortepiano ni, tarie s'il demi clavicytherium horizar*—ah, sorry. Keyboard player. That. Strange, being."

"Frelle Samondel is from a very distant mayorate," explained Martyne. "She is here to learn Austaric."

"You know the playing of keyboards?" asked the waiter.

"Girls must, in royal house—" began Samondel.

"Frelle Samondel would love to play it," Martyne hastily cut in, but the word 'royal' was already loose and free to do damage.

"Please, feel free to play what your fancy takes!" exclaimed Manuel.

Martyne took the waiter very firmly by the arm and whispered in his ear.

"The princess is under my protection, and her presence in Rochester must not be revealed."

"Princess?" breathed Manuel.

"If anyone asks after her, get their name and report it to me. Here is my card."

Manuel read the card, nearly swooned, and was guided to a chair by Martyne as Samondel played a few experimental chords and runs. Manuel read the card again. " 'Dragon Silver Martyne Camberine. Libris. Unattached.' "

"Manuel Ruavez, so much as even *think* of calling her Your Highness, and you will not live to see the dawn, nor will your body ever be found."

"I understand, great and powerful Fras. This place is sacred to lovers, no safer place on earth to be in love than here."

Samondel stopped playing chords and runs, having gained a feel for the instrument.

"This is 'Towers of Condelor,' to play. Two centuries past, Prince Marbeyer courting lady, ah, disguised? Yes, disguised as commoner. Flew sailw—ah, magically enchanted machine amid towers of Condelor, at night. Beautiful towers, beautiful city. Very romantic."

Samondel began to play. For Manuel the café was suddenly floated on a cloud of stardust and was lifted up into the darkening sky. It was a delicate, rolling, almost mathematical piece, like the beating of a huge bird's wings as it carried the two lovers amid the towers of some fairy-tale city. Samondel closed her eyes, and long, red eyelashes shadowed her cheeks. There were tears on Manuel's face as he took them to their table.

"Little sister, I know that piece," said Martyne.

"Know it? How being?"

"Samondel, it is not two hundred years old, it is *two thousand three hundred* years old. My sister's friend used to play it. It is by Scarlatti, I know it as the Pastorale Sonata."

Samondel's violet eyes shone with wonder. "You take most romantic music known, then write it with stars in sky."

She reached out and squeezed his hand. The face before him briefly had brown eyes and black shoulder-length hair. Elsile was alive again, she had been given a second chance at life. He blinked. Again the hair was red and the eyes violet. A divine vision, thought Martyne. This time he would not fail her.

"This place, very strange," said Samondel. "Like . . . not real."

"It is known widely as a lucky place for lovers, little sister. Many come here while courting, some come here after quarrels, or a long time apart."

"Has . . . magic."

"Years before I was born, Overmayor and Highliber Zarvora brought her lover Denkar here, to try to make up after a quarrel. The story is complicated. Very complicated."

"Please tell."

"Ah, well, to simplify it, she had kept him in prison for nine years. She asked for forgiveness, but he would not forgive her. He said someone must suffer for each of his years in the Calculor— well, in prison, that is. She called in her guards and had one of them punch her in the face. She fell back over that table to your left. Then she got up and had him strike her again. She staggered back and brought down that rack of plates, on the back wall there. They are the same plates, although they have ah been patched together again."

"Why is doing?" asked Samondel, frowning.

"Denkar asked her just that. She said that she was suffering one blow for every year that he had been imprisoned. He only let her take those two blows before he stopped the guard. He and Zarvora were married the next day."

"Not believable."

"*Unbelievable* is the way of saying it. That painting over there, of two lovers staring at each other across a table. That is them. Look carefully at the furnishings and seats."

"Is . . . ah, partitions, little doors, in painting. Not here now."

"What else?"

"*This* table! Zarvora and Denkar, are sitting."

"Correct. Manuel must like you indeed if we have been placed here."

It was close to midnight by the time they returned to Villiers College.

"Martyne, a most wonderful day, I have had," said Samondel as they paused before the doors to the Villiers College foyer.

"I am always pleased to be with you, Eyes of Amethyst. While in my care you will be safe and happy."

"Are sure you are betrothed?"

"Yes. There is a big dinner tomorrow night, in the Libris hostelry chambers. Velesti is organizing it, and I am to swear the vows of commitment with my fiancée."

"You love her?"

Martyne hesitated, then shook his head.

"For me, there is other man," Samondel admitted.

Martyne shuddered slightly. "He is the most lucky man in all the world," he said reluctantly, and under his breath.

"Is married man. Am mistress."

"Frelle Samondel!"

"I owe him much. Am thinking, perhaps, I love him too. To tell, is hard."

Another pang sliced through Martyne. "Then be discreet, wives tend not to be understanding about that sort of thing," he said, feeling giddy.

"Is arriving tomorrow, my lover. Are jealous?"

"I am grateful for what I get, lovely Frelle."

"Trusting you."

She trusted him! Martyne felt that he was going to burst with pride. He seemed to watch in slow motion as Samondel wrapped her arms around him and pressed her lips against his cheek. His arms enfolded her. She giggled.

"Cannot offer more," said Samondel. "Am not like other girls."

"I cannot accept more," replied Martyne.

They laughed as they embraced each other again, then Samondel looked into his eyes in Mirrorsun's light.

"Is wrong, what I said. Before. Can offer more, seeing this?" She held up a small bunch of ribbons sewn onto a slipknot cord. "Traditional, giving of colors to esteemed friend or beloved, wear as warrior. On right arm. Can be wearing, Martyne?"

"Why yes, thank you."

"Is ceremony for lady and her champion. If alive you are being, after fight, I say, 'Wings of my Colors, welcome to the ground you have defended.' You kiss my colors, and say, 'Colors of my Wings, in your name, many victories have I won.' "

"The words are very pretty."

"Very old, also."

"I would be honored to be your champion. Will you be mine?"

"What? I—I only learn Baleshanto, one month."

"As I said, will you be my champion?"

Samondel took a moment to decide that Serjon should be thankful that he was soon to be sharing her bed again, and that he did not have a monopoly on certain other things.

"Yes," she replied.

Martyne untied the small black band from his neck and handed it to Samondel. It had a red stripe at either end, and "Brother Camderine" embroidered into the fabric.

"Never wear this around your neck, that is only for your real ranking in Baleshanto."

"Understand. And Colors of Wings only for right forearm."

They both tied the colors to their arms, then stood facing each other in the light of Mirrorsun. Samondel took his hand and squeezed it.

"Soon, am leaving," she said, looking down at her feet. "Forever."

"Good for both of us, perhaps," replied Martyne.

"Not good. Just best."

Samondel put her free hand behind Martyne's head and pressed a lingering kiss as soft as rose petals against his lips.

"Good-bye," she said, then turned and hurried up the steps and through the door of the college without once turning back.

Highliber Dramoren was exceedingly ill at ease as he waited on the street corner, alone, wearing a Dragon Librarian uniform and cloak without his black color of rank, coat, or skullcap, but with a mask. The wearing of masks was not unknown in Rochestrian society, but was generally done when assignations involving adultery, unsympathetic parents, or similar factors were involved. A dozen disguised guards were within a direct line of sight, but still he was uneasy. Another figure appeared in the distance, walking confidently but with a slightly mincing gait. She was wearing a Dragon Librarian uniform as well, and was also masked.

"Overmayor, this is very dangerous!" hissed Dramoren as she stopped before him.

"Highliber, there is no more secure place to have a proper meeting than an unexpected place, and what I want to say is in great need of security. Come, give me your arm."

Dramoren led her to the door of Café Marellia, pushed it open, and escorted her in. The waiter hurried up to them.

"I am sorry, there are no spare tables," Manuel began.

"We have a booking," said Dramoren. "Two. The name is Franzas."

"Ah yes, Franzas," exclaimed Manuel. "Come this—"

Dramoren caught him by the arm.

"Keep your voice down and be very, very discreet," whispered Dramoren. "I am Highliber Dramoren, this lady is Overmayor Lengina, and the couples at tables two, seven, nine, twelve, and fourteen are members of the palace guard and the Libris Tiger Dragons. Breathe a word of this meeting and you will not live to see the dawn and your body will never be found."

Manuel closed his eyes and swayed slightly.

"Great and powerful Fras, this place is sacred to lovers. There is no safer place on earth to be in love than here."

Dramoren winced at the word "love."

"Just take us to our table and shut up."

The meeting was for coffee and chocolates rather than a meal. Manuel noticed now that the couples at tables two, seven, nine, twelve, and fourteen were watching everyone else except each other, were not smiling, and had not touched their coffee, cakes, or chocolates. To his surprise the master of the Commonwealth's infrastructure and the Commonwealth's monarch drank their coffee quickly, then ordered another each.

"Frelle, what could be so important that you could insist on meeting me here?"

"Palaces are full of devices for people to listen and watch, they have been perfected over many centuries. Courtiers want to know things. They are seldom spies, but they like to be part of the great and momentous decisions."

"Libraries are little different."

"Which is why I had us meet here," she said emphatically, grasping his hand. "Try to show some romance, people will get suspicious."

"Suspicious, Frelle Overmayor?" hissed Dramoren. "You are currently defining new extremes in the application of that word. This is about as suspicious as a monk on a nunnery wall at midnight with a bottle of sacramental wine in one hand and a condom in the other. What possibly—"

"I want to provoke a war with the Woomeran Confederation."

Dramoren nearly choked. He gulped down the remains of his coffee and Lengina offered him her mug. He drank half of this as well.

"May I ask why?" he eventually managed.

"I want the Commonwealth unified against Jemli the Prophet and her—what is the new name? Reborn Gentheists?"

"Reformed Gentheists. But the Southmoors—"

"Are hostile to her. They are traditional Islamics. The Central Confederation is mostly Christian and similarly hostile."

"And at war with the Southmoors."

"Secret peace talks have been commenced, or have you not been spying on my diplomatic dispatches lately?"

"Frelle Over—that is, Len—I mean, Frelle, I only—"

"I *expect* you to spy on me, Highliber, so never mind and don't apologize. The only other major group is the Northmoors. They are rural, Islamic, and like to be left alone; they do not even have a strict ruling on fueled engines. We have the chance to show the Reformed Gentheists a solid wall of opposition in the East. At present there is no hostility, so their people come and go from the Commonwealth as they please."

"But why bother? Jemli's Reformed Gentheists are gaining little support. Since Ilyire of Glenellen began preaching tolerance throughout the Commonwealth they have been thwarted further still, and when you had him cut your hair it actually became high fashion to get a haircut and oppose Jemli."

"I want a *solid* wall, Fras Franzas. If I can manage it I do not even want fighting, just hostility. Out of all the overmayorates, only Rochestrian Commonwealth has been able to maintain its structure and economy since Black Thirteenth and the loss of electrical machines. Without our Dragon Librarian Service and paraline engineers Jemli does not have the ability to raise, move, or use an army of any size from Woomera or Kalgoorlie. Even the Alspring Ghan lancers have been softened by two decades of imported luxuries, more liberal lifestyles, and paraline transport."

"I have heard that they now allow women to become lancers," said Dramoren, looking uneasily around at the other genuine couples in the café for signs of suspicious interest.

"Yes, because their men are all busy building paraline tracks and running merchant houses. I only want an incident to close the border, Franzas. Not bloody battles, not victories, just a wall between us and the religious riff-raff."

"I shall work upon it, Frelle—ah, Lengina. A war."

"With no fighting."

Dramoren ran his fingers through his hair. He wondered if a rather hunted look was obvious on his masked face.

"Very well, and while I am at it what about a nice alliance between the Commonwealth, Southmoors, and Central Confederation, and a declaration of neutality from the Northmoors?"

"Well, yes, if you think you can do it."

The wretched woman can't recognize a joke, thought Dramoren as he drained the last of her coffee.

"Is there anything else, Frelle Lengina?"

"We . . . look tense."

"Is this meant to come as a shock?"

"We look as if we are having a lovers' quarrel."

"That's unlikely, we are not lovers."

"My guards will be sad, they care for me."

"What?" Dramoren laughed. "Who cares what guards think? My Tiger Dragons *do* as they are told, *think* when they are ordered to do so, and don't even *screw* unless it's in the service of Libris."

Lengina put her hands beneath Dramoren's jaw, leaned over the table, and pressed her lips against his. After a moment of astonished panic, Dramoren took her arms in his hands. Her tongue flickered teasingly across the surface of his lips.

"I—I take it that our quarrel has been resolved?" ventured Dramoren.

"I admire you greatly, I have done so for a long time," responded Lengina.

"I am, ah, honored. Of course, ah, any man who does not admire you needs a good optician—but my own eyes are very good."

"You have always been so aloof with me."

"Frelle, you are the *Overmayor. Nobody* just asks you out for dinner and a tour of his sleeping accommodation!"

"That is the trouble. I get a lot of fine, formal approaches and proposed arrangements of marriage with great strategic benefits, but no romance. *You* are always so distracted and, well, cool. My advisors say that you meet with two women late at night."

"Frelle Velesti is one. Did some idiot describe her as a woman? Whoever it is needs to be hospitalized."

"Ah, the one that even the guard dogs run from. Oh, well, point taken. And the other?"

"The ghost of Highliber Zarvora. You can walk right through her."

"You are joking!"

"Would you like an introduction? I can arrange it. Lovely Frelle, why bother with me? I am not particularly brilliant or capable, I achieve what I do by working a *nineteen-hour day*. This is the first time that I have eaten anything resembling a meal while sitting down for over a week. Cool? Distracted? Frelle, I am just *tired*!"

"You need someone to look after you."

"I have a lackey, he does a good job. I even paid him a bonus last month."

"Over the past months I have had five princes and mayors propose to me as serious possibilities for consorts."

"And all were found to be unsuitable in major or minor ways."

"I have spies too, and some are better informed than my personal advisors."

"They should have reported that I lead a blameless life and my investigations are above reproach."

"You dedicated two thousand of your staff to uncovering scandals and secrets involving those five men."

"You are deserving of no less diligence."

Lengina opened the top button of her blouse's collar, then another, and a third. Dramoren's hands began to tremble.

"*Please*, Overmayor, our guards are watching," he whispered desperately.

She reached into her cleavage and drew out a folded piece of poorpaper.

"While investigating the latest of my suitors, you instructed the Dragon Gold in charge of the Espionage Constables to, and I quote, 'Find something wrong with the fucker or I shall personally affix your head to the highest lightning rod on the Libris beamflash tower.' What does that mean?"

"Ah, 'fucker' is an ancient term for a very naughty person."

"You were frantic to keep me unwed."

"It was a bad time for a royal wedding—politically, that is."

"You were jealous."

Dramoren opened his mouth. To say no would be an insult. To say yes . . . would be admitting the truth. It would also involve considerable loss of face for him, except that the woman, his monarch, quite obviously fancied him.

"Well, sort of . . . yes."

Lengina removed her mask and flung it over her shoulder. Dramoren swallowed, removed his mask, folded it neatly, and placed it on the table. Complete silence suddenly gripped Café Marellia. Lengina looked around and scowled.

"I command you all to keep talking," she ordered.

Loud, polite, facile banter instantly blanketed the room.

"I love the scar across your face."

"It is not there by design, Frelle—"

"Lengina."

"Sorry—Lengina."

"Franzas, I like to think of the Commonwealth as a body," said Lengina, taking both of Dramoren's hands in hers. "The Dragon Librarian Service is the brain, I am the heart, and you are its right arm. What other overmayorate has that sort of unity?"

"But people are the soul of the Commonwealth. We had better be discreet until they are prepared."

"By the time we return to the palace tonight the greater part of Rochester should know about us, and the beamflash signaling system will be lit up like a bonfire on Equinox Night. Still, I doubt that we shall have anything to worry about."

An hour before midnight Dramoren and Lengina stood embracing in front of Café Marellia, oblivious to the nightlife that hurried, sauntered, staggered, and occasionally crawled past them. From across the darkened street two Dragon Silver Librarians regarded the young lovers through the open shutters of the Rector's Lash.

"Young fools," said the graying, dour-looking woman.

"Don't know what the world has in store for them," replied the sallow, haggard man across the table from her.

"Dangerous, evil people out there."

"Betrayal."

"Death."

"Jealousy."

"Costly child care."

"Poor young fools."

"Think they'll do it?"

"Sure to."

"Lucky young fools."

"Why?"

"In love."

"Futile. Love leads nowhere but dinner, drinks, and bed."

"You can do that without being in love."

"Fancy another drink?"

"Love one."

Martyne stepped out of the pedal train and onto the Rochester terminus platform, stretched for a moment, then walked quickly to the gates. There was nobody to meet him, for he had traveled under a false name and with false papers, but then Espionage Constables cleared for his level of discretion could do that sort of thing.

Once clear of the terminus he went straight to the market, putting on his auditor's hat and sunframes as he walked. The elements of his disguise were minimal, but worn with style and accompanied by all the appropriate mannerisms. Some vendors sneered as he approached, others scrambled to hide goods and registers. One even offered him a bribe, but he held up his hand and shook his head.

"Thank you, Fras, but I am beyond corruption," he said with a smile. "Nevertheless, for the act of offering you must come with me."

Martyne took him by the arm, but the other led the way. They walked in silence through the crowds for a distance, then Martyne's companion stopped.

"Serjon is the weedy-looking one over by Jairlin's Flintlocks," he said. "The one with the black hat and dustcape."

"My thanks," replied Martyne. "Stand shadow."

It was where Serjon had been told to meet with Samondel, but he was somewhat early. For a time he paced restively, drawing a paraline watch from his pocket several times to check the time. Suddenly he hurried away. Martyne trailed a little behind him, blending well with the early evening crowds of the market. Serjon made for a stall with an awning whose skirt reached all the way down to waist level. The words painted above were Amar At'agnine, which translated as The Amorous Sheep. *Well, if he's going there at least he doesn't want her to carry his child,* thought Martyne. *Not yet, anyway.*

After some minutes Serjon emerged. Martyne snapped his fingers and pointed to him but did not follow as the Yarronese hurriedly slipped into the crowd. Martyne felt curiously burned out inside, and disinclined to do anything at all, but almost of their own volition, his feet began to walk. They walked straight to Amar At'agnine. Inside there were two lamps burning within red shades, while a slightly stooped yet widely grinning little man with pop eyes and hair tied back in a tight ponytail stood rubbing his hands and bowing almost continually. Along the top shelf was a row of a dozen pegs of varying length and thickness, while on all the others were packages that could be conveniently enclosed in a fist. Each package had an index number and symbol.

"And, ah, what would Fras require?" asked the vendor, raising his hand to hover before a middle level shelf.

"I am unfamiliar with all this," Martyne said with a flourish. "I am from far away."

"Does Fras require a little advice on company as well?" enquired the vendor. "I can arrange liaisons of a suitable but transitory nature."

Suddenly Martyne's mind made the subtle transition to warrior, although it was shown only by a slight chill in his voice.

"What was bought by the Fras who was in here before me?" asked Martyne.

"Oh, Fras, it is the nature of my trade to repeat nothing that—"

Martyne took the man's hand so gently that there was barely a hint of hostile intent. The pain in the vendor's wrist was, however, so great that he was incapable even of calling out. Martyne eased the pressure very slightly.

"I shall only ask one more time, and if I do not hear an answer that is both realistic and honest you shall not live to see morning and your body will never be found."

Although the threat was formulaic, it was nonetheless not far from the truth. The vendor took several gasps to recover his breath.

"A package of half a dozen of the peg 6 ME, with red silk ribbons attached and a joke of an amorous nature on pink tissue paper with every suit of love's armor."

"Let me guess: 6 M would be six inches in length and indifferent width."

"You have the measure of him, Fras," said the vendor with hurried diplomacy.

"What did he say while here?"

"His Austaric was not good, Fras. His lady had not seen him for a long time, but he felt that she might still be inclined his way. If the mood took her thus, he wanted to appear to have appropriate precautions to hand without seeming to have had lewd intent. The 6 ME pack has 'For Emergencies Only' scripted across the wrapping, and it was this that I recommended."

Martyne released him, then nodded with his eyes squeezed shut.

"Er, a disappointment in love, Fras?" enquired the vendor uneasily.

"Not much love was involved," replied Martyne, opening his eyes and staring speculatively at the 7 M+ peg.

"Perhaps you would consider a free sample?" asked the vendor. "You know, ladies of good breeding do favor a considerate man."

"Thank you, Fras, but by dawn I may be dead, so why bother?"

Martyne emerged from the covered stall, then returned to where Serjon was waiting, watched by Martyne's shadow. Minutes passed. The vendors in the area grew restive at the presence of an auditor for such a length of time.

"Serjon!"

Both Martyne and Serjon whirled at the sound of the voice, but it was Serjon to whom Samondel rushed. They fell into each others' arms, kissing and laughing with elation and relief. They were very much the center of the nearby vendors' attention as well, but when the lovers hurried off with their arms about each other, the lurking auditor was also found to be gone.

Martyne flung his auditor's hat and sunframes into the gutter at the center of the street, resuming the look of an edutor as he walked. He made for the Ugly Friar, ordered himself a mug of wine, and drained it. He ordered another, drank it rather more slowly, then ordered a third, and a fourth.

"He did appear to be quite a decent and handsome young blade, I have to admit," he told the jarmaid about fifteen minutes later.

"Ah, who would that be?" she asked, already having the stirrings of fancy for him.

"My beloved's true love," replied Martyne.

"Ah, silly girl, handsome Fras, jilting one such as you. Not to worry, though. I'll look after you tonight."

The jarmaid returned to the vintner with Martyne's coin, but when she turned back to regard him he was gone, his empty cup left on the table.

Martyne was already in the street, hurrying unsteadily away.

"Looked after, by a woman, in this condition, aye, been there, done that," he mumbled to himself as he walked. "Twice. Apparently."

In the hospitality suites of Libris, Velesti was at that very moment engaged in entertainment of her own. Martyne's parents and Elene Disore were the guests, but found themselves in the most unusual position of sitting at table with Julica. The only person feeling more uneasy was Julica, who had eaten very little of the meal.

"I thought Martyne was to be here?" Elene asked, squirming a little in her chair and looking impatient.

"As I have said time and again, Mother, he was invited but was called away to a monastery in the south."

"What can possibly be more important than being here with his—his loved ones?"

"I have told you."

"In a monastery?"

"Theology and the interpretation of dogma are currently the cornerstones of the continent's politics," said Velesti, leaning back and folding her arms. "Monasteries are where a lot of the Christian side of it is determined."

Elene squirmed again, and looked particularly uncomfortable.

"If you please, I must visit the comfort room," she finally admitted.

Velesti stood up and walked to the door, saying, "Certainly, there is a pot privy at the first floor on the left. Meantime I shall call for dessert."

Elene was gone only a matter of minutes, but Velesti was absent for twice as long. When she returned it was with a silver platter, upon which were three crystal glasses of darkish yellow liquid and a tiny beaker of something clear. Velesti set the tray down on the table, and her guests noted that before each glass were three cards with J, V, and E in cyrello script capitals. Julica sat back with her hands clasped over her swollen abdomen and her eyes cast down.

"I have a little magic show for you, while we wait for the sweetcakes to arrive," declared Velesti, picking up the beaker. "Actually it is not magic, just herbalistry, and as reproducible as any chemistric test."

The guests looked on attentively.

"These three glasses contain a little filtered urine from three ladies. I add a drop of this clear potion to this one, kindly provided by Julica, and behold!"

A drop splashed into the urine, which immediately shaded into a warm, red hue. Velesti moved on to the next glass and tipped a drop into it. This time the color turned blue.

"Now, the Frelle who was gracious enough to provide the contents of the middle glass was myself," Velesti explained.

"Uh, why is there a difference in the two colors?" asked Elene.

"Because Julica is most certainly pregnant, and I am most certainly not. Now, moving on to Mother's sample—"

"No!" shrieked Elene, but the drop was already falling. The yellowish liquid turned blue.

Elene rose to her feet, sending her chair tumbling, then advanced on her daughter. The slap aimed for Velesti's face was caught deftly and Elene's wrist was twisted so that she bent backward. By now the other three were on their feet, but Velesti grasped the hem of Elene's gown and flung it up over her head. A cushion was revealed, carefully strapped over her abdomen. The others stopped and stared.

"Quite an unusual pregnancy, I think it requires an assisted birth," said Velesti, drawing her knife and slashing it across the cushion.

Feathers poured out onto the floor. Velesti released Elene, who swept the gown from her head, then glared at her, her face scarlet with mortification.

"I have the feeling that Martyne walked out of our house a virgin," said Velesti. "On the other hand the idea of carrying his child did remain with you. Trick him into marriage, then begin a real pregnancy. So convenient. Two great mercantile houses united with a single heir. And when were the Camderines introduced to the scheme?"

Graten and Telsa remained silent and sheepish. Julica was so still and silent that she could not even be seen to be breathing.

"Timid, drunken sot couldn't get it up," muttered Elene after a short but poisonous silence.

Velesti pointed, and four pairs of eyes followed her gesture to Julica.

"As you may have noticed, I like to keep track of such things as the dalliances—or attempted dalliances—that are going on around me," said Velesti. "Julica, did you really think I would not have noticed what you did with Reclor?"

Julica shook her head in silence, while Elene sat with her mouth open. Julica got to her feet but Velesti stepped between her and the door.

"There is the future of the Disore household," she concluded with a grand sweep of the knife with which she had cut open Elene's cushion. "Frelle Julica was generous and compassionate enough to lie with Reclor some hours before his duel, so that he did not enter it a virgin. Now she is carrying his child—and your grandchild, Mother."

For some moments nobody moved, then Elene shambled over to Julica and put her arms around her. Elene began to sob, then fell to her knees and pressed her head against Julica's swollen abdomen, crying "Reclor, Reclor, you're still alive."

"I was too ashamed to tell, you, Frelle," explained Julica. "I came here, I wanted to earn enough to raise the child myself, alone."

"Oh, silly girl, good girl."

"Aunt Velesti, the name appeals to me," said Velesti, returning her knife to its sheath.

"Will—will Martyne be coming here at all?" asked Graten Camderine. "We owe him an apology."

"Some of you more than others. Actually, one of my informants told me some minutes ago that he has unexpectedly arrived back in Rochester after only a half day away, but no matter, we can take him out to lunch tomorrow."

"Perhaps a little boat trip where we can talk with discretion," said Graten.

"Perhaps," conceded Velesti. "The preserved meats and sausages of the Camderines may not be united with the wool and hides of the Disores, but then children should not be the currency of commerce, should they, Fras and Frelle Camderine?"

Elene got to her feet and cradled Julica's head in her arms. "You are my foster daughter now, and you are returning to Griffith with me. Everybody will be told, and damn what is whispered. I am so, so proud of you."

"Actually, I checked the civil legislation," said Velesti, drawing a folded poorpaper from her jacket. "The letter of the law states that: 'a coupling preceding a duel presided over by any legally qualified official of a mayorate, city, the Dragon Librarian Service, or the clergy is looked upon as associated with, and bound to, for the purposes of civil law, proceeding, and matters related to the duel, that specifically involve property and property associated therewith.' "

All four of Velesti's audience looked quite blank.

"Could you possibly repeat that a little more slowly, Frelle?" asked Telsa Camderine.

"I shall do better than that, Frelle, I shall translate it. By relieving Reclor of his virginity as part of the preparation for the duel, Julica became technically betrothed to Reclor. Frelle Julica, due to a legal technicality you appear to be my legal sister-in-law."

Velesti left the astounded group to themselves and returned across the alleyways, steps, and plazas of Libris to her room. She removed her jacket and had done sixty-five chin-ups when there was a rap at her door. It was Marelle.

"It's Martyne," she announced.

"Explain," replied Velesti, already apprehensive.

"Remember that girl he's besotted with?"

"Samondel?"

"Yes."

"Well, her long-lost true love has arrived in Rochester. Martyne has taken it badly, very badly—"

Velesti dropped to her knees, put a hand over her head and began pounding the floorboards with the other.

"You didn't know about any of this, did you?" asked Marelle.

Velesti stood up, glared at Marelle, then snatched a dueling shirt from the rack.

"No, I did not," she conceded. "Do you happen to know what Samondel's lover is named, and where he resides?"

"He has a room at the Celestial registered under Serjon Feydamor."

Velesti went curiously blank for a dozen or so heartbeats.

"Thank you for telling me all of that," said Velesti, snatching up her jacket. "I shall be out and about."

"Where are you going?"

"To remove the last of the complications from Martyne's life."

• • •

Highliber Dramoren was working in his study when there was a pounding at his door. He admitted one of his personal guard, who brought with him a request for an audience from Velesti Disore of the Espionage Constables. The priority code was Direct Threat of Invasion. Velesti was hurriedly admitted, and the door closed behind her. Dramoren started the little water-baffle fountain to muffle their voices.

"Now we can talk," he said breathlessly. "What is this?"

"I have been keeping a student of the university under watch for some time, a girl named Corien Meziar. She is actually an agent of the Reformed Gentheists, and she keeps a list of activists for and against their causes and beliefs."

"I am aware of several such agents, herself included."

"She has just sent a coded message to Peterborough concerning a fellow student, Samondel Leover. Frelle Leover is the second of the American flying machine's crew."

"The devil you say! Are you sure?"

"Oh yes, and the tale worsens. Another American agent has just arrived in Rochester, and has joined her. They are passing as lovers, dining and carousing this very night. They are suspected of connections with that Christian Gaia Crusader movement that recently sprang up locally, and of smuggling advanced weapons from the North American continent for Reformed Gentheist use—against us."

"I see," said Dramoren, rubbing his hands together. "But what has she been doing for these two months past?"

"One can do a great deal in two months, but I do not know specifically. However, Frelle Leover is also an American head of state, and her lover is one of their greatest warriors."

"Ignore my last question," Dramoren said urgently. "I want them arrested. Now!"

"Highliber, one does not casually arrest a head of state."

"One does if she is conspiring with other foreign powers to invade the Commonwealth!"

"You do not know that."

"In that case I shall go down to her cell and ask her, in half an hour or so. I shall now repeat myself, which is something that some of my staff have discovered—very painfully—that I dislike doing. Arrest her!"

"At once, Highliber, but . . ."

"But?"

"Might I suggest, Highliber, that very few know what I have just told you. The Americans have fueled engines powering their flying machines, in flagrant violation of the Prophet Jemli's teachings. There is clearly a contradiction to be resolved before we can prove that they are in some conspiracy."

"True, quite true. Arrest them with discretion, then take them to the cloisters of the University Library. There we shall have a private inquest, and possibly a trial by ordeal. Should the worst suspicions be brought to light, they can merely vanish, and we can blame Reformed Gentheist assassins."

"Useful people, those Reformed Gentheist assassins."

"Can I name you as my champion against Frelle Leover's warrior, Frelle Velesti?"

"I can secure you a better champion than I, Fras Highliber."

It is a quite well known fact that most people who go drinking in the hope of finding some more sympathetic company than a barrel will generally find only a barrel. Martyne was, however, only in search of barrels, and he had sampled the contents of several. He stumbled into his room alone with a thumblamp in his hand, looked at his neat but empty bunk in annoyance, then set the lamp down, blew out the flame, and crawled beneath his bunk to sleep. He lay fully clothed on the floor while the darkened room spun around him at a truly distressing speed. After another minute there was a knock at the door.

Martyne did not answer. There was a sharp bang and the door burst open. Velesti stood in the doorway holding another thumblamp. Martyne put his head out from under the bunk.

"Oh, God in heaven, had I wanted female company this night I would have prayed for someone more sympathetic," chanted Martyne in slurred Balesha plainsong.

Velesti entered the room, set the thumblamp down, reached under the bunk and dragged Martyne out. She hauled him to his feet while batting her hand back and forth across his face.

"Get your train back on the paralines, Sensei, the Rochestrian Commonwealth has need of you," she said, dropping Martyne onto a stool.

"Screw the Rochestrian Commonwealth."

"What were you doing beneath your bunk? Were you expecting to be attacked?"

"Frelle Velesti, you are a woman. You cannot understand the workings of men's thoughts."

"Try me," Velesti replied.

She selected a shirt from the peg rack, then removed Martyne's cloak and began to unlace his tunic.

"If anyone happens to ask how I spent this night, I can in all honesty say that I visited Amar At'agnine, drank rather more than was good for me at the Ugly Friar and elsewhere, and did *not* end up in my own bunk. It is highly unlikely that anyone would ask me such a question, but the fact that I have an answer that is both honest and impressive gives me a measure of comfort. Now I can even add that the tunic was ripped off my back by a woman who—ow! You have cold hands! Please, leave me alone, what is this? Give me facts!"

"Fact: Your beloved Samondel is being dined and feted by her American beloved. Fact: My mother is not pregnant. Fact: Julica is pregnant with Reclor's child. Fact: Julica has been adopted by my mother. Fact: In June I shall become an aunt. Fact: You no longer have to marry my mother."

Elation, despair, hope, confusion, and agonized grief flickered across Martyne's features like lightning bolts amid thunderclouds. He fell to his knees, weeping.

"Too late, too bloody late!" he moaned.

"Fact: Samondel and her lover are about to be arrested."

"What? Why?"

"Fact: She is a head of state called an airlord, all the way from the continent of North America. Well-founded speculation: She appears to have been spying on the Commonwealth, conspiring with the Reformed Gentheists, and possibly conspiring against Avian as well. Fact: The Avianese attacked America and stole flying technology from the locals. Fact: The Americans are a bit cross, understandably so, if you ask me. Fact: There is to be a secret trial by ordeal. Fact: Because of your association with Saireme Airlord Samondel, also known as Red Death, victor in six clear air combats, and leader of the secret expedition to this continent, you have been chosen to demonstrate your loyalty to the Highliber, Overmayor, and Commonwealth by standing as champion against her."

The barrage of revelations crushed Martyne's already reeling senses.

"Samondel? My Samondel? Beautiful Samondel?"

"Beautiful and devious Samondel. How much did you tell her?"

"About the Espionage Constables? Nothing—fact."

"Good. You must go to the University Library cloisters. There you will meet the Highliber, who has named you as his champion."

Martyne's head suddenly cleared considerably.

"There is to be a secret hearing, and probably a duel. Dramoren is a good librarian but an average shot. When I suggested that you might be willing to be his champion, he welcomed the prospect of having a former Balesha monk fighting on his behalf."

Velesti hauled him to his feet again and draped his cloak over his shoulders. Taking Martyne by the arm, she marched him to the landlord's bedroom. When the man did not answer her knock she struck the door with the side of her left fist, just above the lock. The door swung open. The landlord and his wife sat up in bed, clinging to each other.

"Fras Martyne's lock is broken," Velesti announced. "Repair it. Now."

"Yes, Frelle Dragonliber, yes, Frelle Dragonliber," babbled the landlord.

Out in the dimly lit street Martyne saw that ten Tiger Dragons were waiting for Velesti.

"Fras Clemento, make sure that my friend reaches the University Library within the quarter hour, and make sure that a strong coffee is within him by then," said Velesti. She put an arm around Martyne and whispered in his ear. "The prospects are good for a very ugly night for all of us, little brother. Just remember that Fortune guards those unlucky in love, and that all is fair in love and warfare."

"What do you mean by that?"

"When the time is right, you will know."

Clemento and Martyne hurried off down the street, and when they came to a corner Martyne looked back. Velesti and the other Tiger Dragons were nowhere to be seen.

"She must have an almighty battle on the brew with someone," said Martyne to the portly but broad-chested Clemento. "I have never known her to need the help of even one Tiger Dragon, let alone nine."

"I have been told nothing, Fras, but doubtless we shall hear the fight all the way from the University."

Serjon returned to his room with Samondel after a delightful dinner at the Banquet and Barrel. They had with them a jar of sweet hargen-wine, and as they entered his room Samondel flopped backward onto his bed with her arms spread out.

"Sorry that I have mugs instead of glassware, but perchance it will have been worth waiting for," he said as he took two mugs from the bedside stand and placed them on the tray.

"We have waited so long, what is a few minutes more?" she replied.

They toasted each other, then swapped glasses and toasted each other again in a traditional Yarronese gesture. The meal had been succulent, and the wine was a curious mixture of chill and heat. Serjon poured the last of the wine into their mugs, then set the tray on his bedside table and stretched out with one leg on the bed and the other on the floor.

"You look uncomfortable," said Samondel. "Come. I'll move over."

She put her arm around his shoulders and drew him over, and they lay side by side for a time, sipping their wine in silence.

"I wonder where Bronlar is now?" said Samondel presently.

"At Lake Taupo Wingfield, alone in her bunk," said Serjon.

"You seem confident of her fidelity," remarked Samondel with a little grin.

"The problems she has with me could only be amplified with anyone else."

"Problems? Yours was the marriage of the century in Mounthaven. How could you have problems?"

Serjon sighed. "As you know, she was tricked into bedding those two mere artisans before our reconciliation. Whether by guilt or whatever, the act of intimacy now causes her considerable pain, even with me. It is a condition known well to students of medicine."

"Terrible, terrible. Have you sought help?"

"I have read books, but other than that, no. How could we have it being known that Mounthaven's two most celebrated heroes of the Great War are miserable in bed?"

There was another short silence.

"So what do you do?" asked Samondel after a gulp of her wine.

"We do very little, aside from warming each other while sleeping."

"No, I mean what do *you* do?"

Serjon laughed. "What do you think I do? I am a great hero, the invincible victor of a hundred and four clear air victories. Women like a hero."

"So, you have been unfaithful to her—apart from with me?"

"Why not? I was unfaithful to you too."

Samondel gasped, then giggled. "Beast!" she squealed, and poured the rest of her wine over his head. He tried to grab her arm, but spilled his own wine over her blouse. They grappled with each other, giggling and laughing for several minutes.

"It must have been Seyret," laughed Samondel. "The dumpy little airlord's daughter that you flew to freedom."

"And you must read minds, ach, I'd better be careful what I think."

"When was it? Before me?"

"No, you were my first, just as surely as I was yours. The night after I'd brought Seyret home I was taken out into the palace gardens by her very fiancé, would you believe it? He said that they both wanted to thank me for freeing her by means of a couple of rather intimate hours with her. When I finally came to be abed with her she had none of the devices that you and I have always used. Perhaps she wanted the chance that her first child might be of Feydamor blood. Everyone wants to be part of the Serjon Feydamor legend."

"Me, Seyret, Bronlar . . ." said Samondel, counting on her fingers and frowning.

"That's all."

"Three, a lucky number. You must keep it at that."

"The others are a long, long way away."

"But I am close, and I love you."

"I love you as well, far more than Bronlar."

Samondel sighed. "What a pity that it is the time of a dangerous moon for me."

Serjon considered. For that entire evening he had told the truth. Why bother to resort to lies now?

"I did have hopes for your favor," he admitted. "Only this evening I bought a packet of suitable devices, just in case your favor might turn to me again."

"Always the considerate one," said Samondel, then she rolled onto him and kissed him on the lips, a hard, greedy kiss.

Serjon rolled her onto her back, reached down and began to run his hand up her left leg, raising her skirts.

"And how many more have there been for you?" he asked.

"Just you."

"Just me? I don't believe it."

He stroked her inner thigh, noting that she wore no underclothes. Perhaps she had been intending to be his all along for this night.

"It's true."

"Not even that ex-monk you told me about?"

"Martyne? Ah, I was just lucky that you came along. A day more and I might have been his."

"Really?"

"Well . . . leave me some secrets. Now here we are and I love you, Serjon." She placed her hands over her left breast. "You have my body and my heart."

"And I love you," Serjon purred in her ear as he unlaced his trousers. "All this time in this strange land, I have bedded nobody else. I knew that you were here, alone. I could not bear the thought of you being alone if I was in company."

Serjon rolled between her legs, but she wriggled out from under him at once.

"First, apply your device," she warned.

"Not even this once?"

"In a fortnight I may consider all reasonable arguments. For now, if it is not on, then neither are you."

Serjon lay on his side, picking at the string binding of the Amar At'agnine, 6 ME package, his trousers tangled around his ankles. Samondel's skirts were around her waist as she lay on her back, watching the operation with considerable amusement and giggling continually. Serjon rolled back onto her.

"And now—"

The door burst open. Framed between Samondel's legs was Velesti, and flanking her were two more women in uniform, both wielding short-barrel, wide-bore flintlocks. The fist with which Velesti had smashed the door's lock was still clenched, and a Morelac was in her other hand. Serjon made a move for the reaction pistol beneath his pillow, but Samondel seized his hand.

"No, Serjon, no!" cried Samondel, grasping at him. "She'll kill you. She's faster than humans, or even featherheads."

Cowering in each other's arms, they faced the Dragon Librarian, who was still standing in the doorway, unmoving.

"Frelle Samondel Leover and Fras Serjon Feydamor, you are

both under arrest and charged with espionage," said Velesti. "Get dressed and come with us."

"Where we are to go?" asked Samondel in Austaric.

"The University Library."

"The University?"

"It is not your place to ask questions," replied Velesti.

Samondel stood up, letting her skirts drop to cover her legs. Serjon stood with his back to the Dragon Librarian while he raised his trousers and laced up again. When they were both ready Velesti gestured to them with her gun.

"Take these two and hold them in the street outside." Velesti said to the Tiger Dragons in the corridor. "I must examine his room."

Alone in Serjon's room, Velesti did a quick but thorough search. As she had expected, there was nothing of interest apart from one Clastini reaction pistol and four spare clips of ammunition. She put the Clastini into her belt and buttoned her jacket over it, and pocketed the ammunition. His papers appeared to be in order, but were probably an expensive forgery. All of his clothing bore the marks of Seymour tailors, and he had five royals in gold and some silver.

Velesti straightened the bedcovers, dropped the remains and contents of the Amar At'agnine, 6 ME package into her pocket, then went downstairs. The landlord was waiting for her, rubbing his hands together anxiously.

"The lock mounting is broken," Velesti told him. "Have it repaired. Now."

"Yes, Frelle Dragonliber."

"And, Landlord,"

"Yes, Frelle Dragonliber?"

"I have made an inventory of the room's contents. If everything is not as it was when the young man returns, you will suspended over a slow fire and asked some very probing questions."

"Oh, Frelle Dragonliber, it will be as secure as your undoubted virtue," the landlord assured her.

"It had better be an improvement on that," Velesti warned.

•   •   •

Dramoren was shown into Lengina's parlor while she was still draping a red flannel dressing cloak over her nightgown. Her handmaids squealed and gathered in front of her, but she ordered them out even as the Highliber was bowing.

"Alarming news, Frelle Overmayor, a foreign monarch has been arrested after two months disguised as a student of the university," he began succinctly.

"From Woomera?" she asked, more puzzled than alarmed.

"From North America. She was in that flying machine that Alarek Andren arrived in. She is called an airlord."

"She? Airlord?"

"There are suggestions that she is behind these Christian Gaia Crusaders in the independent castellanies of the Southeast, and there are further suggestions that there is a conspiracy against Rochester. There are also suggestions that she has contacts with the Reformed Gentheists, and there are even suggestions that these Crusaders intend to arm the Gentheists with very advanced weapons."

"Suggestions, further suggestions, also suggestions, even suggestions? Has anyone in the Espionage Constables ever heard of hard evidence?"

"Frelle Airlord Samondel Leover has been openly associating with a Reformed Gentheist spy and activist."

"Ah. And what does she have to say?"

"She has not yet been questioned. I would bet a bag of royals that it is something along the lines of 'I am innocent,' yet bear in mind that we did fire upon her flying machine without provocation."

Lengina folded her arms beneath her dressing cloak and thought for a moment, but all that she could think of was that her feet were cold.

"Speaking as a fellow head of state, I suppose I would have hidden too. All right, then, Fras Dramoren, I am in the dark without a lantern. Advise me."

"I suggest a judicial duel. Their society recognizes dueling, and I have a suitable champion ready, one who can place a shot on the target so well that she could not go on to a blood duel. We would then have a pretext to hold her for trial, and have a full trial before a magistrate. That way her government cannot be affronted if she is speaking the truth."

"If she loses."

"She is up against a former Balesha monk, gracious Frelle. She cannot win."

Lengina nodded. "Do it. Is there any point in me going back to bed just now?"

"Probably not. I shall send news as soon as it is available."

When they reached the University grounds Serjon was taken to the administration chambers by four of the Tiger Dragons. Samondel continued on with Velesti and the other five.

"We must call past your room at Villiers College, Frelle Samondel," said Velesti in Old Anglian once they were walking across the darkened lawns. "You need to change out of those casual robes."

"I do not understand. Why we are here? Why were we arrested—and how do you know *Old Anglian*?"

"I fought in Mounthaven, against the aviad radicals. As for the rest, there are sensitive issues involved, Frelle. Politics, religion, loyalties, identities, and deception have been mixed into a most unstable and explosive paste. Unfriendly eyes watch Libris, the cathedral, the city watchouse, and even the mayoral palace. The university is safer ground, for all the parties concerned. The Highliber, City Constable, and others are waiting to speak with you in the University Library cloisters."

"But why?"

"Your lover Serjon and you have been named in a plot against the Rochestrian Commonwealth."

"No! We are innocent. And he is not my lover! Well, nearly—again—but not quite, thanks to you. But I am not ashamed—"

"Would you like to stand up at a public trial and speak under oath about just exactly what you were doing with him? I might be inclined to lie on your behalf, but Gellien and Sylendi saw what I saw and will beg to differ."

It took only moments for the logic and full consequences to trace a very alarming set of projections through Samondel's mind.

"You think I am lying?"

"Frelle, Martyne has trained with me for many months. How many Dragon Librarians seriously believe that I have never slept with him?"

"None, quite probably," said Samondel with a trace of annoyance.

"Yet that is the truth. I believe that I forestalled a seduction, but when one is at such an advanced stage of proceedings as we caught you at, does it really matter whether his ramrod had actually been inserted or not? This is unimportant, however. Sex is legal in the Rochestrian Commonwealth, espionage is not, and espionage is what you are charged with."

In Samondel's room Velesti selected a pair of lace-up boots, riding trews, a wide belt, and her dark green satin cloak.

"You have no wide-sleeve shirts," said Velesti, rummaging about as Samondel changed out of her wine-splashed clothes.

"No, I prefer tunic over trews for general wearing, and a blouse with skirts for looking nice."

"That will never do, for where you are going. Here, take mine."

Velesti unbuttoned her coat, then removed her shirt. Samondel gaped, even though she had seen the unbelievable muscles before. She blinked. The muscles did not go away, but Samondel now noticed that her benefactor did have moderately large breasts stretched across her pectorals. Velesti's shirt was loose but somehow rakish on Samondel as she regarded herself in the mirror. Velesti struggled into one of Samondel's white blouses, but it split across her back as she bent over to pick up her Libris jacket. No damage showed once the jacket had been buttoned up, however.

They proceeded to the University Library, and past the reading rooms to the cloisters. At least a dozen lamps lit the scene, and standing at the center on a wide stone path were Martyne and three other men. A steady, chill wind was blowing through the cloisters.

Velesti spoke to the guards of their escort, then went over to the waiting men, undid her jacket, and showed them the Clastini. She spoke softly and quickly so that Samondel did not hear.

"Frelle Leover, do join us," said the oldest of the men finally. "I am dean of this university. This is our Highliber, Fras Dramoren, and this gentleman is the City Constable. Fras Camderine you already know, I am led to believe."

Martyne's face was as blank as a whitewashed plaster wall. Samondel could sense that something extremely serious was about to take place, and could not work out what part a mere edutor in applied theology could have there. Then she realized that he was wearing the jacket of a Dragon Librarian.

Plots. Trickery. Deception. She had fallen for it all so willingly. Suddenly an airlord again, she walked forward.

"My Honor, meeting all," she began. "Intending, I was, to seek audience, with Overmayor. After first reception, rather nervous, however."

"That was not her doing, Frelle Leover," Dramoren quickly assured her.

"I lived, so is not problem. What is now problem?"

"An agent of the Libris Espionage Constables has been conducting investigations into yourself and a certain foreign national named Serjon Feydamor," said the City Constable. "That agent is present, in secret, at this gathering. You and Fras Feydamor were seen in each other's company today."

"In particular, you are both accused of selling certain highly sensitive equipment and designs to enemy nationals on Rochestrian soil," said the Highliber, "and of aiding those nationals in the act of subversion within the Rochestrian Commonwealth.

"A watching order was placed upon yourself and this Serjon Feydamor. You have been heard to converse in an unknown language while keeping company. A search of his room at the Inn of Celestial Dreams revealed a very advanced weapon that fires prepackaged charges with the bullets."

Mortified, Samondel gritted her teeth. A spy. Present, but in secret. Martyne! He had never been courting her, or even been her friend, he had been spying on her all along! He was a Dragon Librarian, and was almost certainly an agent of the Highliber.

"My agents have collected more evidence besides this," said the Highliber, his arms folded as he stared at her. "It is circumstantial, but still alarming. Can you explain yourself?"

No doubt much of it being intensely intimate as well, thought Samondel.

"Cannot! Shall not!" said Samondel sharply. "Am Airlord!"

"That's a type of mayor," said the Highliber to the City Constable.

"Have you brought agents of the Christian Gaia Crusaders into the Commonwealth?"

"Who?"

"An American organization dedicated to the abolition of all fueled engines," Dramoren explained.

"What? Me? Airlord of Highland Bartolica? If meeting Crusader perverts, have them shot for treason—and heresy, and perversion of public morals and insult to all wardens' honor."

The vehemence of her reply seemed to satisfy Dramoren in part.

"Speaking of morals and honor—"

"No more! Having not privacy affairs waved like flag on pole."

"That is why I am here, Frelle," said Dramoren. "As another head of state's representative I can grant you diplomatic immunity as an envoy if you challenge the word of my agent. The most incriminating evidence is circumstantial, you see."

"Not understanding."

"The Highliber is willing to trust your word if you are willing to fight a duel to clear your name, and that of your lover," Velesti explained.

"Do you challenge the honored and sworn word of my agent that Fras, er—"

"Serjon Feydamor," prompted Velesti.

"Fras Serjon Feydamor's actions did violate the security of the Rochestrian Commonwealth?"

"Do challenge accusation. Word of mine, do have, Saireme Highliber."

There was complete silence, and all others but Samondel and Martyne stepped back several paces.

"As champion of the Highliber and thus his agent, I accept," replied Martyne, his words barely audible.

Again there was silence. The silence began to lengthen. The City Constable cleared his throat.

"You must say 'Who will stand with me?' Frelle Leover," he prompted.

"Who will stand with me?"

Velesti took three steps forward and stood beside Samondel.

"I stand with Frelle Samondel Leover," she declared.

Martyne glared at them, his arms folded and his legs apart.

"Who will stand with me?" he asked.

"You stand champion for me, so I suppose I had better be your second," said the Highliber as he joined Martyne.

"I am registered to adjudicate without judges," said the City Constable.

"I was once Academician of Surgery at this university, so I can be the medician," said the dean.

"Seconds, confer with your principals," ordered the City Constable.

Suddenly everyone began walking to apparently prearranged positions, and the City Constable chalked a line across the path. Two Tiger Dragons stood to either side of the line, their muskets' strikers cocked and ready to fire.

"What is happening? "asked Samondel." Is there going to be a hearing now, in the middle of the night?"

"Hearing? §aid Velesti." Don't you realize? You have just challenged a member of the Espionage Constables to a duel."

"What? No! I thought I was agreeing to a trial, an inquest, whatever you have here."

"There can be no trial now. To back out would be an admission that Martyne's charges are true. Your lover would be shot for spying. You might be shot too, or at the very least be held for ransom. What you must do now is name me as champion. Martyne and I are equally matched, but I am in better practice."

"This is . . . just beyond belief. Martyne is your best friend, but now you are going to kill him. How do your minds work in Australica? Are you all insane?"

"Martyne is the Overmayor's champion, neither of us has any choice. I pledge with my life to be an honorable champion for you, Frelle Samondel. Trust me, follow my advice. I can bring him down and save your beloved for you."

"Beloved? Serjon is my friend, Serjon is delightful company, but—"

"Do you want him dead?"

"No."

"Then I must kill Martyne."

"You Australicans really are mad."

"The moderator has his hand raised, we must fight now. Let me do the talking."

Samondel nodded.

"Frelle Leover, do you call a champion?" called the City Constable.

"She—" began Velesti.

"I do not!" barked Samondel.

Velesti's head snapped around, her eyes wide.

"Declare the choice," said the City Constable.

"Miscafis," replied the Highliber.

"Declare the time and place."

"Here, now, in the cloisters of the University Library."

Both Velesti and Dramoren loaded the Miscafi flintlocks, then presented them to the duelists.

"Why did you do that?" muttered Velesti.

"I shall not let you fight your friend," replied Samondel. "Besides, I learned in the hard school of Bartolican politics that I must fight my own battles."

As challenger, Martyne shot at the conciliation target first. He stepped up to the line, extended his flintlock and fired in a single fluid motion. The smoke cleared, and a hole became visible at the top of the outermost circle.

"Frelle, with that shot Martyne is saying that he is a deadly opponent, but he gives you the chance to better him," Velesti explained. "You must hit closer to the heart circle than that."

"I can do better," said Samondel, filling with confidence for the first time since she had been taken into custody.

Samondel stood square on to the target, holding the Miscafi in both hands. She squeezed the trigger. Released from its ratchet, the striker swung through a short arc with a loud, emphatic click, striking sparks with its flint and raising the cover of the priming powder pan. The gun boomed and kicked hard in Samondel's hand. The breeze swept the smoke aside, revealing that her shot had clipped the edge of the heart circle.

Velesti held out her hand for the Miscafi. The City Constable stared at the target and frowned.

"The duel will proceed, and may God have mercy upon you both," he declared.

"I do not understand," said Samondel as Velesti reloaded her Miscafi. "He said the duel will proceed. Was the duel not inevitable anyway?"

"Had you missed the target or hit worse than Martyne, you would forfeit the right to duel with him, and the matter would have had to go to a trial. You bettered his shot, however, so you now have to fight him. Did Martyne not teach you that?"

"No. He taught me to shoot, not dueling protocols."

Samondel's heart sank. A trial would have been public and humiliating, and would put a rumor on public record that she had slept with Serjon after he had married Bronlar. Perhaps the result had been for the best after all. Velesti handed her the reloaded pistol, with the striker cocked back.

"Now you two must duel, but Martyne will call the distance," Velesti explained.

"So he decides the number of paces?"

"Yes. After the last count, you both turn and fire at will. The moderator will actually call out the count, however, as a result of the Cybeline amendment some three decades ago."

Samondel and Martyne stood back to back. She felt the heat of his body against hers through the shirt. All that would now protect her from his bullet would be that white cotton shirt with puffed sleeves.

"The challenged will call the distance," said the moderator.

"Ten paces," said Martyne.

Samondel's heart leaped. Ten plus ten was twenty paces, precisely the distance that the conciliation target had been from the line. The moderator began to count, and Samondel and Martyne walked away from the line, and each other. When she turned, there would be a target and she would have to hit it before it shot back at her. Just a thing, not the young man she had held in her arms and kissed as the moon had been rising only yards from where they now paced. Serjon's life was hanging by a thread, and that thread was being held by *her* fingers. There was a thing to be killed, then Serjon would be safe.

At the word "ten" Samondel whirled, placed Martyne and fired, both hands on her gun. Martyne was standing side on as the bullet hit him, his Miscafi pointed straight up, his left arm hanging limp. The breeze blowing through the cloisters quickly wafted the smoke away and Samondel saw Martyne fall. Exultation surged through her, she had killed him. Killed him. Devastated, Samondel realized that he was dead, and by her hand. Martyne stirred. Slowly, to Samondel's horror, he began to get up. His left arm was bleeding and his chest was a mass of red as he faced her and straightened. In his right hand was the Miscafi, hanging down but still cocked and ready to fire.

Samondel lowered her empty gun. Martyne began to raise his own Miscafi, although in obvious pain. The red continued to spread down his arm and lower chest. Samondel's right leg began to shake involuntarily. I'm going to die now, passed through her mind, but I'll show them all how a Bartolican can die. Her arms at her side, she thrust her chest out and stared steadily at Martyne. For a moment there was silence in the cloisters. Nobody moved, most were not even breathing. The dean was standing with a roll of bandage in one hand and a jar of medicinal whiskey in the other, both extended before him, waiting to rush to the aid of whoever was more seriously wounded—and still alive. Samondel did not move.

"Good-bye, Samondel," said Martyne.

She closed her eyes, then in a blaze of pride she forced them open again. Martyne was aiming deliberately wide.

He fired without taking his eyes off Samondel. The jar of medicinal whiskey burst in the dean's hand and the breeze carried away the veil of smoke from the shot. For a moment more they stood facing each other, both Miscafis empty.

"I love you," said Martyne, then he fell again.

Samondel let the flintlock drop from her fingers and stood frozen with her hands to her face. Then she screamed and took a pace toward him. Velesti darted into her path and seized her.

"No! You may not cross the line. You must leave the cloisters after the moderator's verdict."

"Martyne!" screamed Samondel.

"Samondel! The guards will cut you down the instant you step over the line. You *must* stay here and you *must not* call out again."

"Fras Camderine is unable to fight another round," called the dean as he cut the fallen man's shirt away.

The City Constable produced his own flask of whiskey as the Highliber and dean began to bandage Martyne. He did not flinch as the whiskey was poured onto his wounds.

"The result goes to Frelle Samondel Leover," declared the City Constable.

There was a brief, agonized silence.

"The duel is concluded, both duelists and seconds must leave the path of honor without crossing the line, and must not speak with the opposite principal or second for a dozen days from this moment."

Martyne lay on the ground, his chest and arm a mass of blood and his torn shirt and bandages stained. Samondel continued to struggle in Velesti's grip, and her hair burst free of its pins and cascaded down over her shoulders and dueling shirt.

"Why, Martyne, why?" she cried.

"Come, we must leave the cloisters," said Velesti, finally resorting to an armlock and applying moderate pressure to force Samondel to move away.

They stopped in Mirrorsun's dim light, just outside the cloisters.

It was a windy but mild night, typical of a summer approaching equinox.

"*Tra? Fen cavas indiate des g'vrastin—*"

"I don't speak much Bartolican, just Old Anglian."

"Why? I just don't—"

Velesti suddenly seized Samondel in her arms and pressed her face against her shoulder.

"Don't look," she whispered in Samondel's ear as the stretcher bearers came past them.

"To the dissection chambers," said the dean as he hurried after the stretcher. "At the Faculty of Medicine."

The dean flicked a wink to Velesti as he passed. Velesti released Samondel's head, Samondel turned, saw dark drops of blood on the stone path, then pressed her face against Velesti's shoulder again.

"Perhaps he will be all right," Velesti began.

"I know enough Austaric to understand what 'dissection chamber' means. Martyne is dead."

"There are worse ways to go."

"They said he was spying on me, yet he, he . . ." Samondel burst into another fit of sobbing and it was some time before she could speak again. "Martyne, *Es cor valoricel,* Martyne, oh, Martyne, my love. Why did he fight, Velesti? Why?"

"He—he volunteered, and now I think I know why." Velesti sighed. "He knew anyone else would try to kill you if you chose to duel. If you named a champion, well, champions exist to be shot at. He gave his life to let you win. Now you are established as a foreign envoy, unless further evidence is brought against you. I am your liaison, and you may seek an audience with the Overmayor."

"He died for me?" whimpered Samondel. "Deliberately?"

"Er, yes. The Highliber will be annoyed, but that is hardly Martyne's concern now. I—"

"I killed Martyne! Your best friend. Don't you care?"

"Yes," replied Velesti, her voice a trifle ragged. "He was more than my friend, he was my sensei, my master, my teacher, my edutor, my, my—mentorian, is that the Bartolican word?"

"Warrior teacher, yes. Mentorian."

"I hate my body, I hate my life, I hate filthy, lecherous men, I hate my breasts, I hate the way men's eyes fondle me, and I hate, I hate . . ." Velesti shook her head. "When Martyne was instructing me, when we were sparring together, just for a moment here and there, I stopped hating. I felt . . . as if I had a place. I care about losing *that*, Samondel, and there is *nobody* to replace him."

Velesti looked around. Students on the way home from late-night revels were beginning to gather in small groups and point at them.

"Frelle Samondel, come with me. By tradition, you must now leave the city for a fortnight. I know a place where you can have some peace."

"Where?"

"A research monastery. A very quiet place. But first you must meet the Overmayor, I'll arrange an audience for midnight."

They stopped at the administration chambers, where the four Tiger Dragons were waiting with Serjon. Velesti dismissed Serjon's guards.

"You may go," Velesti said to the Yarronese flyer.

"What is this?" asked Serjon as the Tiger Dragons filed out of the room.

"I have just killed Martyne in a duel," said Samondel quietly. "By law I must avoid my—my opponent's second for a fortnight, so I am leaving Rochester."

"I don't understand. You killed him, yet we are free?"

"Yes. You may return to your room at the inn. In a fortnight I shall join you again, and we can speak directly with the Highliber about open diplomatic ties with Rochester."

"Rochester? But your sailwing was shot down by Rochestrians, you face charges of heresy for using compression engines."

"No, that has changed. The Reformed Gentheists are only one faction here, and they are losing support all the time. The Highliber is interested in trade with Mounthaven. Our venture is about to become a great success."

Serjon stood up and tried to take Samondel's hand, but she pulled it away.

"I shall be at a monastery with Velesti, praying and meditating," Samondel explained.

"But why are you so upset about that monk if he tried to kill you?" insisted Serjon as he snatched for her hand again.

Velesti's hand shot out and seized his, twisting his wrist around and bending it at an excruciating angle. She dropped slightly, so that Serjon doubled over with the pain.

"Velesti, let him go!" exclaimed Samondel.

Velesti released Serjon and folded her arms beneath her breasts again.

"Do nothing to alarm Velesti, she is very dangerous," Samondel cautioned.

"Easily alarmed," said Velesti quietly in heavily accented Bartolican. "Away, fortnight. Leaving, now."

"Yes, we must go," Samondel repeated.

"Er, so what should I do?" asked Serjon.

"You will be safe here. Explore Rochester, enjoy yourself, you can go about openly now but beware of Gentheists. When I return I'll take you to all my favorite places, and we shall move into a nice hostelry with double beds."

"But what about you?"

"Velesti is my bodyguard as well. She is very effective."

Velesti gave a shallow bow, her eyes never once leaving Serjon. Serjon shuddered at the sight of her eyes. They were deep and hungry, and whatever was behind them was definitely not human. Another aviad, concluded Serjon. Samondel came across and kissed him on the cheek, then placed a purse on the table.

"Spend time in the markets and do try the riding school," said Samondel as she returned to the door. "Work hard on your Austaric. Misunderstandings can happen very easily unless one is careful with language."

Lengina lay slumped in her reading chair, her feet propped on a padded stool and warming before a fire. A book of protocol theory lay open on her lap, and three heralds and a magistrate hovered in the shadows behind her, all clutching books on intermayoral law. Before her stood Dramoren, his jacket still stained with Martyne's blood.

"Now, let me repeat this back to you in the Overmayor's Austaric," she said as Dramoren cringed before her, his hands clasped firmly behind him and shifting his weight from foot to foot. "I am Overmayor, after all, so by definition my Austaric should be the finest available to human ears."

"Without doubt, Overmayor."

"Airlord Leover was seconded by the Dragon Librarian who arrested her, Frelle Disore. Your champion was the ex-monk and Espionage Constable, Fras Camderine. You were his second. Fras Camderine allowed Airlord Leover to shoot him in the duel, then declared that he loved her as he fell. Frelle Leover was then led away in tears by Frelle Disore, who then beat up Frelle Leover's American lover before taking Frelle Leover away to . . . somewhere. How am I managing?"

"Word perfect, gracious Frelle."

"Had I found a plot like that in a romantic novel I would have flung it into the fire."

"Justifiably so, gracious Frelle."

"Did anyone think to ask Frelle Leover whether she is at war with my Commonwealth?" shouted Lengina, standing up and flinging her book to the floor.

"That is a rare book, gracious Frelle, please be—"

"Answer me!"

"She has never heard of the Christian Gaia Crusaders. When I explained who they were meant to be, she said that she would have had them shot for treason and heresy had she encountered them in North America."

Lengina kicked the book of protocol theory away across the floor, and a herald hurried to snatch it up. Her shoulders slumped, and she collapsed back into her chair.

"Dramoren, advise me!" she pleaded. "What do I do with Airlord Leover?"

"In a dozen days we can both meet with her, she seems anxious to buy horses and other trade animals and goods, but will probably insist that we not fire upon her flying machines."

"Oh. So she is not angry?"

"No, there are no residual resentments. Americans also think duels to the death are a good way to settle intractable disputes."

"Well, I do not, but what I think does not seem to matter. So we are not at war?"

"No."

"Is she pretty?"

"Oh yes, beautiful. Violet eyes, long red hair, and no more than perhaps twenty years of age."

"Beautiful, young, brave, dedicated, what a woman! I am looking forward to meeting her."

"I am so glad, gracious Frelle."

"Meantime, can I achieve anything by staying out of bed any longer tonight?"

"Ah, well, yes."

"Fras Highliber, you look uneasy. Precisely *what* can I achieve?"

"Well, being a duel disputant I cannot speak with Frelle Leover for twelve days, so I arranged a meeting for her, with you, in approximately ten minutes."

Lengina stood up so quickly that her reading chair flew back and struck a herald.

"What!" she shrieked. "With my hair entangled, and wearing a nightsmock and dressing cloak and slippers, and with no makeup or jewelry?"

"But Airlord Leover is only dressed in boots, trousers, and a dueling shirt—"

"Rouse my maids!" shouted Lengina as she dashed from the room, flinging off her dressing cloak, then her night smock, as she ran.

Dramoren watched her receding, naked figure as it vanished into the shadows of the passageway.

"Now, there's a sight you don't see every day," said the magistrate from behind him.

W e must be at the palace at midnight, but there is plenty of time,"
said Velesti as she walked along with Samondel leaning on her arm.
"Then a special galley train will take us away."

"I must rest, I feel dizzy," said Samondel.

"Over there, we can get the best coffee in Rochester."

"Café Marellia? But Martyne said—"

"He took you *there*?"

"Yes. He said it was only for lovers. *We* can't go there."

"I can be very persuasive," said Velesti.

The door of the café looked just as subtly enchanting as when
she had first seen it. Even though it was nearly midnight the place
was packed, and the waiter hurried across looking harassed and
carrying an ashwood tray with three mugs of coffee and a plate of
butternut shortbreads.

"Ah, sorry, so sorry, all full—Ah, beautiful Frelle Samondel, so
sorry but—"

Although it was the waiter's arm that Velesti's hand closed
around, it squeezed the words from his throat.

"There has been a terrible mistake," said Velesti in a voice that
was not loud, but was absolutely distinct to everyone within ten feet.
"Frelle Samondel has just killed her beloved in a duel and needs
somewhere to sit down."

The waiter dropped his tray of coffee and butternut shortbreads.
Although his lips managed to say no more than an anguished "Ah!"
his face said a great deal more. Velesti's words were transmitted to the
more remote tables within moments, and over a dozen of the closest
patrons bounded to their feet and gestured to their seats and tables.
Soon Samondel and Velesti were seated in a corner, while the displaced couple squeezed onto a bench at a larger table. Manuel had
tears in his eyes as he set two mugs of the finest Northmoor coffee before them, each with a spiral of cream slowly sinking into its depths.

"Beautiful Frelles, eleven people have asked if they can pay for
whatever you have to eat and drink," he reported.

"Pay? Why?" asked Samondel.

"Rochestrians fancy themselves as being very romantic," said Velesti in Old Anglian. "You have just been part of the most intense romantic tragedy possible. They consider that their own ability to feel love is greatly heightened by just being in the same room as you, and that your tragedy blesses their own lives. Nobody will leave this café while you are here."

Samondel put a hand to her face and closed her eyes. "Austral-icans, all mad," she said in Old Anglian, "except that some are mad-der than others."

"Thank them, but I shall pay," Velesti told the waiter. "What we really need is a pedal gig to be brought here to carry Samondel. She is feeling dizzy and—"

"Stop! No more! It is happening."

Manuel dashed off.

Suddenly everything made sense to Samondel. Although Velesti resembled, acted like—and probably was—a dangerous and homi-cidal psychopath, she was remarkably kind, understanding, and loyal to those in her favor. Samondel had somehow joined this quite ex-clusive elite, which had also included Martyne until an hour or so earlier.

"Did Martyne ever speak of me?" she asked after a sip from her mug.

"Continually," said Velesti, staring up at the ceiling with her chin on her fist and drumming her fingers on the table. "Try to have a sen-sible conversation about spinning back kicks and all I ever got was eyes of violet gemstone, hair like a summer firestorm, and a lot a spec-ulation about whether you would be willing to hold his hand. You are apparently also brave, beautiful, charming, sophisticated, witty. . . . This may take a while. Do you really want me to continue?"

Samondel closed her eyes again. "God give me strength. Why did he say all that to *you* instead of *me*?"

"I'm not sure. My eyes are sort of bluish gray and my hair is auburn."

"Do not try to cheer me up, Frelle Velesti. Answer my question."

"It is complicated. Martyne would rather have faced enemy bombards than face you and be laughed at, but also—"

"I *never* laughed at Martyne!" shouted Samondel angrily. "With, yes. At, never! After our last dinner together he walked me back to Villiers College, and I kissed him. I—I really did fall in love with him. I wanted to tell him, but . . . another girl, he had another. Soon after that Serjon arrived. Oh, Martyne . . . yet he spied on me, he denounced me."

"Wrong. I spied on you, I arranged for you to be denounced."

Samondel blinked. Velesti nodded. Samondel's already protuberant eyes bulged with rage. She flung the remains of her coffee in Velesti's face, then backhanded her across the cheek, but as she raised her hand to strike her again Velesti offered her a Morelac, handle first.

"Here, this is quicker," said the Librarian.

Samondel clicked a striker back, aimed between Velesti's eyes—then raised the barrel and fired. Her shot obliterated the price beside SOUP OF THE DAY on the chalkboard. The other patrons slowly climbed out from under their tables and returned to their meals, cakes, and coffee. Manuel hurried out with another mug of Northmoor coffee for Samondel.

"Here, Frelle Princess, compliments of house—"

"Not princess! Airlord! Sort of queen, mayor, general, overhand, and commander. All in one. Understand?"

"Yes, Frelle."

"Thankings for coffee. Now please, leaving. Alone."

Manuel hurried away. Velesti shifted uncomfortably. Strong men fell over themselves to get out of the way when Velesti walked down the street, thought Samondel, yet here she was, running her finger around the rim of her coffee mug and looking as if she would rather be anywhere else but here. Indrawn breath hissed between her teeth.

"When I heard about Serjon being in Rochester with you, I went to visit Martyne. When he did not answer I broke the lock. He was under his bed. He wanted to be able to say that he did not sleep in his own bed on this night."

"Oh, Martyne!" cried Samondel, letting Velesti's flintlock fall from her fingers to the table.

"I tried to comfort him as best I could, but comforting people is not one of my strengths. Besides, the prospect of having a quiet ale with me was no substitute for the prospect of holding hands with you."

"I was lonely! I was alone in a foreign, alien city and Martyne said he was . . . taken!"

"That was all a mistake too. Lies, misunderstandings: Martyne was free, yours for the taking."

"Martyne was all that made Rochester enchanting. Then Serjon arrived. He found me at the market. Serjon had been my lover before he was married, and suddenly I was alone with him. He desired me, I—I love him, in a way. What was I to do? What would you do, were you me?"

"Were I you? Probably much the same. Were I me? Drag Martyne out from under his bed, empty a jug of water over him, march him down to Marelle's Late Night Tavern, sit him at a table with a drink and have a quiet word to Marelle on the way out. They were once lovers, you know."

"Damn you."

"Sorry."

"But thank you for caring about him."

"Think nothing of it."

Forty-three pairs of eyes followed their every gesture, forty-three pairs of ears listened to every word, although only Samondel and Velesti understood Old Anglian.

"Velesti, why did you denounce Serjon and me?"

"Martyne was supposed to be spying on you, but he was shielding you instead. Serjon was being shadowed by another agent, and when you two joined up—"

"Take that back!"

"Ah, *met* each other in the market, your own identity became subject to scrutiny. I submitted a report, Martyne was forced to fight you, and I was instructed to arrest you and Serjon at once. You know the rest of the story."

"You must think of me as a filthy little whore."

"Why so? Why should you and Serjon be different from Martyne and Marelle?"

Samondel was, for some odd reason, very pleased that Velesti had a good opinion of her.

"Sometimes, just sometimes, Velesti, you show that you have the heart of a saint."

"Which I keep in a jar of expensive whiskey on my bookshelf."

Samondel laughed.

"It is pleasant with Serjon. I know him well, there was no tension. I know what he needs, desires, gives, and means. The Bartolican expression is 'we laugh well together.' Do you understand?"

"The Australican term is 'mates.' How do you feel about aviads?"

"There are good aviads and bad aviads. Serjon's feelings are a different matter. At the start of the Great War—"

"I know that story."

"You do?"

"His mother and sisters were raped and murdered when Bartolican carbineers led by an aviad captured the Jannian estate. Several hundred Bartolican honkey-boy carbineers took the estate with scarcely a shot fired, raped the women, then killed everyone except the guildmasters—who they abducted."

"How could you know that?"

"I am a Dragon Librarian. Librarians know everything. I know what Serjon saw, I know . . . more than he has admitted to you."

"You are more frightening as a librarian than a warrior, Velesti. Can you read minds too?"

"You are thinking, 'Wherever you are, Martyne, I love you.' "

Samondel gave a sniffle. "Close. I was thinking, Yonlitor elme stelderen, Es cor valoricel. 'Glory of the starlit sky, my heart is your warrior.' "

"Ah yes, classical Bartolican for 'I love you.' "

8

GUILE OF LIBRARIANS

Rochester, the Rochestrian Commonwealth

Marelle shouldered the student medician aside and burst into the dissection room where the dean was operating on Martyne on a cadaver table. Half a dozen students were holding the patient down.

"Martyne! They told me—" she began.

"Fykart sadist!" cried Martyne, ignoring her. "Dammit, hurry up!"

"Number forty-seven, only two more stiches," said the dean.

With her fist jammed into her mouth Marelle stared down at the man who had been lying in her arms only two months earlier. There was a great deal of blood on the cloth beneath him, and the medician was in the last stages of closing a gash at least ten inches long that ran across his chest, just below his pectoral muscles. The wounds where Samondel's bullet had entered and exited his arm had already been neatly stitched closed.

"Will—will he live?" asked Marelle.

"Unless he gets shot again, yes. Starting stitch number forty-eight."

"Enough, damn you!" cried Martyne, his voice ragged.

"This is professional pride, Fras Camderine."

"Stop it! I'd rather have the scar."

"You enter a duel, you accept repairs."

"Ow!"

"Will someone tell me what happened?" demanded Marelle.

"This young hero presented his left side to his opponent in a duel over some point of honor that ostensibly involved treason, espionage, and politics, but which I suspect also involved a woman, another man, and . . ." He stared at Marelle over the tops of his spectacles, "possibly yet another woman. She shot—"

"She?"

"I'm sorry, Fras Martyne, should this lady know about—"

"Finish that last stitch and leave me alone!"

"Frelle Samondel's bullet passed through his left bicep, hit his torso, broke a rib, tore a very dramatic furrow across his chest, and clipped the top of his right bicep before flying on to lodge in the buffers. It was also coated with a particularly nasty substance known as razor dust, which stings like a thousand wasps. The pain from these impressive but unthreatening wounds made him think he was dying, and certainly made him pass out from shock."

Marelle leaned against the edge of the bench, her head spinning.

"Martyne, you were so, so lucky," she said.

"More than lucky," said the dean. "The bullet was deflected, it must have been badly charged. The shot should have passed through his heart, as straight as a musket barrel."

"And Frelle Samondel? Was she harmed?"

"He chose not to shoot at her, and in a most dramatic fashion." He held up the neck of the shattered whiskey jar.

"So he will definitely live?" asked Marelle.

"Yes," replied the dean as he and the student medicians began to bandage Martyne's chest.

"When I heard he had been taken to the dissection chambers I thought the worst."

"There is no hospital on university grounds, so the dissection rooms are used for emergencies. I thought everyone knew that."

"Everyone except me, apparently. When can he leave?"

"You can take him tonight."

"When can I slap his face?"

"Five days, perhaps a week."

"I thought I was staying here," croaked Martyne.

"You shut up!" snapped Marelle.

"Let us not be too flippant about this young man," said the dean. "In the cloisters of honor he did pass out with pain, shock, and blood loss."

"Martyne, you are going to be nursed by *my* hands."

"Be careful of his stiches," said the dean as he tied the last bandage. "I take it she was the underlying cause of the duel, Fras Camderine?"

Marelle raised her hand, but with considerable effort refrained from slapping the dean's face. Martyne remained discreetly silent.

"Ah, I apologize for that rather tasteless pun, Frelle," said the dean as he backed away.

He has vanished," said Marelle as she and Velesti sat together in a crowded tavern at the serving bench some days later.

"Just as I expected," said Velesti. "He cannot have been seriously hurt."

"His wounds were painful, but not serious. You should know, you put the razor dust on Samondel's lead shot."

"I have a strong sense of theater."

"Especially theater of the absurd."

"Did you roll him again?"

"Velesti, do you know why I could never be his beloved?"

"Early morning Baleshanto training?"

"He reminds me too much of my father."

"Believe me, beautiful and understanding Frelle, he is nothing at all like your father."

"Believe me, baleful and disturbing Frelle, *you* are even *more* like my father. Is Samondel well? Martyne was worried about her, and so am I."

"She will live. I took her to a quiet country place for the dozen days."

"Yet you are back in Rochester."

"There are things to do, things to discuss. Like where Martyne has gone."

"You know?"

"Passage was booked to a lonely, isolated railside about a day by wind train east of Kalgoorlie. The name in the register was a false one, but it was the first time in the clerk's forty years of service that anyone had booked a one-way passage there. A few days' walk to the north is Balesha."

"So, we have driven him back."

"His experiences with women have hardly been encouraging."

Marelle sighed and shook her head. "How do we women manage to do such things to the nicest of men, and why do the real bastards have success with us so easily?"

"I don't know."

"Serjon presents well. He risked everything for Samondel, he braved great danger and traveled right to the heart of an enemy empire to rescue her."

"Perhaps she's gunpowder to lie with?" suggested Velesti.

Presently they returned to Marelle's tavern, and went to the main taproom hall. It was late afternoon, but already people were there, drinking, talking, and striving to be noticed.

"What other things do you have to arrange?" Marelle asked.

"Samondel now loves Martyne, but thinks Martyne is dead. Martyne wants it to stay that way. Serjon is here in Rochester, waiting for Samondel to return. I think Samondel will return to Serjon, and take up with him where I interrupted. But . . . I know a little bird who saw Serjon at the Traralgon Castellany. Would you like to know what else my little bird saw?"

"I am tired of riddles, Velesti. Why not speak plainly?"

"Because, Marelle, I have only riddles," replied Velesti, spreading her arms wide. "Other people have answers, but no riddles. You are one of them."

"Ask for an answer, I shall provide it," replied Marelle.

"What is Serjon doing in Rochester?"

"Have you no eyes, Frelle Velesti?" Marelle sighed, exasperated. "He was bedding Samondel! I know a few little birds as well, Velesti.

One of mine said that Samondel was on the bed and on her back, and Serjon so completely inserted that his toes were barely visible."

"Well . . . it was obvious that they were somewhat more to each other than just good friends, but that is not the point. Fact: Serjon's people must have a secret wingfield somewhere in Traralgon. Fact: the Castellian of Traralgon breeds cavalry horses. Fact: the American flyers are in search of horses. Fact: Avianese intelligence has been very active in the Southeast lately. Fact: Serjon hates aviads. Fact: aviad children are being moved to the Southeast, even though there are supposedly no aviad wingfields there. What do all these facts tell us?"

"That Serjon must have learned to accept and work with aviads."

"Correct, but what I want to know is who Serjon is working *against*?"

"The Reformed Gentheists, people who shoot at people using fueled engines. Is it not obvious?"

"To a live person, yes."

"My mother told me never to play with dead people."

"Dead people can be fun to be with," retorted Velesti. "Take me, for example."

"No, thank you, you are not my type."

"I am dead, Martyne is dead, but is Serjon dead?"

"You, Frelle Cadaver, are talking nonsense, and have lost me. Totally. What are your plans?"

"I should like to vanish."

"Just vanish?"

"Vanish to walk in darkness and danger, in the service of truth, justice, and large angelic choirs singing in sixteen-part harmony."

Marelle put her arms around Velesti and hugged her with real affection.

"Be feared and respected in the dark and deadly places, Frelle Strange One."

Velesti whispered something in Marelle's ear.

"Yes, I can arrange that," said Marelle, who nevertheless looked puzzled. "But I doubt that it will work."

They stood apart, bowed, then Velesti walked away across the tavern hall and through the door to the stairs. When she was gone one of the jarmaids came out into the hall with a polishing cloth.

"That's the Dragonliber, the lady spy," said Nereli wistfully as she began to wipe a tabletop near Marelle.

"I have heard rumors to that effect," replied Marelle, "but then there are such rumors about me as well."

"How exciting, how romantic. Having affairs with rich, handsome, and powerful men, living like a noble, and among the nobility."

"The reality is not nearly the same," replied Marelle.

"That's all right for you to say. I'm just a jarmaid, *you* had first right of refusal when Martyne Camderine was here—and you didn't refuse."

"Sometimes jarmaids make better spies than moderately prosperous tavern mistresses like me."

"I see no recruiting tables at the market."

"Frelle Nereli, if you wish to be part of a covert venture, I can arrange it."

"Me? What can a jarmaid like me do?"

"Take off your clothes for a start. If you impress the enemies with your body yet they have less-than-impressive bodies to impress you, what do you think they will do?"

"Spend money to impress me?"

"More than that. They will try to impress you with their secrets, to show how important they are."

"Ah."

"Would you like a simple assignment?"

Seymour, the Rochestrian Commonwealth

Shadowmouse walked straight from the Seymour paraline terminus to the nearest stables and bought a horse and saddle. At the stables he also asked about caravans, and he was told that one was due to leave later that day. He spoke with the caravan master, and had himself signed up as an outrider guard. For this he would be granted a land plot at the center of their planned town. Outrider guards were, however, the very last word in vulnerability. The shot that would kill Shadowmouse would be the shot that alerted the caravan to a freebooter attack.

Because land was available in what used to be the Calldeath lands, people with drive but limited prospects in mainstream society were flocking there in spite of the dangerous warlords, outlaws, freebooters, aviads, and wildlife. They traveled by horse, dray cart, two-wheeled gig, and even by foot. The better caravans traveled fifty miles per day. The group that Shadowmouse had joined was too big to be vulnerable to most groups outside Rochestrian law and justice, however, and the warlords were not interested in wasting warriors against people who were only passing through. Thus the journey was relatively free of incident for the first few days.

On the fourth day Shadowmouse rode away into the woods. Once out of sight he took a reaction pistol from his robes, checked its action, settings, and ammunition clip, then concealed it again.

Traralgon Castellany, Southeastern Australica

Traralgon Castle was a long, low rambling wall enclosing the store halls, stables, and armory of Galdane's cavalry. The village supplied blacksmiths, leatherworkers, carpenters, and farm laborers, and the entire complex was extremely well patrolled.

Shadowmouse rode along the single path to the village, which was merely a pair of ruts for the supply carts. Galdane's lancers traveled the open country, holding roads in contempt. The warriors felt that only slaves and peasants used roads, and to be seen on one was an admission of just that status.

Three lancers burst out of the woods in the distance, galloping across the field of long grass. Their first shot struck Shadowmouse's gelding, but he rolled as he was pitched to the ground. The warriors bore down on him, expecting him to surrender or run, but Shadow-mouse lay flat with the Clastini held in both hands. He fired.

The incident took place within view of Traralgon Castle, and it was not long before a squad of lancers rode out to investigate. Shadowmouse stood over his dead gelding, the Clastini in his right hand, pointed straight up to the sky. The warlord was at the head of the squad, and had his own Clastini. Galdane reined in his mount, surveying Shadowmouse, the Clastini, and the dead horses and lancers.

"This demands vengeance," began Galdane.

"Who owns these fools?" demanded Shadowmouse.

Nobody had ever spoken to Galdane like that. The intruder had one of the strange and wonderful gun machines. Galdane had used nearly all of his own ammunition impressing his men, but even owning a Clastini gave one a certain aura. Ever anxious not to lose face before either his enemies or warriors, Galdane thought quickly.

"My men were told to watch for a different warrior," rumbled the warlord.

Shadowmouse recognized the lie for what it was.

"I was told only to follow the path to Traralgon Castle," he replied smoothly.

"Everybody knows not to take the road unless wearing the yellow tunic of the slave or peasant—"

"Not from as far away as my people come from!" interjected Shadowmouse. "So, you are the warlord that my servant Serjon selected. Where is the wingfield?"

At the sound of Serjon's name Galdane's doubts collapsed. He ordered one of his lancers to stand guard over the bodies of the fallen while Shadowmouse took his horse. The other lancers were sent back to the castle.

"Those sons of slaves should have checked whether there were papers beneath your cloak before shooting," said Galdane as they set off. "You shall have their weapons, gold, and women."

"Thank you, but I live only to serve my airlord and may own nothing but my clothing and weapons. Has Fras Serjon been an agreeable envoy?"

"Yes, yes, he promised one of these pistol machines and a thousand shots for every five fine, strong young horses. Two male and three female. I—"

"May I?" asked Shadowmouse, holding his hand out for the Clastini.

Galdane hesitated, then reluctantly surrendered the gun. Shadowmouse examined it, checking the clip. The clip was down to five bullets, and there was grit in the mechanism already. Without proper maintenance it would soon fail. The option catch was set to reaction. Shadowmouse took three rounds from his pocket and added them to the warlord's. Galdane's eyes widened with the joy of a child confronted with a particularly large birthday present.

"See this catch?" he said as he handed the weapon back. "Push in and twist. That's right. Now fire."

Galdane aimed at a rock nearby, and a single shot barked out. He held up the gun and stared at it, then fired at the rock again.

"Hah! Now it shoots once for each pull of the trigger," Galdane exclaimed, not sure whether to be pleased or disappointed.

"Serjon should have showed you that option, it saves you wasting shots. In my mayorate, reaction mode is said to be only for battle, or for the unskilled."

"But why did he not tell me?"

"To make you waste shots in reaction mode, to make you pay more horses for fresh shots. Here is a little secret, Fras Galdane. Serjon is a good and brave warrior but his father was a merchant. It is in his blood to haggle and swindle."

Suddenly Galdane caught on, and began to laugh. Here was a true noble from the distant mayorates. He could fight, ride well, he spoke with only a slight accent, and he held merchants in contempt. Soon the warlord was talking freely about Serjon's mishaps while learning to ride, and revealing when the sky machines arrived to carry off horses and certain mysterious people who arrived on foot, by the road.

"The sky machines come down every ten days, and one is due tonight," said the warlord. "Seven children and one guard are waiting at the wingfield."

"And horses?"

"Oh, yes, five fine young horses, just weaned. Young people and young horses, all will fly together."

All will fly, thought Shadowmouse.

They reached the wingfield, which was just a level stretch of land about half a mile long that trailed off into dense woodland. Piles of dry leaves and branches were at each corner of an oblong strip, and these had been built on the ashes of earlier bonfires.

"Listen, Galdane, the children's guard needs to learn the ways of horses and lancers, or he will become like Serjon," suggested Shadowmouse. "Why not take him back to your castle, riding this horse? Give him over to the women of the warriors that I killed, ply him with drink, teach him the way of lancers."

"That is very generous of you, the act of a true warlord. Ach, Shadowmouse, are you sure that you are not a warlord going about in disguise?"

"Truly I am not, Fras, but it is my duty to act as my warlord would because I act in his name."

The group of children was hidden in the trees as Shadowmouse dismounted, saluted Galdane with arms crossed over his chest, then walked over to where the guard stood. The man regarded him uneasily as he approached, but the reaction pistol was visible in his belt and gave him credibility.

"A change of orders, I am to fly out with the children," said Shadowmouse.

"What? It was my turn—I, I was not told."

"You are being told now! Fras Serjon says that Horsebreath over there needs to be watched more carefully. I had to kill three of his lancers on the way here."

"You—How?"

Shadowmouse tapped the Clastini with a finger. "We need an envoy in Traralgon, and Galdane has agreed to accept you."

"But what must I do?"

"Whatever is expected of you! Drink, fornicate, sing about fighting, and vomit when the need takes you. It should not be much longer than a month."

"A month," said the man, stroking his beard as he weighed up the possible virtues of this temporary change in career paths. "No more than a month?"

"One month, and then you get a flight out, a medal, and a bath."

Shadowmouse watched the guard ride away with Galdane, and he hoisted one of the children onto his shoulders to wave. The child was very light, and had a subtle fluffyness about his hair. Pyres were to be lit when a flare appeared in the sky one hour after sunset, the guard had said before leaving. Shadowmouse checked his pocket watch, then shepherded the children back among the trees to feed the tethered horses.

When the super-regal landed, it was all that Shadowmouse could do to keep his senses from giving in and leaving him reeling. A vast, silent blackness swept in over the woodland and came to earth with a squeal of wheels on the ascent strip's surface. The flames of the pyres were already dying down as Shadowmouse hurried over. By now the thing had begun chuffing softly in the darkness, and two darkly dressed men were there to meet him. First the horses were led up aboard, then the children followed.

"I note five horses, seven children, and you," said one of the dark figures in accented Austaric.

"Then you have us all," replied Shadowmouse.

"Give me your hand, feel that handle?"

"Yes."

"Well, start turning it, the hatch needs to be up and bolted before we ascend."

The engines revved, but at first they just taxied around the newly leveled turning circle. Abruptly the engines roared, and they soon had the sensation of speed, then everything tilted and the children screamed. The rumbling of wheels stopped, and there was a smooth, floating feeling, like that of cantering along on horseback at night.

Launceston, Tasmania Island

The flight lasted two hours and a half, which was a lot less than Shadowmouse had expected. The first that Shadowmouse knew of arrival in Launceston was a heavy jolt and squeal of wheels, then they were rumbling along some wingfield. The hatchway was opened, but this time there were lanterns outside. The same two men herded Shadowmouse and the seven children out of the *Albatross*.

Shadowmouse turned back to see ten huge, circular areas of shimmer at the rear of the wing, and the compression engines continued to chug. Two wagons of barrels were nearby, and teams of men and women were hard at work pumping fuel up into the body of the immense wing.

"No need to hurry or hide now; you are in Avian's capital," said a woman who had apparently come to take charge of the children. "There's hot drinks ready, and then you can watch the *Albatross* ascend."

Avian. The American flyers were dealing with the people of Avian. Shadowmouse struggled to make sense of it. The Avianese had no inhibitions about technology and engines, even the Liberal Gentheists among them believed that as long as the fuel came from harvested plants, then steam and compression engines were morally defensible. Shadowmouse sat down with his back against a stack of compression-spirit barrels, staring into space. He was here at last, to die, and soon he really would die. He began to weep with desolation. There was a touch on his shoulder. A child of about six was standing before him, a boy.

"You shouldn't let the other children see you cry, Fras," he said. "They would remember their own mothers and fathers, and how they'll never see them again, and soon everyone will be crying."

Shadowmouse sighed. "Quite right, young Fras. I was thinking of my lost Ladyfrelle. Very selfish of me."

"My mother and father are dead, so I know all about crying. I have had to look after the others for weeks. Cry, cry, cry, that's all they did."

The boy sat down beside Shadowmouse.

"So, what are you going to be?" Shadowmouse asked.

"A flyer," replied the child without hesitation. "And you?"

"Oh, a flyer too. But much sooner, I expect."

A quarter of an hour later Shadowmouse and his young friend watched the immense black patch of sleekness roar up into the now overcast night while the other aviad children clapped and cheered.

"Ah, Fras, forgive me, but I have not been told your name or skill," the woman said to Shadowmouse.

"My name is Shadowmouse, and I am here to see the mayor of this place," he bluffed.

"I am Mariar Lanstor, the mayor's wife," the woman replied. "What is your business with him?"

"I am a coordinator of Airfox, and I volunteered to come here."

"I do not understand."

"My identity has been exposed, and thus I am no longer of use to Airfox. I was told you have a use for the redundant."

"Were you indeed? Well, Fras, you do not look stupid, so you must be very, very brave. Do you have good eyesight, and how are your reactions?"

"Both are excellent, would I have been sent over otherwise?" replied Shadowmouse, wondering what was to be his fate.

The following day Shadowmouse awoke in a room of the mayoral palace of Launceston, which was a low, rambling building of salvaged bricks, abandonstone, and newly cut timber. His bed was a bunk with a tentcloth mattress stuffed with dried eucalyptus leaves, and the blankets were rough woven wool. Breakfast was sheep milk cheese, scrambled eggs, and rainwater, and was at the table of the mayor.

"I'll not say that I approve of you being here," the mayor stated quite bluntly. "We can recruit volunteers for our defence machines from those already here."

"Perhaps I was considered to be a superior recruit."

"Fras, I hope for your sake that you *are* a superior recruit. Two out of three do not survive beyond six weeks. You weigh, say, a hundred seventy pounds in your clothes. That could have been one hundred and seventy pounds of tools, medicines, seeds, fertile chicken eggs, or three children. Every pound of anything that crosses the Strait is a miracle."

Shadowmouse bristled.

"It may not have crossed your mind, but many of my people have died or been captured to make sure that aviad children and artisans reach the secret mainland wingfields," he retorted.

"Do you know how many have died crossing Bass Strait?"

"No! And that is because once your wings are in the air we never hear back from you. Oh, there are letters, tightly cribbed missives along the lines of 'Mama, Papa, I love you, it is wonderful here,' and shared with a dozen others on pieces of poorpaper that would fit onto the palm of my hand with space left over."

"Even those papers cost compression spirit. We have lost nine kitewings in the past half year."

"But there must be thousands of people here. A kitewing can barely carry two adults."

"Originally we had better."

A teenage boy came in to clear away the plates and mugs, all of which had been salvaged from the abandon and were two thousand years old. The mayor pushed away from the table and beckoned for Shadowmouse to follow.

The palace was at the edge of the wingfield. Beside it were the buildings and workshops of the Launceston Technical Academy, and alongside was the Kitewing Research Institute. Thatch-roof shelters for the aircraft were lined up in a row, and some hundreds of yards farther away was the compression-spirit plant.

"Artisans are trained in the Academy, and compression engines are built next door in the Research Institute. Every engine is a work of research, Fras Shadowmouse. In the years before last September we brought thousands of aviads over here using the electrical essence sunwings."

"Those sent down from Mirrorsun?"

"Yes, and most were lost in the Melting. This one was an exception."

In the first thatch-roof shelter was a large and elegant sailwing, but its twin engines and cockpit showed signs of burning. Seven very young-looking aviads were carefully boring holes in the engine mountings.

"This sunwing ferry was on the ground when everything electrical melted. From its condition, you may well imagine what happened to those that were in the air. One of the young artisans has an idea to mount compression engines and control wires and get it flying again. The airframe weighs a fifth of what we can build, and it could carry four adults. The trouble is that it has to be fed with sugar."

"Fed?"

"Yes. In a strange manner that we do not even begin to understand, it is alive."

Shadowmouse looked along to the next shelter, where an edutor was lecturing students on an aircraft that had three tiered wings.

"That is a very advanced-looking machine," said Shadowmouse as he pointed.

"Yes, it is, and it can exceed two hundred miles per hour in a dive. Look there, a kitewing trainer is being readied to ascend."

A chugging steam engine on a trolley was being used to spin up the compression engine on what was no more than a double boxkite on wheels. Once the compression engine caught, the flyer supervised while his trainee strapped himself into the lower of the main wings.

The mayor began walking slowly along the dispersal path, and Shadowmouse fell in with him.

"A long time ago, during the Milderellen Invasion, one of the sparkflash radio units invented by Highliber Zarvora detected messages from a very advanced civilization in the mountains of old North America," the mayor explained. "From the first few messages we realized that they had compression engines and small flying machines. Although it was not a very warlike society, their guns were vastly more advanced than ours, and this inspired certain factions in Avianese politics to propose theft on a grand scale. Theft of weapons, gunwings, artisans, and tools."

"But Highliber Zarvora was supplying far more advanced machines, such as that one back there, using the old Mirrorsun factories."

"Highliber Zarvora had an idea to fly aviads out to empty islands like this one and build aviad mayorates that were independent of humans. Other factions thought to take over Australica instead. The more benign of them wanted the humans enslaved, the extremists wanted them exterminated. When Zarvora was killed, the extremists had a problem. It would take centuries to learn the secrets of the sunwing machines, but the secrets of the guns and gunwings of North America required no more than good teachers and a few examples to allow us to master them. Sunwings, bigger versions of the one we just saw, were used to ferry Avianese agents over to the other side of the world, and after a time guns, aircraft, and artisans began to arrive here. Some of the later artisans spoke on the radio devices of a war breaking out between two mayorates called Yarron and Bartolica, a war that we started. Apparently the war did not go well for our faction, and finally our main base reported being under attack by a vast flock of Yarronese wings. Very soon after that the spark-flash went silent, and some hours later the Melting happened and the Call stopped. We were again very much on our own."

"With only a few stolen air machines left for contact with the mainland," said Shadowmouse, nodding.

"You have it. Much to our surprise, however, an American sail-wing arrived here two months ago. The Americans had forgiven us for the invasion but wanted help transporting horses back to their homeland, to help colonize their former Calldeath lands."

"Of course! They had no choice but to turn to us. All the mainland, human mayorates have religious prohibitions on fueled engines."

"Yes. Our relationship is one of a marriage of convenience, but we are still on honeymoon and there is plenty of goodwill in evidence."

Out on the ascent strip the kitewing's flyer opened the throttle of the compression engine and it began rolling along and gathering speed. After what seemed like a much longer run than the super-regal had needed, it lifted into the air and climbed in a straight line until it was several times the height of the nearby trees. It began a wide circle of the wingfield.

"So why are you using those dangerous string bags?" asked Shadowmouse. "You have at least a dozen stolen air machines under these shelters."

"And we used them, too. We knew that the easy times were over, so we flew tools, books and rare materials across by the wingload. Sometimes we made five flights a day, but then parts started to wear out, highly specialized engine parts that we could not hope to duplicate. Finally a twin-engine wing seized one engine on a flight to King Gate Wingfield and was nearly lost. We began to cannibalize parts to make a few reliable engines out of many, but even these wore out eventually. Other wings were actually lost in Bass Strait so we grounded all the North American wings, but by then sufficient kitewings were in service. They are not much, but they are all that we have and we do know how to build them. The students of the Institute have been slowly rebuilding the worn American parts and restoring the stolen wings to service, but so far only three of them are cleared to ascend. Our facilities are so limited that we have to have many parts forged and machined secretly on the mainland."

"And is this all that you have? This single town and wingfield?"

"Yes, there are no other settlements larger than fifty souls. We cannot afford to waste resources with transport. Farms have been established to grow seeds and grains to make compression spirit, as well as to feed us. As you can see, we are surviving but are in a precarious state."

Shadowmouse was given a tour of the gun workshops, which were producing heavy reaction guns that could be used either by infantry or be fitted to the kitewings. He spoke to many of the children living in the dormitories and working the farms between school classes, and found them to be healthy and generally happy.

"And the North Americans, how do they fit in?" Shadowmouse asked an artisan at the Institute over a lunch of boiled potatoes and goat milk butter.

"The first of them overflew us on the second day of February, and one parachuted down to this very wingfield. They wanted to trade horses for gold, but we wanted engines, tools, and skills—and we had no horses. We made an agreement that we would make horses available on the mainland if they would ferry a few aviads over here before flying on with their horses. They will also be sending tools and artisans to help us build better wings. Why, one compression-spirit artisan has already been brought over, and the efficiency of our plant has been improved fifteen percent."

"The first one to land here, was his name Sair Serjon Feydamor?"

"Why, yes, that was him. Fine fellow, and so young."

"I had the honor of meeting him."

Early in the afternoon Shadowmouse was preparing to ascend to overview the capital, and to experience a kitewing for himself. The flyer helped him strap in, lying flat along the lower main wing.

"Compression-spirit stores are low, due to the volume that the super-regals need, so we make sure that all flights are training flights," he explained. "This kitewing has dual controls, and after we ascend you will take over and learn a few basics."

After a mere two hours Shadowmouse made a solo flight in a tiny armed kitewing. He made several passes at a target kite, shooting at ribbons suspended from its tail. When he landed he was put through a short ceremony declaring him a flyer of the Avian Flock, while a band of two flutes, a trumpet, and two drums supplied the music.

His flyer's badge had not been on his cloak for two minutes when the wingfield adjunct came over to speak with him.

"So, Fras Shadowmouse, you have no sweetheart or children, and your parents think you are dead," declared the adjunct, reading from a slate.

"That describes me," said Shadowmouse.

"Were you to die, none would be told."

"In my case, none would care."

"Splendid. Come this way, now, and see the ancient weapons. They do not need compression engines, and were originally developed in case the Americans attacked."

"But they are intended to stop the Gentheists now?"

"Yes. Gentheist experiments are under way to develop massive galley airships, held aloft by hot air and powered by hundreds of pedaling musketeers. The humans could reach this island and wipe us out, they could make hundreds of those things from just cloth and wooden frames while we struggle to put a half dozen compression engines together. But we also have ancient weaponry, Fras Shadow-mouse. Dangerous, barely understood, highly unstable, but devastatingly effective. In time we shall make them safer, but for now the Skyfire weapons are prematurely in production because we need them. People like you are being asked to die in them for just that reason as well."

Peterborough, the Woomeran Confederation

Whatever one might say about prophets, dreamers, and visionaries, it is fair to say that they do get inspiration from somewhere. Four decades earlier the young Zarvora Cybeline had sitting in the University Library, lamenting the demise of the ancient civilization's intelligent calculating machines and contemplating the vast amount of calculation needed to determine when Mirrorsun would complete itself and unfurl in the skies of Earth. All around her were her fellow students of mathematics, all hard at work with their calculations. Suddenly the thought struck her: she was surrounded by intelligent calculating machines. All that she needed was a system to coordinate them, a few hundred abacus frames and benches, leg shackles, guards with whips, a shift roster, the money to feed the slaves and pay the guards, and sufficient power to put anyone who objected before a firing squad. Six years later she was the Highliber of Libris and the first unhappy components were being chained into the original Calculor of Libris.

Although publically a Gentheist, Zarvora had been an agnostic, and often maintained that she would have been an atheist but she did not have sufficient faith to deny the existence of a god, deity, or any other manifestation of an all-powerful being. Thus she put her inspiration for the first calculor down to sheer intelligence, of which she did have a great deal. The idea had come to her in midafternoon, on a bright, sunny day, and in a public place. She did not leap out of a bath shouting "Eureka!" She merely drew a diagram and wrote down some figures. She then walked across the city to Libris, demanded a Dragon White examination, and passed it with a perfect score. She then demanded to sit the examinations for Dragon Yellow, Dragon Orange, Dragon Red, and Dragon Green. By midnight she walked back to her university college of residence with the color of a Dragon Green pinned to her tunic, and by noon the following day she had killed her first supervisor in a duel over an accusation of fraud. She demanded, and was given, her supervisor's rank.

Thus, although Zarvora's rise through fifteen year's worth of seniority in twenty-four hours might have been considered miraculous, nothing had taken place that intelligence, a sound education, sheer talent, good flintlock targetry, and an absolutely psychopathic dedication to the salvation of civilization could not explain. This was not the case with Jemli Milderellen, four decades later.

A reciprocating clock was clanging out the hour of midnight in the mayoral palace of Peterborough as Jemli sat contemplating a portrait of her sister Lemorel on the wall. Lemorel had experienced the most tragic of romantic losses, then set out to conquer the continent. She had very nearly done it, too, and it had taken the cosmic might of Mirrorsun to stop her army.

"We shared the same room in childhood, we even shared the insufferably obnoxious John Glasken when we grew older," Jemli said to the portrait. "So why are songs sung about you, why do bards recite thousand-verse epics in the taverns about your loves, duels, and victories, yet they call me the Prophet who shall never die because the Deity could not stand having me in paradise? How I hate bards! Burn one and half an hour later you need to burn a dozen more."

Jemli was being very unfair to herself, and her melancholy was in part explainable by the nine tumblers of gin and bitters that she had consumed over the previous hour. Her Reformed Gentheist movement now covered the overmayorates of Kalgoorlie, Woomera, and Alspring, so that she actually had a greater population paying her homage—and taxes—than Lemorel had conquered at the height of her military expansion.

"Why am I a failure?" she demanded of the portrait.

She drained the last of her gin and bitters, then flung the crystal tumbler at Lemorel's portrait. She missed by over a yard, and the tumbler shattered against the limestone wall. Lemorel's affairs had been wildly romantic, Jemli had merely experienced seductions and managed to marry two men with excellent prospects.

"The bards sing that when you got into bed with a man the trees burst into flower, even in the depths of winter, and the birds perched on the roofs and serenaded you and your lover to sleep in sixteen-part harmony. With me it was all grubby fumble, slap, and tickle."

She flung the empty jar of Hawker gin at the portrait, missing by such a wide margin that she hit the portrait of herself in mayoral robes. The portrait fell to the floor along with the fragments of jar. Jemli snatched up the little phial of bitters and threw it too at her sister's image. It smashed through the window, and she was rewarded with a shriek from somewhere out in the darkness. She certainly lacked Lemorel's coordination and skill at targetry.

"Well, at three feet even I can hit a wastrel husband and his giggling hopsicle!" shouted Jemli.

She lurched to her feet, reeled over to a wall, and pressed a panel. There was a clack. She slid the panel aside, took out the Morelac that had once belonged to her sister, and drew back both strikers. Making her way across to Lemorel's portrait, she discharged both barrels into the face at a range of six inches. Moments later two of her personal guards burst in.

"Get out!" she shrieked, flinging the Morelac at them but hitting the reciprocating clock instead.

The guards left hurriedly. Jemli snatched the gun from the wreckage of the clock and returned it to its recess. Slamming the panel back, she leaned against the wall with her arms folded.

"What is it about you?" she asked the ruined face of Lemorel's portrait. "Oh, you were brave, charismatic, and clever, but I am too! I'm cleverer. I conquered quicker, and more souls—and they're alive! Mostly. You killed hundreds of thousands, you put entire cities to the torch, you murdered whole mayorates. I just burned a few heretics . . . and bards. You betrayed your patron Zarvora Cybeline, you smashed her beamflash system, and murdered her librarians. I don't murder. I charm. I'm cleverer than you."

Cleverer. What would a clever person do? Lemorel was clever, and everyone knew what she had done. Jemli returned to her table and picked up the decoded message that her beamflash crew had delivered some hours before.

/ I AM IN A POSITION OF TRUST IN ROCHESTER / I LOVE THE DEITY / I HATE ALL ABOMINATIONS / ALL POWER TO THE WORD / DEATH TO ENEMIES OF THE WORD /

The attached report linked it with the Highliber's office. Obviously a trick, but worth investigation. Perhaps he or she could be used. How? She picked up another report.

/ CHRISTIAN GAIA CRUSADERS OF WARRAGUL PROPOSE ALLIANCE /

Her priests were reporting that the Christian Gaia Crusaders were doing most of their recruiting from her own followers. As Jemli subverted, so was she subverted.

"I get more out of one assassination than you got from ten thousand battle deaths," Jemli snarled at the portrait. "You conquered cities, I conquer citizens' hearts and souls, I—"

Jemli froze, her own words ringing in her ears. No, not her words, the Word. Was she not the lips that spoke for the Deity? The beamflash network. The Dragon Librarian Service. Conquer mercifully. The beamflash network was powered by humans and sunlight! It was blessed, it was meant to be her tool. The human-powered calculors of the Commonwealth had confirmed her prophecy about Mirrorsun not harming the world and being cast away into the darkness. Rochester was made for her to conquer, no other overmayorate was better poised to fall to the Word, Rochester was begging for salvation—and that was it!

Abruptly a mighty vision solidified before her. Jemli shrieked, but this time her guards decided to remain outside. She slammed the door open, lost her balance and fell, but made it seem as if she was dropping to her knees to praise the Deity.

"The Word says that we conquer through salvation and mercy!" cried Jemli to her very nervous guards. "No war, only salvation; no conquest, only mercy! Sing praise to the Deity! Fetch my priests. Fetch my advisors and mayors!"

The guards immediately began to sing the first verse of "Nearer to Thee, Glorious Deity," then four of them hurried away before the others realized that they had missed a perfectly good excuse to put distance between themselves and the notoriously unstable Prophet. By the next day the beamflash network had spread the news far and wide that Jemli the Prophet had been blessed with a new vision. There would be no wars in the Deity's name, the Deity's love and mercy would vanquish all abominations and enemies of the Word.

Rochester, the Rochestrian Commonwealth

Samondel noticed that Velesti was walking differently, still with her swaggering stride, but with more urgency. After twelve days at the monastery, Samondel's Austaric had become not so much fluent as more precise.

"What we must do now is integrate the contacts Serjon has made," said Velesti. "I have not spoken directly with the Highliber again, but his deputy says he is anxious to make diplomatic links with Mounthaven. He has been asking about the volumes of alcohol and vegetable oils that your wings need for compression spirit. Our artisans could even help with some of the simpler spare parts for engines."

"Serjon said his present contacts are not official. They are even a little beyond the law. Dealing with them has been difficult. For him."

"They sound like aviads; they could supply compression spirit as well as horses."

"I cannot see Serjon dealing with aviads."

"I may be wrong. Whatever the truth, an official contact with Rochester would be of benefit to everyone."

"Here is the inn," said Samondel, pushing the door open.

"So, let us see whether Serjon is willing to tell us just who are his associates."

As they climbed the stairs Samondel fumbled in her pockets for the key.

"Serjon is still in the same room," Velesti said. "I saw it on the chalkboard."

"I cannot find my key, and he may already be out for the day."

"I'll get us in."

"Velesti! Don't you dare break down his door. Again."

"I swear on my life that I shall not."

"And if he's in bed—"

"I shall leave very hurriedly," Velesti assured her, "and you may take up the option to stay with your dear lover."

They stopped at Serjon's door, but before Samondel could knock, Velesti slipped the airlord's stolen key into the lock and flung the door open. Samondel was assailed with a multitude of tumbling, chaotic impressions in the dim, dawn light filtering through the closed shutters. A woman with masses of brown, curly hair and particularly large breasts sitting up in bed and screaming. Serjon scrambling for a pistol under the pillow. Velesti's boot flicking the weapon from his hand. Velesti's boot on Serjon's neck and the barrel of her flintlock in his ear. The remains of a meal and several wine jars. A strident perfume. Clothing and underclothes strewn about on the floor and furniture.

Samondel stood in the doorway with her hands on her hips. The woman stopped screaming. Serjon stopped struggling.

"Surprise!" said Velesti in a bright and cheerful tone.

Velesti picked up Serjon's flintlock, then stood back and let him get up.

"You," said Samondel in Austaric, glaring at Serjon's bedmate. "Get dressed. Get out."

The girl slipped from the bed, gathered her clothing, and dressed hurriedly. Not a word was spoken. She began to edge toward the door. Samondel moved aside for her. Velesti held up a frilly garter.

"I presume this is not his," she said with a glance to Serjon.

"Ah, no, Frelle Tiger Dragon," said the girl. "It's mine."

"I know you from somewhere. Your name is Nereli, is it not?"

"Aye, Frelle Tiger Dragon."

Velesti strode across and slapped the garter into her hand, then closed her fingers over it.

"Now go, put it on outside."

"Aye, Frelle, at once," babbled the terrified Nereli, just as she caught the merest flicker of a wink from Velesti.

It was only when she was out in the street that Nereli opened her hand and found five gold royals sharing her palm with the garter. So this is the life of a spy, she thought. An easy seduction, then merely rolling about in bed with a very pleasant young man who barely spoke Austaric let alone divulged any secrets. One moment of intense fright, danger, and humiliation, then a wink for thanks and five gold royals. Thanks and royals for what? "I was once a spy," she would say wearily to some patron in Marelle Glasken's tavern that night, "but no girl can live that way for long. You never knew who you were working for, what you were doing, or if it was for good or evil. The gold, luxury, and excitement just do not make up for the uncertainty." She would, of course, have to cultivate an air of mystery and more languorous speech, but that would not be hard.

Back in Serjon's room, it was as if Greatwinter had suddenly returned. Velesti stood beside the door as Samondel picked up a second garter between her thumb and forefinger. Serjon remained seated on the floor, hugging his knees.

"Who was she?" asked Samondel with a voice as cold as frost under bare feet.

"I, ah, met her."

"Obviously," said Velesti, also in Old Anglian.

"Quite by chance."

"Frelle Nereli Torisen, jarmaid, Marelle's Tavern," said Velesti.

"Quite by chance, in a tavern?" asked Samondel.

"It is known to be the best assignation place in Rochester—" said Velesti.

"Nothing but the best for Serjon Feydamor," snapped Samondel.

"—and center for espionage exchange," added Velesti.

"What?" cried Samondel and Serjon together.

"The Espionage Constables and their agents all drink there, only lower-class spies go to the Filthy Swine. I trust you said nothing of importance to Frelle Nereli?"

Velesti could hear Samondel's teeth grinding. Serjon suddenly realized that Velesti was speaking fluent Old Anglian.

"You seek me out, you shatter my friendship with a man so sweet that he could charm the very birds out of the air, chance alone saved me from the renewed attentions of your penis, then as soon as I am gone you go straight down to the nearest tavern and, and, and—what is the local euphemism?"

"Get a leg over," said Velesti, now opening a sealed square of poorpaper that she had taken from her jacket.

"Get your leg over the first jarmaid to hand—who is probably a spy for heaven knows who? Reformed Gentheists? The Dragon Librarian Service? Why did you bother trying to seduce me again? Was it the feeling of power, bedding an airlord? How many others have *really* been making up for Bronlar's difficulties in bed with you, and for how long?"

"At least five in Rochester," said Velesti, tapping the report that she held.

"No! Not so!" shouted Serjon.

"This is a report from certain . . . associates of mine, left to watch over your welfare," said Velesti, hunching her head forward and putting her hand above her eyes. "I was worried that the Reformed Gentheists might attack you."

"Five?" cried Samondel, parts of her face blazing a deeper shade of red than her hair.

"Jilmer, Metel, Darien, Zoltine, and of course, Nereli."

"Lies!" insisted Serjon.

"Well, yes, I am lying," said Velesti. "I only had you trailed for six days and five nights, so there could have been . . . hmmm, one new girl per night, five nights, another seven nights at the rate of one girl per night is twelve girls in your bed—oh, plus Samondel is thirteen. Very unlucky number, that. I do understand, though. All that unrequited desire building up, after all. Of course were I a man I would have thought masturbation a chivalrous path to take, but—"

"You stay out of this!" shouted Samondel. "Twelve others! And how many more since we became lovers last July?"

"Assuming one per day for eight months, take off a half dozen days to fly the ocean, two hundred thirty-four—ooh, eighteen times thirteen, very unlucky number."

"My love and dearest, she's lying—" began the increasingly frantic Serjon.

"I might never have known about all this had not Velesti mistranslated 'dozen days' as 'fortnight', which led to us catching you here. I was actually *anxious* to see you. I was wondering how to get rid of Velesti so I could tumble into bed with you, and open that 6 ME package again."

"This one," said Velesti, drawing from her pocket the roughly rewrapped packet.

Samondel glared at Velesti for a moment, then decided that Serjon was still a far more worthy target of her hatred.

"Get dressed," said Samondel firmly.

"Not in front of *that*!" snapped Serjon hugging his knees more tightly to his chest and scowling at Velesti.

"I am certainly not going to let it be said that I was alone with you while you were dressing," retorted Samondel haughtily.

Velesti tossed Serjon his clothing, and Samondel flung Nereli's second garter to him as well. Serjon kicked the garter away and began to dress.

"I was going to apologize for going away, plead for your understanding, your sympathy. Bah! Even Velesti has more sympathy that you."

"And that is really saying something," added Velesti as she scooped up the garter.

"But I forget myself, I have other questions. Are the aviads' wingfields in Tasmania Island selling you compression spirit—and in return for what?"

"Samondel, darling, you must have heard this from Velesti. You can't believe her, she's a spy, just like Nereli. They set me up. Nereli was the only one."

Velesti pulled Nereli's garter on over her boot and put her hands on her hips, thrusting her breasts out.

"Definitely not you," said Samondel.

Velesti removed the garter and tossed it to her.

"She's probably an aviad herself!" insisted Serjon.

"Aviad I am not, but Inspector in the Espionage Constables I certainly am, and the agent who seduced you reports to the division coordinator who reports to my deputy!"

Samondel and Serjon gasped together.

"Serjon Feydamor, you are under arrest on charges of espionage and plotting to overthrow the Rochestrian Commonwealth by force. Lie on the floor with your hands behind your back."

"This can all be explained," insisted Serjon as Velesti shackled his hands and feet. "Yes, we have an alliance with the Avianese, but the Gentheists gave us no choice. No harm was intended to Rochester."

Velesti overturned the bed, revealing a crate and several barrels. The crate contained a dozen Clastini reaction pistols and spare clips.

"Can you explain these as well?" asked Samondel.

Serjon did not reply, and his eyes were downcast as Velesti tied him to the grille of the fireplace.

"I believe we have earned breakfast," said Velesti. "My Dragons will come up here and tidy things away while we eat, meantime he can sit here alone and contemplate his sins. Would you care to visit the eatery downstairs, Frelle Samondel?"

"I would be delighted, Frelle Velesti."

"You will be attended to shortly, Fras Serjon. Just practice sitting there quietly. I expect you will be sitting quietly in small rooms for a very long time to come."

There were neither errand boys nor runners in the taproom, so they went out into the street. Velesti hailed someone Samondel had never seen before, and whispered something to him. The man set off for the inn.

"So you were an inspector in the Espionage Constables all along," said Samondel.

"Well . . . it certainly frightened him into confessing," said Velesti, avoiding the question.

Samondel doubled over with laughter, clinging to Velesti's arm for balance.

"Frelle, Frelle, you are the most delightfully clever and wicked woman I have met in my entire life."

They were knocked flat by the explosion that blew the inn apart, fountaining tiles, boards, plaster, and smoke high into the air. They lay with their hands over their heads as fragments and dust poured down around them. Both had their guns out as they got to their feet and surveyed the damage. The Celestial was just a pile of burning wreckage, and the buildings to either side were burning too, and partly collapsed. Screams were already coming from within the ruins, and every Constable's Runner within the radius of a mile was blowing his whistle.

The search of the ruins took the rest of the morning, and nobody was surprised when no identifiable pieces of Serjon's body were found. It was only in midafternoon that Velesti began to track down sightings of someone answering Serjon's description fleeing through the city and across one of the bridges immediately after the explosion.

"He thought I was downstairs," Samondel kept saying over and again. "He tried to kill me."

Samondel walked past Marelle's tavern twice before finally entering. It was early in the evening, and several jarmaids were cleaning tables and sweeping the floor while a carter and his apprentice carried jars and barrels in. Samondel stood waiting for someone to approach her. One of the jarmaids looked up. Nereli. The girl squeaked and dashed out of the room. When she returned, it was with a disheveled but nevertheless glamorous-looking woman in her midtwenties who was wearing a bathrobe of green silk. Nereli was cowering behind her.

"I doubt that you're here for a drink or a job," said Marelle Glasken.

"Actually, no," replied Samondel slowly.

"Well, you have before you the two women who have slept with the two most recent men in your life, Frelle Samondel. What can we do for you?"

"Talk. Please."

Marelle turned to the other jarmaids "That's clean enough, go." She indicated a table and the three of them sat down. Samondel sat with her hand on her chin for a moment, then pointed at the quavering Nereli.

"Where?" Samondel asked.

"I, I met Fras Serjon at the Celestial, in the taproom. I was having a drink by myself. When he came down to dinner I caught his eye, we started talking, then, ah, ah—"

"Usual proceedings took place, I am imagining. Who sent you?"

Nereli half turned to Marelle with her mouth opened, then she stared down at the table. Samondel looked to Marelle.

"Who, ah, did tell you to send Nereli . . . on mission?"

"Martyne is still alive," answered Marelle smoothly.

As a diversion, the tactic worked superbly. Samondel's composure cracked.

"Where? Must—I must, er, see him," she said eagerly.

"He vanished over a week ago, he said he was never returning to Rochester."

"Was dead. Taken to, ah, dissection rooms."

"The dissection rooms are the University's emergency hospital. Didn't your second tell you?"

"No," replied Samondel, looking thoughtful.

"His injuries were dramatic, but were not fatal," continued Marelle. "Your gun must have been badly charged, otherwise he would have died."

Badly charged? thought Samondel. Velesti could no more mischarge a gun than she could kiss a man. Unless . . . A "fortnight," a "dozen days."

"Velesti lies, plots, schemes and manipulates as easily as others breathe," Samondel muttered, her teeth grating.

"Sorry?" asked Marelle.

"Go," Samondel said to Nereli, who pushed away from the table hurriedly, almost knocking her chair over in the process. "And Nereli," Samondel continued.

"Ah, ah, yes Frelle?"

Samondel smiled broadly. "Good work. Thank you."

Samondel turned to Marelle as Nereli dashed through the door.

"Nice girl, reminds me of my mother," said Marelle.

"Velesti has paid . . . did instruct you, ah, to have Serjon seduced. Particularly on day eleven. Correct, I am?"

"I'm not going to lie to someone as astute as you, Frelle. Velesti arranged it."

Samondel sat back with her eyes closed, the breath hissing in her nostrils.

"Why?"

"She did not say."

Samondel opened her eyes again.

"Nereli's report. Contained what?"

"Not much, Serjon didn't say a great deal. His story was that he was a wine-and-spirits merchant, investigating Rochester's distilleries. They spent the nights together, he vanished during the day—"

"How many nights?"

"All those while you were gone."

"Velesti! Damn her, she is the devil!"

"He was going to go south after he left here. Hunting. 'Hunting birds,' were his words. 'Make feathers fly,' he would say, then laugh."

Samondel considered again. Serjon was a deadly shot in a gunwing, but clumsy with carbines and had never gone hunting in his life. Hunting birds—featherheads! Aviads!

"He did say, where he is— was—from?"

"Just 'far away,' and that he was soon leaving on a whirlwind hunting trip."

"Whirlwind? What is?"

"Wind that swirls in a circle, picks up leaves and dust."

Tornado! Featherhead hunting. Everything was suddenly very, very clear to Samondel. Horrifyingly clear.

"You know, concerning me, with Martyne," Samondel said.

"Yes."

"You love him?"

"Love? What a giggle. He amused me for a while, and I may have amused him."

"Martyne, I do love."

"Alas, Frelle, that show has left town. He faced certain death, but when he survived—thanks to Velesti, I suspect—he decided to leave, vanish from your life as if he were indeed dead. To leave you and Serjon together and return to his monastery. Martyne had become free to be your beloved, but your heart was Serjon's—"

"I would have left him for Martyne!" shouted Samondel.

The carters carrying in the jars and barrels stopped to stare at them. At a gesture from Marelle's thumb they returned to their work.

"Did you tell Serjon you loved him?" asked Marelle.

"What else you telling someone in bed?"

"*I* usually say 'Wake up, I can't sleep.' "

"Frelle, am not . . . what is multiple-lovers word?"

"Promiscuous."

"Am not promiscuous. I loved Martyne, but thought he was not mine. I was so, so lonely. What to do? Leave Serjon? Pine for Martyne while he lives with wife? Would you?"

"Never!"

"I opened my heart, just an instant. Let love for Martyne blaze out like, ah, meteor, then closed it again."

"You really loved him?"

"Yes! Still! Martyne taught me what love really means! Now I chase Serjon, kill Serjon, clean up mess he has making, then follow Martyne to Balesha, tell Martyne I love him like sun blazing in summer sky. Perhaps he can be returning. If not . . . end of everything."

"No man is worth that, silly Frelle."

"Then is something I have felt and you have not, wise Frelle." Marelle stood up.

"Frelle Samondel, believe it or not, I would kill to feel what you have felt for Martyne, but I suspect that you will always have the advantage of me. Martyne and you were well suited. I like you both."

"Am feeling . . . no grudge. To you. But to Velesti . . ." Samondel spread her fingers and tilted her hand back and forth. "Am not sure."

Marelle held out her arm. "Come now, visit my kitchen, meet my cook, and sample my coffee."

Velesti was oddly subdued when Samondel found her, and sat listening quietly as the undeniably annoyed American airlord related all that Marelle had said.

"After I exposed Martyne's betrothed, I went to my room and exercised for a time," she confessed.

"You what?"

"How was I to know about Serjon arriving?"

"You arranged that whole, ah, ah, what is the local term? Carnival of blood, perhaps?"

"Bloody circus?"

"You arranged the whole bloody circus to get rid of Serjon?"

"Ah . . ."

"No lies!!"

"Yes."

"God in heaven, please tell me this is dream! Why? You lie to the Highliber, lie to me, lie to your Overmayor, lie to the Espionage Constables, provoke a duel, risk starting wars, change the destiny of continents, but *why*?"

"To cool your passion for Serjon, to give Martyne a real chance with you."

"I cannot believe this!" cried Samondel, pulling at her red hair.

"He's my mate. In Australica you do that sort of thing for your mates."

"Mate, I know the word now. Good friend. Best friend. No love, only loyalty. Very strange. Usually only men are mates."

"But not always. As you said, Martyne is my only friend. I was a fiend, and he saved me. I owe him everything. I would never sleep with him, but I would die for him."

"And me?"

"You're his beloved, so I'd die for you too."

"No, I mean—ah, thank you—I mean, you are not jealous? Of me?"

"No. I don't love him."

Samondel sat with her head in her hands for a long time. Presently she looked up, her eyes bloodshot and red rimmed.

"Velesti, I am only a damn ignorant American, so . . ."

"So?"

"Can you help me do something—oh, and explain some local terminology to me?"

"I owe you that. All right."

"Help me find Serjon, but . . ."

"But?"

"*I* am to kill him!"

Velesti considered this for a time.

"You may have the first shot at him. Even as your friend I shall promise no more."

"That will be enough . . . but tell me this: You are Martyne's 'mate.' "

"But you are my 'friend.' "

"Yes."

"But we are not mates?"

"Of course not. We're girls, we are far too sensible to be mates."

Samondel closed her eyes and pinched the bridge of her nose.

"All right, all right, I give up. Where do we start looking for Serjon?"

"With this report on the Celestial. Fifteen killed, dozens injured. If we had been eating in the taproom . . . well . . ."

"We would be dead."

"The explosion happened on the top floor, then the whole inn crashed down."

"Serjon tried to kill us. Damn him! Less than a fortnight ago we were rolling about on his bed in each others' arms. How could he? *What* is he?"

Velesti seized her by the shoulders. "Serjon is someone who likes to help a victim. He first lay with you when you were both victims, but now look at you: independent, strong, resourceful, and growing into a legend that will soon eclipse him. Airlord Sartov has great influence, and he is known to want Avianese air power destroyed."

"You are saying that this whole venture, *my* venture, was an excuse to mount an attack on the Avianese on Tasmania Island?"

"I am saying nothing, but I am *asking* a great deal. Serjon will try to go to Traralgon, Frelle. Can he ride?"

"He told me he could not."

"Then he must use the paraline trains or go by horse coach. I shall use the beamflash towers to have every train and coach stopped and searched. We can catch him."

The following day Velesti was not quite so confident. A report came in about a lone bandit who had committed murder in Seymour. Velesti and Samondel were summoned by Dramoren.

"I thought you said he couldn't ride?" exclaimed Velesti.

"*He* said that!" retorted Samondel.

"Well, *someone* who could ride quite passably well just killed a stableman at Seymour, stole a fresh cavalry horse, and used something that sounds suspiciously like a reaction pistol to kill three of the five lancers who went after him. So, he can ride, and he must have ridden cross-country. I should have checked at the Rochester stables! Damn his duplicity. He was heading southeast, according to the survivors."

"What do you wish to do?" asked the Highliber in Austaric. "Traralgon is outside Rochester's control, our authorities cannot pursue him there."

"Samondel and I shall go after him," announced Velesti.

"I can requisition a galley engine for you and order the lines to Seymour cleared," said the Highliber.

"Good," replied Velesti. "Please beamflash for fresh horses to be waiting for us at Seymour as well."

·   ·   ·   ·   ·

Serjon was gone by the time Samondel and Velesti reached Traralgon Castle, but he had left his mark. The warlord and five of his men had been shot down and their new reaction pistols stolen. The angry but confused lancers said that the latest group of children and their guardian were gone too, along with another five horses. Selvintan, the aviad who had been appointed envoy to Traralgon ten days earlier, confirmed that Serjon had done the killing. Green eyes and wavy black hair, all of them had agreed on that. The envoy aviad did not need any persuasion to come with them, and he rode Serjon's stolen horse as they left the castellany.

"Now that we are clear of the castle, you must tell us everything you know of the flying machines," said Velesti as they rode.

"They fly in from the east, pick up five horses and up to twenty children, then go south."

"Where?"

"All that I know is that I was meant to fly with them on the flight before last. Obviously Avian is to the south, on Tasmania Island. The research academy and kitewing workshops are at the capital, Launceston."

"Where else might they go?"

"Nowhere, Frelle. The other five wingfields are mere strips of grass with a windsock, a box of tools, and a pile of compression-spirit barrels."

"You are good informer," began Samondel.

"My lady, never!" exclaimed Selvintan.

"She means that you are well informed; I was about to say the same myself," explained Velesti.

"I am actually a distiller. My wife and family are already on Tasmania Island, and I lived there for a time myself. I was sent back here to oversee certain distilling operations run by unsuspecting humans, then suddenly I was called back to Launceston."

"Expanded need for compression spirit," commented Samondel.

"I arrived at Traralgon wingfield and was given charge of a

group of children, then another aviad arrived and took my place. He told me to stay and act as envoy to Traralgon. I must admit to some confusion, but it is my place to obey orders, so here I am."

"Who told you to stay?" asked Velesti.

"The young aviad. He had dark hair and a beard. He killed three lancers who tried to jump upon him. That impressed the warlord mightily. When the air machine ascended, he was on it."

"Five horses, so many people," said Samondel, switching to Old Anglian. "Even a super-regal would be struggling, it definitely could not carry spirit for fourteen hours with such a load . . . unless they take on more spirit at Tasmania Island, after the passengers are dropped off."

"This does not calculate," remarked Velesti. "I thought you said Serjon hated aviads, yet he seems as thick as treacle with them."

"I do not know what to think. He is working with them, ferrying passengers to Tasmania Island in exchange for spirit and horses. Perhaps I misjudged him."

"Frelle, over the past days Serjon has also killed more people than I have in as many months. He intended you to be one of them."

"I cannot explain that."

"Then perhaps we should pray for divine guidance."

"You? Pray?"

"I *am* joking, but nevertheless there is a fine new Reformed Gentheist church at the frontier settlement of Warragul. We are going to pay it a visit."

"But I am a Damarite Christian."

"Oh, but I think you should see this church, Frelle. It has been blessed with signs and wonders."

Warragul, Southeast Australica

The wonder that was the central feature of the Church of Celestial Balance was a small, enclosed boat with stubby outrigger pontoons and a harness over a hundred feet long. After accepting a donation the lay preacher was delighted to relate how it had been found in the tidal marshes, and how a tracker had discovered the Envoy nearby. He was known only as the Envoy, and in broken Austaric he said he had been towed all the way from North America by cooperative cetezoids. The people of North America had apparently overthrown their heretical engine builders and aviators, and the cetezoids had wished to bring them to Australica to help humans crush the aviad mayorate on Tasmania Island. Reformed Gentheists were making pilgrimages from everywhere to see it. Even the Prophet Jemli was considering a trip there.

"The Envoy, does he have green eyes and black, wavy hair?" Velesti asked. "In his boots he is about six feet tall?"

"That is him, Frelle, I see you are a devout and well-prepared pilgrim," replied the preacher.

"That is all a fake!" said Samondel to Velesti as they left. "After six thousand miles the paint of that boat thing should be worn where the harness rubs against it. Instead, it looks as if new. It's Serjon's doing. What is his scheme?"

"To me it seems that he is playing aviads against both warlords and Rochester, while working with the Reformed Gentheists," speculated Velesti. "You have a military background, yes?"

"Yes, it comes with being an airlord."

"Then consider this. Launceston is what, in calculor circles, is called a single point of failure for Avian. Everything depends upon it. Serjon could get the Avianese into his confidence, then smash them in a single raid from the air, then tell the Reformed Gentheists that North American musketeers traveled by sea to do the fighting. Thus North America restores its monopoly on aircraft, Avian is annihilated, and the Reformed Gentheists are free to overthrow the Commonwealth with smuggled reaction pistols—if Prophet Jemli can explain why they are not fueled machines. The aviads left on the mainland would be caught between the sea and a very hostile Reformed Gentheist government."

Samondel did not have to think about Velesti's words for very long. She turned to Selvintan, who was whirling a little model of Serjon's boat that he had bought at the church's kiosk.

"Flying to Avian, can be arranged, yes?"

"Flying! Frelle, there is a list of people waiting for the few kite-wing flights that is longer than a taxation auditor's memory."

"Who determines the list?" asked Velesti.

"He is known only as Terian."

"Ah, yes, I know him," she said casually.

"You—you what?" exclaimed Selvintan. "Even Fras Terian's own shadow does not know who he is."

"Well, Fras Terian's shadow is obviously not a member of the Espionage Constables, but I am. Frelle Samondel, I shall contact Terian from the Seymour beamflash tower, then we three shall take the paraline to the Bendigo Abandon. Fras Selvintan here will escort us to one of the secret wingfields, and you shall be flown to Launceston to warn the mayor of Serjon Feydamor's plans."

"Why me?" asked Samondel.

"Because you are American, because you can speak with as much authority as Serjon, and because you may even be able to help with their defenses."

Seymour, the Rochestrian Commonwealth

Velesti and Samondel visited the Seymour bathhouse as they waited for a galley engine to be prepared and crewed for them. Velesti's body caused no small amount of consternation among the other patrons of the women's section before they realized that she was definitely female. They bathed quickly, more anxious to be hurriedly clean than to luxuriate in warm, soapy water, but as they were toweling Samondel took Nereli's garter from her jacket pocket and drew it onto her thigh. She struck a heroic pose, with her foot on a bench. Velesti glanced at her, raised an eyebrow, and returned to lacing her boots.

"Nine," she decided.

"Only nine?" asked Samondel, sounding genuinely worried.

"I deducted one for the silly pose."

"How *could* he prefer her to me?"

Velesti blinked. "Speaking as a woman: he was a bastard. Speaking as a man: she was there and you were not."

"So you would excuse what he did?" exclaimed Samondel, now sounding puzzled.

Velesti stood up, snatched up her sports bra, sniffed at it, shrugged, and put it on. She stood before Samondel with her arms folded beneath her breasts.

"Muscles or no muscles, I am undeniably a woman," she pointed out. "I can understand his behavior, but that does not mean I approve or sanction it."

"So is this all there is between men and women?" demanded Samondel, extending the leg with the garter horizontally. "Lies, lust, and trying not to get caught?"

"What would Bronlar have said, had she been with me when I surprised you with Serjon?"

"I know, I know," admitted Samondel, lowering her leg. "Perhaps I am just as tarred as Serjon."

"Yet would you have ever betrayed *Martyne*?"

"Never!"

"And Martyne was prepared to die for you. Even now, he thinks that he has left you to be happy with Serjon."

"True, true."

"So there is hope."

"But Martyne is gone."

"Martyne is alive, and that is a vast improvement over being dead. Go to Tasmania Island, Frelle, help the aviads survive against your people. Then return here and I swear I shall bring him to you again."

Samondel removed the garter and tossed it to Velesti. Velesti twirled it on her finger.

"Kindly return that item of uniform to your loyal and diligent agent," said Samondel, "and yet again give her my thanks."

The Southeast Coast, Australica

An hour after nightfall a kitewing descended to Apollo Wingfield as silently as a black owl, with its engine idling through a maze of baffles. The flyer handed out bags of mail and small, heavy packages without unstrapping himself from the flight bunk.

"Return mail?" he asked the adjunct.

"No, adult passenger."

The flyer cursed softly, but Samondel heard. She had not eaten all day, and was wearing only cotton trousers and a blouse under a featherdown jacket, but her one hundred and thirty pounds was at the limit of what could be managed for a stealth ascent with the early model kitewing. The standard seventy pounds of mail, infants, or small tools was far preferable.

"I shall make inquiries about Martyne," said Velesti in Old Anglian. "If he has returned to Balesha that may take time, however. The monastery is deep within Reformed Gentheist territory, and the beamflash system is less than reliable without the Dragon Librarian Service to operate it."

"Shall I ever see you again?" asked Samondel, staring at the dark shape that was Velesti's head.

"I have to haunt someone, and if she decides to test whether I am really a ghost it could prove bad for my health."

"You have a way of staying in good health."

"Then try to emulate me."

Samondel had been in Velesti's company for long enough to know that she made no farewells. The American skipped forward, flung her arms around her, and squeezed for several heartbeats.

"Go your way, and do something unspeakable to someone deserving of it," she said as she kissed Velesti's cheek.

"Go your way, and do something that I would approve of," replied Velesti, cuffing her head.

"That leaves me a lot of scope, Frelle Incredible."

Samondel climbed onto the wing and strapped herself down as

the handlers pushed the aircraft to the end of the ramp. Velesti was already gone.

"First time?" asked the flyer.

"Flying, very much," replied Samondel. "American. Six kills."

There was very little that the flyer could say to that. The handlers began to run with the kitewing as it descended a steep slope. What had once been a road curved sharply to avoid a sharp drop, but the kitewing glided out into open space. The flyer eased the throttle forward and the kitewing's downward glide curved up into level flight. The idling of the compression engine was little louder than the air's rush past them.

"Past those two hills and we're over open sea," said the flyer. "About five miles out I'll open the baffles and let it roar. It takes an enormous lot of spirit to push past the muffling."

The extremely low stall speed of the kitewing also meant a very low cruising speed. Thus the thermals around the hills buffeted them heavily, then they were out over the water.

"Wingfield to wingfield it's seventy miles, Frelle; coast to coast it's sixty. The kitewing has a glide ratio of twenty to one and the engine can be dropped if it fails so we can glide maybe ten miles. There's really only forty miles in the middle that could kill us. We try to avoid rough weather, so engine failure is the main risk."

"Kitewings failing often?"

"Fairly often."

"Am sad. Death certain."

"Not always. One floated for two days, and washed up on King Island. The flyer lived, the mail got through. I suppose the cetezoids thought it was a floating tree and ignored it."

At five miles the engine's baffles were opened and the engine roared loud as it put them into a steeper climb. Samondel had never been in a wing that lumbered along at a mere forty miles per hour, or been sustained by such a ragged-sounding engine. The cold seeped into her clothing and she began to shiver. She had left everything back on the mainland: her gun, ammunition, watch, and gold. Even her forged papers and flight jacket were safely locked in her room at Villiers College. Then she remembered. Around her neck was a gold locket with her name, office, and crest engraved into an iron disk inside. Serjon had bought her the locket in Condelor, what seemed like centuries ago, but what was in fact less than a year.

"Half hour to go!" called the flyer.

With numb, fumbling fingers she drew out the locket and popped it open. The disk was like a small, thin coin in her hand as she slipped it into her pocket. She tugged at the chain and snapped it, held the locket and chain out over the leading edge of the wing, then let it go.

"Lot of folk do that," called the flyer.

"Do what?"

"Drop things at halfway point. Drop bits of their lives that they want to get rid of into the one place where there's no return."

"Was rat, drowning," shouted Samondel.

Suddenly the engine lost power. Samondel froze.

"Powering down for the approach to King Gate Wingfield," the flyer said above the much quieter engine. "Spirit is always in short supply, we can't afford to waste it."

"Sensible," agreed Samondel, greatly relieved.

"Present from a lover?"

"Is what?"

"Whatever you dropped back there."

"From him, no love involved."

King Island

King Gate Wingfield might almost have been in Mounthaven, for there were marker pyres all along the ascent strip, and a flare trailing smoke to indicate the wind's direction. Handlers were sprinting along the ground and steadying the wings even while the kitewing was still in the air, so low was its stall speed. Samondel slid from the wing, numb and stiff. The wingfield was a stone inn, several tents, and a fuel store. Samondel identified herself to the wingfield adjunct, and he arranged for a steam cart to take her south overnight, in spite of her pro-

tests that she could not afford the time lost. But thirty miles that could
be traveled by burning wood was several gallons of spirit saved.

Tasmania Island

As the sun was rising Samondel ascended in another kitewing, this
one with a louder and far more powerful engine. Within an hour she
was on Tasmania Island and arguing with the wingfield adjunct of
Smithton. Once more, there could be no kitewing spared to take her
to the Avianese capital at the Launcestion abandon, but a steam gig
had just arrived towing a tank of diesel spirit, and she was invited
to ride the hundred miles to Launceston if she helped with the stok-
ing and wood cutting. This time the driver was even friendlier than
the one on King Island, and at sunset insisted on stopping to camp
for the night by the roadside. There was a short but one-sided scuffle
before the driver lit the mutton-fat headlamps and drove the last two
hours through darkness with his own flintlock pointed at his back by
Samondel, who was seated on the wood tender.

Euroa, the Rochestrian Commonwealth

Brother Nikalan went where he wished, whether it was in the Monastery of St. Roger, the Mayorate of Euroa, the Rochestrian Commonwealth, or anywhere on the continent of Australica. Like Jemli
the Prophet, or Liaisary Ilyire, he was seen as a skilled juggler employed for entertainment at a family revel: excellent value for an
afternoon, but one hoped he would move on quickly and let life
return to normal. With Rangen, however, it was different. He ad-
mired Ilyire greatly and aspired to be like him.

"I have been reading about births, deaths, and lynchings for the
past three hundred years," declared Ilyire as he walked into the phys-

ics workshop where Rangen was ordering a team of his own superiors about.

"I have been sucking water through pipes," replied Rangen.

"I have also been to Libris."

"I have stayed here."

Half a dozen monks sat back on benches, while others began to hurry in from outside. They hissed at each other for silence.

"I have used the Libris Calculor to make a discovery," explained Nikalan.

"I have developed a new calculor," replied Rangen.

"Did you know that I have discovered something about aviads?"

"Did you know that I can calculate by sucking?"

Nikalan unrolled a scroll on the bench beside a very complex arrangement of several hundred pipes, levers, wheels, dials, and valves. Rangen lifted a pail of water from the floor and poured it into a cistern held above his apparatus by three stout wooden legs carved with ornamental spirals.

"Tell me how to live in peace with the aviads," said Nikalan.

"Screw the aviads. Pose me a simple exercise in calculation."

"Correct. Ah, the square root of four thousand, eight hundred seventy-two, rounded to the fourth decimal place."

Rangen began working levers and valves, then he turned a stopcock below the cistern and released a governor spun by clockwork. His labyrinth of pipes began to chatter softly to itself.

"Aviads must intermarry with humans, else they become childless after the fourth generation. You know what that means?"

"The weight of water in pipes forms an excellent method of opening and closing logic gates. You know what that means?"

"You should have dalliance with a fourth-generation aviad woman."

"And you should use water for your calculations."

"It would be an act of harmony between species, God would approve of it."

"It would be a humane alternative to human-powered calculors,

God would approve of it. Have *you* had a dalliance with a fourth-generation aviad?"

"I have indeed. Have you the square root of four thousand, eight hundred seventy-two, rounded to the fourth decimal place?"

"I have indeed: sixty-nine point seven nine nine seven."

"Correct."

"Did your experiment with the fourth-generation aviad Frelle prove fruitful?"

"I cannot say, it was only last week."

"There is a chemical test that will provide proof either way."

"Good, I like binary arithmetic. Why have I not heard of it?"

"You have neglected to read *Beamflash Abstracts* this month."

"Careless of me."

"Give me her name, I shall test her."

"How?"

"She must piss in a beaker."

"She is sure to cooperate. She is a medician, a woman of science. May I test your hydrocalculor?"

"Yes. I shall write instructions."

"Instructions? Instructions? Only fools read instructions. Here is her name and address."

"And here is another bucket of water."

Three dozen monks, the abbot, nine Dragon Librarians, a member of the Espionage Constables, five nuns, and an off-duty beamflash transmitter burst into applause. Nikalan and Rangen turned to their audience and bowed, then Nikalan took Rangen's seat and Rangen walked out of the workshop. The abbot tapped the beamflash transmitter on the shoulder as they were leaving.

"Come with me to the beamflash tower, I have an encoded message to send to Rochester," he said urgently.

"At once, Reverend Abbot. What is the content?"

"Those two brilliant lunatics have just changed the universe. I think that our leaders ought to be told before they read it in *Beamflash Abstracts* or else the Highliber will probably demand my admittedly redundant balls on a silver platter."

Launceston, Trasmania Island

Samondel was blindfolded before being taken into the rookery, as the Avianese called it. They were ruled by the mayor, but he was in turn advised by four experts and six representatives elected by those living off the mainland. The experts were selected according to the issue. Samondel counted 310 steps, mostly on hard paving. There was also one short stairway of fifteen stairs. A door was opened and she was ushered into a room that echoed slightly and smelled of burning olive oil.

"Fras Mayor, advisors," said one of her escorts. "Permit me to present Airlord Samondel Leover of Highland Bartolica."

"Thank you, Fras, you may go."

"Your word, Fras Mayor."

The voice sounded like that of a man in his early sixties, mature and well intoned, but with its edge starting to fray. Samondel put her hands to the blindfold.

"No! That stays on," barked the mayor. "You may not learn either our names or faces, because if you are who you say you are, there is a chance you will go free again. You may call me Fras Mayor. Present are my marshal, Fras Gun, my spymaster, Frelle Eye, my flockleader, Fras Wing, and a member of the mainland underground, Fras Shadowmouse. We have all read the deposition that you presented to the Constable of Launceston two hours ago, and we have discussed it. It has caused no small amount of alarm."

"Fras Mayor, every word true, being," Samondel assured him.

"You could not be expected to say anything else, but there are matters to be clarified. You say that Fras Feydamor plans to return here tomorrow with the super-regal *Albatross* and at least four armed sailwings. He plans to seize the wingfield, murder all of our artisans, flyers, and leaders, then burn the workshops, kitewings, stores, and compression-spirit distillery."

"A venture, name of Tornado. Meant to be, for seizing of horse farm, by force. Carry off horses."

"But as you point out yourself, Fras Feydamor, ourselves, and the Warlord of Traralgon have already cooperated to fly twenty-five young horses to your American dominions by peaceful means. Why should Fras Feydamor suddenly turn against us, especially when everybody is benefiting so greatly?"

"Because the Mayorate of Avian is only other air power in the *world*. And Avianese hated in Mounthaven, so much. Your Radical Aviads starting a terrible war there. None so bad in two thousand years. American airlords want to shatter your tiny mayorate. They can do it."

"True, we are only a few thousands, compared to the millions on the mainland, and even compared to your American mayorates, but how many musketeers can be flown on the *Albatross*? Six? Eight?"

"Thirty, Fras Mayor! Fly here, just enough spirit to reach. Thirty finest carbineers from Mounthaven with reaction guns. Four best wardens in armed sailwings, having firebombs. Catch by surprise, seize wingfield. Refuel. Fly to Smithton, King Gate, destroy there, too."

"Fras Gun, what do you think? Can it be done?"

"Two or three dozen highly trained musketeers with reaction guns could indeed set us back by years with such an attack," agreed the marshal.

"Fras Wing?"

"I could check with Traralgon, but it would take days. They only expect a wing to land every ten days, so the wingfield is only cleared of sheep and horses then. Trying to land there without beacon pyres, unexpected, with livestock on the ascent strip, could easily lose us a kitewing and flyer."

"Frelle Eye, have you an opinion? Have your heard anything?"

"Nothing, Fras Mayor, but some of the girl's story has a disturbing consistency with known facts. Frelle Airlord, have you heard of Equinox Day?"

"No."

"A week after the Call ceased and all electrical machines burned, a faction of Avianese rose up against the Radical Aviads. Most of the Radicals' leaders and best warriors were in Mounthaven, so under the leadership of Fras Mayor and with the aid of one of the Radicals' leaders—me—the Equinox Day revolution was successful. Before you ask, I then had myself put on trial as a war criminal, was found guilty of crimes against your own people, and I now direct our spies from a cell in this palace."

"Integrity, are having, Frelle Eye."

"In the Radicals' files we found transcriptions of radio messages from Mounthaven. One concerned the killing of the entire royal court of Bartolica by one Yarronese super-regal and two gunwings. It struck unexpectedly, in a very, very long-range attack. It was led by Serjon Feydamor, and it marked the beginning of the end for Bartolica and the Radicals. Are any patterns apparent to you, gentlefolk?"

Samondel assumed that glances, nods, and winks were being exchanged in the silence that followed.

"Fras Feydamor has toured our wingfields and inspected them," admitted the marshal. "He knows our strengths and weaknesses in considerable detail. You say an attack is expected tomorrow, Frelle Airlord?"

"Yes," said Samondel. "Is little time, for to prepare."

"Prepare? How?" asked the marshal. "We could move our artisans and academicians to the woods, we could even disperse the kitewings, but experts and kitewings without fuel, workshops, and the Academy are about as useful as fins on a bird. I suppose we could drag logs across the ascent strip to stop the *Albatross* landing."

"Parachutes, firebombs, reaction guns, can use," said Samondel. "Landing not needed."

"If Fras Feydamor is blameless and arrives to find the wingfield on battle alert, it could be very bad for the relations between our peoples," said the mayor. "I call for a show of hands. Who is in favor of telling Frelle Leover what has been arranged for tomorrow?"

There was apparently a show of hands. The verdict went in Samondel's favor.

"When he came through here seven days ago, Fras Feydamor

said that the first of a flock of armed sailwings would be traveling here with the *Albatross*," said the mayor. "These would be given to Avian, along with the artisans to maintain them and train our own people. We had a big revel planned to welcome them, a wing show with flypasts and demonstrations of all our kitewings. There was also to be an exhibition of sailwings and gunwings brought here during the war, although most of those are no longer airworthy. There are Welcome signs everywhere, and leafy vines strung up in the work-shops—we cannot spare paper for streamers. Every senior and junior artisan in Avian is currently within a mile of where we stand. All will be on the wingfield tomorrow."

"Suspicious," was Samondel's opinion.

"In more ways than one," said Frelle Eye. "You might not be American at all, you could be a Rochestrian with a fake accent, here to destroy the pact between Avian and Mounthaven. We have heard that the Inn of Celestial Dreams was bombed, and that you shot one of our agents in a duel in Rochester—"

"What?" cried Samondel. "Martyne is aviad?"

"Why, yes, didn't you know?"

"He never told me."

"Indeed! So now you turn up here, with a pass of transit from the Airfoxes that might have been taken from a dead body. Why are you so anxious to help us, especially after what our misguided Rad-icals did to your homeland? Or are you an Espionage Constable, trying to provoke a battle so that the Americans take their trade and skills to the humans of the Commonwealth? Can you give us real proof of what you are saying?"

Samondel hung her head and clasped her hands in front of her.

"I have no proof," she admitted.

"Do you know where Martyne Camderine is now?" asked Fras Shadowmouse.

"Balesha, am told."

"And you disliked him?" asked Frelle Eye. "You shot him?"

"No! Loved him. Loved him. Then too late. Forced to fight him. He was Overmayor's champion, Serjon's life threatened. Now know truth. Should have shot Serjon."

Samondel paused. There was a rustle of clothing as someone folded their arms.

"I realize this is difficult for you, Frelle Airlord," said Fras Wing, "and I sympathize with the cruel trick that was played upon you, but what has all this to do with the prospects for tomorrow? Do I tell my flyers to prepare for a revel or an attack? I need hard evidence."

"Confusing," said Frelle Eye. "What did Serjon do to betray himself?"

"After duel, came 'dozen days.' Returned early. Found Serjon, ah . . . with woman. Had met in tavern. Big giggle, big tits; think expression is 'all arse, no class.' Yes?"

Samondel's emotional involvement in the matter was all too apparent. She heard titters of mirth being stifled.

"Do go on," said the mayor.

"Found also, box of reaction guns, he had. Had him arrested, left him with guard. Guard died in bomb blast, Serjon escaped, fled to Traralgon, then here."

There was a longer and more awkward pause.

"Fras Eye, can you confirm any of that?" asked the mayor.

"Apart from Serjon passing through here on the last flight, no."

"Fras Shadowmouse, what about you?"

"No."

"Well, then—" began the mayor.

"But one more question," interjected Fras Shadowmouse. "The dozen days leaves no scope for confusion. Why did you return to Serjon early?"

"Friend lied to Serjon, said *fortnight.* Same friend searched room, found weapons. Same friend paid girl to seduce Serjon."

"What is your friend's name?"

"Frelle Velesti Dis—"

"She's telling the truth!" exclaimed Fras Shadowmouse. "That is our proof."

"How so?" asked the mayor.

"If you are ever unlucky enough to be helped by Velesti Disore, Fras Mayor, you will know."

There was more rustling of cloth, but nobody else had an opinion.

"Well, then, the rookery will vote," said the mayor. "The motion is to accept Frelle Leover's story. Second? Thank you, Frelle Eye. Accept? That's five. Reject? Five against, leaving the decision up to your long-suffering mayor. Fras Shadowmouse, just one more clarification. How do you know this Frelle Velesti?"

"She is my operational contact with sympathizers in the Espionage Constables."

Samondel heard the hiss of indrawn breath, followed by a gusty sigh.

"Very, well, I vote yes, the motion is carried."

Samondel felt as if she could almost float into the air with relief.

"The compression spirit and civil kitewings will be moved to safety," the mayor decreed, "as will the artisans, technical library, and any tools that cannot be easily carried. Fras Wing, what can you do against what is coming?"

"The Americans are fast, deadly, experienced, but outnumbered. We have nine armed kitewings, and three American aircraft that are still airworthy."

"Combat experience?" asked Samondel.

"Only training practice."

"Will be slashed to pieces," was Samondel's verdict. "Hide them."

"We have Skyfire, of course," added Fras Wing.

"Which may kill more of our people than Americans," replied the mayor. "Fras Gun, what can you do on the ground?"

"I can muster ninety militia with reaction carbines, and three hundred more with bolt-action carbines or flintlocks. All have seen action. The academy also has three experimental heavy reaction guns mounted on handcarts."

"Frelle Airlord, what do you think?" asked the mayor.

"On the ground, good chance. Likely that *Albatross* will descend peacefully, taxi to adjunct, then carbineers burst out among you. Maximum impact, wanting. In the air, suicide. Armed sailwings will your flock, cut to pieces. Two leaders alone have twelve dozen victories. On our side, six, all mine. I volunteer, fly for you."

"Frelle, our kitewings are very different to your aircraft and you would need more hours training in the air than we have left," said Fras Wing. "Aside from that we have two sailwings and a Yarronese triwing, but the bearings and rings are worn in their compression engines."

"*Starflower* was Yarronese triwing. Have fought in the type."

"*Hellfang* was meant to be mine," interjected Fras Wing.

"Oh. Sorry. Have been presumptuous."

"But my loyalty is to Avian and my flock and you are a better flyer. *Hellfang* may be old and tired, but she is the fastest thing with a compression engine on this wingfield. Check her tonight with the artisans, take her up at first light, then fight in her when the enemy comes."

The meeting soon concluded, and Samondel was led out by Fras Wing. He took her part of the way to the wingfield before removing her blindfold. He turned out to be a fresh-faced young aviad with blond hair.

"My real name is Flockleader Bretallus, and I have two hundred hours in the air. Are the enemy really as dangerous as you say?"

"Worse. They are twice faster than your kitewings, and even *Hellfang* will be straining to catch them. Odds of ten to one, maybe a chance. Less? Do not bother."

"Then why *are* we bothering? I am not going to lead my men and women to certain death if the result is going to be exactly the same."

"Because of *Albatross*. Capture *Albatross* intact, then can fly *dozens* of aviads from the mainland every night."

After checking over *Hellfang* and giving instructions to the artisans, Samondel was taken back to the institute's buildings. She was locked inside a small but comfortable room, with an aviad nurse staying with her.

"Should be sleeping near *Hellfang*."

"You were told to sleep here by the mayor, Frelle Airlord."

"Artisans, they may be needing advices."

"Then they know where to find you."

From outside came a low rumble. Thunder, thought Samondel at first, but the sound was continuous and smooth. Slowly it faded, then was cut off suddenly.

"What is that?" asked Samondel.

"A storm, perhaps, Frelle Airlord."

"The weather was clear only ten minutes ago."

"I am only a nurse. I do not know of those things."

The rumble started again, smooth and continuous, then suddenly there was a loud snap followed by a very loud explosion.

"You are attempting, for to tell me, that was thunder too?"

"No, Frelle Airlord. That was the sound of a very brave youth dying."

"Youth? Dying?"

"I can tell you little more, Frelle Airlord, because I know little. On dark, cloudy nights there are lights in the sky. Very, very fast lights, impossibly fast lights. Sometimes there are balls of fire too, and twice I have seen . . ." The nurse shuddered and hugged her folded arms against herself. "Twice I have seen pieces of bodies. Burned, mangled pieces."

Samondel tried to sleep, and occasionally the rolling thunder sounded outside. The Avianese had something that they had not talked about, some sort of flame thrower bombard, perhaps. Perhaps even something left over from millennia past. Some dangerous, un-reliable, but highly effective thing that killed one's own people but killed even more of the enemy. That may have been why they were curiously cooperative about loaning *Hellfang* to her the next day. She tried to puzzle out what it might be, but after counting eleven peals of thunder she was none the wiser.

9

TALONS OF MICE

Launceston, Tasmania Island

It was two hours after sunrise that the tethered watch balloon's bell began clanging. Samondel had slept badly, worried about the roughly running compression engine powering *Hellfang*. She walked the stiffness out of her joints and drank coffee while the six aviad artisans checked the steamers that were keeping her compression engine warm. The instant she heard the bell she began running across the grass while all around her signal whistles sounded. As she reached *Hellfang* the compression engine was spluttering into life while signalers called directions, windspeeds, and profiles.

"Signal mirror message from the balloon," called the adjunct, hurrying along with a megaphone. "Eleven sailwings and five super-regals. Repeat, *eleven* sailwings and *five* super-regals."

Samondel's heart seemed to sink into her stomach. This was an overwhelming attack, and by vastly superior numbers and flyers. She ascended alone and then flew out lower than the tallest of the trees to circle away from the wingfield to the northeast. If she could come out of the sun, she might do some serious damage before the inevitable. Away in the distance were the super-regals, slowly circling the wingfield in preparation for landing. A smoke rocket streaked into the air, welcoming the enormous wings. The first of them descended, and was lost to Samondel's sight. From what she could tell, it had not been a bombing run, and it had been too low to have been dropping parachutists. That either meant a rather more bold plan, or that Samondel was about to look very foolish. One of the sailwings descended with the super-regals as well.

The last super-regal descended. Ten sailwings were still in the air, but one of them was sure to contain Serjon, and he was worth a hundred. Samondel began a spiraling climb. Still no second smoke rocket from the wingfield. Was she a fool? Had Martyne been wrong? Were a lot of embarrassed Avianese officials on the ground trying to explain to the Mounthaven flockleader why he had been welcomed by a wingfield on battle alert?

The wingfield adjunct stood watching the super-regals approach, awestruck by the sheer spectacle of five of the enormous aircraft together in procession along the dispersal path. Out on the ascent strip a sailwing had landed, but the flyer had just turned the aircraft around and stopped. One of the two propellers was spinning more slowly than the other, and as he watched the flyer got out, crawled to the cowling, and opened an access hatch. There was undeniably a problem with one of the engines.

"Armik, take an artisan and two strong militiamen to help move that wing off the ascent strip," called the adjunct. "We can't have it there when the other sailwings start to land."

His assistant hurried away, with three other men jogging behind him. They waved to the super-regals as they passed them. The crowd around the adjunct cheered and threw eucalypt leaves into the air as the *Albatros* stopped. The next super-regal was in the same class as the *Albatros.*, the third and fourth were the smaller, older models, and the fifth was some sort of hybrid. The hatchways opened and began to wind down, but the propellers continued to spin. The adjunct had his first pang of doubt. Normally the *Albatross*'s wingcaptain turned the engines off the moment it stopped moving, as compression spirit was priceless in this remote area.

Out on the ascent strip there was a burst of gunfire as the sailwing flyer lost his nerve and turned on Armik and his men with a reaction pistol. They went down as one, but not before one of them managed to shoot back. The flyer jerked, staggered, then fell into the starboard propellor. The adjunct hesitated. An accident, perhaps. A misunderstanding. His finger trembled on the flintlock lever that would fire the smoke rocket. The other sailwings circled lazily at about a thousand feet. One of the wingcaptains waved to the crowd from his cockpit, but the compression engines continued to idle.

Carbineers with reaction carbines bounded down the ramps of each super-regal at some signal unseen by the adjunct, opening fire as they ran. The adjunct blew his whistle and triggered the smoke rocket together. Three carts disguised as floats draped with leaves, vines, and ribbons transformed suddenly into heavy reaction gun carriages, as the gunners opened fire on the cockpits of the super-regals. The wingcaptains and navigators were riddled within moments through the fabric of the aircraft. The cheering crowd abruptly dropped into three lines, lying, kneeling, and standing, and three volleys slashed into the carbineers who were already charging them. Ninety elite Mounthaven carbineers, most of them from royal guard squads, fell, staggered, or dashed onward while firing. The murderous fusillade continued for no more than twenty seconds before the survivors of the two groups merged. Smaller squads of aviads skirted the fighting and dashed up the hatch ramps of the super-regals with their reaction carbines at the ready.

By the time the smoke rocket was in the air Samondel was with the sun at her back and still climbing. Her flock was also close enough to be noticed by the approaching sailwing flyers. The enemy wings had drop tanks, and were painted sky blue beneath and red on top. Hard to see against the sky, easy to see from above if they crashed. There were no other markings apart from numbers from 01 to 11. No heraldic crests, no serial numbers, no names, no decorations. Some had three engines, some had two. Samondel closed as pairs began forming up to cover each other.

"That's not the way to greet your welcoming party," she whispered.

Her own triwing was still painted in Yarronese camouflage, but had the Avianese serial number AX-09, red flames, and a pair of fangs painted on the engine's cowling. It also had a more recently painted symbol on the side: a starflower.

The original *Starflower* was probably still at the palace wingfield in her tiny domain of Highland Bartolica, but that did not matter. There was a message to be conveyed here, and if anyone was feeling nervous, they might well see the starflower, assume the worst and—

Panic. The leading sailwing rolled into a dive, belatedly shedding its drop tanks. Samondel opened her throttle and began a turn that stood the gunwing on its starboard wingtip, and she came around just in time to see the trailing sailwing discard its tanks, looking for all the world as if it had just exploded. Samondel came around still on her wingtip and firing side-on. The other sailwing banked and came around. Faster. Samondel was in a stolen gunwing, serviced by amateurs who had learned by trial and error, and which was as badly worn as a carbineer's bootheel. The enemy flyers had been fifteen or more hours into the mission, but their sailwings would have been tended by guildmasters who had been flown to Lake Taupo. The sailwing smoked, trailed flames, then exploded in a gaudy fireball.

The second sailwing was pouring compression spirit from its wing tanks as she turned to chase it, and it banked away and into a dive. He was trying to lose weight, but already her bullets were among the blades of its propellers. A propellor shattered, the flyer panicked, flung open the hatch, and jumped at no more than three hundred feet. His parachute was still in the process of opening when he hit the trees. Samondel had already turned away.

Smoke suddenly billowed out along the ascent strip, like a rolling explosion. A smokescreen rocket, thought Samondel, but then she saw that the thing was wedge-shaped, red, as big as a kitewing and climbing almost as fast as her gunwing could dive. It closed with a sailwing, the sailwing began to trail smoke, then rocketwing rolled into a dive. The rockets on the red, wedge-shaped wing died and fell away, but another red wing was ascending by now.

Samondel banked, looking for a target. A larger group was wheeling about a quarter mile away. Two sailwings began diving at the wingfield, but two more red wedges were ascending on pillars of smoke and flame. There was a head-on pass, then a wedge and sailwing collided. The other sailwing slammed into the wingfield, while the surviving rocketwing continued on upward. Samondel began a long turn to come at her targets out of the sun.

The Avianese had bypassed the limitation of sophisticated compression technology, they had instead bolted simple rockets onto high-speed gliders. They could only ascend for a short time, but during that time they were lords of the air.

A Mounthaven sailwing banked into an angled convergent pass with the other Avianese rocketwing, and in spite of fifteen hours in the air, the enemy flyer calmly fired a long burst into the Avianese aircraft. The rocketwing seemed unaffected. Incredibly, the enemy numbers had been halved, but the survivors were not to be taken lightly. Samondel dived out of the sun at a knot of three sailwings that were forming up to dive on the wingfield, but her attack was cut off by a fourth making a very accomplished head-on attack. The number was 01: it had to be Bronlar or Serjon. A kitewing trailing smoke swirled past her, then bullets thudded harmlessly through her gunwing's fabric and empty wingtanks. She rolled and dived, saw a parachute with Avianese markings. Another pass from sailwing 02, a sensible, considered pass. Bronlar

Samondel did not see the next pillar of smoke and flames erupt on the ascent strip, nor did she see the red rocketwing streaking into the air on a trail of smoke. It banked slightly, climbing unbelievably fast, then the smoky flames ended and the wedge began to slow. Two stubby, dark things fell away. A new streamer of smoke appeared and another wedge could be seen climbing up from Launceston Wingfield. The three sailwings held together, preparing for a head-on pass, then at a combined speed of nearly four hundred miles per hour an Avianese rocket interceptor collided with the middle sailwing. The other two broke away, but now another rocket was climbing and shooting, and this time its target began to trail smoke, then it stalled.

Two more streaks of flame and smoke lanced out along the ascent strip, but at no more than five hundred feet the trailing rocket lost a wing. Wrenched around under full power, it disintegrated, but somehow a parachute appeared amid the descending wreckage. A Mounthaven sailwing blundered into the path of the wreckage and a tumbling fragment of wing smashed all three propellers. Higher up, a sailwing pursued a descending, unpowered rocketwing, only to be cut down by his wingman on his last solid fuel rocket.

Samondel had seen none of this, she was in a chasing circle, with sailwings 01 and 02 bracketing her. She could turn more tightly, but her engine was becoming sluggish and the heat gauge was off the scale. The triwing slewed through a stream of fire and rolled away to dive out of the circle. Sailwing 02 rolled out to pursue, but Samondel's gunwing continued to roll a moment longer, then dropped after the sailwing. The huge, shallow V shape and pusher propellers of sailwing rose up through her reaction guns' sights and she pressed the firing key. Lines of bullets walked across the starboard wing to the compression engines, then off into empty air.

Samondel plummeted past. The other sailwing slashed at her with his reaction guns, then swerved to avoid the stricken sailwing. They broke off in different directions, Samondel came around more sharply because of her lighter weight and three wings, and she fired at the descending 02 again. Suddenly shots tore up out of her instrument panel and past her head, oil splashed over her face and goggles. Blinded, she rubbed at them with her free hand, shots thudded against wood, fabric, and wing tanks, Samondel rolled and tried to dive vertically with no more than a vague idea of whether she was at a safe height, pulled down her goggles, and saw something red loom up in front of her with twin reaction guns flashing. It shot past her, blanketing her in smoke, then Samondel was trying to pull out of her dive and trees were before her, individual branches distinctly visible. She was down among the treetops before she had leveled out, and as she climbed again she saw sailwing 01 with one compression engine dead and a red rocket wing with R5 painted on it dropping unpowered above it. Another burst of reaction gun fire hit something within the sailwing's structure, for the port wing buckled and tore away. The sailwing was in a wild, gyrating fall when a parachute streamed out but tangled in the wreckage, then it hit the trees, not far from the wingfield's perimeter.

               •   •   •

The super-regal had been inspected and all crewmen declared dead, but then, this was a battle, and people tend to work in haste. Someone had been in haste when feeling for a pulse at the neck of the wing-captain of the super-regal *Moonwing*. No controls had been disabled, because nobody knew any functions, and everyone was fearful of traps that would set off hidden firebombs.

Suddenly the entire bank of engines were throttled up and the *Moonwing* began to roll away toward a dispersal track. Fire from dozens of guns raked the body of the super-regal, but not the engines. Every aviad warrior had been forced to recite over and over that engines were more precious than gold, and that engines were not to be targeted under any circumstances. With compression spirit streaming from bullet-riddled tanks, the *Moonwing* gained speed, but two aviads sprinted after it and leaped for the open ramp at the rear. The super-regal roared on at full throttle as the aviads clambered toward the cockpit. One stopped, his reaction gun at the ready to cover the other as he flung the internal cockpit hatch open.

"It's empty, the thing started by itself!"

"Wrong," said the wingcaptain as he opened fire from a storage locker.

Both aviads went down, and the wingcaptain scrambled through the cockpit hatch and grasped for the controls with blood-slick hands. The super-regal rotated while still on the dispersal track, was airborne as it crossed the ascent strip, snagged a treetop with one of its wheels, then slowly leveled out and began a gentle bank to come around on a heading north.

The wingcaptain expected the sound of more bullets thudding through fabric and splintering wood at any moment, but there was nothing but the drone of the compression engines. Through sheer luck the rocketwings were all gliding back to the wingfield, their charges spent. Some flyers saw the *Moonwing* escaping, but assumed that Samondel's gunwing could catch it. Samondel's gunwing had experienced a massive bearing failure, however, and was struggling to maintain even a sixth of normal power. It was left to two little kitewings to take up the chase, but even the lumbering super-regal had a twenty-miles-per-hour edge over their maximum speed. Realizing that they could do nothing but lose ground, the two Avianese flyers opened fire with their reaction guns at a range of half a mile. At that distance even a lucky shot was out of the question, and once their guns were empty, they both turned back for Launceston.

The *Moonwing* reached the open sea, still heading north. The wingcaptain locked the controls and pulled open a medical kit. He had three wounds to his legs and one to the lower abdomen. All that he could do was wrap bandages over the bloody rents in his trousers and flight jacket to slow the bleeding. Next he began to check the condition of the super-regal. There was fuel left for seven hours, but the levels in two tanks were dropping even as he read the gauges. He pulled down on levers, diverting compression spirit so that the leaking tanks were used first.

Nobody was pursuing, he had somehow escaped amid the confusion. If they shot him down now, the super-regal was lost to the Avianese, and even though he had barely enough fuel to fly a quarter of the way back to Lake Taupo, there was a chance that he might find one last way to hurt the enemies that had destroyed the rest of the attack flock. He changed course to several points to the west of north, then locked the controls again and washed down a near-overdose of stimulants. He switched back to the only undamaged tank, noting that three hours of compression spirit remained.

"That's enough to pluck and gut you featherhead bastards," he gasped. "All I need now is three hours of blood."

Samondel's compression engine was laboring even to maintain level flight as she approached the wingfield. She counted nine pillars of smoke nearby, and there were fires burning amid the buildings near the super-regals. All four were intact, in fact most of their engines were still idling. Crowds of aviads swarmed over the wingfield, dragging the rocket wings off the ascent strip as soon as they had come to rest. Her engine missed, caught again, then evened out into a shuddering idle as she enriched the mixture and dropped to approach the ascent strip.

Once on the ground Samondel's body automatically attended to all that was needed to be done. The dying compression engine dragged the gunwing onto the dispersal path, then Samondel threw the cutoff lever. Nothing happened. She flicked it again, then again. Finally the engine died of its own accord and ground crews ran up to drag it clear. Covered in oil and soot but unharmed, Samondel climbed to the ground, then dropped to her knees to wait for everything to stop spinning.

"Are you all right, Frelle?" asked a medician carrying a white bag with red crosses painted on the sides.

"Death was so near, I felt the feathers of her wings brushing against me," she said in Bartolican.

"Your pardon?"

"Not hurt, help others."

Samondel glanced at her watch as he hurried off. Just fourteen minutes had passed since the smoke rocket had been launched but now R1, R2, R3, and R7 were lying idle beside the ascent strip. The flyers of the incredible rocketwings were gathering, still wearing their numbered black jackets as they removed their leather balaclavas. Samondel shakily got to her feet and approached the loudly babbling flyers.

"Look at that! Peed my pants."

"Me too."

"I didn't."

"You're too stupid to be frightened."

"Elcrin got a synthetic funeral."

"Took one with him."

"That was safer than training. Remember that day we lost three?"

"Told you nobody'd give us a welcome."

"And the crowd roared!" shouted the flyer with R1 on his jacket.

"Roar!" they shouted together.

"And the crowd cheered!"

"Cheer!"

"And the crowd was bitterly disappointed!"

"Ah, shyte!"

Flyers, flyers like her, thought Samondel. Boys, half-hysterical with relief and surprise at still being alive, and even being victorious. Each had colors from aviad girls on his right arm. Samondel stroked Martyne's black band on her own arm, then hailed them.

"Gentlefolk, good to see you having colors," she said, slapping R3 on the back, then draping her arms over the shoulders of flyers R7 and R3.

"Hie, it's royalty," said R2, doing an exaggeratedly low bow that turned into a somersault.

"Remember, bad luck to kiss a girl of colors before reporting to the adjunct," she warned.

"Get any, Princess?" asked R1.

"Got three, but R5 stitched up last one before I am turning."

"No consideration!" cried R3.

"Now we go to pennant pole, tell adjunct kills and losses. Big tradition."

"Wait, here comes Shadowmouse in R5."

"What of escaped super-regal? Someone chasing, yes?"

"No, but fuel was pissing out of the wing tanks."

"Both wings?"

"Port and starboard, Frelle."

"Then is not enough to reach Taupo. That wing is lost."

Through the drifting clouds and swirling streamers of smoke came the R5, red and sleek, unpowered yet faster than most Mounthaven gunwings in level flight. Its single skid slammed into the grass; it bounced, tipped, straightened, and bounced again before sliding to a stop in the middle of the grass ascent strip. It was resting on its starboard wingtip as they ran over, followed by the handlers with a trolley and jacks.

"He's our newest," said R1 as they ran over.

They helped the handlers attach a trolley to the rocketwing and drag it clear of the ascent strip. The flyer opened the hatch in his canopy and jumped clear as they stopped.

"Fras, am owing you big favor." Samondel laughed.

Martyne removed his leather balaclava and shook out his hair.

"Think nothing of it, Frelle Airlord."

The silence between them spread to the other rocket flyers and the handlers. The two stood motionless, staring at each other.

"*You* are Fras Shadowmouse?" said Samondel at last.

"Yes."

"Why—you did not tell me?"

Martyne shrugged. "How?"

The rocketwing flockleader was aware that the tension in the air was extreme, but he had no idea why and even less idea of how to defuse the situation.

"Wings of my Colors, welcome to the ground you have defended," declared Samondel.

Martyne blinked, then touched the bunch of ribbons tied to his arm. Attached to Samondel's arm was a small strip of black.

"Wings of my Colors, welcome to the ground you have defended," he echoed.

She brought her right arm up, bending it and draping Martyne's black band over her forearm before touching her lips to it.

"Colors of my Wings, in your name, three victories have I won," declared Samondel.

Martyne raised his arm to kiss the bunch of ribbons draped over his forearm.

"Colors of my Wings, in your name, three victories have I won," he responded.

"Ah, you know each other?" ventured R1.

Samondel and Martyne reached for each other, but the spell was broken by the other rocket flyers, who seized them by the arms and dragged them farther apart.

"Back, you two, back!" cried R3. "Bad luck to kiss before you report to the adjunct."

They began to walk toward the pennant pole, but Samondel and Martyne gradually dropped behind.

"Sorry I shot you," said Samondel. "Big mistake."

"Think nothing of it," replied Martyne.

"Velesti! Know not whether to kiss her or strangle her."

"Don't kiss her, you'd be poisoned."

"Hey, remind me what I'm supposed to say to that daft Frelle of mine when I see her!" R1 called back to them.

There were bodies scattered all around the pennant pole area, and the adjunct stood beside his tent taking statements from the five surviving kitewing flyers. Aviad guardsmen were everywhere, their reaction guns raised and their eyes alert. The flockleader hurried among them, his arm bandaged roughly.

"Frelle Airlord, are you all right?" the adjunct shouted as Samondel approached.

"All the blood I ascend with, I bringing back," replied Samondel. "What of here?"

"We lost ninety, they lost ninety-seven. Four captured, but one will not live more than minutes. Ten sailwings destroyed for two rocketwings lost. One sailwing and four super-regals captured."

"Careful, if please. Traps, yes?"

"None, actually. The artisans have already checked the super-regals. Looks like our Mounthaven friends thought they were invincible."

The flockleader arrived and hurried Samondel away to the medicians' tents to identify the living and dead.

"This one is from 02," said the medician, drawing back the blanket. "Your third."

Bronlar's body looked like a rag doll that had been pulled out of a fire and then fought over by two terriers. Her neck was stretched and twisted, and the reek of burned hair hung on Samondel's nostrils as she looked down.

"Warden Bronlar Jemarial, Yarronese. Was dead when found?"

"Never saw anyone in that condition and still alive," replied the aviad medician.

Serjon was alive, with his clothing torn and his face scratched, but incredibly he had no other injuries that she could see. His hands were bound and his feet hobbled.

"So, you beat Bronlar," Serjon croaked. "That will make you famous forever."

"She was just my ninth victory," replied Samondel. "Just as *you* are some rocket flyer's victory."

"Filthy featherhead tricks—and you are a traitor to Mounthaven."

"Traitor? You betray me, Mounthaven, *and* Bronlar, then you talk about traitors!"

"You never saw my mother and sisters. Dead . . . raped . . . cold."

"And what makes up for that? How many deaths? I'll tell you. *All* the aviads that exist, all the males, females, the children, the infants, but there is more, Serjon Warden Killer, because dozens of human Bartolicans were at work alongside one aviad leader. How many Bartolicans have you killed, how many Bartolican deaths do you need? You wanted revenge, so you *became* the enemy, calling down apocalypse on everyone. What were you doing in bed with me on those nights in Condelor and Rochester? Pretending to rape all Bartolican women?"

"Featherhead lover! I rode you, like Yarron rode Bartolica."

Samondel could scarcely stop herself from dashing out of the tent, but she stood her ground as tears ran down her cheeks.

"In sheer hatred, Serjon, I am outgunned and outclassed. You are a pig, and I will not roll in the gutter to fight you."

"You already rolled with me." Serjon began to laugh.

"Yet even the mighty Serjon Feydamor was outgunned and outclassed today."

"Featherhead shytehead."

Samondel's mind formed a gunsight around Serjon's head as she regarded him. He was now a thing, as Martyne had once been. *Can he resist the temptation to boast?* she wondered. *Probably not, that's all he has left.*

"So, the Council of Airlords voted to attack Avian," she said.

"That flock of sparrows?" exclaimed Serjon. "You know nothing. Yarron, Cosdora, and Dorak have the only *real* airlords in Mounthaven."

"And I suppose you are the venture's leader?"

"I would have fought a thousand duels for the privilege. All of us were volunteers, we were handpicked among those who had lost loved ones."

"*That* is all I need to know," said Samondel as she turned away.

"What do you mean?" called Serjon as she strode from the tent.

She found the mayor after a short search. He was congratulating the surviving rocket flyers, one of whom was Martyne. The situation was less than ideal, but Samondel knew that her hatred was like the rocketwings. It would only be deadly for a very short time, and there was still one enemy in the air.

"Have questioned Feydamor," interjected Samondel. "All this, not from Council of Airlords' orders. Terrorist attack, being."

"Are you sure?" asked the mayor. "They must have had a lot of resources behind them."

"Council resources, misused."

"Frelle Leover, ah, Airlord, are you aware of what you are saying?"

"Yes. And as member of the Council of Airlords, I turn them over to your authority. You know what that means."

"Yes, yes," he replied slowly. "Very well, then."

The mayor hurried away, and soon aviad musketeers began moving people about and clearing a space beside the abandonstone wall of the Technical Institute. Samondel stood close to Martyne, her hands clasped tightly together. Aviad artisans knocked three short poles into the soil with mallets. The three surviving Mounthaven prisoners were led out of their separate tents, still bound and hobbled. They were tied to the poles.

Two dozen musketeers now marched up in good order and formed into two rows, one standing and the other kneeling. By now the prisoners had realized what was happening.

"Stop! Prisoners of war!" shouted Serjon.

The mayor raised his hand. Silence descended.

"Having determined through the duly appointed envoy of the Mounthaven Council of Airlords that the attack on this city was an act of terrorism, and thus wholly outside the authority of the Council, it is my melancholy duty to carry out the sentence prescribed for acts of terrorism under both Mounthaven and Avianese law."

"No, am warden!" shouted Serjon.

"Make ready," ordered the mayor.

"*This* is terrorism, Mounthaven will never forgive or forget you filthy mice," cried Serjon, now in Yarronese.

"Take aim."

"Didn't kill enough of you featherhead bastards. Bronlar, I always loved you—"

"Fire."

Samondel did not move, even when the crowd had dispersed and the bodies had been cut down and dragged away for burial. Martyne stood beside her, not moving either.

"Martyne," said Samondel. "I could have saved him. Terrorism sanctioned by state, maybe act of war. No precedent here."

"Australican humans have run a genocide against aviads for millennia," replied Martyne. "I had no vocation to Balesha, Samondel. When I was discovered to be an aviad I was sent there to hide from lynch mobs. Do you think I hate humans after all that?"

"Hoping not."

"Serjon and the others were executed under Avianese law. To punish our own war criminals for what was done in America, we drafted laws specifying the death penalty for voluntary acts of terrorism, whether in the name of states, secret groups, or individuals. As we punished our own people, so did we punish yours. The issue is closed."

"Martyne, am frightened. Frightened of being as Bronlar or Serjon. Were twisted, full of hate. All their compassion, just act."

"Were Serjon or Bronlar frightened of being like that?"

"Is obvious. Not so."

"Velesti was like them, but slowly she learned to fear what she was. That was when I began to lead her back from the edge. If you fear it too, you could never be anything like Bronlar and Serjon. They were proud of what they were and what they were trying to do today. That was real evil."

"Wise words," conceded Samondel with a sniffle. "Must think on them."

Rochester, the Rochestrian Commonwealth

Dramoren stood before the assembled masses that were the Libris Calcular's components, his arms folded firmly behind his back. To his right was the system herald, to his left the system controller, and behind them all were three dozen armed Tiger Dragons.

"I wish to announce that experiments conducted by the Dragon Librarian Service under contract to the experimental research monastery of St. Roger have resulted in the development of a water-powered calcular," he began.

A rustle of whispers greeted the words.

"Obviously this will not be subject to the same afflictions as unshielded electrical-essence calculars, and will need only a staff of regulators to maintain and operate it. Of all those in Rochester, I thought you components should be the first to know. Your work here has held the Commonwealth together during dark and dangerous times, and is appreciated. The date of your release from service has not yet been determined, that will depend upon how long it takes to build a water calcular the size of Dolorian Hall, and at present only a small model is in operation. Please be patient and work hard. Soon you will be released, honored, and compensated. You are dismissed."

Dramoren was given three cheers quite spontaneously as he walked from the calcular hall, and the voices of the jubilant components were in his ears as he was met by Lengina in a courtyard outside.

"So, they took the news well," she observed.

"Oddly enough, yes."

"A pact with the Avianese will be more difficult to announce. The Reformed Gentheists will denounce it as a lie that pretends to link the destinies of our two species."

"But our destinies *are* linked."

"Truth, like childbirth, provides a lot of pain along with its blessings."

"The Avianese probably knew about this for decades. That is

why they are so obsessed about breeding and eugenics, and why they work so hard to transport newly discovered aviad children to Tasmania Island."

"But this is all wrong, we should live in peace!" said Lengina, beating the air with her fists. "Our species are interlocked, just like men and women."

"Are you trying to tell me that men and women live in peace?" Dramoren sighed.

"Men and women display a lot more harmony than humans and aviads just now. Perhaps it is time that we take over the research of our learned monks and use the whole of the Commonwealth as a workshop for developing ways to coexist."

Launceston, the Rochestrian Commonwealth

Samondel insisted that Serjon and Bronlar be buried together when the first of the graves were dug in the early afternoon. The surviving long-range sailwing turned out to merely have a fuel blockage in one atomizer, and Samondel was able to take it up for a test flight. After that she had another meeting with the wingfield adjunct.

"I need to tell of this, all in Mounthaven," she said. "Else they will try again. I am saying, terror flock wiped out by Avianese, never had a chance. Mighty warriors, are Avianese, with invincible wings. Ours were best, best they have sent. Total patriots. Suffered greatly from aviads. Best flyers, finest wings, fought here. Still defeated."

"You said you wanted to use the captured sailwing," said the adjunct.

"Needing to reach wingfield, at distance. Having severe words for Lake Taupo wingfield adjunct. Then Mounthaven."

"In the captured sailwing?"

"How else?"

"But it is needed here."

"I have given four super-regals, to you."

"But we are desperate for wings."

"Teaching super-regals flying, I can. Without lessons, how many are crashing, to learn?"

The adjunct conveyed Samondel's request to both the overhand and mayor. They did not take long to decide that they were of the same mind on the subject.

"The sailwing is worth its weight in diamonds to Avian," the overhand decided. "She wants to use it to take on perhaps dozens of her own warriors, with no more than a reaction pistol and her own authority. After that, she wants to fly on to North America."

"I agree, we might as well light a fire under the sailwing and stand back to watch, for all the good it will do," agreed the mayor.

"Yet I would point out one minor but important detail," said the adjunct. "Airlord Samondel alone has had experience with flying both advanced sailwings and the super-regals. Speaking as a flyer, I would dearly prefer a short training course from a qualified instructor rather than an extremely short course in self-instruction."

"This is true," said the overhand, "but Frelle Samondel may prove less than cooperative."

"We shall tell her she can have the sailwing, but she must show us how to fly the super-regals first. After that, what can she do if we break our promise?"

"We must certainly keep her safely away from the wingfield once the lessons are over," said the overhand. "Fras Adjunct, have the wings especially well guarded tonight, and tell all flyers that she must not approach any wing while alone."

Martyne was no longer required for any of the hearings. As the sun was setting he made his way to his accommodation hut, lit a fire, and removed his boots. He took off his shirt, contemplating the slight chill on his skin from the midautumn air. I am alive to feel the chill, he thought, stooping over and rubbing his hands before the flames in his stone grate. His left arm was still stiff and tender, and blood had seeped and dried from a torn stitch in the wound in his chest, but he could raise his hand to his face, he could see his fingers. Serjon certainly could not.

Everything manufactured was in short supply in Launceston, and Martyne had arrived in just the clothes he was wearing. Following his nightly ritual, he removed his socks and underclothes, washed them in a bowl of rainwater, then hung them to dry by the fire. Lastly he washed himself, then hunched shivering beside the fire to dry. There was unlimited firewood and water, but cloth for underclothes was unobtainable. The cloth that did not go into aircraft fabric went to clothe children. Even his blankets were roughweave dry grass; they were scratchy, but nevertheless warm. Presently he was lying on his back, his eyes closed and his arm draped over his face, trying to think of nothing, but thoughts kept slipping past his guard.

Red Death, even the other Avianese flyers were now calling Samondel that. At last Martyne began to descend into a haze of dark, contented stillness, more through sheer exhaustion than his skills with meditation and relaxation control, but time and again Samondel's image took his hands, drew him close, and pressed her lips against his.

"Martyne," she would say as she drew back a little.

He could say nothing, but he smiled.

"Martyne, I love you."

Still he could only smile, and now she looked sad. *Can't say anything, she might get the wrong idea*, some imbecile voice kept warning him. What wrong idea? That he loved her, that he desired her, that he wanted to flout all aviad conventions and marry her? Still he could not reply. Yes he loved her, but she might think he desired her as a great and powerful noble from the distant, glittering, magnificent mayorates and cities of North America. Samondel began to fade.

"Martyne?"

Yet again the voice dragged Martyne back from the balmy blackness.

"Yes?" he slurred, on the verge of sinking again.

"Room for me, yes?"

Martyne removed his arm from his eyes—and found himself looking up at the unbuttoned flight jacket, liner, blouse, and bare breasts of Highland Bartolica's monarch.

"There is always room for you," tumbled unbidden from his lips.

Samondel stripped in the dim light from the grate's coals, never once taking her eyes from Martyne.

"Have seen your chest at training," she said as she sat naked on the edge of his narrow slat-mortice bunk. "Longing for to show you mine."

"We shall be packed very close," said Martyne, lifting the woven grass blanket for her.

"Whole idea," she replied, drawing the blanket back over and settling carefully on top of him. "Not hurting scar, I hope?"

"*Those* are unlikely to hurt anyone," replied Martyne, hugging her down against him, "but is this a safe thing for you to do?"

She looked down into his eyes and caressed his hair.

"Chivalrous to the end," she purred admiringly. "Is time of the safe moon, for me. Is need for nothing. For me, is new thing."

Martyne was still drowsy in the early morning as Samondel lay with a leg across him, looking at the scar that her bullet had torn across his chest.

"Can never be apologizing enough," she said, running her fingers delicately along the scar below his pectorals.

"Once is sufficient."

"With you, have dispensed with, ah, devices. Serjon, to use, always had to."

"Leave him alone, he's dead."

"Had to give you what he never had. Even if myself not in the time of safe moon, would do all again. Understand?"

"Time of the safe moon, what a charming and beautiful expression," said Martyne, reaching up to caress her face. "And I am truly flattered."

"Today I train Avianese to fly super-regals. They will be a great help for refugees."

"Will you stay here?"

"Wish to stay with you, but . . . wherever I go, always is you only. Forever. Love you only, never have another."

"But I see nothing that could come between us."

Samondel frowned and shook her head.

"Must go home, shout 'Attack on Launceston' from tops of palace towers. Guilty airlords deny everything, they will, but not possible they can make new conspiracy, if revealed. All others then watching. Closely."

A pang of sorrow burned through Martyne as the implications of her words unfolded.

"Would you really leave me for that?"

"Are preferring a new war with Mounthaven, yes?"

"No, but—"

"Need to save your people, enough damage and suffering, has been. Am airlord. Airlord means sacrifice for greater good."

Martyne shivered and drew her close. "All of us flyers have been told not to let you near a wing while alone, especially after the training is over. You must realize what that means. Those in charge need you, but they want to keep every wing they can get."

"They agreed, letting me have sailwing."

"Do you believe them?"

"No, I suppose."

"We could steal the sailwing together, though, and go to Mounthaven."

"No. As aviad, in Mounthaven, you soon are being shot."

"So I stay here, even if I help you steal a wing?"

"Please."

"Well . . . I seem rather short on options."

Samondel closed her eyes and lay against him for a while, savoring the moment.

"What you are doing without me?" she asked.

"Being very sad."

"I mean, without me, pastime?"

"Oh, dine with Velesti in taverns, then wander the streets looking for bully boys to beat up. Climb onto hostelry roofs and hang upside down at windows watching couples at dalliance and calling out suggestions. Then sleep alone and remember you."

"Sounding more merriment than reigning over Highland Bartolica, then sleep alone, thinking of you. So you will helping me leave, really?"

Martyne thought for a moment, but only to think of the most suitable words.

"Would I keep a bird in a cage?"

They washed in the chilly waters from the cistern, rubbed each other dry with grass brushes, then built a fire and boiled up a soupy mixture of dried meat, nuts, and potatoes, and toasted each other with rainwater. The wreckage on the wingfield had been cleaned up by the time they arrived there, not particularly well rested but very happy. Samondel was wearing an embroidered flight jacket from one of the dead Yarronese, and a dozen Australican flyers were already waiting for instruction at the adjunct's pennant pole.

Each of the super-regals was in turn ascended, and Samondel spent the entire morning teaching the Avianese flyers to control them. All through the lunch break she taught the artisans what she knew of the new engines and mechanisms. The adjunct was reluctant to let Samondel ascend in the captured sailwing, given her plea the night before to fly it to Lake Taupo, but when Martyne volunteered to ascend with her he relented.

It was in the late afternoon that they finally did ascend, with Martyne at the controls and Samondel lying in the navigator's bunk. The aircraft was in good condition, and Martyne noted that it was very easy to fly.

"There will be times, when apart, we are living," said Samondel as they made a wide, leisurely circle of the capital of Avian.

"If you return early, you will find me alone," said Martyne.

Samondel pressed the stud that lowered the headrest, pulled herself forward, and wrapped her arms around his neck.

"Myself also. Sleep alone, it is incentive, for to keep trying, ah, to return. But . . ."

"But?"

"But one promise."

"Yes?"

"You will promise?"

"Promise what?"

"Promise first. Then hear. Is possible, for you."

Martyne sighed.

"Very well. Now, what have I promised?"

"Is never, never, setting foot in rocketwing again."

"What?" Martyne laughed.

"Rather surprise you with whoopsicle girl than have to bury you."

"Frelle, I've survived fourteen Skyfire flights, two of them in combat. I'm currently Avian's greatest gunwing ace. How can I—"

"*Please* Martyne! Damn, bloody things *climb* faster than gunwings can *dive*. Not natural. Dangerous."

"Samondel—"

"Highly unstable below two hundred miles per hour. Flies like brick at stall speed. All this, told by you! In bed. Last night."

"Well, perhaps I was exaggerating a little."

"Think of you with other woman, annoying. Think of you in rocketwing, terrifying! Not to be tolerated. I—"

"Yes, yes, yes, all right. No more rocketwings, I promise. No other women either, for what it's worth."

She squeezed him, then rested her head against his.

"Then forever I am yours."

Martyne reached down and drew his reaction pistol. He handed it to Samondel, along with three clips of ammunition.

There was a small access hatch just behind the headrest. It was cramped in the cockpit, too cramped for a rapid exchange of positions between flyer and navigator in an emergency. Thus another set of controls had been provided, rudimentary but adequate. Samondel pushed the emergency throttle forward, then steered for the east. The Skyfire rocketwings were much faster, but they were not now on standby and had an extremely short range. By the time they could be armed and fitted with rockets she would be well outside their operational circle.

Martyne slid the hatch open. After giving Samondel one final, lingering kiss, he jumped.

Samondel locked the emergency controls in a shallow climb heading southeast, then crawled into the cockpit. She began a careful examination of the compression spirit floats. The tanks had been neither drained nor added to since the sailwing had been captured, and it had a little under half of its compression spirit remaining. With the prevailing winds behind her, this would probably be more than enough to reach Lake Taupo.

After adjusting her heading with the float compass and solarac, Samondel waited until she was out of sight of Tasmania Island, then turned due east and brought the sailwing to its optimal cruising altitude. Finally she throttled back the compression engines and locked the controls. The sun was on the sea's horizon for her, but at ground level it had been night for some time. Samondel now began to weep, and had not ceased weeping by the time dusk had faded completely from the sky and Mirrorsun was well above the eastern horizon. She checked the sailwing's course, made a minor correction, then lay back in the seat again with her hands over her eyes.

Lake Taupo, New Zealand

Red-eyed from the fifteen-hour flight from Australica and from almost as many hours of mourning the loss of Martyne for a second time, Samondel did a slow circuit of the Lake Taupo wingfield before coming in for her descent. There were bodies visible beside the ascent strip, and all of the shelters had been burned. Nothing was moving.

No sign of any burned-out wings, observed Samondel grimly to herself as she wound down the flaps. *But no bodies actually on the ascent strip, no damage to the surface, and nothing rolled across it to hamper any wings coming in. Very significant.*

Samondel began winding the wheels down, and there was an emphatic clack of the lock pins snapping into place. The wheels screeched briefly, then she was rumbling along the surface toward the burned-out shelters. Samondel taxied off into the staging bay, then stopped the compression engines. There had been nine bodies visible in and around the ruins, but she treated the carnage as if it had been as normal a thing as a pre-ascent inspection. Three men appeared from beside the compression spirit shelter as Samondel slid back the canopy hatch. They were armed, but looked to be at ease as they walked over. She jumped to the ground.

"So, how did it go?" asked one of them in Yarronese.

"Seventeen kills, no losses," replied Samondel through the scarf shrouding her face, raising both thumbs into the air.

"Good hunting! And what do you think of all this?"

"Impressive," said Samondel as she began to untie the scarf.

"All our own work, I think we made things look like quite a convincing Avianese attack. When the others arrive we must go over our story. How far behind are they?"

"Twenty minutes."

"That's not Warden Hareak, that's a girl!" shouted one of the men.

"Correct," said Samondel quietly as she drew the Clastini from her jacket and opened fire.

With the reaction pistol in one hand Samondel examined her victims. All were dead. She walked to one of the other bodies and saw that it had been dead some days. The fiction was obviously that aviads from Tasmania Island had mounted a sneak attack and destroyed most of the wingfield facilities and stores before being driven off. A counterattack was sent to Launceston to destroy their capacity to fly or build wings. The Council of Airlords would sanction an alliance with some human faction to establish a base on the mainland and mount further raids on the Avianese survivors.

All very clever, Samondel concluded, looking down at the dead.

Launceston, Tasmania Island

Let me clarify this yet again," said the Overhand of Avian. "You say she reached down and drew your reaction pistol, then pressed it against your head."

"Yes," replied Martyne.

"Did you not struggle? Did you not try to stop her?"

"I was making my first flight in a new wing, I was giving it all my concentration."

"And you took six hours to return to the wingfield after parachuting out."

"I had no say in where to jump."

"You were seen to perform some ceremony with her after the battle," said the adjunct.

"The American colors salute, yes. We carry each other's colors."

"Might I suggest that you were less than reluctant to give her your gun?"

"You might, but I shall deny it."

"The wingfield guards cannot say where the airlord slept on the night after the battle, Fras Shadowmouse. Would you have any suggestions?"

"No more than for where you slept, Fras Adjunct."

"You seem of good humor," said the mayor, "especially for one facing a charge of treason. Do you really appreciate your position?"

"Somewhat better than the three of you," replied Martyne, his face and voice suddenly hardening. "Yesterday you promised the Airlord of Highland Bartolica the use of the sailwing after she had instructed us in the flying of the super-regals and sailwing. I acted within the parameters of that agreement."

"And you had my direct order not to let her escape with the sailwing," shouted the overhand.

"Your *secret* order, Fras Overhand."

"You can also be *secretly* shot, Fras Shadowmouse."

"Not so. Frelle Samondel agreed to fly via the mainland, refuel, and leave a message before ascending for Taupo. That message is for the Highliber of Libris, consort of that well-known and highly placed aviad sympathizer, the Overmayor of Rochester. It explains everything, Fras Overhand, and it includes a personal plea from Airlord Samondel that the Overmayor make diplomatic representations to have all charges against me revoked—and make me a flyer instructor on the ferry flights to the mainland."

Martyne's audience of three took some time to assimilate this news.

"*I* have authority here," said the mayor.

"Would you like to test your authority against that of the beloved of the Overmayor of the Rochestrian Commonwealth? She who could grant a treaty? She who could order secure wingfields built? She who could authorize the building of distilleries to supply unlimited compression spirit? Yield to the logic of the situation, gentlemen. You have lost one sailwing in return for benefits to Avian exceeding your wildest dreams. Would you endanger all of that for the sake of one petty act of revenge?"

Martyne walked from the room a free man, and the Avianese leaders' secret decision to betray Samondel was sponged from existence. By the time that the mayor, overhand, and wingfield adjunct of Launceston learned that Samondel had made no descent to the mainland, and that the message to Dramoren had never existed, their emotions had cooled somewhat and they were content to let the matter rest.

Lake Taupo, New Zealand

After sleeping for the best part of the day, Samondel awoke in the late afternoon, and refueled her sailwing. With a cloth tied over her face, she dragged the decomposed bodies to the compression spirit store, then took her three victims to the firewood stack. Soon everything was blazing fiercely while Samondel stood flinging reaction guns and carbines as far into the lake as her strength would allow. She stood watching the blaze for a time, rubbing a mixture of glycerine and charblack into her hair, then she tied it back tightly.

At last she returned to her sailwing, pulling a little steam engine on a trolley behind her. Once it was stoked up and chugging strongly she strapped it to her compression engines and spun them into life, then stood back and fired a short burst from her reaction pistol into its boiler. She ascended with a pall of black smoke rising into New Zealand's overcast skies.

Samoa

As she approached the Samoa Wingfield, Samondel noted a smoke flare rising to welcome her, and she wound down her wheels and banked into an easy approach in almost windless conditions. Three men were waiting for her as she stopped her engines.

"Aye then, Sair, what news?" asked the leader, who was wearing an adjunct's jacket embroidered with silver thread and set with onyx plates.

"Semme, if you please," said Samondel as she unstrapped.

"Semme Bronlar, my apologies," responded the wingcaptain.

"We had complete success, and we even arranged direct trade links with the Rochester humans," continued Samondel. "Thus we still have a supply of compression spirit and horses."

They began to whoop and cheer as she climbed out of the hatch. "And our losses?" asked the captain.

"Heavy, heavier than expected."

"Defeat would have been worse."

Samondel jumped to the ground.

"Now, then, who is still alive here?" she asked.

"As of last week, just us three."

Samondel drew her reaction pistol and sprayed them with fire until the clip was empty. She slapped another clip into the gun.

"And as of now, just me," she said to the bodies.

The following day Samondel refueled her sailwing. Ascending, she circled the wingfield, noting that from the air all was identical to when she had arrived the day before.

"I truly am sorry," she said softly to the three lying dead below her, "but you chose the wrong side."

She turned the sailwing for twenty degrees past north and began a long, slow climb to cruising altitude.

Rochester, the Rochestrian Commonwealth

Vorion was not the type of man to defy his superiors, but neither was he liable to shirk from telling Dramoren any unpalatable truth. He handed the Highliber of Libris a closely written sheet of poorpaper and stood back while he read. Presently Dramoren looked up.

"Who else knows of this?" he asked.

Vorion snatched the sheet from his hands, crumpled it, and tossed it into the fire.

"Only me, Highliber."

"You spied on me?"

"I filled holes in your security, through which the like of this might have leaked."

"Thank you."

"Highliber, you cannot do this! Your name will be reviled by both aviads and Rochestrians."

"The Reformed Gentheists will probably make me a saint."

"But you will die, then be hated forever. It will break the Overmayor's heart when she learns that you were a traitor."

"Better one broken heart than the death of my species."

Tears began to trickle down Vorion's cheeks, and his face contorted with sobs before he covered it with his hand.

"Overmayor, don't do this. It makes me so sad. You are the finest person I have known since Frelle Zarvora died, your name deserves to be remembered in honor and glory, just as hers is."

"Vorion, if the truth that I am an aviad is revealed, Lengina's enemies will say that her humane policies toward them were whispered by my lips into her ears. She will lose credibility, and there will be more massacres and lynchings. No, I must play the role of traitor. She will be filled with hate for all Reformed Gentheists, and she will bring the Commonwealth down on them like a brick on a peanut. I have already arranged for Avian to offer help to Rochester once . . . well, when I am gone. It will be the start of the first aviad-human alliance. My death and disgrace is worth that."

The little librarian wiped his tear-streaked face and stared defiantly at Dramoren.

"Service to the Highlibers has been my life, but now I must make a stand. Make me part of your plan or kill me, Highliber. Otherwise I shall reveal your schemes to the Overmayor this very hour."

Dramoren closed his eyes and thought through both the offer and alternatives. It did not take long.

"Very well, you give me no choice. You are recruited."

"Thank you, Highliber. I swear to betray Commonwealth and Dragon Librarian Service with dedication and diligence."

Dramoren laughed softly as he stood up. "Go now, I shall have instructions for you at the stroke of the next half hour."

Vorion pulled the door shut behind him as he left, then set off for the little office that had been his for nearly four decades.

"And I swear to betray you too, Highliber, and to become a saint," he whispered as he walked.

Hawaii

By the time Samondel reached Hawaii her nerve was beginning to fail. There would be more people to kill face-to-face, more bodies to drag away and bury in a shallow trench. The flight had been perfect, with strong, consistent tailwinds. She had made near-record time and had ample compression spirit to spare.

She circled the wingfield and tiny settlement. All but one house had been burned, and bodies were visible even from several hundred feet. A streak of smoke speared up, clearing her to descend, and she could see a single sailwing on the dispersal track with two figures beside it. She made a low pass, the pair on the ground waved. She came around, wound down her wheels, and approached more slowly. Those on the ground could not see her unlock the sailwing's reaction guns.

The spray of gunfire cut down the two figures on the ground almost before they realized that anything was amiss. Samondel wound her wheels back up and came around again, this time strafing the sailwing, from which fragments scattered. Nobody came rushing out to shoot at her. She brought her sailwing around to a heading for the North American mainland. She noted that the winds continued to favor her, and hoped that it was a sign of divine approval.

Rochester, the Rochestrian Commonwealth

It started with the traditional Alms Day ceremony, in which the mayors of all mayorates in the Commonwealth went among their people to distribute alms to those most in need. The day had no specific date, for past experience had shown that all manner of people in very convincing beggars' robes would be present if advance notice was given. Overmayor Lengina simply appeared in the streets, trailed by several lackeys and escorted by a dozen of the palace guard. Also present in the background, and attempting to look inconspicuous, were several members of the Dragon Librarian Service. Present, but succeeding in not being noticed at all, were representatives of the Espionage constables. The latter were taking notes on people encountered by the Overmayor and how they behaved.

Lengina's route had been determined on the Calculor, so that the most beggars were encountered while she was visible to the most people in the smallest time, while walking the shortest possible route—and thus being vulnerable to the least number of assassination opportunities. Amputees, the blind, and the visibly diseased tended to be interspersed. The alcoholics, older orphans, and slow of wit were more mobile and mixed in with the crowds to beg in the markets, and so were not well represented. This was Lengina's first Alms Day, and she approached it with unease.

The first few amputees and blind were approached without incident. The young Overmayor handed the coins over, asked about their circumstances, and was told that she was as generous as she was young and beautiful. Meantime an orphan managed to cut the strings to her purse and slip away with it, only to be caught by the Espionage Constables once out of sight of the mayoral party, relieved of the purse, and handed over to the Constable's Runners. In the wake of the mayoral party were the shadowboys and protection guilds, intent on a share of the mayoral largesse, and watching them in turn were the Espionage Constables. Widows and young orphans followed the mayoral party, not so much to get a second coin as to gain the protection of the mayoral guard until they could slip away from the street predators before being robbed.

Lengina was listening to a three-part-harmony chorus of drunks singing "Rochester the Brave and Learned" when the catcalls began.

"Why's you cut your hair?"

"Live for the Word!"

The Constable's Runners were quickly in action to move the offenders away, but the numbers of Reformed Gentheist sympathizers grew quickly.

"Jemli for Overmayor!"

"Blasphemer!"

"Aviad!"

Rotten fruit and stones began to fly, but the Calculor had allowed for this as well. Several houses, workshops, and merchant houses had been flagged as good routes to escape through in order to meet with a heavier escort that was following in parallel. The palace guardsmen and Constable's Runners laid into the offenders in the crowd, while Lengina was surrounded by Tiger Dragons and led away. Nordy's Nut House was briefly turned into a thoroughfare for one Overmayor and eleven armed librarians, and Fras Nordy had scarcely time to thrust a bag of almonds oven-roasted with cinnamon at the Overmayor before she was hurried through his back door. Fras Nordy then chalked 'By Appointment to the Overmayor' on his shop door, only to have his shop smashed, looted, and set on fire by the mob conducting the religious riot that was now in control of the street.

Lengina was not a great orator, and spent little time in contact with the lower social orders of her subjects. Overmayors were, after all, high-level rulers of rulers, rather than rulers in tune with the people who were actually ruled. Zarvora had been so formidable that none dared raise a voice of dissent against her, and the first two who followed her were steady administrators with no particular interest in people. Lengina was, in a quite real sense, the first overmayor to take a heartfelt interest in the welfare in the lowest of her subjects. Thus it was that she took the insults, missiles, and the riot personally, and was deeply disturbed by the time she was hastened back into the palace. Dramoren had naturally been alerted, and arrived as a gaggle of servants with bowls of scented warm water and towels were cleaning the fragments of fruit from the Overmayor's face and hair. Her soiled robes had already been removed, and she wore only a dressing cloak.

"They hate me," she said bleakly as he knelt before her.

"Only failures are hated by nobody," replied Dramoren.

"Oh. Who said that?"

"I did, just now."

"Ah. So it's not some wise saying?"

"Do I have to be long dead but in print before my sayings become wise?"

A screen was placed between Dramoren and Lengina while her servants and chambermaids changed her into clean clothing. By the time the screen was removed yet another group was washing her hair.

"They threw things," sobbed Lengina.

"Lucky they didn't shoot things," replied her beloved without much concern evident.

"They were waving sticks."

"Ah, then you cross-block with a nice little arc-parry, then cut across to the temple. A very underrated target, the temple."

"Dram! I've just been attacked!"

Dramoren now knelt beside her recliner and took her hand in both of his. "Dearest Frelle, the average Dragon Silver in the Dragon Librarian Service currently has 1.64 deaths on his or her hands. For Dragon Gold it is 2.78 deaths, and the averages are slightly higher for women. On my way to Dragon Black I fought eleven duels and killed six senior librarians and the champions of another two, as well as inflicting some rather serious wounds. Speaking of wounds, I have more like the one on my face."

There was a tittering among the maids, who now realized that Lengina had never seen her beloved with his clothes off. This affirmation of her virtue felt more like a loss of face to Lengina, who ordered them from the room and began to towel her hair dry by herself.

"Jemli can sway people, she can reach into their hearts," she said dispiritedly.

"So can a vendor of chocolates."

"Be serious!"

"I am being serious."

"I went out at a random time, on a random date, into a street chosen at random by your Calculor. Even so I ran into dozens of militant Reformed Gentheists. If that is a sample of Jemli the Prophet's support, then half of the Commonwealth must be ready to take up stones on her behalf."

"Frelle Lengina, there are any number of people who knew that route up to ten minutes in advance. Preliminary tallies show twenty-eight people arrested. Twenty-eight! How hard might it be to keep twenty-eight, thirty, even three dozen men and women at the ready, waiting to rush to your Alms Day ceremony as soon as the traitor alerts them? Actually only five or six were probably behind today's mob, and I would be surprised if more than one or two of the real leaders have been arrested."

"You have only fought duels, this was a mob. Being set upon by a mob is different. It is like being judged by the voice of the people."

"Do you really think so?"

"As of today, I know so. Jemli has something about her. Perhaps it is God's will. I don't know, but I did feel as if a greater thing had judged me today. I plotted to turn the Commonwealth against Woomera, but no matter what I do, peace breaks out. God is judging me, and finding me wanting."

Dramoren walked across to the shuttered window, pushed the shutters open, and looked out over the city. By now order had been restored, and it was as if the incident had never taken place.

"I disagree," he said without turning. "Woomera is going out of its way to be a good neighbor to the Rochestrian Commonwealth, and in affairs of state, a good neighbor is a neighbor who wants something."

Dramoren was cloaked and masked as he strode down the darkened street in the rain. An identical figure fell into step with him.

"The righteous are within the palace," the stranger reported.

"Can they be detected?" asked Dramoren.

"They carry nought but their convictions and instructions. What of your task?"

"The device is in place and cannot be detected. It has Southmoor markings aplenty, so they will be blamed. What of the Woomeran Overmayor?"

"A worthy sacrifice, one life to save millions. This is the Word as revealed to the Prophet Jemli, the Enlightened One."

"All praise to the Deity and the Word from the Prophet Jemli. One life to save millions."

Martyne spent as much time in the taverns of the commoners as he did in the more refined establishments such as Marelle reigned over. The Filthy Swine was actually a lot cleaner than the name implied and served a special wood-brewed beer whose reputation was known right across the Commonwealth. Having helped train several flyers to fly the super-regals and having completed a dozen trips to the mainland and back, Martyne had been granted a few days' leave from service in the Avianese Civil Flock. He decided to visit Rochester.

"Beer off the wood," he said to the jarmaid as he sat by the first fire of the season.

The man rubbing his hands before the flames wore an eye patch, and the skin of his face had either been diseased or burned in the past.

"Brave scar on the arm," he remarked as Martyne reached out to accept his beer. "You'd be a veteran, then?"

Martyne's scar had not been visible to the man. This was his contact.

"Got it in action," Martyne admitted.

He had been told that his contact would guide the conversation, and that he should not flinch from any subject or suggestion.

"Aye, then, you'd be in Rochers for the One Day of the Year?"

Martyne thought quickly. "Yes, but just to watch."

"Why? All march in the ANZAC parade, even old foes, even aviads."

By now a circle of drinkers had either fallen silent or were speaking more softly.

"But not a veteran of the Avian regulars."

The room fell totally silent. Nobody had ever heard of an official Avianese fighting force, although they were suspected to exist.

"Then who were ye fighting with, and where, young Fras?"

"The Skyfire Flock during the Battle of Launceston against the Yarronese Americans. I shot down three of their wings. Now I am with the Second Armed Kitewings, although on secondment to—"

"Fras, Fras, march back a little!" called a genuine veteran, sauntering over with his beer. "D'ye mean flying machines?"

"Yes."

Martyne expected a dangerous confrontation over matters of fueled engines and heresy. The actual reaction of the company took him by surprise.

"There's been a war in the air?" exclaimed the veteran.

"Yes, but it only lasted fifteen minutes. Things move very fast, you see."

"Americans attacked Avian?" called a rather overweight, bearded bombardier who was smoking a pipe.

"Yes, but we stopped them."

"Bastards! Teach 'em to attack our aviads."

There were mutters of assent. Martyne could scarcely believe his ears. *Our* aviads?

"It was only one American faction, most others are rather nice," he now explained. "One of their flyers is my sweetheart, she fought alongside us."

"A *human* fought with you?" asked someone from behind Martyne.

"Yes, a Bartolican."

"Young Fras, this seems to smell of a lie, dressed to get you free drinks for the rest of the night," said Martyne's contact. "Now, a real flyer would wear his sweetheart's colors just below his right elbow, a sort of bundle of ribbons. That's what I got told by the Dragon Librarians who questioned that American fella shot down last January."

"Oh, you mean these?" said Martyne, throwing back his cloak and holding his arm up to display Samondel's colors.

There was a loud, involuntary cacophony of gasps, oaths, and cries of amazement.

"Young Fras, is your girl close?" asked the jarmaid. "We must meet her."

Martyne lowered his arm and stared at the floor.

"She is missing in action, Frelle, and that action was three weeks ago."

In a matter of hours Martyne found himself to be the toast of Rochester. In a city overflowing with veterans for the ANZAC parade, he was a veteran of a type not seen for two thousand years. The next day he found himself standing before the parade committee, and beside him was Terian.

"If you insist that there is goodwill in Rochester, then we Avianese are willing to march," Terian was saying.

"Second Armed Kitewings and Battle of Launceston are to be

the two banners, yes, we'll have those completed in time," said the secretary. "Will you accept human youths to carry them?"

"The Avianese veterans would be honored, Fras," said Terian. "I can arrange three for the parade."

"Three flyers?" asked the committee president.

"Yes."

"Ah, and one of them is yourself?"

"No, I am of the Fifth Wingfield Lancers, Outrider Guards."

"Fras Harbean, another banner," the president ordered, turning to the secretary. "Did you catch the title?"

Forian, North America

On the other side of the world another veteran of the same conflict was not being similarly honored. Samondel was standing before the eleven other members of the Council of Mounthaven Airlords who had been willing or able to gather in Forian. The mood was one of impatience and distraction, and while they had actually met to discuss the Australican venture, the matter of the disintegration of their own domains weighed far more heavily on their minds. Most had oil-stained hands from having to help maintain their own compression engines. That was a bad sign.

The sudden availability of a frontier the size of a continent with no human population at all, practically limitless ancient cities to mine for resources, and the availability of game and farmland that put Mounthaven to shame meant that the ancient American states were hemorrhaging citizens. The majority of those who were leaving were young, strong, bright people who otherwise had no more prospects than inheriting a family cottage, while following a trade producing some minor component of some warden's gunwing. By comparison, the idea of owning a wilderness freehold the size of a warden's estate, living in a newly built cabin, and calling nobody master had scarcely less allure than a bag of gold lying in the middle of the road.

Many workshops now contained only guildmasters and a few children. Fields of fuel crops lay untended, and wardens often worked in their own fuel distilleries just to stay in the air. Among the ancient trades, only the gunsmiths were prospering, but even these were packing their workshops and stock onto carts and setting out for the frontier settlements where new markets were booming. The demand for hunting rifles was particularly strong, while the guildsmen producing bullets were accumulating wealth to rival that of their former wardens.

All of this was at the back of Samondel's mind as she spoke, however. Airlord Sartov's conspiracy to attack the Australican wing-fields was a matter of honor that she gave even higher priority than that of Highland Bartolica's disintegration.

"I have seen stupidity on a scale that I did not believe possible," she cried, slamming the butt of the speaker's mace down on the floor. "Resources wasted that could have been used to bring hundreds of young horses across the ocean. Instead the Avianese annihilated your sailwings with their rocketwings. It took minutes! They can climb faster than sailwings can dive!"

"Where did they get those things?" asked Sartov, furious yet unsettled.

"They developed them from ancient texts; do you think nobody but us can fly? They have the ultimate defensive wings, Airlord Sartov of Yarron: limited range, exceedingly high speed, and very simple to build. They only need our artisans and skills for developing civilian transport wings."

"Transport of featherhead brats, transport of bombs, transport of carbineers, it is all the same," said Sartov.

"You never change, do you? A carefully planned, secret raid over an impossible distance against seemingly overwhelming odds, that is your way. Well, it might have worked against Bartolica, but Avian stopped you."

"We have twenty-five horses, and the two oldest are with foal," said the Airlord of Cosdora, anxious to end the debate and move on to the loss of most of his worthwhile subjects to the former Callscour frontier. "A young bull and four cows as well. Surely Venture Australica can be declared a success?".

"The Airlord of Highland Bartolica should be commended for a most remarkable feat," added the Airlord of Senner.

"The Airlord of Highland Bartolica has killed over ten dozen of our finest and bravest wardens and air carbineers," retorted Sartov.

"Your terrorists," countered Samondel.

"The wings and compression spirit belonged to us all," said Sartov. "You betrayed us, you sacrificed them to the featherheads. You have cost us more in handcrafted wings, compression engines, and fuel than the entire featherhead war!"

"You organized the conspiracy that cost us all that!" shouted Samondel. "Without you we would have kept every wing, and gained as many horses as our explorers and carbineers could ride."

"Wardens Jemarial and Feydamor are dead because of you."

"Fact! I shot down Warden Jemarial in a Yarronese triwing. Fact! Serjon Feydamor, Mounthaven's greatest flyer, was shot down by Martyne Camderine, Australica's greatest flyer."

"Fact! Sair Camderine was flying one of those monstrosities that moves faster than the bullets from our reaction guns! It was no fair or chivalric fight—"

"Fine words from the airlord who organized a terrorist attack on Launceston Wingfield."

"That was not a civilized wingfield, just a strip of grass that barbarians ascend from—"

"In wings vastly superior to ours. My lords, think upon what I have told you, and upon the reports sent back earlier from Sair Feydamor himself. The Avianese now have adjuncts, pennant poles, colors, wing names, champions, and standards of chivalric honor."

"But they have no airlords or wardens," the Airlord of Cosdora pointed out.

"And we have no Highlibers, Dragon Librarians, or beamflash captains," replied Samondel. "That makes *us* barbarians to *them*."

"Powerful barbarians," warned Sartov. "Remember what happened to Greater Bartolica in the war."

"And remember what happened to your one hundred twenty-one terrorists, Airlord Sartov. All dead."

"They were betrayed."

"Wrong. They were killed before they had a chance to betray. Their motive was based in hate, just as yours is. You perverted our venture, you wasted our resources—"

"Not *our* resources, *my* resources!" shouted Sartov, standing up and waving his fist. "We Yarronese designed and developed every sailwing and super-regal that was used to cross the ocean. Without Yarron, Venture Australica would not have happened. All that the rest of you contributed was compression spirit, engines, and a few flyers—ah, yes, and one very dubious leader."

"Sair Speaker, I wish to move a motion of censure against the airlords of Yarron, Cosdora, and Dorak for their conspiracy against the Mayorate of Avian," announced Samondel.

"Yarron does not need this council," warned Sartov.

"Does anyone second Airlord Samondel's motion?" asked the speaker of the council.

The four Bartolican airlords voted affirmative, while Yarron, Dorak, and Cosdora voted against and the others abstained. Clerks ran in and out of the chamber with messages to and from advisers, then order was called. The clerks were sent out again, and the doors were closed. Sartov was grim faced as he rose to reply to the vote.

"I have instructed my advisers to begin gathering my wardens for a general council," he said with no trace of emotion. "There I shall move a motion that Yarron withdraw from this council. I have no more to say."

He sat down. After some moments of uneasy muttering the Airlord of Dorak rose to make a similar statement. Samondel could hear the sound of the compression engines of a sailwing warming up outside. Her sailwing. She closed her eyes, lowered her head, and squeezed at the bridge of her nose. A muffled explosion cut off the compression engines, and all airlords but Samondel rushed to the windows.

"Airlord Sartov, I do wish that you would consult with your fellow airlords before taking rash actions," said Samondel.

Furious, Sartov turned back to her.

"You sabotaged my sailwing!"

"Like a loyal Mounthaven airlord I set governor detonators that would explode if the engines were revved to ascent speed without my authorization keys inserted. We cannot have one of Yarron's finest sailwings falling into the wrong hands, can we?"

Sartov stayed only long enough to hear the airlord of Cosdora declare his intent to withdraw from the council, then he led the other two from the council chamber. Within a half hour all three airlords were in the air and bound for their domains. The others passed a vote of thanks to Samondel, and made administrative arrangements for the sharing of the horses and cattle. Samondel proposed that a new guild of artisans be set up, but could get no more than a promise that each of the remaining airlords would send one representative to the meetings. There was no interest at all in pooling compression spirit for a future venture to Australica. As her last act in what turned out to be the last meeting ever called of the Council of Mounthaven Airlords, Samondel read out the lists of the Adjunct of Launceston Wingfield, detailing the participants, deaths, and victors at the Battle of Launceston. A vote was passed to include the Australican wingfield in the Mounthaven Register of Chivalry, although Samondel's amendment denouncing the raid as an act of Yarronese terrorism was defeated.

The next day Samondel flew out for Condelor in the luggage store of the sailwing flown by the South Bartolican airlord, Loring.

"Where is your gunwing?" she asked as they climbed northwest, with Medicine Bow Peak to starboard.

"I retired my gunwing flock, converted them to twin-engine sailwings to ship hunting carbines and ammunition to the frontier settlements," her fellow airlord replied. "That's where the money is. Very light, very valuable cargos."

"But what about the defense of your realm?"

"I have carbineer mercenaries for that. I only need to defend my capital, wingfield, and compression spirit estates."

Already degenerated into a petty warlord, thought Samondel.

"What of Highland Bartolica?" he asked after a time. "How many wings do you have?"

"One gunwing and five sailwings belonging to the realm."

"Would you consider selling them? I need to expand my merchant flock."

"Me, an *airlord*? Sell my own flock?"

"Saireme, the airlords of Towervale, Friscon, Omelgan, and Senner no longer own any wings at all. Their compression engines are in my merchant flock, the airframes are firewood, and they lease their personal sailwings from me. Tell you what, keep the gunwing for personal use and sell me the sailwings. Think on that as we fly."

Samondel thought a great deal as they flew. Avian was safe, for without the combined resources commanded by the entire council, the ocean could not be crossed. Avian might as well have been on a distant planet—but so might Martyne.

At Montpellier, the capital of Highland Bartolica, they inspected the royal flock while the courtiers and nobles looked on uneasily. Airlord Loring agreed to buy four sailwings, and to pay for an option on the remaining gunwing. Once he was gone Samondel called together the guildmasters of her domain and led them to the only sailwing remaining to Highland Bartolica.

"I want this wing rebuilt," she explained. "You are to halve its weight, double its fuel capacity, and render its engine into the lightest and most reliable in history."

This was far more easily said than done. Even though she had enough money for the work, there were only guildmasters and apprentices available, no experienced artisans. Nevertheless, the work was begun. A reserve store of compression spirit was established, and armed carbineers assigned to guard it. Thereafter Samondel spent most of her time locked away with maps, globes, performance tables, and calculation slates.

Rochester, the Rochestrian Commonwealth

The ANZAC Day parade was always preceded by a meeting of the mayors of the Rochestrian Commonwealth, for all of them always attended the parade and took the salute beside the Overmayor on the palace balcony overlooking Libris Plaza.

"I wish to open this meeting with the announcement that High-liber Franzas Dramoren and myself are to be married on the afternoon of the winter solstice, here in Rochester," Lengina announced.

There was an immediate round of applause.

"I should like to point out to you, the mayors of the Commonwealth, that this is an arrangement of great convenience as well, and combines the offices of Overmayor and Highliber once more, following the lead set so successfully by Highliber Zarvora."

"And no romance at all is involved!" called the Mayor of Seymour.

Extended and rowdy laughter followed, ended finally by three cheers for the happy couple. The business session that followed had a rather long agenda. There was widespread dissent about the continued conscription of numerate people for the Libris Calculor, yet considerable gratitude that the paraline and beamflash networks were operating normally while those of neighboring overmayorates were practically crippled. The electrical-essence trades had been annihilated, yet people remained prosperous thanks to new industries.

"My people hear plenty of travelers' tales from over the border with the Southmoors," declared the Mayor of Rutherglen. "Riots, battles between factions of the nobility, towns isolated, farms looted and burned. My own people are frightened of the anarchy spreading to Rutherglen, and the membership of the Rutherglen Mayoral Militia has never been higher. Why, only last week when a Reformed Gentheist orator exhorted his listeners to take up arms and burn the houses of heretics, he was nearly lynched—and by an audience of Gentheists!"

"The Dragon Librarian Service reports similar behavior across all mayorates," agreed the Overmayor. "Even the castellanies in the west have increased lancer patrols on the borders with Woomera."

"Is there a danger of invasion?" asked the mayor of Seymour.

"The danger is more from a surfeit of refugees," explained a castellian observer. "They come seeking food and work, then start preaching the way of the Word. Some have been attacking known aviads."

"I propose that those convicted of disturbing the peace should be subject to mandatory deportation in the case of foreign nationals," said the mayor of Rutherglen.

The matter of recognition of Avian was raised next, but dealt with quickly. Terian had been sent as an envoy, proposing trade links, and claiming a sliver of land in the south covering the Otway Mountains. The land was of no particular worth, and was only to give the Avianese a secure wingfield on the mainland. A motion to recognize the claim and begin negotiations on a treaty with Avian was passed with little discussion.

The ANZAC parade had been held on the twenty-fifth day of the fourth month for over two thousand years. Nobody was even sure what ANZAC meant. The Meridian Avenue was the longest and widest street in Rochester, and ran five miles from the edge of the outer city, due north to the lake, across the thirty arches of a stone-and-brick bridge, through an arched gate in the wall of the old inner city, and ended at the plaza in front of Libris.

Jemli had pronounced the march to be an affront to the Deity, because it commemorated wars fought using machines. Only religious wars could be commemorated in good conscience according to her, and even then only those who had fought on the sides opposing machines should march. To this end, some three hundred Ghan lancers, veterans of the Milderellen invasion, were sent to march if Jemli's conditions were met. This turned out to be a very unpopular move. Not only were the Ghans a former enemy that was close to becoming a current enemy again, but the tradition of marching was one of the few that had managed to transcend religious and political divisions. Preparations for the march continued, however, and massive numbers of veterans and their families were arriving.

Faced with the prospect of not being represented in the march at all, the Reformed Gentheists of Rochester decided to instruct the Ghan lancers to participate.

The morning of the 25th promised a clear, cool, windless day. Children had been gathering baskets of colored autumn leaves and evergreens for days to fling onto the marchers from rooftops, and Rochester's citizens turned out in numbers that were estimated to exceed a hundred thousand.

The Ghans had insisted on being first, riding camels and horses. This had been calculated to strew piles of dung into the path of the marchers who were following, but the veterans were still quite capable of matching wits with an enemy. Grandchildren with hand shovels, brooms, and sacks were stationed every hundred feet, ready to dash out and clean up.

Mobile bombards rumbled past next, artillery rockets rolled by on their trolleys, then came their support crews. After these came the ranks of infantry and lancers, and there were vast numbers of these.

Dramoren and Lengina stood together on the palace balcony, at the center of the row of leaders and dignitaries. Children on the palace walls flung colored leaves onto the marchers, and the bands of the palace and Libris took turns to play the anthems of each group of nationals that passed. A wave of cheers rolled along the street in slow motion as one particular group of infantry came marching along, each with his musket held across his chest with both hands, while two young women marched out in front. One was playing "Campbell's Farewell to the Red Castle" on a zurna, the other carried the colors high on a T-shaped pole.

"That's the hundred and fifth Overmayor's Heavy Infantry, John Glasken's old unit," said Dramoren.

"Glasken, yes. He was the chivalrous hero whose enemies started a legend of him being a rake and lecher," replied the Overmayor.

"Well, you know what they say. Those who are remembered well must have done some good."

"Why is there a dead chicken tied to each man's belt?"

"Tradition, but I can't say why. I was a child when they fought the Battle of Ravensworth. I do know that Glasken started a tradition that two women should carry the colors and pipe them along, in memory of Lieutenant Dolorian Jelveria. See, the one playing the zurna is his daughter by his second wife, Marelle is her name."

Following the 105th was the First Alliance Radio Corps, led by the survivors of *Starflash 7*. Their carefully restored wagons were making their annual pilgrimage out of the museum, and after two decades of loving care by conservators they looked better than they had when they were new.

Now there came a new wave of sound: cries of amazement followed by renewed cheers. Hats were flung into the air, and even into the path of the marchers. Lengina raised a small telescope and read the approaching banners.

"Aviads!" she exclaimed, even though both she and the entire city had known that a handful of Avianese veterans would be marching. "Second Armed Kitewings from the Battle of Launceston, there are two of them. The other is Fifth Wingfield Lancers, Outrider Guards. There are five, all mounted."

The Avianese entered Libris Plaza, and approached the point for the salute to the balcony filled with leaders while bands blared and the crowds cheered. Suddenly the Mayor of Seymour pointed, and they all turned. There was a large speck in the sky, flying at rooftop level above the Avenue. Above the bands and cheering they could hear the drone of a diesel engine.

"A kitewing, a real kitewing!" shouted Dramoren.

"A kitewing, the Avianese envoy promised me a flight in one at the banquet last night," squealed Lengina, clapping her hands.

Martyne was a lot happier to be flying the kitewing than the Skyfire rockets. Its speed was sufficiently low to forgive mistakes, even if in combat it was heavy, underpowered, and clumsy. From well beyond Rochester's outer walls he aligned himself with Meridian Avenue, which cut right through to the center of the city. The kitewing

flew over countryside mottled with woods and farmland, then above
an untidy tangle of outlying streets and cottages. The Arch of Return
commenced the Avenue, and was a four-point stone arch resting on
the heads of fifty-foot-high statues of a musketeer, lancer, nurse, and
bombardier, each facing away from the center. Behind the arch was
a park where crowds of veterans were milling about, preparing to
march, but on the other side the former warriors were in orderly
ranks, marching away between rows of onlookers. Ahead was the
massive beamflash tower of Libris, and to the left was the mayoral
palace, both overlooking Libris Plaza and the Memorial to the Fallen
at its center. Traveling at a hundred feet and forty miles per hour,
the kitewing was only a score of yards from the roofs of some of
the taller houses.

None but the Avianese had seen a kitewing before, and true to its
name it resembled nothing more than a large, double boxkite making
a loud droning sound. As it passed along the Avenue people shouted
and pointed up, then cheered. The veterans did not stop, although
many broke ranks to stare. The Avianese marchers now saluted the
leaders on the balcony, Martyne saluted from the kitewing—and a
burst of fire pattered out from the northeast tower of the palace.

At first it was taken for a salute, then everyone saw black smoke
belch from the kitewing and the note of its compression engine lowered and began to miss. The flyer banked away to starboard over
Libris, narrowly missing the great beamflash tower. Cheers turned
to screams across Libris Plaza. Dozens of outraged veterans in the
crowd opened fire on the palace tower, and Overmayor Lengina ordered the palace guard to seize the place at once. Out in the square
the Ghan Lancers fired a volley at those shooting at the tower. The
dignitaries and leaders scrambled from the oration balcony of the
palace, but Dramoren remained behind, holding up a mirror and
flashing a signal across the plaza to Libris.

In the northeast tower the captain of a squad of Reformed Gentheist
infiltrators dressed in the uniforms of palace guardsmen held up her

flintlock as two of her men pinned her lieutenant to the wall by his arms.

"Why in the name of all hells did you order that volley?" she screamed in near-hysterical fury.

"Frelle Captain, when I saw that blasphemous abomination flying past I could not help myself—"

She fired, hitting him squarely between the eyes.

"*That's* what happens to anyone who can't help himself or obey orders!" she bellowed to the others.

From below there was the sound of pounding on a door that was barred from the inside.

"Hurry, get the bombards forward and bring down the beamflash tower!" the captain ordered.

"But Captain, the balcony has not yet—"

"Screw the balcony! Obey me! Now!"

Part of the tower's bombard gallery burst inward as the first of the shots from the Libris ceremonial bombards landed. The captain picked herself up.

"Open fire, bring down the tower," she cried.

Dramoren crouched below the balcony railing, holding up his mirror and signaling to the Libris gunners to keep firing. A bombard shot thudded into the beamflash tower, punching a dent into the heavy stonework, then another clipped a corner and knocked out a shower of stone blocks and fragments.

What do you mean, you've never fired a shot-loaded bombard before?" Lengina demanded of the captain of the southeast palace tower.

"The tower has been purely ceremonial for two hundred years, Frelle Overmayor."

"Pick up one of those balls, push it into a bombard, and fire!" shouted Lengina, pointing at the northeast tower.

"I don't know how to aim!"

"There's a plate on the mounting," suggested one of the bombard crew.

The captain dropped to his knees. " 'Congratulations, you have just purchased a Talini Brothers bombard . . . nine-inch balls . . . iron or lead-iron composite—' "

"Just point it at the tower!" said Lengina.

"—only certified bombardiers with a scroll from the Mayoral Commissioner of Armaments—"

"Point and fire!" shrieked Lengina. "At this range you cannot miss!"

The bombard was fired. It flew off its mounting with a fume-choked thunderclap, crashed into the wall behind it, and came to rest on its side in a cloud of sulfurous smoke and dust.

Hit from the side by the shot from the southeast tower, the roof of the bombard gallery of the northeast tower collapsed. Several tons of stonework and bricks crushed the Reformed Gentheist bombardiers, although the musketeers in the stairwell below survived.

Fighting was still raging down in Libris Plaza as Dramoren straightened. He watched guardsmen smash down the northeast tower's door with an improvised battering ram. There was a burst of gunfire as the guards streamed in.

"Dramoren!"

He could see a figure in white robes waving to him from a bombard arch in the southeast tower. Dramoren inserted his foot into a small niche in the stonework, felt for a lever, and flicked it up. *What a bonus, no need to feign a bomb scare to evacuate the balcony,* he thought.

"And as Martyne Camderine once said to Airlord Samondel Leover, I love you," Dramoren whispered to the distant figure of Lengina. He pressed the hidden lever down with his foot.

The blast that followed gouged out the center of the entire east wall of the palace, demolishing the oration balcony and sending a cloud of dust and smoke billowing out across the plaza where Ghan lancers still battled Rochestrian veterans.

Martyne managed to nurse his kitewing out over the lake before the damaged compression engine seized. He skimmed the glassy water, lost speed, then dropped heavily to the surface. Martyne unstrapped himself, flung off his jacket and boots, and jumped. The water had a pronounced mid-autumn chill, but at least nobody shot at him as he waded ashore.

Vorion watched the fighting from the roof of Libris, then returned to the Highliber's study and stepped through the leadlight window. He picked up a note written by Dramoren and began reading.

> I, Franzas Dramoren, Highliber of Libris, do offer my death and the deaths of the heretical heads of state to the Deity so that Prophet Jemli may be free to lead the righteous of the Rochestrian Commonwealth into the light of salvation. Death to all heretics, death to aviad abominations, a curse upon Mirrorsun and all fueled engines.

Vorion crumpled the poorpaper and dropped it into the fire.

"No, my Highliber, that will never do," he said as he sat down to compose his own note.

> I, Vorion Poros, lackey to the Highliber Dramoren, do affirm that I have betrayed my Highliber, the Dragon Librarian Service, the Overmayor, and the Rochestrian Commonwealth in the name of the Deity and for the greater glory of the Word, and with the help of the blessed faithful of the Woomeran Confederation. My only regret is that some demon or abomination drove the mayors from the balcony before my bomb exploded, and that the great beamflash tower did not fall to

the cannons of the righteous. All power and glory to the Word, long life to Jemli the Prophet.

Vorion signed his name, dripped wax beside the signature, and pressed his seal into it. His hands were shaking almost beyond control as he drew his small, ceremonial flintlock. He pressed the barrel hard against his temple to make sure that he could not miss.

You know there is no other way, I must do this to clear the Highliber's name, he prayed as he squeezed his eyes shut. *God forgive me, God forgive me—*

With all the shooting that was going on outside, nobody paid any heed to yet one more muffled shot.

10

CHILD OF THE MIRROR

Peterborough, the Woomeran Confederation

Jemli was conducting her afternoon's meditation when she noticed that a girl had entered her chambers, a girl with the coldest expression that she had ever seen. She stood with her arms folded and stared unblinking at Jemli, who was seated on a huge, embroidered cushion. There was something familiar about her, something about her manner, attitude, bearing, expression, and even the smirk on her lips.

Unfolding her arms, the intruder now walked across to a wall, her boots making no sound at all on the flagstones. She pressed a panel without taking her eyes from Jemli. The panel clicked softly. The intruder slid it aside, reached into the recess behind it, drew out a Morelac, then closed the panel.

"Mine, I believe," said the intruder in educated Austaric that retained a slight Rutherglen accent.

The words had the impact of a snakebite upon Jemli.

"Guards!" she called, and immediately the doors at the end of her meditation chamber were flung open. Two guards entered, their muskets held ready.

"Guards, take her away from me," Jemli called fearfully.

One of the guards crossed the room and stood beside the intruder.

"Come, you are in trouble beyond telling," said the guard, reaching out to seize her.

His hand passed right through her arm. The guard cried out, recoiling back and firing his flintlock. The ball passed through the intruder, ricocheting from a stone column and lodging in a panel. The intruder held up the Morelac twin barrel.

"I shall go," said the intruder to the guard, then she turned back to Jemli. "For now."

She walked silently across to a stone wall and stepped straight through. Both guards exchanged glances with Jemli.

"It is a vision, sent by a demon to shake our faith," she said quickly. "Go, go. My solitude is my strength."

When the guards were gone again Jemli locked the double doors behind them and made straight for the secret panel where the Morelac that had once belonged to Lemorel Milderellen was concealed. She pressed the panel. It clicked. She slid the panel aside. The space behind it contained a pistol rack, but no pistol. Jemli reached in and picked up the rack, she held it up to the light, turned it before her eyes. Suddenly she screamed, dropping the rack as she fainted. This time the doors had to be smashed open by the guards. They found Jemli lying on the ground, an open panel in the wall and the gunrack beside her. A stretcher, medician, and nurses were sent for at once and Jemli was carried out, surrounded by a dozen men and women.

Only when the room was empty did Velesti step from behind a screen, wearing a guard's uniform and holding the missing Morelac in her hand. She slipped it into her belt and buttoned her coat over it. An image of a guard with Zarvora's face materialized in the air before her, floating a foot above the floor.

"Thank you for your help, Frelle Mirrorsun," said Velesti. "Now, would you escort me through the palace, or must I fight my way along?"

"That would spoil the illusion, Frelle Disore. And after all my hard work with those illusions, too."

"And mine."

• • •

Jemli lay resting in her bed, now surrounded by eight guards, two medicians, three Reformed Gentheist priests, and five of her personal maids.

"I had a vision, the Invincible Lemorel appeared to me," she was telling the priests. "She held up her favorite pistol, the one our beloved papa gave to her. She said that she had returned to be sure that I was making no mistakes. I did not recognize her at first, it has been so long since her death. I called the guards, and it was only when one put his hand through her that I realized who was before me. She said she would go, I think she was satisfied."

Jemli realized that nobody was watching her anymore, they were looking at a woman who was standing to the right of the bed with her arms folded . . . and halfway through the wall. Jemli screamed and sat up.

"I have been talking to Glasken, we dead have a lot of time to chat," said the image. "He was wondering if it was you who arranged Mayor Bouros's murder. He was not dead then, so he could not watch you as closely."

Jemli's mouth hung open and her jaw was trembling, but she did not reply.

"I see, I hear," said the guard on her right, gesturing to the wall and phantom. "I cannot stand it."

He began to back toward the door. Most of the others began to follow.

"No! Don't leave me!" shrieked Jemli.

They stopped, but did not return to where they had been.

"We *do* know it was you who denounced Glasken and sent the militia into the underground University," continued the image of Lemorel softly.

"Stop it!" shouted Jemli. "Lies!"

"Denkar said he died there, with all the other engineers. Strange, I only knew Denkar as FUNCTION 9 while he was alive. He was a component in the original Calculor."

Jemli looked from the image to her guards and other staff.

"A demon, here to baffle and confuse us with lies," she assured them. "We must face it together. None of it is true."

"Oh, but your last husband, the Overmayor, told us. He was rather cross that you killed him, by the way. Cross with himself, that is, for not bothering to have you removed earlier."

"In the name of the Deity, begone!" shouted Jemli, standing up on the bed and gesturing at the image with the heel of her hand.

It was an imposing sight. With the extra height of the bed her head was eight feet from the ground. The image of Lemorel was not moved, and did not move.

"The Deity is at my right shoulder!" shrieked Jemli. "The Deity will cast you back into hell!"

The image unfolded its arms and spread its hands, looking around.

"Here I am, waiting to be cast," it said, then folded its arms again and glared at Jemli. "The dead are watching you, Jemli Milderellen. Fart in your bedchamber and we hear it. Preach abominations, death, and hellfire to a hundred thousand of your faithful, and we hear it. Bomb the Rochestrian Overmayor's palace balcony during the ANZAC parade in Rochester and we hear it all the way from here."

"Get out!" Jemli now snapped at her staff and guards. "It's trying to divide us by lies laced with truth. I must face it alone."

Laced with truth? thought everyone else in the room.

The image watched the others hurry out. The duty captain of the guards pulled the door shut behind him and looked around. All the others had already hurried off, including his fellow guards. Only a single guard remained at her post, by the double doors at the end of the corridor. She saluted as Jemli's duty captain approached.

"Watch that door, but do not approach it," he ordered. "If the Enlightened One calls out or screams, send for her priests."

Velesti nodded. The captain opened the left door, then stopped again.

"She is battling a demon," he whispered. "I saw it."

Velesti nodded again, but did not allow herself a smile until the door had clicked shut behind him. The duty captain thought for a moment how similar to Lemorel's image the guard's face had been, but did not hold the thought. He no longer had much faith in what his eyes told him.

Back in Jemli's room the image of Lemorel sauntered clear of the wall. Jemli watched, still standing on the bed.

"The bombing of the palace was about a minute ago, by the way, and congratulations, your agents managed to kill Highliber Franzas Dramoren and shoot down one Avianese kitewing. Unfortunately all the other leaders survived, and are very, very angry. The great beamflash tower of Libris survived as well, and is currently transmitting a declaration of war on Woomera to the border forts and garrisons."

Only now did the image fade. Jemli collapsed down onto her huge bed, desperate to have peace, to sleep, to rest, to just lie still with a blank mind, yet aware that the image had told no lies at all. At least nothing that she knew to be lies, at any rate. The Dragon Librarian Service was to be crippled, the Commonwealth left leaderless, the Southmoors blamed. They were the only neighboring power not to have a representative on the palace balcony, she had even sent the unsuspecting Overmayor of Woomera to die there. It could not fail, she had decided. The presence of her own Overmayor was to be her proof of innocence.

Hours later reports began to arrive by the Gentheist-controlled beamflash system that reached to the border with the Commonwealth. The paraline and road bridges had been blown up on the river border, and trenches were being dug across the roads on the Commonwealth side. Woomeran barges and river galleys were being seized in Commonwealth river ports, and others had been shelled and sunk by shore-based bombards. Another report spoke of a battle raging between two squadrons of river galleys directly outside the river harbor at Morgan. The two forces were evenly matched and were flaying each other to matchwood. The same agent in the beamflash tower of Morgan reported mobs shooting Gentheists regardless of whether or not they had affiliations with Jemli, and every Gentheist shrine in the port was burning. Soon after that message the beamflash transmissions ceased, after an announcement that war had been declared and the border was closed.

Jemli now had a dilemma. Her army of lancers, officials, priests, and newly trained beamflash operators was ready to rush into the Commonwealth and save it from anarchy. It was not an army of invasion, however, and was not intended to deal with coordinated, determined, and sustained opposition. Worse, from Morgan onward, the beamflash towers were all on the Commonwealth side of the river border.

In a strategically canny move, Jemli sent a message to the Burra tower to dispatch three riders to Wentworth, a Woomeran town on the junction of the Southmoor Emirates, the Commonwealth, and her own lands. The thousand lancers there were to make a dash into Southmoor lands, then cross a nearby bridge into the Commonwealth. The riders covered the distance in a single day, and the thousand Ghan lancers were on Southmoor land by midnight and in the Commonwealth by morning.

One of the lancers swam back across the river and staggered into Wentworth five days later. The brigade had been annihilated.

Burra, the Woomeran Confederation

The report of the surviving Ghan lancer was given to a dispatch rider at once, but it was a further day before he reached Burra, which was now the eastern terminus of the Woomeran beamflash network. The priest in charge of the tower read the report in disbelief before giving it to the transmitter.

/ WENTWORTH LANCERS WIPED OUT / ALL COMMONWEALTH TOWNS AT SIEGE STATUS AVIANESE KITEWINGS DIRECTING COMMONWEALTH AND SOUTHMOOR LANCER BRIGADES FROM THE AIR / THREE CAVALRY BATTLES AGAINST SUPERIOR ODDS/

"Why is this happening?" asked the transmitter. "Peterborough said that it was the Southmoors who bombed the palace in Rochester."

"The leaders of the Commonwealth and Southmoors think differently," replied the priest, "but faith and the Deity will defeat them. Besides, our people are born and raised as warriors, we learned from the mistakes of the Milderellen Invasion. . . ."

His voice trailed away. The sound that had caught his attention was like the drone of a large bee, but this bee was drawing shouts of amazement from the gallery on the other side of the beamflash tower's gallery. Hurrying across, the priest was confronted with something like a kite approaching from the southeast at much the same altitude as the tower's gallery.

"Abominations in abominations," declared the priest. "They think to spy on our territory as they spied on our lancers."

It was then that the reaction gun aboard the kitewing opened fire on the beamflash tower, with the firepower of a hundred musketeers. In two passes it shattered every mirror, telescope, and lens in the gallery, then turned north. His face flayed by flying glass, the priest staggered back across the beamflash gallery to the northern balcony.

"Warn the capital, that thing might attack their central tower!" he cried, but the man working as transmitter had been killed in the attack.

The priest knew enough code to send basic, unencrypted messages, but the mirrors, telescopes, and even semaphore switchboxes were riddled with half-inch holes. He picked the dead transmitter's binoculars up off the floor and looked for the kitewing. It was barely visible already, flying low and straight for Peterborough. It was fast, it would take no more than twenty minutes to reach the capital.

Thinking quickly, the priest opened the flare locker and ignited a smoke flare, then he selected the largest fragment of mirror in the gallery, took a sighting on the sun and began flashing his warning to Peterborough.

/ ALERT / AIR GALLEY ATTACK IN THIRTY MINUTES / TOWER DISABLED / NINE DEAD / MIRRORS DESTROYED /

Peterborough, the Woomeran Confederation

In the central tower in Peterborough the faint twinkle of the priest's message was noticed a few minutes after the first smoke flare had been sighted. The supervising priest was called, and he ordered that a request for clarification be transmitted. None was returned, but the desperate warning continued. The interval being flashed in the warning now was five minutes.

"There is nothing at all on the paraline," reported the shift's observer.

"He must mean a galley engine has attacked," the priest decided. "He is not a trained transmitter."

"A galley engine would take an hour to cross from Burra. Anyway, the line is clear."

"Transmitter, alert the paraline guardhouses," ordered the priest. "Receiver, is his message the same?"

The receiver peered into his telescope again. "Yes, and a second flare—"

The image of a huge and ungainly kite rose up into the receiver's field of view with its reaction gun already sparkling. Bullets tore through the tower, tearing through flesh and shattering equipment. A lamp was hit, and the olive oil spilled and ignited. In this tower the priest was one of the first to die, and most of the operators who were still alive scrambled for cover. As the kitewing made a second pass the guards on the ground opened fire on it, but they had no way of estimating its true size and speed, neither were they trained to aim slightly in front of a fast-moving target. On its third pass the kitewing was confronted by a lone, brave operator who fired two shots from his flintlock pistols, but to no effect. The flames had taken hold of the tower's gallery by the fourth pass and the operators were already escaping down the stairs.

Jemli herself saw the kitewing empty its reaction gun into the gallery in its last strafing run, then assume a course southeast and slowly gain height. All across Peterborough the tower and church bells were ringing their futile alarms. It was hours before musketeers ceased shooting at anything that dared to take to the air above the Woomeran capital, by which time five military messenger pigeons had fallen to friendly fire. That evening a galley engine arrived with the news that the Southmoors had formally joined the war and had taken Wentworth in a single battle.

Jemli called a meeting of her Assembly of Priests, then vanished with them behind closed doors until the ninth hour. When they did emerge the criers were roused to go through the city, proclaiming a mighty rally for midnight of the following day.

In the main marketplace of Peterborough two figures walked together as evening faded from the sky. One was a woman wearing a uniform of the palace guards, the other was dressed only in a kilt and cloak, and was assumed to be a visiting hermit.

"You are in great danger, there are now priests following you and listening to everything you preach," cautioned Velesti.

"Oh, good, I might convert them," replied Ilyire.

"You are also unique. How else can we communicate with the cetezoids except through you?"

"I have trained some of my best students, they are already able to carry on in my absence. I am not important."

"What can be achieved by dying?"

"Nothing in particular, but do not worry. I am not planning to become a martyr."

Highland Bartolica, North America

For Samondel, the problem was that her enemies happened to be the most highly skilled at making what she wanted. The guildmasters who remained loyal to her had begun to reduce the weight of her sailwing by removing its reaction guns and armor and replacing its skin with a much lighter silk, but a difficulty remained. It had been built very much in the traditional style, long before the war with Yarron. It was aerodynamically stable, and reliability had been built into every aspect of its construction, but it was still heavy compared to the Yarronese sailwings that she had used to conquer the Pacific Ocean. The same applied to its compression engine, which was currently in hundreds of pieces, with the guildmaster under orders to halve its weight and double its efficiency.

"Fourteen hours," declared the guildmasters' spokesman proudly as he stood before her throne.

The court hall was empty, apart from the two of them. It was nearly midnight, and only one lantern was burning.

"That is twelve hundred miles in calm air," replied Samondel. "I need two thousand."

"We could bore and plane a little more wood from the airframe, Saireme Airlord, but that would save only a few more pounds before the strength became compromised, even for handling the most benevolent weather. You could gain another hundred miles at most."

"Then do it. Has your esteemed colleague an estimate on when the compression engine will be rebuilt?"

"Three weeks, he told me. We could be test flying before the end of May."

Alone again, Samondel pondered capacities and distances in her little throne hall. A sailwing leased from South Bartolica could tow her out over the ocean for as many as five hundred miles. The rebuilt engine might just be light and efficient enough to bridge the remaining gap.

She could reach Hawaii, but what then? There would be no second sailwing to tow her for the next five hundred miles, although there was fuel . . . but there *was* a second sailwing, a Yarronese sailwing. She could spend months there, repairing the sailwing with the tools that had been flown out already. The more efficient Yarronese sailwing could easily reach Samoa, and then beyond to Australica's north. After that, it was a mere thousand miles by land to Rochester. A little gold would buy a horse.

Her mind conjured a suggestion of a cloaked figure to stand before her throne.

"You need never have returned here," Martyne chided.

"My dearest, how was I to know that Mounthaven could lose its arts of flying so very fast?"

"You could have taken me with you."

"You would have been tested and identified as a featherhead within moments of descent. Then shot."

"Well, can you return to me?"

"The kindest of figures say yes."

"Soon?"

"It must indeed be soon. I have sold everything to rebuild the sailwing and buy compression spirit. One of my wardens wants to buy my abdication and his nomination as airlord, and after that I have nothing more."

"Then when?"

"A month, and I shall reach Hawaii. A few more months, then Australica's north. Three months after that, Rochester."

"I shall be there, alone and waiting. Good-bye."

"Good-bye."

The vision vanished. Alone within her thoughts, Samondel dozed on the throne. Outside, the two palace guards sat with a bottle of wine between them.

"Saw her talking to thin air again," said one.

"She's mad."

"Heard she's to abdicate next month."

"None too soon. She's not airlord material."

"But a good leader. Many wardens would still follow her to hell."

"Trouble is, that's probably where she's going in that sailwing of hers."

His comrade gestured up to Mirrorsun.

"Well, that thing's building up to no good. Scholars say it's spinning too fast. Some say it's a doomsday engine."

"A what?"

"Something that kills both you and your enemy if your enemy defeats you."

"Daft idea. Who would have built it?"

"Dunno. Australicans, maybe."

Soon they were dozing too. The lamp in the throne hall ran out
of oil and winked out. It had been the last lamp alight in all of
Highland Bartolica on that particular night.

Rochester, the Rochestrian Commonwealth

The entire Commonwealth was plunged into mourning in the days
leading to Dramoren's funeral. The flower-smothered coffin was
drawn the length of Meridian Avenue on a bombard trolley at noon,
preceded, flanked, and followed by musketeers, Dragon Librarians,
beamflash crews, and even calculor components and regulators. The
Overmayor herself led the horse pulling the trolley. Dressed in a
black jacket and walking, the most powerful figure in the Commonwealth looked very small to the onlookers. They noted the flintlock
in her belt, however, for they were now at war and she was the
supreme commander of the military.

As the coffin reached Libris Plaza a loud rumble became audible
from above the city, and four enormous flying machines appeared in
the south. They flew high above the Avenue, their shadows sweeping
along the crowds and marchers, and colored leaves streaming from
their open loading hatches. As quickly as they had appeared, they
were gone.

The front of the palace was still a gaping ruin as the Overmayor
led the bombard trolley to the gates of Libris. Dramoren had been
Highliber, after all, and was entitled to be buried in the vaults deep
beneath the vast and ancient library. The bombards of the palace
began to boom a salute, one shot for every mayorate in the Rochestrian Commonwealth, and each shot was echoed by the bombards of
Libris. A closed service in the Libris chapel followed, then the coffin
was taken to the burial vaults below ground level.

The crowds were still there when the Overmayor emerged over
an hour later, and she walked alone across the plaza to the cheers
and applause of almost the entire city and thousands of travelers from
the other mayorates. At the foot of the memorial at the center of the

plaza a group of Gentheist priests took off their robes, poured olive oil on them, and set them afire, then cut their hair and flung the severed locks onto the flames. A brigade of lancers on the way to the Woomeran border was mobbed by well-wishers, and their way had to be cleared eventually by the Constable's Runners.

At last Lengina reached the palace gates. She walked inside, then climbed to the top of what remained of the wall and faced the crowd.

"My subjects, loyal citizens, Rochester has always stood for progress," she began. "Progress in the sciences, progress in theology, progress in administration, progress in trade, and progress in tolerance." She gestured to the shattered front of the palace. "There are those who think that tolerance is weakness, and that it is a signal to conquer the weak. The aviads have tolerated our attacks for centuries, but they are not weak. After my true love's death I appealed to the Avianese envoy for help to avenge him. Very soon an Avianese kitewing flew to Peterborough and silenced the voice of the greatest and most important beamflash tower of the Reformed Gentheists."

A rumbling groundswell of cheers greeted this news, washing back down the Avenue slowly, as her words were shouted in relay.

"Are we going to let our Avianese allies do all our fighting for us?"

The roar of "No!" blasted back from the crowd.

"The Gentheists have tried to exploit our tolerance, but tolerance does not mean standing back and accepting defeat. Tolerance means fighting for the right to live as we wish to live. Tolerance means serving in the Commonwealth army. Tolerance means serving in the Libris Calculor, beamflash network, and Dragon Librarian Service. Tolerant Gentheists should turn upon their Reformist preachers and slay them where they stand because those people hate tolerance. Tolerant Gentheists will embrace aviads as victims of the Greatwinter War's legacy, not as abominations. Tolerant Gentheists will teach our engineers and artisans to run their steam and compression engines in harmony with the world created by their Deity, not condemn them cynically for political gain."

The crowd was with her as she paused for breath, and to wipe away her tears.

"The man who I was to marry, the man whose leadership and genius held the Commonwealth together after Black Thirteenth, is dead. He had one last message for us all, however. Ilyire of Glenellen taught us that Mirrorsun means us no harm, that Mirrorsun destroyed machines of electrical essence because they caused it ill health. Franzas Dramoren now calls to you from his grave below Libris. The research that he sponsored says that tonight, at midnight, you will see why part of Mirrorsun spins, and you will be *joyful*. Go your way now, and my thanks for your good wishes."

Although the cheering began to subside after a half hour, the crowd did not disperse. The words "midnight" and "Mirrorsun" were on the lips of everyone, and they were determined to be together to see what was to happen.

Vorion's body was burned without ceremony, and his ashes scattered scattered on a dungheap outside Rochester. However, it was soon reported to Jemli that he had been the secret contact within the Highliber's office. Within weeks he was declared a Reformed Gentheist saint.

The dungeons of the Overmayor's Palace in Rochester were clean, dry, and whitewashed, for their prisoners tended to be of a reasonably high social standing. The Overmayor of Woomera was certainly the most senior inmate ever to inhabit them, but he was not particularly impressed with the clean surfaces, warm blankets, cooked meals, and lack of lice. When the key turned in the lock to his door, he was on his feet at once, drawing breath for a barrage of invective. The warder opened the door to reveal Overmayor Lengina.

"Why were you not on the balcony for the ANZAC parade salute?" she asked as he stood speechless.

The Woomeran's astonishment gave way to sullen resignation.

He looked down at the flagstones, thought through the facts yet again, then spoke.

"Armed masked men and women came into my quarters in the palace guest suites, just before the parade was due to begin. They held me in silence until there was a distant explosion, then left without leaving a trace. After some minutes I went in search of a guard, a servant, anyone. I was arrested by your guardsmen, and have been held here ever since. The magistrate questioned me about a bomb, and why I was missing from the balcony during the ANZAC parade salute. What is going on?"

"The palace oration balcony was bombed, but by chance it had been evacuated only moments earlier. Were it not for that chance, dozens of leaders would have died, including me."

"Thank the Deity—"

"Silence! One leader did remain behind, and died. The Commonwealth's Highliber, my fiancé."

The Woomeran swallowed. This was serious, more than politics was involved.

"The Rochestrian Commonwealth and the Woomeran Confederation are now at war. The act of terrorism from which you would have been spared even if chance had not led to an evacuation, was *before* the declaration of war. My Council of Mayors has considered the magistrate's report on you, and has condemned you to death for terrorism."

"What?"

"God have mercy on your soul. Guards, take him out to the firing squad."

Lengina was signing papers in her administration chambers when the blast of musketry reached her ears. Her advisors, clerks, and lackeys froze for a moment as she looked up.

"Returned to his Maker," muttered the Christian Bishop of Rochester awkwardly.

"With a complaint," added Lengina, reaching for the next document.

"Ah, now, this is my pastoral clarification regarding fueled engines," explained the bishop. " 'Engines are only hateful in the sight of God if the fuel consumed in the service of humanity is not in balance with the restoration of fruits of the Earth consumed in its production.' "

"In other words, if you grow it you can burn it in an engine."

"Well, er, yes. But we would like your endorsement, in the cause of good church-state relations."

"Strike out 'in the service of humanity,' it could lead to misinterpretations that could insult our Avianese allies."

Without another word the bishop drew a line through the words and initialed the change. Lengina now scrawled her approval to the bishop's text.

Peterborough, the Woomeran Confederation

In Peterborough there were also rumors about Mirrorsun. A Ghan prophet was in the city, addressing people in the markets, preaching at street corners, speaking from the steps of buildings, and even preaching as an invited guest in churches and shrines. His messages were simple and clear. The tolerant have nothing to fear from Rochester or Avian. Mirrorsun's rotation would cease a half hour before midnight. Science without conscience is evil. Religion without conscience is evil. Finally, he began to add that Jemli the Prophet was a fool. The last statement was naturally the occasion for quite a degree of comment, and it quickly reached the ears of Jemli. Very soon Ilyire himself was brought before her. He was still wearing a threadbare cloak over his kilt.

"I have been told about the heresies you have spread throughout the Rochestrian Commonwealth," she said as Ilyire stood before her flanked by guards, with his hands bound.

"Hearing about the lies you have been spreading inspired me to action," replied Ilyire, then he turned to a guard and winked. "I was once her lover, you know."

The outraged guard backhanded him across the face. Ilyire staggered, then shrugged.

"You preach tolerance for lies alongside truth, evil beside good, cons͵iracy beside justice," said Jemli. "I preach the Word of the Deity."

"For whose truth people have to take *your* word."

"People are not fools, they know, their hearts tell them."

"Their hearts tell them about everlasting love, as well. While courting Frelle Darien I loved her more than life itself, but after three years of living with her . . . sheema sheesh! Hearts are fools, I should know."

"My heart knows the Deity's voice."

"Your heart fell to Glasken's charms—but maybe the Deity has a sense of humor."

Jemli's lips became a thin, tight line, and her eyes narrowed. Ilyire knew that look only too well.

"Which you obviously don't share, Frelle. Just like Lemorel. She was always too serious for her own good, and the good of about a quarter of a million who died early, thanks to her."

"Lemorel had no message, she was just in search of power. I have the Word."

"Does the Word tell you Mirrorsun will cease to spin tonight?"

"I have consulted the mathematicians and natural philosophers who are among my faithful. What you say is impossible. It is called conservation of momentum, and Mirrorsun has a huge amount of momentum."

"Impossible even for the Deity?"

"The Deity does not do tricks, the Deity gives signs. The Deity tells me what you are planning. You think to trick me into predicting that Mirrorsun will stop, then Mirrorsun will not stop. You want to make the Enlightened One seem not so enlightened. Very clever."

"I do not believe in a Deity that would tell you a lie like that, Frelle Jemli. Perhaps demons lie to you, in the guise of the Deity."

"I know the Word, and the Word is the truth!"

"Or perhaps a little half-truth, just like you are only Lemorel's illegitimate half sister—"

Jemli was not so much enraged as panicked at the prospect of her followers knowing that her fraternal connection with the great Lemorel was less than perfect. Almost without thinking, she drew a small-bore flintlock from her sleeve and shot him through the heart. Ilyire collapsed in the grip of the guards, then fell facedown to the floor as they released him.

"I had to protect you from the demon that twisted his tongue," she explained. "It was not what I wished to do."

"But he died happy, telling a truth."

A figure in a Dragon Librarian's uniform stepped out of the shadows. It was of an old-fashioned uniform, and her rank was Dragon Silver. Her Morelac fired twice, and the two guards fell. A knife stapled Jemli's shoe to the floor, narrowly missing her toes.

"Every time I appear I become a little more real," said the apparition.

"Lemorel?"

"You do not sound convinced. How may I convince you that I am now completely real?"

The apparition lashed a slap across her face. Jemli tried to back away, forgetting that her foot was pinned to the floor. She overbalanced and fell heavily.

"No, no, no!" Jemli moaned. "At home it was always you, best at everything! Go away! It's my turn now."

"Shut up with your whining, Jemli Milderellen. If you wanted what I had then you should have studied and worked as hard as I did!" the wraith Lemorel shouted. "I used to get so sick of you as a girl. I still do. You make up your own histories, then believe them real. Now you have learned to make other people believe as well."

"Guards!" screamed Velesti.

Two guards flung the door open and rushed in, followed by their captain. They saw Jemli lying on the floor, and the ghost standing not far away. Ilyire and the other two guards lay still beside Jemli.

"Kill her, she's real," cried Jemli.

"Gen'gi, you were only nine when I last saw you!" Lemorel's reincarnation exclaimed to the captain.

"Frelle—Frelle, are you . . ."

"You wanted to ride with us, to invade what was then the Southeast Alliance, but your father said no, and I agreed. Remember what I said?"

"There will always be wars," said the captain.

"Ah, not quite. I said there will always be wars, so be patient."

"Frelle Lemorel. But you were shot."

"And I am dead, but I am here. Death is no problem."

She touched Ilyire's body. He got up, and she untied his hands. Next she raised the guards she had killed.

Jemli drew her gun again, but the striker clicked sparks into an empty flash pan. The toe of her half sister's boot flicked the gun from her hand.

"Are many of the old ones here tonight?" she asked Gen'gi.

"Many of them, Frelle."

"Then let us see them, come."

They left Jemli lying on the floor, and walked out into the palace hallways. Ilyire and his two guards dropped back, then their images faded into nothingness. The real Ilyire stepped out from behind a pillar and hurried to catch up with them. They entered a hall where several dozen mayors, overhands, and priests were gathered. Those who had known Lemorel two decades earlier gasped with astonishment.

"I'm afraid I have not changed in twenty-two years, but the rest of you are older," the reincarnated Lemorel said to the silent crowd.

A Ghan elder came forward and peered at her intently.

"Baragania," Lemorel said. "Yes, you were right. When I was alive, I made mistakes. I wanted power for its own sake. I conquered in the name of conquest. I avenged for the sake of revenge. Now I see it happening again. Do you really want to pour your blood into foreign earth because of my stupid young half sister?"

"You have the *flesh* of Frelle Lemorel," said Baragania. "Why are you here? To restore our ways to the Deity's path, to preserve *the protection*?"

Lemorel unbuttoned her coat, then started on her blouse. She pulled it open to reveal a modest amount of cleavage.

"Does my nakedness offend you?" she asked.

The elder's nerve wavered. Not only did she look like Lemorel, but she had a strangely similar charisma.

"No, Frelle Lemorel."

She backhanded him across the face, sending him sprawling, spitting teeth.

"Then why impose your religious cloistering and bondage, which *the protection* is, on your family's women?" she demanded.

She strode around him, slowly doing up her buttons again.

"You disgust me, following that clown Jemli after the lesson of my death. If you want to learn from me, come to Rochester. Come with your women. One female pilgrim with every male. Come and learn from the diversity there."

She swept her eyes across them all.

"I did not appreciate being brought back from the dark, cold serenity of death to undo what Jemli is doing in the Deity's name. Stupidity makes me very angry."

"Frelle Lemorel, we are afraid," began Gen'gi.

"Of what? Of me? Of Mirrorsun? You follow a clown with a loud voice and long hair because you are afraid?"

She turned back to Gen'gi.

"My half sister has just reloaded her gun, and she is on her way here. Disarm her."

Gen'gi hurried out, followed by most of the guards who were present. There was a gunshot. Gen'gi returned, bleeding from his right shoulder. He was followed by the guards who held Jemli. Her arms were pinned behind her back and she was missing a shoe. Her calf-length hair was in much need of grooming by now.

"Hold her here," Lemorel's reincarnation told the guards. "The rest of you come with me."

They walked out onto a balcony, below which the citizens of Peterborough had gathered in their thousands. Many were holding lanterns, and the city authority had rigged many more lanterns to hang from buildings that ringed Oration Square. *So far so good and I have never even had an acting lesson*, thought Velesti as she looked out over the crowd. *But can I feign Lemorel's charisma as well?*

"Citizens of Peterborough, some of you may remember me," she began in a voice that was not unnaturally loud so much as exceedingly penetrating. "Rumors have been spreading that I am again alive, and that I have been haunting my half sister. Well, they are both true. I am Lemorel Milderellen."

Thousands of mutters and murmurs rustled through the gathering. What she said was fantastic, yet their leaders were standing with her. *I don't have them yet*, thought Velesti.

"The Southmoors are coming. They have taken Wentworth. The Rochestrians are coming. They have destroyed your river galleys. The Avianese are coming. They have already struck your beamflash tower with their canvas birds and reaction guns. Do you want to be saved?"

The muttering from the crowd was generally along the lines of "Yes."

"Make a grant of Wentworth to the Southmoors, in exchange for a truce. Your Prophet has killed the Overmayor of Rochester's beloved, so while she lives here you will never have peace. Expel her to Kalgoorlie."

There was something reassuringly sensible about her words, and the listeners wanted reassurance.

"Tonight my sister, Jemli, killed the Ghan holy man, Ilyire of Glenellen, who has been preaching in your city."

Again she paused. The news shocked some, but Ilyire was not yet highly regarded except among the Alspring Ghans.

"I restored him to life."

This time there was immense shock evident in the immense groundswell of noise. *I think I have them, I think I have become Lemorel*, thought Velesti in triumph.

"Jemli will not get rid of Ilyire's teachings so easily, either. I could kill Jemli now, but *her* teachings would remain and strengthen. You must reject her. You, her followers."

Now Velesti pointed to the sky.

"You fear Mirrorsun. Part of it spins, part of it does not. My half sister preaches that the Deity will shatter it and scatter the fragments. I say to you, look up at the sky. The part of Mirrorsun that spins will burst and sail harmlessly away across the void to become Mirrorsun in the skies of Venus. Remember too, that your false prophet Jemli never predicted this."

As if on cue, there was a bright flash in the sky, just to the side of the solar reflection that gave Mirrorsun its name. There were screams from the crowd as part of the huge celestial band began to peel away, catching the sun's rays from a thousand highlights as its rotational energy gave it the speed of escape velocity from Earth. The pressure of sunlight caught by immense, lightweight paddles for nine months and stored as rotational speed now began to propel the flaccid band into a transfer orbit that would take it to Venus in four months. The band slowly peeled open across the sky like a fast-moving comet, its twisting, rippling surface undulating and catching light. A small Mirrorsun band remained, however.

The broken band's two arms eventually set slowly on either side of the sky, then were gone without any afterglow or twilight. Only the much reduced inner Mirrorsun band remained. Velesti had slipped away during the celestial show and was riding hard for the border by the time anyone thought to look back to her, but people just assumed that the reincarnated Lemorel had probably vanished back into the spirit world. Jemli was allowed to go free by the guards, now that Lemorel was gone. As charismatic as ever, Jemli now led a large and faithful part of the crowd in prayers of thanks to the Deity for sparing them from Mirrorsun.

Some people may be fooled all of the time, but not *all* people. Within the palace behind her, the Alspring Ghan elders and Woomeran mayors were deciding to break away from Jemli's influence.

In North America it had been daylight when the wide, outer band of Mirrorsun had burst. The sight had thus been far less spectacular, just a peeling off and receding of Earth's outer cosmic girdle, which gradually faded until it was lost in the blueness of the sky. Throughout Australica the scenes were very different indeed because the night view was truly spectacular. A great deal of prayer was sent skyward by both aviads and humans, yet people also crowded about the beamflash towers in search of a scientific opinion, even while seeking divine intercession. There was always a chance that the researchers at one of the monasteries would explain why the band had ruptured so very early. Most expected that the monks at Siding Springs would have the most plausible answer, but it turned out to be the Monastery of St. Roger that provided the answer.

"Look at the point of the break!" exclaimed Brother Nikalan as several hundred monks and nuns from the night shift in the monastery calculor stood staring up at the night sky where the outer band of Mirrorsun was writhing and scintillating as it slowly peeled back and receded into space.

"Very significant," declared Rangen.

"You should have guessed," admonished Nikalan.

"And so should you," retorted Rangen.

"This day is perfect for a transfer orbit, just perfect."

"And I could not think of a better host world than Venus."

"Just perfect for a mirrorsun."

"Very significant."

"Brilliantly conceived."

"Thank you."

"Mirrorsun, not you."

"Will someone tell me what is going on!" demanded the abbot, stepping between them and thrusting them apart to arm's length.

"Mirrorsun was pregnant," said Nikalan.

"It took nine months," continued Rangan.

"It built up its speed using solar paddles, yet stayed in the same place, where the sunlight remained at a constant strength. Very efficient. Even the ancients never thought of that."

"Then it burst at the perfect day for a transfer orbit to Venus."

"Today."

"So it's going to Venus," said the abbot.

"Venus was said by the ancients to be very hot," said Nikalan.

"Just the place for another mirrorsun," added Rangan. "It will cool the place down."

"Humans may even live there one day."

"And aviads."

"See, *our* Mirrorsun is a lot narrower now," said Nikalan pointing to the sky.

"It eclipses fewer stars."

"We need less cooling."

"Mirrorsun Child will slow itself down by dipping into the air of Venus."

"The ancients used that method to slow their spacewings."

"Mirrorsun is a mother?" asked the abbot.

"Yes," answered Nikalan and Rangen together.

By now the abbot had come to a most important realization. The two madmen whose cassocks he was grasping were quite possibly the only mortals in the entire world who had the true explanation for Mirrorsun's fantastic behavior. Right across the continent the news would be more welcome than cartloads of free gold. The Reformed Gentheists would be dealt a body blow, their Prophet would be made to look a complete fool.

"Let me through!" he suddenly shouted, scrambling through the crowd toward the monastic beamflash tower. "I must contact the Overmayor."

Nikalan and Rangen stared after him.

"Did I ever tell you that your aviad medician friend is pregnant?" Rangen asked Nikalan.

"No, you did not. You should perform an experimental verification with some suitable partner."

"Not even in the name of science," replied Rangen. "I am disillusioned with women."

The western border of the Rochestrian Commonwealth

The kitewing descended awkwardly in a gusty wind, coming down quite hard on the ascent strip and bouncing twice. The handlers were beside it within seconds, and even before Martyne had unstrapped they were wheeling it to its tent. Out here on the front there were no adjuncts, heralds, or other keepers of traditional flight ceremonies, and Martyne was not surprised to find the overhand of the Commonwealth's entire western army waiting for his report. This he delivered as they followed the kitewing into its tent.

Martyne always watched carefully whenever anything was being done to his kitewing, because he was by now acutely aware that one day he might be forced down somewhere with nobody to work on it but himself. His several patrol and strafing missions over Woomeran territory had left a number of holes in the airframe, and even a streak of lead on the compression engine.

The wingfield was no more than a straight strip of road not far from the riverbank, with a large tent for the kitewing, tools, and compression spirit, yet this modest installation had a hundred lancers and twice as many musketeers assigned to guard it. Only a single kitewing was on loan to the Rochestrians from Avian, but the value of its flights over Woomeran territory was beyond calculation. To compound the little aircraft's value, the numbers on its wings were repainted every day, to maintain the illusion of a larger flock.

"That shot to the compression engine could have been a disaster," said the aviad engineer as they inspected the kitewing with the overhand.

"So might a shot to me," Martyne pointed out.

"Had it hit the atomizer, it might as well have been you. That is what is known as a single point of failure. You brought back eleven hits this time. What were you doing?"

"I attacked a wind train, and set it burning with trace bullets. There were, however, a lot of Woomeran musketeers aboard and they all fired their muskets together."

The overhand rubbed his chin as he stared intently at the holes.

"Fras, far be it for a human to tell you what to do, but as your client I can tell you that knowing where the Woomerans are moving is of far more use to us than one kitewing attacking an occasional train. Were you to fly at two or three thousand feet you would be a very poor target, yet bring back to me information about Woomeran troop movements that I value more than half a dozen extra divisions—as well as antagonizing the Woomerans, which is always a good idea."

Martyne reluctantly agreed after the engineer declared that the repairs would take two days. He left the tent with the overhand.

"We had two new arrivals from over the river last night," the overhand reported. "One was Ilyire."

"Ah, a great, wise, and holy man," responded Martyne.

"Indeed, and said to be invulnerable to the Prophet Jemli's gunshot. He has already left to preach to my troops. His friend said that he seems to have caused the beginnings of a schism in Prophet Jemli's ranks."

"So easily and quickly?"

"It's hard to say. The Ghans and Woomerans seem to think that Lemorel Milderellen has come back to life. Many have seen her, talked to her, and even touched her. She has given Ilyire great credibility. Some say she raised him from the dead. He has introduced doubt to the Reformed Gentheists, and people tend not to fight well when they have doubts. The other one, the Dragon Silver, says she knows you. She is waiting with my escort."

Velesti greeted Martyne with a nod, then got down from her horse.

"What news from Avian?" she asked as they walked alone down the center of the ascent strip.

"Well, the battle at Launceston—"

"I know about the battle, and the truce, and about how Samondel stole a sailwing and flew east alone. Did she not want you?"

"Ah, yes, she did, but she had duties. Now we are apart."

"As you may know, I have a secret link to Mirrorsun, and Mirrorsun can see very clearly from the skies. She returned to America."

"So?"

"Why did she not take you with her?"

"America is a very dangerous place for aviads, and I am an aviad. She had to return home and expose the conspiracy, to tell the truth about us over here. She is going to try to get back, and I am going to wait."

"Ah. Good. Nobody is better qualified to fly the ocean than her."

"Indeed. I also have some additional information about Avian. It was doomed anyway."

"Doomed?" responded Velesti, doubtful because she made it her business to hear significant things first, and she had not heard about this.

"Ever wonder why so many children are flown across there?" asked Martyne, looking appropriately smug.

"To keep them safe, is what I would have said."

"And you would have been correct, however did you know that after four generations of aviads breeding with aviads the offspring are infertile? Even after three generations the couples have to hammer away at it daily for two or three years to conceive."

Velesti shook her head. "I'm not sure I understand."

"As Jemli keeps reminding people, we aviads were built by the old civilization. It seems that we were also designed not to become independent of humanity. Every two or three generations we must intermarry with humans again to produce offspring."

"Of which some are aviads and some are human, presumably?"

"Exactly. From the point of view of breeding, it would have made great sense for me to marry Samondel."

Velesti was unaccustomed to hearing so much from Martyne, rather than telling him instead. It was as if he were growing up, and leaving an older sister behind.

"How have Avian's leaders taken to this news?"

"Badly, but with resignation. There is considerable interest in the reforms of Overmayor Lengina and the fostering of tolerance in the Commonwealth. That is why I myself, my kitewing, and my ground crew are here on loan."

"In the long run it would make more sense for aviads to live in the Commonwealth than to go to all the trouble of keeping an air link with Tasmania Island open."

"That debate is currently raging, believe me."

"Ilyire would love to hear that. Just imagine, be tolerant or become extinct."

"I intend to tell him."

They reached the end of the ascent strip, turned, and started back. Velesti looked uncomfortable, and made several attempts to speak before finally succeeding.

"Martyne, I am truly sorry about Samondel. If I could do anything, you know I would."

He shook his head.

"Frelle Velesti, only the super-regals can rebuild the link to Mounthaven, and the Avianese now seal a clockwork bomb aboard before each flight. It has to be disarmed by someone with the right key, on the ground, before six hours have elapsed, or else there is one very large bang. To cross the Pacific I need four jumps of twenty hours, plus multiple flights to ferry huge stores of compression spirit, plus the problem of finding Samondel on a continent bigger than ours."

Velesti shook her head and folded her arms behind her back.

"The Avianese are liable to be less than sympathetic to a project like that. You certainly have a habit of getting yourself into impossible situations."

"True."

"Well, look on the bright side," she suggested.

"Is there one?"

"You still have me."

"There isn't one."

Rochester, the Rochestrian Commonwealth

Velesti stood at the leadlight windows of the Highliber's office, looking out over the roofs and towers of Libris. A leather folder was in her hand. Across Libris Plaza masons were already at work repairing the damage done to the palace by both the bombing and the Libris bombards, and in the distance a dark speck that was a super-regal was moving slowly across the sky. Presently Lengina entered, a sheaf of papers in her hand. Velsti turned and gave a shallow bow.

"Pleased to report that Prophet Jemli has been expelled from the Woomeran Confederation, and has returned to Kalgoorlie," Velesti reported. "The new Woomeran overmayor wants to open peace talks with you."

"That is good news, Frelle Disore. Arrange a date and place."

"At once, Overmayor."

"Wait, I have good news too, Frelle Disore," the overmayor said brightly. "On my recommendation, and after reading the late High-liber's reports on you, the Libris Dragon Gold Council is to make you a Fellow."

"I'd like to see them try," mumbled Velesti.

"Sorry?" asked Lengina.

"Nothing, esteemed Frelle. But why should I sit on the Gold Council?"

"Because of what is in my latest declaration."

She handed a sheet of illuminated poorpaper to Velesti. Velesti scanned it and looked up almost at once. She considered feeling faint, but that was much too silly. She considered laughing, but it was no laughing matter.

"Why?" she eventually exclaimed, staring steadily at her over-mayor and tapping the paper.

"Because you are brilliant, fair, frightening, vindictive, merciless, brave, cunning, devious, unpredictable, and as pure as wind-driven snow in the eastern highlands."

Velesti read the paper's words again.

"I have a very, very high price to demand before I agree," she announced.

"Well, then, let us discuss it," responded Lengina, taking her by the arm and guiding her in the direction of the waterfall courtyard.

•   •   •

Manuel had seen thousands of couples pass through Café Marellia's doors, but on this particular night he had a pair of patrons that nothing could have prepared him for. One was Velesti, which was bad enough in itself. The other looked a lot like Zarvora, except that Zarvora was dead. On the other hand, the one who looked like Zarvora was also semitransparent. Manuel set the tray down on their table, gave them a forced grin, then left hurriedly.

"You are not drinking your coffee," said Velesti, after taking a long sip from her own mug.

"I am trying to cut back," said Zarvora, waving her hand through the mug. "Have you an answer to my proposal?"

"I do, and it is no."

"What?" exclaimed the hologram.

"I said no, I can't put it more simply than that."

"But you are female."

"So? I have always enjoyed the company of women, and being one myself removes a lot of social barriers."

"But I have just offered to restore you to being Glasken—or at least male."

"No thank you."

"Velesti, this is no trick. There is a youth, a sailor, who was aboard a river galley during the recent battles. He was trapped when the galley sank, and was only rescued after a quarter hour underwater. His body lives, but his mind does not. We can obtain Theresla's interface collar from Ilyire, we could install it on the sailor's neck."

"But I like *this* body. Being female liberates me."

"I cannot believe what I am hearing!" snapped the hologram. "I know you too well. You're *never* going to let any man have any sort of access to what you have to offer."

"True, but there is more to life than sex."

"Fras Glasken, has living as Velesti driven you mad? Don't you remember? You hated being female."

"Only at first, but then I began to grow. Now I am more than Glasken could ever have been, and I could never go back. Could *you* give up being Mirrorsun?"

"No, but a body would have its uses. I had planned to take over Velesti, but not to imprint on her brain as you have. I need access to eyes and hands, your services have become too unreliable."

"Besides, your experiment with me proved it could be done in safety," Velesti pointed out.

"Well, yes," Zarvora admitted sheepishly.

"So? Why not make the sailor with the dead mind your hands and eyes, but without giving up Mirrorsun?"

"But he is *male*," said the hologram, distaste on its face.

"Indeed he is, Frelle Zarvora."

"But I want to be Velesti! She is highly placed in Libris and the Commonwealth."

"But I say no. Er, could I have your shortbread, seeing as you can't eat?"

"No!" Zarvora snarled, putting a semitransparent hand over the plate. "Glasken, I'll wipe your mind archives from Mirrorsun, you will be stuck as a girl until the day you die."

"Do it," said Velesti, taking the shortbread through her hand. "I'm fully imprinted on this brain by now, and quite independent. Besides, we agreed that you would wipe the archives anyway. When this body's life is over I'd like to die, thank you."

"This is just bare-arsed revenge, Frelle Velesti."

"Oh, yes, Frelle Zarvora."

It was only to be expected that Alaxis Sandar's mother seriously contemplated slamming the door and running to an upstairs window to scream for the Constable's Runners after opening it to find Velesti on the doorstep. Before she had been able to make the decision, however, Velesti had stepped inside the doorway, where she now stood with her arms folded behind her back. Behind her, still in the street, were several Tiger Dragons.

"I am the Overmayor's representative," Velesti explained without a great deal of interest in the woman, her husband, their three younger children, or the family medician—who happened to be paying a visit. "I am here to visit Fras Alaxis."

"Ah, of course, Frelle. His galley captain said that he might be granted a medal," responded the youth's father.

"Medician, I want a jar of medicinal spirits," said Velesti. "Frelle Sandar, I want a piece of clean cotton cloth and a half hour alone with your son."

"What do you mean, esteemed Frelle?"

"I may be able to revive him."

"Revive—"

"And in return he is to join the Dragon Librarian Service. Do you agree to that?"

"But of course, Frelle. He can only breathe and swallow—we'll agree to anything that may improve his condition."

Alaxis was lying on the lower level of a double bunk in a small room, which he was sharing with his younger brother. His eyes were closed, and he was breathing evenly. He gave no response at all when his mother squeezed his hand.

"He joined the Rochestrian Mayoral River Navy to see the Commonwealth, and to help with the family debts," said Fras Sandar as Velesti drew back the youth's eyelids, then snapped her fingers before his face. "He was just seventeen."

There was no response. The medician handed her a jar of spirits, then Frelle Sandar came in with a clean cloth.

"I have a very advanced medician's device," Velesti explained. "I can bring him back, but he will have no memories, only skills. He will be able to walk, eat, speak, and write, but he will not remember any of you or any of his past life. Are you willing to accept that?"

Alaxis Sandar's parents nodded.

"Then get out and close the door after you."

Once they were gone, Velesti peeled the band away from her neck but it remained attached at the back. She began to tug gently. Blood began to trickle down her skin. In the mirror she could see long, lank filaments coming out of her neck. The last of them came free and hung limp, then they began to slowly retract into the band.

Velsti steadied herself with a hand on the frame of the bunk. The room was spinning and all of her movements seemed faster than her mind was used to. It was several minutes before she felt confident enough to let go of the frame, and several more before she was able to swab the inner lining of the band. She examined a little patch at the back. It seemed to be a collection of tiny needle points.

Tearing a strip from the cotton cloth, she soaked it in spirits, and swabbed the back of her own neck. Wincing with the sting of spirits on the patch of broken skin, she wrapped the strip around her neck and buttoned her collar to hold it in place.

"How are you feeling?" tinkled a tiny voice from the band on her lap.

"Terrible," she admitted as she turned the sailor over and splashed spirits on the back of his neck.

"The filaments of the collar are more efficient than the nerves of your body. Now that you are without them, you will take some days to get used to moving about. You body will not feel like your own."

"I have had plenty of experience with my body not feeling like my own," replied Velesti. "What about my image in Mirrorsun?"

"All sponged away, and the storage space prepared for better things. I have been short of space ever since I fissioned. All that remains of you is in your head."

"I would have thought you had room for dozens of people's images in Mirrorsun's fabric."

"Most of the human body is not brain, just as most of Mirrorsun is not what the ancients called neural transaction fabric. But even if space were plentiful, I would not want company. I learned that by trying to share Mirrorsun with you, when you were Glasken."

Velesti lifted the band and applied it to the neck of the sailor. As she rolled him onto his back again she noticed that the band was growing hot. Almost at once Alaxis's eyelids fluttered, then opened.

"Adequate," whispered Zarvora through the youth's lips.

"Then I shall leave you to his family."

"Appreciate . . . help."

"But I want you to suffer."

"Bastard."

Velesti stood up too quickly, reeled, and nearly fell. For several minutes she paced the little room, getting used to walking while unaided by the neck band. Zarvora's voluntary control was improving quickly as well.

"This penis, how does it work?" asked Zarvora as she explored beneath the blankets.

"Really well, if you are that way inclined. Now, try to think male thoughts. Your new family awaits you, and remember, you are Fras Alaxis Sandar."

Velesti helped the youth from the lower bunk, and he stood swaying in his nightshirt as she opened the door. His mother, who had been waiting outside, took one look at her revived son, shrieked, then fainted. His father rushed in and embraced him as the other children tried to revive their mother.

"Have him report to Libris for induction as a Dragon White Librarian tomorrow," said Velesti as she stepped over Frelle Sandar's body.

She walked quickly from the house and hurried off down the street with her squad of Tiger Dragons.

"Did the procedure go badly?" asked the Dragon Blue in charge of the squad, noting that she was in haste to get away.

"It went perfectly, Fras."

"But then why are you so anxious to leave?"

"I cope very badly with gratitude. Next time I promote you, be sure not to thank me."

"I'll be sure not to," replied the Dragon Blue diplomatically.

Siding Springs, the Central Confederation

The monks at Siding Springs were very much aware that the world was watching over their shoulders as they in turn watched through the largest operational telescope in the world. It was the twenty-first of August, and Venus had been under observation for a full week. As it happened, Brother Tontare was at the eyepiece. The abbot was pacing the floor some distance below.

"Any sign of a flash of fire yet?" called the abbot.

"Nothing," Brother Tontare called back. "The Mirrorsun child might have arrived while Venus was beneath the horizon. It was due to arrive yesterday, after all."

"Keep watching. I *want* a flash to be seen, I *need* a flash to be seen, I *will* have a flash seen. Anything else bar the Mirrorsun child arriving at Venus will be a victory for the Reformed Gentheists."

"They will deny that any flash was seen by us, even if we saw one. You know what religious people are like."

"That had better have been a joke, Brother Tontare," warned the abbot, ceasing his pacing and glaring up.

"If you say so, Reverend Abbot. But why concentrate on a mere flash that is gone a moment after it happened? Why not the shadow of the Mirrorsun child on Venus, after it has formed up and unfurled? That would be there forever, for all to see. Well, those with a big enough telescope, anyway."

"The theoretician from Euroa, Brother Rangen, has argued that it will not be visible from Earth."

"Well, he is wrong, I can see it now, on the crescent of Venus."

"You what? Why didn't you say so earlier, you wretch!"

The abbot scrambled up the steps, and saw exactly what the monk had reported. The report of the discovery was quickly dispersed into the beamflash network, but other observatories in other monasteries had seen the shadow on the distant planet as well by now. Jemli denounced the observations as the work of devils in all telescopes. The monks had an exorcism performed on their largest telescope, but the mark on the face of Venus remained. The Mirrorsun child would not return to smash into Earth.

Once more the world breathed easier, and those in search of any reasonable or unreasonable excuse for a revel opened their jars of beer and wine at venues across the continent. Reformed Gentheists held prayer vigils outside those venues against what they denounced

as blasphemous acts of debauchery, while revelers bared their
breasts, buttocks, and genitalia from the rooftops and windows, and
flung down empty jars.

Back in Siding Springs the abbot and monks in the observatory
toasted Venus with jars of unconsecrated altar wine liberated from
the cellar by the abbot himself. Venus dropped below the horizon.
The monks had by now begun singing the more tuneful hymns in
organum. By midnight they had added lewd words at strategic
places, and by the time the bishop arrived in the morning to con-
gratulate them, they were all so sick that they regretted ever having
been born.

Rochester, the Rochestrian Commonwealth

Although Velesti was still Overseer of the Rochester University Baleshanto Guild, a real monk from the Balesha order was now sensei.
She and Martyne stood watching the monk take a training session
on the university lawns, noting certain subtle refinements in style
that had evolved since they had last trained in the monastery.

"He is good, but he is not coping well," said Velesti.

"I think he is training them extremely well," replied Martyne.

"I mean with the girls. What are the odds that he will lose his
virginity within a lunar month?"

Martyne shook his head. "I know the man. He is pious, temper-
ate, ascetic, dedicated, and has a very highly developed sense of self-
discipline."

"Truly?"

"I'd give him two months."

Velesti smirked, then turned to the youth at her side. "What do
you think, Fras Alaxis? Would you like to learn Baleshanto?"

The newly promoted Dragon Orange thought for a moment.
"Might it improve my coordination?"

"Sure to."

"Then I shall join."

"Sensei Ortano, another recruit for you," called Velesti as she took Alaxis over to be introduced.

Presently she returned to Martyne, and they began to walk away across the lawns.

"We should mark the half-year anniversary of Samondel leaving you," Velesti suggested, with no sense of tact whatever. "She has been gone six months today."

Martyne had come to expect nothing less, and took no offense.

"She adored me," he said, "and I adored her. I still adore her."

"Once, long ago, someone adored me," said Velesti. "*I* betrayed my adoring lover."

"Congratulations."

"Given my time over again . . ."

"You would not have betrayed him?"

"Her, and I would not have entered the liaison in the first place. Martyne, any reasonable person would say that Samondel is dead as far as you are concerned. Perhaps in fact, as well."

"Are you telling me that it is time to stop waiting for her?"

"Well, yes."

She draped an arm over his shoulders, then drew him close and whispered something in his ear. The astonished Martyne pulled away, his eyes bulging.

"You cannot possibly mean it!" he exclaimed.

"Oh, yes, I do."

"But how?"

"Because I am on good terms with the Eyes of the Mirrorsun Calculor. Will you be my companion?"

"How can I refuse?"

Condelor, North America

The dray cart was towed by a team of thirty men and women, and was loaded with eleven rotary compression engines that had either been recovered from old gunwing and sailwing wrecks or had lain unused in the gunwing halls of now abandoned wingfields. All but one were rusted, and some even had grass growing from between their cooling vanes. The country was dangerous, yet what the draymen had for sale was heavy and not easily stolen. Only in Condelor would the engines command a price for being what they were. Everywhere else they were scrap metal, to be melted down into tools, nails, and guns.

One welcome feature of the east road into Condelor was that it was downhill, and while the team pulling the dray had to remain at their push bars, much of the work was done by the two men working the brake blocks on the wheels. A sign appeared ahead, and a cheer went up from the team. Glory Bend was near the end of the journey, and as they rounded it they saw Condelor and its palace sprawled before them. The sight was truly glorious, all towers, spires, arched coronet fancies, and domed cathedrals. Flying low over the city was a merchant sailwing, clawing for height with four engines roaring, weighed down with a rich cargo of bullets, hunting rifles, medicines, and tools.

"Give a sixmonth, these engines will be ascending on a few o' those wings," said the draymaster to his two brakemen.

The last fifteen miles tended to be where the drays lost most members of their teams. It was not due to accidents, outlaws, exhaustion, or disease but to the fact that Condelor was in sight. Those travelers pulling the heavy dray were mostly there for the security of numbers against the outlaws and petty warlords who were rapidly taking over the mountains between Highland Bartolica and South Bartolica's capital. Those travelers who could not afford to ride the steam trams had to walk, and those who walked alone were always bailed up. If they were lucky, they would just be robbed, if they were less lucky they would be abducted and sold into slavery. If they were very unlucky or put up a fight, they would be shot. On this particular dray the packs of all those in the team were carried with the engines, and they were not to be returned until they had reached the walls of the city.

Fifteen miles is seven hours if one is walking at the pace of a dray pulled by people, and although the sunrise was behind them when they rounded Glory Bend it was midafternoon before they dragged the dray through the gates and drew up beside a canal. Here there were barges and cranes, and the first of the engines was loaded onto a barge. The members of the team that had brought them from Montpellier and past Bear Lake claimed their packs and began to disperse. One woman, still shrouded against the dust of the mountain road, paused to put her hand out and touch a fire-blackened cylinder of one of the compression engines. When the draymaster barked a caution at her, she walked away without another glance.

"Best of the batch," said the draymaster to the guildsman who was in charge of the barge. "A little singed, but when rebuilt it will sing like a guitar."

"What happened to it?"

"The airframe burned. Bought it from the former Airlord of Highland Bartolica."

"Samondel?"

"That's her."

"I hear she vanished."

"Aye, probably into a six-foot hole. Same Yarronese contractor that chopped her also torched her sailwing, I'd say."

Once away from the dray, Samondel removed the gloves, hat, scarf, and dust cloak that had disguised and protected her for the trip's duration, found a stall in a gateside market, and sold them for a few coins. Walking through the streets with her carbine, she now looked like an artisan's daughter returning from a day's fruitless hunting in the nearby mountains.

All around her were the signs of a civilization that was, if not in decay, at least in severe trauma. People now lived in Condelor not because it was a desirable place but because of the banditry beyond its walls. The city no longer had a mighty empire whose taxes kept it well maintained and beautiful. The place was a mixture of poverty and fortune, and there was a quite unfamiliar cocktail of stale scents on the air: rotting vegetables, swinelet droppings, urine, unwashed people, and pools of stagnant water from blocked and broken drains. Samondel hurried on.

The grounds of the airlord's palace were something resembling a wilderness more than a garden, but they were still well guarded. Several of the priceless horses from Australica could be seen grazing there, while carbineers took riding lessons on others. Samondel reached the gates. When the guards challenged her she produced papers and a scroll.

"Samondel Leover is my name, I am a warden in the employ of the airlord," she explained when she was brought before the seneschal of the palace. "The airlord is leasing my gunwing, *Starflower*."

"Yes, all of that is understood and in order," the seneschal replied. "And what brings you here?"

"I wish to claim my right to fly *Starflower* in the service of the airlord."

She was allowed to bathe and provided with clean clothing. When she was taken for her audience with the airlord she was wearing her new flight jacket, one that she had just spent months embroidering.

"Such a pity you sold your rank," the airlord said as they had drinks together in an overgrown little courtyard. "We could have married, and merged our domains."

"But we did not, and now I am a warden without lands," she replied. "And I claim the right to serve in *Starflower*."

"Former wardens are thick on the ground, while gunwings are not. I can only give you lodgings, food, and an allowance as a reserve flyer."

Samondel had expected this. At least she would remain on a wingfield, and would occasionally be flying. One night she might steal a fully fueled, unloaded sailwing and fly to Hawaii. Such dreams were all that she had.

"Flight preserved my pride, and I value my pride. I shall fly for you."

"You have been missing for a long time since your sailwing burned."

"I was in mourning for it."

"A stranger was looking for you, a foreigner. Money was offered for your location."

A Yarronese agent, thought Samondel. Sartov's man, seeking to kill her body after having wounded her soul.

"Well, I am safely in your service now, Airlord Loring."

Loring raised his right hand and waved it in a horizontal circle. A squad of guards converged on Samondel.

"So, I am neither safe nor in your service, Airlord Loring."

"I was offered a great deal of money as well as a treaty, Warden Samondel. I made a mecantile decision."

Samondel was held under guard for some hours, and although she was treated well, she was kept under close watch. Evening came, and the scent of roasting meat wafted through the palace. Samondel was taken from her room and marched through the corridors until she was just outside the great hall where she had once presided over feasts as Airlord of Greater Bartolica. That had been less than two years ago. How much more could happen in another year, she wondered.

"I propose a toast to our former enemies but future merchant allies," Airlord Loring was saying. "We have fought too long as clever and dedicated adversaries. It is time that we pooled our wealth and wits to form the greatest alliance of domains the world has ever seen. An alliance of air merchants! We are the only two major air powers left, but we shall grow, and we shall dominate the trade in the air, and on the ground. To the air merchants!"

A new alliance of South Bartolican and Yarronese air merchants, Samondel suspected. She knew what was going to come next. She had been in the wilderness, pushing a dray, for too long. She had forgotten how fast the world could change in mere months.

"And now, most honored guest and partner, for your last night in Condelor I have arranged a present for you. You have, as we all know, offered a huge reward for a certain woman who has proved very elusive, even to the finest of Yarronese and South Bartolican agents. Rest easy, however, for she is here, and securely held by my guards."

The company gave a cheer.

"Rest even easier, for in honor of our new mercantile alliance, I now present her to you to take home when you ascend at dawn—

and I shall claim not one single gold coin of your generous reward, only your esteem and goodwill."

"And most favored trading domain status!" someone called out, and they all laughed.

"Bring in Warden Samondel Leover," Loring ordered.

Once again, I am led into my own hall in captivity and humiliation, thought Samondel. She was led between two rows of feasting tables, mostly bordered with merchants, traders, and even a scatter of wild-looking men who were quite obviously petty warlords from the nearby mountains. Loring was seated and smirking at the high table, but the place at his right was empty. A woman in a familiar but grossly out-of-place Dragon Librarian's uniform was coming around the table and descending the steps.

"Velesti!" Samondel screamed in astonishment, then she ran from her guards and flung her arms around her.

The entire company rose, cheering, hooting, and applauding.

"Is this your idea of a bloody joke?" Samondel demanded in Old Anglian.

"Well, yes, as a matter of fact," replied Velesti.

"You're *here*! How?"

"That is a long story, but we shall have a lot of time for explanations tomorrow, on the flight to Australica."

The following day they were still over the North American continent as Velesti related how the *Moonwing* had appeared low in the sky over the Monastery of St. Roger, its compression engines already misfiring as the compression spirit ran out. The wingcaptain brought it down in an open pasture, and although the rough ground damaged the wheels, the super-regal came to rest in one piece. The monks had entered the dauntingly large flying machine and found the wingcaptain dead but still warm. Written in blood on the bulkhead fabric was the message, Holy Artisans, a Gift to the Featherhead-Hating Humans of Australica. Ferry Your Warriors over the Water. Burn the Featherheads in Their Nest.

"So this was a gift made in hatred?" asked Samondel.

"Yes. The idea that humans might *not* hate aviads was unthinkable to the wingcaptain. It took a very long time for the monks and artisans at St. Roger's to make the *Moonwing* airworthy again, but at least they had money from Rochester and advice from Alarak. He was made a Dragon Green Librarian for that, and for training all our navigators. He now works in the Libris map archive. Martyne made the first ascent from the newly built St. Roger Wingfield. The whole *Moonwing* venture was kept secret for a long time. Theology, you know. Theological theory had to be approved to allow *Moonwing* to be operated, but that has obviously been done."

"I thought Martyne would have been on this flight," said Samondel wistfully.

"The command of this venture was offered to him, but he declined. Both he and Alarak feared a warm reception in Mounthaven. Alarak for being a traitor, and Martyne for just being an aviad."

They shared time at the controls, and nineteen hours after crossing the coast they were within sight of the Hawaii wingfield.

"So many days between us still, so much flying to go," Samondel sighed as they descended. "Still, it is for the best. I am tired, grubby, smelly, and ill groomed from the long flight, and I want to be bathed and brushed to perfection when I meet Martyne again."

What Velesti had not told her was that Martyne had commanded the compression spirit ferry trips from the new Northmoor Wingfield in Australica to Samoa and Hawaii. It was a well-scrubbed, fully rested Martyne who was waiting at the Hawaii wingfield to greet Samondel.

"Sorry, should have warned you to clean up," said Velesti to Samondel as the former airlord pointed through the cockpit canopy and took a very deep breath.

"You beast!" she shrieked. "You knew all along!"

"Well, sort of."

"Beast, beast, beast! Why didn't you tell me?"

"Er, surprise?"

"Look at my hair! What am I going to do?"

"There's a comb in the chart drawer."

The following morning Martyne and Samondel were lying in each other's arms in a tent on the edge of the Hawaii wingfield. Although spartan as accomodation went, it did feature real sheets and pillows flown all the way from Rochester.

"Fras Martyne?" whispered Samondel.

"Frelle Warden?" he responded.

"Months ago, to kill you, I attempted."

"Not this again."

"You are not, ah, annoyed?"

"For the thousand dozenth time, no. Fortune favors those unlucky in love, so I was sure I would not die."

"Know feeling. Now of true, real love, I learn, for first time. I love you. Always."

Martyne squeezed her hand. "And remember what I said after you shot me?"

"Remind me, Martyne, my only, my dearest."

"I said 'Ouch.' "

Samondel snatched up a pillow and pounded at his head.

"Beast! Beast, beast, beast! Horrid, smelly, Australican beast!" she cried as Martyne burrowed down under the sheets to escape her. The pillow burst as she slammed it down at the shape under the coverings, showering the inside of the tent with feathers. After wrestling each other for some minutes they lay still once more.

"Martyne, I love you," said Samondel again.

"And I love you, Mayoress of the Skies. All the pain was worth it, just to be in your embrace again."

A week later Samondel and Martyne stood kissing outside the door to Café Marellia in Rochester. The moon was just clear of the rooftops, and the air was slightly too cool to be comfortable.

"I remember first time we were kissing," said Samondel. "Moon was ascending, we had been at Café Marellia."

"But this time there is nothing between us," Martyne assured her.

"Soon married to you or wanting to know why not," she said as they began to stroll hand in hand down the darkened street.

Martyne opened his mouth, closed it, then swallowed.

"My parents, ah—and I, that is, would like that," he managed.

Samondel laughed.

"Next summer. Yes?"

"Yes. Did you know that aviad-human marriages are now encouraged by both the Commonwealth and Avian?"

"Very sensible."

They stopped and embraced for a time, indistinguishable from any of Rochester's other courting couples. The two Espionage Constables and Balesha monk who were loitering nearby knew who they were, however, and they were closely but discreetly attended all the way back to the safety of their suite at Libris.

Velesti and Lengina watched Martyne and Samondel arrive back in Libris from a tower window in the gatehouse.

"Are you happy now?" asked the Overmayor of Rochester.

"Yes," replied Velesti.

"Then sign this," she ordered, holding out a sheet of illuminated poorpaper.

Velesti began to read.

"I, Velesti Disore, Dragon Gold in the Dragon Librarian Service, do hereby accept my nomination to the position of Highliber of Libris and Commander of the Dragon Librarian Service—"

"Go on, sign!" snapped Lengina. "You've already read it twice."

Velesti signed, then returned the acceptance to Lengina. "I must have the Dragon Orange, Alaxis Sandar, as my personal lackey," she warned.

"Why tell me?" said Lengina. "Your appointments are your own business."

"I want ready access to him, he has . . . very useful contacts."

For a time they sat watching the moon climbing over the rooftops of Rochester. Lengina cleared her throat.

"I have arranged for a portrait of you to go with the diplomatic dispatch to Kalgoorlie announcing your appointment," she said.

"Jemli will think that Lemorel's ghost has become Highliber."

"Yes, the one person in all the world that Prophet Jemli really fears," said Lengina, rubbing her hands together. "That should dampen her ambitions to conquer the East."

"Is that why you made me Highliber?"

"Well . . . it was one of several reasons. But, Velesti, when you said your price for accepting the Highliber position was high, I never realized how high."

"Still, you paid."

"Unbelievable! You had me fund repairs to the *Moonwing*, build wingfields, build compression spirit distilleries, then pay for you to fly spirit and artisans to the abandoned wingfields on Samoa and Hawaii, so that you could establish a trade link to Condelor to hold trade talks. And why? Not for your greater glory, not for intercontinental peace, not even to improve the Commonwealth's balance of payments situation—"

"Which it did do."

"—but to get Samondel Leover and Martyne Camderine back into each other's arms!"

"I like a nice romance. Between others, anyway."

They lapsed into silence again. In the distance someone rang a bell and cried that all was well.

"Good to see you out of black," said Velesti.

"My six months of mourning for Dramoren are long over."

"But are *you* over *him*?"

"He will always have a place in my heart, but . . ."

"But?"

"I'm young, pretty, and single," declared Lengina. "I'm also bored."

"Good, that means that the Commonwealth is running well," responded Velesti.

"I'm still bored. Suggest something exciting that we can do."

"Loring, the young American airlord of South Bartolica, hosts rather good revels in Condelor. I thought he was a lot of fun."

"Condelor? It's half a world away."

"Samondel and Martyne managed."

Lengina considered this. Monthly trade flights to Condelor had been established using *Moonwing*. The prospect of a very exciting adventure was suddenly laid out before the young overmayor.

"And if I happen not to like Airlord Loring . . . he will be half a world away when I return here!" she concluded aloud, looking very pleased with herself.

"Which is why I made the suggestion," replied her new Highlibcr.

EPILOGUE

No society is ever completely stable, just, fair, or enlightened, but as the moon rose over Rochester that clear, windless night the world was in fact entering a period of relative stability, steady progress, and general prosperity. Diversity and tolerance had been found to have value, and until that lesson was again forgotten, the four intelligences sharing Earth would live in something resembling harmony.